"There's no doubt about it: Thomas Harlan is a marvelous tale-spinner. . . . What's to come? Well, Volume Three will be *The Storm of Heaven*, and there may be more to follow. But this is no standard continuing fantasy series, endlessly recycling clichés. Thomas Harlan sinks his teeth into some very meaty subjects, and it's a pleasure to join him at the feast." —*Locus*

Praise for THE SHADOW OF ARARAT

"Set in a world in which the Roman Empire survives the barbarian invasions, Harlan's first novel features powerful and evocative prose as well as a strong cast of characters, a wealth of vivid detail, and a conclusion that leaves plenty of room for sequels. Highly recommended for fantasy collections."
—*Library Journal*

"Harlan's command of military strategy and tactics is thorough and vividly realized. When Roman and Persian armies clash in these pages, we can feel the dust sting our eyes and the ground shake beneath the rush of cavalry charges. . . . *The Shadow of Ararat* is not only an ambitious debut novel, but a first-rate alternate history by any standard." —*Amazing Stories*

"How long has it been since a writer has managed to begin a large-tome, multi-volume epic fantasy giving alternate history the vividness of the real thing and magic the combination of visceral and intellectual impact of the hottest new science—in a first novel? Well, Thomas Harlan has done just that in *The Shadow of Ararat*."
—*Locus*

The DARK LORD

Tor Books by Thomas Harlan

THE OATH OF EMPIRE
The Shadow of Ararat
The Gate of Fire
The Storm of Heaven
The Dark Lord

The DARK LORD

Book Four of
The Oath of Empire

Thomas Harlan

TOR®
fantasy

A TOM DOHERTY ASSOCIATES BOOK
NEW YORK

THE DARK LORD: BOOK FOUR OF THE OATH OF AN EMPIRE

Copyright © 2002 by Thomas Harlan

Edited by Beth Meacham

A Tor Book
Published by Tom Doherty Associates, LLC
175 Fifth Avenue
New York, NY 10010

www.tor.com

Tor® is a registered trademark of Tom Doherty Associates, LLC.

ISBN: 0-812-59012-0
Library of Congress Catalog Card Number: 2002019000

First edition: July 2002
First mass market edition: August 2003

Printed in the United States of America

0 9 8 7 6 5 4 3 2 1

ACKNOWLEDGMENTS

A considerable debt is owed to the men and women of the Barrington Atlas of the Greek and Roman World project, who have produced an exemplary reference to the ancient world. Without their labor of love, this book would be far poorer.

NOTES ON
NOMENCLATURE

The Roman mile is approximately nine-tenths of an English mile.
A league is approximately three Roman miles in distance.

MAPS

The Roman Empire
Roma Mater
Egypt and the Nile Delta
Alexandria

OATH OF EMPIRE ON THE WORLD WIDE WEB
http://www.throneworld.com/oathofempire

THE WESTERN ROMAN EMPIRE

**Partial EASTERN and WESTERN
ROMAN EMPIRES
(625 AD)**

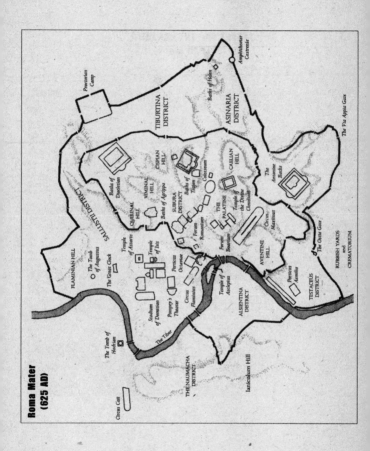

Roma Mater
(625 AD)

Praetorium Camp

TIBURTINA DISTRICT

SALLUSTIUM DISTRICT

FLAMINIAN HILL

QUIRINAL HILL

Baths of Diocletian

VIMINAL HILL

CISPIAN HILL

Baths of Agrippa

SUBURA DISTRICT

ESQUILINE HILL

Baths of Trajan

Colosseum

CAELIAN HILL

ASINARIA DISTRICT

Baths of Helen

Amphitheater Castrensis

THE PALATINE

Temple of the Divine Claudius

The Aurantine Baths

Temple of Astarte

Temple of Isis

Forum Romanum

Circus Maximus

The Via Appia Gate

The Tomb of Augustus

The Great Clock

Porticus Octaviae

Forum Boarium

AVENTINE HILL

Porticus Aemilia

RUBBISH YARDS and CREMATORIUM

The Ostia Gate

Stadium of Domitian

Pompey's Theater

Circus Flaminius

Temple of Asclepius

ALSENTINA DISTRICT

TESTACEUS DISTRICT

The Tomb of Hadrian

The Tiber

THE NAUMACHIA DISTRICT

Janiculum Hill

Circus Gaii

EGYPT AND THE NILE DELTA
(625 AD)

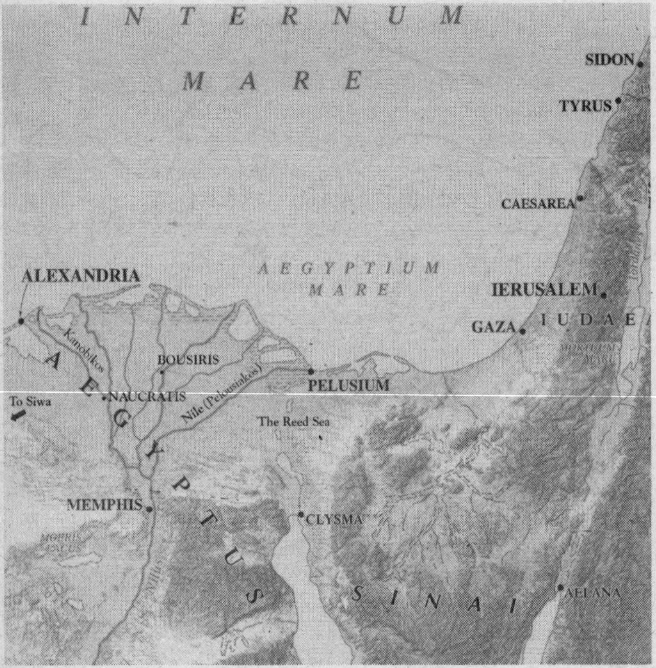

INTERNUM
MARE
SIDON
TYRUS
CAESAREA
AEGYPTIUM
MARE
ALEXANDRIA
IERUSALEM
GAZA
IUDAEA
Kanobikos
BOUSIRIS
PELUSIUM
To Siwa
NAUCRATIS
Nile (Pelousiakos)
The Reed Sea
AEGYPTUS
MEMPHIS
CLYSMA
SINAI
AELANA

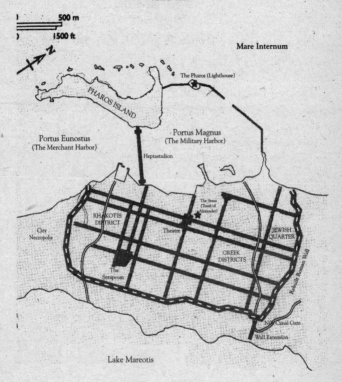

ALEXANDRIA
(625 AD)

500 m

1500 ft

Mare Internum

The Pharos (Lighthouse)

PHAROS ISLAND

Portus Eunostus
(The Merchant Harbor)

Portus Magnus
(The Military Harbor)

Heptastadion

The Sema
(Tomb of Alexander)

RHAKOTIS
DISTRICT

Theatre

JEWISH
QUARTER

City
Necropolis

GREEK
DISTRICTS

Rebuilt Roman Wall

The
Serapeum

New Canal Gate

Wall Extension

Lake Mareotis

DRAMATIS PERSONAE

THE ROMANS AND THEIR ALLIES

GALEN, Augustus (Emperor) and God of the now reunited Roman Empire. A thin, driven man; the eldest of the three Atreus brothers, sons of the Latin Roman governor of Narbonensis (southern France). Formerly a Legion commander, and Emperor of the West for eight years.

AURELIAN, Caesar (prince) of the Empire. The middle brother, a cheerful, burly, redheaded man with a talent for engineering, mechanical toys and horse breeding. Commander of the Roman defense of Egypt and Galen's heir while little Theodosius is underage.

MAXIAN, Caesar (prince) of the Empire. A priest of the temple of Asclepius the Healer, youngest of the three Atreus brothers. Gifted with the rare ability to heal, and an unexpected and dangerous talent for necromancy. Not yet grown into his full power, Maxian is the strongest thaumaturge to ever serve the Roman Empire. A normally cheerful lad now grown somewhat morose and distant under the weight of ever-mounting responsibilities.

HELENA, wife of Galen, Empress of Rome. An inveterate writer and socialite, the sharp-tongued Empress is the last of an ancient house and a throwback to the Empire's days of glory. Confidante, coconspirator and friend of the Duchess De'Orelio. Mother of Theodosius, Galen's infant son.

ANASTASIA De'Orelio, Duchess of Parma, former Minister of the Western Office of Barbarians. Widow of the elderly Duke of

Parma, a semiretired spymaster for Emperor Galen, and secret priestess and agent of the forbidden cult of Artemis the Hunter. Orphaned as a child by Visigothic pirates and sold as a slave, Anastasia was taken in by the Thiran priestesses of Artemis and has risen high in their councils as the "Queen of Day."

BETIA, the Duchess's Maid. Young German novitiate of the cult of Artemis. The Duchess's eyes and ears in the City of Rome.

THYATIS Julia Clodia, Agent of the Office of Barbarians. Adoptive daughter of Duchess Anastasia, her heir, novitiate of the cult of Artemis and centurion in the Roman Legion. She has also served, for six years, as the Duchess's primary sicarius, or assassin. The eldest daughter of the ancient and (sometimes) respected Clodian gens in Rome. A distant descendant of Mark Antony, via his marriage to the daughter of Clodius Pulcher, an enemy of Julius Caesar during the last days of the Republic.

NICHOLAS of Roskilde, Agent of the Office of Barbarians. A Latin child purchased as a slave by the Stormlords of the Dannmark, Nicholas returned to the Empire as a mercenary and freelance agent for the Eastern Empire's secret service. With the Eastern Empire in disarray, he and his boon companion Vladimir are at loose ends.

VLADIMIR, a wandering K'shapâcara (or "nightwalker"), Agent of the Office of Barbarians. A cheerful barbarian exile from the Walach tribes in highland Carpathia, forced into the Empire by the vicious expansion of the Draculis tribes.

GAIUS Julius Caesar, formerly Dictator of Rome. Revivified by Maxian's power, the cunning, lecherous, brilliant ancient now serves as the prince's spymaster and advisor. Imbued with new life, he intends to take advantage of every grain of time passing through his fingers.

ALEXANDROS, descendant of Zeus Thundershield, former Emperor and last of the Agead kings of Macedon. Like Gaius

Julius, the youthful King owns new life from Maxian's hand. Though still brilliant, rash and headstrong by turns, the weight of centuries has taught the Conqueror a tiny fragment of caution. And now, there is a new Persia to defeat. . . .

THE CAT-EYED QUEEN, an ancient sorceress of uncertain antecedents. The ruler of the K'shapâcara tribes dwelling in the human cities of the Eastern Empire and long-standing enemy of the demon Azi Tohak and his inhuman masters.

THE PERSIANS

SHAHR-BARAZ, Shahanshah (King of Kings) of Persia. A former farmer, rebel and lately General of the armies of Persia. Known as the "Royal Boar" for his vigor, enormous mustaches and relentless headlong success on the battlefield. The Boar previously served Chosroes Anushirwan, but with the great king's death, Shahr-Baraz has reluctantly occupied the Persian throne, declaring himself protector of the Twin Radiances, the princesses Azarmidukht and Purandokht. In their name, he rules a weakened, divided yet victorious Persia.

KHADAMES, a Persian General. An old friend and subordinate of Shahr-Baraz, Khadames serves both the King of Kings, and his brother, Prince Rustam—otherwise known as the sorcerer Dahak—as aide and chief of staff. Weary, and worn down by the enormous effort of the sorcerer's vast plans, Khadames continues to labor in the service of a beloved Persia.

DAHAK (Rustam Aparviz), a Sorcerer. The younger brother of the dead shahanshah Chrosoes, Rustam has trafficked with dark, inhuman powers. In this way he has gathered many servants both fair and foul to his service. Through his powers, Rustam intends to see Persia restored and Rome destroyed.

C'HU-LO, yabghu of the T'u-chüeh (Western Huns). First among Dahak's lieutenants, the T'u-chüeh khan has fallen far since the days when he ruled an empire stretching from the Rha (the Volga) to the Chinese frontier. Now he commands a small, but growing army of expatriate kinsmen and is the voice of Dahak in the wilderness.

PIRUZ, Prince of Balkh. Greatest of the Aryan feudal lords along the northern frontier of Persia, Piruz—a young, aggressive noble—seeks no lesser prize than the hand of princess Purandokht, and by that means, his sons on the throne of Persia.

THE COMPANIONS OF MOHAMMED (THE SAHABA)

ZENOBIA VI Septima, Last Queen of Palmyra, lineal descendant of Emperor Aurelian and Zenobia the First. Though her great desert city has been destroyed and the Queen herself struck down by the might of Persia, Zenobia lives on in the memories and thoughts of her kinsmen and allies. The heart and soul of the Decapolis—the Greek and Nabatean cities of the Middle East.

ODENATHUS, Prince of Palmyra, the Queen's nephew. A Legion-trained thaumaturge, the young prince now commands the armies of Palmyra-in-Exile as Queen Zoë's second-in-command. Close friend of Khalid al'Walid and many of the Arab captains.

ZOË, Queen of Palmyra, Zenobia's niece. Heir to the Palmyrene throne and a powerful thaumaturge in her own right. Like Odenathus, she was trained by Rome, and fought in the great war against Persia. The leader of the revolt of the Decapolis and the Arabs against the tyranny of the Eastern Empire. In her, most of all, the memory of Zenobia burns bright.

KHALID al'Walid (the "Eagle"), General of the Arab armies. Dashing and handsome, the young Eagle has risen—with the presumed death of Mohammed—to command the Sahaba and the armies of the Decapolis. Accompanied always by his silent companion, Patik, al'Walid intends nothing less than the establishment of a Levantine Greek-Arab empire in the ruins of the Roman East.

JALAL, a Tanukh bowman. Former mercenary, now risen to command the Arab qalb, or heavy horse. One of the few surviving companions of Mohammed who fought at the siege of Palmyra.

SHADIN, A Tanukh Swordsman. Like his old friend Jalal, a former mercenary. Commander of the Arab *muqadamma,* or "center." He too served under Mohammed at Palmyra.

URI BEN-SARID, captain of the Mekkan Jews. Boyhood friend of Mohammed, and the leader of the various Jewish contingents in the army of the Sahaba.

PATIK (the "silent"), Persian mercenary, formerly the Great Prince Shahin. Once a grandee of the Persian Empire, close relative of shahanshah Chrosoes, and commander of the Persian armies in Syria—the tall, powerfully built Patik has been reduced to a wandering sell-sword, finding service in the ragged band of men following Khalid al'Walid. By this circuitous route, he finds himself once more in the service of Persia, under the rule of his old rival, Shahr-Baraz.

MOHAMMED AL'QURAYSH, a merchant of Mekkah. After a long life of wandering on the fringes of the Empire, unable to find his destiny, Mohammed fell into the company of an Egyptian priest and into the crucible of war. Embattled and trapped in the destruction of Palmyra, Mohammed encountered true evil made flesh. Soon after, distraught at the death of his beloved wife Khadijah, he attempted to end his own life. Instead, a voice entered him and gave him new purpose and direction. Guided by the voice from the clear air, Mohammed set forth to punish the treachery of the Eastern Emperor Heraclius, precipitating a new war.

THE KHAZARS

SHIRIN, Empress of Persia. Wife of the now-dead shahanshah Chrosoes Anushirwan, Shirin is a young Khazar woman, forced into exile in Rome. Secreted for a time on the Artemisian holy isle of Thira, Shirin has escaped both the order and the clutches of the Eastern Empire. Lost in the ruin of the Vesuvian eruption, she searches for her lost children and her friend, Thyatis.

JUSUF, tarkhan of the armies of Khazaria, Shirin's uncle. A lean, laconic horseman who has variously served as Thyatis' second, Anastasia's lover and commander of the Khazar armies. In his youth, he spent time as a hostage in the Avar *hring,* and the T'u-chüeh court of the reviled khagan Shih-Kuei. Widely traveled and an expert with horse, bow and lance.

DAHVOS, kagan of the Khazar nation, Shirin's uncle. The youthful son of the late kagan Zeibil Sahul. Now the weight of his responsibilities presses upon him, and he must choose whether the Khazar realm will continue to stand against Persia and beside Rome, or if they will strike their own path.

What Has Gone Before

In the year 622, the Eastern Roman Empire was close to destruction, the capital of Constantinople besieged by the Avars in the west, and Persia in the east. As told in *The Shadow of Ararat,* the Emperor of the East, Heraclius, and of the West, Galen Atreus, launched a daring attack into the heart of their Persian enemy. The half-mad Persian shahanshah Chosroes was taken unawares, and after great battles, he was defeated and his empire given as a wedding gift to the Eastern prince Theodore. At the same time, while the two ancient powers strove to overthrow one another, two critical events transpired.

First, in Rome, the young Prince Maxian Atreus discovered an ancient thaumaturgic pattern—the Oath—constricting the lives and dreams of the Roman people. Aided by the Nabatean wizard and Persian spy, Abdmachus, Prince Maxian embarked on an audacious quest to find the sorcerous power he needed to break down the lattices of the Oath and free the Roman people from their invisible slavery. Second, while the prince exhumed and revivified Gaius Julius Caesar as a source of thaumaturgic power, a young Roman mage, Dwyrin MacDonald, was swept up in the chaos of the Eastern war.

Attempting to find and save his pupil, Dwyrin's teacher Ahmet left the ancient School of Pthames on the Nile and struck out into the Roman Levant. By chance, in the ancient rock-bound city of Petra, Ahmet encountered an unexpected friend in the Mekkan pottery merchant Mohammed. Together, the teacher and the merchant found themselves in the service of Zenobia, Queen of Palmyra. At the urging of the Eastern Emperor Heraclius, Zenobia and the princes of the Decapolis and Petra gathered an army to resist the advance of the Persian army into Syria, under the command of the Great Prince Shahin. Unaware of Heraclius' intention to see the independent cities of the Decapolis sacrificed to divert Chosroes' attention,

Zenobia clashed with the Persians, was defeated and then besieged in Palmyra itself. Despite furious resistance, the City of Palms fell to the monstrous power of the sorcerer Dahak. Zenobia and Ahmet perished, and Mohammed only escaped with a small band of his followers through sheer luck.

While Persia collapsed, the Roman agent Thyatis, accompanied by the Khazar tarkhan Jusuf, entered Ctesiphon and stole away with mad Chosroes' second wife, the Empress Shirin, Jusuf's niece. Though she was supposed to deliver the Empress to Galen, Thyatis chose instead to disguise her escape and flee south, making a circuitous and eventful return to the Empire via southern Arabia, the East African coast and the black kingdoms of Meröe and Axum. A dangerous decision, not only for the terrible peril of the voyage, but to thwart the desires of an Emperor . . .

Not far away, in the ruined Persian city of Dastagird, Prince Maxian found the last piece of his puzzle—a crypt holding the stolen, hidden remains of Alexander the Great. As he did with Gaius Julius Caesar, the prince revivified the Macedonian and felt his power was at last sufficient to break the Oath strangling the Roman people.

In the year 623, as told in *The Gate of Fire,* the Roman armies of East and West returned home, and both nations rejoiced, thinking the long struggle against Persia and the Avar khaganate had at last come to an end. Great plans were laid, both by Heraclius and Galen, and many legionaries rested their weary feet. Yet, all was not well, neither within the Empire nor without. Heraclius' attempt to return home in triumph was spoiled by a sudden and unexpected illness. Galen's return was more joyful, for he found his wife Helena had at last borne him a son.

Worse, in Arabia the merchant Mohammed reached Mekkah to find his beloved wife Khadijah cold in the ground. Devastated, Mohammed climbed a nearby mountain and attempted to end his own life. As Mohammed lay poised between death and life, between the earth and sky, a power entered him, speaking from the clear air. The voice urged him to strive against the dark powers threatening mankind. Heeding this voice, Mohammed—after a brutal struggle in the city of his birth—set out with an army of his Companions, the Sahaba, to bring the treacherous Emperor Heraclius to justice. To his surprise, he found many allies eager to overthrow the tyranny of the Eastern Empire. First, the rascal Khalid al'Walid, then the lords of Petra, and finally the exiled Queen of Palmyra, Zoë. With their aid, Mohammed raised the tribes and the cities of the Decapolis to war against Rome. Heraclius' treachery would be repaid with blood and fire.

Indeed, even in Persia the enemies of Rome did not lie quiet. The sorcerer Dahak had escaped from the Roman victories with an army and made his way to the ancient, remote fortress of Damawand, high in the mountains of Tabaristan. There, in a shrine once held holy by the priests of Ahura-Mazda, the sorcerer began to muster a great power—not only of arms and men—but of darkness. Deep within the fortress lay a door of stone, a door holding inhuman, implacable gods at bay. Risking his life and the earth itself, Dahak opened the stone door to capture the power of the ancients. By these means, he shed the last of his humanity and became a true master of the hidden world. At last strong enough, the sorcerer made his way to ancient Ecbatana and there—with the aid of his servant, Arad—placed the great general Shahr-Baraz on the throne of Persia. Now, a reckoning would come with Rome and Persia's lost glory would be reclaimed.

In Rome itself, events rushed to a devastating conclusion. Prince Maxian, flush with the strength afforded him by the legends of Julius Caesar and Alexander, strove again to overthrow the power of the Oath. Unwilling to sacrifice his brother Galen, the young prince failed, nearly killing himself and wounding his companion Krista. Fleeing to the safety of his mother's ancestral estate on the slopes of Mount Vesuvius, Maxian struggled with his conscience. Unwilling to wait for his decision, Krista fled, bringing news of the prince's whereabouts and fatal plans to the Duchess De'Orelio—the Western Empire's spymaster and secret priestess of the Thiran Order of Artemis the Hunter. Her hand reinforced by the return of Thyatis, Anastasia ordered the prince murdered.

Thyatis, Krista and their companions found the prince on the summit of Vesuvius and after a deadly battle failed to kill him. The prince, mortally wounded, opened himself to the power in the mountain, bringing himself back from death and inciting the somnolent volcano to a staggering eruption that destroyed the cities of Baiae, Herculaneum and Pompeii. Maxian escaped aboard his iron dragon, while Thyatis chose to plunge from the flying craft into the burning wasteland rather than become his servant. Only the two survived, all else having perished in the cataclysm. Far away, in Persia, Dahak became aware of the prince and his growing power, realizing a rival had emerged to contest him for the world of men.

These bleak events omened further evil, and the year 624 proved devastating for Rome. As told in *The Storm of Heaven,* the Eastern Empire suffered disaster after disaster. In the Levant, the armies of the Sahaba, relentless under Mohammed's guidance, destroyed prince Theodore's Eastern legions at Yarmuk, captured the city of Hierosolyma after a long siege, and seized the critical port of Caesarea Maritima. In Mesopotamia, the armies of Persia marched west again, recapturing their lost provinces as well as the great city of Antioch. The Persians and Arabs, now allied, launched an invasion by land and sea into the Eastern heartland, besieging Constantinople once more.

In Rome itself, a direly wounded Thyatis struggled to reclaim herself in the face of abject failure. Despite the help of a troupe of Gaulish holy performers, she fell into the clutches of Gaius Julius, now entrusted with the execution of enormous and extravagant funeral games for those slain in the eruption of Vesuvius. Forced into the arena, Thyatis proved herself more than a match for man and beast. At last, thought dead again, she was spirited away by Anastasia and the Empress Helena. The successful culmination of the games also provided the prince Maxian—working behind the scenes and without his brother's knowledge—with victory over the rigid and inflexible structures of the Oath. The prince, setting aside his desire to destroy the ancient spell, instead ingratiated himself with the all-encompassing structure. By these means, he hoped to direct its power and free Rome slowly and subtly from its invisible master.

In the East, Alexandros raised a new army among the Gothic tribes and marched towards Constantinople. Before he could reach the Eastern capital, a monumental battle evolved before the gates of the embattled city. Western legions, Eastern troops and a contingent of Khazars under the command of the new kagan Dahvos attempted to break the Persian siege. Despite the awesomely destructive powers of the young firecaster Dwyrin MacDonald, they failed and the combined host of the Decapolis, Persia and the Avar khaganate drove the Romans from the field in disarray. In the ensuing confusion, Heraclius reclaimed his throne and prepared to lead a final defense of the Eastern capital. The end came in darkness. Dahak's infernal servants shattered the gates and an army of the risen dead stormed into the streets of the city. Dwyrin, exhausted in a fruitless attempt to stem the attack, was struck down. The Roman troops trapped in the city fled, evacuated under a burning sky by the Western fleet.

Even the sudden arrival of Prince Maxian and his brief alliance with the Cat-Eyed Queen are not enough to stem the tide of defeat. The prince and the surviving legions slink away, broken and battered. Persia and her allies stand triumphant, poised to invade the Roman heartland. After two thousand years, the Empire slides down to destruction. . . .

ALEXANDRIA, CAPITAL OF PTOLEMAIC EGYPT,
LATE SUMMER, 30 B.C.

)H(

Grimacing, the Queen turned away from a casement window, sleek dark hair framing her elegant neck and shoulders. Outside, the roar of shouting men filled the air. Beneath her slippers, the floor trembled with the crash of a ram against the tower doors. The room was very hot and close. Swirls of incense and smoke puddled near the ceiling. For a moment the Queen was silent, considering the array of servants kneeling around her husband's funeral bier.

"Antonius Antyllus," she said, at last, as a fierce shout belled out from the courtyard below and the floor shook in response. "You must take my son."

The stocky Roman, clean-shaven face pinched in confusion, half turned towards the back of the room. At the Queen's arched eyebrow, a slim young man in a pleated kilt stepped forward. The boy was trembling, but he raised his head and met the Queen's eyes directly. Antyllus made a questioning motion with his hand, brow furrowed. "Pharaoh, I cannot take him away from you . . . where will he go? Where would he be safe from your enemies?"

"Home," the Queen said, stepping to a silk and linen-draped throne dominating the room. As she moved, her attendants drew a gown of shimmering black fabric from a chest. A blond handmaiden knelt and raised a headdress of gold and twin scepters. Beside her, a dusky maid bore a jeweled sun disk, ornamented with an eight-rayed star in bronze. "To your home, to Rome, as *your* son. His Latin is excellent. He has been raised, as his noble father wished, a Roman."

Antyllus shifted his feet, unsure, but finally nodded in surrender. There was a huge crash from below and the drapes swayed. The legionary tried to summon a smile, but there was only bleak agreement in his fair, open face. "Another cousin," he said, looking upon the young man, "among dozens of our riotous family. . . ." His eyes shifted to the corpse on its marble bier and grief welled up in his face like water rising in a sluice. "Father would wish this, my lady, so I will take your command, and his, to heart. Your son will find sanctuary in the bosom of my mother's family—they are a huge clan and filled with all sorts. . . ."

"Go." The Queen raised her chin, sharp sea-blue eyes meeting those of a man in desert robes, his lean, dark face half shrouded by a thin drape of muslin. "Asan, you must take Antyllus and Caesarion to safety—a ship is waiting, at the edge of the delta. Will you do this thing, for me?"

The Arab bowed elegantly and stepped away into the shadows along the inner wall of the room. Antyllus did not look back at the Queen, boots ringing as he strode to the hidden door. Caesarion did, looking to his mother with bleak eyes. His youth seemed to fade, as he ducked though the opening, a weight settling on him, and the Queen knew the boisterous child, all glad smiles and laughter, was gone forever.

Voices boomed in the corridors of the tower and the shouting outside dwindled, replaced by the clashing of spears on shields. The Queen did not look out, for she was well used to the sight of Roman legionaries. Instead, she settled on the throne, long fingers plucking at the rich fabric of her gown. Narrowed eyes surveyed her servants and councilors, a meager remnant of the multitude who once clung to the hem of her glory.

"Get out," she rasped, voice suddenly hoarse. Sitting so, facing the closed, barred door to the main hall, she could look upon the shrouded, still body of her last husband, laid out in state at the center of the chamber. "All of you, out!" The Queen raised a hand imperiously, golden bracelets tinkling softly as they fell away from her wrist.

They fled, all save fair Charmian and dusky Iras. The Queen listened, hearing the tramp of booted feet in the hall, then the door—two thick valves of Tyrian cedar, bound with iron and gold and the sun disk of Royal Egypt—shuddered. A voice, deep and commanding, shouted outside.

The Queen ignored the noise, leaning back, letting her maids

fix the heavy headdress—a thick wreath of fine golden leaves
around an eight-rayed disk—upon her brow and place hooked
scepters in either hand. The doors began to boom as spear butts
slammed against the panels. She closed her eyes, crossing delicate fingers upon her chest, then took a deep breath.

"I am ready to receive our conqueror," she said quietly, looking sideways at the blond maid, who knelt, tears streaming
down her face. "Where is the god?"

Iras lifted a wicker basket from the floor, then removed the
fluted top. Something hissed within, thrashing, bulging against
the sides of the basket. The dusky maid grasped the viper
swiftly, just behind the mottled, scaled head. The snake's jaws
yawned, revealing a pink mouth and pale white fangs. Iras
worked quickly, squeezing the poison sac behind the muscular
jaw with deft fingers. A milky drop oozed out into her hand. A
brief spasm of pain crossed the Nubian's impassive face as poison burned into her flesh, then the maid tilted her hand and the
droplet spilled onto the Queen's extended tongue.

Kleopatra closed her mouth, clear blue eyes staring straight
ahead. The door splintered. Ruddy torchlight leaked through,
sparkling in clouds of dust puffing away from the panels with
each blow. Then she closed her eyes, long lashes drooping over
a fine powder of pearl and gold and amethyst. At her side, Iras
broke the snake's back with a twist, and then dropped the creature onto the floor, where the serpent twitched and writhed for a
long moment.

The two maids knelt, bowing one last time before their
Queen, and then they too tasted the god's blessed milk and lay
still, as if asleep, at her feet.

The ruined door swung wide and the legionaries stepped back,
tanned faces flushed, the chin straps of their helmets dark with
sweat. For a moment, as they looked into the dark room, no one
spoke. There was only the harsh breathing of exhausted men.
The centurion in charge of the detail glanced over his shoulder,
a question plain in his sunburned face.

"Stand aside," a quiet, measured voice said. "There is nothing to fear."

A young man, his hair a neat dark cap on a well-formed

head, limped across the threshold. Like the soldiers crowding
the hallway, he wore heavy banded mail, a red cloak, and
leather boots strapped up to the knee. His sword was
sheathed—indeed, the man claimed to have never drawn a
blade in anger—and even on this day, he did not wear a helmet.

Gaius Octavius, defender of the Republic of Rome, the victor—now, today, in this singular moment—the master of Rome
and Egypt, looked down upon his last enemy with a pensive
face. Nostrils flared, catching the brittle smell of urine and
blood, and he nudged one of the slaves sprawled below the
throne with the tip of his boot. The girl's flesh was already
growing cold.

For a moment, standing over the body of the Queen, the
young man considered calling his physicians, or discovering if
any Psyllian adepts were in the city. But then he saw the
woman's cheeks turning slowly blue and knew he had been denied a great prize.

"Khamûn," Octavian said in a conversational voice, "come
here."

There was movement in the doorway and without turning the
Roman knew the frail, spidery shape of the Egyptian sorcerer
knelt behind him, long white beard trailing on the mosaic floor.
No one else entered the room.

"Royal Egypt is dead." Octavian stepped up to the throne itself, one foot dragging slightly. "She is beyond us, her flesh so
swiftly cold, joining her Dionysus in death. . . ." Octavian
barely spared a glance for the dead man in the center of the
room. He was already quite familiar with the strong, handsome
features—he had no need to look upon them ever again. "Your
gift to me, as you have so often called it, has vanished like
dew." Octavian turned, one eyebrow rising, his eyes cold. "Has
it not?"

Khamûn bent his head to the floor. "Yes, my lord. Alive,
alive she . . ."

Octavian turned away, back to the dead Queen, who sat upon
her throne in the very semblance of life, save for the patent stillness of her breast and the inexplicable failure of the vibrant energy, wit and incandescent charm that marked her in life. The
Roman bowed to the dead woman, acknowledging the end of

their game. "Pharaoh is dead, Khamûn. But I am content. I will rule Egypt, even if I may not possess her."

The sorcerer nodded, though he did not look up. Octavian looked to the doorway, where his soldiers were waiting, afraid to enter. "Scarus—find those servants who remain and bring them to me. They have unfinished business to attend."

"Here is your queen," Octavian said, standing on the top step of the dais. He looked down upon a clutch of Egyptians the legionaries had dragged from the tower rooms. Others would have escaped, he was sure, but these slaves knew their mistress well. "She has joined her husband and sits among the gods. Look upon her and know Rome did not stoop to murder."

The servants, faces streaked with tears, looked up, then bent their heads again to the floor. Octavian stepped down, careful to lead with his good foot. A wreath of golden laurels crowned him, and his stained soldier's cloak had been replaced with a supple white robe, edged with maroon. The lamps were lit, joining the fading sunlight in illuminating the death chamber. Both maids had been carried away, but the man and the woman remained, each in their chosen place.

"Has a tomb been prepared for your mistress?" Octavian's voice rose, for more Egyptians stood outside, in the hall, the late Queen's ministers and councilors among them. "A place of honor for her and for her Dionysus?"

One of the slaves, a broad-shouldered man with a shaggy mane of blue-black hair, looked up. His limbs gleamed with sweat, as if he had run a great distance, and he spread his hands, indicating the room. "Yes, great lord, this tower is her chosen tomb."

The Roman pursed his lips and looked out through the tall window, across the rooftops of the houses and temples of Alexandria. Even here, within this great edifice, he could feel the mournful chanting of the crowds, the restless surge of the city. Alexandria was a live thing, filled with furious, fickle energy. Octavian swallowed a smile, acknowledging the Queen's foresight. *Let you sleep within the walls of your beloved Alexandria? That will not do!*

"This place will not suffice," he said, looking down upon the slave. "You must take her away—far away—into the desert. Prepare there a hidden tomb, safe from the eyes of men, where these two may lie in peace for all time. Let them have each other in death, for eternity, for their time together on earth was so short."

Many of the slaves looked up in wonder and Octavian saw the black-maned man's eyes narrow in suspicion. The young Roman raised a hand, stilling their questions. "Rome does not wish to know where you place her—nor should you tell another, for tomb-robbers will dream of Kleopatra's treasure with lust. Take her far from the dwellings of man. Let her find peace."

Octavian turned away, looking out upon the city again, and he waited, patient and still, until the slaves and servants bore away the two corpses. Then he smiled and laughed aloud, for he was alone. *Fools! Let Rome be magnanimous in victory—it costs nothing—and the witch-queen will be well hidden, far from the thoughts and dreams of men.*

Drums boomed, a long rolling sound drowning the constant chatter of the crowds, and a pair of bronze horns shrilled as Octavian dismounted from his horse onto the gleaming marble steps of the Mausoleum. Three ranks of legionaries stood between him and the crowd, the men sweating silently in their heavy armor and silvered helmets. The young Roman raised his hand in salute to the crowd and to the city fathers, who crowded onto the edges of the steps like buskers at the races.

Without a word, he turned and took his time climbing the ramp. The drums continued to beat, slowly, in time with his pace. Their heavy sound made the midday heat fiercer, the polished sandstone and marble buildings reflecting the full weight of the sun upon the street. When Octavian disappeared into the shadowed entrance, the horns shrilled once and then drum and *bucina* alike fell silent.

Inside, in blessed cool gloom, a bevy of priests and Khamûn's spear-thin shape were waiting. Despite the fierce protests of the clergy, legionaries with bared weapons stood in the shadows, their eyes glittering in the poor light, watching their commander walk past, into the center of the tomb.

An opening had been broken in one wall, leaving plaster and

brick scattered on the floor. The wall had been painted with a colorful mural—all gold and red and azure—showing a mighty king in battle, throwing down his enemies. A gilded sarcophagus lay on the floor, gleaming in the light of lanterns and a dim blue radiance from windows beneath the roof. Octavian frowned, turning towards the Egyptian wizard. "I thought the Conqueror was entombed in solid gold."

Khamûn bowed, wrinkled face creased by a sly smile. "My lord, one of the later Ptolemies found himself short of coin—he had the body removed, the coffin melted down, and the god's corpse placed in crystal instead."

The Roman snorted in amusement, then knelt by the head of the sarcophagus. A sheet of heavy glass covered the top of the coffin, allowing a distorted, milky view of the body within. Octavian grunted a little, running his fingers over the surface of the lid. The glass was of exceptional quality, with few bubbles or distorts. He raised his head and gestured to the legionaries biding in the shadows. "Bring levers and my grave gift."

The priests in the hall stiffened as two burly legionaries stepped up to the sarcophagus, iron pry bars in muscular hands. Octavian ignored the Egyptians and their half-choked cries of protest. "Open it up, lads, but carefully—I want nothing broken."

The two Roman soldiers grinned, but slid the pry bars under the glass with practiced ease and—after a moment's effort—popped the lid free. Grunting, they managed to get the cover loose and placed aside on the ground. Another man—one of Octavian's aides—opened a box of enameled pine. The smell of freshly cut flowers and incense rose from within.

Octavian knelt again, leaning beside the coffin, staring down at ancient, withered features. The man within—in his breathing life—had been of middling height, broad-shouldered and narrow-waisted. Now all of his body save the face was carefully wrapped in layers of fabric and even now, after hundreds of years in the tomb, embalming spices and unguents tickled Octavian's nose. Curly hair lay matted against the skull, and the eyes were closed, as if the man were merely asleep. The young Roman frowned, reaching out with a questioning hand, then withdrawing before he touched the ancient flesh.

Carefully! He reminded himself, *he's old and fragile— wouldn't do for the great Alexander to lose his nose from your clumsy touch!*

"Curious . . . he looks nothing like my adoptive father." Octavian's voice was sad.

The old Egyptian, Khamûn, raised an eyebrow in question. Octavian did not turn, but straightened up, remaining on his knees. "My adoptive father, Julius Caesar, believed himself the reborn spirit of Alexander." The young man's voice was soft and contemplative.

"He felt a great pressure throughout his life," Octavian continued, "and it made Caesar mad, I think, always racing to match the achievements of Alexander. Sometimes he complained of urgent dreams, and never accounted he had matched his *old glory.*"

Khamûn said nothing, though his face turned pensive. Octavian continued to speak softly and quietly, musing on the past. "He sent me a letter from Alexandria, soon after Pompey the Great was defeated. He too looked upon the face of Alexander . . . he said the visiage was *familiar* but not his *own* face. That Woman played to his obsession, I think, plying Caesar with tales of reborn souls. She wanted him to be Alexander."

Octavian looked up at Khamûn, eyes narrowed in suspicion. "Are the souls of the great reborn, wizard? Could Alexander's spirit have dwelt in my father's body?"

"I have heard this said, my lord." Khamûn took a moment to still his racing heart. A terrible thought had occurred to the old wizard, chilling his blood. "Many men, and women, too, oft claim the blood of the great heroes and kings runs in their veins . . . mostly those who hope for descent from some heavenly power. Alexander, I have heard, claimed his own house of Aegea descended from Hercules, and through him from Zeus Thundershield. I do not know if that is true."

Octavian stood, his expression turning cold. "You are not answering my question, wizard."

Khamûn swallowed, but managed to speak. "There are some great spirits, my lord, which maintain after a man or woman dies. We call them the *ka*, and they do not die with the defeat of the physical body. Such a man as Alexander? His spirit might live on for a long time . . . but from what I have seen and read, it will be drawn like to like. In his own descendant, perhaps, he might live again. But the great Caesar is a trueborn Roman, yes? Born of Latin blood? Not a Macedonian . . . and everyone agrees Alexander's children perished, strangled or murdered by his successors."

Octavian continued to fix the old Egyptian with a cold stare, but at last relented, turning back to the coffin on the floor. "True," the young Roman mused, "his line ended in blood. So my father's dream was just that—a dream—though he was carried far on those wings! Just the memory of the man was enough. . . ." Octavian's voice trailed off into silence.

A long moment passed and Khamûn, seeing the young Roman deep in thought, did not venture to disturb him. Finally, Octavian roused himself, looked around and gestured to his aide. The youth unfolded a cloth in the box, and removed a golden diadem, surmounted by the eight-rayed star of the Macedonian kings. Octavian, moving with great care, settled the crown upon the ancient leathery head, then saluted the corpse as one Roman general might another. He followed the diadem with the petals of many flowers, strewn artlessly in the coffin.

"It is done," he said, and the two legionaries—under his careful eye—replaced the glass lid and drove thin wedges of lead into the spaces around the edge to hold it fast. Octavian turned away, grinning at Khamûn. At the same time, he put something in a pocket inside his cloak.

"My lord?" ventured one of the priests, "would you like to look upon the mausoleum of the Ptolemies?"

Octavian laughed at the man, now seemingly in great good humor. "I came to see a king, not a row of corpses!"

With that, Octavian strode out of the tomb, with his legionaries and aides in a crowd around him, leaving the priest sullen and red with anger.

"Now, Khamûn, where have you hidden the boy, Caesarion? I would like to see him for myself." Octavian slouched in a field chair in his great tent outside the city. Full darkness had come, revealing a vast wash of stars girdling the heavens. All around the young Roman, his Legions were bedding down for the night, here on the plain just east of Alexandria. In the gloom, their lanterns and torches made a bright orchard along the banks of a canal. "Her children by Antony I have already looked upon—charming and well-featured, but useless—where is Caesar's child?"

The old Egyptian stood at the door of the tent, staring out into the darkness. Now he turned, long wrinkled face filling with despair. "Gone, my lord. None can say where, and I have cast about in my thought, seeking to gain this knowledge. The boy has vanished. Some . . . some say he has fled south, to Axum or the dark kingdoms at the source of the Nile. . . ."

Octavian stood abruptly, his usually calm face twisted in anger. "You purchased your child's life and freedom, master Khamûn, with promises of power over Egypt and Rome alike! Now, what do I have? Nothing! You are a weak tool, a chisel that slips too many times from the cutting groove. Why should I keep you, when you fail so often? Do I mistake the passage of events? Each thing I desired, I have taken *myself*."

The Egyptian paled, seeing raw fury in his master's face for the first time. The young Senator was not a man of great passions and the change was startling. Khamûn knelt, swiftly. "My lord . . ."

"Be quiet." Octavian stared out at the dim lights of the city, a constellation of pale yellow and orange crashed upon the earth. "My agents, my men, will search for the boy. I will set Agrippa upon the task—he has never failed me! This child of conjoined Rome and Egypt will not be allowed to live. I am Caesar's *only* heir and I *will* have Rome for myself."

Octavian gestured for the Egyptian to rise. "Yet there is a task I have in mind for you, something I hope is within your skill! My reach is long . . . wherever you have hidden your beloved will not be far enough away, if you fail me again." The young Roman smiled suddenly, teeth white and feral in the half-darkness. "I will make a new Rome, a glorious, eternal Rome. You will help me. I have not ignored the little you have taught me of power and this hidden world you claim to master."

Khamûn watched his master warily, though the Egyptian breathed a thankful prayer he still had some use. He did not want to die under the burning tongs—his ancestors would have laughed at such threats, but the blood of Khem was thin in these later days. "Of course, my lord, I am your servant."

🔲〇-〇🔲

A STREET, NORTH OF THE FORUM BOVARIUM,
CONSTANTINOPLE, LATE SPRING A.D. 625

)-(

Afaint groan issued from beneath a heap of corpses. Pale sunlight fell on dead staring eyes, picking out faint gleams from buckles and rusted links of chain armor. The entire street was filled with scattered bodies—most of them burned beyond recognition—though many still held the semblance of life. There were no flies, no rooting, bloody-nosed dogs, no scavenging peasants, no crows or ravens or seagulls feasting on the flotsam of war. Empty windows stared down onto the sloping street, shutters scorched black by some awesome blast of flame that had raged up and down the avenue.

Bodies shifted, heavy gray arms falling away, thighs encased in armor clanging to the ground. A man clawed his way out of the corpse midden, face streaked with dried blood, armor dented and scratched. He stood, trying to muster the spit to clear his mouth. Dark eyes, almost black, took in the wreckage all around and the soldier grimaced. There was nothing moving, certainly nothing alive as far as his eye reached in either direction.

A great stillness pervaded the houses and crouched in the doors of the little shops. The soldier realized nothing lived, even in the dark, close rooms behind the facades. Grunting, he tried to climb up over the heap of half-naked bodies—part of his conscious mind registered Slavic spearmen, long hair stiff with white clay, their bodies intricately diagrammed with whorled signs in black and dark blue dye—and found his right arm weak. Frowning, he looked down on his forearm and realized a huge gash ripped from his wrist to the elbow, tearing through a sleeve of linked iron rings.

"Merciful gods!" The man hissed. Something had shattered his arm, cleaving right to the bone. *An axe?* He remembered something bright flashing towards him.

The soldier reached to undo the buckle at his shoulder and his left arm caught on something. Cursing, the man realized a long black-shafted arrow had wedged itself through the center of an iron link and clear through his forearm. The stubs of two more arrows were buried in his chest. Snarling, without even words to express his rage, the man broke the shaft of the arrow off at the base, rewarding himself with a popping sound and the slow welling of thick, dark blood around the wound. He ignored the arrows in his chest for the moment.

With swift, experienced motions, Rufio unbuckled the straps holding the armored sleeves to his shoulder plates, then jerked the heavy iron hauberk off over his head. The arrows in his chest snapped with a wet sound and he hissed with pain. A pale, welted body crisscrossed with terrible scars was revealed. The street remained silent and desolate. Even the sky was empty of birds. The uncanny stillness weighed on the soldier's mind. He assumed the city had fallen—but where was the occupying army? Where were the oppressed citizens?

Blunt fingers gripped the head of the arrow in his left arm, then dragged the shaft out through the muscle. The point emerged, slick with reddish-yellow fluid, and Rufio tossed the arrow away. He bent over, feeling abused muscle and bone creak. Two arrows were buried deep in his chest. Squatting, bracing his shoulders against the nearest building wall, Rufio lifted a spent shaft from the ground. Another dead Slav, lying facedown, flesh distended and purple, provided him with a moderately clean knife. Ignoring the throbbing pain in his left arm, Rufio cut the head from the arrow, then trimmed the resulting shaft, notching the blunt head into four quarters.

Clenching his jaw, Rufio wedged his trimmed arrow against the broken butt of the one in his shoulder, wiggling it until the notched head settled properly against its new friend. Then, holding his body as still as he could manage, the soldier bore

down, pushing the arrow lodged in his body through, feeling it
grind past bone and muscle, until it punched through the skin of
his back. Tears streamed down his cheeks, cutting tracks in
dried, crusty blood. Despite being half-blind, his entire body
shimmering with pain, he carefully withdrew his dowel. With
the iron head of the shaft sticking out of his back, Rufio managed to reach around and snag it with his thumb. Some wiggling around managed to slide the bolt free.

One more to go. Rufio lay back, panting, staring at the pale
sky. A haze seemed to lie over the city, making even a clear
bright sun, high in the bowl of heaven, seem faded and washed
out. *Oh, you cursed gods,* the soldier thought bitterly, *I never
asked for this . . . to see nothing but an eternity of ruin and destruction! You should have left me safely dead, cursed physician!*

But he remained alive, and though his entire body was trembling, he fitted the dowel, again, to the broken stub jutting from
his chest and began to push. A long agonized groan escaped the
soldier's lips as the arrow punched out his back.

NORTH OF THE REED SEA, LOWER EGYPT,
EARLY SUMMER, A.D. 625

)⊫(

The stand of cane waved softly, moved by some zephyr of
the upper air, creaking and rustling with quiet voices. A
thin little man, wiry body given desperately needed bulk by layered leather armor, crouched at the edge of the thick green
stalks, his lower body tugged by a sluggish current. The Roman
peered through the foliage, ignoring the flies buzzing and crawling on every surface and the gelid sensation of leeches squirming against his legs. One of the man's hands was raised, bidding
other men—hidden still further back among reeds and rubber
trees thick on the banks of the canal—to wait, to be patient.

Beyond the screen of cane was a ford where the ancient brick
sidings of the canal slumped away with age and use, leaving a

high sandy bank cut by a rutted wagon path. Here in the lower delta of the Nile, silt filled old passages and the river—in times of flood—cut new channels on its way to the sea. From where Frontius was crouched, skin itching and nostrils filled with an overpowering stench, he could barely make out the paving stones that had once joined a proper road—a Roman road—to a bridge across the canal.

Frontius clenched his fist, feeling the water stir. Little dimples began to appear in the thick brown surface. A sound rose over the constant buzz and hiss, a thundering roll of hooves on sand and broken paving. A man appeared, jogging along the old road, leading a small tan horse. The new arrival was swathed in white and ochre, mail glinting through his robes, and a conical helm wrapped with a green flash. The scout, careful, probed the muddy water with a spear, then—even at this distance, in this heavy, nearly opaque air—Frontius could see the man smile. The old bridge had collapsed into the muck, making a firm, sandy bottom. The Arabian high-stepped through the water, but there was little need—the slow current barely covered the mare's fetlocks.

After a moment, the Arab disappeared back the way he had come. Frontius opened his hand, making a signal to the others, then settled himself lower in the muck, letting the tepid water lap up around his torso until only his head and shoulders were revealed, pressed against the heavy black loam anchoring the reeds. The thundering in the earth was growing stronger, making the surface of the canal ripple and bounce. Then the scout reappeared and the Arabian splashed lightly across the stream and scooted up the far bank. Within an instant, the road and ford were filled with men. Dozens, then hundreds of mounted men picked their way across the canal, surging up the western bank.

In the cane break, Frontius bit at his knuckle, counting and watching, praying the footing of the ford would hold—they had not expected *so many* of the enemy to come this way! A troop of men with green banners splashed past, then they too were gone. For a moment, there was silence, then the croaking of frogs and the honking cries of marsh egrets and cranes returned. Frontius rubbed furiously at his ears, crushing a feathery carpet of mosquitoes. His hands came away bloody and gray.

He bent his head, listening. A grain passed, and then another, then most of a glass, before he heard the rattling din of battle suddenly brew up to the west. Horns called, echoing mournfully over the swamplands and the screaming of horses grated across his nerves. Now he stood, arm raised again, mud oozing from his armor, and watched the high bank where the *banda* of Arabic cavalry had passed. The sound of the fighting grew closer—shouts, the clash of metal on metal, cries of pain, the *snap* and *hiss* of arrows. High in the broadleaf trees, Frontius could see branches moving in some breeze, but here, down in the muck, there was only a close stillness. Sound carried far over this stagnant water.

A horse burst from the top of the western bank, slewing down the slope, throwing up a spray of sand and brown water as it hit the canal. The Arabian staggered, then came up, leeches clinging to its flanks, saddle askew. There was no rider. A moment later, a man—his face covered with blood—limped down the sandy bank, then managed to cross the ford, using his spear as a cane. Off to the west, there was a sharp *boom* and leaves fluttered out of the cottonwoods. Frontius smiled: the Legion thaumaturges weighed in.

The Roman engineer turned, opening and closing his hand twice. Off through the thick brush, reeds and white-barked trees there was an answering flash of light. Frontius closed his nose, trying to keep mites from crawling in, then began wading back up the canal. The mud was deep and thick under the thin sheet of water, slowing his progress. His heart started to beat faster, hearing a low rumbling sound upstream, and he veered towards the bank. Here, under the tree roots, there was a course of fitted stone. He reached the bank as the first wavelet passed, pushing gently at his legs. Frontius swallowed a curse, then grabbed hold of one of the clinging roots and started to climb out of the canal.

Another, higher wave rushed down, more of a rolling hump in the brown water, but when this one passed, the level of the canal did not drop. Instead, the water began to sluice past, running faster and faster, swirling around Frontius' boots. The wiry little engineer struggled, trying to scramble up the stone, cursing the enormous weight of mud and water trapped in his armor.

Someone shouted in anger behind him and Frontius risked a look over his shoulder. The ford was filled with Arabs afoot and a-horse, crowding through the crossing. The hump of water crashed into them unexpectedly, throwing some down, fouling others. The sky above lit with a searing bolt of flame, followed by a resounding *crack!* Some of the Arabs on the far bank turned and loosed arrows in quick succession over the heads of their comrades. Horns shrilled on both banks.

Gritting his teeth, Frontius lunged for the top of the stone wall, catching the lip with his fingers. Desperate—for the water was rising very swiftly now—he clawed at the roots and loose soil. A clod of dirt came free and broke apart on his face, blinding him. "Gods!"

The Arabs shouted, voices filled with fear. The canal was surging up around them, boiling white around the horses. More men fell down and were pushed away, into the deeper channel where the canal cut behind the blockage of the fallen bridge. Another shout joined them, the basso roar of the Legion advancing. The clash and clatter of men in combat was very close.

Frontius felt the swift water drag at his legs and his left hand slipped from its purchase. He cried out, feeling his right elbow twist in the joint, then managed to clutch at an overhanging branch. The Arabs, driven back into the rising canal, fell into the water, where a huge crush of horses and men jammed the sunken bridge.

An arrow shattered on ancient stone beside Frontius' waist and he yelped. On the opposite bank, one of the Arab archers crawling through the underbrush had seen him. Without sound, neck bulging and arms twisted with agony, he heaved himself up, out of the canal, now running close to the top of the bank, and clawed his way into the sumac and thornbush lining the old canal. Arrows whipped past, hissing through leaves and clattering off the trees.

Frontius crawled away, shaking with effort. *Sextus will pay for this! I'm sure his dice are loaded.*

Roman legionaries in grimy, mud-spattered armor appeared on the western bank of the canal, heavy rectangular shields forming a solid wall. Golden eagles shimmered in the heavy afternoon air, rising above rows of iron helms. Clouded blades licked down, stabbing at Arabs still clinging to the sandy bank. Javelins plunged down into the mass of men and horses trapped in the canal. Wounded and dying, the bodies were shoved off into the rushing stream. On the eastern bank, the Arabs fell back, their arrows suddenly intermittent, darting only occasionally out of the murky white sky. Their horns blew, sounding a general retreat.

"Caesar, a courier from Pelusium!"

Aurelian looked up from his field desk, covered with rolls of papyrus bound in black twine and stacks of fresh parchment. The walls of the tent had been raised as the day lengthened, extending welcome shade against the brassy glare of the late afternoon sun. Dozens of scribes, couriers and soldiers waited nearby, squatting or sitting on the hard-packed earth. The big Roman ran a scarred hand through his beard, smoothing thick red curls, and motioned for the man to approach. Shaking a cramp out of his fingers, Aurelian set down his quill and handed the parchment—covered with an intricate drawing in fine black lines—to one of the scribes. The man, an Egyptian like most of the imperial staff, whisked the drawing away to be dried and then copied.

"Ave, Caesar!" The messenger was young and drenched in sweat, lank yellow hair plastered to an angular skull. He shrugged a leather courier bag from his shoulder and removed a kidskin packet. Aurelian nodded in thanks, then unwrapped the message and quickly read the letter. As he did, his bluff, open face grew long and when he finished intense irritation sparked in his eyes. "Lad, how old is this news?"

"Two days only, Caesar," panted the soldier. "I left as soon as the Greek attack broke."

Aurelian made a sharp motion with his finger, and one of the scribes was immediately at his side with a waxed tablet and stylus. The powerfully built Western prince, the second brother of the Emperor of the West, bent his head a little towards the brown, shaven-headed scribe. "Here are my words," he growled, "for the attention of the Legate Cestius Florus, who commands at Pelusium. Sir, you will hold your line and prevent incursions of the barbarians into the delta by any means at your disposal *save* that of flooding, or the use of dams or prepared canals. These directions have already been given to you, you *will* follow them, or you will be replaced."

The scratching sound of the stylus in the wax continued for a moment, then ended. The scribe, knowing his master's desire, held up the tablet for Aurelian to read. The red-beard was not a scholar, but he owned a handy grasp of Latin, Greek and some Persian. Aurelian nodded, then motioned the scribe away. "Lad, go with Phranes here—he is my aide—and get something to eat and drink. I will send you back to Cestius, with my reply, and I hope you will take great haste in reaching him."

The soldier nodded, then saluted. Phranes led the boy away, calling for food, for watered wine, for a place in the shade. Aurelian did not return to his working table, moving instead to the eastern side of the tent and staring out, glowering at distant Pelusium, across leagues of field and farm and canals and the distant bright ribbon of the Nile itself. The air was thick and gray here in the humid lowlands. Vast flocks of birds rose and fell like living smoke above the slaughter yards and granaries surrounding Alexandria. The prince's camp sat atop an ancient tell rising from the depressingly flat plain of the delta. Old columns, bricks and shattered slabs of paving stone crunched under his feet.

At the base of the ancient mound, thousands of men labored in the sun, digging with spades and mattocks in the dark earth. They made a line arcing around to the north and west, running along a low ridge marking the eastern border of the sprawling, profligate metropolis of Alexandria. In the time of the Ptolemies—the Greek dynasty that ruled Egypt before the coming of Rome—the city itself had boasted a wall of sandstone and marble. The intervening centuries, under an enduring Roman peace, saw the ancient wall engulfed by the city, then demolished block by block for building material. Now there was no rampart, no bastion, no powerful towers to hedge the city in. Only miles of villas and shops and warehouses and little gardens. There was only one gate of any size, completely surrounded by a dyer's district, and entirely useless for defense.

Aurelian had levied sixty thousand laborers to build a line of fortifications from Pelusium at the eastern edge of the Nile delta south to the edge of the Reed Sea. Though the Roman had every confidence in his men, he was also cautious. The enemy *might* break through the defenses sixty miles to the east. Alexandria *might* be threatened.

So nearly a hundred thousand men sweated in the blistering sun before the provincial capital, with two full Legions of Western troops to guide them. A wide ditch was being gouged from the earth, from Lake Mareotis a mile south to the shore of the Mare Internum a mile north. The earth from the excavation was being hauled in cloth bags—one to a man—up to a wide, heavy berm behind the ditch, along the crest of the ridge. A rampart thirty feet high would loom over the ditch, and it would be faced by a thicket of stakes and fitted stone. A fighting wall twelve feet high would run along the length of the rampart, with square towers jutting up every half mile.

All the land for a half-mile before and behind the wall was being cleared; the villas knocked down, the houses broken into brick and timber, the shops emptied and demolished. Brick, mortar, stone, cut timber—Aurelian's enterprise swallowed building materials at a prodigious rate.

The eastern horizon was a flat green line, shrouded with haze curving up into a simmering blue-gray sky. Somewhere out there, four Roman Legions were squared off against the Greek rebels and their Arab auxiliaries. Aurelian did not expect there to be a battle—the enemy army was far too small to force its way past the fortifications spidering out from Pelusium. He did not want his hand to be tipped, though, and this fool Cestius may have done just that.

"Lord Caesar?" Aurelian turned, and sighed, seeing another messenger arrive, this one in the armor, cloak and sigils of the Eastern Empire's fleet.

"What news?" The Western prince had little hope it was good. Then he saw the messenger's face, and felt a chill steal over him. The man was haggard, worn to the bone, with badly healed wounds on his face and arm. In his eyes, Aurelian saw a reflection of horror.

"Phranes! Bring a *medikus*!" The prince took the sailor's arm and led him to a chair. The Easterner moved like a puppet, jerkily, without life or animation. Aurelian prised the message packet from his fingers. The man did not seem to notice. When one of the priests of Asclepius arrived, the sailor was carried away without complaint. Aurelian paid no mind, squatting on the ground, ignoring the surprised expressions on the faces of his staff. He took his time reading each page, cribbed in a scrawl, tightly spaced, obviously written in great haste.

When he was done, Aurelian rose, shaking out a cramp in his leg. The sun was beginning to set, a vast bloated red sphere wallowing down through the haze and murk. Already the east was drenched in deep purple and blue as night advanced. The prince gestured for his Centurion of Engineers, then waited until old Scortius had come close enough to hear a low voice.

"How many feet of water are behind the Reed Sea dam?" Aurelian turned away from the crowd of people waiting in the tent. Scortius raised a white eyebrow, but answered in a low voice. "Thirty feet, lord Caesar. As you planned and, frankly, the best we can manage in this flat country!"

"Good." Aurelian's face was tight and controlled, odd for a man usually open and expressive in all his dealings. "You must be at the dam tomorrow. Take four centuries of the best men you can find—no one is to trouble our project there, no one! Let nothing—not a bird, not a dog, *nothing*—within sight. I will signal you, when I am ready."

Scortius nodded, chilled by the venom in the prince's voice. Where was the affable commander? The big cheerful red bear, so beloved of his troops? "Aye, my lord. We will leave immediately."

Aurelian turned away, striding back to his field desk. As he did, the eyes of every man in the tent turned to follow him, poised and waiting for his command. The Western prince stared down at the diagrams and notes scattered across the wooden table. Then he began putting them away—the bottles of ink, the rulers, the stacks of designs and diagrams, the small wooden models. Scribes crept up around him and took each thing away. Busy in his own mind, and concentrating on the simple task, Aurelian barely noticed them. When the field table was clear, the prince looked up.

"Bring the priests of every temple and thaumaturgic school within a day's ride of Alexandria. I will speak with them at noon tomorrow. If a man refuses my command, which is given with the voice of the Emperor, then that man is to be slain. His second, or heir, will come instead. Do this now!"

Thin high clouds and an oppressive pressure in the air marked the following day. Aurelian rose before dawn and spent the morning standing at the edge of the tell, watching the fortifications rising below him with relentless speed. Slabs of basalt in twelve-by-eight-foot sections—looted from an abandoned temple on the outskirts of the city—were being placed along the fighting wall and driven home with padded mallets. The sight gave him no ease, for he could feel the wind turning to come out of the east. Phranes had forced him to choke down some food, but now the flat bread and boiled grain lay in his stomach like a ballast weight.

"Lord Caesar?" It was Phranes again, venturing out from the great tent. "The priests have come, as you commanded. The Legion commanders are here, too."

Aurelian did not turn around. "Has the commander of the Fleet arrived?"

"Yes, my lord, as well as the senior captain of the Eastern ships in the harbor."

The prince nodded, then turned and climbed back up to the tent. The space under the awnings was full, priests and soldiers and clerks packed shoulder to shoulder. Though the day was cloudy, the sun seemed much hotter than usual, making the air simmer. Slaves moved through the tight mass of men, filling cups and passing trays of pastry and cured meat. Only the space directly behind the field desk was open, and Aurelian passed through the press of men slowly, meeting the eyes of many, speaking softly to others.

By his command, a map of the delta, carefully inked on sheets of parchment, lay open on the table.

"I have news," he began, without preamble, looking out over the sea of faces. Everyone was sweating, even the Egyptians. "It is poor. Constantinople has fallen to Persia."

The murmur of men speaking in low voices stilled. There was only a faint creaking of ropes and canvas. Aurelian nodded, looking from face to face.

"This news came last night, by sea. The Eastern capital has been destroyed. The Persians, with their Greek and Avar allies, have overthrown its walls and slaughtered—yes, I say slaughtered—its citizens. The army of the East has been broken and can no longer be accounted upon the field of battle." Aurelian paused and bowed his head, placing his palms flat upon the table.

"The Emperor Heraclius . . . the Emperor is dead, and his brother, the great prince Theodore, has also fallen. The Eastern fleet has been scattered and only the remains of the Western Legions, supported by Khazar and Gothic auxillia, stand between the Persian army and Greater Greece."

Aurelian looked up and saw a cold, stunned silence had fallen over the gathering. Even the priests of the temples—usually a stoic and sullen lot—seemed surprised, even fearful. They were, however, listening very closely. The prince did not smile, though he was pleased to see that his harsh words had woken them to attentiveness. "There is more. The Persians have employed the foulest sorcery to—"

"Rubbish!" One of the priests made a loud snorting noise, sticking out his chin pugnaciously. "Roman lies! The mobehedan serve the lord of light, they would never—"

Aurelian made a slight motion and one of the legionaries in the crowd slammed the butt of his spear into the priest's back, knocking him to the ground, gasping for breath.

"There is no time for discussion," the prince barked at the crowd. "By the eyewitness account of soldiers and priests within the city, it is all too clear the Persians have brought a monstrous power against us. The great gates of Constantinople were toppled by something which cannot be described." He picked up the parchment and read aloud: "*A storm of darkness, writhing with obscene movement*—and within the city the soldiers were overwhelmed by hosts of the risen dead. Yes, the Persians own a necromancer among their number."

Aurelian paused, letting his words hang in the air. The priests stirred, incredulous, and began to speak, their voices rising up like a flock of gulls.

"Be quiet." The prince did not repeat himself. The priests fell silent, cowering under the stern visage of the legionaries among them. "You may read the accounts yourself, when I have finished, but I have not misled you. Know this—the Eastern Empire has fallen, its emperor dead, its army scattered, its fleet broken. Emperor Galen, Lord of the West, has placed all Eastern lands under his direct authority. You may dispute my conclusion, but I *know* the enemy will turn upon Egypt, and we will be sorely pressed to withstand him."

Aurelian turned to the east, gesturing out into the murky haze and the endless green fields. "Within the month, the Nile will begin to rise. By the end of Augustus it will be in full flood, making an impassible barrier between us and the east. That leaves the enemy only two months in which to break through our lines at Pelusium. I believe he will make that effort with every power at his disposal."

The prince turned back, a grim smile on his face. "Every power." He stabbed a thick finger at the priests. "The day has come for you to leave your temples and schools. A black tide rushes toward us and you will have to bar its passage."

"Us?" One of the priests, a spindly little acolyte of Sebek the Crocodile, squeaked in alarm. "We are not battle magi—"

"You will have to be. We need thaumaturges desperately. Too many have already been slain in Thrace or Syria. You will have to fill the gap and stand against the foulness Persia brings. Have you heard me? The Persians have cast aside every covenant and restriction—they will wake the dead of Egypt to destroy us. They have summoned the forbidden onto the earth to throw down their enemies! This has become a war of great powers, not just of men!"

Aurelian's voice rose, trying to force his point across by volume. Some of the priests were nodding, ashen-faced; others spoke agitatedly among themselves. But too many of the shaven-headed men stared at him in confusion or outright disbelief.

"Your gods," he barked, temper fraying, "demand you stand and fight! This is the oldest enemy—you may call it Set or Ahriman or Typhon—but it is the foe of all that lives! Wake up! Rouse yourselves—if we fail, if Rome fails, if *you* fail, then Egypt will be destroyed, as Constantinople was destroyed. The temples will be cast down in fire and ruin, the people enslaved, your own heads will be upon a stake, and death itself would be a welcome release from the torments you will suffer.

"Know this, priests and captains: Rome will fight to the last to hold the enemy from Egypt. Without Egyptian grain, Rome will starve. If Rome fails, then Egypt will die too. You *must* come forth with all your strength—you are learned men; many of you can wield the power of the hidden world, you own ancient secrets passed down from the Pharaohs—you must bend all your will and power to this enemy's defeat.

"Know this, too; there is no escape from this war. If Egypt falls, there will be no place to flee, for the enemy will grow ever stronger, and Rome ever weaker. In the end, if you hide, the enemy will find and consume you. You must fight, and we must win."

The prince ceased speaking, a little surprised at his own vehemence. In the night, he had spoken with the Legion thaumaturges and their words filled him with raw fear. The power unleashed upon Constantinople still echoed in the hidden world, jolting furiously outward, and where such foulness passed, men with the sight quailed. A truly horrific power—something out of ancient legend—was loose in the world, and allied with Persia—if not its master!

Aurelian did not think he could hold Egypt against such strength. In truth, if the enemy fleet controlled the sea, he was not sure he could hold Egypt against the Persian army, much less this power. More than half of his men were new recruits and the rest had never faced such a terrible enemy. *But I will not yield. I will buy time, at least, for Galen and the Empire.*

Aurelian did not dwell on his brother's situation. The Emperor had his own concerns.

"Lord Caesar." One of the priests rose—a very old man, bald, with smooth, dark brown skin and a neat yellow-white beard. He leaned upon a hawk-headed cane and the sign of Horus the Defender was worked into a clasp holding his tunic at the shoulder. "I will speak frankly. Egypt has never loved Rome, even under the 'good' Emperors. You are foreigners and conquerors. Your taxes are heavy and your demands in labor worse. There are some among us who might hope Persian rule would sit lighter upon our necks. . . ." The old priest looked

around, grinning, showing gappy white teeth. "But they are
fools. Even without this . . . dark power . . . the Persians would
ignore our traditions, trample our gods and squeeze the farmers
for every last coin. This is the way of Empires."

The grin faded and the old priest leaned even more wearily
upon his cane. "I have felt the power—the destroyer—moving
in the hidden world. It is a black sun, swallowing all light.
Many here, I am sure, have had troubled dreams of late—
strange visions, seductive promises, disturbing vistas of dead
drowned cities and lost realms. This—if you have not the wit to
ken it yourselves!—is the work of the enemy. He seeks to
frighten or seduce us."

The old priest met Aurelian's eye with his own bright gaze.
"Nephet of the house of Horus the Strong will stand by you,
Pharaoh. We are few and weak, perhaps, but we will not flinch
aside from battle, or flee. Long ago, at the beginning of days,
Lord Horus strove against such an abomination as this . . . he
won through. I pray that we can do the same, though our
strength is much diminished." The priest paused, laughter in his
eyes. "So many centuries of Roman peace have made us weak!"

The Roman prince nodded, some small hope welling in his
chest. Then he looked upon the faces of the others and saw
naked fear, or avarice, or anger . . . anything but honorable assistance. Aurelian kept his face still and unrolled a scroll his
aides had prepared. *Very well* . . .

"Each temple," he began in a carrying voice, "will be assigned to a Legion . . ."

🬀🬀🬀🬀🬀🬀🬀🬀🬀🬀🬀🬀🬀🬀🬀🬀🬀🬀🬀🬀🬀🬀🬀🬀🬀

THE RUINS OF BAIAE, BELOW VESUVIUS

)=(

A patch of grass remained, on a hillside facing away from
the mountain. Vesuvius still loomed in the eastern sky, a
vast smooth cone, but her tapering green crown was gone. Now
a jagged summit smoked and fumed, sending up a thin, con-

stant spiral of ashy smoke into a blue Campanian sky. The slopes, once lush with orchards, farms and vineyards, were black and gray, scored by massive mudslides. Snaky black trails of hardened lava spilled from the flanks of the volcano, puddling down onto the plain below.

On the grass, a young woman was digging in the rich, dark earth.

Beside her, wrapped in woolen sheets, were four small, twisted figures. The homespun was caked with ash and soot. Tiny charred, blackened feet poked from beneath the cloth. This slope—turned away from Vesuvius—had escaped the billowing clouds of burning air, the waves of poisonous vapor and fiery meteors, which rained such destruction upon the land below the mountain. Just over the crown of the hill, lined with skeletal, leafless trees, was a sprawling villa. The children had been sleeping in the great house when the volcano woke in darkness and exploded with such terrific violence ships at sea were swamped by the shock in the earth and nearly everything within a hundred miles of the mountain had been smashed down, burned and then suffocated by choking, invisible vapors. The roof of the villa had been stripped away by howling wind and the interior had burst into flame.

All four children died almost instantly.

The young woman was digging in the black soil with a spade taken from the gardener's cottage behind the villa. The grass— puzzlingly green and living amid the ruin surrounding the hill on all sides—parted under the metal edge. The woman's lithe, muscular arms were smooth and brown. A mane of black hair, shining like ink, was tied behind her head in a ponytail. A traditional Roman *stola* and gown was neatly piled beside her on the grass. For the moment, she was digging in her under-tunic, ignoring the sweat matting the thin cloth to her back.

Shirin had placed her children—these tiny bodies—in the care of a dear friend who had promised them safe haven in a dangerous world. Her shoulder muscles bunched as the spade cut into the earth, turning up grass roots and fat earthworms and tiny black beetles. Shirin had trusted her friend's judgment and sent her children to be hidden from the agents of the Emperor of the East, Heraclius, who had designs upon the mother, but no regard for her two little boys and two little girls.

The first grave was finished: deep enough to keep dogs away, long enough and wide enough for the curled-up, charred, body of a nine-year-old boy. Shirin stood up, wiping her brow, and stepped aside two paces. The edge of the spade bit into the earth again. Heraclius had promised Shirin in marriage to his brother, Theodore, as part of a greater prize—the whole of the Persian Empire. Not two days ago, in the half-burned, but still bustling port of Misenum, Shirin had learned both Heraclius and Theodore were dead, Persia restored and the Eastern Empire in ruins.

So the lord of heaven gave, and the lord of heaven took away.

Mechanically, she lifted blocks of turf away with the spade, then began to dig out the soil below. This grave did not need to be so big, only enough to hold the corpse of a six-year-old boy who loved bears and horses and a drink called cold-water-with-ice. Shirin's arms and shoulder burned with effort, but she continued to dig, her mind carefully empty. In the end, there had been no need for mother and children to be separated. The attentions of the Eastern Emperor were diverted by the revolt of the Decapolis cities, even before Shirin's children reached Rome.

They did not have to be dead. She did not have to be alone. Her dear friend did not have to be a monster.

Shirin finished the second grave. Sweat stung in half-healed wounds across her back and side. A thin golden chain slithered on her neck and the heavy egg-shaped ruby hanging between her breasts bounced each time she drove the spade into the ground.

When Vesuvius erupted, she had been on the deck of a merchantman in the great half-circle of the bay. A wave rolled up out of the deep and smashed the Pride of Cos onto the shore. Shirin leapt from the ship, taking her chances in the midnight sea. Something struck her, leaving long cuts on her back, but she was a strong swimmer and managed to reach the pebbly beach alive.

By great good luck, an offshore wind followed the great

wave, driving the choking air away from the beach. By the time Shirin had crawled out of the surf, the sea was filled with corpses. The strand was packed with stunned people, the citizens from the beachfront villas and little towns dotting the rim of the bay. Flames filled the night and the people watched in silence as their homes burned furiously. The sky billowed with huge burning clouds, streaked by plunging comets trailing sparks and fire. Shirin, bleeding, staggered south along the beach, wading at the edge of the surf, pushing her way through drifting bodies. The water thrashed with violence—great gray-bodied sharks tore at the dead, jagged white teeth sparkling in the red air. It seemed wise to flee the glowing, thundering ogre of fire filling the eastern sky.

The third and fourth graves were still smaller. Both of her girls had been little sprites with curly dark brown hair, like their father. Shirin, arms caked with ash and loam, laughed bitterly at the thought of dead Chrosoes, king of kings of Persia. He had been an Emperor too and he had been cold in the ground for more than two years. She felt nothing, thinking of him now, though she had loved him dearly in life. His passage into madness had suffocated their love. Shirin grimaced. The spade clanged against a root. Relentlessly, she hacked away, metal biting into the soft yellow wood. The blows echoed up her arm, but she was young and strong and her back had healed well.

Royal Ctesiphon seemed like a dream; a faint memory of luxury and glorious splendor. Today, under this bright sky, sweating, digging the graves of her own children, her marriage and husband were distant phantoms. Memories of her youth were brighter, as clear as a swift river or a still pool among mossy rocks. The faces of her uncles were sharp in her mind; and racing horses, or hunting ermine and fox in the deep snow, or the sight of storm-heavy clouds winging up over the black peaks of the Kaukasoi.

Shirin leaned on the spade, weary and gasping for breath. Her arms and legs were numb. A breeze drifted over the hill, carrying the acrid smell of wet ash. Months had passed since the mountain vomited fire. The stinging yellow rain had stopped, the sky washed clean of a bitter haze. Now the green shoots of grass and flower buds poked up from the gray earth. In another year, a carpet of green and yellow and orange would cover the hills. She frowned, supple lips twisting into a grimace.

Chrósoes had tried to keep her—a beautiful, singing bird in a gilded cage. He had died, hacked to death by Roman soldiers in the burning ruin of the Palace of the Swan.

Heraclius and Theodore had desired her, to seal the conquest of Persia and bind her royal blood to theirs, cutting the root of Chrosoes' dynasty. Both had perished in the wreck of their own grasp for power.

Thyatis had tried to set her away, a perfect crystalline beauty, in the prison of Thira. For safety. So that she would be unchanged, unblemished when Thyatis returned. Shirin spit to clear her mouth, bile rising in her throat.

There were four graves in the ground, and four little corpses to fit them.

Thyatis was gone, wrenched away by fate and transformed beyond recognition. Shirin's hands trembled and she clasped them firmly around the haft of the spade. The same madness, which filled Chrosoes, distilled into the shape of her lover, like wormwood settling into wine.

The day had been blindingly hot. Now night came, bringing close stifling air. Within the oval domain of the Flavian amphitheatre, Shirin was crushed into a narrow marble seat, pressed all around by sweating, anxious Romans. The entire city was in a fever, enthralled by the newest, most ferocious fighter to ever enter the arena. Every tavern and bath was filled with men and women praising the killing speed and ferocity—the art—of the Amazon Diana. Down on the white sand, lit by thousands of gleaming white spheres, it was butchery.

An axeman leapt in, hewing wildly. Thyatis skipped back, parrying and parrying again. Sparks leapt from her blade as it caught the edge of the axe. The man screamed, a high wailing sound that flew up into the air and vanished into the constant roar of the crowd. Blocking, Thyatis caught the haft of his axe on her hilts, and they grappled, faces inches from each other. The man was still screaming, tendons bulging, eyes bugged out. Thyatis let him charge, taking his full weight upon her. She twisted gracefully and he flew, slamming into the ground. She kicked the weapon away, knelt, reversing her own blade and driving a convulsive blow into his chest. Ribs cracked and splintered, blood bubbled up through his armor, and then the body stiffened and lay still.

Thyatis stood, unsteady, limbs trembling with desire. She turned towards the crowd, oiled muscles streaked with scarlet. Thyatis' expression was wild, ecstatic, transported by blood lust. Shirin shrank back in her seat, the entire world focused down on the face of her friend. The expression there was all too familiar.

"Are there more?" Thyatis' scream echoed back from the marble walls. "Are there more?"

Shirin stabbed the spade into the soil, letting it stand, then bent and dragged the first corpse to the grave. Carefully, she rewrapped each body, tucking in the wool all around. For a moment, she considered placing her knife beside her son.

You will need a hunting knife, in the green fields and forests, to skin your game and cut the fat from sizzling meat above the fire. Then Shirin remembered the blameless dead, the children taken before their time by accident or sickness, were watched over by the *elohim* and all the servants of the lord of the world. *Rejoice my son*, she thought, drawing great consolation from the thought of her children among the bright ones. *You will not wander in torment, among the uneasy dead.*

Beside her neat pile of clothing sat an urn of lime, and she sprinkled each corpse before turning the soil back over to fill the little pit.

"The lord of heaven gave you to me and the lord of heaven has taken you away," she said, softly, bending her head to her knee. "Blessed be the name of the lord of heaven."

When the graves were filled, she worked, kneeling, and fitted the cut turves back into place. There was quite a mound of soil left, so she scattered it across the grassy sward. In some future spring, flowers would bloom and saplings would rise out of the ash.

The plants would grow swiftly and well in such rich soil.

I do not think I am accursed, Shirin thought, *but my choices have been poor*.

She felt very old, standing on the hillside, looking down at the sparkling blue arc of the bay. The sky was filled with racing clouds, puffy and white, and she watched their shadows pass over the land. After a time, the sensation of emptiness grew too great and she drew on the *stola* and gown. The Roman garments were hot and binding, but she desired no undue attention, not in this place and time.

> *The rocky beach ended in cliffs, but Shirin found a narrow path and followed it up onto a headland at the end of the bay. The sky was still black with ashy cloud and a constant gray rain of soot drifted out of the heavens. The promontory held a small temple and she took shelter there, suddenly realizing she was bleeding from a dozen unnoticed cuts. Many women were already huddled under the arched dome, for the hill was sacred to Minerva. When the sun returned, after days of gloomy darkness, the priestesses came and took them all away, out of the devastation. A larger temple sheltered them, and in time, Shirin's back healed and she could move without pain.*
>
> *Then she set out for Rome, in search of her children, who were supposed to be staying with Thyatis' guardian, the Duchess Anastasia De'Orelio. She located the residence of the Duchess, and made inquiries, but found the servants close-mouthed and suspicious. A placard in the Forum had caught her eye next—a towering Amazon, redhaired, stood over crudely drawn opponents—Diana, read the legend. The Emperor promised a greater spectacle than ever beheld by Rome. Shirin stared and stared, finally succumbing to curiosity, spending her last coins.*

Shirin climbed the crest of the hill, spade over one shoulder, the urn of lime tucked under her arm. Her cloak and gown

seemed very heavy. It seemed doubtful a gardener would ever
tend the ruins, but Shirin was no thief and she returned what
she borrowed. The dead pines made a strange palisade of blackened trunks, but the path was clear. When she came down to the
low fieldstone wall marking the top of the kitchen garden, she
paused.

There were voices, people speaking in the ruins of the big
house. Shirin laid down the tool and the urn, then turned up her
hood. The thought of seeing another person, much less a sur-
vivor of this devastation, was repugnant. This was a private day,
her grief not for public display. She would have welcomed a
priest to sit by the evening fire and hear her lament. Bile rose in
her throat, almost choking her. Shirin hurried away, following
the line of the wall, and disappeared over the crest of the hill.
There was a road not far away, an easy walk on this brisk afternoon, and it led down to the shore and the ruined port.

"You're sure they were here?" Thyatis pushed aside a fallen
timber, letting it crash to the smoke-blackened tiles. Her long
limbs were filled with nervous energy and she walked heavily,
sending up puffs of ashy dust from the ruined floor. "Not away
at the seaside—not returning to Rome? Not lost, among the
crowds of refugees, nameless, without a guardian?"

The tall Roman woman looked around, rolling slightly from
foot to foot. In better days, the villa had sprawled around a big
central courtyard ornamented with fountains and a running
stream. Red tile roofs and whitewashed walls, climbing trellis
of flowers and fragrant herbs—only a shell remained, gutted,
the walls crushed in by falling stones, the tile blackened and
broken. She paced through the remains of the great entrance
hall, clouds of black ash rising and settling as she moved.

"They were here." Her companion answered in a lifeless
voice. The older woman did not enter the ruins; she remained
on the bricked entranceway, one slim hand raised to hold a veil
of gauzy silk between her eyes and the sun. "They sent me a letter—all scrawled and covered with paints and fingerprints—the
day of the eruption. The messenger was found on the Via Appia, asphyxiated, by one of my men."

Thyatis turned, red-gold hair falling short around her lean

head. Freshly healed scars shone white against tanned skin on her shoulders, arms and neck. Her face was blank, thin lips compressed into a tight line. Her fingers settled on the hilts of the sword slung on a leather strap over her shoulder. They were uneasy there, but the touch seemed to calm the tall woman. "I will look, for myself. I must be sure."

"Of course," the older woman answered, still refusing to enter the burned house. "I will wait here."

Thyatis nodded, her thoughts far away, and then moved quickly off into the ruins.

Anastasia watched, her own mind troubled. The crushing depression afflicting her after the events of the eruption had recently eased. Her efforts had turned askew on the mountaintop that dreadful night—many men and women she treasured had been killed. For a time, she had feared Thyatis—whom she had come to care for as a true daughter—lost as well. The prince Maxian, whom she had hoped to kill, survived. A disaster. At least—*at least*—it seemed the prince, whose sorcerous talents had seemed so implacable a threat, such a monstrous, unforgivable abomination, had righted his path.

The Duchess considered biting her lip, but forestalled the impulse. Her maid would take great exception if the carefully applied powders and pigments were disturbed. Instead, the Duchess contented herself with making a sharp corner out of the silk of her *stola* and rubbing the crisp edge against her thumb. Her eyes, shadowed by the veil, followed Thyatis' movements among the fallen, burned timbers and the soot-stained walls. In happier times, they would have gleamed violet, sparkling in wit or delight.

Now she had seen too much, lost too much. Despite Betia's best efforts, her eyes were smudged and dark, revealing exhaustion and despair. The Duchess looked away from the ruins, driving away fond memories—idle summer parties, long twilit dinners, the intoxicating aroma of jasmine and orange and hyacinth in the spring—and looked out across the rumpled, tormented plain towards Vesuvius.

The mountain loomed, dark and shrouded with smoke. Jagged and broken, its smooth flanks rent by the vomitus of the earth and terrible mudslides. All the land around its feet—once some of the richest in Campania—was abandoned, haunted, dangerous in poor weather. Anastasia sighed, thinking of the wealth destroyed and the Imperial resources now consumed, trying to set right the wound. Gold and men and time were desperately needed in the East, where disaster tumbled after disaster like a summer flood.

Anastasia felt old and tired. With an effort, she walked back to the horses they had ridden down from Rome and sat—ignoring the damage to the dark gray silk and linen of her *stola* and cloak—by the roadside. The gentle cream-colored mare bumped her with its big nose, and Anastasia responded by rubbing its neck. The horse was disappointed—no apples, no biscuit were forthcoming.

"Someone was here." Thyatis appeared out of the twilight, long bare legs streaked with charcoal, strapped sandals black with ash. "There are many bodies among the ruins, all burned or rotted. A young man in boots came into the little house by the garden and rooted around. They may have taken something away—but the light is failing and the signs were unclear." Thyatis squatted down, peering at the Duchess, who had her head buried in her arms.

"Are you sleeping?" Thyatis brushed the Duchess's hair with the back of her hand. "Shall I carry you back to the city?"

"No." Anastasia's voice was muffled, hidden behind her round white arms and the huge pile of curls Betia had pinned up in the morning. "I will be fine."

"Surely," Thyatis said gently, her voice soft. "Come on, stand up."

Anastasia allowed herself to rise, thin white fingers standing out in the gloom against Thyatis' darker skin. "Have you seen enough?"

Thyatis looked back at the ruin, now all but hidden in shadow. Beyond the hill rising above the villa, the sky was still bright, filled with glowing orange thunderheads set against an overarching field of sable and purple. High up, out over the sea, long thin clouds gleamed like bars of molten gold. Here, in the hill's shadow, the villa walls gleamed like phantoms in the dim light. She felt drained of the nervous energy that had driven her down from Rome in such haste. "Yes, I have seen enough."

"What will you tell her?" Anastasia removed her veil. In the twilight, she did not need to protect her pale skin. "What can you say?"

"Nothing." Thyatis' jaw clenched and she began to make a chewing motion. Then she stopped, aware of the nervous tic. Instead she captured the big stallion's traces and pressed her hand against his muscular shoulder. "I dreamed . . . I dreamed she was drowning, her face was in the sea and there were flames and lights upon the water. I think she is dead, and I hope—no, I pray to the gray-eyed goddess—they are together, with Nikos, and the others, and every man who followed me into death, in the golden fields."

Anastasia nodded, though her face was almost invisible, only a pale white shape in the gloom. "You believe in the gods, then. You think there is a life after this one. A place without care and suffering, in Elysium and the gardens of the blessed."

Thyatis snorted, swinging up onto the horse. She leaned over and helped Anastasia onto the mare. "I hope, Duchess. I hope. Do you?"

"No." Anastasia arranged her *stola* and cloak to cover her legs, then twitched the reins. The mare, amiable and hopeful, turned away from the ruins and the blackened trees and began to clop down the hard-packed road leading down the hill. "I think there is only a black void, a nothingness. But that too is free from the weight of this world."

Thyatis said nothing, and the stallion followed the mare down the road and towards the distant dim lights flickering in the ruins of Baiae.

The night deepened, yet Thyatis did not feel weary. Her exhaustion lifted as the heat of the day faded. The horses were happy to set an easy pace and the two women turned north, on the road towards Rome. The wasteland stretched away into darkness on either side. Without the lights of farmhouses, or inns, it seemed they rode on the mantle of night itself. A small paper lantern, carrying a candle inside a screen, hung from the end of a long pole in front of Thyatis' horse. In that pale, flickering light, they kept to the via. The land was quiet and still, lacking even the whisper of night owls or the chirping of crickets.

The *clop-clop-clop* of the horse's hooves seemed to carry a great distance.

A mile marker passed, a granite tooth momentarily visible on the roadside. Then another.

Thyatis stirred, uneasy. Her thoughts turned to the face of her enemy and she felt anxious. Time was slipping past, invisible grains spilling from a phantom glass. She looked over at the Duchess, who rode with her head bowed, cowl drawn over glossy curls. Thyatis wondered, suddenly, if all these deaths lay as heavy on the Duchess as in her own mind.

"My lady?" Thyatis' voice was faint, and she coughed, clearing her throat.

Anastasia raised her head and turned. In the faint candlelight, only the pale oval of her face was visible, the cloak, the horse, the road all swallowed in darkness. Her dark eyes did not catch the light and Thyatis felt a chill fall over her. Had a ghost ridden up beside her, some spirit of the dead? *Had Shirin come up, a distraught soul lost in the darkness? But the sound of the horse's hooves is real!*

Thyatis blinked, and saw a tired smile on the Duchess's face.

"I am still here," Anastasia said, softly. "My own thoughts are weary and far too familiar. What troubles you?"

"The prince." The redheaded woman's face tightened unconsciously. Her shoulders stiffened and she sat up straighter in the saddle. "I have sent my dead to the blessing fields with great sacrifice—twenty men, or more, I offered up to the hungry spirits on the arena floor. Red blood was spilt, ghostly bellies filled and their way lighted in the darkness. That sacred duty is discharged—but he still lives, in all his monstrous power, still young and hale. I must kill him, I think. But I cannot see how . . ."

Anastasia brushed a curl from her face. She seemed relieved, her mood lightened. "Do not trouble yourself with the prince. More urgent matters press us—he has sworn himself anew to the Empire, to serve his brother. We will need his strength against Persia."

Thyatis' eyebrows rose in surprise and she turned in her saddle, staring at the Duchess. "Do not trouble? He is monstrous, foul, a necromancer—the murderer of tens of thousands of citizens! We ride in devastation of *his* making! These things you declared yourself—when you set me upon him, a hound upon his fox, with strict orders to murder him by any means at hand." Thyatis stopped, unable to continue. The enormity of the prince's crimes rendered her speechless.

"I know what I did." Anastasia looked away, out into the night. "It was very foolish. I acted rashly, without consideration. Fear drove me, and you see this"—she lifted a hand—"is the result."

Thyatis reached over and took the reins of the mare. Obediently, the horse stopped, shaking its head in question. The redheaded woman leaned close, her face stricken. "Are you mad? This is the prince's doing—he was on Vesuvius for a reason—he *is* a monster." Thyatis stopped, a suddenly clear, terrible thought forcing its way into her consciousness. "No . . ."

Anastasia's eyes were still in shadow, but Thyatis felt the pressure of their gaze. "Yes, daughter. You have read the reports from the East; you have listened to the tales of those who escaped. A *thing* has risen up—something inhuman, insatiable, so far beyond the prince's blundering crimes as a man is above the worm. By the gods, child, the entire Eastern Empire has been shattered like a clay cup! The West is still weak, our numbers depleted by plague. Already, we have lost two Legions at Constantinople—"

"Oh, this is foul!" Thyatis ripped the cloak away from her shoulders, suddenly flushed with sweat. Her stallion started to buck, then danced sideways, disturbed by the violent motion. "Now the fair, pretty prince is an ally, a tool, a weapon against the Persians? What of all the Roman dead? Does all this"—her finger stabbed out into the dark—"mean nothing to you? Prince Maxian is a *murderer*—where is Roman justice now? Are you the judge of the twelve tablets?"

"You will be silent!" Anastasia's voice was sharp in the darkness. Thyatis recoiled, and the Duchess rose up in her saddle, face fully visible now, eyes flashing. "I am not a judge, but I have a duty to the Empire, as do you. Emperor Galen accepted his brother's return—in *full* knowledge of what occurred on Vesuvius—and he, and I, find no pleasure in the act. Maxian is terribly dangerous, but he is still a human being. He loves his brother, he loves Rome, and—*look at me!*—we need him desperately. He fought the dark spirit to a standstill, far from home, without any aid or support. Persia will press us—I know this—and we will need the prince and all his power."

Thyatis made to speak, but the grim look on the Duchess's face stopped her cold. "Very well." Thyatis nudged the stallion into motion again. "Very well."

Anastasia's breath escaped in a hiss and the mare began trotting to catch up. "Daughter, listen to me. You saw the wheel of fire, in the Emperor's library? The portal opened upon Constantinople?"

Thyatis nodded, though she did not look at Anastasia. The Duchess sighed, quietly. "There are things I must tell you—here, far from Rome and all its spies—there is work for you, if you will take it up."

"What kind of work?" Thyatis glanced over her shoulder, frowning. At the same time there was a tickling sensation in her stomach, a quickening pulse, the bright spark of interest. "I think I've had enough of the Emperor's business."

"This is not for the Emperor," Anastasia said quietly, her tone somber. "This is for the Archer."

"The Archer?" Thyatis was nonplussed. *Who is the Archer—oh!* "For the goddess?"

"This is Thiran business." Anastasia reined her horse in and motioned for the little light to be doused. Thyatis slid the pole back, then blew gently on the wick. The candle fluttered out, settled to a glowing stub and then died. There was no moon and the desolation was utterly dark. Only the stars glimmered down between silent, rushing clouds.

Anastasia waited, listening, until the night felt still and empty.

"The Daughters of the Archer have a sacred purpose." Her voice was soft in the gloom and Thyatis bent closer, straining to hear. "One part of our task is to ensure certain ancient secrets are not allowed to trouble the world of men. The thing you saw, the wheel of fire, is part of one of those secrets. That device, a *telecast*, is very old. Until I looked upon it for myself, I would not have believed the Emperors of Rome had come into possession of such a . . . weapon."

"A—" Thyatis felt a finger press against her lips and fell silent.

"I have learned there is—there was—a second telecast in Constantinople. The mechanism allows an adept to look upon faraway places, to see and to hear what transpires there. If two of the telecasts are conjoined, as the prince effected, a man can move swiftly, instantly, from one device to another. Of itself, this is a powerful tool. But there are more than just two of these devices."

The Duchess sighed again, and shook her head, cursing herself for letting such a critical matter escape her attention. *I knew Galen and Heraclius were carrying on secret correspondence! I should have marked its speed, and efficacy, and wormed out this secret . . . then there might have been time to do something. Before the Prince learned of the thing . . . before he stepped through the burning door!*

"I do not know how many telecasts existed before the Drowning, but there is at least one more, hidden within Thira itself. That telecast has not been used in centuries and I pray it will escape detection. But I fear . . . I fear the prince and the Emperor will see the great use and advantage in war of these devices and they will seek to find more. If they do, then they may stumble upon Thira itself."

Thyatis laughed, an humorless acid sound. "You will wield one weapon—the prince—but not another? Isn't Rome worth it? What about your duty to the Empire?"

"You are insolent." Anastasia's voice turned cold. "I am a Daughter of the Archer, first, and a servant of Rome second. At the moment, I balance a precarious burden. Listen to me and think upon my words—what is the first edict of the Order? That *no man* ever be allowed to set foot on holy Thira itself. There is a reason, and the telecast held safe there is a great part of it.

"Possession of the telecasts will neither win nor lose this war for Rome, but their use might destroy Thira and the Order. The prince, if he were aware of the Thiran device, could call upon its power and step through, leaping across the leagues in a thought's instant. He would stand inside the depths of the mountain, within a chamber where no man has ever set foot. My sworn duty—*your* sworn duty as a Daughter of the Archer—is to prevent just such an event."

"Why? What will happen?"

Anastasia felt a sinking feeling, hearing the simple curiosity in her adopted daughter's voice. "I will not say," the Duchess said. "It is enough for you to know we must contrive a way to destroy the telecast now in the Emperor's possession and prevent any other such device from ever falling into his hands."

"Of course." The Duchess ground her teeth, hearing the smirk in Thyatis' voice. "Stealing from the Emperor isn't a crime. . . ."

⊞〇[〇]〇[〇]〇[〇]〇[〇]〇[〇]〇[〇]〇[〇]〇[〇]〇[〇]〇[〇]〇[〇]〇⊞

THE PYRENEES, THE WESTERN ROMAN
PROVINCE OF NARBONENSIS

)(

Rain drummed on mossy stone, sluicing down out of a leaden sky. Clouds clung to the mountainside, slowly rolling across the crest of a narrow ridge. Among massive granite boulders, dwarf trees clung to the slope, glossy green leaves pointing downhill. A path wound among the stones, itself a tiny running stream as the sky rumbled and cracked with distant thunder.

A figure appeared out of the mist, head bent, a thin white hand gripping a tall bone-colored staff. Water beaded from a heavy woolen cowl and the woman climbed slowly, exhausted by the steep ascent from the valley floor. Mud beaded on her bare white feet, slipping away from the skin like oil separating from water. The path ended, opening out onto a narrow way surfaced with fitted stones. Fallen limbs and broken stones lay scattered across the road; grass, flowers and long-rooted shrubs grew in cracks between the slabs. No one had dared use the road up the mountain in a long time.

The sky grumbled, flashing intermittently with muted silver light. On the road, the woman made better time, striding wearily along, her will refusing to admit exhaustion, flat tendrils of sleek wine-red hair peeking out from under the hood of her robe.

The road wound around the shoulder of the mountain, rising steeply, then twisted back like a snake and ended in a looming, dark gate of scarred and blackened stone. The peak itself ended in a massive wall of granite and shale rising up into the mist. Once, a heavy gate closed the tunnel mouth, but the portal had been torn away long ago and hurled down the mountainside in anger. Without a pause, the woman strode into the passage, deftly stepping over and around blocks of fallen masonry and a scattering of ancient, rusted metal.

"Children!" The woman's tired voice whispered through the tiny yard beyond the gate passage. Slit windows stared mournfully down into the court. Blooming roses and dark green ivy climbed the walls, slowly eating away at the mortar. A ramp of steps led up onto a battlement on the left and another tunnel opened out to the right. "Attend me!"

The woman grimaced, dried rose-petal lips sliding into a frown. *Where are the wretched creatures?*

Standing in the shelter of the tunnel mouth, she flipped back her hood, revealing an elegant pale neck and colorless eyes. Despite the humidity, her hair did not tangle or run riot, but swept behind her head and over her shoulders like a bird's wing.

"If you do not come out to greet your Queen," she said, voice rising and carrying over muted thunder, "I shall come into this house and root you out, each and every one."

The soft padding of feet whispered out of the nearby tunnel. Yellow eyes flickered in the darkness, first one, then a dozen. A musky smell suffused the air and the Queen nodded, tucking the staff under one arm. "Come here, children, let me see you."

Something like a wolf, but with a longer, rangier body and larger head loped out of the tunnel and sniffed the Queen's feet. She smiled, teeth white in the dim light, and the creature whined and licked at her hands. Three more of the creatures slunk out of the tunnel, heads low, tails dragging on the cobblestones. The Queen laughed and pulled their ears and whispered to them, growling deep in her throat. At the sound—a merry greeting in their rough language—men and women crept out of the tunnel. Their hair was long and sleek, their tunics and shirts and woolen trousers simple and unadorned. They too bowed before the Queen.

"You are a ragged lot," she said, looking them over with a sharp eye. Rain continued to spatter out of the sky, but she ignored the soft mist beading on her porcelain skin as she went among her children. With care, the Queen examined their teeth, poked a long blood-red nail into their ears checking for mites, ran fine thin hands over their pelts, growled and bit at them. At last, she seemed satisfied. "Take me to my things, you rascals."

Grinning wolf grins, long red tongues lolling, the creatures coursed around her, leading the way into the depths of the old fortress. They did not howl or bay, but ravens and crows nesting in great numbers under the eaves of the castle fluttered up in a black cloud, cawing and wheeling in the dim white mist.

High above the storm, day reigned, the sun smiling down on a vast sweep of mountains buried in cloud.

The Queen stood at a window high on the side of the ruined fortress, looking out upon the surrounding peaks. The rounded granite helmets were bathed in sunshine. The storm had settled down into the lower valleys, drenching the little human farms and towns. Here, among the summits of the ancient peaks the air was pure as crystal. Below, in the courts and passages of the castle, there were intermittent sounds of banging and hammering. The Queen made a half smile. Her children needed pointed direction to complete complicated tasks.

The great ravens and crows nesting in the broken towers were far more willing to abide by her will—quartering the bright sky and spying on everything moving among the rumpled peaks and steep-sided valleys. The Queen was pleased with her refuge, a desolate, isolated land widely accounted to be worthless and hard. *Suitable . . . suitable for a long rest*, she thought.

"O Queen?" A gruff, rumbling voice intruded on her contemplation. Herrule stood at the door, massive shoulders brushing the stone frame on either side. "There is a man at the gate. He wishes to speak with you."

"Is there?" The Queen's eyes narrowed to slits, glittering like pearls. "Bring him to me."

The room was little more than a shell, with three mossy walls and a partial roof. At some distant time, a terrible fire had raged through the entire fortress, cracking the foundation stones and destroying anything supported by wood. Still the outer wall of the chamber remained and the simple arched shape of the remaining window pleased the Queen. Through its vantage, she saw the world framed and confined. She had not walked openly in the sun for a very long time—that would not have been prudent in her previous domicile—and the vast sweep of the world was dizzying.

"O Queen? Your guest, the man Shemuel." Herrule's voice rolled and rumbled and the Queen nodded, turning to look upon her visitor. The big Walach stepped out of the door and a small, round-shouldered man stepped into the room, his face rigid with tension. Graying curly hair hid under a small cap and a heavy dark wool cloak lay over his shoulders. His body showed the effort of climbing the mountain—shins caked with mud, an exhausted tremble in his hands—but his eyes were bright and aware. The Queen made a polite bow. She knew how the daywalker male felt.

"Good day, *rev*. Please, sit and take your ease. Herrule! Bring us wine, bread, something to eat." The Walach, still looming in the doorway, nodded and disappeared down the stairs.

The Queen remained standing by the broken wall, one slim hand on the windowsill.

"Why have you come to this place?" Shemuel's voice rasped—he was still breathing heavily from the climb. With an unsteady hand, he sat on a stone bench along the inner wall. "What is your business here, on this cursed mountain?"

"I seek privacy," she said, smiling faintly. Despite an almost automatic instinct to bend her will upon the man, to blind him with the glamour that was part and parcel of her as breathing was to him, the Queen restrained herself. To his eyes, she hoped to be only a thin, tired-looking woman of later middle age. "I assure you, *rev*, I will not trouble your village, your house of worship, even your shepherds in the forest meadows. My . . .

friends . . . can find what they need among the high peaks, or in the secret places where your people do not go."

The man grimaced, brushing sweat from his forehead with the back of a white hand. The Queen saw he was near complete exhaustion. His hands could not stop trembling, yet he showed no signs of losing his focus. "Last week, one of your . . . friends . . . came down into the high pasture and took four good sheep. We are a poor community! Such a loss . . ."

The Queen raised a hand and Shemuel found his tongue cloven to his mouth. His eyes widened, unable to speak. Herrule entered, shouldering through the door, and laid a wooden board, polished and carved with interlocking designs of leaves and flowers and running dogs on the end of the stone bench. There was wine and fruit and fresh bread. Steam curled away from the golden loaf. At a motion from the Queen, the Walach left again. When he was well gone, the Queen's fingers tightened into a fist and Shemuel blurted out "—cannot be borne!"

He stopped, rubbing his jaw and glared at the thin woman. The Queen laughed, delighted by the outrage in his face and the way his eyes bulged out when he was angry. She had not intended to laugh, covering her mouth with a hand. Shemuel looked away, blushing furiously, and the Queen schooled her face back to impassivity. A little irritated with herself, she dampened the slowly rising glow around her, and banished the subtle scents of rose, coriander, myrrh beginning to pervade the air. *Silly girl! How much trouble has this brought you before? Ages of strife are on your head! Leave this tired old man alone.*

"Rev Shemuel, I will make good your loss, and be assured, I will restrain my children. They *will not* bother your herds or dwellings again. Will you say the same, for your people?" She bent her attention upon him, expression intent, watching the twitch of his eyes and marking the pattern of his breath. Shemuel recoiled from her scrutiny, but mastered himself and shook his head.

"They call you a queen. What is your name? Who do I treat with?"

"A fair question." The woman brushed a fingertip along the line of her jaw, beetle-red enamel bright against pale flawless skin. "If a name will ease your mind, then you may call me Aia, which is long familiar to me." She almost laughed again, thinking of distant youth, but then her face shadowed and became grim, thinking of what had come after.

"Aia . . ." Shemuel's face also turned, and she saw he was thinking furiously, dredging old memories. Then he looked up, gaze fierce and he tried to stand. His legs betrayed him, weak and depleted by the long climb through rocks, mud and slippery pine. "That is not a name to inspire confidence in me," the *rev* gasped, "but if it *is* your name, then you are a Queen and I will treat with you as such. I have never heard *you* broke an oath, when given."

"Are you a king?" The Queen tilted her head to one side, looking upon him with bright eyes. "Do you rule, with a scepter, with laurel, holly and gold in your hair?"

"I speak for my people, lady Aia, but I am not a . . . king. We have no king, not now."

The Queen's nostrils flared slightly, intrigued, and she stepped closer. Shemuel froze, remaining quite still, and the woman—hair hanging long around her face—circled him, tasting the air.

"You are lying." Her voice was intimate and he shuddered involuntarily. The Queen stepped away to the window. She looked down, upon the white clouds and the pine-clad slopes, her arms spread wide, hands resting on the chipped, dark gray stone. "We could strike a bargain, *rev* Shemuel. My aegis could watch over your people, my children could run in the woods, watching and listening for your enemies. Would that ease your mind? Make you feel safe?"

The man laughed, though it cost him carefully husbanded breath to do so. "As safe as any baker's pie! No, Queen of Aia, we will look after our own business and let you to yours. Let us say this—the people of the valleys will say nothing of what they might see on the peaks, and those living among the clouds will say nothing of what transpires below."

One of the Queen's eyebrows inched up, an alizarin wing on a white unwrinkled forehead. "You are a scholar, *rev*, but you make me wonder—is there aught to see below, in your villages and farms? This has ever been a land for those seeking sanctuary. Do you conspire, down under the clouds? Do you plot? Do you dream glorious, violent dreams, there in your whitewashed houses?"

"No." Shemuel met her eyes. "Do you?"

The Queen shook her head and for an instant, as the moon might break through racing clouds, there was great weariness on her face. "I am done with such follies," she said.

"Very well." The *rev* stood, swaying slightly. "Then nothing moves in the ruin of old Montsegur."

The Queen took Shemuel by the arm, lifting him effortlessly. "And below, among the hidden valleys, there is no 'beloved one.' I will keep your secret, *rev*, as you keep mine."

The *rev* nodded, then walked to the door. Herrule was already waiting, a looming dark shape.

"Carry him," the Queen said. "Take him home, safe and swift."

The Walach nodded and, despite Shemuel's weak protests, swung the old man up onto his broad back. The Walach grinned, then sprang away, taking the steps two and three at a time. Shemuel was clinging tightly to the furry pelt, eyes screwed shut, when the Queen lost sight of them on the mountain path.

"So . . ." muttered the Queen. "Dare I rest?" She went to the window facing the east. By rights, she should not yearn for sleep. An ancient enemy was awake, prowling the world, growing stronger with each day. Yet, such exhaustion filled her limbs and dragged at her thoughts, she could not stomach the thought of the struggle to come. "That daywalker child will be alone. . . ."

Not too long ago, the Queen matched her power against the Lord of the Ten Serpents and only barely survived. Their test of wills had been an unwelcome revelation. Centuries had passed since the last time she bent her power to its destruction, and in that long endless time, her own strength faded, while the old enemy grew.

Is my time past? The Queen bent her head, unwilling to admit the years might tell upon her, as they did upon the daywalker children. *Is there a length to my days? I should not have matched strength against strength with that . . . thing. Not alone. But who could help me? The others are all dead or passed away. . . .*

Even the thought of battle made her weary. She longed to sleep, to rest and let the world pass on, without her watchful eye. Below the broken tower there was a crypt and a tomb, where a scented bed already lay, girded round with signs and symbols of her own devising. There, on silk and golden thread she might take her ease, far from the brilliant sun, while her children kept a vigil over her.

If darkness comes this far . . . then Rome is overthrown and the boy has failed. Will there be life, then? I might drown in night, while I sleep, and never feel the passing day. And I am so tired.

The grim thought offered release from the cares of the world. The Queen turned away from the window in the ruined wall, and descended the stairs, thin arms wrapped across her chest. Around her, the fortress groaned and creaked with ancient voices. The faint residue of ghosts lingered, shimmering with pain and a terrible death in fire. She ignored them and continued to descend, down into close, clammy darkness.

I will sleep, if only for a little time, and regain my strength.

CONSTANTINOPLE, AMONG THE RUINS

Stone ground against stone, spilling fine granite dust into the pit. A dozen men, stripped to the waist, hauled on guide ropes twisted around the huge block. Above, a wooden crane towered over the ruins, secured to old marble pillars rising towards a vanished ceiling.

"Heave!" The foreman cracked a short whip in his hand. The block trembled, swinging to and fro, casting a long shadow down into the recess of the excavation. Sections of broken floor—all sparkling tesserae and geometric patterns—jutted from a rubble of brick and roofing tile. Everything was stained and blackened by fire. Down at the bottom of the pit, men were digging, filling leather buckets with scraps of leather, dirt, moldy books, sections of splintered wood. "Heave!"

The granite block—twelve feet long and two-by-six in cross-section—rose up. High above, heavy cables squealed through pulleys greased with pig fat. Out of sight of the pit, hundreds of men strained against the cables, bare feet digging into the rubble, muscles stiff with effort. The block rose jerkily, and the foreman's face beaded with sweat, watching the stone sway back and forth. "Keep 'er steady!"

The block rose up, swaying over the lip of the pit, and more men were waiting, drawing ropes tight, easing the granite over solid ground. The foreman stared up, blood draining slowly from his face as the sharp-edged shadow drifted across him, and then the granite block was gone. It was dropped clear, shaking the earth with a dull *boom* as it crashed down into some useless part of the ruin sprawling in all directions from the huge pit.

The foreman steadied himself against a translucent sheet of green Cosian marble. The elegant stonework was badly damaged and spidered with long, milky cracks. A statue's arm emerged from the tumulus nearby, lifelike pink hand raised towards the sky. The debris pile groaned, shifting with the shock of the granite falling into an abandoned ornamental pool. Dust spurted from cracks in the rubble, then drifted hazily in the air. The foreman wiped his brow, glad the day's work had gone without injury. *So far*.

Below him in the pit, men crawled over every surface with brooms and shovels, carefully sifting through the rubble. Another crane carried a long succession of leather buckets, suspended from iron hooks, swaying, up out of the excavation. At the top of the pit, two scrawny bald men worked ceaselessly, catching the buckets, slipping them from the hooks, then dumping the contents—dirt, gravel, shell-like marble fragments, broken tile, wadded-up pages of papyrus and parchment, twisted bits of leather and metal—onto the top of a long, sloping wooden frame. The frame sat on stout legs and the bottom was covered with a mesh of closely set metal wire—in itself worth a

vast sum. Ten men shook the frame from side to side with a
rolling motion. Dirt rained out of the bottom of the mesh, and
all of the detritus of the excavation tumbled and slid down towards the end of the sieve.

At the bottom of the frame, under the watchful eye of a
dozen brawny men in full head-to-toe armor—the closely set,
overlapping enameled plates of the Persian *clibanarius*—four
women bent over a large circular bronze bowl. Fragments of
stone and glass and metal spilled into the bowl in a constant
stream, making a tinny, ringing sound. The women's hands
were busy, sorting metal from wood, leather from parchment.
Everything not metallic was pitched downslope, onto a swiftly
rising midden spilling away across the smashed, burned gardens of the Bucoleon Palace.

The metal—bronze, iron, copper—was tossed into a fluted,
elegant urn, which held a steadily accumulating collection of
metal bits and pieces. The women worked quickly, trying to
keep up with the endless stream of buckets.

One of them caught a gleam of bronze in the spillage and
snatched it up. The fragment was triangular, with a blunted tip,
and four well-polished sides. Her dead eyes registered the gear
tooth, and then her hand—spotted with patches of black hair-
like spores—flipped it unerringly into the urn. When the urn
was full, a pair of *diquans* hoisted it with a rope and, straining,
picked their way to the south, along a walkway of boards and
chipped slabs of buff-colored marble, towards an arcade of
arched pillars.

A vase of red porphyry replaced the urn, immediately chiming with the sound of falling metal.

All around the ruin, at the eastern end of the dead city, the
army of Persia was busy, swarming like ants across a giant's
tumbled larder. There were other excavations underway, sorting
through the destruction. A forest of cranes loomed over the old
palaces. Thousands labored feverishly, for their master had bid-
den them to haste, and those still living desired only to continue
breathing and seeing the blue sky.

The dead did not care, and they worked all the harder, for his
will was upon them.

*   *   *

The two *diquans* reached the edge of the ruins, where a long arcade of pale white marble was still standing atop a seawall. Blue water sparkled through the arches, slim pillars framing a view of the Asian shore of the Propontis. Many ships with triangular sails and low, sleek hulls moved on the waters, busy ferrying the loot of the Eastern capital across the strait. In the shade of the domed roofs, the *diquans* set down their burden, then tipped the urn, spilling hundreds of tiny fragments across a smooth floor.

Scraps and broken bits of bronze and copper bounced across black-and-white squares, some sliding to the foot of a heavy wooden table topped with a travertine slab. A figure stood at the head of the table, brown arms braced against the cool stone. The Persian knights did not look upon the shape—a man, muscular and bronzed by the sun, his head enclosed in a iron jackal mask—and bowed nervously to the shadows before hurrying away. Beneath the arches and domes, the air was very cold, and the bright sunlight on the water seemed dim.

The broken tooth bounced across the floor and then sprang into the air as if seized by a ghostly hand. Unerringly, the metal piece flew up, shining in the dim light, then settled onto the tabletop. The travertine was covered with concentric rings of bronze and iron, eight in all, radiating out from the smallest arc—barely the width of a woman's hand—to an outer layer, incomplete, almost four feet across. The gear slowed, drifted this way and that, then rattled to rest along the fringe of a bronze wheel, joining an even dozen of its fellows. The fragment fit perfectly.

The jackal remained still, though the air around him shimmered and trembled as a heat haze does upon the open desert. The remainder of the debris on the floor rustled, sliding across the marble tiles, then drifted up like a cloud of flies and fell, sparkling, into the sea below the palace. Waves lapped against house-sized blocks of granite and limestone, and golden lions stared down from alcoves among the pillars surmounting the seawall.

"Ah . . ." breathed a laughing voice in the shadow. "You must be patient, dear Arad, our enemy took some pains to destroy this treasure. Many days of sorting may pass, before your task is done."

The jackal-headed man did not respond, remaining still and silent at the head of the table.

In the shadows, the speaker moved, rising and gliding to the table. A handsome fine-boned face looked down upon the ruined device, thin lips quirking up in amusement. Long-fingered hands drifted over the surface of the corroded, scorched bronze, a thin gold bracelet circling one wrist. The skin was dusky, olive, but mottled and sometimes—as the figure passed slowly around the table—gleamed and rippled, as if fine translucent scales lay just under the skin. "But soon this will be complete, and you may turn your attention to other tasks."

Dahak, the Lord of the Ten Serpents, beloved servant of the King of Kings, Shahr-Baraz, smiled with genuine humor, looking down upon the broken fragments of the ancient device. "This pretty will be sent east, to the forges of Damawand and there—by my foresight—workmen wait, ready to restore it to working condition."

"And then, my lord? How will this trinket serve you?"

A second figure emerged from the shadows; a young woman, hair dark and glossy, high-cheeked face turned dark by the sun. Her eyes glittered, reflecting the blue waters. Armor clinked as she moved, gliding to the opposite edge of the table. A dark silk cloak lay over her shoulders, and a corselet of silver girded her breasts. She watched Dahak with a calm, even placid expression. "So much effort is poorly spent, for a toy."

"Something old, dear Queen, something I thought lost." Dahak answered genially, though an air of irritation suffused the line of his body. "Not a toy, but a tool. A powerful tool." The creature in the shape of a man passed his hand across the fragments and they gleamed with an inner light. The radiance filled in the missing pieces of the disks, the teeth and gears and rotating mechanisms. For a brief moment, the thing seemed whole and complete, but then the light faded away again and there was only a profusion of broken parts on the tabletop.

"This device—in my youth they were called the *duradarshan*—allows an adept to look upon that which is far away, even if hidden or concealed. Each Circle of the City held a sanctuary, and in each Temple of Sight stood an Eye, whirling and golden." The creature's voice changed subtly as it spoke, gaining a different timbre and tone, suggesting enormous age.

The young Queen watched the sorcerer with masked, clouded eyes. At times they seemed to be an electric blue, at others a soft brown. Though she stood beside the jackal, she did not acknowledge the beast-man's presence. "You may look upon your enemies, then, and spy out their intent, their plans, their dispositions . . . all in safety."

"Yes, and more may be accomplished, if this one's siblings may be found." Dahak grinned, and the air around him clouded with a faint haze. A whispering sound, the faint speech of myriad insects, filled the air. The thin hands drifted over the debris again, and the light flickered down. "I can almost feel them, though the connection is weak, very weak. But in time, this one shall be whole and the others will be revealed to me."

"Can they see you, my lord?" The Queen's chin rose, a faint challenge in her voice. "Isn't it dangerous to reveal yourself by such means?"

Dahak's eyes narrowed to slits and his nostrils flared. Again, the air trembled around him. He moved a hand. "I am shadow, slave, where I move nothing marks my passage! A ghost leaves no trace, seeing all secrets, knowing all things!"

The Queen staggered, her face twisted in pain. Soundlessly she turned, though her fingers clutched at the edge of the table, and faced the jackal. Arad turned as well, also against his will, and the dark eyeholes of his mask stared upon the Queen. Dahak laughed and clapped his hands in delight. His good humor was restored, seeing the jackal kneel, and the Queen's face crease in sorrow, thin silver tears streaking her high cheekbones.

"I am the master here, dear Zenobia. Do not make yourself tiresome."

Dahak turned to look out over the sprawled, tumbled ruin of the palaces of the Eastern Emperors, and beyond, to the ranks of red-roofed houses and the colorful red and orange and blue gleam of temples on the hills of the city. "I do not need either of you, though it warms my heart to see you, at last, reunited."

Zenobia gasped, unable to move her head. Her eyes were a

clear blue, pinched at the edges and filled with sorrow. "You'd discard useful . . . tools . . . because they took skill . . . to use? Your will is . . . our will . . . yet we have eyes to see and minds to think . . ."

Dahak's face contorted in disgust, and he hissed. "I have learned this lesson! Loyal Khadames taught me well—I have not forgotten the sacrifice of the Sixteen—but you . . ."

"I . . . what?" Zenobia managed a sickly grin, tears streaming down her cheek. "I . . . challenge you, lord of darkness? I . . . question and argue? You have need, lord, of more than servants. You *need* allies or . . ." She coughed, bright blood flecking her lips. Dahak relented, seeing the girl's body was failing between the pressure of his will and the Queen's. ". . . you would already possess the world."

Dahak spat on the floor and turned away, brow clouded with anger.

Another pair of knights approached, moving with a heavy step up the walkway, shoulders bent under the weight of the red vase. The jackal rose stiffly and resumed his position at the head of the table. The Queen gasped and fell against the tabletop, supporting herself with a white-knuckled hand.

"You should thank me," the sorcerer continued, "both of you longed to be reunited. And here you are!"

The Queen did not bother to hide her fury. But her eyes still avoided Arad.

The King of Kings sat on the steps of the Senate House, eating olives and cheese from a basket. Shahr-Baraz was a huge man, well over six feet in height, with broad, powerful soldiers and a trim waist. Despite the heat of the afternoon, he was clad in a hauberk of gilded overlapping steel plates and long, woolen leggings. Big boots, scuffed with wear, the leather turned almost black, stuck out in front of him. The olives were sharper tasting than in his homeland, far to the east, but he ate them by handfuls, spitting pits onto the paved oval forum surrounding the milestone at the heart of Constantinople.

He was watching rows of men hauling crates and boxes and trunks out of the front of the ruined Great Palace. A series of violent explosions had ripped through the huge structure, collapsing domes, setting fires in many portions of the sprawling complex. The forum had also suffered—great craters yawned in the limestone paving—exposing hidden tunnels and sewers. Despite the destruction, the Persian army was busy both in the ruins and in those buildings that had survived intact. The Emperors of the East had ruled from Constantinople for almost three hundred years—rarely stinting in ornamenting their residences with treasure. Shahr-Baraz spit out a pit, then smoothed down his long, tusk-like mustaches. He grinned, mentally counting load after load of gold and silver coin, the rugs, the tapestries, the bolts of raw silk, the jewels, the fine statues and paintings—all the loot of a vast Empire.

Six men staggered past, carrying a section of smooth-planed wood, painted with an intricate and detailed map of the land between the two rivers. The shahanshah snarled quietly at the sight—the map was loot from the old palace of the Persian kings at Ctesiphon—then laughed, a deep booming sound that startled the soldiers and slaves laboring in the huge forum. *So is dead Chrosoes revenged*, Shahr-Baraz thought, *with his enemy thrown down, cursed Heraclius dead, his capital fallen, his people in chains. . . .*

A fleet of barges and merchantmen toiled in the strait, hauling all the loot of the city across to the Asian side of the "cattle crossing." A powerful army—a loyal *Persian* army, not this Hun or Avar rabble!—stood watch over the treasure accumulating among the summer villas of Chalcedon. The King of Kings wanted to ensure the systematic and thorough sack of Constantinople was not wasted. The Romans had taken their time looting Ctesiphon, and he planned to return the favor fivefold. Footsteps echoed on the walkway behind him and the King of Kings looked up, smiling in greeting to the man that approached.

"Hullo, Khadames." The Boar held out a handful of olives. "Hungry?"

"No, my lord," the older man smiled, beard streaked white, face lined with age and care. Khadames, general of the armies of Persia, sat on the step beside his friend and ruler. "This Greek food is too rich for my taste. . . . I'm still digesting last night's feast."

Shahr-Baraz grinned and nodded, feeling remarkably content. It was a beautiful day and his enemies were scattered and in disarray. Old wrongs were avenged and he—the son of poor frontier nobility—was victorious ruler of the greatest Empire in the world. His grandfather would have approved; old Ohrmuz would not turn up his nose at so much good red gold, or so many slaves to work in the rocky fields below his drafty fort.

A long way, grandfather, a long way ... Shahr-Baraz felt great regret, thinking of all the old friends who had perished— from plague or spear or axe—in the decades since he had left home. Somewhere he possessed palaces vast enough to swallow grandfather's hall. He had never seen these palaces. They were far away and the Boar was a man who had no time for idleness.

When the mantle of King of Kings had settled upon him, Shahr-Baraz had determined he would spend his reign—be it long or short—in the field, moving, under an open sky. Let these courtiers and ministers attend him! He would not mew himself up in some stifling palace. At one time he had known the name and face of every soldier, groom and ostler in his army. Such familiarity was impossible now, with the host of the King of Kings grown vast beyond counting, and there were the Serpent's allies and pawns to consider as well. Anger welled for a moment, but Shahr-Baraz admitted, at least to himself, the massive triple walls of Constantinople would not have been easily breached, save by the sorcerer's power.

"Does *his* work leave a foul taste your mouth, as it does in mine?" Khadames asked softly, looking at his king out of the corner of his eye. "Was it worth it, to pay such a price for victory?"

"We have what we wanted," Shahr-Baraz sighed, rubbing his long face with muscular fingers. "That is what matters. We have broken the Eastern Empire and reclaimed all Chrosoes lost. . . ."

Khadames smiled faintly. "And now? What now, oh great king who bestrides the world? O modern Xerxes?"

The Boar made a face at the mocking tone in the general's voice and turned to face Khadames. "We part ways, my friend. This victory must be secured with another—we now hold the

Levantine coast from Gazzah to Antioch. Our army here in Constantinople is isolated from the rest of Great Persia by the breadth of Anatolia—provinces still nominally held by Rome—and supplied only by sea. Thanks to the strength of our Arab allies, we enjoy a fleet and the ability to move freely along the Asian coast. The Roman fleet is scattered or captured."

"But this good fortune cannot last," Khadames said, nodding in thought. "Soon they will press us again—with fresh ships from the West—and this ruin will be a trap, if we cannot leave and cannot feed ourselves!"

"Yes." Shahr-Baraz stabbed out his hands, miming the thrust of a blade. "The line of attack has changed, shifted south. To our west, Greece is still recovering from the Avar invasions, to the east, the Anatolian *themes* are little more than bickering princedoms. With this stroke, the Eastern Empire has been set at naught, but the West—ah, now—the West still has strength. Our seizure of Constantinople, of the Propontis, is a mighty blow. Roman trade and messengers cannot reach their allies in Khazaria, and we stand poised to drive—aided by our Avar friends—into Thrace and Greece. Yet the West still holds a dagger pressed hard against the Levantine coast."

Against our strong arm, he growled to himself, *all exposed, extended in the blow . . .*

"Egypt." Khadames said. "Where—if the lord Khalid's spies can be believed—there are no less than six Western Legions encamped, under the command of Prince Aurelian."

"Even so." Shahr-Baraz nodded, a clenched fist against his jaw. "Consider this, Khadames . . ." The King of Kings sketched a swift diagram of the Mare Internum in the dust on the walkway. The eastern end of the middle sea made a fat *U*-shape running left-to-right, joined by a second *U* on the upper arm. At the crown of the second *U*, he placed a fat black olive. "Here we stand, at Constantinople, looking down upon the Mare Aegeum." He placed two more of the ripe fruits—one opposite the first, at the bottom of the first *U*—"and here is Egypt, and here Antioch." He placed the third in the upper depths of the first *U*, making a triangle of the three. "All our supply must either come, swiftly, by sea from Antioch, or slowly over two great mountain ranges and the interior plains of Anatolia. Our army, in turn, may sail back to Antioch in a month, perhaps two, while marching overland will take at least six. In the same time, the Western Legions in Egypt may strike north. . . ." His blunt finger moved up the curve of the first *U*, towards Antioch, "reaching Antioch, easily, in three months."

Khadames nodded, lips pursed. "There is an Arab force at Gazzah, on the Judean coast, but I believe it numbers no more than five or six thousand horsemen."

"Lightly armored lancers and bowmen," Shahr-Baraz mused. "Against the Western Legions the Arabs could delay and harry and raid, but they will not be able to stop a concerted effort. Indeed, they would be hard-pressed to hold any of the coastal fortresses. . . ." The Boar's finger stabbed in succession along the curve of the *U*. ". . . Gazzah, Caesarea, Akko, and then there is Tyre." Shahr-Baraz grinned ruefully. ". . . which is still held by a Roman garrison."

"Our fleet?" Khadames raised a hopeful eyebrow. "It could strike behind the Roman line of advance, slowing them down?"

Shahr-Baraz shook his head, troubled. "What is our fleet? Arab and Palmyrene crews in captured and refitted ships, a few more than a hundred of them. We have some war galleys, true, taken from the Empire, but our victories at sea—I think—have come with a great helping of luck. When the Western fleet comes at us again, it will be ready for the lady Zoë's sorcery and for all manner of tricks and stratagems."

At the mention of the Palmyrene Queen's name, a shadow flickered across Khadames' face. Shahr-Baraz stopped, a questioning look on his face. "What is it?"

"Nothing, my lord. Nothing worth speaking of here, at any rate."

The Boar essayed a smile, but it did not touch his eyes. "You've marked the change, then? Some subtle difference in her voice, her gait, the way she holds her head?"

Khadames nodded slightly, though he was wary and said nothing aloud.

"Some of our allies," Shahr-Baraz said slowly, looking away, out across the oval space of the forum surrounding the blackened, shattered stump of a great marble column, "are not what we might wish, yet with them has come victory. For the moment, I am content to let these things be."

"And in future?" Khadames ventured, trading on old friendship and a lifetime spent in campaign and battle beside his king. "Will the Peacock Throne be ever shadowed by the Serpent?"

"I cannot say." Shahr-Baraz looked back, meeting Khadames' eyes with a rueful expression. "I cannot divine what will come. Can you?"

"Perhaps," Khadames growled. "I have looked upon Damawand, lord king, and you have not. That foul place—all smokes and fire and the roar of the forges—may be our future. There is a power growing at the lord Dahak's hand, something beyond the reach of kings. Do not think that he is your servant!"

Shahr-Baraz nodded, though his expression was closed, and he looked down upon his crude map and sighed softly. "Our ways will part soon, my friend. I have decided to take the bulk of the army—the *diquans*, the Huns, the Arabs—south on the fleet, to Caesarea Maritima. I have sent letters, informing the governors of Antioch and Damascus and those further east, to direct our reinforcements to meet me there. You, I leave here, to hold this flank and keep the Romans penned in Thrace and Greece. You shall have a goodly portion of our heavy horse, those Armenian lancers, the whole of the Avars. This should suffice to fend off any Roman raids."

"What about the infantry, the siege engineers?" Worry crept into Khadames' voice.

"They will accompany the treasure train east, as guards. I do not think that there is anything in Egypt needful of their attentions—at last report the Roman fortifications there were lacking—and Dahak has promised he will bring forth his own strength against anything the West can raise."

"How will I hold the city, then?" Khadames bit his thumb, measuring distances on the sketch map with his eyes. The thought of having to hold a position with more barbarians and mercenaries than Persians made his stomach turn queasy. "If the Romans press me, I may be driven back into the ruins. The Avars will be useless for that kind of work—I doubt the plainsmen would enter the city if driven with whips!—and I won't have enough men to cover the whole length of wall."

"Don't bother," Shahr-Baraz said with a decisive tone. "Within the week we'll have looted everything but the bathtubs. You'll have all those barges and the other boats we captured— you can flit across the water to safety! We don't *need* to hold this place, though it warms my heart to stand in the house of our enemies."

The older general made a face, but he knew the Boar's temper and did not press the matter. The King of Kings did not need to worry about the lading of boats and turnaround times for troops loading and unloading on the further shore. That was Khadames' business and—quite to his own disgust—he found himself unexpectedly skilled in such matters. If he must evacuate the city, then he would, and that was all that mattered.

The lines of men hauling loot continued to trudge past, loading wagons carrying the treasure of an empire down to the docks. Khadames and the Boar sat, letting the fading afternoon sun warm their bones, and dreamed quiet, simple dreams of the things they would do with such wealth, when at last they were home again.

A blustery dawn wind came up out of the north, carrying the smell of rain down from the Sea of Darkness. The massed fleet of the Arabs and Palmyrenes rode at anchor in the Military Harbor, preparing to cast off and begin the journey south as soon as full light settled on the waters. At the end of one long stone quay, a sleek-lined merchantman—a Palmyrene ship with broad sails and a high prow—was loading a great number of wooden crates and wicker hods holding amphorae in latticed, straw-stuffed containers. Torches hung in the rigging, casting a fitful light. The name of the ship had once been *Jibril*, but its new owner replaced the fluid Arabic cursive with blocky letters in an ancient script. To the learned, who might chance to decipher the spiky characters, the name now read *Asura*.

The tramp of booted feet echoed on the quay and a strong force of armored men appeared, swords bared and glittering in the lamplight. The sailors and longshoremen crept aside, for a jackal-headed man preceded the little procession and the appearance of the uncanny figure presaged the arrival of something worse from the darkness.

Behind the jackal, thirty heavy-set barbarians—long hair led in queues behind their heads, faces scored with tattoos and half-healed scars—labored under the weight of a heavy iron box, incised with thousands of signs and symbols on every surface.

Beside it, tanned fingers resting lightly on the solid metal, walked the lady Zoë, dressed not in her habitual armor, but in a clinging silk gown shimmering like a flame, raven hair swept back behind her head, jewels winking at her throat. Many of the Arab seamen looked away, startled and embarrassed by the plunging neckline of the dress. In previous times, before the dreadful and unexpected death of the lord Mohammed, the young Queen had never exposed herself in such a way. Even the Palmyrene sailors goggled, for they had never seen such a wanton display either. At least, not upon a noble lady. . . .

Many of the Sahaba—those who had been the companions, in life, of the Teacher—muttered among themselves and felt great unease. Things had changed since the great, glorious victory before the Roman city. They still reeled from the death of the kindly man, the one-who-listened, their friend and teacher, Mohammed, lord of the Quraysh. Now even Zoë—whose fierce, martial demeanor gained the loyalty of many a soldier—was changed, transformed. Those watching in the dim light drew away, ashamed and afraid. From the corner of her eye, the Queen marked their furtive movement, and found some small consolation in their guilt.

The iron box was carefully carried up, onto the ship, and then fitted with hooks from a crane. In the damp air, the box steamed and smoked with frost. The barbarians lowered it with much grunting and straining into the hold of the ship. When the sarcophagus was secured below, Zoë climbed to the rear deck of the ship and looked to the east. The sun had risen fully over the distant shore, flaring up through low-lying mist and clouds. In the pearly gray light, she saw a flash of light, blazing from a ruined window in Chalcedon.

So our master took wing with velvet night, and we stoop to carry his baggage. The Queen looked to the hold, her heart filled with disgust and bilious fear. *So do slaves serve.*

"Set sail," she commanded, voice sharp and assured. The captain—a Palmyrene—jerked at the sound, staring around in astonishment. He started to say something, but Zoë glared at him, her expression icy, and he quailed and slunk away. The jackal looked up at the Queen from the deck below, as motionless and silent as ever. The Queen ignored him, for the moment, her head canted as if listening, then called out in a clear voice: "Signal the fleet! We sail. The winds will speed us."

By midday, the fleet cut through the dark waters of the Hellespont, heading south onto the placid waters of the Mare Aegeum. White spray blew from the prow of the *Asura* and her sails bellied full with a fresh northerly wind. Behind the flagship, the wings of the fleet spread wide across the green waters. The morning clouds had thickened into stray white puffs, casting intermittent shadows on the low waves.

The Queen stood near the prow, one tanned, muscular hand on a cable, staring out over the sea. A hundred yards away, a pod of dolphins leapt among sparkling, brilliant waves, pacing the ship. Their slick gray backs flashed, catching the sun, and spumes of water leapt up as they plunged again into the azure water.

"My lady?" The jackal's voice was hollow, ringing metallically from within the mask. The woman did not turn, though her face tightened. The man made to touch her shoulder, but the stiffness in her body warned him from such familiarity.

"Go away," she said, closing her eyes, hand tightening on the cable. "Our master is far away, rushing through the rarer air, but his thought is still upon us, even now. I will not speak to you, save at his command and about his business." The Queen's voice was hoarse and barely intelligible.

The jackal raised a hand, fingers touching the enameled metal shrouding his face. Then his fist clenched. "Do I offend?"

"Go away!" The Queen hissed, half turning, the sea wind blowing tangled, thick hair around her face. "Isn't it enough, that we are his chattels? Let us not be actors on this foul stage, amusing him with our desperate thoughts. I may be a slave, but I will not please him!"

The jackal flinched back from the bitter anger in the Queen's voice, then bowed jerkily and moved away, across the smooth pine planks. The Queen leaned heavily on the cable, fixing her gaze upon the leaping dolphins, trying to ignore the so-familiar smell of the man's body. She willed her heart not to race, and after a time, it settled and she felt a calm sense of distance enter her.

As it did, her eyes clouded, and soft brown spilled in, occluding the sky blue. Yet the loss and pain on the face of the Queen did not relent, though her expression softened, seemingly younger than it had been before.

〔回〕-0-〔0〕-0-〔0〕-0-〔0〕-0-〔0〕-0-〔0〕-0-〔0〕-0-〔0〕-0-〔0〕-0-〔0〕-0-〔0〕-0-〔0〕-0-〔0〕-0-〔0〕-0-〔回〕

THE CURIA JULIA, ROMA MATER

〕〔

Maxian, youngest brother of the reigning Emperor of the West, Galen Atreus, halted at the threshold of the Senate House. A great wave of noise met him—the voices of more than a thousand senators, all packed into the hot, close confines of the ancient building—a chattering roar echoing from the vaulted ceiling like angry gulls. On either side of the prince, burly Praetorians in gleaming golden armor halted as well, spears held sideways to hold back the crowd. Maxian was sweating, the heavy formal toga chafing his neck and arms. The wool trapped heat close to his skin and he blinked, feeling his eyes sting. Despite the presence of the legionaries, he felt a knot of tension in his gut. The prince had never formally addressed the Senate before.

An elderly man, his long face pinched and sour, pushed his way through the crowd of citizens to the edge of the Praetorians. Maxian stepped forward, schooling his face to polite impassivity. His brother Galen tended a careful relationship with the Senate, while Maxian had always taken pains to avoid the actual mechanisms of Imperial rule. Everyone knew the Senate was a snake pit of awesome proportions, filled with sly and cunning men, where treachery suckled fat on corruption and vice.

"Caesar Maxian," the clerk growled, squinting in the sunlight gleaming from the marble porticoes of the Forum buildings. "You wish to address the Senate?" The man's tone of voice made it seem Maxian was nothing but a lowly petitioner, little more than a barbarian or slave. The prince's nostrils flared, but he remembered Galen's parting admonition.

Be polite, piglet. The Senate has been grumpy for a thousand years . . . putting up with a day of their airs will not harm you. They do not rule, but they do annoy!

"Yes, a matter concerning me will be discussed today." Maxian kept his voice level.

"Very well," the clerk sniffed, looking at the Praetorians. "You and your clerk may enter. Unarmed."

This was expected and the Praetorians stepped aside, opening one side of their ring of spears allowing the prince to enter the Curia itself. The long rectangular hall was illuminated by light streaming down from tall windows set just under the eaves. Colored marble and stone patterned the walls where they were not streaked with soot from lantern sconces. The center of the long room was cleared of chairs or seats; a patterned mosaic of the world, a huge map of the lands surrounding the Inner Sea, covering the floor. The map was relatively new—added in the time of Diocletian the Great. During his reign, a fire had swept the Forum, damaging or destroying many buildings.

Diocletian had rebuilt everything on a grand scale, and in the case of the Curia, the Senate hall had been expanded. In his time, the Senate had grown so large there were no longer enough seats for everyone, so the Emperor widened the hall, installed deep ranks of stepped wooden benches on either side, with a gallery rising behind them supported by marble columns. Alcoves were spaced along the gallery, holding statues of the gods, dressed in fine linens and garlanded with flowers. Only senators and select petitioners were allowed on the ground floor. Aides, ambassadors and guests contented themselves with the gallery, where they stood in a great crowd behind a screen of carved, pierced marble.

The hubbub did not die down as the prince entered—indeed he wasn't even noticed—just one more young patrician come to see about the doings of the Empire. Maxian took his time, moving slowly forward, through and around groups of men, young and old alike. He heard every kind of accent—Hispanian, Gaulish, Briton, even Greek—and all of their words, flowing around him in a muttering river, were of gold and power and land and trade. The prince became amused—no one here knew him—though they would have flocked around his brothers like bees to water in the desert.

"Lord Prince!"

Maxian turned at the sound and smiled warmly in greeting. An old friend, leaning heavily on a cane, approached and the other senators parted before him like the sea wave before the prow of a ship. Maxian extended his hands, clasping the old man's. The terse knot in his stomach began to ease. "Gregorius Magnus! It's good to see you."

"And you, my lord." Gregorius dipped his head, smiling through his neatly-trimmed white beard. "You too, Master Gaius, though we see enough of each other already, I think."

At the prince's side, his lean, gray-haired shadow bowed deeply to the senator. Gaius Julius was very simply dressed in a plain toga, unadorned with gold or silver edging or any kind of flash. With his thinning silver hair and patrician nose, he seemed no more and no less than a man of the city, one among thousands filling the Forum each day.

"Senator, time spent in your company is never wasted." Gaius Julius' voice was a rich baritone, trained and schooled in this very arena. When he spoke, men listened. Gregorius nodded amiably, waving the compliment away with a frail hand.

"Lord Prince, come and sit with me and I will speak for you to this *august* assembly." The old senator's eyes were twinkling and Maxian felt his apprehension fade away. With Gaius Julius at his side—even half-invisible—and Gregorius to speak for him, Maxian was sure the petition would go well.

Gregorius led them to the front row of the wooden seats. As they approached the end of the room, a wave passed through the crowds of talking men, and many turned to look at them. Then, at some unknown, unseen signal, the Senators began to take their seats. Gregorius sat down on a small cushion set at the end of the first row of seats, very close to the podium dominating the far end of the room.

On the podium was a simple folding stool, quite plain and very old, made of yellowed ivory. Two men stood on either side, dressed in archaic-looking garments, holding bundles of bound rods in the crook of their arms. An axe blade jutted from each bundle. The seat was currently empty. Maxian sat next to Gregorius, in a place held by one of the other senior senators. That man—an ally of Gregorius', Maxian supposed—moved aside, smiling in greeting. A shuffling went down the row as each senator on the bench was forced to move over.

Somewhere a junior senator would be forced off the benches to stand against the rear wall. Gaius Julius disappeared into the crowd—he was no senator now!—and Maxian supposed he would secure himself a good vantage. The old Roman was very good at that kind of thing. Maxian found the seat hard and uncomfortable.

"They are supposed to be that way," Gregorius whispered out of the corner of his mouth. "So some business gets done each day and we hurry home!"

The room quieted, even the chattiest of the senators at last getting the word to *shut up*, though the sound of so many men breathing and rustling in their heavy robes seemed very loud. Maxian felt nervous again, but Gregorius' heavy, solid presence beside him was a great comfort. A banging sound suddenly came from the entrance doors off to his left. Everyone turned, some craning their heads to see. Outside there was a faint roaring sound and the beating of drums.

"The princeps wishes to sit among his peers, the Senate of Rome." The clerk's voice boomed through the quiet room, echoing back from the vaulted ceiling. "Is he given leave to enter?"

"Aye!" Gregorius said, his old voice—once powerful—carrying in the still, hot air. "Let the princeps enter and sit with the Senate of Rome."

A huge chorus of "Aye!" followed, along with more rustling and shuffling. Maxian saw sour expressions on the faces of the men seated across the walkway from him, but in all everyone seemed to welcome the presence of the Emperor. The center of the room was now clear and after a moment, the swift rapping of a man in boots echoed around them and then the Emperor of the West appeared, striding purposefully along the length of the chamber.

Galen Atreus was a thin, nervous-looking man with a cap of

dark hair hanging down over a high forehead. The Emperor
looked very businesslike, smiling tightly to his enemies in the
seats, nodding to his friends. Today he was wearing a dark
cloak and toga, with deep maroon edging. A gold clasp held his
cloak at the shoulder and his laced boots were red. This was a
new part of the Imperial regalia, added in the past month, as the
Emperor of the West had declared himself the Avtokrator of the
East. Maxian frowned slightly, seeing the pinched, tired look
on his brother's face.

Too many disasters and too little time to react to them, Maxian thought mournfully.

Galen reached the podium and turned, seating himself on the
lone chair. He looked out over the huge crowd of senators and
nodded, as if to himself. "Senators. I thank you for allowing me
to sit among you, in such a noble company. I will not waste
your time in idle chatter. . . ."

So don't waste mine, Maxian continued the thought with
amusement. His brother was notoriously brisk.

". . . are there matters in which the princeps may advise the
Senate?"

For a moment there was silence, with Galen sitting at ease in
the chair, and the senators eyeing each other with interest. Then
Gregorius stood, knuckles whitening on the cane, and cleared
his throat. Everyone looked at him and the Emperor raised his
chin in acknowledgement.

"Princeps," Gregorius said, bowing, "you honor us with your
presence. A matter has arisen, a petition to fill an ancient and
noble post, long left vacant. This is not a trivial matter and I
think the Senate should consider the situation carefully. Your
wisdom and guidance in this matter, my lord, would be of great
use. . . ." Gregorius turned, ancient eyes sharp, and the cane
made a sharp rapping sound on the mosaic floor. "Fellow senators, you have all heard of the disasters in the East. You have all
heard rumors and wild tales from the refugees who daily enter
the city or crowd the southern ports, fleeing the advance of the
Persian armies. You have all heard a great evil has risen among
the Medes, and this foe bends its dark will against Rome."

Gregorius' statement was met with scattered laughter and a
general murmuring. Maxian felt a chill, realizing many of the

senators did not believe the stories. The prince made to rise, intending to deal sharply with these fools, but the older men on either side of him caught his elbows and held him firmly in the seat. Gregorius did not notice and continued to speak.

"There are poor omens all around us—some say the eruption of Vesuvius heralds a time in which the gods will turn their faces from Rome. Calamities and signs trouble both the heavens and the earth. You are all learned men, you have heard, as I have, of these unmistakable portents: an ape entered the very temple of Ceres in the midst of ceremony and caused great confusion; an owl—in broad day—flew into first the temple of Concord and then the Capitolium, evading all efforts at capture and restraint. The blessed chariot of Jupiter that once graced the Circus Maximus with its golden splendor, has recently been destroyed amid the troubles and riots. Coupled with these distressing signs, a flaming torch has creased the eastern heavens, hanging over Greece like a fiery brand. Even in the south, where Mount Aetna smokes and fumes, the earth has been restless, crying out with the voices of the uneasy dead."

As Gregorius spoke, he moved across the surface of the map, indicating each place in turn.

"Our Legions have been defeated before Constantinople, tens of thousands of our citizens have perished in ash and fire, entire cities in Campania are tenanted only by corpses! Men have reported to me, swearing by the twelve tablets and by the great gods themselves, that a two-headed serpent of *no less* than eighty feet in length has lately appeared in Etruria and caused great harm, ere lightning struck it down. The serpent's husk now journeys to Rome, so all may look upon the omen for themselves.

"Now, Egypt is threatened by our enemy and with it the corn supply for Rome. Yes! I see your doubting faces—I speak truly, my friends—we are faced with a powerful enemy and one wielding inhuman powers."

There was another murmuring and many of the senators looked at each other in disbelief. A few scattered shouts of "lies!" and "impossible" were heard.

"This the truth!" Gregorius barked sharply, widening the eyes of many senators. They had not seen him so animated or so grim in years. "Rome has slept for a long time, ignorant of the malefic power Persia has harnessed. The nature of our enemy, my friends, has *changed* and not for the better. For a very long time, the Persian mobehedan served a power they call Ahura-Madza, a deity of light! I assure you they no longer turn their faces to the sun in worship. No, our great victories two years past have made them desperate."

Gregorius paused, catching his breath. A disbelieving murmur rose in the quiet, then fell away again as the old senator glared at his fellows. It was clear to Maxian many of the older men were beginning to wonder what the point of all this was. The younger senators simply did not believe the warning. *Why should they?* Maxian realized. *They've not seen these things for themselves.*

Gregorius began to pace along the length of the hall, glaring at individual senators as he moved. Few men met his gaze and none could hold it.

"We have all heard rumors—as children or as adults—of demonic powers who oppose the great gods, Jupiter and Minerva and Juno. Over the centuries our philosophers have claimed these gods *do not exist*, that they are the superstitions of a credulous, ignorant people. Some men point to the abilities of wizards and sorcerers and say; 'there are your gods of old, the men who first wielded such power.' We have been blind, my friends."

The walking cane rapped sharply, punctuating his words. The senators did not stir, bending all their attention upon the old man.

"There are dark powers, things that should remain nameless, deities desiring only destruction and the enslavement of all human life. I do not know if the great gods exist, or if they will help us, but I *do* know we are locked in a struggle to the death with the servants of darkness. Rome has never—I say never—faced a more terrible enemy, even in the war against the Egyptian Queen."

Gregorius turned to the Emperor, face filled with foreboding. "Augustus Galen, you are the protector of the state and the Senate and the people. Above all, you are the bulwark of civilization, both against the barbarian tribes and against impious darkness. We are embattled, matching our mortal strength against this supernal power—I beg you, in the name of the people, to raise a shield, an aegis, against these enemies."

Galen stirred, sharp eyes flickering across the crowd. "What more would you have me do, Senator? The Legions and the Thaumaturges are already upon the field of battle, striving to turn back the Persian tide. There are no more men to call up, no more armies to raise. . . ."

"There is an Imperial post, princeps, which has never been filled. I beg you to fill it now."

Maxian was surprised—he knew full well what Gregorius had in mind—yet now he felt his throat constrict. A complete silence fell upon the assembly, and many of the senators tensed, staring at Gregorius as if the old man had become a monster himself. Maxian's eyes drifted over them and he saw calculation and ambition alike shining in their faces. For a moment, he felt sick, filled with revulsion at their reaction.

Where is your love for Rome, the wise city who nurtured you? he cried to himself, heartsick. *You see only opportunity and a chance for greater wealth, power, fame . . . Is this the Rome of my fathers?*

"It is," a cultured voice said in his ear. Maxian started, but he did not turn. Instead he berated himself for speaking aloud, or wearing his thought so openly on his face. "These are only men, not gods," whispered the voice.

"What is this post?" Galen leaned forward, intent upon Gregorius, and Maxian swallowed a laugh. Both the old senator and the Emperor had gone over their little speeches to the Senate in past days, yet now, in this electric atmosphere, it seemed each word was new, wrung from circumstance for the first time. "How may a single man aid us in this desperate strait?"

"Princeps, in the first days of the principate, the Divine Augustus in his wisdom established the sacred and honorable post of *custos magus imperium*, intending for the greatest of the Thaumaturges to not only defend Rome on the battlefield, but to serve as a protection for the Empire as a whole. The *magus* was to defend the Empire from those threats that come unseen, as the Legions defend the frontier, and the Emperor oversees all, guiding the people as a wise father. My lord, I beg you to fill this post now, for we have great need of such a man, and such a bulwark against the sorcery of the Persians."

In the silence that followed, eager voices began to rise, but Galen raised a hand sharply and everyone subsided. The Emperor remained sitting in the chair, seemingly deep in thought. The moment stretched and Maxian began to fidget, but again the men on either side of him held him in place. Finally, Galen raised his head and looked upon the Senate with a grim expression.

"I am loath to fill such a post," he said, frowning, "for Rome has never placed its faith in wizards or anything but our strong arm, iron will and the blessing of the gods. In this way Rome brought civilization to many benighted countries and raised up a great Empire. The men and women of Rome have always placed their faith in things that can be seen and done by eye and hand." Galen stood up, his face severe, and stepped down onto the open floor.

Maxian suddenly felt a foreboding chill, fearing Galen had decided against the plan without informing his brother or Gregorius or anyone. *But we must take this step!*

"Fellow senators," Galen's voice was low, but it carried to every ear. "If a wizard is raised to the *magus imperium* then we will have changed Rome forever. We will turn down a path traveled by the nations of the east—where long ago god-kings and sorcerers ruled over men. This is dangerous, for who can say what a man will do, if given such power?"

Galen turned, seemingly staring right at Maxian. The prince stiffened, but the Emperor's eyes traveled over him without stopping. "This is a desperate measure, but the esteemed Gregorius has spoken truthfully. We are overmatched in the east. Our Thaumaturges cannot stand against the dark powers the Persians have unleashed. We must consider new weapons if we are to defeat them. I fear Rome has slept too long, ignorant of these matters, relying on our Thaumaturges, yet not giving them rein enough to develop the strength we are now desperate for."

"Understand!" Galen reached the far end of the hall, by the entry doors, and his voice boomed loud from the ceiling as he turned to face the distant chair. "We must find a man, a wizard of great strength. We must give him *more power* if he is to repel this foe. Many old traditions will be overturned and our Thaumaturgic Legion will be vastly changed. We cannot know where this path will lead, but . . ." The Emperor paused and Maxian perceived enormous weariness in the line of his body, in his face, in the tenor of his voice. A great rush of fear threatened the prince and again he nearly leapt up to run to his brother, who suddenly seemed so old. Galen shook his head, throwing off the fatigue with a visible effort and stood up straight. ". . . we must do something. This path, perhaps, offers a hope of victory."

"Is there such a man?" A voice called out from the crowd of senators, though Maxian could not see who spoke.

"If there is," Galen responded, drawing the cloak over his chest. "I will not name him. This is a critical matter, and one that I lay at your feet, Senators." The Emperor looked around again, then walked slowly to the outer doors of the hall. "I will abide by your wishes in this matter. I pray you choose wisely."

Galen stepped up into the threshold of the bronze doors and they opened, flooding the chamber with brilliant sunlight. A solid rank of Praetorians closed around the Emperor and then he was gone, swallowed by the noon sun. The doors swung closed again with a dull *boom*.

Everyone began to speak at once, in a rush of excited noise and shouting and general clamor. Maxian remained sitting, realizing he was sweating, and found Gregorius sitting beside him once again, smiling quietly, his bushy white beard spilling over both hands clasped on the head of his cane.

"Rest your feet, young prince," the old senator said, "this will take some time."

Gaius Julius stepped away from the marble screen, quite pleased with himself. Part of him wished he had delivered the little speeches, but his conscious mind—which learned at least one lesson in his abruptly interrupted life—was content to remain unknown and unremarked. The gallery was crowded with all manner of citizens, though slightly oily-looking men with particularly sharp togas and tunics predominated. There were large numbers of provincial and city representatives—a dizzying array of Nubians and Goths and Gauls and even some

Britons—milling about in traditional costume. It all made a colorful scene, but Gaius was not interested in rural politics, not today. With the ease of long practice, he weaved through the crowd and found a man selling wine. The old Roman pressed a few copper coins into the peddler's hand and took a cup. With the chipped clay in his hand, he wandered slowly the length of the gallery, idly watching the discussion on the floor of the Curia.

After a moment he stopped and stepped sideways behind a cluster of Axumite merchants. Their tall feather headdresses made suitable cover and he took another drink from the cup, eyes narrowed over the rim. A woman he recognized entered the gallery and he felt a certain trepidation in being seen by her. They had never exchanged more than a few words; in his guise of a hardworking patrician bureaucrat there was little reason for him to engage in lengthy discourse with an Empress. Helena might not recognize him, but approaching her now was reckless.

Unfortunately, he found her particularly attractive. He knew from palace gossip she was strong-willed, sharp-minded and carried on a voluminous correspondence. Once or twice, he managed to overhear her conversations and she wielded a dagger wit with aplomb. Gaius Julius checked the drape of his toga, then mentally ground down on his ambition.

This is not the time for seduction! He wanted her though, and vivid imagination yielded up delightful, tempting vignettes. He started to step forward, desire convincing his limbs it would be perfectly reasonable for him to go up and speak with her, breathe in the air around her, look into sparkling dark eyes, bandy wit and wordplay with her. Gaius Julius caught himself and turned away, forcing himself to look down onto the Senate floor again.

The senators had gotten themselves into a furious argument. From the raised voices reaching the gallery, Gaius saw the awareness of the possible patronage and graft attendant upon an important new Imperial post was spreading through the white-haired old men like blood on the sea. Gaius suppressed a grin, unconsciously flicking his robes into an even straighter line and checking his hair. The smell of fear and power in the air was heady and he felt his pulse quicken.

Stop this. You're getting jittery. Gaius paused by one of the pillars and took a moment to calm down. He craved this—the lunge and parry and brutal verbal combat of the Curia and the Senate. He wanted to step down on the floor—as was his *right!*—and set his mind to the influence and control of others. There was a physical pain in his gut, like a rat was squirming among his organs. Against this desire, thoughts of Helena disappeared. *Impossible, you old fool! You must be patient. Quiet. Like a mouse.*

Gaius breathed out, slowly, and looked around, avoiding the flushed, sweaty faces of the men talking and exclaiming on all sides. He was not sure he approved of the renovations to the Curia—he had taken pains, in his breathing days, to see the building was just small enough. This gallery was new and there were more seats than he remembered below. Gaius frowned, counting rows of benches. There must be room for almost fifteen hundred senators. That, he thought, was too many. Even in his day—so long ago now!—he had ordered the architects and builders to make the Senate house just a little smaller than it needed to be.

The old Roman grinned, forgetting his own advice to remain impassive. With a constant shortage of seats, the junior senators stood in the back of the hall, or even outside. That kept them helpfully out of the debate, and gave them incentive to compromise so they could move inside. Now this expansion had made a muddle of everything, and this too-convenient gallery allowed anyone to watch the Senate at work. *How . . . republican . . .*

"Master Gaius?"

The old Roman turned, smiling genially. Three men approached him out of the crowd and the middle one—a stocky, balding white-haired "twenty-year man," if ever Gaius Julius had seen a Legion veteran trying to be inconspicuous in civilian clothes—was also carrying a *krater* of wine. The man's pockmarked face seemed habitually grim and his attention was in constant motion, watching the crowd for enemies. Gaius guessed the man was forty or fifty years old.

"I am Gaius Julius. Welcome to Rome. You must be Sergius."

The soldier nodded, flashing a bit of a wintry smile. "You're welcome sir. It was good to hear from you."

Gaius nodded, turning his attention to the other two men. Both of them were young and alert, with the air of those used to violent action. "This would be Nicholas and Vladimir?"

Sergius nodded, motioning the other two forward. "They are. A pair of right rascals, but I was never gladder than to find them alive after our disaster." The old soldier shook his head in dismay.

Gaius clasped wrists with the thinner one, a whipcord-lean man with dark brown hair and peculiar mauve eyes. The lad had powerful wrists, well-used and corded with muscle. Like his companion, he was wearing a nondescript military cloak over a tunic and some kind of armored shirt. The hilts of a heavy, *spatha*-style longsword rode at his trim waist. Nicholas grinned, matching Gaius' gaze, and made a little bow. The young man's mustaches were very sharp, twisted to points beside a thin nose. Gaius nodded in welcome. "Nicholas. Where are you from?"

"I don't know, sir. I was raised a slave in the Dannmark."

"But you are surely a Latin—taken in a raid by the Scandians?"

The young man shrugged. "I don't remember any of that, Master Gaius. My first memory is of a gray sky, and ravens crying, and then entering the fortress of Roskilde." His expression changed, growing feral. "Everything after that is rather cruel. At least, until I entered the service of Rome."

Sergius nodded, seemingly pleased with himself. "True enough, Master Gaius, and we've had good service of young Nicholas. He and Vladimir have gone into and come out of some tight places in the name of the Empire."

"So I have heard." Gaius maintained a lengthy correspondence with Sergius. The old centurion was a field officer for the Eastern Empire's Office of Barbarians. Over the years, Sergius had decided a close relationship was needed between—specifically—himself and the Western Office. Some small-minded men might have termed the stoutly built centurion a traitor, but Gaius thought of him as a man who could tell which side the loaf was going to fall on.

Before Gaius Julius involved himself in such matters, a woman—a beautiful, powerful woman named Anastasia De'Orelio—had been the secret master of the Western Office. Over a year ago, however, she abandoned her post and Gaius Julius—at something of loose ends at the time—took the opportunity to gather up some of the responsibilities she let fall. In fact, the small-minded might also accuse Gaius of theft and outright falsehood. Some privy letters, he allowed, might have gone astray, but if they did—well, the world was filled with troubles—and one of those letters led him to Sergius and then, in the full course of time, to these two admirable young men.

"You are Vladimir, then, the Walach." The corners of Gaius Julius' eyes crinkled up and he clasped wrists with the young barbarian. The Walach—a riot of dark curly hair, a creamy white complexion over rippling muscle, brilliant dark eyes—took his hand tentatively and Gaius could see the boy's nostrils flare. "We are all friends here, Vladimir, do not worry."

Ah, but I must smell strange to him, Gaius thought. *I should not have met them here, in this public place . . . in private, I might allay their fears with honest words.*

"Master . . . Gaius." Vladimir looked down, unwilling to meet Gaius' direct gaze. "Thank you for your patronage and support."

"My assistance," Gaius said, "is only what you deserve, for such loyal service."

All three men nodded and Gaius saw honest appreciation in their faces. With the collapse of the Eastern Empire, a huge flood of refugees hurried west. Rome was crowded with out-of-work ministers, logothetes, clerks and their families. The soldiers were immediately incorporated into the Western Legions, but everyone else was having a difficult time just finding food to eat and a place to sleep. As it happened, Gaius Julius had recently invested in blocks of apartments, warehouses, taverns, smithies, brick factories and all manner of other businesses. He could easily find lodgings for a few dozen Easterners at loose ends. Better, he had plenty of work for men like these three.

Gaius clapped a hand on Sergius' shoulder and looked down into the main hall of the Curia. "As it happens, my friends, I have great need for men who are swift and alert. Do you see that young man—the dark-haired fellow in the first row—sitting by the graybeard?"

Both Nicholas and Vladimir peered down through the screen.

"Yes," Nicholas said, squinting between the marble legs of a titan wrestling a giant serpent. "Thin-faced, long hair tied back, looks like he hasn't sleep in a week?"

"The very fellow." Gaius said. "His name is Maxian Atreus, the youngest brother of the Emperor Galen. He is a . . . powerful . . . young man, but not in the way most people think. He is also my patron, even my friend." Gaius Julius stopped, thinking about what he had just said. *Is that true? Sometimes it seems that the boy is barely aware of me, as if I were a chair or a table. Does it matter? I am alive!*

"As you might imagine, he has enemies." Gaius chuckled suddenly. "Some of them are very beautiful. He needs bodyguards and I think the two of you will do well in such a post."

"Bodyguards?" Vladimir's nose wrinkled up and he ran long sharp nails through his beard. The Walach seemed displeased by the prospect. "Don't the Praetorians handle such things? As the Faithful Guard did in the East? This sounds like a lot of standing around inside . . ."

"Sometimes." Gaius spread his hands, indicating things were *different* in the West. "I will surely sleep sounder at night if I know he has guardian spirits to watch over him. He has been attacked at least once before, and came close to death. Things would turn poorly for everyone if he were to die now."

Nicholas looked intrigued, thumbs hooked in his belt. "What kind of *beautiful* enemies does he have?"

Down on the floor of the Curia, Gregorius rose and spoke to the crowd. The other senators took the cue to sit and listen. Gaius Julius felt the pang of regret again—why couldn't he be the one to speak? The one to stand at the center of all attention, the world turning on the lever of his actions? He stifled the feeling, contenting himself with being the playwright, not the pantomime.

"Watch," Gaius Julius said, his expression changing subtly. All life seemed to leach out of him. "You will see more than you desire. Not all our enemies are fair to look upon."

* * *

Maxian felt his gut twist at the realization he would have to stand and speak. He didn't expect to be so nervous, but this was the *Senate!* The faces in the hall blurred into a mass of indistinguishable white ovals. *Why can't Galen do this? He's the Emperor. . . .*

Suddenly a memory swam up out of the past and into waking thought. He was in the great teaching hall of the Asclepion, below the hill of old Pergamum, and a stocky, brown-bearded priest was speaking. Tarsus—his old friend, his teacher—was explaining a simple process all his students were to learn, a mnemonic pattern to induce a settled, focused mind. Maxian felt calm flow over him, just remembering the voice like a soft murmur in his ears. The words and the mental pattern became clear in his thoughts and the prince felt his anxiety fall away.

"Fellow senators," Gregorius said, looking about with a stiff, grim expression. "We must agree, and swiftly, to give a man the power of the *custos magus imperium*. This man must be a powerful wizard and we, the Senate, as guardians of the people, must trust him to defend Rome." The old man's voice rose sharply and some of the younger men in the back rows, who had been falling asleep in the heat, jerked awake in surprise.

"In a simpler time, we would summon the magister magorum of the Thaumaturgic Legion before us and anoint him with this post. But these times are *not* simple. I have already spoken with old Gordius and he has declined this duty. A new man must be elevated to the custos."

Gregorius paused, leaning on his cane, drawing a breath. He was tiring rapidly with the effort of trying to convince so many, all at once. "Is there a man we can trust with this task? A man strong enough in the hidden arts to pit himself—with hope of victory!—against the darkness Persia has summoned up?"

One of the older senators stood up abruptly, disgusted. "Get on with it, Gregorius! We've listened and listened, while you wend and weave—get to the point! If you've a candidate, set him before us!"

Gregorius smiled genially and waved for the senator to sit down. "There is something you must see first, my friends." The old man turned, his white beard bristling out. He made a sharp motion to the Praetorians loitering at the back of the hall. "Close the doors! Clear the gallery! What now transpires is for the Senate alone."

There was a commotion in the vestibule where a huge crowd of clerks and aides lolled about, eating sausage rolls heavy with garlic and oil, chatting in low tones while the senators declaimed in the main hall. The Praetorians herded everyone out with the butts of their spears and the main doors were closed with a dull thud. More soldiers cleared the gallery; the complaints and cries of protest were muted by the marble screen. When, at last, silence had fallen and the centurion in charge of the guard detail signed to Gregorius everyone had been herded out, the old senator turned to Maxian.

"Fellow senators, I have brought a young man before you. He has seen our true enemy and he has, by his own skill and power, lived to bring us warning. This—for those of you who have not gotten out of your wine cups enough to know—is the Caesar Maxian Atreus. My lord, would you tell us what you faced in the ruins of Constantinople?"

Maxian stood up and the unsteady roiling sensation in his stomach was gone. He felt rather light-headed and perfectly calm. At the edge of his vision was a storm of color, like blowing snowflakes in every imaginable hue and shade. With an effort, he focused on the physical reality around him, allowing the faces of the senators to become solid again.

"I will do better than tell, good Gregorius, I will show you." The prince raised his hand and at the center of the hall a mote of light sprang up over the mosaic plains and mountains of Anatolia. For a moment the little ball spun and hissed, lighting the dark corners of the Curia and throwing long shadows behind the senators. A mutter of fear and surprise rose from the assembly.

"I entered Constantinople, Senators, even as the great gates fell, broken by a power far beyond anything I have ever felt before. Something rose up out of the earth, under a baleful sky, and tore down the gates and sundered the walls. I raced across the city, hoping to forestall the doom rushing over the Rebel's city, but I was too late."

The glow swelled and then passed away, leaving the hall

dark. Even the light of the late afternoon sun, which should have fallen in long, slanting beams through the high windows, was absent. Only a faint spark remained, drifting over the map on the floor, illuminating—by turns—mermaids and ships and cities and mountains. The slow movement ceased, spinning slowly over the coast of Morea, and then the light unfolded, growing huge, and in its depths; fire and smoke and the distant, muted screams of the dying and the dead.

"I came into the forum of Constantine, from which the Easterners count the miles, and there, clad in night, I saw . . ."

. . . a deserted street under a black and starless sky.

Maxian steeled himself, his face settling into a tight mask as visions of defeat welled up in the light and his shadow image struggled in the broken city against an unimaginable enemy.

". . . this was how I left Constantinople, in ruins, a broken wasteland." Maxian dropped his hand and the phantasm passed, light streaming in once more from the windows. A thousand throats gasped for air, for every man had been holding his breath in horror, and a complete, stunned silence filled the hall.

Maxian sat down, sweating again, his pulse racing. Even the simulacrum of his battle against the Persian was far too real. Again, he summoned up the calming meditation and settled his mind. When he was aware again, Gregorius was standing in the open space, leaning on his cane, watching the assembly slowly regain its color. A few servants were moving along the benches with wine. Not a single senator refused the offered cup, or failed to drain the thick, unwatered contents.

"That is our enemy," Gregorius said at last, when he judged his words would be understood. "This young man, our own prince Maxian, is the only wizard within the reunited Empire strong enough to confront him. I say we invest Caesar Maxian with the powers and duties of the custos magus imperium, so he might be our shield against this Persian monster."

There was no immediate response and many of the senators stared at Maxian with new interest and naked calculation. The prince sat up straight, meeting their gaze. Gregorius was silent as well, waiting. He seemed content to wait forever, frail old body leaning on the cane, eyes in shadow, neatly trimmed beard covering his hands. Maxian forced himself to sit patiently.

"Can we defeat this enemy?" The senator who had spoken before rose to his feet. He seemed haggard, drained, but his eyes were sharp with an indomitable will. "The prince failed to destroy it in the vision. . . ."

"I was unprepared, Senator." Maxian stood and—again—all fear and concern faded away. "Before that instant, I had never seen our great foe, or felt his power. I was lucky to escape alive. But their advantage is lost. When next we meet, I will be ready."

"Will you?" The senator's tone was pure curiosity, but he waved the question away even as it crossed his lips. "Senator Gregorius, in truth, do we have any other choice? Ours is not a nation of sorcerers, we are not the Chaldees of old, or even Egypt in its time of power. Is this young man our best chance of victory?"

"He is, Livius," Gregorius said, nodding, though his hand was trembling and he barely squeaked out the words. Maxian moved to catch his elbow, but the old man steadied himself.

"Then," Livius said, spreading his hands in acceptance, "we must seize this reed, though it seems terribly frail . . . shall there be a vote?"

A rumbling chorus of "aye" answered him.

Maxian helped Gregorius sit down, filled with great relief, though a sense of inevitability seemed to surround the event. The old senator was trembling. The prince thought of his work in the hidden world, and of the grim king on the throne of stone, and an unassailable feeling of *rightness* came over him. *This is what is supposed to be*.

The rear doors of the Curia opened, grinding loudly on ancient hinges, and a flood of haggard-looking senators poured out, clogging the steps down into the old Forum. Gaius Julius, with Nicholas and Vladimir in tow, waited patiently while the patricians streamed past. The old Roman was openly smirking, enjoying the deflated, defeated looks on the faces of the "powerful."

"They've seen something today," he muttered, "they won't soon forget."

Neither Nicholas nor Vladimir said anything. In Gaius' company, they had remained in the gallery and seen the prince's little show. Both men were rather pale themselves, with a pinched look around the eyes and mouth, but Gaius Julius was impressed with their reaction. Unlike many of the senators, they had not cried out or been reduced to weeping. A party of slaves with litters ran up the steps and entered the Senate hall.

"Follow me." Gaius Julius stepped in, nodding to the Praetorians standing back from the door. The guardsmen nodded in recognition—Gaius had recently struck up a profitable friendship with the two prefects of the Praetorian Cohort over the matter of some vineyards in the south whose owners had died in the eruption of Vesuvius—and let the three men pass. Inside, there was a peculiar chill in the air and the hall still seemed quite dark, though the high windows remained open.

Prince Maxian knelt at the end of the benches on the right-hand side of the hall, his young face filled with dismay. Lying on the bench, hands clasped on his chest, was Gregorius. Gaius Julius hurried forward, sandals slapping on the mosaic, and felt a growing dread.

"What happened, my lord?" Gaius bent down, eyes searching the old man's face. Gregorius met his searching gaze with a faint, weak smile. The old senator's color was very poor, and Gaius was disturbed to see the blue veins showing so clearly through the skin. "You are not well."

"I am not," Gregorius whispered. "I was . . . unprepared for such terrible sights and sounds. Ah!" The senator's hands trembled with a palsy, and he jerked forward. Gaius, speechless, pressed him gently back onto the bench. Nicholas, standing close, handed the old Roman his cloak, folded into a pillow. Gaius nodded in thanks, tucking the pad under Gregorius' head.

"Sir, I can help you!" Maxian's voice was a harsh whisper, and Gaius—looking sidelong at his master—saw fear and dismay and guilt war in the prince's face. "Let me exert my power upon you. I can restore your heart, your lungs . . . all the vital humors."

Gregorius shook his head slowly. His left hand fluttered like a bird and Maxian grasped the cold fingers. The prince was as pale as death himself. The senator tried to smile, but stiffened with pain instead.

"Lord prince," he whispered after the spasm passed, "do not anger the gods. I am very old. I should have died years ago. If nothing else, the plague should have taken me. I have done enough, I think, for any man. . . ." Another spasm rippled across his chest and throat, muscles jumping. Maxian laid a hand on the senator's forehead, his brow furrowed in concentration.

"No," Gregorius said, batting weakly at Maxian's hand. "Listen to me, Caesar, you must accept the finality of death. Not everyone . . . can be saved." The old man's eyes fluttered and then, suddenly, he lay still.

The prince, with a ghastly expression on his face, stared down at his old friend, and there was a trembling in the air, some musical note just past hearing. Gaius Julius jerked back, staring around. Many voices were singing, filling the hall with a beautiful harmony. Nicholas and Vladimir stared at Gaius in alarm. The lean northerner's blade was half-drawn from the scabbard. The old Roman shook his head in puzzlement. The hall was filled only with the muted laughter of slaves lifting those senators who fainted onto litters.

"My lord?" Gaius knelt next to Maxian, his voice low and fervent. "You must bring him back."

"I cannot." Maxian's hands moved gently on the old man's face, smoothing back the white hairs, pressing stiffening eyelids down over dead, clouded eyes. Both wrinkled hands were carefully crossed on the sunken chest. The prince was crying, though he seemed unaware of the tears streaking his cheeks. "He has already crossed over the Black River."

"My lord, we need him." Gaius Julius gripped the prince's shoulder. "Without his support in the Senate, our efforts will be stymied in discussion and argument at every turn. You saw how they are today? Can't you bring him back like . . . well . . . like . . ."

"Abdmachus?" Maxian turned, eyes glinting with anger. "As a puppet? As a shape without life, but something to recite the words you devise?"

"Yes," Gaius Julius said, jutting out his chin. "Please, my lord! He is the most powerful man in the Senate; a leader, your *friend* and your brother's staunchest supporter. His death means the Empire is weakened—the Emperor will have to work even harder, take more on his shoulders—which we cannot afford, not with the Persians bearing down on Egypt like a storm."

Maxian grimaced, thinking, and pushed Gaius Julius' hand away. The old Roman moved away, staring at the prince with a determined expression, but he said nothing. Maxian stood, his whole attention fixed on Gregorius' body. After a moment, he raised his hand in the beginning of a gesture, then shook his head abruptly and turned away.

"He is gone," Maxian said to Gaius Julius with a fierce look. "Do you understand?"

The old Roman started to speak, trying to marshal a new argument. Maxian continued to glare at him, and finally Gaius raised his hands in surrender. "I'll not mention it again, Lord Prince."

"Good," the prince said, smiling thinly. "Who are these men?"

Gaius rubbed his bald crown, still shaken by the unexpected death of his onetime patron. "My lord, this is Nicholas of Roskilde and Vladimir, a Walach. They are soldiers from the Eastern Empire. They too were in Constantinople. . . . I have taken them into your service."

"My service?" Maxian was taken aback and looked at Gaius in open amusement. "What on earth do I need them for?" The prince turned to Nicholas, embarrassed. "Your pardon, Master Nicholas, and you too, Master Vladimir. I mean you no disrespect. Gaius . . ."

"My lord," the old Roman interjected firmly, "these men will be your bodyguards."

"My what?" Maxian seemed nonplussed, but Gaius plunged on, keeping his voice low.

"Lord Prince, you have many enemies. Have you forgotten how close you've come to death before?" Gaius paused, searching the boy's face. Maxian made to speak, then paused and Gaius sighed in relief, seeing his patron was *at last* thinking about his situation. "Yes, my lord, you have enemies—some of them, I am sure, are still in Rome. And what of the Persians?

What of the *thing* you confronted in Constantinople? It will be looking for you too, and I am sure he will not balk from poison or murder sent in the night!"

"No . . ." The prince's face screwed up into a grimace, as if he had bitten into a rotten olive. "We know the shahanshah has spies in Rome. And there is the . . . ah . . . our *beautiful* friend. . . ."

Gaius Julius nodded somberly. "Will you accept their service, my lord?" The old Roman drew a copper chain out of his tunic, letting the prince's eye catch on the flat black amulet dangling from the end. Maxian's eyes widened, but he nodded, understanding.

Ah, Gaius thought, *a single ray of hope* . . . The old Roman took a moment each day to mentally thank Alexandros for discovering those in Gaius' peculiar state did not need sleep or food. Having those extra hours in each day meant all the difference when you had to clean up behind a rash young man like Prince Maxian.

Maxian touched the amulet and there was a faint, muted spark. "Nicholas, Vladimir. I see from your expressions that you are new to this idea of bodyguarding too."

"Yes, Caesar," Nicholas said, the set of his mouth speaking volumes. The Walach looked even less comfortable with the idea. "We're not professionals . . . not in that way. We've always, ah . . ."

"—worked outdoors," Vladimir put in, his Latin thick with an indefinable accent. "Keeping an eye on things, you know, or quieting troublesome people."

"I understand." Maxian said. "I don't like being cooped up either." The prince peered at Nicholas' sword for a moment. Then he managed a half-smile, eyes shadowed by unruly hair. "You're on good terms with your blade? You have some skill?"

"Yes." Nicholas answered the smile with a grin, fingertips resting on the hilt of the blade. "I do."

"Good." Maxian glanced at Gaius with a considering air. "We'll need larger quarters."

The old Roman nodded. "Already secured, my lord. A quiet little place on the Cispian Hill."

"Really?" Maxian looked very dubious. "I suppose I will have to see it for myself."

The prince smoothed back his hair and looked over his shoulder at Gregorius' corpse. Sadness washed over his face, making him seem much younger. "I am going to tell Galen what has happened. See the body is taken up, in a state befitting a great and noble Roman, and placed in the vestibule of the temple of the Divine Julius. Inform his family immediately. I will pay the expenses of his funeral myself."

"Of course, my lord." Gaius swallowed a groan. *Those are my hard-earned sesterces you're throwing about, my lad!* But he said nothing, only bowing and motioning for Nicholas and Vladimir to follow him. The thought of entering the Temple of the Divine Julius made him feel a little ill. Gaius made a sign to avert evil fortune, his quick mind already distracted by the delightful prospect of writing Gregorius' funeral oration. Sadly, he supposed the prince would deliver the speech, though Gaius Julius could make sure he had an excellent text.

"Nicholas, Vladimir. I will speak with you tomorrow. There are things you need to know." With that, the prince strode away, heading for the main doors to the Curia and the swiftest path through the crowds of the Forum to the Palatine and his brother.

Vladimir jogged along a narrow street plunging down the side of the Caelian Hill, feeling his skin prickle and grow damp as each step took him closer to the heart of the city and deeper into the fetid close heat pooling among the brick buildings. He wiped his face, sweating furiously, and cursed—not for the first time, or for the last—this business of cities and buildings and putting so *many* people cheek by jowl. The Walach did not like Rome at all, and he did not bother to disguise the fact.

As he passed, matrons walking with their children flinched away and men in doorways scowled. Vladimir ignored them, tugging restlessly at the tunic's tight collar. The house servants had taken away the loose linen shirt and checked pantaloons he favored and he was sure he would never see them again. In return, he had these city clothes—no more than a tunic and undershirt—and a funny-smelling bronze dolphin amulet on a leather cord around his neck. The prince had given him the signet, telling the Walach it would "keep him out of trouble."

Nicholas seemed impressed by the cool halls and high ceilings of the villa, but Vladimir preferred forest and glen and a high mountainside, wet with summer rain.

At the bottom of the hill, the street twisted into a maze of ramshackle buildings set even *closer* together and now there were people everywhere, shoulder to shoulder, pressing and pushing. The low roaring became a din of shouting voices, ringing metal on metal, the creak and growl of machines, singing, cook fires, boiling steam, the lowing of cattle. Vladimir winced, ducking under laundry hanging across the street, and clamped a thumb and forefinger firmly over his nose.

The smell of Rome was the worst, a stew of unwashed bodies, sweat, fear, mucus, urine, offal and rotting flyblown meat. Head down, Vladimir plowed his way through the crowds of the Subura, ignoring angry shouts and glares from the citizens. All he cared about was reaching someplace open and clean where he could see the sky. He looked up, hopeful, but found cliffs of soot-stained brick and plaster looming over the street. Lines hung with wash, curing hams, plucked chickens and pigeons, lengths of dyed wool, obstructed any possible view of clouds or even the sun.

At the edge of the Subura, the crowds grew thicker as the street approached a deep gate set in a mammoth wall of brick. Vladimir accounted himself a strong man, with thickly muscled forearms and broad shoulders, but in this mass of people all he could do was inch forward. The sides of the road were lined by burned out, wrecked buildings. Vladimir could see people sleeping or sitting in the ruins. Others were selling trinkets, amulets, little copper idols from the steps of the burned houses. Close to the gate, crews of slaves were busily clearing the wreckage, hauling bricks, rotted corpses and charred lumber out hand over hand. The Walach frowned, seeing the labor overseers wearing Gaius Julius' dolphin blazon.

The dead man has been busy . . . clearing the ruins, building new blocks of flats, offering reasonable loans . . .

It took nearly a half hour to pass through the tunnel, where cold-eyed soldiers watched the mob with bared weapons. The brickwork facing of the gate was black from the fire that had swept away the blocks of apartments. Beyond the gate tunnel, Vladimir sighed in relief, though he was half-blinded by the sun glittering off the vast sweep of the Forum. He crossed a huge plaza thronged with well-to-do men in long cloaks or togas, lined with monumental buildings faced with marble and brightly painted plaster. The glare hurt his eyes, as did the gilding on the myriad statues standing before the temples. He hurried on, hoping to get into some shade as soon as he could. The Roman summer leached moisture straight from his skin.

Following the directions given by the prince's majordomo, Vladimir passed between a small temple on his right, filled with chanting priests, and a long columned passage on his left. Through the columns, he could see some kind of a garden or park. The sight of trees and grass trapped in the middle of this huge hive made him feel a little ill but he did not stop. Instead, he continued on, across a paved courtyard and through a vaulted hall the size of a whole village and three stories high. Hundreds of men and women were standing around in the gloom, examining goods set out on tables. Huge bundles of wicker cages stood on poles, holding pigeons, sparrows and rabbits. The trestle tables were groaning under the weight of cured sausage and bags of millet and wheat and rounds of cheese.

Beyond the market, Vladimir finally caught sight of his destination, another hill completely obscured by more enormous buildings. These were rather plain, though as he approached he saw they were solidly built and utilitarian. His lips twitched into something like a smile when he noticed there were no windows on the first and second floors. He spied a gate to his left and approached. The crowds petered out, leaving only a brace of very large and well-armored legionaries in the shadow of the gatehouse.

"Ave," Vladimir said, coming to a halt. "I am looking for the Office of the Legions."

The centurion in charge of the guard detail stepped away from the wall, flipping a half-eaten apple into the street. "Papers," he grunted, still chewing.

Vladimir produced a letter from Gaius Julius—won rather easily, the Walach thought, but it was of no matter to the dead man, he supposed—and handed over the paper. The soldier cracked the seal and glanced over the writing inside, then nodded. "Fourth building up, barbarian, with crossed spears over the door."

The Walach nodded and recovered the letter. He pressed coins into the soldier's hand and stepped inside. The centurion grinned, then settled back against the wall. His mates clustered around, eyeing the money.

Vladimir didn't expect much, but he was disappointed to find the Office of the Legions very small and cramped and filled with pale, round little men smelling of ink, dry sweat and unwashed feet. He thought about pinching his nose closed again, but decided they might be insulted. The clerk sitting in the vestibule was reading his letter of introduction for the fourth time. Vladimir tried to keep still, but he only managed to keep from clawing furiously at the door. Large brown water stains marked all four walls and a ceiling thick with spiderwebs. A brief fantasy of seizing the spindly little man by the neck and squeezing until his eyes burst, spilling red, and Vladimir having bit through his throat distracted the Walach for a moment, and then passed.

"I see your master has a sense of humor," the clerk said, holding up the letter with an approving air. "He perfectly captures the Great Caesar's brisk efficiency and clarity of thought." The clerk stared at Vladimir, who bared his teeth, and then sighed in regret. "Never mind. You want to find the whereabouts of an Eastern soldier—one Dwyrin MacDonald? Attached to the Eastern Thaumaturgic Corps, in Constantinople?"

"Yes," Vladimir nodded eagerly. "Is he alive?"

"How, may I ask, would we know?" The clerk made a face. "All of the Eastern records were destroyed, or lost, and the most we've received are partial reports of men who have survived and fled with the fleet to Athens. It would take weeks just to sort through those!"

The Walach squatted down, so that he was on the same level as the clerk. The man inched back, surprised at the swift motion. "Will you look?" Vladimir tried not to growl, but the words rumbled back from the walls. "I will pay you."

The clerk made another face, then threw up his hands. "You're not supposed to bribe me! Not yet. That's for later, after we've dickered for a bit—*urk!*"

Vladimir dragged the man up, claws digging through his tunic. "My friend is missing," the Walach rumbled. "If you look through your bits of paper, and find out if he lives or not, I will pay you." Vladimir's nostrils flared and he leaned close, sniffing the clerk's ears. "I will come back later."

Then he leaned the man against the wall. There were some coins left in his purse. Vladimir placed them carefully on the writing desk, then went out. The smell of dusty paper set him on edge. He hurried out, hoping the prince would decide to leave the city soon.

A GLADE, IN AN ORCHARD OF FRUITING TREES

Mohammed struggled for a moment, then threw back a heavy cloth binding his face and arms. Flat, harsh sunlight struck his face and he turned away, eyes smarting. When, after a moment, he opened them again, he was lying on his back, staring up at a perfect blue sky, unmarred by clouds. The spreading branches of a tree obscured a quarter of his vision.

A fig, he realized, recognizing the hand-like leaves. *Not a good omen.*

He tried to sit up, but found his arms weak and stabbing pains shot through his back. The merchant subsided, letting his head rest among the roots of the tree. He lay in the shade of the fig for some time, trying to gather his thoughts, but found a terrible, ripping hunger dominating his consciousness. Worse, his limbs were utterly drained of strength. With an effort, he raised his left hand and was shocked to see the flesh shriveled and tight on bone and sinew like some dry creeper clinging to ancient stone.

"How long did I sleep?" His voice rasped like a bellows and

he felt his lips split with the motion. A drop of blood slowly oozed from the edge of his mouth.

"A long time," a voice said, drawing Mohammed's attention. A man—dressed in a simple woolen tunic, flat, black hair brushed over his shoulders—was squatting nearby. "Are you hungry?"

"Yes," Mohammed whispered as he tried to sit up again. This time, by leaning against the trunk of the fig tree, he was able to ease up, though the pressure of the bark on his skin was painful. The leaves rattled a little and their shadowy pattern rippled across his face. Now Mohammed could see his legs. Like his hand, they were parched and gaunt, old leather stretched over knobby bones. The skin of his stomach was shrunken, as if it clove to his backbone, and his ribs pressed against pale, translucent flesh like the rafters of a dilapidated shed. "Do you have something to eat?"

The man nodded, then pointed with a slim hand. "There is food in the city."

Mohammed's eyes followed the pointing, well-manicured finger.

The fig tree stood at the edge of a neat forest, filled with tall, slender trees, evenly spaced, with cleared ground and low grass between them. Beyond the trees was a grassy sward, cropped short, leading down to a long, low wall. The rampart seemed to glisten in the sun, shining a dark purple color. Mohammed raised an eyebrow. He had never seen so much porphyry in one place before. Domes and towers rose beyond the wall and the merchant was reminded of Mekkah, in the district around the temples and the holy well. A gate stood open in the city wall and he could see people bustling about their daily business.

"I am too weak," Mohammed said, "to walk so far."

"Would you like me to help you?" The man stood up, moving with ease. He bent down, holding out a hand. "I can carry you into the city."

Mohammed raised a hand to grasp the offered wrist, but then he paused in surprise.

He had not noticed—over the gnawing pain in his gut and the terrible lassitude in his limbs—the silence pervading the park and the trees and the grass. There was no sound, save his own harsh, gasping breath. He turned his attention inward, clasping his hands on his chest. A prayer settled his nerves, and he let the common, simple words lull his mind to quiet, until even the stabbing hunger faded away. There, in the quiet in his heart, he sought out the voice from the clear air, which had guided and accompanied him for such a long time.

There was nothing. No invisible voice, ringing like a trumpet to welcome the rising sun.

Mohammed realized he was alone, and his eyes flickered open.

The man was still standing, waiting, a hand held out to lift him up. The city still beckoned from beyond the meadow, filled with fountains and tables—he was sure—groaning with food and drink and good company.

Mohammed, prince of the Quraysh, merchant of the city of Mekkah, realized he had been betrayed and captured by the enemy.

"Do you have a name?" he rasped at the man standing over him.

"Yes," the man said, smiling cheerfully as he stepped away. Now he seemed very tall, his limbs in perfect proportion, his visage filled with strength. "You may call me Mōha, if that pleases you. Are you hungry or thirsty? I can bring you water."

"No," Mohammed said, lying back against the trunk of the fig and closing his eyes. "I am not hungry or thirsty."

"Do you wish to go into the city? There is a physician there and a soft bed. You could take your ease in comfort."

"This bed is soft enough for me," Mohammed said. One eye fluttered open a little and he looked up, at the flat, blue sky, undisturbed by clouds or wind. Only the leaves of the fig moved softly in the still air. "I have enough comfort already."

"Are you sure?" Mōha knelt again, his beautiful face filled with concern. "You are terribly thin, malnourished; your buttocks are like a buffalo's hoof; the pupils of your eyes seem sunk deep in their sockets like water shining at the bottom of a well; your scalp like a bitter gourd cut unripe becomes shriveled and shrunk by sun and wind; the hairs on your arms and legs rotting at the roots and falling away from your body."

"I am content," Mohammed said, closing his eyes again. "I will abide here, waiting to see what may transpire."

"Very well," Mōha said in a genial voice, rising. "If you need anything, call my name and I will hear. I am always within earshot."

Mohammed felt the man leave, though there was still no sound. He prayed and waited, lying under the tree, feeling its soft, wrinkled bark behind his head. The sun shone down upon him, but the light did not warm his withered flesh, and no breeze or wind stirred his hair.

THE PORT OF MISENUM, CAMPANIA

✠

Where will I go? Shirin pondered, holding the corner of her cloak across her face. Ash billowed up in the sea breeze, driven off the docks and warehouses of the port. The answer came to her swiftly, as if on the sooty wind. *I will go home. Dahvos and Jusuf will be waiting for me.*

Misenum had been a bustling port before the eruption had roused the sea to wreck the warehouses along the stone quays, grinding the ships to kindling along the oval bay. Now the port was twice as crowded as before, with work crews swarming over the ruins, and barges and dredging ships in the channel and harbor. Shirin walked down the central avenue, keeping to the tufa-slab sidewalks, mind distant from her feet.

The roads were crowded with wagons and soldiers, all inching their way down to the harbor. Legionaries watched with interest as she passed, stepping lightly among their piled gear, the bundles of stakes and shovels, tents of spears, bawling donkeys and sullen mules, white faces and black. Shirin wore a vaguely priestess-like robe and gown, her thick black hair held in place by copper pins. The garments were bulky, disguising her lithe figure. Soot and weariness stained her face. She passed a rank of standards, shining gold-and-silver eagles lashed to the sides of a wagon and made a fleeting bow. The centurions and aquilifers sitting in the shade of a storefront noticed the motion and frowned or smiled, as conscience demanded.

Few would think to pay respects to the spirits of the dead thronging around the Legion standards, hungry for blood and sacrifice, thin voices keening hopelessly. Shirin's people held similar beliefs, and she had been raised among warriors. No soldier wanted to be forgotten and the men carrying the Legion standards took their duty very seriously. Every battle was remembered and the names of the dead were scrupulously recorded in leather-bound books. Those who lived took strength from the memories of the fallen. Every legionary knew Rome herself watched over them.

Brilliant sun glittered from the harbor, illuminating sea-green depths. Drowned ships lay on the floor of the bay, leaning masts still jutting above the waves. Colored banners flapped on the mastheads, marking the wrecks. Of sixteen quays, only three were in operation and Shirin frowned, seeing the only ships in harbor were massive grain haulers, wooden flanks rising two or even three stories high. Their masts towered over the buildings and rivaled the twin pharos at the entrance of the bay for height.

Spying the harbormaster's office, Shirin turned towards the low building, though her quick eyes saw only soldiers boarding the huge ships. She entered the offices of the port, relieved to escape the heat. There were a dozen men inside, sitting at low tables, scribing furiously on long parchment sheets. Drawing a veil over the bottom half of her face, Shirin stepped gracefully past them, to a raised platform where a very thin little man was working among a pile of wooden tablets filled with beeswax inserts. Two centurions were standing at the desk, muttering angrily to the little man in low tones.

Waiting, Shirin saw everyone was drawn and haggard, exhausted by the weight of their labors. *I feel the same way*, she thought. *Who here has not lost his family, or part of it?* Even the floor was sticky with ash. Shirin had given up hope of being clean weeks ago. The feeling settled into her skin, coupling with grinding exhaustion and an endlessly hollow space in her gut. The centurions departed, disappointed, ignoring her as they argued in harsh voices.

"Yes, my lady?" The thin little man did not look up from his work. He was counting tallies from the wax tablets with sets of glazed pottery beads. His fingers were quick, shuffling the beads from one pile to another.

"Are those ships heading east?"

"Yes." The man looked up briefly, his eyes dark brown on brown, with barely any white around them. The tone of his skin matched his eyes. "All shipping goes to Alexandria by the Emperor's orders! Grain and refugees out, soldiers and supplies in."

"Nothing going to Ephesus or Pergamum?" By Shirin's reckoning, the old Greek cities were the closest she was likely to get to the Sea of Darkness, at least without entering the Hellespont. With the Persian army and fleet crouched at Constantinople, her easy road home was blocked. However, if she could make her way to the Asian shore then she could make her way overland to the Pontian coast on the southern rim of the Sea of Darkness. From there a ship might be found heading for the northern shore, and Khazaria. And then, at last, she would be home.

The thought of seeing her aunts again and sitting in the great round yurt and eating among the cheerful, bickering crowd of her family overcame her with longing. Her knees felt weak and she gripped the edge of the work table.

"No." The man shook his head sadly. A smear of ink underlined one eye like a bruise. "The Asian shore is too dangerous . . . quartered by Persian pirates and every kind of evil. We've not had a ship from beyond Egypt for months."

"Which ship can take me to Alexandria, then?"

The harbormaster finally looked up and actually saw her. One eyebrow raised, and he pointed at her with his chin. "You are not a Roman."

Shirin nodded. "I am a priestess of Artemis, from the great temple at Ephesus. I was sent here just before the eruption, to tend a shrine above Baiae." It was easy to bring a desolate tone into her voice and to let her face fill with grief. "It has been destroyed, and all the priestesses, save myself, killed. I must go back, and tell the high priestess what happened."

The harbormaster nodded, his own dark eyes distant. "I understand. The *Bast* is the nearest ship. She will leave in the morning, once all of these cursed soldiers are aboard. Her sailing master is named Calvus—he will want a fee from you. Do you have any money?"

"A little," Shirin allowed, looking worried.

"You will need to eat." The harbormaster rummaged on his desk and found a punched copper ticket. "Take this scrip," he said, pressing the token into her hand. "Calvus should be happy to have a priestess on board; it'll bring good luck. If he makes trouble, show him the scrip and tell him you're traveling on municipal business, on *my* business."

The harbormaster stared at her for a moment longer, then shook his head. "Good luck."

"Thank you." Shirin tucked the copper scrip away and hurried out. The *Bast* seemed very large, though she supposed the grain-hauler would shatter like any ship, if a large enough wave roared up out of the deep to swamp her. The Khazar woman was not happy at the prospect of going aboard—the quarters would be cramped and hot, and filled with soldiers. One slim hand crept under her cloak and touched the hilt of a long iron knife she had taken from the ruins. The cold metal made her feel better. The heavy weight of the jewel between her breasts was comforting too, though thinking of the gift turned her thoughts onto an unhappy path.

Gangs of shallow-draft tugs herded the *Bast* out to sea when the wind turned in late afternoon. Shirin managed to find a spot on the upper deck among some lashed-down crates. She was watching the rowers straining at their oars, bare backs glistening with sweat. The grain-hauler edged out to sea, passing between the pair of pharos. The wind was light, but it bellied the sails enough to let the heavy ship make headway. Shirin watched the Latin coast drop away, still dominated by the ragged cone of Vesuvius. Her memories of the ruined villa and the little graves already seemed faint, clouded and indistinct. She turned away, looking out to sea, watching the blue waters flash in the sun.

The sailing-master of the *Bast* hadn't troubled her, not when he saw she bore the sign of the Huntress. Shirin was very glad—she didn't know enough about this foreign religion to deceive a real believer—but her time on Thira had acquainted her with the basic themes. Despite what she'd told the harbormaster, she did have enough coin to purchase food during the voyage to Egypt. But it was not wise to boast of such things, not to a stranger.

"Mistress?" Shirin turned, hand automatically sliding around the hilt of her knife. A legionary, a very young one, was standing beside her at the rail. His brown hair lay flat on his head like a leather cap, and his warm eyes were filled with worry. "Will you say a prayer for us, for the voyage? To keep this flimsy boat from splitting open and spilling us into the sea?"

Shirin looked where he pointed and saw a group of soldiers sitting not far away. They already looked bilious and pale, which almost made Shirin smile. Until Thyatis had snatched her out of the burning ruins of Ctesiphon, she had never been on a boat larger than the hide coracles her brothers made to fish in the Rha or in the marshes along the Salt Sea. Three months in a dhow dogging the coast of Arabia and Africa exposed her to the real ocean, and against the heavy waves and tides of the Mare Erythraeum, this Inner Sea of the Romans was a flat, placid lake.

"What is your name?" she said, keeping her voice and face solemn. She supposed some priestesses might smile, but was not a good idea, not for a single woman on a ship filled with legionaries. She did not feel like smiling anyway. The soldier swallowed visibly, then bobbed his head.

"I'm, ah, Marcus Flaccus, my lady. We're from the *Immortal Bulls*, the Legion Fifth Macedonia."

"Do you have a sacrifice, to placate the gods and Poseidon Sea King?" Shirin knew her voice was cold and forbidding, but the little spark of fear in the soldier warmed her. "A hen, a lamb?"

The soldier shook his head sadly. "No, lady. We hoped you would spy out any poor omens . . . and avert them, you know, by speaking for us to the god."

Shirin nodded, looking out to sea again. The sky was clear and the horizon a slightly bowed line of dark blue. She turned back to the boy and fixed him with a gimlet eye. "The captain had omens cast, before we boarded?" Marcus nodded, looking a little queasy. "They were poor?"

"Oh, no!" Marcus raised a hand to his lips. It veered close to bad luck to mention poor omens aboard ship. "They were good, very good. The priest sneezed—to the right—during the ceremony. A good sign."

"Then why are you worried?" Shirin essayed a thin smile. "If you are not impious while aboard, if you do not swear, or curse the gods, and suffer no dreams of dark water, then all will be well. We will be in Alexandria in a week or a little more. I will watch for signs the gods have changed their mind."

"Yes, my lady. Thank you." Marcus bowed and scurried away. Shirin watched him with interest. She had not been raised to be particularly religious; she was the daughter of a kagan, not a *rev*, and the hand of omen and portent lay lightly upon her. These Romans, though, they seemed a frightened lot, filled with concern over the flight of birds, or the color of the sky, or whatever phantoms of drink and poorly cooked meat plagued their dreams. Hiding a smile again, she settled on one of the heavy crates the Legion had brought aboard and wondered what she would do about food and water. She did have some money, but it occurred to her that on a ship of soldiers, there might not be anyone to purchase food *from*. Usually a big ship like this carried at least one merchant, selling tents, capes, sun hats, food, wine and fruit to the passengers. She scowled, wondering if she would have to beg from the crew.

The sun plunged down into the western sea, filling the sky with a glorious clear light. A few clouds crept across the heavens during the long, hot day and they gleamed like polished bronze. The *Bast* made good time, it seemed, down the Latin coast. Even with night falling, the captain was pleased enough with the weather to keep sailing after dark. On the shore, lights were beginning to wink on, tiny and orange against the deepening gloom. Shirin supposed there were towns and villages all along the coast, providing simple wayposts for passing ships.

She sat cross-legged, as Mikele might do, picking at the hem of her robe in irritation. An hour or so ago, she had taken a turn around the long deck—the *Bast* was almost two hundred feet long, with a deck forty feet, or more, wide. Every conceivable space was crowded with soldiers and their gear. The sailing master had mentioned nearly two thousand soldiers were aboard. Belowdecks, she supposed it was worse, with the cavernous cargo holds crowded with animals, more equipment and those men who hadn't managed to find a place to sleep up on the deck. She hadn't found anyone to sell her food. Now the Legion cooks were busy around a stone hearth behind the main yard, and the smell of frying sausages and bacon, meal cakes and fresh biscuits filled the air. Shirin's stomach growled and she clutched her middle, surprised by the pang of hunger shooting though her.

She closed her eyes and sent up a prayer to the great god watching over her people. *Please don't let my mother know I had to beg for food from a foreigner!* The thought made Shirin a little ill, but eating was far better than not eating, as her belly reminded her. Then a brief, intense series of memories plagued her—every glorious feast she had ever presided over while in Ctesiphon—the details of the roasts, the golden-glazed hens, the acres of cheese and baked breads and sweetmeats and wine, all presented themselves for her inspection. She desperately missed being an Empress.

"Foulness . . ." she whispered, staring gloomily out at the sea. A grunt answered. She looked around and found a grizzled-looking man with stout arms, a barrel chest and broad, stump-nosed face standing nearby. He was wearing the undertunic and leggings of a legionary and his bare arms showed puckered scars and welts like a blacksmith's anvil. Shirin felt a chill, seeing his flat eyes and the way they traveled over her.

"Your . . . pardon, lady," the man said, squinting. Shirin tensed, gaining the impression this soldier might not believe her story. "My lads wanted to know if you would join them at dinner, bless the food and the like, set their minds at ease."

"You are not at ease?" Shirin's nostrils flared. The soldier was staring fixedly at her breasts. She stood up, drawing the cloak around her. He blinked then, meeting her eyes.

"Can't say I like traveling on the water, no," he allowed.

Shirin nodded, looking over at the soldiers sitting on the deck. They had their food on wooden plates and they were watching her, faces pale ovals in the growing darkness. "Will you join us?"

"I will," Shirin said, hunger blunting the edge of her suspicion. "My name is . . . Ruth. I serve Artemis, the Hunter. What is your name?"

The soldier blinked again, then rubbed his nose. "Florus, centurion of the Twelfth of the Fifth."

Shirin nodded somberly. "Well met, then, Master Florus."

Full night had fallen by the time Shirin finished stuffing herself with fried meal cakes and honey. The soldiers watched her with amusement and then in a little awe. They hadn't eaten so much—but then they'd had a meal in the morning too. When she was done, the Khazar woman set the plate on the deck, swallowed and looked around at the men with a calm expression. Inside, she wanted to shout or cheer with relief, before curling up and going to sleep. She had not eaten so well since diving off the *Pride of Cos*. Grubbing in the ruins, or accepting handouts from the Imperial troops sent into the devastation were poor sources of food. In Rome, the stink of the city, its strangeness, awesome size and the howling roar of the Collo-seum crowd had crushed her appetite. Sitting in the darkness, only faintly lit by a candle lantern, hearing the rigging creak and feeling the cool night air wash over her, reminded her of the long trip around Arabia and up the African coast.

She clenched her teeth, biting back tears, missing the solid warm presence of Thyatis at her side, and her cousins Kharmi, Efraim and Menahem, and her children. . . . She felt a terrible pang, like a knife twisting in her diaphragm, fearful the voyage might prove to be the only happy time in her life. A vision of Thyatis laughing, red hair bound back behind her head, a little boy hanging from each arm, shrieking as the Roman woman spun them about on the deck, swam up into her memory.

"Thank you," she managed, driving away the cruel image. "May the Huntress's luck be with you, in war and in peace."

There was a pleased murmur from the soldiers. "Thank you,

lady, we'll need it with these Persians! Though they've not faced the Fifth, by Jupiter!" Heads nodded, half-seen in the darkness.

Shirin looked over at Florus, sitting at the edge of the circle, his hands busy with oil and a cloth and a file. His armor lay out in front of him, each segment carefully arranged, the wire and leather thongs removed. The soldier was carefully cleaning each bit of metal, rubbing away rust, coating them with oil. Some of the other men did the same, though they were not paying such close attention.

"There will be fighting in Egypt, then," she said.

"Yes," Marcus answered her, sitting up. His young face caught a little of the light from the candle lantern. "They've been lucky so far, thrashing the Easterners, but they've not fought the West, not yet, not under a real general like the Caesar Aurelian!"

The other men nodded and some laughed. "We'll show them a steady line," they said.

"Have you fought the Persians before?" Shirin was curious. She had spent a long time in Persia and knew what the *diquans* said of Rome. What did their enemies think? "You've faced the *cataphracts* and the *clibanarus*—the oven-men, I think you call them—in full battle array?"

"No," Marcus admitted, grimacing. "Well, the centurion has, right Florus?"

There was a grunt from the darkness, but the centurion did not look up from his work.

"If you follow his orders," Shirin said, seeing the soldiers were very young and brave, but afraid to admit they had not faced an enemy as fearsome as the Persians. "You will do well, and fight honorably."

"Have you seen the Persians in battle?" Marcus failed to keep both curiosity and disbelief from his voice.

"I have," Shirin said, then stopped, wondering if anything she might say to these boys would matter. Soon they would fight and live, or die, by their own merits on some Egyptian field. "When I was little, before I became a . . . priestess, I lived near the Persian frontier. More than once, I saw the Persians ride against . . . my people. They make a great show on the march, bright banners and flags and great horns blowing, and they are all a-horse, great chargers with round chests. Their spears are keen, I remember, and wave like a forest of shining reeds."

"But Rome has always beaten them," Marcus interjected, his voice concerned. "Off their horses they're no match for us, not on broken ground!"

"I hope so," Shirin said. "The Huntress would be pleased to see you live. When I am home again, I will sacrifice for you, and your safety."

That pleased the young Romans, who raised their cups in salute. Shirin felt a little odd, as if she'd pulled a mask across her face and suddenly spoken with someone else's voice. Marcus lowered his cup, his face suddenly grim. "We shouldn't be too quick to discount them, though."

"Why?" called some of the other men. Shirin noticed Florus raise his big square head to watch the younger man with interest.

"They have arts we lack," Marcus said, looking around at his fellows, mouth thinned to a sharp line. "They did not throw down the walls of Constantinople by strength of mortal arms! No, their foul priests summoned up some fiend—"

"Their priests are not foul!" Shirin was surprised by the vehemence in her voice. "The *mobeds* and *mobehedan* are pious men, who serve a god of light, not darkness. Their god may be different from yours, but he too rules justly in heaven. I fear—" She stopped, throat choked closed by old anger. Her face seemed to shutter, as if a door closed on a lighted room. In dark memory, she looked upon almost-forgotten pain and turned the scenes and voices over in her thought like glittering bits of glass. With an effort, she returned her attention to the present, and the stunned, questioning faces of the young soldiers.

"I am little older than you are," she said, voice falling into a cadence she'd first heard in her father's voice, around the campfires of the people. "But I have heard a tale out of Persia, one you have not, I think. Your enemies are only men and women, like yourselves, and they are prey to many failings. They are prey to evil, and not the simple evil of lies or theft, but the kind of evil that makes the gods turn their faces from men."

Shirin stopped, looking up at the sliver of the moon and the thick wash of stars carpeting the heavens. It was very dark between the glittering lights. The Romans were silent, the pale glow of the candle lantern shining in their eyes, Florus setting down his tools and oily cloth as they watched her, as she once watched her father sitting under a Khazar sky, telling the old stories of the people.

"Many years ago, before you were born, the king of kings—the shahanshah—of the Persians was growing old. He endured a troubled reign, much plagued by barbarians called the T'u-chüeh who raided and burned and caused much grief along the northern frontier. At last the old king rode out against them with a great army, and in the way of such things, fell into a trap, and was slain. He left two sons, but they were still very young, and neither was yet a man. The greatest of the old king's generals was a stiff sort of fellow named Bahram, and his enemies called him *choban*, which means 'made of wood', when they thought he could not hear them, and behind his back.

"Bahram seized the throne of Persia and claimed he ruled in the name of the eldest of the two boys, whose name was Khusro—in Roman lands, you call him 'Chrosoes.' But no one saw the young prince, or heard him speak, for the Wooden King sent him away, to live in exile in a fortress, far from the eyes of the court and the great nobles. The younger son vanished completely and everyone was sure he had been murdered. Bahram was not a good king, but he was greatly feared, though in all matters the realm grew weak and filled with petty evil.

"Young Khusro was imprisoned in a castle set high on a mountain, near the northern frontier, and in the custody of an old and very loyal *diquan*—you would call him a knight. The old knight was loyal to a fault and he'd sworn an oath to the Wooden King and, by all the gods, he intended to keep his word. In the castle, however, lived a strapping, powerful young man—his grandson—and this boy would one day be known as Shahr-Baraz."

A low whistle went up from the legionaries. They did not set any stock by the heroes or kings of other lands, not and be Romans, but this was a name they knew and respected, for the Royal Boar was legendary even in Rome, where few barbarians gained such renown. No enemy had ever won so many victories against the Empire.

"Yes, you know him for his famous beard. The Boar was still young then, and green as spring grass, but he was restless in his grandfather's castle and yearned to see what lay beyond the barren fields and the desolate hills. Too, there was this other young man, also trapped, also eager to make his way in the wide world. This was prince Khusro, the son of the dead king, a prisoner in the old keep. They became fast friends and practiced constantly in the fighting yard, growing stronger and faster with each day. Never have there been two friends like these—each strove to best the other in all things—and each swore mighty and secret oaths they would escape their dull prison and restore Khusro to his rightful throne.

"Winter approached, one bleak year, and the old *diquan* fell ill and died. A messenger was sent to Ctesiphon to bring this news to the Wooden King. The Boar, however, did not wait for the royal courier to return. He had, as yet, sworn no oath to the king of kings on his distant throne. Instead, with a boldness that has only grown with age, he bent his knee and neck to his friend, Prince Khurso and called *him* king of kings and made himself the prince's sworn man. Now Khusro set himself against his regent and Shahr-Baraz was a rebel lord.

"Together they fled from the drafty old fort and made their way south and west by secret ways, into the great central plateau of Persia, where all her true riches lie—for there among wide plains and grazing fields are the domains of the *diquans* and their knights and the very strength of Persia. Khusro intended to find support amongst old friends of his father and raise an army to reclaim his throne. But the prince, though brave, was still young and Bahram was old and sly with treachery. Some of the great nobles rose up for the young king, but more joined the armies of the Wooden King and the prince's revolt was violently suppressed.

"Khusro escaped, and lived, only because there was no man upon that field, or on any other, who could match Shahr-Baraz with lance or sword or spear. The Boar hewed his way from the melee, slaughtering hundreds, and the two rebels escaped into the mountains. This time, the Wooden King found a body resembling the prince and carried the dead boy back to Ctesiphon in a great funeral procession. That boy was buried, as if Prince Khusro had died, and Bahram Choban made himself truly king of kings. Everyone wept, thinking the young prince had fallen.

"Secretly Bahram's men searched everywhere, quartering the mountains and the hills, urgent to find the Boar and the prince. By luck and skill, they failed, and the Boar took the prince north, beyond the mountains of Persia and into the great grasslands surrounding the Salt Sea, where terrible savages roam and the winter is nine months long."

Shirin paused, thirsty, and drank from her cup. When she looked up, she saw more men had come out of the darkness and squatted or stood around the little circle of light from the candle lantern. No one spoke while she drank again and settled herself more comfortably on the deck.

"They would have died in that cruel winter, both the prince and the Boar, if they had not been found by a hunting party of the Khazar people, who rule those lands. Now, know this—the Persians and the Khazars are old enemies, who long fought over the land called Albania, and there was long enmity between them. Yet, know this as well; there have never been two braver men than Shahr-Baraz and Khusro. The two were taken to the camps of the Khazar kagan and made his guests and they spent a long winter there, in peak-roofed Itil, on the banks of the black-watered Rha. Khusro was without fear and he put his case to the kagan and asked him for help to reclaim the throne, which had been stolen from him by the Wooden King.

"Now, in those days, the Khazar people were ruled by a kagan whose name was Sahul Ziebil and despite his short years, he was very wise. Sahul saw Khusro was a man of honor, with a great heart, and—perhaps—peace might be struck between the two nations. Sahul himself was not without daring and when spring came he sent a strong party of riders to guide the prince, and Shahr-Baraz, to the Roman port of Chersonessos. With them went a letter, for the Khazars and the Eastern Empire long maintained a correspondence, particularly in regards to matters of Persia, their common foe.

"So it was that Prince Khusro and his champion, Shahr-Baraz, came to Constantinople, the city of gold, and met in secret with Emperor Maurice. The Emperor was astonished—he had thought to be meeting a Khazar delegation—not the lost king of Persia! Yet he treated Khusro with honor and as an equal, placing a seat at his side for the young prince. All three realms were exhausted by endless war and longed for peace. Maurice and Chrosoes made a pledge that summer in Constantinople and Maurice sealed the pact with the marriage of his daughter, Maria, to the young prince. An Eastern army, and Maurice's aid, were her dowry. Khusro would yet be king of Persia."

Shirin stopped speaking, her voice grown hoarse. It had been years since she told such a long story. The crowd of young Romans had grown again and some sailors hung from the rigging to listen. She smiled at Florus and Marcus. "Your pardon, I am tired and my voice is failing. I will finish the story tomorrow."

With that she stood and left the circle of faces. In the darkness outside of the lantern light, Florus stopped her, his face shadowed and indistinct. Shirin stiffened, wondering if he would try and overpower her. The iron knife was in her hand, hidden under the robe.

"That was well told," Florus said gruffly. "Takes their mind off this cursed voyage. Here."

Shirin felt something thick and woolen press into her hands and she took the blanket. "Thank you."

The centurion mumbled something, then padded off into the darkness on his bare feet. The centurion looked a little bilious in the poor light. Shirin curled up among the crates, glad to lie out under a starry sky, in the open air, the blanket folded under her head as a pillow. Sleep stole over her gently, and for the first time since she woke on the *Pride of Cos* to a vast rumbling sound, like giants banging on a bronze gong, she slept without nightmares.

Shirin settled on the deck, at the edge of a rough circle made by Florus' soldiers. Marcus, blushing a little and ignoring the comments of his fellows, passed her a blanket for a cushion. Shirin was a little disappointed the great crowd of soldiers and sailors who listened the previous night were nowhere to be seen. But, really, it didn't matter. The group of young soldiers fed her

again and she felt pleasantly full. That was welcome change
enough!

"So," she began, "Prince Khusro invaded Persia at the head
of a Roman army, accompanied not only by his boon companion Shahr-Baraz, but by his father-in-law Emperor Maurice and
many other Persian exiles. The Wooden King was not well
loved and as Khusro marched against Ctesiphon from the west,
many lords who loved his father flocked to his banner. There
were battles in the land between the two rivers and Bahram
Choban was defeated, his supporters scattered, and Khusro set
upon the Peacock Throne, adorned with gold and pearl.

"There was peace too, between Persia and Rome—for
Khusro found a new father in Emperor Maurice—and between
Persia and the Khazars, who had rendered him such timely aid.
Khusro became a great king—he restored order and law to the
Persian lands—and he defeated the T'u-chüeh who so plagued
his father. He was happy with his wives and Empress Maria
bore him a son. The wise men of the court named him 'Anushirwan'—he of the great soul. In all things, it seemed the young
king would preside over a glorious age of peace."

Shirin's face darkened, and she stopped, taking a drink from
her copper cup. There was a sour taste in her mouth.

"One day, a messenger arrived in haste from the West. The
man brought terrible news—Empress Maria's father, Emperor
Maurice, had been overthrown and murdered, along with his
entire family. A base-born centurion named Phocas seized the
Eastern purple. Khusro was outraged—a man he honored as a
father was dead—and Maria was distraught. Her own brothers
and sisters strangled, her mother hacked to bits on the highway,
their heads displayed in the Forum. She demanded Khusro punish the murderer Phocas. He demurred—there was a treaty, an
honorable peace . . . Maria did not care, she wanted vengeance
and more, she wanted her son Kavadh-Siroes to sit on her father's throne."

A stir went through the circle of Romans and Shirin heard
them hiss in surprise.

"Yes," she said softly, "the boy was heir to the Eastern
throne, the grandson of an Emperor, son of the king of kings. In
him, by blood, both Persia and the Eastern Empire united. Yet

Khusro heeded his advisors, who counseled peace. Shahr-Baraz was first among them, urging his oath brother to abide by the treaty. Phocas, as fate revealed, was a cruel and rapacious man and quite mad. Shahr-Baraz believed the Romans would soon overthrow him. Then, said the Boar, when Phocas was dead—Kavadh-Siroes might be welcomed as Emperor.

"So Khusro waited and watched events in the west, and Maria became angrier and angrier. One day she was walking in the Imperial gardens, which stretch along the Euphrates for miles, filled with every kind of flower and tree and glorious bird, and she found a young man sitting under a tree. He seemed very familiar to her, but he introduced himself as a stranger, and said his name was Rustam. He said he was a priest and he could help her avenge her father's death."

Shirin took a breath, and made a sign before her, a warding against evil. She looked around at the tense faces of the young soldiers and her face settled into grim lines.

"You are young, but you must know there are gods not spoken of by pious men. There are monstrous powers who act in opposition to the great gods in heaven. The old Greeks called them the Titans. In Persia they name the king of darkness Ahriman. And he is locked in eternal battle with the lord of light, Ormaz. Now this young man speaking to Empress Maria in the garden was a priest of this same Ahriman and a vessel of dark powers. He was not a priest, as you might think of them, but a sorcerer instead.

"Rustam lived in secret in the palace for some time, while Maria accepted his instruction in the dark arts. Khusro at last relented in this matter of the war against Rome—Shahr-Baraz was sent west to raise an army and test the frontier defenses. Heraclius, who had been nothing but the son of a provincial governor, overthrew Phocas. Khusro wrote to the young general, urging him to accept Kavadh-Siroes as his Emperor, as was proper."

The Khazar woman essayed a small smile, seeing incomprehension on the faces of the soldiers.

"You must understand," she said, "that in Persian lands, the king's descent of blood must be pure. The usurpation of Bahram Choban—who was not of the Imperial line—had caused great outrage. Khusro knew this, as he knew his own lineage for thirty generations. For him, to see a base-born man ascend to the Roman throne, when his *own son* was the rightful ruler, was a grave insult. Heraclius denied the boy's claim and Khusro determined to see Kavadh-Siroes rule on his grandfather's throne.

"Shahr-Baraz smashed the Eastern armies and broke through the frontier like a maddened bull. He drove on to Constantinople, only halted by the Imperial fleet in the straits of the Propontis. Despite his victories, however, Maria was not satisfied. The sorcerer filled her thoughts with poison, and she conspired with the dark man to raise a terrible spirit, a winged shade to cross the leagues to Constantinople and murder Heraclius. Maria did not think the new Emperor any better than the murderer Phocas.

"She and Rustam set about their blasphemous ceremony in secret, in the old River Palace, but they had not counted upon the sudden appearance of Khusro himself, who had been warned trouble was afoot. The ceremony went awry and there was a great fire. Maria perished and Khusro himself was nearly blinded, his face disfigured and burned. Rustam the sorcerer escaped, carrying the king of kings out of the inferno. Then, gasping for breath in the gardens, as pillars and towers shattered in the tremendous heat, Khusro looked upon the face of his rescuer—whom he had never seen before that moment—and saw his long-lost younger brother yet lived.

"Yes, Rustam the sorcerer was the missing prince, Khusro's own brother, who had vanished so long ago. The king of kings was filled with despair and delight in equal turns. No one knows what passed between the two men that night, but thereafter the king of kings possessed a weapon no ruler had ever dared wield—a sorcerer unbounded by conscience or fear of the gods—a dark spirit to do the king's bidding without thought of remorse or mercy. In this way, my friends, the Persians gained a terrible weapon."

A hiss of breath met Shirin's last words and the soldiers shrank back from her and from the light of the candle lantern.

"But," Marcus whispered, "Chrosoes, king of kings, was

killed, slain by his own men in his own house. . . . We've never heard of a brother . . . surely he was killed too?"

Shirin raised a hand and halted his words. "Men who taste the power of the dark one will not set the draught aside. It is said Chrosoes himself came to rely more and more upon his brother's power. It is like the lotus—one taste and a man thinks of nothing else. Shahr-Baraz may be king of kings in name, but I think Rustam is at his elbow."

"That is bad news," grumbled Florus from the darkness. "If this Rustam is what broke into Constantinople. How can we stop a sorcerer?"

"Bravery," Shirin answered and a strange feeling came over her, a hot flush flooding her chest as if she plunged into steaming water. She looked down, distracted. Distantly she heard herself saying: "Men can stop such horrors, if they do not yield to fear."

Between the smooth olive curve of her breasts, the jewel was glowing softly, shining red like a rising star.

PERINTHUS, ON THE COAST OF THRACE

W hat is this?"

Alexandros of Macedon, *comes* of the Western Empire and commander of the Legions in Thrace, stopped abruptly, his leather boots sinking into soft, muddy ground. Without waiting for his train of aides and bodyguards to stop, he seized the bowstave of the nearest soldier between his thumbs. The soldier, an archer and swordsman in Alexandros' Gothic legion, stiffened in fear. Alexandros ignored the man, his entire attention on the heavy laminate of horn and wood and glue comprising the long limb of the bow. As he had passed a discoloration in the cream-colored horn caught his eye. The Macedonian's thumbs ground at the thick laminate and sud-

denly the glue gave way and cracked and the long arm of the
bow toppled over, hitting the soldier on the head.

Alexandros hissed in anger, one hand brushing unruly hair
out of his face. He wrenched the remains of the bow out of the
man's wooden bow case and split it lengthwise with ease. All of
the glue was rotten and the bone turned a sickly green. Mold
was growing in the laminate. Anger washed across the Macedonian's clean-shaven face, then vanished.

"Syntagmarch!" Alexandros' voice was a harsh, deep shout.
The Macedonian had an unpleasant voice, but it carried clearly
across a battlefield. A tall, thin man at the end of the column
turned sharply and jogged down the line of legionaries to
Alexandros. The file-commander loomed over Alexandros, but
he seemed pale and uncertain. "Your name is Valamer. You are
responsible for this syntagma?"

The Goth nodded, unable to speak, his throat tight. Alexandros' face was a blank, eyes snapping with anger. "I want to see
every man's bow and arms. Now."

Valamer nodded, then turned to face the syntagma. Four
ranks of forty men stood in a rough rectangle along the side of
the road. Their attendants were clustered behind them, holding
horses and pack mules and sitting on the biscuit wagons.
Valamer took a deep breath, then bellowed out: "All ranks! Present arms for inspection!"

Alexandros watched the legionaries carefully, seeing hesitation in their movements as they set their bow cases on the
ground. Many of the men looked sick, or ill, and one young
Goth, long blond hair hanging on either side of his face in
braids, was trembling as he drew out his bow and laid it on a
cloth. Others seemed more composed, drawing long swords
from their scabbards and laying them out.

Behind the Macedonian, his aides clumped up, puzzled. The
road through the camp was clear for the moment, but men from
other syntagma would soon pass by. Rumor flickered through
the sprawling camp like a fire in dry grass and soldiers were
more curious than cats. Keeping his face entirely impassive,
Alexandros paced to the beginning of the first row of men. He
was already displeased, just seeing the fear in their faces. At the
same time, there was a cool sense of relief in his stomach—he

could already guess how things were and he would take appropriate measures immediately, and then—*perhaps*—such a problem would not recur. He took his time, walking slowly, letting the men fidget and sweat.

A dozen soldiers from other units were loitering in front of the log buildings the army had thrown up in the fields around Perinthus. More were coming and Alexandros wanted everyone to see what happened. By the time he reached the head of the first line of men, at least two-dozen curious onlookers were watching.

"Soldier," he growled, "show me your bow."

The lead man—a senior noncommissioned officer, what the Western army would call an *optimate*—held out a long, curved bow in stiff hands. Alexandros took the weapon, and ran a hand along the smooth upper limb, tracing the *S*-curve and digging the corner of a nail into the thin lines of glue holding the bone and willow laminate together.

The weapon was modeled on the Hunnic horse bow, but heavier and faster to produce. The "Alexandrine" bow was not designed for use from horseback, but rather while standing in serried ranks. The Macedonian knew, from stolen books, a trained man could loose six shafts within a minute's time. An arrow flung from this recurved bow, driven by a strong man's shoulder and arm, could punch straight through the heavy pine laminate shields favored by the Legions or even the overlapping iron armor of the Persian or Roman heavy horse. Alexandros imagined a battle line of nearly a thousand Peltasts supporting his main body of pikemen. Arranged in three or four ranks, the Peltasts fill the air with an unceasing, constant rain of arrows. Should an enemy cavalry charge manage to break through the arrow storm, they would face the *hoplites* and their eighteen-foot spears, also arrayed in ranks.

Alexandros knew, from long experience, the phalanx was unbreakable if composed of disciplined, veteran, properly trained men. He was also sadly aware a gulf of nearly seven hundred years separated him from the last true phalanx army. Rome had eclipsed the Greek city-states and their armies of *hoplites*. This little army was a ghost of the power he once employed. Still, he would do what he could with the time and materials at hand.

He finished his inspection of the bow. The glue and laminate seemed sound. The centurion's sword was well oiled and free from rust. Alexandros grunted, gave the man his weapons back, then moved on to the next soldier in line. This time, as he bent the bow in his hands, he heard a creaking sound, and—sure enough—the laminate was cracking, warped by moisture. Alexandros made no comment, returning the shaking, pale-faced soldier his weapon. So he went along the lines of men, testing each bow with his own hands, examining their armor, sword and dagger. Some men carried axes or maces as well, and these weapons were also subjected to a close scrutiny.

"You men," he shouted, at last, when he stood before them, "are soldiers in the army of the Republic of Rome. You have sworn oaths to the Emperor, to serve faithfully, to stand your ground, to obey the orders of your superior officers."

The sun had climbed far into the sky, and the day was hot and very humid. Standing at inspection, in their mailed shirts and leather bracings, the men sweated furiously and some looked rather wilted. Alexandros, himself, did not feel the burning sun and many of his men had remarked, quietly, and only to close companions, the general seemed tireless and it was widely known he rarely slept.

"You are not children," Alexandros barked, cold voice ringing in their ears. "More than half of your weapons are useless, pitted with rust or split in this damp climate. Your armor is likewise rusted, with loose or rotted straps. You have *failed* to follow my direct orders: that each man's kit be spotless, that his arms and armor be kept in readiness, clean and free of rust, at all times, that he draw a heavy bow sixty times a day in practice, that by every third day each man should loose ten times forty arrows against a target."

The cold dispassionate tone struck each man like a physical blow. In the back ranks, one of the younger men—a Gepid by the look of his wild red hair—staggered and nearly fell.

"The lives of every man in this army are placed in peril by your failure. There must be a punishment, for I will not have men's lives spent uselessly. Syntagmarch Valamer, step forward!"

The syntagmarch stepped away from the line, his face a

mask, and stood before the Macedonian. Alexandros saw the man's weapons and armor were in moderate condition, though his sword hilt was chased with gold and his tunic was of fine-quality linen. Pride struggled with fear in the Goth's face and Alexandros remembered something of his history. Valamer was a chieftain, one of the Gothic *amali*—their most noble tribesmen. A man used to command and assured by an ancient tradition of unquestioning obedience.

He knew the bows were ruined, the Macedonian thought, *and could not bring himself to seek aid from the armorers, or from me.* It was not the first time such a thing had happened. Caring for the bows was especially difficult in these humid lowlands—they needed to be stored, when not actually in use, in specially heated wooden boxes. A damp bow was useless.

"You have failed me, soldier," Alexandros said, his voice carrying into the ranks. "My father once said this to me, and to my half-brother: there are no bad legionaries, only bad officers. You are at fault here, for you knew your duty and you did not carry it out."

Alexandros gestured for the man's sword, and Valamer, face turning sickly gray, removed the spatha from its baldric and presented it to the general. The Macedonian hefted the sword in one hand, then removed it from the sheath in a quick, fluid movement. He raised it over his head.

"This man, Valamer, a Goth, has shown himself unworthy of being syntagmarch! Therefore, until he redeems himself by deeds, he shall be no more than a common soldier, an attendant, who will hold the horses and gear of other men, while they fight!"

The Goth blinked and breathed again, then his mouth settled into a tight line. In common course, only camp followers, or the wounded, or raw recruits held the horses of men in the line of battle. He was shamed, but he would not be killed out of hand. Alexandros did not return the sword, though he sheathed it again. The general did not look at Valamer and the Goth remained standing, swaying slightly, weaponless.

"Many of you," Alexandros continued, his voice still cold, "followed this poor example and have not kept your bows dry, your arms and armor clean. I know this discipline is new to you, for many of you have come from brave nations, but those nations are not Rome. You will, therefore, learn to keep those tools which sustain life and bring victory as if they were a dear child."

Alexandros' voice suddenly rose and his anger leaked through in a biting, acid tone.

"Each man whose kit has failed inspection will be provided with new weapons and armor from stores, but his pay will be docked to account for this waste. Further . . . men know how to follow orders and do their duty; but children, boys, are oft remiss, for they have not learned the ways of men. Therefore, each man who has failed his duty will have his hair shorn and his beard shaved. You have acted like boys, now you will look the part, until you have learned discipline!"

At these words, the soldiers gave out with a groan of fear. The Goths, Germans and particularly the Franks in the ranks were devastated. Some men, heedless, fell to their knees and began crying out, begging for forgiveness. Amid the tumult, Alexandros beckoned to Chlothar, the commander of all the Peltasts in the army. The big Frank's face was tight with anger and his liquid blue eyes were filled with pain. He too came into Alexandros' service with short, shorn hair—disgraced. The Macedonian saw the look in his eyes.

"Chlothar, put your best syntagmarch with this unit for a few months. He should carry this sword while he commands. It is too fine a weapon to be wasted on a common soldier." Alexandros paused, lips quirking in an almost-smile at Valamer. "Take heart, if this were truly Rome, then one man in ten would be put to death for such failure. Chlothar, send this man Valamer to your best syntagma. He must learn he is no longer a chief, but a Roman soldier."

Chlothar nodded, then beckoned over his under-officers. The wailing among the soldiers died down a little under his glare. The big Westerner enjoyed being forbidding and Alexandros encouraged him to be the "strong hand."

The *comes* did not look back, but continued on with his inspection. As ever, he walked swiftly, head held a little to the side, looking sideways at the rows of tents or log buildings. It would be a long day, for he intended to inspect not only his own troops, but each Khazar and Eastern Empire regiment as well. He commanded a polyglot army, parts of which had suffered a terrible defeat. The Easterners, in particular, were demoralized. Alexandros had drilled them relentlessly, hoping to restore their spirit, but it was slow going. Soon the combined army would take the field to drive the Persians back into Constantinople, or even beyond, and Alexandros was impatient to begin.

Dahvos, kagan of the Khazar people and *bek* of the war host fighting for the Emperor of the East, stared gloomily down at the harbor of Perinthus. His curly blond hair was tied back behind his head, though the damp air encouraged an untidy sprawl around his shoulders. Out of habit, even within the presumably safe confines of the town, he wore a heavy shirt of overlapping iron wedges over a thick felted shirt. He carried a round iron helmet with a tapered crown and ornamented chin guards under one muscular arm. A dark green cloak hung from broad, well-muscled shoulders and the worn bone hilts of a long sword hung from a leather baldric at his side.

Below the Khazar prince, the harbor was busy with barges and boats swarming around the flanks of square-sailed merchantmen. Lines of men crowded the docks, boarding amid a confusion of wagons and horses and longshoremen and bales of goods. Tall standards surmounted by golden eagles and wreaths of silver laurel were being carried aboard the ships. Clusters of red-cloaked officers huddled among the throngs of men, deep in conversation. Soon the motley fleet would put to sea for Egypt.

"What ails you, brother?"

Another Khazar, this man taller, older, leaner, with rumpled black hair, leaned against the wall. Merriment danced in his blue eyes. Dahvos grimaced at Jusuf, then turned his attention back to the port. "I see our strength fleeing, and I wonder what the boy-king Alexandros is thinking. With the departure of the Western troops, only these Goths, our lancers and the Eastern Legions remain. Barely half the strength just defeated before Constantinople."

Jusuf nodded, though he did not seem as disturbed as his half-brother. "You heard what those fishermen said—the Persian fleet left the city, and many soldiers crowded the decks of their ships. Don't you think most of the Persians have left as well? Even the Eastern officers seem convinced the *dreadful Boar* has turned his attention elsewhere."

"Perhaps. But why? They have the upper hand here— Shahr-Baraz could tusk his way into Greece with ease. Even with the boy-king's touted Goths, I wonder if we could stop a determined attack. Where is the wisdom in letting a wounded enemy live?"

Jusuf raised an eyebrow and tried to keep from laughing, but mostly failed. "You're not smitten with our young *comes* and his battle wisdom, are you? You call him a boy—yet he's older than you! What sets you on edge about him?"

Dahvos' expression contorted into a grimace and then a snarl. The subject of Alexandros did not lie easy with him. He failed to note the mischief in his half-brother's eyes. "I don't know, but I dislike this Alexandros as much as any man I've ever met. He is ill luck for us, Jusuf. He is a bent arrow."

"Hmm. Well, with the pace of foraging and scouting, I'd say he intends to march against the Persians within the month."

"Yes." Dahvos' expression grew ever more sour. "The *comes* desires to see the mettle of the Persians for himself—to foray up the Imperial highway to Selymbria or beyond—to see if the enemy will come out of his camps at Constantinople. This— with only his own troops, untried and untested in battle, with these Easterners, whose spirits are as low as a grave, and as muddy, with our own horse—by which, he tells me, he sets great store."

"We have given a good account of ourselves," Jusuf said quietly. "But we will suffer if the enemy has kept his heavy horse in Thrace. Our arms, our armor, the weight of our horses, are not a match for the Persian *diquans*. But our men are game for the chase—they will not shy away from battle."

"No, they will not! Not when the memory of defeat is so fresh!" Dahvos turned away from the port, eyes glittering in anger. "But the Eastern *cataphracts* have been ground up and spit out already and our men are the only ones with the nuts to match the Persians—so we will pay a heavy price to reclaim lost honor."

"What about the Gothic spear wall?" Jusuf raised his chin in challenge, then turned and motioned out beyond the roofs of the town, towards the outer wall and the camps covering the countryside above the port. "Lord Alexandros never fails to express confidence they can stand against any cavalry charge in the world."

"Have you seen them stand in battle?" Dahvos walked along the wall, cloak thrown behind him. The day was cloudy and a constant wet haze lay over the rumpled green hills and the flat, dark waters of the narrow sea. With summer far advanced, it was far too hot. The eastern horizon was a gray line marking the shore of Chalcedon. "I have puzzled through the old books—Hieronomyus of Cardia's *Historia* and Polybius—and once upon a time the Greek phalanx could withstand any cavalry charge, and break it, drenching the field with blood. Now? Those Goths can barely find a privy pit to piss in . . . much less march in order and keep those pig-stickers straight."

"They are getting better." Jusuf tried to keep his tone level. "Their skill improves daily and even the Eastern troops are starting to regain their color. I doubt the Eastern foot has been drilled so fiercely in generations!"

"Fine." Dahvos made a sharp motion with his hand. He was still very angry. "What about their *cataphracts*? Do they drill? No—they mope about the camps, drinking until they fall down, cursing the gods—as if the lord of heaven had *anything* to do with Great Prince Theodore's idiocy on the Plain of Mars—and acting the lackwit. Listen to me, Jusuf, if we meet the Persians again in full battle, those Eastern knights will break like a rotten trace and spill us all on the cold ground."

Jusuf rubbed his long nose in response, and tapped his chin with his knuckles. "Do you think that the next battle will be decided by the actions of *cataphract* and *clibanarus*?"

"Yes," Dahvos snapped, "how else?"

Jusuf shrugged, then leaned an elbow on the battlement again. "I wonder . . . I think our new commander, this same *comes* Alexandros you dislike so much, smells the wind changing. The heavy horseman with lance, mace or striking sword in hand, girded in armor from head to tail, his horse likewise barded all about with heavy padding or even iron, has ruled the Eastern battlefield for what? Three centuries?"

"Since Emperor Valens bled out like a trussed pig at Adrianopolis," Dahvos grunted, scowling. "A little less than three hundred years . . ."

"Yet," Jusuf interjected smoothly, hooking a thumb down at the busy chaos in the harbor, "in the West, Rome has ridden out shock after shock, losing whole provinces and then wresting them back from the barbarians. Where are their clouds of horsemen, their cohorts of knights? They have kept their traditional Legions—oh, supplemented by barbarian horse, surely—but the core of their armies, which have been victorious for more than *seven hundred years*, remains the foot soldier with his shield, his stabbing sword, his weighted javelins."

"What does this have to do with Alexandros and his Goths?" Dahvos winced, hearing a surly whine creeping into his voice. "He's brought a mishmash of men on foot, men that ride then fight afoot, archers, that bastardized outdated phalanx, lancers . . ."

"More than that," Jusuf said, laughing, bending close. "Did you know Alexandros has appropriated all those loose horses we gathered up during the retreat from Constantinople? His quartermaster levied every wagon he can find in Thrace. He even stole all the mules that should be going with those Western troops—said they didn't have enough hulls to carry them away."

Dahvos' scowl faded, slowly replaced by a considering look. "How many horses and mules does he need?"

"Enough," Jusuf said, grinning at the audacity, "to put every man in his army on horseback, and all their biscuit, gear and arrows on mule or wagon. He marched down here from Magna Gothica with half his men on horseback and it took them two months. I was breaking bread with that big moose tarkhan of his—Clothar Shortbeard—and he guesses they could make the return trip in half the time."

"Huh." Dahvos' eyelid twitched. He did not seem impressed. "But can they . . . no, can *he* fight?"

"He can." Jusuf seemed very sure. "If that is your worry, set it aside."

"You're so sure? Why?"

"You'll see." Jusuf was still grinning. "You will see."

Dahvos didn't see how his half-brother could be so sure, but Jusuf was so confident he let the matter drop. The kagan had enough work of his own to do, getting his own troops ready to take the field. Jusuf, on the other hand, seemed to be looking forward to a battle.

Jusuf was letting his mare trot along at an easy pace, enjoying clear blue skies and a warm summer day, when battle presented itself. Five weeks had passed since the conversation on the town wall, and true to his word, Alexandros marched his army—ready or not—out of their camps at Perinthus and up the northeast highway towards Constantinople. The Goths and Khazars broke camp with admirable efficiency and got under-way the first morning. The Eastern troops struggled manfully for most of the day, finally being forced to march by torchlight into late evening to catch up with the rest of the army. Jusuf had been out watching with the picket when they straggled into the main camp. As he expected, the Eastern infantry arrived in good order, wagons packed, gear stowed and kit in fighting trim. The cavalry had not, in fact, arrived until the next day, heads low and banners furled.

Alexandros had not been pleased, but despite everyone's expectation, he did not punish the cavalry officers. Instead, the army had been roused the following day by horns and bucina-call before dawn and they marched for three straight days at what amounted to breakneck speed for the legionaries. Forced to keep up with everyone else, the Eastern horse shrugged off their ill-humor. Faced with obvious loss of face to some mud-footed infantry, the cataphracts rose to the occasion. The Khazars, laughing behind their hands, tried not to jeer the Eastern horsemen, but it was difficult. The Eastern legionaries and Gothic foot had shown no such restraint.

This morning, Alexandros had deployed the Khazar light horse under Jusuf's command in a wide-ranging screen in front of his main advance. Everyone expected to reach the large town of Selymbria today, through which they had fled in such haste four months before. Jusuf's memory of the place was poor—rain, exhaustion and a wagon hanging from the road, wheels spinning uselessly in the mud. He remembered straining, packed shoulder-to-shoulder with a dozen other men, pushing it back onto the road while rain bit his eyes and his boots slurped into clinging black mud.

A shout of alarm and the peculiar whistling sound of arrows plunging from a high shot roused Jusuf from his memories. His riders were turning, swinging away from the road and into a field of wheat stubble. Other men—in darker clothing, with tubular, trailing dragon banners—appeared across the lot, pouring out of two lanes cutting through thatch-roofed houses. Jusuf clucked at the mare and she picked up the pace, high-stepping down the bank. Black arrows flickered in the air and one of them struck the road a wagon's length away, then sprang back up, flipping end for end, before rattling onto the paving stones.

"Avars!" Shouted one of Jusuf's men, wheeling his horse around to face the tarkhan.

"Quite a number of them," Jusuf said, shading his eyes with a hand. The crowd of Avar horsemen was growing bigger. Now some had appeared on the main road and they spilled out into line on either side of the highway. A few of the stronger Avar archers were shooting high, hoping for a lucky hit. Jusuf nudged his horse to the side. She whickered at him questioningly, then skipped away as a black-fletched shaft sank into the earth inches from her fetlocks. "Ride back and find Alexandros," he said, watching the Avars pour around the farm buildings like water from an opened sluice. "Tell him we've found about, oh, six thousand Avars—mostly light horse, but a goodly proportion of their knights."

The man rode off in haste, kicking up a cloud of dust. Jusuf moved himself under the shade of a big willow standing beside the road above a culvert. He was pleased to see his riders spread out into a skirmish line, loosing long shots from their bows when they spied an interesting target. Three couriers found him under the tree, riding up with their young horses streaked with sweat.

The Avars continued to arrive. Now Jusuf spied tall horse tail banners and golden horns and a thick cluster of men in bulkier armor. He whistled, standing in his stirrups, peering at the enemy.

"Avi, you ride back and find *comes* Alexandros and tell him the Avar khagan—or at least his household guard—is on the road in front of us."

The boy bolted off, like a good courier, and Jusuf called to his singnaller to blow retreat in good order, which produced the skirling wail peculiar to Khazar horns. More arrows lofted into the air, the sun glittering from their points and Jusuf and his command cantered away, back towards the line of trees on the southern side of the stubbled field. *The Roman army will arrive soon*, he thought.

Behind the retreating Khazars, the Avar columns continued to spread out, slowly forming a solid body across the road, and two heavy wings stretching across the fields. Despite the poor quality of their Slavic allies—well, subjects really; a motley aggregation of Croats, Moravians and Sklavenoi—the Avar officers were excellent and they did not brook disobedience from their vassals.

Despite Alexandros' eagerness to test himself against the Persians, Jusuf spent the rest of the day falling back field by field, keeping the Avars busy while waiting for the Roman army to arrive. The skirmishing was desultory, since the Khazars easily kept at long bowshot, save when they fell back through an orchard or woodlot. All of the land around Selymbria was heavily built up, filled with farmhouses and fieldstone walls. By nightfall, Jusuf had lost only a dozen men, and at least two of those might have gotten lost in the maze of tracks and lanes. As soon as the sun dipped behind the western hills, the Avars halted their advance.

Jusuf told off his men to keep a picket line across the main road and through the trees and brambles on either side. He let his horse rest, browsing on thin yellow grass under the olives. His courier riders squatted down among the gnarled trees and ate some legion biscuit—a hard, flat bread like a meal cake and as solid as old leather—and washed it down with wine they had appropriated from one of the farmhouses. Jusuf had been surprised, as the long day unwound, at the absence of any farmers, or stock, or even chickens. He wondered how the locals knew to flee. The absence of men among such signs of their industry—for these Romans were industrious, if nothing else, and

Jusuf felt a little trapped to be in such a close, cluttered land-scape—lent everything an ominous air.

"Ho! Tarkhan!" Jusuf looked up and his guards relaxed a lit-tle, lowering their bows. One of the courier riders assigned to Dahvos rode up, ducking his head under low-lying branches. His horse seemed rested and filled with mischief—it bit at Jusuf's mare, earning a wall-eyed glare in return. "*Comes* Alexandros wishes to speak with you."

"Fine." Jusuf levered himself from the ground, grunting, and took one of the fresh horses. "If anything happens, send two riders to find me and don't lose track of the enemy," he said to the men still squatting under the trees. "Otherwise, I will be back before dawn."

It was full dark by the time Jusuf passed through a picket of le-gionaries on the road and reached the main camp. The *comes* followed standard Eastern practice, choosing a big triangular section of waste ground filled with brambles and Scythian this-tle between a road junction and two fields filled with ripening melons. Despite the irregular space, the Easterners were busy, digging a long ditch first facing the road, crossed by two earthen ramps, and then around the other two sides of the camp. As was customary, the army engineers marked the boundaries with ropes strung on stakes. The ditch lay on one side of the boundary rope and a palisade of sharpened stakes and cut logs on the other. Where there had been insufficient time to build the fence, army wagons were lined up to close the gaps.

Bonfires burned cheerfully at each gate and along the av-enues leading into the camp. Some men were awake, either on guard duty, or just sitting in front of their tents, as Jusuf rode through to the praetorium at the center of the encampment. Everyone else seemed to be asleep, or at least pretending to sleep. Jusuf had heard many soldiers boast of being able to doze anywhere, but most men, he knew, would be praying, or thinking of home. There would be battle soon and only the lord of heaven knew who might live and who might die.

Grooms ran out to take his horse as Jusuf dismounted and he smelled stew bubbling on the fire and lamb and mutton roast-ing. The air was filled with the soft sound of thousands of horses munching oats and grass. All the stable tie-lines were set at the center of the camp, within a protective shield of infantry cohorts. Alexandros was still awake, which came as little surprise to the Khazar. *When did the general ever sleep?* He ducked into the tent.

"Tarkhan Jusuf, welcome." Alexandros was sitting on a backless, tripodal chair. A large rug covered the floor of the tent, and the other commanders—Chlothar Shortbeard, Dahvos, an Easterner named Valentinius who commanded the Roman foot, and lord Demetrios, who was responsible for the rabble of Eastern cataphracts—were arrayed on either side. Jusuf nodded to them, then hooked over a camp stool and sat down.

"*Comes* Alexandros," he said in greeting.

Alexandros smiled, brushing a long lock of hair out of his face. It was a habit and Jusuf saw the Macedonian was in good humor. "I received your messages by rider, Jusuf, as to the advance of the enemy and their encampment for the night. Is there anything else? Have you seen any Persian troops afield, or only Avars?"

"No, *comes*," Jusuf answered, seeing that a fuller report was expected. "We've seen a large number of Avar horse—both light horse-archer and knights—as well as, late in the day, a quantity of Slavic foot on the main road. They were bringing up wagons at dusk and lagering—as the Goths would say—about a mile from our positions. With the addition of the Slavs, there must be at least twelve thousand men. I saw the khagan's banners and his guardsmen, though I did not set eyes upon Bayan himself."

"You know him by sight?" Alexandros leaned forward, quite interested.

"Yes," Jusuf said. "As a youth I was sent to the Avar court as a hostage. I know the khagan Bayan well."

"Excellent." Alexandros slapped his knee. "Tell me about him. What kind of man is he? Does he favor one hand over the other?"

Jusuf paused, marshalling his thoughts. His time among the Avars now seemed quite distant, though less than a decade had passed since he'd been sent to live among them. There had been talk of an alliance then, between peak-roofed Itil and the *hring*—the triple-walled Avar capital at Serdica in Moesia—but nothing came of the matter. In the old days, the T'u-chüeh would have forbidden such an alliance—they despised the Avars and called them slaves—but the T'u-chüeh empire had lately fallen into disrepair.

"My lord," Jusuf said at last, having summoned up old memories and arranged them to his liking, "this khagan is named Bayan, after his grandfather. Unlike his father Jubudei, he is neither patient nor wise; he is reckless and given to bold maneuvers. Bayan is stout, shorter than most of his kind. He hides his right arm—an arrow cut the elbow in a border skirmish, making the limb weak. So he fights with his left hand. When he was a young man, he won many victories over the Gepids in the west, over the Bulgars and the Slavs. Even the Blue Huns pay him tribute."

"Do you think he will lead in battle himself?"

"No, *comes*, not with a weak arm. He will stay back, and let his *umen* commanders handle the line of battle."

"Good." Alexandros' curiosity was satisfied. "Tomorrow we may fight, if the enemy has the stomach for battle. All of you have seen the ground—very poor for horses, filled with streams and fields and orchards. If we fight here, matters will be decided by our infantry in close quarters."

The Macedonian smiled broadly and stood, filled with nervous energy. He paced the circumference of the tent, harsh voice ringing. "I cannot think of a better place to fight this enemy. Our men, on foot, are the match for two, three, even four times their number in these barbarians. It may be the Avar khagan has tired of sitting at Constantinople and has taken the field to loot, to pillage, to forage for his men. Therefore, we will rise up before dawn and attack, straight up the road. My Goths will lead, and your men, Valentinius, will follow close behind. When we come upon the Avars, you shall deploy on either flank."

"And my men?" Demetrios wore a remarkably foul expression on his face. "What shall we do—hold your horses?"

Jusuf raised a mental eyebrow at the man's truculence, though his face remained impassive.

"You, Demetrios, will be waiting on our far left wing, waiting for the kagan Dahvos here and his lancers to draw the attention of the enemy. They will cover the left flank of the legionaries, as they advance. You will wait for certain news to reach you."

"What news?" The cataphract's ill temper did not abate, a purplish flush rising at his throat. Jusuf watched with interest, wondering if the man might burst a vessel right there in the tent and expire. The Eastern nobleman was certainly choleric enough. . . .

"You will wait," Alexandros said in a genial tone, "for the Avar knights to try and swing wide to our left, around the brawl that will inevitably develop in the center, and then you will fall upon them like Zeus' own thunderbolt and destroy them."

Demetrios blinked, then sat back, rendered speechless. He had not expected to be given a place in the line of battle.

"But you *must wait*," Alexandros continued, "until the enemy—goaded beyond anger by our slaughter in the middle—unleashes all his dogs, not just a few, and they are intent upon their prey. Do you understand?"

"Yes," Demetrios said, choking, suddenly aware of the fierce look on the Macedonian's face and the way Alexandros loomed over him. "We will wait until the moment is right."

"Good." Alexandros' face was very hard and Jusuf wondered if the *comes* had been drinking. There was something about the quicksilver change in his emotions that brought the grape to mind. "If you charge too soon, or not at all, indeed—if you fail to perform adequately, Demetrios, then you will find yourself unable to perform at all."

Sweating with fear, Bayan, son of Jubudei, khagan of the Avar nation, woke in darkness. Heavy quilts lay across his body and silken pillows cushioned his head. Concubines, comfortably warm, curled on either side of the Avar. In the gloom, he could hear the girls breathing softly, deep in sleep. The khagan's face twitched and he squeezed his eyes shut, trying to keep from crying out. Though the night covered his right arm, Bayan could feel the limb lying stiff beside him, the flesh cold and inert. Grunting with an effort, he groped across the quilts with his good arm.

Beside his bed, on a folding lacquered table, his fingertips brushed across a bow stave of horn and springy wood. Something like a hot, bright spark flashed in the darkness. Bayan gasped, and felt a hot, warm rush of strength flood his body. Ignoring the sleepy complaints of the two girls, the khagan threw back the quilts and rolled out of the bed. Outside, lanterns hanging from the eaves of his great tent shed a faint illumination.

Bayan watched his right arm, streaked by pale bands of light, and the limb trembled with suddenly flowing blood, with the flush of life, and then stringy muscles swelled and firmed with visible speed. The khagan felt joy fill him, even as his arm grew stronger and stronger. He clasped the tall bow, glittering and dark in the faint light, to his breast. His right hand clenched into a fist.

"What a gift!" He breathed, barely audible even to himself. "What a gift."

Even the bearer had been delightful, the perfect emissary to catch Bayan's attention. . . .

The T'u-chüeh bent one knee, neck exposed between his oily black hair and the top of his laminated armor. Bayan snorted, turning from his place at the edge of the raised wooden platform. He did not deign to look fully upon the ambassador. "Rise, Persian slave."

The T'u-chüeh stood, his temper admirably leashed. Bayan was in a foul mood, as were his advisors, a grizzled set of older men standing close by. They glowered at C'hu-lo, fingering their weapons. Persia was no longer a friend of the Avars, not after the disasters of the previous spring. Sending one of the eastern lords to treat with them was daring—had not the Avar broken free of the T'u-chüeh yoke a hundred years before? Didn't the eastern Turks call the Avars "slave" and "beast"? But Bayan acknowledged, silently, the sight of the single-braid kneeling before him was pleasant.

"Great lord, my master sends you warm greetings, offering you gifts and tokens of his friendship." C'hu-lo pulled a *gorytos* from his back in a smooth motion, laying the bow case down on the rough-hewn planks. In the bright sunlight the case gleamed a rich dark red. The horsehide was carefully treated, rubbed with preserving oils, the nap of fine hair arranged just so. Leather edging surrounded the mottled red-and-white hide, punched with signs representing the sky, the wind, the gods, the horses and the people. "The king of kings thinks you will find this small gift, the least of gifts, pleasing."

Bayan did not look at the case, his face turning dark with anger. The khagan was a stout man, shorter than his advisors, with one arm hidden in the folds of his fur vest. His other hand, his left, tugged at a thin patchy beard. Like his captains and advisors, he was wearing a long peaked cap of green felt and a fur-lined cape. Armor of riveted iron rings covered his barrel-like chest and hung down past his waist. His features echoed C'hu-lo's own—a flattened nose, high cheekbones, a slant to his eyes. To the Eastern eye, there were subtle differences; the Avar khagan wore his long black hair in two plaits, where the T'u-chüeh favored one.

"You are not pleased, lord of men? Has the king of kings given offense in some way?"

The Avar advisors growled, bristling, and one of them drew his curving cavalry sword. The T'u-chüeh did not respond, watching Bayan with a patient, stoic expression, one hand flat on the platform.

"What is the cost of Persian friendship?" Bayan looked down upon C'hu-lo. "You offer a single bow and the swords of the Romans will take ten thousand of my subjects. You offer fine words and promises of victory, but the Romans will deliver fire and death. Three years we strove against the walls of the City. We took nothing but windrows of the dead. Where is the glory there? The prizes? The slaves? Cold and rotting in the ground with my sons, with the sons of my sons."

C'hu-lo remained impassive; though the fury and hatred in Bayan's voice was hot enough to set wood alight. In response, he unhooked three clasps holding the bow case closed. Deftly, he opened the case, revealing the bow and arrows within to the sky. The Avars surrounding him hissed in surprise.

The bowstave was a sleek dark wood on the inner face, then glossy bone on the outer. It was of a full length, the "man" bow of the Huns, with a long curving topstave and a shorter, thicker foundation. Coiled strings, shining with oil, sat in leather hold-ers on the inside of the case. A sheaf of arrows, the shafts painted in blue, the fletching white-and-gray goose, filled the other half of the case. C'hu-lo stood, holding the weapon in his hands. "This is the bow of a king, of a hero."

Bayan's face darkened, turning a muddy red color. C'hu-lo matched his stare. Bayan thought his heart might burst, so fiercely did it hammer in his chest. "Here, lord of men, take it, draw it, set your sight upon a pleasing target."

Bayan could not bring himself to speak. His right arm, hidden in the vest, slipped out. The limb was withered, scored by a long curling scar lapping over the elbow. C'hu-lo took the moment—the advisors averted their eyes from the khagan's shame—and stepped close, looking slightly down on the man. "Lord Bayan," he whispered, "put your hands upon this weapon, feel the power! The king of kings offers you not insult, but a great gift."

Bayan glared up at him, but then paused, seeing a strange pleading in C'hu-lo's eyes.

"My arm is too weak," the khagan whispered. "You insult me before my men!"

"No, great lord," C'hu-lo's voice was low and urgent. "Here is the string, well waxed, a shaft, straight and true. Do as your fathers have done, string, draw, loose! Trust me and you will be delivered from shame."

Bayan shook his head, refusing to touch the weapon. C'hu-lo knelt again, holding the bow above his head. "If you do not find the weapon sufficient, great lord, then strike off my head."

C'hu-lo thrust the bow into Bayan's hands, forcing the man to take the stave, lest the weapon drop. No T'u-chüeh, or Avar, would allow such treatment of a bow. The T'u-chüeh bent his head to the planks, dragging aside his hair with one hand, exposing a tanned neck. His voice muffled, he said, "This thing is in your heart, great khagan—your ancestors look down. See the pride in their eyes!"

Bayan grimaced, but the bow felt good in his hands. He looked around, seeing his advisors—the lords of the Avar clans, the chiefs of the towns under his sway, his kinsmen, the friends of his youth—still looking away in embarrassment. Among their people, it defied the gods for the khagan to be crippled or flawed in the body. But Bayan's affliction came late in life, well after he had established himself and sired many strong sons. Each day he cursed the chance Roman arrow. It had been such an insignificant skirmish in the depths of winter too. There had been many victories in his youth and his legend was strong among the yurts and campfires of the people. His recent failures ate at him like a cancer. *The Romans would be his slaves!*

The khagan looked out on the marshlands, squinting into the sun. The land was green and verdant, filled with stands of aspen and willow, cut by hundreds of channels, sparkling bright under the sun. Egrets and herons filled the air, sweeping and darting in numberless flocks. This was a rich land, filled with game. It pleased the khagan to know true men hunted in these willow breaks and fished in these plentiful streams. In the distance, there was a thundering of wings and a flock of geese suddenly bolted into the sky. Doubtless one of the wild cats hunting in the estuaries startled them up.

Bayan swallowed, then put the bow to his knee. A leather pad was sewn into his legging for just such a purpose. His fingers remembered what to do, at least, and he slipped the tightly wound string loop under the base of the bowstave. The other end hooked over the top and the wood of the stave began to flex. Despite gnawing fear, Bayan put the arrow to the stave, then—in a sudden hush—pushed the string away from him, drawing, sighting, seeing the geese climbing into the summer sky, leading the first bird, then—*snap!*—the arrow was away, lofting into the sky.

The khagan shuddered, feeling nauseated, but the arrow rose and rose and then, reaching the top of its arc, fell gently, piercing the goose through the center of its great white-and-gray body. There was a burst of feathers and the bird fell, plummeting, into the marsh below. Bayan's mouth was open in surprise. He could not bring words to his lips.

"See," C'hu-lo whispered, rising and leaning close, "the king of kings is mighty. His strength flows to your arms from his heart. In this way, all his friends are exalted."

Bayan watched as half-naked boys ran out from the base of the hill, leaping amongst the pools, running between tall stands of green cane. Soon they would bring him his kill, the first of the season, and it would roast over a stone pit, a delicacy for all the warriors thronging to his tent.

"Feel your arm, lord of men, is it strong?"

Bayan nodded, flexing the fingers of his right hand. The bowstave felt good in his hands, right and proper. His hand seemed powerful, not so weak and pale. Strong, like the Avar nation.

"Hey-yup!" Jusuf pointed with his lance, rear strap wrapped around his arm, through the crowd of legionaries jogging along the road, and the column of light horse following him swerved like a flock of birds turning over a lake. The mare whickered, found the footing on the side of the road suitable and half-trotted, half-slid down the bank into high grass. Jusuf let the horse find her own way. He turned in the saddle and watched his men pick their way down the slope.

On the road, long lines of Eastern infantry moved north at step-and-a-half time. A column of nearly a hundred men tramped past, long rust-colored tunics hanging down to their knees, broad-toed boots ringing on the paving stones. Each man had a leather quiver slung on his back, heavy with arrows, his bow in hand, half-strung. A small, round wooden shield—painted a solid color and bossed with iron—bounced on his shoulder. Most of the archers carried axes thrust into broad leather belts, or short swords hung from a strap. In the Eastern manner, their hair—most of them were bareheaded, though some sported straw hats against the sun—was cropped short in a style the Khazar heard called "leonine," though they looked nothing like any species of lion Jusuf had ever seen.

The Khazar light horse trotted through high grass, stirring up a drifting cloud of dust and seeds to hang in the air, glowing in the early morning light. The entire Roman army had started moving before dawn, and Jusuf was hurrying, trying to get into position before the battle started. Dahvos and the main body of the Khazar horse were somewhere behind him, held up on the road or trying to pick their way through the maze of farm tracks paralleling the highway. The high grass suddenly fell away and the mare splashed through a shallow stream and up a stony bank. Almost immediately, Jusuf shouted to his trumpeters to sound a warning call.

"Time to cut wood," he said, chuckling to his aides.

Long wide-mouthed horns of beaten bronze wailed.

A hundred yards away the Avar camp was awake and alarmed, with men pouring out of a farmhouse and leaping up from the ground like ants disturbed from a nest. A huge crowd of Slavs spread out across the open fields, hair hanging lank around tattooed shoulders, the rising sun winking on iron caps and the points of their spears.

"Deploy in loose order!" Jusuf shouted, turning and riding towards the highway on his right. The Khazar lancers advanced to the left of the Eastern infantry, providing an appetizing target for the Avar knights. All around Jusuf, his men rode up out of the stream in a steady wave, lances unlimbered or bows laid across their saddles. A hundred feet away, as Jusuf trotted to the end of the line, a cohort of Eastern Empire heavy infantry splashed across the stream as well. Between the stream and the houses was a long section of open, flat ground. They advanced with a measured step, heavy oval shields facing the enemy. Each man marched forward with a long spear angled up and ahead, steel helmet shining, a tuft of cloth—matching the color of his shield—dancing at the point. The tramp of their boots boomed in time with a shouted cadence.

Beyond them, barely visible against the bright eastern sky, ranks of Goths filled the main road. Jusuf ignored them for a moment and cantered up to the edge of the Roman infantry. A dozen paces from the edge of the formation, a grizzled-looking veteran was walking backwards, his red cape swirling around his legs, watching the alignment of the men.

"Centurion!" Jusuf called as he rode up. "Good day!"

The officer looked up, scowling, then made a face to see some barbarian looming over him. "What do you want?"

"To wish you and your men good luck," Jusuf said, leaning on his saddle horn. He felt a little giddy with battle imminent, and the air was clear and sharp and the morning birds were singing. With luck the day would be gloriously clear, though at the moment a haze drifted among the trees. "We'll watch your back."

The Roman officer stared at him for a moment, walking backwards, one eye gauging his men's advance. Then the man grunted and waved in acknowledgement.

"Good hunting!" Jusuf shouted, saluting to the men in the ranks, some of whom were looking over at him curiously. Then he clucked at the mare and turned back to see to *his* lines. The Khazars had crossed the streambed and fanned out in an easy trot. Across the fields—studded with individual trees and piles of stones gathered by farmers—the Avars were pouring out of their encampment in a black flood. Horns blew and drums beat furiously. Jusuf looked off to his left and frowned. There was no sign of the Eastern cataphracts lurking among the brush and trees.

"Signal advance at a walk!" Jusuf signaled to his banner and trumpet men. Flags fluttered in the air and there was more wailing and honking. Mindful of Dahvos' warning to stay out of trouble, Jusuf tossed his lance to one of the couriers behind him, then drew his striking sword. "Advance!"

"My lord! The Romans . . ."

"I can hear them." Bayan was watching the morning sky, chin raised while servants bustled around him, strapping greaves and armored plates to his legs, his arms. A light fog was dissipating, leaving the sky a clear blue. A few thin clouds streaked the face of Tengri's heaven. A broad leather belt was cinched at his waist and he lowered his arms, letting the armorers slide a back-and-breast of laminated iron strips over his arms. The khagan pursed his lips, finally considering the *umen* commanders kneeling before him. "What do you see?"

The young man kept his face impassive, though Bayan could see a vein throbbing on the side of his neck. "A Roman army, lord of the world . . . a large force of infantry is astride the road, while cavalry is forming up on either wing."

"Their numbers?" Bayan shifted his bow from one hand to the other, allowing the armorers to secure the straps on his right arm and slide an armored glove over his fingers. The khagan flexed his fingers in the glove, finding the mesh of iron rings firm. He nodded absently to one of the servants, who opened a small box and took out a steel ring, incised with interlocking geometric shapes. The thumb ring fit snugly over the armored glove and Bayan turned the ring slightly, ensuring the smooth inner surface sat under his thumb.

"Three thousand foot in the middle, my lord. Four thousand Khazars on the right, and another four thousand Roman horse on the left." The *umen* commander made a face at his mention of *Roman horse*. Bayan understood—the men of the Stone City might have a rich empire, but they were not *horsemen*. At least the Khazars could draw, loose and ride at the same time. "But more men are still coming out of the woods."

Bayan scratched his beard, thinking. The color of the sky promised a beautiful, clear day. Even the damp closeness of the woods and fields did not weigh on him as it usually did. "I will command the right wing," the khagan said briskly. "My household guard and the heavy horse will be under my banner. The Sklavenoi and Slavs and other lesser men will hold the center, among the buildings. Place Jujen and his *umen* on the left, to screen the flank. I doubt the Roman horsemen will be able to dislodge him!"

The *umen* commanders laughed, rising and bowing to their khagan. Bayan was pleased to see their faces filled with eagerness for battle and honorable glory. The sky father would bless them today!

An hour passed with Jusuf keeping a weather eye on the Roman lines. His riders wheeled and darted towards the slowly assembling Avar lines, loosing clouds of arrows into the Slavic spearmen. This drew shouts of rage and occasional warriors burst from the ranks of their fellows, running out to hurl a spear or a javelin at the Khazar riders, who danced away, laughing. The enemy maintained his line, though Jusuf saw at least a dozen Slavs—wild white hair, thick with grease and clay, barely armored in leather jerkins or woad-blue tattoos—cut down by their Avar officers.

Jusuf bit his thumb nervously. *Those Avar beki jegun are good. They'll kill a hundred men to keep the rest in good order . . .*

The huge mass of the Slavs was being reinforced by troops of Avar horse—glinting mail and horsetail plumes and tall spears—and moving forward. There were a lot of Slavs on the field today, and behind them, half-hidden by the mass of spear- and axe-men and the cloud of dust they raised, bands of cavalry were forming up. Jusuf began to get a feeling the full weight of the Avar nation had come down the road from Constantinople.

He suddenly felt foolish. His appreciation of the *comes* Alexandros' tactics had blinded him. Soon enough, the Avars were going to storm right into his line and try their best to kill him and his men. Jusuf shook himself, like a soft-mouthed Charka hound rising from some prairie lake. A trickle of fear pulsed through the Khazar and he took a firm grip on his sword-hilt.

Then a shrill of *bucinas* and a thunderous kettledrum roar sounded from the center of the Roman line. Without Jusuf noticing, his portion of the line had carried forward beyond the axis of the Roman advance and now, looking off to his right, he could see back into the center. The lines of round Eastern shields had parted, folding back like a clockwork, and a great host of men advanced up the highway, pikes swaying above like young saplings. The Goths advanced on the Avar center with a deep basso shout and the *tramp-tramp-tramp* of their hobnailed boots.

The haze shrouding the field faded and Jusuf wheeled his horse, riding back, shouting for his banner commanders. "Fall back! Re-form on the Roman line!"

Down on the road, the Goths deployed with surprising ease, flooding out across the highway and falling into twelve deep ranks. The drums continued to beat, shivering the air, and Jusuf saw a stillness fall across the Avar front. Every man was staring at the apparition emerging from the Roman lines. The Gothic ranks continued to deploy, pikes upright, swaying almost in unison as the men below marched forward. At the edges of the phalanx, more Goths ran forward, a mixture of armored men with bows and some with swords and maces.

Horns wailed and the phalanx rippled like a snakeskin, the long spears dipping as one and suddenly the Avars were faced with a solid wall of iron points. The first five ranks held their spears low, underarm, while those behind remained raised. The maneuver developed effortlessly and the phalanx swept forward without so much as a missed step.

From his vantage, Jusuf suddenly felt a chill and the hairs on the back of his neck stand up. *Oh, lord of heaven*, his mind raced, *Anastasia was right—this is no actor playing the king of kings, this is the very man himself!*

Moments later, the phalanx ground into the center of the Avar line at a swift walk and there was a resounding crash of metal on wood and flesh. The Avar host reeled back from the shock and Jusuf could see men screaming, dying, pierced through by eighteen-foot spears. The Goths stabbed overhand, leaf-shaped points licking into throats and chests. The first three ranks stood their ground, holding the Slavs back with a thicket of iron. A drum boomed, a single deep note, and the phalanx advanced a step.

Terrible confusion gripped the Avar center. The phalanx was hungry and it ate into the crowd of barbarians—armed with axes, short spears, javelins, swords—who could not come to grips with the iron-faced men in the twelve ranks. At the same time, the flanks of the Roman advance filled with lines of Peltasts, running up with their great bows to take a shooting stance.

A deep roar brewed up from the center, mingled screams and battle cries and the ceaseless *stab-stab-stab* of the phalanx grinding forward, a step at a time, into the enemy. Avar officers ran out on the sides, lashing the Slavs and drawing their own weapons. The black mass of the enemy began to draw away from the forest of spears and rush forward on either side.

The first rank of archers loosed, the *snap* of their bows singing across the field. Jusuf flinched as if he had been struck himself. The air was suddenly dark with arrows. The Avar advance staggered and there were more screams. Dozens of men fell, pierced through by yard-long shafts. The second rank of Peltasts loosed hard on the heels of the first and the Slavic line staggered. Then the third rank loosed, shooting high, lofting a black hungry cloud over the heads of their fellows. The first rank had already plucked a fresh arrow, drawn, sighted and loosed again.

The Avar officers screamed, urging their men to stand, but the lightly armored Slavs were being forced back by a constant rain of arrows, loosed at point-blank range. The wicker shields were thick with shafts. Their own archers were trying to shoot back, but everything was in chaos, with men surging back, trying to flee, and more men hurrying up.

The phalanx continued to advance, step by step.

Jusuf tore his attention away from the slaughter. "Stand ready!" His own men formed up, readying arrows. Any moment now the wings of the Avar host would come into play. . . . Jusuf looked back and saw, to his great relief, Dahvos and the heavy Khazar horse surging up out of the streambed, banners snapping in the breeze, their own standards flashing in the morning sun. The Khazar wheeled his horse, surveying his lines and seeing that there wasn't enough space for Dahvos' *umens* to deploy on this side of the streambed.

Need to clear some room to maneuver, he thought.

"Lancers!" he shouted, voice booming across the field. "With me!"

Surrounded by a thick crowd of nobles on horseback, Bayan rode through a stand of evenly-spaced lemon trees. Thick, glossy leaves brushed his helmet and plucked at his lance. Dappled sunlight fell on dark gray armor under by a shining silk coat printed with a pattern of russet leaves. The khagan felt light, almost exalted. The rumble of four thousand hooves, the creaking of armor and the mutter of men praying or talking surrounded him. The royal guard swept out of the orchard and into the confusion behind the line of battle.

"Clear the way," shouted Bayan's outriders, spurring their horses forward, lances lowered. Crowds of Sklavenoi parted before them, the mountain barbarians staring at the khagan as he passed. Many of the blond and redheaded men watched Bayan pass with ill-disguised anger. The khagan ignored them, for they lived in huts of wattle and daub in the high mountain valleys. Though they were sometimes brave, they could not withstand the practiced efficiency of Avar soldiers.

Horns blew, ringing in the air, and the royal guardsmen began to form up by rank and file, shifting around Bayan like a cloud of dark birds. The *hring* banner came forward and the khagan raised a hand in salute. Other banners—long dragon-mouthed tubes of cloth, or square blazons holding images of the sun and the lightning—surrounded him.

Ahead, beyond clumped *umens* of spearmen and axemen, Bayan heard the sound of battle. The earth quivered and he could see arrows in the air, flashing bright as they fell.

"The Khazars," he said, caressing the stave of the bow laid across his saddle horn. "Are they attacking in earnest, or only flourishing before our lines?"

"They harass the foot soldiers," barked one of the beki jegun, quilted armor spattered with dust. The man's voice echoed from behind a full face mask. "Like Huns themselves."

"Very well." Bayan raised the black bow and every man within sight focused on him, their eye drawn—willing or no—to his face. "Form wedge and prepare to attack! We will drive off these slaves of the T'u-chüeh and show them how real men fight! You, messenger, inform the commanders of foot we will be moving up. They will clear a lane through their mob for us!"

Men wheeled their horses, eager to do his bidding. Bayan smiled, then laughed aloud.

The day was perfect. His quiver was filled with arrows, fletched with gray goose, and each shaft, he knew, would find destiny in a Khazar heart.

Jusuf slashed his arm down, pointing with the sword, and his line of horsemen bolted forward, hooves drumming on the stubble. The Khazars swung out, riding hard at the Avar line and clumps of high grass, isolated trees and marshy wet ground flashed past. Jusuf held his mare back a bit, letting the first wave of lancers sweep on. A clot of couriers, young faces gleaming with sweat and wild grins, swerved with him and his own bannermen and trumpeters held themselves close, hands tight on their standards and horns, mounts guided by knee pressure.

The lancers swept diagonally across the front of the milling Slavic infantry. There was a great angry shout and the mass of spearmen lunged forward, breaking ranks. The Khazar riders loosed at the gallop, bows singing and arrows flashed down into the ranks of the enemy. Another, angrier, roar smote the air. The lancers nipped in, stabbing overhand, and men toppled backwards along the frontage, faces and chests smeared with blood. Jusuf grinned in delight, letting the mare course across the ground. The Khazars wheeled away, throwing clods and dust into the faces of the Slavs. The Avar infantry ran forward, disintegrating into a mob, screaming and shouting. Even the Avar beki jegun were charging, swords whipping around their heads.

Jusuf turned, letting the dust drift past, then his hand shot up and the flagmen tensed. The Slavic roar was building, growing louder and louder. Out of the corner of his eye, Jusuf saw his lancers swing back and regroup, forming around their *umen* banners, checking their armor, binding wounds and drawing new weapons to replace those they had lost.

"Again!" Jusuf shouted and his banner-men dipped their flags. The trumpeters winded, sending up a hair-raising noise. The lancers began to trot forward. Dust settled out of the air, and Jusuf felt an almost physical shock. The Slavic infantry was still screaming and shouting, raising a huge noise, banging spears on shields and yelping like a vast pack of demented wolves. But they had not continued their pell-mell, mindless charge. Instead the beki jegun checked their wild rush and the entire mass of the enemy split open like a melon.

A solid mass of horsemen—armor gleaming, twin queues bouncing on armored shoulders, lances glittering like stars, their tube banners stiff in the air—was advancing at a quickening trot, straight for Jusuf and his couriers.

The Khazar's heart stuttered and his mouth went dry. The Avar heavy horse—two, maybe three thousand men in full armor of iron scales sewn to leather and backed with felt, mounts likewise protected on head, neck and forequarters, helms flared and throats protected by an iron gorget—thundered towards him. They were perhaps a hundred yards away, erupting from the mass of infantry with frightening speed.

Dahvos, he gibbered to himself, *will only need a moment, just a grain of time. . . .*

"Charge!" Jusuf howled, spurring his mare forward. All thought of keeping himself safe fled, and the couriers and banner-men leapt forward with him. In an instant, in a cloud of dust filled with the war cries of a thousand men, the Khazar lancers sprinted forward, spears leveled. Jusuf cursed leaving his lance behind and spared a half-grain to wrap a strap around his wrist and through the hilts of his sword. He shrugged his left arm, feeling the shield strapped there. Wind keened in his helmet and everything became terribly clear.

The Avars spurred forward as well, voices raised in a single huge shout, and the tiny distance between the two lines of men vanished in the blink of an eye.

Jusuf staggered, feeling a wrenching blow on his left arm, and his mare jinked to the side. An Avar lance sheared across the shield, ripping through the first layer of wood and tearing away the iron boss. The Khazar turned hard in the saddle, hacking down with his sword. The lance flicked away as the Avar knight flipped his weapon out of harm's way. Jusuf reversed his blow and blocked desperately with the shield. The lance stabbed past his head, missing his left eye by inches. Shouting, Jusuf slammed his shield out, knocking the long spear away. The Avar's horse, a nimble black creature, snapped at the mare's head and she shied, dancing back. Jusuf cursed again. He needed a lance of his own.

Arrows whistled overhead. A great din stormed at his ears, deafening him with the roars and shouts of men, the whinnying of horses, the clang of metal on metal and on wood. Jusuf spurred, and the mare responded, leaping forward. The Avar knight was already trading blows with another Khazar and Jusuf rushed past, stabbing across his body. The triangular tip of his sword plunged into the man's armpit and came back slick with blood.

There was no time to see if the wound was mortal. More arrows sleeted out of the sky. A Khazar within Jusuf's field of vision jerked and then slid from his saddle, leaving a wide smear of red across mottled gray horsehide. Three arrows jutted from his chest. Jusuf tried to turn, trying to see what was happening, then furiously parried an Avar mace. The blow rocked him against the rear saddle plate, but he wrenched the mare's head around, turning the whole horse and the mace slithered away along his blade. Without thinking, Jusuf punched the Avar knight in the face, his metal-studded glove sparking on a bronzed metal face mask. Pain jolted up to his elbow. The Avar clawed at his mask, trying to adjust his helmet.

Jusuf whipped his sword sideways, cutting into the man's hand and then, as tendons popped and finger bones split under the blow, into his throat. The sword belled, ringing back from an iron gorget around the Avar's neck. The Khazar cursed, laying in another heavy blow. This time the man jerked back, still blind, and the sword blade wedged between chest plate and helm. Another arrow smashed into the shield on Jusuf's left arm, punching through the laminated wood.

The Khazar cursed, blood turning cold, and tried to wrench his sword free. The blade was stuck. He pulled with both hands. The Avar got one eye lined up with an eyehole and it went wide. The man scrambled to draw a sword from a sheath at the side of his saddle. Jusuf abandoned his stuck blade and smashed the Avar full in the face with his shield. As he did, he leaned far over, falling almost off his horse, and across the neck of the Avar stallion.

A gray-fletched arrow flashed above him and cracked through the armor of one of the Khazar banner men fighting through the press to aid his commander. The boy's eyes went wide, he spat blood and toppled backwards. Jusuf caught the death from the corner of his eye and scrambled back up into his own saddle, the Avar's sword in his left hand. The enemy knight fell out of his saddle and hung upside down, shouting for help.

Jusuf wrenched his horse around, the mare snorting in anger at such rough handling. Another arrow blurred past and another of the Khazar banner men jerked violently in the saddle. Jusuf blinked, staring across the riot of the battlefield. He was only peripherally aware of the Avar charge smashing through the lancers, scattering them, then swinging with full force into the oncoming ranks of Dahvos' *umens*.

A hundred feet away, khagan Bayan was sitting easily on horseback, face serene and untroubled. Jusuf blinked and saw the Avar prince raise his bow—a gorgeous black horn-bow nearly five feet high, gleaming in the sunlight—draw, sight and loose in one fluid, powerful motion. The Khazar's eye could barely follow the flight of the arrow, though his head snapped around instantly, and he saw one of the *umen* commanders in Dahvos' ranks stagger, pierced through by the shot. Jusuf looked back, aghast, and felt a terrible chill.

His arm was ruined! Jusuf's mind struggled to reconcile present sight and past memory. *I saw it, all withered and weak! This is impossible.*

Bayan plucked another arrow from a quiver slung at his knee and fitted it to the string. The movement was very clear to Jusuf and he could see the powerful fingers of that right arm curling around the grip on the bowstave.

A wave of pigtailed horsemen charged past, long banners fluttering, and Jusuf lost sight of the khagan. Seconds later, he was furiously engaged, trading blows with two Avar knights coming at him from either side. His broken shield took another hammer-blow and shattered, shedding splinters and fragments of wood. Jusuf threw the remains at the man on his left side, then barely blocked a thrust at his leg from the right. The tide of battle swept around him, pushing him away from the khagan.

Another gray arrow flashed through the melee, and another Khazar died.

Chlothar Shortbeard, Alexandros' commander of the phalanx, cursed, pulling off his helmet. The heavy iron bucket spilled sweat and the Frank gasped in relief to be able to breathe. Without thinking, he flipped the leather strap around his saddle horn, letting the *spangenhelm* bounce against his thigh. It was dangerous to go bareheaded, but he needed to be able to see. The day was getting hotter and he felt he was swimming in this dreadfully hot, wet air. In the last thirty minutes, the center of the slowly expanding battle had congealed. Chlothar snarled for his standard-bearer to come up, and the man did, urging his own horse forward, wither-to-wither with the Frankish captain's.

The main body of the phalanx continued to advance up the road at a steady walk, but they were running out of open ground. Now they were on the verge of the Avar's overnight encampment—a scattering of farmhouses—thatch-roofed, plastered walls over withes or a timber framework—and scattered high-sided Avar wagons. Thankfully, the Slavic infantry had disintegrated and the barbarians were fleeing in a mob through the leather tents and bundles of sleeping hides. A scattering of bodies lay on the road and the embankment.

"Sound halt and re-form!" Chlothar rubbed his chin in disgust, feeling short prickly hairs under his fingers. Beside him, the bucinators immediately began blatting out a stentorian wail. The ranks of the phalanx began to halt, their file leaders howling commands and using rattan canes freely on any man failing to follow the halting drill. The rear ranks stopped first, squaring themselves and shifting their pikes back, out of fouling distance of those ahead. Within a minute the entire mass slid to a halt. Chlothar didn't watch, knowing someone would foul up.

There was a mighty rattle of wood on wood, and then yelps as unfortunate *hoplites* caught it from their file leaders. Chlothar turned his horse away and trotted along the rear ranks. The Frank stared through the spears, hand shading his eyes against the brilliant sun. The Avars were regrouping among the farmhouses and behind scattered wagons. Some of the Slavs stopped running and Chlothar cursed again, seeing a solid line of shorter men, in darker, heavier armor, appear among the buildings. Brightly colored square banners flapped in the air above them. The Slavs stopped, then turned, shouting defiantly at the Romans.

"Peltasts forward on either side of the road," Chlothar bellowed. "Keep them from forming up!"

Couriers dashed off from the cluster of men around the Frank. Chlothar rose up in his stirrups, straining to see the left and right wings of the army. To the left, there was only a huge, confused, swirling mass of men on horses. Banners jutted up from the field in every direction and the swirl and surge of cavalry in battle was raising a huge cloud of dust. What he could see, however, indicated the Eastern infantry on his flanks holding steady. A distance of at least fifty feet separated them from the Avars, and the opposing lines were staring at each other, waiting for someone to break ranks and attack. The Roman line matched the left edge of the phalanx. Just as it should.

Impressive, the Frank allowed, grudgingly and only in the privacy of his thoughts. The Eastern Legions—the infantry at least—seemed to be every bit as professional as the Western armies. Personally, he was praying desperately to keep from making some irretrievable mistake—Chlothar had only risen to command the *hoplites* when Prince Ermanerich had been forced to remain in Magna Gothica. He'd felt sick all day.

To the right, however, both armies had collided, with the Eastern foot soldiers engaged in a sparking brawl with the Slavic spear- and axe-men. There the barbarians were stiffened by many Avar knights fighting on foot with long swords or heavy spears. Beyond the melee, where the *comes* Alexandros and the Companion cavalry were supposed to be in action, Chlothar could see nothing but treetops. Grunting, he turned back to observe the Avars on the road. Given a moment's respite, they were busily dragging wagons across the paved surface of the highway and making an impromptu barricade. Men behind the wagons exchanged bow shots with the Peltasts as they ran forward.

About half of the Peltasts had unslung their oval shields and stood armed with sword, mace or axe. The rest continued to wield the big recurved bow and were shooting at any target of opportunity. Most of the buildings were on fire and smoke billowed up in white clouds from the damp thatch. The Frank shook his head in dismay. *Soldiers and fire! Those buildings must be empty by now*.

Figuring he had seen enough, Chlothar raised his hand. The runners and signal flagmen tensed. Avar arrows hissed down out of the sky as more of the nomads crowded up to the barricade. Now they were shooting high, trying to hit the men in the phalanx or behind. Their own horse bows could easily make the range.

Chlothar raised his own shield, not a moment too soon. Arrows shattered on the road around him and one of his lieutenants took one in the throat. The Goth choked to death as his companions tried to pull him from the horse and cut it out of his neck. Men died in the phalanx too, but the rest held their ground. Behind the wagon laager, the Avars jeered the approaching Romans. Chlothar ignored them, watching the Peltasts dodge forward through the buildings. In moments the sword and shieldmen would be at the wagon barricade. Arrows continued to flick down out of the smoke. Two of the big Frank's bodyguards moved forward, screening him with long, oval shields.

"Sound advance!" Chlothar barked at the *bucina*-men and the runners. "Attack!"

Horns bellowed and the file leaders began a marching chant. The phalanx rippled, pikes lowering from rest position and the men began to walk forward. Chlothar watched them uneasily, a sick feeling percolating in his stomach. The *comes* had once mentioned, in an offhand way, he hoped the *hoplites* would be able to move at a jog soon, but Chlothar couldn't see them getting up to much more than a fast walk. Not today, anyway. The pikes lowered again in a rippling, rustling motion, which reminded the Frank of trees bending in a high wind.

The phalanx ground forward, flowing inexorably down the road. More arrows flicked out of the smoke. The Avar archers could see them moving, even through the smoke.

Jusuf leaned wearily on the front of his high, four-cornered saddle. His arms felt like lead and sweat streamed out of his helmet and gloves. His left hand burned with pain and he was afraid he'd shattered a knuckle on the Avar's face mask. By some chance, the swirl of battle moved away from him, leaving a cluster of Khazar lancers panting in the drifting clouds of smoke. Most of the men he'd led into the teeth of the Avar charge were dead or scattered across the field, but Dahvos' heavier knights had piled in and were currently locked in a ferocious melee to his left.

Shaking his head to try and clear away the fog of exhaustion, Jusuf stared in disgust at the leather straps hanging on his left arm. The shield was long gone. He needed another.

"Keep an eye out," he said to the lancers on either side of him. Clambering down from his horse was a slow, painful process, but Jusuf spied a fallen shield only a few feet away, spattered with mud and crimson streaks. He *oofed* when his feet hit the ground—his abused thighs flashed with needle-points of pain—but he managed to reach down and drag the round, iron-bossed shield out of the muck. He flipped it over and muttered a curse. One of the straps was missing.

"Useless!" He cast about for another and saw with surprise he was on the far side of the village. The village itself was now burning merrily, sending long, wispy trails of smoke curling across the battlefield. Somehow, in the struggle, he and his men had cut their way through the original enemy line. Disturbed, Jusuf grabbed onto his saddle and managed—by luck—to get the point of his boot into the stirrup.

"Tarkhan!" One of the lancers pointed back the way they'd come. "The kagan is coming this way."

Jusuf stared at the sight of his half-brother trotting towards him, then clambered up into the saddle. Dahvos was at the head of at least a hundred guardsmen—their armor made in the Persian style, with conical backswept helms and a full mail coat from neck to thighs, with sleeves and leggings of overlapping iron lozenges. Each man wore a green surcoat as well, the linen or wool sticking to the metal in the damp air. A flutter of banners and standards completed a martial picture.

"My lord!" Jusuf called out and urged his horse to move. The mare was very tired, but game, and she managed to amble forward. Dahvos heard the call and turned towards him, raising a hand in greeting. Jusuf waved, feeling some of his exhaustion lift—the kagan would take charge now, and tell them all what to do. Just the sight of his commander was a relief.

Something gray flashed past the tips of Jusuf's fingers.

Dahvos caught the blurring passage of the arrow out of the corner of his eye. His shield swung up, covering his face, and then cracked with a pealing ring as the bolt shattered wood and twisted the iron strap around the rim. The kagan toppled backwards, face wild in surprise at the power of the blow. Two guardsmen caught him before he could fall out of the saddle. Jusuf saw a smear of blood on Dahvos' surcoat, but he was already wheeling his horse towards the enemy.

"Bayan!" he screamed, the shrill sound rising above the tumult of battle. His lancers moved with him, almost as one, and their war cry rang out loud and clear. To the east, the melee among the heavy horse broke open and a thick mass of Avar knights swept free, turning towards Jusuf. Among the riders, the Khazar caught sight of Bayan in his dark gray armor and saw two banners flapping behind the khagan—one was the *hring* banner of the Avars, three golden rings on slate—and the other was new to him—a mottled red circle on a black field.

"We must kill the man in gray," he shouted to his lancers.

The horses surged forward, though their poor hearts were close to bursting. Jusuf ignored the trembling in the mount under him and urged her to leap a marshy section of ground. Arrows flashed past overhead, falling among the Avars, and the enemy shot back. Jusuf's standard-bearer cried out in anguish, but the Khazar couldn't spare a glance sideways. Instead, he thrust the captured sword forward as if it were a spear, thundering into the midst of the Avar knights. Two of his lancers rushed forward, stirrup to stirrup with him.

A wall of Avar knights loomed up, lance tips burning with sunlight. Jusuf's mare continued at the gallop and then she swerved violently, nipping past the first of the Avars. The nomad thrust with his lance and Jusuf flung himself sideways, swinging behind the mare's body, clinging with one hand to the saddle horn. The lance slashed overhead and there was a tremendous crash as one of the Khazar lancers slammed his own spear into the Avar's exposed chest. Jusuf swung back up, slashing sideways at another Avar charging past. The tip of the blade sparked from the man's shoulder plate, but did not penetrate the heavy iron.

The mare continued to gallop forward and Jusuf passed a wild moment as she bolted through another crowd of Avars. Two of the enemy hacked at him—he could only block one blow, and the other bit into the mailed sleeve on his left arm—but then he burst past them as well. Blood slicked his arm where the stroke drove iron links through the woolen shirt and leather into muscle. Blood roared in his ears and the sky faded to gray.

Bayan was only yards away, smiling serenely into the melee swirling around him. He held the black bow high, the top stave well over his head. The khagan drew another gray-fletched arrow to the string. Jusuf spurred the mare and she gave one last, game effort, spurting forward. Jusuf ignored the crowd of Avar guardsmen turning their horses towards him, their arrows flashing through the air, the scream of battle rising steadily on all sides. He even ignored the blowing horns in the distance and the trembling in the ground as thousands of hooves beat the earth.

"Bayan the cripple! Face me, coward!" Jusuf's voice boomed,

distorted by the helmet, but the khagan's head snapped around, bow swiveling and his dark eyes widened in recognition. All this, Jusuf saw in a blur as the mare plowed heedlessly, blind from exhaustion, into the flank of the khagan's horse. The Avar steed leapt back, surprised, and kicked violently. The mare reeled drunkenly, stunned by the impact of running headlong into the larger horse's armor and she collapsed, whinnying in pain.

Jusuf leapt free, dragging a dagger from his belt and left hand clutching his sword. Bayan had not fallen—he was far too good a horseman to be thrown by his own horse—but he was forced to seize the reins and bring the big black under control. Gray-fletched arrows littered the sandy ground. Jusuf dodged in as the Avar horse swung towards him and rolled nimbly under the foam-flecked chest. Bayan shouted for his guards, but when the Khazar came up from his roll the saddle strap parted neatly and the khagan slid helplessly to the ground.

Bayan came up furious, eyes glittering. The bow was still clenched in his right hand, but a long single-bladed saber rasped from his sheath with the ease of long practice. Jusuf did not wait for stirring words, or even an insult, but leapt in, slashing at the gleaming black bow with the point of his blade.

The khagan shrieked in fear, snatching the bow back from danger, and Jusuf stabbed with the dagger at the man's face. Unlike his guardsmen, Bayan was wearing an open-faced helmet, which gave him good vision but lacked the full-face protection of their iron masks. The Avar flinched away from the blow and the tip of the dagger scored across his cheek. Face streaming with blood, Bayan blocked wildly. The curved blade of his sword jarred against Jusuf's dagger hilt. For a moment, they swayed back and forth—strength pitted against strength— then the Khazar jumped back, letting his dagger drag, binding along the blade for an instant, and he whipped the longsword in a flat cut at Bayan's head.

With his right hand clutching the precious bow, Bayan could only leap back himself. The tip of Jusuf's sword blurred past his nose. The Khazar swarmed in, his enemy out of balance, smashing heavily at the khagan's guard. Bayan parried furiously, sliding backwards on the soft ground, blocking one stroke, then two. Jusuf drew back, panting, and the Avar got his feet under him. Bayan said nothing, gasping for breath himself, but Jusuf could see undiluted hatred and recognition flare in the khagan's eyes.

I should have left him to die in the snow, the Khazar thought in a still, motionless moment. *I had my chance.*

Bayan's eyes flickered sideways—searching for his guards—mouth opening to shout, and Jusuf struck. He lunged, the longsword shearing the air beside the khagan's left ear, then slashed down, turning his whole body into the blow as Bayan threw himself to the side. Jusuf's blade bit into the khagan's wrist and ripped through muscle, flesh and bone with a cracking sound. The black bow flew away into the grass and Bayan screamed like a lost child. A long wailing sound, filled with utter despair.

Jusuf stepped in over the khagan, his sword flicking up, the sun burning on droplets of blood spilling from the edge.

"Drink, my friend, and tell me what you saw."

Alexandros pressed a leather water bottle into Krythos' hands, tipping up the heavy bag, letting water mixed with vinegar spill into the scout's mouth. The Macedonian waited patiently while Krythos drank. One of the Companions took the bottle when he was done. A ring of men clad in iron surrounded the general, their helmets doffed and held at their saddle horns. The Companion cavalry was armed and armored in the Eastern fashion, with long coats of mail and numerous heavy arms hanging from their saddles. Most of them favored a flanged mace for close combat and lances for the first shock of battle. Most swords would not penetrate the laminated, overlapping armor favored by their traditional enemies.

Like the scouts he commanded, Krythos was clad only in a light shirt of iron rings and his cloak and tunic were mottled, streaked with gray and brown. The scout jerked his chin, pointing back to the middle of the field. A haze of smoke and dust hung over everything. Within the white mist, flames leapt up from a cluster of buildings. Alexandros and his heavy horse stood at the far right end of the Roman line, well beyond the knots of struggling men and the clash of arms where the Eastern infantry drove their enemies back near the center.

"The phalanx," Krythos said, "is fighting among the buildings, in the smoke. The Avars have made a barricade of wagons and the *hoplites* and Peltasts are trying to break through. The situation is confused. There was too much smoke for me to see who was winning."

Alexandros frowned, eyes thinning to disgusted slits. "That fool Chlothar! The phalanx will be disordered among so many obstructions. What of the Romans on the wings?"

Krythos shrugged. "They advance steadily on this side of the buildings. On the other, they were not fighting, nor was the enemy. The Khazars are locked in furious combat with the Avar right."

"But Chlothar holds the enemy's attention, from all you have seen?"

"Yes, lord. Many Avar banners were clustered at the center."

"Good." Alexandros lifted up his helmet and fitted it over golden curls. "Banners only, no horns! We will attack their flank, with all speed and power. Once we break through, curl to the left. We will drive these barbarians like sheep in the pasture!"

The Companion battle flags dipped and the commanders-of-one-hundred began to move, rounding up their men and the entire mass of horses and riders began to congeal. Fifty feet or so in front of the Companions, a screen of light horse was also in motion, keeping their horses moving in a constant, distracting swirl. Alexandros tugged the chin strap of his helmet tight, then hoisted his lance, finding a good grip on the cornel-wood shaft. The Companions fell into place on either side, forming a wedge trailing back to the left and to the right. The bannermen at the head of each cohort held their flags at an angle, keeping them low.

"Prepare!" Alexandros shouted, and lances rose up all around him, leaf-bladed tips shining. "Ready at the walk!" He nudged his horse and Bucephalas pranced forward, eager, big black head tossing, mane sliding like silk over a powerful neck. At the signal, the ranks of the Companions shifted and began to move forward. The wedge rippled forward as men adjusted their spacing and the horses picked their way over the tufted grass.

"My lord . . ." Krythos ran alongside Alexandros, his hand on the general's left boot. "You must stay back."

"What?" The Macedonian stared down in surprise—Krythos had never taken such a tone with him before. The scout's brown eyes were filled with worry.

"You're thinking you'll lead the wedge into the enemy." Krythos shook his head in bemusement. "You think you'll crash into them like a hammer, blade and lance drinking blood like some ancient hero." The scout's eyes narrowed and Alexandros was shocked to see amusement flicker across the man's face. "Like Achilles."

"I . . ." The Macedonian paused, leaning down towards the man. "I will prevail," he bit out, angry at such impertinence. "You've seen me fight—there's no Avar who could withstand my sword."

"I know, I know," Krythos said, nodding in agreement. His fingers curled around the stirrup strap. "I saw you fight the Draculis lord, remember? I saw you take a wound that would have sundered any other man. Aye, and a fine price you exacted from him. . . ."

Alexandros leaned back a little, remembering. Yes, Krythos had been at his side when the *lamia* had run him through, then lost his head in return. Suspicion darted through his thoughts— what did Krythos think of that strange event?—but he pushed it aside. Time was fleeting, even for men who did not feel death hurrying up behind them. The Avar noyan minghan in command of the facing wing was sure to notice their movement at any moment.

"Then rest easy and *take your hand away*—I must attack. The moment is right. I can feel it in the air."

"No, my lord. You are not Achilles, slayer of men. You are *our general*. You must stay out of the fray, watch over the battle and see—like a god looking down from on high—what men locked in combat cannot."

"Take your hand from my stirrup," Alexandros hissed, suddenly furious. His carefully cultivated patience frayed and then he cast it aside entirely. The Macedonian had never accepted any guidance save his own. The man's advice—no doubt well intentioned—goaded his pride like a hot brand. Krythos flinched back from the black look on the general's face, jerking his hand away from the stirrup.

"*Hai!*" Alexandros spurred the black stallion and the horse bolted away. As he moved, so did the assembled mass of Companions and suddenly they thundered across the grassy field, banners and horse manes streaming in the wind of their passage. Alexandros raced ahead of them, gripped by petulant anger, his face terrible and he bore down upon the Avar flank guards like a lightning bolt.

Krythos stared after him, rubbing his right hand as if burned. Then he shook himself and looked around. His scouts had ridden up and were looking at him with interest.

"What do we do now?" Semfronius asked, stringy black beard jutting out at an angle from under his helmet. Krythos ignored him for a moment while he swung up onto his horse. The scout could feel the earth trembling a little. As he turned his horse, there was a burst of noise—shouting, screams, the wild screaming of an injured horse, the clash and rattle of metal on metal. Krythos didn't bother to look—he had seen men fight before—and waved his hand at the edge of the field.

"Spread out," he called to his soldiers. "We'll cover the far edge of Lord Alexandros' attack, to make sure no one is sneaking about in the orchards. The *comes* will take care of his own business, I'm sure."

Clouds covered the sun by the time Jusuf limped up to the field hospital. He was glad to see the canvas awning and the bustle of men in priestly robes working among the wounded. There was a thick smell, but the Khazar was used to death, and the stench of drying blood and flesh no longer provoked stomach-churning nausea. A ring of tall willow-wands surrounded the hospital and there was a subtle change in the air as Jusuf passed between them. Inside the invisible barrier, he noted at once there were no flies or insects. Men lay in long rows on the ground, wrapped in woolen blankets. Most of the soldiers were bandaged on the arms or chest, a few in the leg. Some peered up at the gray sky through linen wrappings on their faces. Jusuf knew how they felt; he had lost part of an ear once, in a border skirmish with the T'u-chüeh. Any kind of a head wound bled furiously.

He accounted the Eastern troops very lucky. Among the Khazars, priests with the healing arts were rare and highly prized and no one thought of gathering them together and sending them out with the army. The Romans, however, had an efficient and well-regulated *medikus* traveling with each Legion. The rare priests of Asklepios were supplemented by a large number of orderlies—brawny men easily capable of carrying a wounded man on their shoulders—who gathered the fallen from the field of battle and tended to their simple wounds.

"Jusuf!" Dahvos, kagan of the Khazar people, sat under a lemon tree at the edge of the *medikus* encampment, his arm tightly bound to his chest. Jusuf smiled broadly and jogged up to his half-brother. Two heavy bundles, one long and one short, banged against his hip. Dahvos did not get up; content to sit with his back to the tree, in the shade. "You look . . . battered," the kagan said in a tired voice.

"There was some dispute over the field," Jusuf replied in a nonchalant tone, squatting down beside Dahvos and laying down his packages. "How is your arm?"

"It was bad," Dahvos said, frowning down at the bandaged limb, "but the priest laid his hands on and now he says it will mend properly. Did you see me fall? That shot destroyed my shield like a stone falling from heaven! The point tore clear through my mailed sleeve too." Dahvos shook his head in dismay.

"I saw you fall," Jusuf admitted, running dirty fingers through his hair. His helmet was tied to the back of his belt. The rest of him was stained with soot, mud and ground-in dirt. "I saw blood and thought you'd been killed."

Dahvos nodded, eyes hooded by the close passage of death. He fingered his chest, tracing the outline of an enormous bruise. "I thought I was too! But my luck held and an iron strap blunted the arrow's flight. Did you see whose arm drove such a bolt of lightning?"

"Yes." Jusuf ran his hand over the silk-wrapped bundle on the ground. His fingers brushed over embroidered leaves, rusty with fall colors and tinted with gold. "I saw the man shoot, more than once. He killed many men—most of them our *umen* commanders."

Dahvos frowned, seeing a strange look in his half-brother's eyes. "Who was it?"

"It was Bayan himself." Jusuf did not look up and his voice was soft. "But I rushed him with my lancers and brought the dog to sword strokes before he could take a shot at me. I killed him, Dahvos, with my own hand and took his head as your prize."

Jusuf picked up the smaller package—not bound in silk, but in rough woolens, now matted and dark—and untied the simple knot. The cloth fell away and the crown of a head was revealed. Blood and bits of bone were interspersed with stringy black hair. Pale skin, now the color of yellowed parchment, was revealed and then the face, frozen in a look of horror and surprise, as Jusuf rolled the skull over. Dahvos looked down with cold eyes, then reached out and turned the head so that he could look carefully upon the cold features.

"You knew him," the kagan stated absently. "I remember, you were sent away as a hostage."

"Yes." Jusuf's voice was flat. "I was."

"You're sure, then? Wasn't he supposed to be crippled?" Dahvos looked up and Jusuf nodded. The kagan smiled. "Well done."

"My duty, kagan." Jusuf wrapped up the head again. They might need it later, to parade before the army. "Did you see the end of the battle?"

"No." Dahvos grinned ruefully. "I saw some blue sky and my guardsmen carrying me from the field."

"The *comes* Alexandros crashed into their left about the same time I cut down Bayan. I think our Macedonian expected to rout them himself—but then, he's never fought the Avars before. . . . The Avar wing held, his charge was repulsed with loss, and the enemy withdrew in good order."

"Their casualties?" Dahvos scowled, thinking of his own dead.

"Many of their allies perished in the center—but they are only spear- or axe-men. Slav or Sklavenoi vassals . . . no real loss." Jusuf tugged at his chin, thinking. "Of his heavy horse, perhaps one or two thousand men fell. Their true casualty was Bayan."

"Yes." Dahvos squinted at the trees beyond the *medikus*. "Both the khagan and time—they will have to retire to Serdica and the *hring*, to quarrel and discuss and ultimately elect a new khagan to lead them. The rest of the year, at least, will be wasted in quarrels and feuds. The great families will need to decide which whelp of Bayan's rises to the throne."

"His eldest sons are dead . . ." Jusuf mused. Then he felt a sharp stab of elation. *That will be a vigorous discussion! And I killed him and set them in confusion!*

"What is this?" Dahvos poked the long bundle with a finger. "That's beautiful cloth."

"Nothing," Jusuf snapped, drawing the bundle away from his half-brother. "The khagan's tunic and my weapons."

"Good enough," Dahvos said, giving Jusuf a considering look. The tarkhan stood abruptly, looking down at Dahvos.

"I am going to round up the men," Jusuf said, feeling strangely skittish. "And number our losses. I fear we bled freely today. Will you be here?"

"No," Dahvos grunted and levered himself up from the ground. "I will be with the *comes* Alexandros, I think. We need to decide what to do next. I have things I wish to say to him, about his conduct in this . . . battle."

Jusuf nodded abruptly and then walked quickly away, the long bundle held tightly across his chest. Dahvos stared after him, a little unsettled.

THE PALATINE HILL, ROMA MATER

Galen Atreus, Emperor and princeps of both East and West, entered a lofty-ceilinged room high on the Forum side of the Palace of Tiberius. Large square windows admitted cool northern light, making the marble and tile gleam. A circular fan turned slowly, moved by ropes passing overhead into a nearby room. The Emperor ignored the Praetorians beside the door and strode quickly to a dark mahogany swan-wing chair at the head of the table. He sat and nodded briskly to the men and women already seated. In polite society men would recline on couches and women sit, but the Emperor was far too focused on matters of state to care for social propriety today.

"Good morning," he said, opening a wooden folder on the table in front of him. The packet was filled with parchment sheets covered in small, neat handwriting. Galen's secretaries had risen before dawn and spent a hurried hour as the eastern sky lightened, trying to condense everything about everything onto the square-cut pages. The Emperor grimaced, looking at the first sheet. *Persia*, he thought glumly. Despite his assured entrance, he felt completely exhausted, bled by thousands of minute, invisible mosquitoes. The Empire had never suffered a shock like the fall of Constantinople—not at Adrianopolis, not at Cannae, not even when fool Crassus threw away six Legions in the Mesopotamian desert.

Why does it fall to me? he thought bleakly. *Have I angered the gods?*

The Emperor sighed, arranged his papers again and looked up, face hard and mask-like. Everyone else straightened up a little and Galen counted noses to make sure everyone was present. His own brother, Maxian, sat somberly to his right, young face paler than usual above a dark tunic and dark brown robes. Beyond the prince, the elderly and nondescript Gaius was doing a good job of being invisible. Galen's eyes passed over him without pausing. The man did a centurion's work with any project, though he had not proven to be innovative, only dogged past anyone's expectation. The Emperor had not warmed to the bureaucrat—he couldn't say why, really. Normally he valued a hard-working, prudent man above all else—but there was something about Gaius . . .

In earlier, better times, Gregorius Auricus would have held a chair, speaking and listening for the Senate as he had done for nearly fifty years. Now his duties had fallen to Gaius Julius—his aide and executor for the past year. Galen tried to ignore the absence and made mental note—not for the first time—to ensure someone appropriate assumed the old man's mantle of Speaker in the Senate. The Duchess De'Orelio sat almost opposite, her perfect face framed by demurely coifed curls wound with gold and emerald. A single booklet lay on the table in front of her and the Emperor did not bother to hide a grimace. The chapbook was simply for show—Galen often wondered if there were anything written on the pages inside—for he could not remember the last time she had consulted the book in the course of business. The Duchess relied on her memory, which was prodigious.

Beside the Duchess's cool elegance, looking very much like a plump brown wren trapped on a ledge beside a hawk, sat Empress Martina. Her presence here was both a personal concession from Galen, who had extended her every courtesy and honor, and a political one. Though Galen had assumed the title Avtokrator of the East, reuniting both halves of the Empire for the first time in almost three and a half centuries, there was no way he could administer the rump provinces of the East without the willing support of their remaining governors.

Those men, as numerous letters and private meetings had revealed, considered him not their Emperor, but merely a regent for Martina's son, Heracleonas, who was probably crawling around in the palace gardens with Galen's own child, Theodosius. Galen knew Martina's residence-in-exile was now the natural and expected gathering place for the huge crowd of dispossessed Eastern nobles, their wives, children, and retainers who had fled the fall of Constantinople. Through her, he hoped to gain the assistance and trust of the Eastern nobility. Galen needed their assistance badly and he hoped she understood the desperate nature of their situation.

"We must," Galen said, clearing his throat, "discuss Persia and Egypt. Lady Anastasia, please relate the current state of affairs." He suppressed a twinge of disquiet. Despite years of working with the Duchess, he still felt uncomfortable allowing a woman to hold such a powerful position. She knew things he did not, which bothered the Emperor a great deal. At the same time, he needed her and the sprawling network of agents she commanded.

* * *

"Lord and God," Anastasia began, bowing to the Emperor and inclining her head to the others. "Our situation in the East is poor. We have lost the provinces of Lesser Syria, Phoenicia and Judea to these rebels out of the old Greek cities in the Decapolis and their Arab mercenaries. Greater Syria and the city of Antioch have fallen to Persia, as well as portions of Anatolia and, of course, the city of Constantinople itself. Worse, we have suffered the loss of nearly the entire Eastern fleet and the Eastern Legions have been roughly handled not once, but twice by the enemy."

The Duchess paused for an instant and opened her notebook. Out of the corner of her eye, she saw surprise flit across the Emperor's face and she repressed a smile. The others watched her with varying attention—Maxian seemed entirely absent, his attention far away, and Anastasia noted his hair was unwashed and his clothing rumpled. She wondered if he slept at all. The lean old man at his side, unfortunately, was watching her with rapt attention. Anastasia did not find being desired by a dead man a pleasant sensation. However, she did not allow herself to show revulsion. There was business to be done here. At her side, Empress Martina was trying to stay awake and plucking at the hem of her very expensive and rather over-ornamented gown.

"Word has reached us," she continued, "of the enemy fleet—captained, we believe, by Palmyrene and Arab merchants—leaving Constantinople." She touched a sheet of parchment in the notebook with the tip of a well-manicured fingernail. "A ship friendly to us sighted the enemy fleet bearing east from Rhodes under full sail. I believe—and this, Lord and God, is only a guess—the fleet is aiming to make landfall at Caesarea Maritima, on the coast of Judea. It is quite likely the fleet is carrying those Arab and Decapolis contingents who fought at Constantinople home again."

"Not the Persians?" Galen leaned forward, narrow chin on his fist. "If this is so, where is the Persian army itself? Where is the Boar?"

"Luckily," Anastasia responded, "the Persian attack on Constantinople, like the campaign three years ago, is really only a very large raid. Despite crossing the breadth of Anatolia, they have not actually conquered the Roman provinces between the Persian frontier and the Eastern Capital. However, there are no Roman armies to keep them from moving freely through those lands. Indeed, reports from the larger coastal cities of Pergamum, Ephesus and Myra report no Persian or Decapolis threat at all!"

The Duchess turned to Martina, who was slouching in her chair. "Your husband's empire, dear, is still greatly intact. We, however, cannot rest easy—the Persians are sure to occupy as much as they can, as soon as they have the troops and time to do so."

Anastasia looked back at the Emperor. "My lord, we have received letters indicating the *comes* Alexandros has reached Perinthus on the Thracian coast, where the remains of the Imperial armies have gathered. He intends to muster those formations still infused with fighting spirit and to press towards Constantinople. I understand he seeks to forestall any further Persian advance into Thrace and to observe the deployments of the enemy for himself.

"When he has done so, we will know where the Persian army lies. Then, I believe, we will be able to tell where the next blow will fall."

Galen grunted, shaking his head in disagreement. "They will strike at Egypt," he said.

"Their forces in the desert before Pelusium are weak," Anastasia noted. "A dispatch ship has come from your noble brother, indicating a raid was made into the defenses at the edge of the delta and easily turned back."

"Those are only scouts,"Galen said, scowling at the Duchess. "Do we know anything about the leadership of these Arabs and Greeks? Do we know if they are firm allies of Persia or only of convenience? Indeed—do we know what they *want*?"

Anastasia hid a sigh behind a pleasant smile and shook her head delicately. "We do not, my lord. But—my apologies, Martina—I believe the spark of the rebellion in Judea and the Decapolis came from the . . . poor use . . . of Palmyra in the war against Chrosoes. Queen Zenobia and her city were widely respected in the area, and she had many allies and friends among the Arab tribes, particularly the Tanukh. We have no proof—we do not even know who is in command of the rebellious army—but I suspect they are Palmyrene nobles and they are very angry."

The Emperor nodded, his face drawn and closed. He seemed to be looking back into memory and he did not like what he saw.

"So," he said, after a moment, "we are still fighting smoke. What about the Persians?"

"There, my lord, I can tell you a little more. By good fortune, there are merchants friendly to the Empire plying the Indian trade in the Mare Ethraeyum and they often visit the Persian port of Charax at the mouth of the Tigris and the Euphrates. By these means, greatly delayed, we have learned two daughters, Azarmidukht and Purandokht, survived the lamentable Chrosoes King of Kings. Both are young, of marriageable age, and unwed. Their mother, I must report, was the Empress Maria, Chrosoes' first wife. Apparently, in the chaos following the sack of Ctesiphon, the two princesses fled to Ecbatana in the Persian highlands and declared a new government.

"Now, our agents relate they found little support initially but then two things happened—first, a man named Rustam appeared, claiming to be Chrosoes' younger brother. Second, our old friend Shahr-Baraz arrived at the city, in the company of the remnants of the Persian Imperial guard. Reports of his death at Kerenos River, it would seem, were premature."

Anastasia spread her hands slightly, palms up. "What happened next is confused—there were reports Shahr-Baraz married Princess Azarmidukht, but when an official proclamation was made, the Boar was King of Kings and *protector* of the two princesses. I think the general decided the two girls were worth more to him as marriage tokens than as wives. We have heard nothing to indicate the princesses have, in fact, been married off. The mysterious Rustam has disappeared. He may have been murdered by Shahr-Baraz."

Maxian stirred, head rising and he focused on Anastasia. The Duchess felt a queer prickling sensation wash over her and struggled to keep from shivering. The prince looked to his brother for a moment, then back at the Duchess. "What about the dark man? Have you heard anything about this 'power' who fights on their side?"

"My lord Maxian," Anastasia replied, bowing to him, "we have received many rumors, but you of all our sources, have seen him most closely. Can you tell us anything about him?"

The prince scowled at her, pressing both palms over his eyes in exhaustion. Then he clasped his hands and said: "Though our enemy might seem to be a man of middling height, long hair, Persian features and complexion, there is something entirely inhuman about the creature. It is like . . . like the man is only a shell hiding darkness . . . and cold, he seemed colder than ice, or frost."

"Is our enemy a god?" The Duchess's tone made the question seem perfectly reasonable.

Maxian looked up, his eyes desolate. "I have never seen a god, Duchess, but this man might make himself one, over our corpses. I fought the Persian to a draw, so his power is not infinite. I suppose . . ." He paused, thinking. "It may be the cold spirit was first invoked by a human sorcerer and the summoned power now rules the body, yet is still restricted by its human shell."

"Can you kill him?" Anastasia cocked her head to one side, violet eyes intent on the young man. "Can *we* kill him? Can he be harmed by the spear, the knife, a scorpion stone?"

"I don't know." Maxian shook his head in dismay. "He felt pain and suffering from my blows. But sorcerers can be difficult to kill."

The prince's eyes narrowed as he said this, meeting Anastasia's eyes with a frank, cold look.

"You should," he said, speaking to her—and only to her, she realized with a chill—"leave such things to me. I have some thoughts as to how his power can be contained."

"Not destroyed?" Galen sat up straight, staring at his brother.

"I'm not sure he *can* be destroyed," Maxian replied wearily. "If a summoned power entered this world, and now inhabits—controls—this man, it could be entirely outside of death and even life. It may be the *power* cannot be destroyed, in which case our best hope is to trap and contain him. In this way, we may preserve ourselves, the state and the people from further harm."

Anastasia suddenly remembered something—a fragment heard on Thira long ago—and brought a hand to her mouth to cover a flinch. Neither the Emperor nor his brother noticed, though Gaius Julius' pale old eyes flickered to her, then away. The Duchess made a discrete cough, then forced her hand back down to her lap. Fear percolated inside her like water rising in a field screw, inching higher and higher with each turn of the handle. *Could this be? Could the Serpent have returned? No . . . that is impossible! My worries about the telecast are clouding my thoughts with old legends.*

Galen, meanwhile, was staring at Maxian with a rather sour expression. "What happens if we destroy the man?"

"In that case," Maxian said, slowly, "I believe the power will only retreat and begin looking for a new host to occupy. There are surely many men of low character in the world, some with power and some without, whom it might entice, thereby finding a new servant."

"Very well. We will discuss this further when we know more. Duchess, are we sure the Persians and the rebellious Greeks have separated their armies?"

"Sure? No, my lord, we are not sure. But it is very likely the fighting men of the Decapolis took ship with their fleet and are returning to Judea. It is *possible*, though I think it unlikely, a portion of the Persian army moved with them. Surely, they will not abandon Constantinople, not after seizing a bridgehead in Thrace. This leaves us with two opposing armies—one in the north and one in the south."

Galen nodded, thin lips compressed into a tight slash. "And their fleet is still loose."

"Yes, my lord."

"Gaius Julius, what Legions and fleets can we move East?"

The older man sat up, blinking away pleasant daydreams, but his hands were quick and selected a wooden folder from the pile in front of him without hesitation. He opened the folder, though Anastasia didn't think he read anything from the pages. Like her, he used the moment of action to marshal his thoughts and compose himself.

"Lord and God," he began, "our situation is rather parlous. We have already stripped the Legions in the west of every spare man. The Legions raised last year have been poorly handled in Thrace or are already in Egypt under your brother's command. Those formations remaining in the West are hard-pressed to cover the frontier or to maintain order in the provinces."

Gaius sighed and everyone at the table could see his weariness. Anastasia's nose wrinkled up, but she made no comment. Everyone was stretched thin.

"A letter was dispatched," Gaius continued, "to the Gothic *reik* several months ago, requesting he raise a Gothic Legion to assist the Empire. That force was raised and one portion of is now in Thrace, under the command of the *comes* Alexandros. The other portion, under the command of Prince Ermanerich, has been engaged in an unexpected campaign along the Danuvius against the Gepids and their Draculis overlords."

The Emperor grimaced and rubbed the side of his head. "And?"

Gaius Julius shrugged. "The matter is still in doubt. I imagine the success of the Avar khagans in the Balkans has inspired the Draculis, and other tribes beyond the frontier, to test our strength. Reports have come from Noricum as well, indicating the Bulgars and Franks in Germania are growing restive."

Galen looked to Anastasia, his face tight. "Duchess? Will Noricum be attacked?"

Anastasia blinked, though she kept control of her expression. Noricum was a roughly rectangular—and the only remaining Roman—province on the further side of the Rhenus and the Danuvius. Rich and prosperous, the region was exposed to attack from north, east and west. Only the southern Alpine border was safe from raids. *I have no idea what passes for thought in the minds of Duke Frigard or the Bulgar khan! How does he expect* . . . The Duchess felt cold. Of course the Emperor expected her to know—hadn't she always known before?

"Lord and God," she said, keeping her voice even. "Reports from beyond the Danuvius are sparse, though our strength in Noricum is drawn down. . . . If Ermanerich defeats the Draculis soundly, then the other tribes will mind their manners. If he fails, or is openly defeated, they will become bolder."

"Very well." Galen made a dismissive gesture. "Gaius, what of Gaul and Britain?"

"More troubles, my lord," the old Roman said. "The Frankish lords in Gaul are upset by the confiscation of the coward Dagobert's estates and possessions. He was well regarded among them—it seems they do not believe he abandoned his command, or fled from battle."

"What *do* they think?" Open anger flooded the Emperor's face. The abject failure of the Frankish lord Dagobert struck him hard—Galen had trusted the man and promoted his career.

"They think, my lord," Gaius said, keeping his voice very calm, "he was pushed aside so a Goth could command the army in the East. They think *comes* Alexandros stood higher in your favor than did Dagobert. The matter is complicated by Dagobert still being at large . . . he may even be back in Gaul, now, and I doubt he will admit to defeat and flight!"

The Emperor raised a thin eyebrow, and his eyes narrowed and swiveled towards Anastasia. "Duchess? Have your agents found our missing general?"

The cold tickling in Anastasia's stomach got worse, and the impression of mounting irritation in the Emperor grated on her nerves.

"No, my lord." Her own eyes narrowed, seeing an almost indefinable smugness on Gaius Julius' face. "The Empire's eyes are in every port, every city, every temple. But he has not surfaced since fleeing the port of Perinthus in a commandeered Imperial galley. I have heard these rumors he returned to Gaul, but he has not appeared in public, and he did not contest the seizure of his lands and estates."

"Where else would he go?" Gaius Julius leaned forward, expressing professional interest. "The Goths and the Franks hate each other with a passion, so he won't have found refuge in the East. Italia would be equally hostile to him . . . this leaves only Spain and Gaul."

"Unless he is dead." Anastasia's voice was cool. "But I fear he has survived, and is in hiding."

"Would you like help finding him?" Gaius Julius smiled, though he did not show his teeth. "I have some acquaintances among the merchant class who could keep an eye out for him."

Yes, Anastasia thought bitterly, *you are thick with the lords of crime and the underworld . . . and through them with every grain hauler, merchant ship, bordello and gambling den in Italy.* "That is very kind, Gaius Julius, but my own informants are already on the hunt."

"Of course." Gaius settled back in his chair. Nothing about him suggested anything but well-meaning intentions and a desire to perform his duties with dispatch and efficiency. "So, Lord and God, even Gaul is unsettled while this matter remains unresolved. Now, when the Duchess's men find our wayward general, and he is brought to trial, and confesses his cowardice before his peers—then public sentiment will swing in our favor. But until then—and, Duchess, I hope you find him soon—Gaul is of concern to us."

"And Britain?" Galen continued to sit stiffly upright in his chair, but his frown grew deeper with each word. "I have seen the monthly reports—the efforts to dislodge the Scandians have failed?"

"Yes," Gaius admitted and Anastasia took a pinch of solace from the glum look on his face. "A collection of local militia, Imperial troops and auxiliaries from Germany made an effort three months ago to drive the Scandians out of their enclave at Branodunium. Unfortunately, the Imperial officer in command of the expedition—a veteran named Uthar—was ambushed and killed by Scandian raiders while observing the defenses of the port. His second-in-command failed to press the enemy vigorously. So things remain as they were."

"That is not acceptable," Galen snapped, right hand clenching unconsciously into a fist. "Find another general, a competent one, and dispatch him to clean up this mess."

Gaius Julius nodded, but—wisely—said nothing. The Emperor stared out one of the windows for a moment, his expression forbidding. Anastasia waited patiently, as did the others. Beside her, Martina started to fidget and the Duchess touched her hand softly, shaking her head in warning. Out of the corner of her eye, Anastasia saw a sour look cross the young Empress's face, but the girl hunched her shoulders and stopped tapping her foot against the table leg.

*   *   *

After a seemingly endless moment, Galen's nostrils flared and his breath hissed out. Pursing his lips, he looked around the table. The Emperor did not seem pleased. "We have no reserves to send Aurelian in Egypt, until either Ermanerich settles this Draculis matter, or Alexandros reclaims Constantinople from the Persians. My brother will have to make do with what he has."

Gaius Julius and Anastasia nodded, reluctantly. The Emperor's expression did not improve.

"Lord and God?" Anastasia's throat felt tight, but remaining silent would not improve her situation. Risk was necessary, as was forward motion. "We *are* stretched thin, and faced with many challenges. Despite the best efforts of our networks of agents and informers, we still know too little about the dispositions and maneuvers of our enemies. Therefore . . ."

She paused, feeling her stomach roil. An acid taste bit her tongue. *What did I just say to Thyatis? What would she say to me, now?* She stifled a bitter laugh, then managed to continue speaking: "Princeps, may I have use of the device that sits in the Imperial Library?"

The Emperor frowned, brows furrowing, but then his face cleared and he looked at her with frank approval. "An excellent idea," he said. "With such long eyes you will be able to fill in the gaps in our too-poor knowledge of the enemy."

Anastasia inclined her head in thanks and out of the corner of her eye, saw Gaius Julius' lips twitch and then a disagreeable expression settle over his face. *Ha!* Gloated Anastasia, *he didn't think of the power the telecast might grant, to those willing to use the* duradarshan *to its fullest.*

"Thank you, my lord," she said, smiling at the Emperor. "We will not stint our labors. It is my hope that, by means of such swift and immediate news, we may be able to derive the work of many Legions from those few we own."

"Good." The weight on the Emperor seemed to have lifted, a little. "Good. Now—yes, Maxian?"

The prince stirred himself and Anastasia thought his attention had been far away, as if roused from some waking dream. Maxian rubbed his eyes and focused, slowly, on his brother.

"Before the Duchess has her way with the telecast," the

prince said, "I think we should use the device to find the Persian sorcerer. We must devise a means of defeating him if we are to win."

Galen frowned, shaking his head. "Are you ready to face him? The matter of the Persian fleet and the disposition of their armies is far more urgent."

"How can that be?" Maxian sat up straight in his chair, staring at his brother in concern. "While the sorcerer is free to act against us, the Empire is in immediate danger! This *creature* is more powerful than armies, deadlier than fleets!"

"Is he?" Galen returned Maxian's puzzled expression with his own. "The Persian mage is only one man, true? He cannot hold cities, or provinces, or exact taxes or tribute by himself. While Shahr-Baraz has a fleet and powerful armies, we are in danger, whether this sorcerer is present or no."

"What?" Maxian's face screwed up in astonishment. "Don't you grasp his power?"

The Emperor's eyes narrowed and Anastasia shrank back a little in her chair. The others drew away from the prince as well, but Maxian did not seem to notice.

"This Persian," the prince continued, voice rising, "shattered the walls of Constantinople—the most formidable city in the entire Empire! He smashed the Eastern fleet to kindling! He nearly killed *me*, never having faced me before in a test of wills."

"Yet," Galen interjected, his voice cold, "you fought him to a draw, all unprepared. Yet, when he broke down the walls of the Eastern Capital, it was Persian soldiers who entered the city, who hold the city. If he scattered the Eastern fleet, it was the Greek rebels who benefited."

"Foolishness!" Maxian broke in, interrupting his brother. "We cannot ignore him!"

"I am *not* proposing we ignore this Persian," Galen snapped. "We cannot focus upon him as our sole enemy. If we do, then his compatriot the Boar will tear out our gut. The Persian sorcerer is a *tool* and he can be forestalled, he can be distracted, your presence can neutralize him. He is one part of a larger puzzle. The Persians and the Greeks are the other pieces and they must be accounted for as well."

"You don't understand. . . ." Maxian looked away, slumping back in his chair again.

"I do," Galen said, softening his voice. "This is not a single combat between you and the Persian sorcerer. This is a war between empires. The outcome of a single battle will not turn the balance between Rome and Persia. The victor . . . the victor will be the empire whose will to fight endures. Exhaustion, not valor, will decide the matter."

The Emperor looked around the table, his visage grim. "Rome will endure. We have suffered worse before and won through. We will do so again. Now, here is my desire: Anastasia, you and your clerks will have immediate and full access to the telecast. You must find the Persians and detail their formations to me. Further, you must discern if these other threats—on the Danube, in Germany, in Gaul, in Britain—are worthy of my immediate attention. Gaius Julius: you carry a heavy load with Gregorius dead. I must ask you to shoulder it a little longer, until the Senate elects someone to replace him. From you, I desire an accounting of every ship, every soldier, every farm, every amphora of oil, every bushel of wheat, every yard of cloth in the empire."

The old Roman grimaced, playing with one of his notebooks. Anastasia was afraid the same sick, grim look was creeping into her face as well. Gaius Julius looked up, staring at the Emperor with a troubled expression. "My lord, you think rationing will be necessary?"

Galen met his eyes with an unflinching look, his face cold and remote. "If Egypt is lost, then Rome cannot feed herself, not without strict regulation. We will be prepared. Maxian . . ."

The prince was staring into emptiness, head cocked to one side.

"Maxian!" The Emperor raised his voice slightly and the prince turned, brow furrowed. Galen swallowed a sigh and the timbre of his voice changed. He bent close to his brother. "I need you to be able to defeat this Persian sorcerer, but I must balance many demands. You and the Duchess will share the telecast—but, pray the gods, do not attempt to deal with this enemy without consulting me!"

Maxian's lips, drawn into a tight line, relaxed a little and he shook his head in a nervous tic. "Gales, I understand. Don't worry, I won't try anything rash. I just . . . this sorcerer is the real enemy; I can *feel* it. If we defeat him, we defeat Persia." Maxian coughed and Anastasia realized he was trying to muster a laugh. "I need to find out who, or what, he is. So—that will be my task, along with the work at Fiorentina—one fitting the *custos*, don't you think?"

"Yes." Galen tried to smile warmly, but could only manage a shadow of good humor. "Let us know what we face, before we give battle." The Emperor turned back to the others. "That is good advice for all of us . . . we face a bitter struggle. Let us know what strength we own and what strength is in our enemies' hand."

Galen stood, and his movements were stiff and slow. He gathered up his folder and nodded to them all. "Good day, my friends. May the gods grant us victory."

Everyone rose, bowing as the Emperor strode out of the room.

"Empress? Is something troubling you?" Gaius Julius bowed slightly to the young Greek woman. Martina was slouched deep in her chair, scowling at the doorway. Such obvious bile did not improve her round features.

"What do you want from me?" Martina's light green eyes narrowed suspiciously, her lip curling slightly. "Don't you already have a position, wealth, power?"

"Ah . . ." Gaius smiled affably. "Empress, I am not blind. Does the Emperor's plan displease you?"

"Am I allowed to be displeased?" Martina made a sharp flinging motion with her hands. She bared her teeth, though Gaius suspected she didn't realize how feral it made her look. "I'm supposed to sit quietly, perhaps nod approvingly when he acknowledges my presence! How delightful!"

"Empress . . ." Gaius shook his head slowly, casting a brief look over his shoulder. The Emperor had stopped in the hallway, deep in conversation with the Duchess De'Orelio. A brace of guardsmen loitered around them, looking studiously away from the pair, ignoring their discussion. *Interesting*, Gaius thought. *I'll have to find Motrius a new toy—then he'll let me know what they were talking about. . . .*

The old Roman turned back to Martina, who was glaring at the wall while she tore tiny seed pearls, one by one, from the hem of her gown. The old Roman placed himself between Galen and the Empress. "You are unhappy with the way you've been treated?"

Martina looked up and her nostrils flared. Heavy makeup disguised, but did not completely hide, dark smudges under puffy eyes. "I am grateful, Master Gaius, for being saved from the ruin of my city. I give thanks to the Gods each day my son lives. I live in a palace—attended by servants of all kinds, guarded by the Praetorians—and my son spends his days playing with Emperor Galen's son. What more could I ask?"

Gaius hid a grin at the venom in the woman's voice. He thought, for a brief instant, of how things stood between himself and the prince, between the prince and his brother. A constellation of impulses ran riot in his thoughts and he weighed them all in turn, sorting swiftly through long memories. Possibilities presented themselves and were discarded. Others rose into consideration, then fell. One avenue revealed itself to him, filled with all manner of delights and riches. He considered an Eastern Empire restored, ruled by a wise Regent and a young, pliable Empress, in the name of a young king with many years to pass before he came into his patrimony. *Very fine*, he thought. *But I will abstain. It is not time to be greedy, not yet.*

His face still genial, open, approachable, Gaius let sympathy show, his eyes crinkling up. "Ah, Empress, if bread were enough to satisfy our souls, if circuses stilled desire, then Rome would be the most content of cities. You mustn't hate Emperor Galen—he is doing his best for you and for your son. But he is a man plagued with worries, faced with crises on every hand. I assure you, Empress, he does not covet your son's inheritance. In the fullness of time, after the Persians are driven back, you will dwell in Constantinople again and your son will sit on his father's throne."

"Will he?" Martina's expression darkened dangerously. "When? Can you name a day?"

"No." Gaius Julius shook his head sadly. "Many years may pass before that transpires. This war may be long and difficult, a struggle of decades."

"Decades . . ." The Empress's hands clenched, ripping the cloth bunched between them. Her eyes were fixed over Gaius' shoulder. "What will be left, then? Each day new edicts and writs go forth from his offices, signed with his name, to set taxation, to raise troops, to appoint judges and praetors—in *my son's domain!* In ten years, who will remember Heracleonas is Emperor of the East? Who will remember his father?"

Who will remember you? Gaius Julius thought in amusement. *No one. Another exiled queen, without lands or treasure, reduced to living on the whim of a distracted Emperor. . . .*

"My lady," he said aloud, "listen to me. I have spent many years in the service of Rome. More years, in truth, than you have lived. I have seen many things. I have risen high and I have fallen low. You must have patience, and you must not set yourself against the Emperor. He is your friend. He is your son's protector and guardian. What you must do, if you wish to see young Heracleonas sit upon his father's throne, is *help.*"

"What could I possibly do?" Martina forced her fist open and shredded bits of cloth drifted to the floor. "I have nothing, no friends, no power, no armies. Why would I want to help *them*?" She pointed with a round chin at the Emperor and the Duchess, who were still standing at the far end of the hallway.

"I was not speaking specifically of the Duchess De'Orelio and Emperor Galen."

"Who then?" Martina looked directly at Gaius for the first time.

"You should help *him*." The old Roman gestured with his head, indicating Prince Maxian, still sitting at the big table, his expression distant, forefinger pressed against his lower lip.

"Maxian?" The Empress's expression softened and Gaius felt a stab of delight in his crafty old heart. "I can't help him either. He's like a god. . . ." Martina broke into soft verse, some old words that she remembered from stories of her childhood. ". . . down from the mountain's rocky crags, Poseidon stormed with giant, lightning strides—and looming peaks and tall timber quaked, beneath immortal feet as the sea lord surged . . ."

Oh, my, a poetess, Gaius thought, riding hard on his expression, keeping it kind and just a little distant. *What vistas unfold now!* "Empress, Maxian is not a god. He is not the lord of earthquakes. He is a young man carrying an enormous burden. Now, if I remember correctly, you are a historian?"

"I was." The Empress pouted a little, which made her round cheeks blush. "All of my books, my writing, everything was destroyed. Why does that matter?"

"I assure you," Gaius said, entirely truthfully, "the libraries of Rome are without equal. Consider the prince's dilemma now—he must find a way to defeat this Persian mage—and he is only one man. I have dabbled a little in history myself—written a few small dissertations on obscure subjects—but he will need to delve into all that we know of Persia and the east, seeking to find some clue to the provenance of this enemy. Is our foe wholly new? Have the Persians raised such a power before? How can it be stopped? You can *help him*."

"I suppose." Martina shrank back a little. "But he's so busy all the time. . . ."

"There is a great deal of work to be done." Gaius beamed. "He'll be very glad of your wise assistance. Just . . . let him know. He's really a very approachable young man."

Martina bit her lip, dithering, but Gaius stepped away, barely restraining a grin. He hoped the prince would have the wit to be nice to the girl.

So straight flies Cupid's arrow, he thought smugly. *Alexandros will be pleased to rule green Macedon again.*

"My lord?" Anastasia hurried, one fine-boned hand holding up her skirts. The Emperor turned to face her, his expression distant. At his sign, the Praetorians parted, allowing the Duchess into a circle of iron-armored chests and flowing red cloaks. "May I have a moment? There is something you need to know."

One of Galen's eyebrows rose and the weariness hiding behind his mask-like expression was plain. "What is it?"

Anastasia brushed dark, glossy curls out of her face as she

looked back over one shoulder. The others were still in the meeting room, leaving the corridor empty. "Lord and God, may we speak in private?" She indicated an alcove, flanked by towering marble gladiators and potted palms.

"Do you have a knife?" Galen cocked his head to one side.

The Duchess recoiled slightly at the suggestion, a hand rising to cover her breast. "No!"

Galen's lips twitched into a half-smile. "Imperial humor, my lady. Very well."

The Praetorians parted again, shifting into a line blocking the alcove from the rest of the corridor. The Emperor leaned against a wall, fine, thin hair hanging limply over his brow and crossed his arms, staring morbidly at the Duchess. "Another plot?" he asked in a resigned tone.

"No, my lord," Anastasia said, suddenly reluctant to continue. The impulse to speak was fading as quickly as it had sprung into being. Now she felt a little foolish. "Do you remember the accusations I made last year, against the prince?"

Galen leaned forward a little, trying to catch her soft voice. Anastasia cursed her recklessness. *Too late now* . . . "When I accused your brother of trafficking with spirits, with raising the dead to do his bidding?"

"Yes." The Emperor motioned for her to continue.

"Master Gaius Julius, to whom you entrust so much," she said, keeping her voice low, "is one of his . . . experiments."

Galen's head rose in surprise, and both eyebrows crept up under his bangs. "He is?"

"Yes, Master Gaius is . . . my lord, he is Gaius Julius Caesar, formerly dictator of Rome."

"What?" Galen laughed aloud, thin shoulders shaking. His face split into a wide grin and he stood up straight. "The famous . . . *the* Caesar?" He laughed again, his face brightening, exhaustion shedding from him like leaves from fall trees. "Really? It's really him?"

"Yes," Anastasia answered dubiously, drawing away from the Emperor.

"That is marvelous!" Galen looked down the hallway. The man in question was standing in the doorway of their meeting room, talking affably with Empress Martina. "The scholar? The playwright? No wonder he has such a flair for the games!" The Emperor rubbed his chin, still grinning. "How delightful!"

"My lord!" Anastasia was alarmed and dared place her hand on his arm. "This is *Julius Caesar* we are taking about! A man who never once in his life set aside the pursuit of power, of the throne, or all the power he could gather into his own hands! Do you realize he will take Gregorius Auricus' place in the Senate, if you do not take immediate steps to prevent him? He will plot, bribe, inveigle, scheme and spy until his power rivals your own!"

Galen nodded, still smiling, but now his expression shaded into something like melancholy. "I know. You know . . ." He paused, tugging at his lip. "He has seemed so familiar for so long, I'm amazed I didn't grasp the fact myself. But who would think to see the dead live again? This is an age of wonders. . . ."

"My lord!" Anastasia hissed in alarm. "He is not a curiosity to be displayed at a garden party!"

"I know." Galen was unaccountably sad. His good humor vanished, leaving a bleak expression. "But Duchess, he is a fine poet, a playwright of repute, a cunning statesman, a fine administrator, even a beloved and victorious general. He was the best of us."

"And the worst!" Anastasia tilted her head, trying to catch Galen's eye. Grief crept into the Emperor's face, and the Duchess was startled to see his eyes shining with incipient tears.

"And the worst . . ." Galen mastered himself, blinking. "How can such a man be trusted, once he tasted a heady Imperial vintage? He should be imprisoned or strangled. Certainly not left to run riot in the Senate, or walk the streets speaking with whom he chooses. Not left free to serve the State, or to pen witticisms in his spare time, or write histories, or . . . do anything the things I would love to see spring from his mind and hand." The Emperor shook his head.

Anastasia cursed herself—why tell Galen this now? She could have just seen to the quiet, discreet removal of the dead man. Then all this would be moot and a viper plucked from the bosom of the Empire. She felt a creeping sense of dread, as if she had unwittingly made a terrible mistake. "My lord . . ."

Galen covered her hand with his own, shaking his head. Melancholy distilled in his eyes. His brief joy was gone. "You did the right thing, Anastasia. I will decide what to do with the esteemed Gaius Julius. That, if nothing else, is my duty."

"Um . . . Prince Maxian?"

A soft, tentative voice penetrated the prince's thoughts and he made a brushing motion near his ear. Faint whispering faded away and he looked up into the leaf-colored eyes of a worried young woman. Her hair was elaborately coifed and curled, sparkling with tiny golden pins. A heavy embroidered stole lay over white shoulders, gleaming with pearls and Indian rubies.

"Hello, Martina," Maxian said. He became aware of sitting in a chair. The ghosts in the room dissolved bit by bit, slowly disintegrating until their translucent bodies shone like glass and then were entirely gone. The marble walls and painted ceilings reasserted themselves and the prince found himself alone with the young Empress. "Is something wrong?"

Martina looked poorly with circles under her eyes and a sallow complexion to her round face. "Have you fallen ill?" The prince took her hand and was surprised at how cold she felt. He frowned, concentrating. "No . . . your humors are in balance . . . but you must sleep more. You're tired."

"Oh." Martina sat down abruptly, her eyes wide. "I felt that!"

"Yes." Maxian smiled, "sometimes you can feel the power as it passes through you. Was it unpleasant?"

"Oh no," she said, blushing furiously. "I didn't mind."

"Good. How is your son?"

"He's well," Martina said, staring at the floor.

Maxian realized he was still holding her hand. He let go and sat up straight in the chair. "I'm glad. I'm sorry we couldn't save more of your people . . ." He grimaced, thinking of the devastation he had seen during the brief time he was in Constantinople. "It won't happen again."

"I'm sure it won't . . . my lord," Martina said in a rush. "Master Gaius said you needed help with some historical research and I'm a historian and perhaps I could help if that's not too much trouble."

"But aren't you . . ." Maxian stopped before he said *busy*. He looked around for Gaius Julius. The old Roman was nowhere to be seen. He looked back at the girl, giving her his full attention. She was still looking at the floor and he could feel her nervousness in the air like the half-heard chime of a temple bell. *What is there for you to do*? he mused, considering her. Ghost images of the Empress unfolded in his sight—laughing, afraid, cowering in the basement room under the palace in Constantinople, clutching her baby to her—then disappeared as he willed them away. *Alone in exile, living on the mercy of others, directionless . . . bored.*

"You're a historian?" he said, curious. "What kind of histories do you write? Can you read Greek or Persian?"

"I can," Martina said, smiling. She dabbed at her eyelashes, smudging charcoal powder on her cheek. "I was writing a history of Constantinople, from its founding by Queen Medea as Byzantium in ancient times to the present day. . . . Heraclius approved, he thought it would keep me out of trouble."

"Medea of Colchis founded the city?" Maxian was surprised. He'd never thought of the woman as anything but a character in a play. "I thought colonists from Corinth made the first settlement."

"Rubbish!" Martina's face changed, her shyness falling away. "I've seen the founding stone of the city myself—and Medea is listed as Queen, under the aegis of her patron, the goddess Hecate. You can ignore Eusebius—he had *no* idea what he was talking about."

"You read old Greek too?" Maxian grinned. He did not relish the thought of plowing through mountains of Achean scrolls, searching for some vague fragment that might bear upon the current matter. Someone to help him would be very welcome indeed.

"Yes," Martina smiled back. "Being an Empress is usually very dull. It would be nice to do something useful for a change."

"Then you can help me," he said, pleased. "I must go up to Fiorentina tomorrow, to oversee some projects. If you'd like to come along, I'll show you what we've gathered."

BENEATH A FIG TREE

)(

The sky was still perfectly blue. Mohammed opened his
eyes to cerulean heavens unmarred by cloud or wind and
a round yellow sun. Despite the brightness, his skin was cold
and the falling sunlight brought him no warmth. He was unsure
if any time had passed while his eyes were closed, but he forced
himself to sit up against the bole of the tree. The sound of his
parched skin rubbing against the skin of the fig was very loud.
His movement made the hand-shaped leaves tremble, and they
rustled softly, disturbing a perfect silence.

Pale-barked woods surrounded him on three sides. On the
fourth, a grassy sward led down to the walls of the city. He
looked through the open gate, seeing men and women passing
by, going about their daily tasks. As he watched, the sounds of
their conversation and business swelled around him. The smell
of roasting meat, of fresh-baked bread, of decanted wine assailed his nostrils and he began to salivate.

Mohammed wiped his mouth, then looked down at his hand.
A fine white dust covered his palm. He raised his hand, squinting, and saw the dust was composed of tiny, broken hairs.

"My beard." He coughed and felt his lip split. Tentatively, he
touched the wound and his finger came away clean. Even his
blood was parched and dry. Yet, he thought, *I have not died of
thirst, or of hunger. What is this place?*

"You are outside the city of Iblis," a gentle voice said. "In a
wood."

Mohammed looked up and saw the well-featured man who
had spoken to him before. Mōha knelt on the grass, strong-
limbed body clad in jewel-colored silk. As before, he smiled
and nodded in greeting. "You are not well. I can bring you water, from the city, or food, if you are hungry."

"I am not hungry," Mohammed said, looking the man over very carefully. "You are the guardian of this place? A servant, who watches over those within?"

Mōha shook his head, puzzled, and his golden eyes danced with laughter. "I am not a jailer," he said. "I keep a watch upon the wood and the city. Sometimes—though not, I must admit, in my lifetime—a disturbance might rise in the wood to trouble those who live in the city. I am . . . a shepherd."

"Your flock seems content," Mohammed said, indicating the bustling crowds in the city only by the movement of his eyes. Even this much effort left him drained and weak. "What happens if they wish to leave?"

"I don't know," Mōha said, standing up and brushing off his tunic. Mohammed watched closely, but did not see grass, leaves or dust fall from the man's clothes. "No one has ever wished to leave."

The man turned, looking back at the city. A procession was passing the gate, holding aloft banners and gaudy icons. Drums and pipes sounded, making a merry noise. The people were laughing, carrying a golden idol on a platform of glossy wood. Mohammed started in surprise, then felt a chill creep across his arms. The face of the idol was his own.

"I'm sorry, but there is poor news," Mōha said, turning back. Now his perfect face was troubled, creased with worry and anguish. "A message has come for you."

Mohammed blinked, looking away from the idol and the cheering crowds filling the streets of the city. Many of the faces were familiar—his friends and neighbors—even those he had not seen since he was a boy. *Was that Khadijah, in her wedding veil?* "A message?"

"Yes." Mōha squatted, clasping his hands. He seemed worried. "You are sorely missed, at home. The young Khalid al'Walid—he has betrayed you—taken your army, your woman, even your name. Did you know he was of the Makzhum tribe?"

Mohammed frowned for a moment before his face cleared and he remembered his father, speaking vigorously in the house of the black stone. "The Makzhum . . . they were driven from the Zam-Zam by my grandfather. They fled the city, into the desert in shame." The face of Khalid wavered into his memory, and now—thinking back across many years—Mohammed saw the resemblance to those proud, hawk-faced chieftains. "Was he even born, when they were driven from Mekkah?"

"No," Mōha said, shaking his head in sympathy. "He was whelped in the sand, among scorpions and snakes. His people wandered in the desert for a long time, without a home, without lands or flocks . . . forced to banditry. The last of the Makzhum were betrayed and ambushed by the Banu Hira. Khalid, still a child, was taken prisoner. In time, he was a slave, and then a scout in the Persian army after Bahram Choban destroyed the kingdom of the Mondars."

"Yes," Mohammed whispered, remembering. "He was at Palmyra. He saw our final battle . . . Uri said . . ." Mohammed fell silent and his mind became entirely clear. A shadow fell away from his sight and he looked upon the man, Mōha, with a piercing glance. "Your master is known to me, creature. I will take nothing from you, or from this place."

Mōha ran slender fingers through his dark hair, sighing. He seemed concerned. "My lord Mohammed . . . Khalid has seized control of the Sahaba, your boon companions. He urges and guides them to fight for Persia, for your ancient enemy. Your teachings are being ignored and forgotten. The lady Zoë is under his spell, his servant. Even such stalwarts as Jalal and Shadin follow him. They continue to fight against Rome, heedless of the danger to their own lives."

"What would you have me do?" The Quraysh was curious.

"Leave this place!" Mōha gestured at the pale-barked trees and the short-cropped grass. "Go home! Take up the banner of your moon and star—drive out the traitor, as your father drove out his fathers. Take back what was yours . . . Look, there is your future. She is waiting for you." The man pointed, off through the trees.

Mohammed closed his eyes, turning away from golden sunlight falling through the clouds. A man and a woman were riding on fine, brightly caparisoned horses. They were laughing and the air around them was clear and filled with song. Their companions followed at a discreet distance, road-weary but smiling, for soon they would be in the city and many old friends would be reunited. Mohammed banished the image, driving glorious brown eyes from his memory.

"No," he said, though his chest was being crushed by an enormous weight. "The world will continue to turn without me."

"But . . . look at her!" Mōha's voice was anguished. "Look . . ."

Light blossomed upon Mohammed's face and this time, to his surprise, he felt real warmth and smelled the sea. The sound of water curling away from the prow of a ship was loud in his ears. Startled, unwary, he opened his eyes.

Zoë stood at the prow of a sleek, lateen-rigged ship, racing over a blue-green sea. Raven hair flowed over brown, tanned shoulders, and her eyes were closed, cheeks streaked with tears. Heavy gold ringed her neck and her strong arms were circled by silver and brass. Her image swelled and Mohammed beheld encompassing grief in her face. She was crying, and each heave of her shoulders cut at his heart. Anguished, he reached for her.

Zoë's eyes opened, and they were brilliant blue, the shade of crushed sapphire swirling in milk. Mohammed froze, hand— seemingly—only inches from her face.

"No," he said aloud and turned away. The light went out, and the cold stillness of the forest folded around him. He hid his face with his hands. For a moment, hidden from Mōha and the forest, he allowed himself a tiny dram of grief. Burning like a hot iron, a single tear oozed from his dusty eyes and puddled in his hand. "Go away."

Some time passed. Mohammed opened one eye a fraction. Mōha was watching him, chin resting on his arms. "I said . . . go."

"You need to go back," Mōha said, spreading his hands imploringly. "She needs you. Your friends need you. Won't you help them escape Khalid's snare?"

"Each man," Mohammed said, "is responsible for his own fate. The creator of the heavens and the earth has set us here, each alone, to find our way to him, or to corruption. Zoë will choose her own way, as will Khalid, and the others. They have free will. I will not take the gift from them."

"Very well." Mōha stood, shaking his head in dismay. The

tight ringlets of his hair cascaded over broad shoulders. "But if they die, or fall into dark places, the fault will be upon you, who could have saved them."

"They will save themselves, creature, by following the straight and righteous path. Or they will fail, by themselves." Mohammed paused, his throat hoarse from speech. Mōha looked down upon him with pity, great compassion on his perfect face. "The great and merciful one," Mohammed managed to gasp out, "keeps a ledger of all our days and acts, and each man and each woman's tally is their own. For good or ill, when final judgment is made and every soul weighed on the balance of good and evil, each of us stands alone. This is the gift of the lord's breath upon the clay, and it is precious."

"So you say." Mōha was unconvinced, his mouth tight with concern. "I see my brother in the desert and his foot is upon a scorpion's back—I run to give him aid—to stand by his side. Would you let him die, if your swift action could save his life?"

"Each man—and even *you*, spirit—must make his own choice. I may save my brother, but I will not imprison him to keep him from danger."

Mōha shook his head in disbelief. "Then return home and take your own path—never see them again—wander the earth, friendless and alone!"

"*No*," Mohammed said. "I will rest here, under this tree, and see what may transpire."

Distressed, Mōha turned away and descended the grassy sward towards the city.

Mohammed waited until the man was gone. When he was, at last, alone, he relaxed minutely, weary with grief and loss. He missed Zoë terribly. He was not surprised Khalid had become chieftain of the Sahaba. This was the way of the world, for the young to supplant the old and with each passing generation the world changed. The tides were unceasing, the sun rose and set, even as the lord of the wasteland desired.

He opened his hand, and the tear glittered on his cracked, seamed palm like a drop of mercury. Mohammed, seeing the liquid quiver and roll in his hand, became very thirsty. Even a moment's respite from the dust in his throat would be a blessing. The Quraysh leaned back against the tree and felt the trunk bend with him. Above, leaves rattled in the branches. They were turning yellow, curling up at the edges, and the buds were small and hard. "You are thirsty too," he said to the tree.

He closed his parched lips, trying to swallow. Dust filled his nose and mouth. Mohammed tilted his hand and the tear slid onto the roots of the fig. The drop of water vanished instantly into the mottled gray bark. Mohammed closed his eyes. *I am so tired.*

CAESAREA MARITIMA, ON THE COAST OF JUDEA

K halid shaded his eyes, squinting into a brassy Levantine sky, and gritted his teeth. One of his horses—a dappled, strong-legged mare—dangled from a ship's crane above the dock. Though a mask covered her eyes and a canvas sling was snug under her round chest, the horse kicked furiously. A Palmyrene dock—foreman waved commands to the men working the winch and she swung back and forth, then lighted on the sandstone surface of the quay. Khalid breathed out, relieved.

"I'll take her!" He shouted at the longshoremen holding the cables, preparing to slip the mare free of the net. They stepped back and Khalid eased up, clucking softly. "Here girl, here's an apple. . . ."

The mare snuffled wildly, tossing her head. Khalid nipped in and caught her bridle. She flipped her big square head to the side, but the apple was waiting. Cautiously, a soft nose snorted around the crisp, red fruit, then the apple disappeared into a horsy mouth with a crunching sound. "There, see, not so bad . . ."

Khalid rubbed the horse's neck until she quieted, then led her—still hooded—down the long dock. The air was filled with noise; the squeal of ropes through pulleys, the shouts of men, a dull boom as wooden crates swung from ship holds onto the quays of the port, shrieking gulls wheeling among the masts.

Sixty ships were moored in the inner harbor of Caesarea, hiding from a constant, tugging wind surging out of the northwest. Beyond the calm oval of the main harborage, beyond a pair of towering sandstone lighthouses, the sea boomed against a marble-faced breakwater three miles long. The Judean shore, particularly here, was open and desolate, without any kind of natural harbor. Only the awesome power of Rome had lifted Caesarea from the sand. Another fifty ships of the Sahaba fleet were tied up on the southern docks, outside the breakwater, protected from the constant wind and a wicked current by the bulk of the port itself.

Khalid reached the end of the dock, weaving his way through lines of men in loincloths and plain white headdresses laboring in the burning sun. They were hauling wicker amphorae frames out of a fat-bellied Roman troop transport. Wine and oil and salt and olives. Khalid grinned, watching the men with an eagle eye—they were working hard, heads bent, moving with quick, jerky motions. They were afraid.

As well they should be, Khalid thought. *They have a hard master. Not one so lenient or so familiar as Rome.*

Atop the harbor towers, looming over a narrow channel filled with angry water, two flags fluttered in the strong breeze; the golden sunburst of Persia and the green field and white moon of the Sahaba. Al'Walid grinned again. *That is my banner now. Mine.*

The horse bumped him again, trying to get nimble lips into the pockets of his cloak. Sadly, there were no more apples. He rubbed her nose, then untied the hood and let her blink away the sun. Satisfied she had her land legs, Khalid swung onto her back and nudged the mare to follow the main street of the port. The road was crowded with wagons, but men parted before him, and the Sahaban fighters policing the port recognized him.

"Make way!" they shouted, pressing back the crowd with their spears. "The Eagle passes! Make way!"

Khalid flashed a smile at two kohl-eyed prostitutes leaning on their balcony and the girls waved, giggling. His heart soared, seeing fear and desire alike in their eyes. *But not today, there is work to be done.* He urged the mare on, and she was glad to pick up the pace, clattering up the long boulevard bisecting the

Roman town. The young chieftain was glad to feel hot, dry wind on his face. The ships were close and cramped, filled with the noxious smell of sweating, unwashed soldiers. Even the strength of the sun, burning on his face, was welcome.

Caesarea was crowded, filled with soldiers disembarking, marching in long columns up from the docks. The Arabs and Greeks were happy, laughing and chattering like blackbirds. A vast quantity of loot was being hauled ashore. When Khalid reached the Capitolina gate, he found the passage jammed with wagons stacked with bundles of spears. Not all of the treasure torn out of Constantinople was gold or ivory. Khalid had spent three days walking through armory rooms in the old Imperial fortress of the Golden Gate, counting bushels of arrows, suits of mailed armor, swords, spears, daggers, scorpion engines, axes, bows, mangonels, shovels, picks, iron helms, shields, sheaves of javelins, bales of tunics, boots, barrels of hobnailed sandals, cornicens in copper and bronze, *bucinas*, even a water organ built on a wagon. . . . He laughed aloud, filled with furious exaltation. *My army is stronger every day. Every day!*

"Clear the gate," he shouted and the Sahaban sergeants trying to control traffic turned. Seeing him looking down from an eager horse, his dark face silhouetted against the brassy sky, they redoubled their efforts. Khalid was restless and each grain while the teamsters strained to get their wagons through the portal was an eternity.

Outside the city, the dappled mare stretched herself, galloping along a broad military road arrowing up into the hills. A mile beyond the dusty white walls of the city, a huge camp sprawled on either side of the road among scrub and salt trees. Dozens of banners snapped in the offshore wind and Khalid cantered down a broad lane lined with tents on either side. Persians and Huns looked up as he passed and the swarthy-faced nomads shouted their appreciation of his horse. Khalid flashed a grin, then rode on.

The arrival of the fleet in Caesarea had found not only the Sahaban garrison Khalid expected but fresh regiments of Persian troops. While the armies of Persia, Avaristan and the Decapolis struggled before Constantinople, the King of King's empire—still weak, but gathering strength—amassed a new army and sent it west. Al'Walid knew the faces of men better than most and he kenned the Persian numbers were greatly swollen by mercenaries. Beside the long-mustached Huns, there were Bactrians with their silk banners and huge-chested stallions; countless numbers of Arabs from the eastern fringes of the great desert; thousands of hill-men—Kushans?—with brocaded tabards and leaf-bladed spears; even Indian knights from the hot lands beyond the great sea. Seeing the vast tent of the shahanshah rising above the lesser tents of the *diquans* and the feudal lords, Khalid slowed the mare, ignoring her whuffling protests and prancing hooves. The day was hot and Al'Walid thought she had sweated enough.

Shahr-Baraz' tent rose three stories high, a monstrous confection of silk and canvas and colored banners. A great gate stood open at the front, revealing a vast interior space filled with muted light and endless numbers of thick rugs. Khalid swung down from his horse, tossing the reins to a groom—one of a huge crowd of servants loitering around outside, jockeying for shade near the door. The entrance itself was empty, save for—just within—two dark shapes, one on either side.

Khalid strode past the Shanzdah, ignoring the unsettling emptiness of their helms, suppressing a shudder as he felt some nameless, cold effluvium wash over his exposed skin. He slowed his pace, letting his eyes adjust to the filtered, golden light falling from translucent panels set into the upper storeys. Shahr-Baraz might be a man of action, a king ruling from the saddle, but his empire had a vigorous bureaucracy and court that rushed here and there, trying to find the Boar and pen him safely in elegance and luxury.

A throne of sandalwood and mother-of-pearl glowed in the falling light. Khalid passed through knots of men—nobles, soldiers, merchants, great lords and small—to approach the center of power. He slowed, watching the faces of those he passed with careful eyes. He schooled his expression to a calm smile, eyes glinting with secrets. He stopped, stepping in front of the hulking swordsman, Shadin. The grizzled, white-bearded Sahaba looked aside and nodded in greeting. Khalid's eyes flicked across the tableau before him and he was forced to suppress a snarl.

How has this happened? She was leaving, a penitent on a long journey into emptiness!

Shahr-Baraz, the Royal Boar, Emperor of the Persians and the Medes, stood beside the throne, one booted foot lodged carelessly against the precious wood. His massive torso was girded in mail, his long salt-and-pepper hair tied behind a thick neck with rawhide.

"Within the week," Shahr-Baraz boomed, his voice a little less than a roar, "the fleet will have completed unloading our men and goods. Within two weeks, our wagons will be filled, our regiments ordered. I say, my friends, in four weeks we shall move south in full array."

Standing on the other side of the throne, her hair combed back in a glossy wave, stood Zoë, queen of Palmyra. She eschewed the Boar's martial display, her neck framed with gold and electrum, smooth arms kissed with silver circlets. Khalid hid a sneer, seeing her brilliant blue eyes enhanced with powdered pearl and antimony. Even her gown, clinging like a skin to her young, lithe body was opulent—a golden-hued silk, like the sky at dawn, cinched with supple kidskin. The Queen was smiling, watching Shahr-Baraz declaim. Beside her, the Palmyrene prince Odenathus leaned on a staff. Khalid tried to catch his friend's eye, but the Palmyrene's attention was focused on the King of Kings.

"Our goal is this," the Boar said, voice settling into a basso rumble. "To strike down upon Roman Egypt like a storm, overpower her defenses and seize the great port of Alexandria. We do not aim to capture the whole of the country, not yet, but we *must* secure the port of Pelusium—the first barrier we will encounter—and then Alexandria. With both harbors under our control, we choke off the flow of grain to Rome." Shahr-Baraz smiled, showing fine white teeth amid the thicket of his beard.

Khalid nodded absently, turning his head a little. Where was—a cold shock made him flinch. Behind the king, hidden in shadow, surrounded by four more of the Shanzdah, stood a slim, dark figure.

Prince . . . Rustam. Khalid's heart hammered, then slowed. He licked his lips. *My . . . ally.*

The prince was watching the King of Kings as well, standing at ease, hands clasped behind his back. Khalid's eyelid twitched. A gleam passed across the prince, making his skin shimmer and twist, as if scales caught the light of a candle. Al'Walid forced himself to remain upright, though a terrible, pressing desire to kneel came over him. He swayed and Shadin—his gruff face pinched in disapproval—caught his arm and held him upright. Khalid wrenched his attention back to Shahr-Baraz.

"The fleet," Shahr-Baraz continued, "under the command of the noble Odenathus, will parallel our course. I expect—no, I *know*—the Roman fleet has regrouped. They will come against us as soon as we show our intent. Odenathus, you will have to fight, and perhaps you will have to flee."

The Palmyrene was surprised by the shahanshah's sober tone and he shook his head. "My lord, we will not abandon you!"

"You will," Shahr-Baraz said, raising a hand to forestall further protest. "The fleet is our only advantage; it *must* be preserved. Because of this, the army will march on land with all supplies necessary to cross the desert to Pelusium. Once we are within the Nile delta, we will forage for what we need. But while we engage the Romans ashore, the fleet must keep out of danger."

"Very well." Odenathus nodded dubiously.

"Good!" Shahr-Baraz beamed at the assembly, tugging at the ends of his mustaches. "Now, the rest of you . . . the lands between here and Pelusium are harsh, with little water, no feed, no browse for our horses. Therefore we must march swiftly, taking advantage of the fine Roman road along the coast. We must reach and take Pelusium before we starve." The King of Kings smiled broadly.

Khalid frowned at the various commanders around him. *These fat Persians make such a bold march? I think not . . . my Sahaba have been tempered on the An'Nefud, the anvil of the lord! The Huns are canny men and used to long days in the saddle with few rations—they will pass the test. Even the men of the Decapolis are hardy and used to the sun . . . but these di-*

quans *from their fat, well-watered land?* He stifled a derisive laugh.

"You *will* be ready in three weeks and your men *will* keep up. If they do not, they will be left behind, without wine or grain." Shahr-Baraz drew a long knife from his belt. He considered his profile in the mirror-bright blade. "A man might live a day without water, perhaps two, under this sun. His death will be slow and agonizing as his skin burns black and ants consume his eyes. This pleases me—I would not want to sully my steel with the blood of a fool or a coward!"

Off to Khalid's left, a tall, broad-shouldered Persian stepped out of the crowd. "Great king," the man declared, sweeping the assembly with a fierce gaze. "We will reach Pelusium at your side and we will crush the Romans as your lightning arm! Nothing will stop us!"

"Well spoken, Lord Piruz." Shahr-Baraz smiled at the man. Khalid looked closer, disturbed by the gaunt features of the Persian lord. There was a brittle spark in the noble's eyes and the Arab found his attention drawn to a flash of black silk at the man's throat. *Ah, one of Purandokht's suitors . . . then he is mad, and reckless for honor too.*

"Consider this," Shahr-Baraz said, stepping away from the throne. His voice took on a considered tone, as if he spoke to children in the temple. "The army of Persia can usually travel ten to fifteen miles in a day. Pressed, my old army of Syria—veterans every one—did twenty. A Roman legion—men accounted throughout the world for their stamina and speed of march—account twenty-five miles a day excellent progress. Between Gazzah, the last town of note before the desert, and Pelusium are no less than one hundred and twenty miles of sand and barren stone. There are no wells, no *qanats*, no oases. Once we reach the edge of the delta, we must fight our way through the Roman army to the arm of the Nile. Our wagons and pack camels can carry enough food, water and feed for our strength for seven, perhaps eight days."

Khalid whistled, impressed. That was an enormous amount of baggage. The army encamped at Caesarea numbered sixty or seventy thousand men. *How many skins of water will a man drink, unused to this sun? Too many.* The Al'Walid had seen men, overcome by the heat, drink so much from a well their stomachs burst. He hid a grin. *Soon they will all look like the lovesick Piruz,* he thought, scratching his short-cropped beard.

"Great king?" Khalid turned to the voice, unable to help himself. Zoë stirred, stretching, and smiled in a languid way at Shahr-Baraz. "Many of these men—the princes of the Decapolis, the Sahaba, even the T'u-chüeh—are used to swift movement over poor ground. But your Persians . . . how will they make twenty miles a day? They have so much baggage, so many servants . . ."

The Persian *diquans* bristled at the Queen's tone, and she smiled at them like a cat, eyes half-closed. Khalid felt a stab of anger, then quelled his temper. *She taunts us, with her body, with her place of favor . . . does she kneel for the King of Kings, or*—Khalid snuck a glance sideways at the dark corner where prince Rustam stood—*for him?*

"We do not need servants," Lord Piruz barked, one lean hand sliding to the hilt of his sword.

"Really?" Zoë cocked her head to one side, considering the northern prince. "Who will bathe you, Lord of Balkh? Who will tend your wounds, or repair your boots after the sand wears away the stitching?" She smiled lazily, the pink tip of her tongue appearing for an instant between white teeth. "Who will cook your food and keep your tent warm at night? Your squire?"

Piruz snarled and took a step forward. The rasp of metal on metal was very loud as his sword slipped from the sheath.

"Peace, Lord Piruz. Peace." Shahr-Baraz' hand was on the prince's wrist and the sword clicked back into the scabbard. "Do not taunt brave men, Queen Zoë. They are unused to this land."

Zoë bowed her head gracefully, inclining her body towards the King of Kings in obeisance. Khalid bit back a hiss as her gown slipped aside, exposing the smooth curve of her breasts and her flat stomach. He felt a shock in his gut and forced himself to look away. When he did, he saw Prince Rustam smiling from the shadows.

"You are both right," Shahr-Baraz rumbled, clasping both hands behind his back. "Our army cannot cross the desert in time enough if we are burdened by camp followers, servants, maids and pleasure women. Yet—we cannot fight, we cannot campaign—without their skills, their goods, their labor. But all these things are known to me. Prince Odenathus and his fleet supply our answer."

The Palmyrene prince's eyebrow rose, then a quick smile flashed across his lean face. He nodded in appreciation.

"Our soldiers will march," the King of Kings said, pacing back to the throne. "Our servants will ride—in the fleet— which, by happy circumstance, escorts a large number of shallow-draft boats that can easily land on a sandy beach. And between here and Pelusium, my friends, there is no lack of beach and sand!"

Khalid laughed with the Boar, grasping the careful planning and foresight required to resolve such a thorny problem. The other lords laughed too, but they only laughed because their master did. Khalid felt a weight ease from his shoulders and he realized he had been worrying at the same problem in the back of his mind. *And who*, he chided himself, *is the master general here? Who has campaigned for thirty years or more, ever victorious? Not I! Not yet.*

"Now, noble lords," Shahr-Baraz said, voice booming again, "to your commands! You all have a great deal of work to do. Do not disappoint me."

Khalid waited, watching the other lords and captains flood out of the tent. He hoped to have a word with the King of Kings, but Shahr-Baraz had already slipped out. Prince Rustam and the Shanzdah were also gone, and the tent felt warmer, more open, for their departure. Only Zoë remained and the young Arab stiffened as she approached.

"Lord Al'Walid. Are you well?"

"Yes," Khalid said, his skin prickling with unexpected heat. The Queen touched his sword hand and her fingertips seemed hot. "Why do you ask?"

"You have such a look on your face . . . are you angry with me?"

"No," he managed to say, though he *did* feel a spark of fury gutter in his stomach. *I should rule the Sahaba and the De-capolis alike!* He was surprised at himself. He was angry with her. Everything he had won, she was taking away. "I . . . you've changed, Lady Zoë. What has happened to you?"

"Me?" Zoë bit her lower lip, staring up at him with concern. Her eyes were very, very blue. Khalid shook his head, suppressing the urge to brush something—gnats?—from his face. She was still touching his hand and her warm fingers slid over his. "Have I? Perhaps."

Zoë paused, looking away, into some abyss of memory. "Yes. You are right. I was very angry when we first met . . . but the Teacher showed how to leave that behind." She met his eyes again, and such genuine warmth and good humor was shining there Khalid smiled back reflexively, though a bitter, oily feeling swirled in his stomach.

She's stealing my kingdom! part of his mind growled. *I could kill her . . . reach out and crush her throat . . .*

"It seems strange," she said, pressing closer. "I grieved for my city, for my aunt. I don't anymore. I know . . . the lord Mohammed showed me things . . . I know Palmyra will live again. And Zenobia . . ." The Queen laughed softly, nails digging into Khalid's hand. "I feel her close to me, every day."

Khalid blinked, eyes tearing, and he stepped back. His feet seemed to drag through mud or deep, heavy sand. Her fingers slipped softly from his wrist. "My lady . . . I need to see . . . to my troops."

"You are a wise commander, Lord Al'Walid. The King of Kings is lucky to have you as a friend, as an ally."

"Yes." Khalid felt speech return and his mind starting to work again. He thought of Shahr-Baraz and the plan for the campaign. There was so much to do . . . he would need to meet with Jalal, Shadin and Uri immediately. *We must see to our own supplies*, he thought, narrowing his eyes. *These Persians will run out . . . and they will be begging for charity in the wasteland.* "Good day, my lady."

"Good day, Khalid," Zoë said, hands clasped at her waist. "Oh, the lord will have need you later—after dinnertime. There are some private matters to be discussed."

"Very well." Khalid nodded.

"He will send for you when he needs you." Zoë said, turning

away. Again, he was struck by the brilliance of her eyes as she looked back over her shoulder. She drew a cloak over smooth brown shoulders, then padded away across the carpets. He noticed she was barefoot and frowned, unaccountably uneasy. Servants were entering, bringing long tables and benches. Khalid watched the Palmyrene girl until she disappeared through one of the curtains.

Then he shook his head, brushing away the gnats tickling his face, and strode out.

The King of Kings will summon me? When he needs me . . . am I his servant? I am a king!

"You will come with me."

Khalid looked up in irritation. One of the Shanzdah filled the door of his tent. The cowled shape was black against the night sky, barely illuminated by lanterns hanging from the tent pole. Khalid sat cross-legged, the sword of night at his right hand. Jalal, Shadin, Uri ben-Sarid and the big Persian mercenary Patik were also in the tent, squatting or sitting around a confusion of parchments, papyrus scrolls and counting boards. Shadin's mouth closed with a snap. The burly swordsman had been accounting the cavalrymen in his *qalb*, their arms, armor, mounts and provisions.

"Will I?" Khalid put down a waxed tablet. He was already tired, though the night was still young. Shahr-Baraz tasked them vigorously with this march on Egypt. "Who asks for my presence?"

"That one," the Shanzdah continued, its voice a cold hiss, pointing at Patik, "will also come."

Khalid settled his shoulders, glaring up at the shape. The messenger's eyes could not be seen in the deep recesses of the iron helmet. Patik rose and shrugged on his cloak. The desert night was cold, even with the day wind died down to a mild breeze. Without a word, the Persian stepped past the armored shape of the Shanzdah and into the night.

"Curse this . . . we've work to do . . ." Khalid grumbled, but the creature was not going to leave. He too rose, slinging the sword of night over his shoulder on its leather baldric and ivory-and-cloth sheath. Already in a poor temper, the Al'Walid frowned at his captains. None of the three men looked pleased. "I will be back as soon as I can."

"Oh, surely," Uri said, a thread of mocking laughter in his voice. Khalid's eyes glinted in response, but he said nothing, controlling his anger. The ben-Sarid chafed under his authority. The friction was intermittent, but it grew with each day.

Not now, Khalid promised himself, *but soon. The ben-Sarid are eager for glory—they will have their fill, once we are at grips with the Romans . . .*

Khalid's disquiet deepened as the swift, dark shape of the messenger passed among the tents. Patik, with his long legs, kept pace easily, but Khalid was forced to hurry. They did not turn in the direction of the great king's tent, but rather to the east. After a little time they reached the watch fires at the edge of the camp. The Persians and their allies had not bothered to build a palisade or ditch, relying instead on regularly spaced bonfires, tended by a mixture of sentries. There were other lookouts too, hiding in the darkness or loitering on the nearby sand hills. The land around Caesarea was quiet, almost devoid of settlements. There were few men able to scratch a living out of the sandy soil and barren coast. Any approaching enemy would be visible miles away.

The Shanzdah vanished into the darkness beyond the campfires and Khalid followed more by hearing than sight. Thorny brush tugged at his clothes and spiked plants stabbed at his boots as they crossed the plain. Khalid's night vision slowly settled and he found himself approaching another camp, unlit by fires or lights. Even the stars seemed dim. The moon was down, making the land ghostly in faint starlight. The night grew colder with each step and Khalid steeled himself, recognizing their destination.

Your ally, a girlish voice laughed in his head, making Khalid blink, trying to drive a vision of the Queen from his memory. *The . . . prince.*

The messenger paused, raising a hand in the darkness. Starlight gleamed from a mailed fist. Patik stopped as well. After a moment, Khalid became aware of a soft noise—something like crickets or beetles rustling on the ground. A very faint sound of chirping flirted with the edge of his hearing. The messenger moved sideways and Patik followed. Khalid peered ahead in the gloom and made out a tall iron pole thrust into sandy ground. Black against black, the metal rose to head height.

Shaking his head again—the intermittent chirping grew louder—Khalid followed the others. The Shanzdah weaved off to the left, stepping around bushes and stones, then back to the right. They passed another metal pole, then two more. Khalid felt chilled and drew his cloak tight around his shoulders. Then the chirping stopped and the cold deepened.

A dozen yards away, a black wagon sat within a cluster of felt tents.

The T'u-chüeh, Khalid thought, wrinkling up his nose. Even in this winter-like air, he smelled rancid butter and urine. He closed his nostrils, then put his head down as they walked swiftly through the encampment. Nothing stirred among the yurts, but Khalid caught glints of metal and lamplight out of the corner of his eye. He did not see any horses, which was puzzling. *But what animal could stand to exist within this dread circle? How can these barbarians? Yet more arrive each day . . . flies drawn to rotting meat.*

The wagon loomed up, easily twice the height of a tall man, and Khalid saw wooden steps—ornately carved with spiky letters and coiling, eye-dizzying designs—leading up to a door. The Shanzdah stepped aside, his mailed arm raised.

"They are waiting," the creature said. The voice was very faint, rasping and scuttling inside the iron helmet.

Khalid tried to clear his throat, grimaced and mounted the steps two at a time. Patik followed, quiet as a shade. For the first time, the young Arab did not feel safer with the Persian at his back. Instead, his shoulder blades crawled with a prickling sensation.

"Lord Al'Walid, come in!" A cheerful voice greeted the Arab as he stepped into warm, golden light. Inside the wagon was a spacious room, rich with bright carpets on the floor, the walls hung with heavy embroidered fabric. Lamps hung from the ceiling, burning bright with scented oil. The slim, elegant figure of Prince Rustam sat cross-legged behind a low writing desk. He had set aside his cloak, wearing only a slate-colored shirt. His hair was loose, falling behind his head in an ebon cloud. "Please, sit."

Khalid looked around, quietly calculating the cost of the golden lamps, the fine carpets, the polished wood paneling. Still in the doorway, he eased off his boots, as was polite, then knelt on a plush, deep-woven Samarkand. Long-bodied hounds intertwined with flowering trees on the carpet. The silk threads felt like fine glass under his fingers. "Good evening, my lord."

"Do you thirst? Do you hunger?" Rustam gestured to one side and Khalid almost hissed aloud in surprise. Zoë knelt against the wall, leaning on one hand, cheek resting on her shoulder, watching him with a smile. Her hair fell behind her shoulder and arm in a black wave. In this golden light, her skin seemed to have grown pale—almost alabaster—with a milky shine. For a moment, Khalid couldn't speak, then he seemed to come back to himself, from far away.

"No?" Prince Rustam nodded gravely. "Lord Shahin, please sit. It's you I've summoned, in truth. But since you have been so ably serving Master Khalid, I felt it best to speak with both of you at the same time."

"Who?" Khalid looked around again, but found only Patik kneeling beside him. The Persian's expression was bleak with unexpected despair. His high cheekbones were pronounced and Khalid realized the mercenary was gritting his teeth. "Who is . . . Patik? You . . . you *are* the Great Prince Shahin!"

"Yes," the big Persian said, deep baritone filling the room. He looked sideways at Khalid, then away. "Do not laugh."

"Why would I laugh?" Khalid put a hand over his mouth. He was trying not to guffaw. The man was his friend. They had shared wine, water, bread . . . thousands of miles in wretched desolation. Khalid did not want to offend Patik—*no, Shahin*, he reminded himself. "You've always been a mystery! So the secret of your so-extensive education is revealed. Well. Well, well."

Rustam coughed politely, and both men froze, then turned to face him. The prince's affable manner remained and Khalid breathed a little easier. Even Shahin relaxed minutely. "There is business to discuss," Rustam said. "You know the shahanshah intends to drive the Romans from Egypt."

Khalid nodded, darting a glance sideways at Shahin. The matter seemed very obvious now—Khalid had even been one of the Great Prince's couriers, during the Persian invasion of Syria three years previous. There had been trouble—the Persians had nearly blundered into a fatal trap at Lake Bahrat. Shahin's command was stripped away by the fortuitous arrival of the Royal Boar himself, arriving all unexpected in the middle of the night, in the company of . . . Khalid's eyes slid back to Prince Rustam, who was watching him with a slight smile. A peculiar pale light gleamed in the prince's eyes and the brief moment of comfort vanished. Khalid shuddered, meeting the burning light in the prince's pale, translucent gaze.

"Khalid . . . do not trouble your mind. True, Shahin was relieved of his command. True, he has lost his rank, his titles, his lands . . . even his family is sure he is dead. But—as you have seen—he has won back his honor." Rustam lifted a long fingered hand, his fingertips broad and flat, like some kind of a climbing lizard. Shahin stiffened, transfixed. "He may grow a proper beard again, and oil and curl his hair, as he once did. Perfumes, perhaps, will be made available, and pomades. My lord, do you desire such things?"

"No," Shahin growled, still meeting the prince's lambent stare. "I do not."

"You choose this life? Sand and dust, a rough bed among thorns? Only steel for comfort, not silk, not down pillows?" The prince's voice was soft, caressing. Khalid shuddered again, feeling his flesh crawl.

"I do choose this," Shahin said, narrowing his eyes. He seemed unaffected by the prince's glamour. "I will fight beside my friends. For my king. For Persia."

Rustam leaned back and Khalid could feel the heat of the lamps again. He could hear Shahin and Zoë breathing. "You surprise me, Prince Shahin. And I am glad."

Khalid thought his heart would stop, hearing—*seeing*—honest appreciation in the face of the prince. *How . . . how can . . .* He tried to stop from babbling, even in the privacy of his thoughts. The prince stared at Shahin and the odd, mottled quality of his flesh faded. The queer light in his eyes died, leaving them a pale amber color.

"You have become an honorable man, Shahin." Rustam managed a half-smile. "You were such a . . . fop, a dandy, a fool! Zenobia nearly trapped your whole army, because you could not be troubled to set watches, or pay your guides, or keep on the mercenary scouts Chrosoes King of Kings gave you! You prevaricated, you lied, your stole the wages of your troops . . . you were a coward."

Shahin's face grew colder and colder with each word, the tendons in his arms stiffening, his face slowly filling with a dark flush.

"Where is that man?" Rustam raised his hands, amazement clear on his face. "I do not see him now. I see a Persian *diquan*, a worthy man, a man the King of Kings can respect. That I can respect. Welcome, Shahin. Welcome."

The prince bowed his head in greeting, and silently Zoë walked forward on her knees, a wooden platter in her hands. Gracefully, she placed a simple bevel-rimmed bowl on the carpet between the two men. Beside it, she laid a loaf of flat, slightly burned bread. Salt trickled from her hand, making a small pile.

"Water from my wells," Rustam said, raising the bowl. He drank, then passed the cup to Shahin. The man drank. The bowl itself was turning dark with water oozing through the cheap clay. Khalid saw a vein at Shahin's throat throb, then settle. As the Arab watched, tension drained bit by bit from the nobleman.

"Bread from my fire," Rustam said, breaking the crumbling loaf in half. He chewed the heavy, unleavened bread, then swallowed. Shahin did likewise, his hands trembling for a moment. Then this too passed.

"Salt." The prince pressed the white grains against his teeth. Shahin did so as well. Rustam offered his hand and the Persian gripped his wrist, still tentative.

"This is your name: Eran-Spahbodh Shahin Suren-Pahlav." Rustam enunciated the words slowly and deliberately. "Son of Shapur and Erandokht, grandson of Soren-Nersi, scion of the house of Frataraka, let there be peace between us. Let all past wrongs be stricken from the tablets, all harsh words forgotten. Know, Prince Shahin, the King of Kings remembers you and accounts you a friend."

The big Persian blinked, then released Rustam's hand slowly, as if in a dream. "That is not my name . . . not anymore. I am only Patik."

"Yes, it is your name." Rustam drew a roll of fine parchment from his writing desk. A heavy wax seal and Tyrian purple string closed the document. "Here is your name, Shahin, and your family, returned to you by the grace of the King of Kings, Shahr-Baraz."

Rustam pressed the papers into Shahin's hand. The big Persian shook his head in disbelief. "But . . . why now?"

"Yes," Khalid said in a dry voice. "What do you need from him?"

Rustam's head turned slightly, fixing Khalid with a cold glare. "I did not give you leave to speak, Arab." The prince blinked and the angles of his face subtly changed, a pale gleam entering his eyes. Khalid recoiled, seeing something of the prince's true nature shining through. "But you too have served well. This is why I have summoned you both. Lord Khalid, this man Patik is no longer yours to command. He is, once more, the great Prince Shahin. I tell you this in courtesy, for you are a fine general, and tonight I rob you of an able captain."

Khalid's nostrils flared and he fought down a reckless urge to protest. *How do you deny the moon? Or a meteor?*

Rustam's forehead furrowed and he pinched his lip. He began to speak, then fell silent. Khalid watched in slow, growing amazement. The sorcerer seemed to be at a loss for words. At last, the prince made a gesture with his hand, as if he threw something away.

"Lord Shahin, here is what you must do," Rustam said. "Gather a few men, no more than five or six. You will take a ship we have lately captured down to Egypt. The ship, and you, and your men, will be disguised as Tyreans. That island city is still in Roman hands—this will allow you to enter Roman territory without undue trouble." The prince grinned, showing long white teeth.

"Once you are in Alexandria, a man will find you. He is a

servant of the king. You will know him, by certain signs, when you meet. He will lead you to a device." Rustam lifted a ragged bit of papyrus from his writing desk. Khalid saw part of a diagram on the ancient paper, some kind of interlocking mill wheel. "This device is buried in a secret place, perhaps a tomb, certainly somewhere desolate and remote. Be careful! In earlier times a rather dangerous order of priestesses watched over the *duradarshan*. They, or their degenerate cult, may still abide. Regardless, you will secure the device and return to Alexandria and the ship. You will bring me the mechanism as swiftly as you can."

Shahin looked down at the bit of papyrus, eyes narrowing. "How large is this?"

"Large." The ghost of a smile flitted across Rustam's lips. "Large and heavy."

"Can two men carry this . . . device?"

"No." Rustam was still smiling. "The *duradarshan* is made of bronze and gold, and likely affixed to a block of jadeite the size of a chest. You will need assistance."

Shahin placed the paper back on the edge of the desk. "How many of the Shanzdah will accompany me?"

"None. They are already busy." The prince grimaced. His thin hands rustled on the desk like large white spiders, finding two clay tablets, each the size of a palm. He lifted them gingerly, regarding them with an ambivalent expression. Then he made a queer half-smile and placed them in a metal box by his side. The lid closed with a snap, and he handed the box to Shahin. "When you reach the *duradarshan*, smash one of these tablets on the ground. A . . . servant . . . will come forth to carry the device."

"What kind of servant?" Shahin and Khalid spoke as one. The Arab felt a creeping sensation on the back of his neck and turned suddenly, looking behind him. There was nothing, only the door, now closed. He turned back, his gaze lingering on Zoë, who was still kneeling beside the wall. She smiled at him, eyes half-closed, white hands resting on silk-wrapped thighs.

"Nothing which need concern you," Rustam said. "As long as you hold the other tablet you will be quite safe. Once you reach the port, throw the box and the remaining tablet into the sea. The servant will depart."

"Very well." Shahin bowed. "I will do as the King of Kings commands."

Rustam's face darkened. Khalid tensed. "You will do as I command," the prince hissed.

Shahin regarded him levelly. "I am the king's man, my lord. Not yours."

"Wait," Khalid said, before Rustam could respond. "I will go in Lord Shahin's place."

"No," snapped Shahin and Rustam at the same time. The two men glared at one another. Shahin's jaw clenched, then released. "I will find the eye . . . the device, lord prince. For Persia."

"I see," Rustam said, but his voice was thick with anger. Khalid, watching the two men, thought the sorcerer might strike down the nobleman. But the creature controlled himself. "Leave tonight. One of the Shanzdah will show you the way to the boat."

"I will." Shahin stood, pocketing the metal box. "Lord prince, my lady." He bowed courteously to Zoë, nodded to Rustam and left. Khalid flashed a half-smile at the Queen, bowed to Rustam—still fuming, his eyes hooded—and hastily departed.

Zoë stirred and closed the wagon door. The cold air raised goose pimples on her arms. With her face turned away from the sorcerer, anguish showed plain for an instant, then her face composed into a calm mask once again.

"You taunt the Arab," Dahak said, sibilant anger in his voice. "Why?"

"Why not?" The Queen turned, settling to the floor in a smooth motion. The sorcerer shed his pleasant guise. The room filled with odd shadows in the corners and the lamps guttered down to a dim, pale flames gleaming on his mottled, slick skin. "If they fear me, they will obey. Your will is my will, is it not? If they fear me, they will fear you more, for you are the master."

Dahak's eyes narrowed and the Queen shuddered, feeling his thoughts upon her like snakes squirming over her skin. She swallowed, forcing down bile, and remained impassive. The sorcerer's eyes gleamed with a feral yellow light. "They look upon you with desire, with lust. You move your body to entice them, you fill their minds with confusion and dreams. This distracts them from doing my will."

"No," she managed to gasp. "The Greeks and Arabs scurry to do your bidding. They abase themselves before you. Armies and nations move as you command. I only occupy their idle moments—when thoughts of treachery might creep in—yet do not, for daydreams of my lips, my thighs, my breasts are there instead. I am a trophy, a prize to flaunt, even as their desire for the Twin Radiances drives the Persian knights to such furious bravery."

Dahak's lip curled up, exposing long, chisel-like incisors. "True . . . but a waste of time! A crude tool. Men are moved by fear best of all. I may seize their minds myself, if they stray!"

The Queen swayed, feeling tremendous relief as the sorcerer's will receded. She hissed, supporting herself with trembling arms. Her hair came loose; spilling in rich, dark curls around her shoulders. "But, great lord . . . I am your willing servant. If you are distracted, gone on more important business, then I can control them. Your reach is the greater, your will refined, focused."

Dahak laughed, the black tip of his tongue flickering between pointed teeth. He leaned back against the pillows. "Yes . . . you did crawl before me, begging for life. Do you enjoy your new body? Does it please you to breathe, to walk under the sun, to see the living, green world?"

"Yes, great lord." The Queen pressed her forehead into the carpet. Tears seeped from the corners of her eyes, but she squeezed them shut until no moisture escaped. "Thank you for this gift."

"A pleasant sentiment," he said, pleased. "But you should not have to rely on these tricks and ploys—this flesh wields true power, can reach into the hidden world. The child you ride has some strength . . ."

"Yes, great lord," the Queen said, forcing her voice to sound complaisant. "But these things are new to me. In life, I owned no talent for sorcery. Forcing these secrets from her is difficult. A long road, filled with false turns and trails fading in the sand."

The sorcerer rose up, anger lighting in his eyes again. One hand curled into a claw. "You chose to live, proud queen! If you cannot master the girl and wield her strength in my service, then what use are you to me?"

"I am a willing ally," the Queen said, keeping her eyes downcast. "While she will struggle and fight every moment. You will have to drive her with whips, with pain. I go willingly where you bid."

"Perhaps . . ." Dahak rose, his attention turned away from her, into the night. "So you gain a day, perhaps two. Make yourself useful or I will discard you." He smiled again and the lights flickered even lower. The Queen began to shiver, feeling all heat leach from the air. "I have many servants, of which you are the least."

"Yes, great lord."

Dahak raised his chin. "The King of Kings desires my counsel. Arad! Attend me."

The air beside the door shifted and a man's shape resolved from nothingness, his head enclosed in an iron jackal mask. Without a further word, the sorcerer swept down the steps, his servant, silent as ever, close behind. The Queen kept her face to the floor, though when they were gone, she slumped against the carpet, shaking with relief. Alone at last, she unclenched her hands, letting tiny points of blood seep from where her nails had cut into the flesh. As she did so, her skin shaded back to an olive tan. Her eyes clouded with brown.

Shahin was already at the edge of the camp, following the swift dark shape of the Shanzdah. Khalid hurried to catch up. Moments later, they trudged together across a sandy plain, squinting in the dim starlight. At least the night seemed very warm after leaving the palisade of iron wands.

"Who," Khalid gasped, a little short of breath, "are you taking?"

Shahin was only a vague outline in the night. "Asha, Tishrya, Amur and Mihr. The men who crossed the desert with us."

And helped us murder Mohammed, Khalid realized with a start. *Very wise. I wonder if they will return?* He squinted at Shahin, trying to make out some expression on the man's face.

"I will miss you at my side. This campaign will be dangerous without your steady hand."

"I would rather stay, Lord Al'Walid." Even in the gloom, Khalid thought the man was smiling. "But I will do this thing. How can I refuse?"

The young Arab was curious. "Could you have refused, before your name was restored?"

"Yes," Shahin said. "Then I was only Patik, a mercenary, a man without honor or a noble name. Now . . ."

"Now you must do *his* bidding." The land began to slope down under their feet, and Khalid could hear the surf booming on an empty shore. "Do you know what this thing is? This . . . eye?"

There was a soft chuckle. "I made a mistake to say even so much."

"What is it?" The last of the salt brush fell away behind them and Khalid could see waves glowing as they broke on the wide beach. A light winked in the darkness, bobbing up and down.

"I do not know . . . only what the old word means."

"The dura . . . dashani?"

Shahin stopped, his boots sinking into wet sand. Surf hissed towards them, the front edge bubbling white. The water stopped a yard away, then receded. Khalid could see the outline of a mast against the stars, and a single lantern illuminating a wooden prow. "The *duradarshan*. The 'eye of shadow.' An ancient word, one I have never heard spoken aloud before tonight."

Khalid pointed at the metal box. "Like the writing on those tablets? You can read the spiked letters?"

"I can." Shahin began to walk forward again, his cloak bunched in one hand to keep it dry. "My house is very old and some knowledge of the beginning of things has not been lost."

Khalid stopped, water surging around his ankles. The sea seemed terribly dark, even compared to the abyssal empty sky. He did not want to go any further. He did not like the water. "Perhaps we will meet again, at Pelusium or beyond."

Shahin turned, his head silhouetted against the lantern. "You're not rid of me yet, Al'Walid. I will be in camp later, to gather up those men."

Khalid wanted to say more, to tell the big Persian he had redeemed his honor with brave service, but could not. Something held him back from saying those things aloud while Rustam's servants waited in the darkness. The Persian turned away and splashed through the waves. On the boat, men lowered a ladder and Shahin scrambled up the wooden rungs, sea foam spilling from his legs. Khalid splashed back towards the shore, throat tight. Then he cursed, muttering in the darkness. There were still accounts and rosters to review.

"Lord ben-Sarid?"

Uri raised his head, sweat running in thin streams down his neck. He was bare-chested, the sun gleaming on a whipcord-thin body. The lady Zoë stood only a few feet away, her tanned face shaded by a loosely wrapped burnoose. Despite the sweltering heat, she seemed perfectly at ease, long hair tucked up behind her head, slim body shrouded in voluminous desert robes. "My lady?"

Uri let the horse's leg down and stepped away, out of range of a bite or kick. The mare tossed her head, disgusted. He palmed his hoof pick and flipped a stone off into the sand.

"Are your men ready to ride?" Zoë's eyes gleamed over a thin lace veil. Uri shook his head, trying to focus on her words. Her eyes were very blue, like the sky, or the deep sea.

"Yes," he said, wiping sweat from his brow. He squinted across the camp. The noon sun was very bright, among the sandy hills. His men were sleeping under dun-colored tents or sitting quietly in the shade. "Khalid says we're the advance guard and must be ready to ride tomorrow . . . he wants us to clear the road to Gazzah and secure the town before these Persian sluggards arrive." Uri's lip curled slightly. "Easily done."

"There has been a change," Zoë said, stepping closer. As she moved, a trim foot in thin leather sandals appeared from her robes, revealing a smooth ankle. Uri wrenched his eyes away, focusing on her chest, which was decently covered. "The matter of the Hierosolyma garrison has come up."

"What? Did something happen?" Uri's idle daydream of a pert bosom and nut-brown nipples vanished like dew or honey cakes at a wedding.

"No," Zoë said, eyes crinkling up in a smile. "I fear something *will* happen. These foreigners are not familiar with the long history of our land. Who knows what might happen if a Persian or Arab garrison is left in the city? Certain holy places . . . might be entered and despoiled. That would cause a great deal of trouble."

"Yes," Uri breathed, suddenly feeling a little sick. *The temple!*

"You are the best man to watch over the city," Zoë said, putting her hand on his arm. She was standing very close. A faint, sweet smell of orange blossoms tickled his nose. "Take your men to Hierosolyma. You must make sure nothing is disturbed and proper veneration is paid to the temples and shrines."

"Yes . . ." Uri felt a cold knot grow in his stomach. *I will rule our city,* he thought, stunned. *For the first time in five hundred years. . . .* "Does Khalid know?"

"I will tell him," Zoë said confidently. "I am the Queen and Shahr-Baraz approves. When can you set out?"

"Soon," Uri said, frowning and rubbing his noble nose. "We are almost ready. By dark, or morning at the latest, we will be on the road."

"Well done." Zoë smiled again, squeezing his hand. Impulsively, she leaned forward and pressed her lips to his cheek. "The city will be in excellent hands. You must write me if anything happens."

"Yes, my queen," Uri said, breathing in a heady perfume of spices, oil and sweat. "I will."

⌑⓪⌐◊⌐◊⌐◊⌐◊⌐◊⌐◊⌐◊⌐◊⌐◊⌐◊⌐◊⌐◊⌐◊⌐◊⌐◊⌐◊⌐◊⌐◊⓪⌑

THE HILLS ABOVE FLORENTIA, ITALIA

)⍑(

Vladimir crept across a drift of leaves, stomach close to the dark earth, nose up, ears flat against his angular head. Despite a thick litter of twigs and leaves under the oaks, he made no sound. Long-fingered hands set down softly on bronzed stones and sharp toes dug into black soil. The oaks were singing softly to themselves, leaves rustling, wrapped in slanting, golden light. The sun was setting, drifting towards the western horizon through ruddy smoke-stained air. Below the hill and west across the river, a city sprawled across the valley. In this deepening purple light, thousands of fires winked, filling the air with tapering gray plumes. The Walach eased to a halt, eyes slitted against the dying light, his nostrils flared.

He caught a familiar spoor. Musty, catlike, redolent of walnuts and soot and unopened houses. Vladimir smiled, skin stretching over a long jaw, exposing sharp, white teeth. He settled lower against the ground, lean body melting into stone and brush. He had been waiting all day for this moment, creeping inch-by-inch across the hillside, trying to catch furtive and wary prey.

A stand of honeysuckle stirred and something small and gray-pelted with a white chest peered out. Black eyes flicked to the left and right, then the tiny creature scuttled forward, hurrying, short stumpy legs blurring as it flitted across the slope. A bulging cloth bag was clutched in a three-fingered paw. As it ran, patterns of leaves and fallen branches flowed across the smooth fur. In the dimming light, the creature faded in and out of visibility.

Vladimir sprang, soundless, and crashed to earth, claws sweeping through the air. The little creature bolted with a squeak, springing across a downed tree, eyes wide. Long, white claws snapped fruitlessly in the air. Dirt spewed away from Vladimir's fleet. He skidded down the slope, crashing into a thicket of brambles. Hissing with pain, he tore himself free. The creature sprang up-slope, walnuts spilling from the bag. Vladimir scrambled up, leaves flying behind him. Branches lashed at his head, drawing red streaks across his muzzle. He burst out of the oaks.

The creature faded from sight as the Walach loped across a meadow of tall, stalk-heavy grass. Clouds of tan dust and feathered seeds puffed up around him. Vladimir snorted a noseful of pollen, sneezed, then came to a complete halt. Sparkling motes flooded the air, catching the sunset. They burned gold and amber as they rose, swirling around him. Heavier seed pods broke loose, flung from long stalks crushed under his feet. They drifted through the trees, shining in golden columns of light.

The gray-and-white creature was gone. Vladimir crouched down, ducking his head repeatedly. Pollen drifted from his face, falling onto crumbling, dry soil. He breathed out steadily through his nose, clearing his nostrils. The Walach slipped forward through the grass, brittle yellow stems bending away as he passed. Clusters of seed-heads swayed, but they did not break.

Ahead, near the edge of the trees, something moved. Vladimir rose up a little, craning his neck. A subtle discoloration against a low wall of fieldstone caught his eye. He focused, ears flattening, teeth baring. *There!* The gray-and-white creature's eyes opened, black pupils in white irises. Trembling, it looked slowly from side to side.

The crisp, clear tone of a bell rang through the twilit woods.

The creature blinked in surprise. Triangular ears canted towards the unexpected sound.

The Walach bolted forward, smooth, controlled. This was no wild leap, but a calculating lunge. The little creature bleated in surprise, faded to nothing and Vladimir's hand flashed out to the right, closing with a *snap* on squirming, wriggling fur. Snarling aloud, the Walach clutched the forest spirit in both hands, then stuffed it violently into a leather bag. The bag thrashed about for a bit, as Vladimir held his captive high in the air, then the creature quieted down. Panting, he tied the sack closed.

Quite pleased with himself, the Walach padded off through the oak and scrub forest. Behind him, walnuts and a ripped cloth bag lay on the ground among dry grass and faded summer flowers.

Vladimir jogged down a faint path past huge, wrinkled oaks. The forest giants arched overhead, crowns glowing with the last touch of sunlight. Below, night filled the green tunnel made by their trunks and spreading branches. Despite the gloom, he passed swiftly over round stones and broken paving. The way opened into a shallow dell atop the hill. Vladimir paused, crouching against a moss-covered plinth. Another tall stone stood on the opposite side of the path.

The Walach tasted the air, and grinned in the gathering darkness. Still clutching the bag to his chest, the quivering warm shape inside pressed against the soft nap of his fur, Vladimir slipped behind the menhir, then up through a hedge lining the edge of the clearing.

Nicholas sat in darkness, his back to the bole of an enormous, ancient oak. The Walach crept up beside him, then squatted with the leather bag in both hands. He could smell the human female—crushed rose, pressed oil, hyacinth and lavender layered over sweat and the peppery smell daywalker women wore like a wreath. His toes dug into the earth, feeling roots and dampness.

Vladimir's tongue pressed against the backs of his incisors. He was very happy to be outside.

Lights drifted in the hollow, dancing over lines of age-worn stones. They shone cold on short grass and gleamed from the woman's diadem. Empress Martina sat on a huge, toppled slab at the center of the dell, legs drawn up sideways beneath her. Silver bracelets circled both arms and her dark gown made a sable firmament for chains of jewels and gold hanging around her neck. Dragonflies blurred past and glowing motes danced and spun, rising and falling around her in gossamer veils.

Vladimir could hear the earth singing and he pressed himself against the ground, burying his head in the loam. Martina laughed, voice soft, raising her hands to catch the fireflies winking, shimmering, darting in the air. Full night came striding over the hills and the forest quieted.

The Walach rolled on his back, looking up. The stars burned—keen as a sword blade—between the branches of the oaks. The stiff leaves were shining, taking on their own glow from the faint light spilling down from the heavens.

Nicholas raised a finger minutely. Vladimir rolled over, soundless on the loamy ground.

A greater light entered the hollow, spinning down on starlight. Sharp-edged shadows drifted across ancient stone. Martina turned her head, alabaster neck shining, pale, psymithion-painted face radiant in the golden light. She seemed frozen, unable to move, though the Walach saw her lips part as if she spoke in greeting. Her brown hair, carefully curled and coifed, spilled back over her shoulders. Her round face, in this glamour, was suffused with beauty.

The light drifted closer, spinning and darting. The Walach squinted and then let out his breath in a soft hiss. A tiny woman, only a hand tall, swept past the Empress, jeweled wings blurring in flight. The sprite was naked, clean limbs in perfect proportion, flowing hair like gold, blazing green eyes wide in interest. Martina's eyes sparkled as she turned, following the arcing flight of the fae. Flower petals were strewn around the Empress and a wreath of holly crowned her head. The sprite darted down, finding clear water shining in hollow leaves. Keeping a safe distance from Martina, the sprite knelt to drink.

Vladimir blinked. Shadow rose behind the tiny creature, looming up out of the darkness behind the slab. A hand appeared, corpse-pale in shimmering golden light, and caught the sprite gently as she toppled over in sleep. The water on the leaf trembled, beading into rainbow pearls. Maxian—his thin face thrown in high relief by the sprite's radiance—cast the night aside like a cloak. Brilliant white refulgence spilled out, making Vladimir blink tears, and Nicholas turn away. The prince caught a sphere of perfect crystal drifting in the air with a fingertip. The glass surface swirled open under his hand. Gently, Maxian slid the sleeping sprite into the globe. Then the crystal, singing with a high, tremulous note, flowed closed again.

Martina laughed softly as she rose. Rose petals, lilies, honeysuckle fluttered to the loamy soil. The prince clasped Martina's waist, then swung her to the ground. From his vantage atop the hollow, Vladimir could see the woman blush, see the heat rise in her skin. Her fingers trailed on the prince's arm.

"I think we are done here." Nicholas rose, unfolding his lean frame from the ground. "Six iron skeletons rise in the city and now there are six shining hearts, one for each."

Vladimir growled softly, but he also stood, the bag—now quiet and still—still clutched to his chest. Together, the two men picked their way down the slope, to join the royal pair sitting on the edge of the slab.

*   *   *

"Good hunting?" Maxian pointed at Vladimir's bag. The prince looked a little tired, though in such brilliant, unwavering light everyone looked drawn and sallow.

"Something quick and quiet," the Walach said, feeling shy. "Not so beautiful as the starlight."

"Let me see," Maxian said, curious. He held out a hand for the sack.

Vladimir was suddenly sorry he'd spent the day hunting on the slope. He didn't like the prince capturing the moon maids. It felt wrong—the prince wasn't even going to eat them! He drew back, hiding the bag behind his back.

"Vlad." Nicholas' eyes were in shadow, the cowl of his cloak drawn up to keep him from being blinded. "Show the prince what you caught."

The Walach swallowed, hearing a strange distance in his friend's voice. "Here."

"Don't worry," Maxian said, laughing. "I won't hurt it."

The prince slid his hand into the bag, inciting a squirming bulge. He bit his lip in concentration, then slowly drew the creature out, held tightly by the ears. Maxian considered the creature, face lighting with a slow smile. It stared back with huge, frightened eyes. "An oak gardener! It's good you didn't hurt him, Vlad. They're good luck. They take care of the forest."

The Walach's eyes slid sideways to the crystalline spheres lined up beside the slab. Weighted nets held each one to the ground, else they would drift away through the trees. The moon maids were still sleeping, each one curled up at the bottom of her clear prison.

"Quiet, little one, quiet . . ." Maxian knelt, setting the furry creature on the ground. "We're sorry we bothered you. Martina, stroke his fur."

The Empress knelt too, brushing long tresses behind her ears. The gardener squirmed fearfully in Maxian's hands, but he whistled softly and the creature became still. Round, white eyes drooped half closed. Martina's round fingers brushed over the gray-and-white fur and she beamed in delight. "It's so soft! Softer than ermine or sable. . . ."

"Yes," Maxian said, opening his hands. The gardener's eyes

snapped open and it trembled for a moment, frozen. "Go on now."

The creature flashed away across the hollow, vanishing in the space of a breath. The prince stood, brushing clods of dirt from his tunic. Martina rose too, clutching Maxian's hand for support. Vladimir stared off into the forest, feeling queasy.

"A fruitful afternoon," Maxian said, "and the moon's not even up yet. Well, we should get back." He let go of Martina's hand, turning to his prizes laid out on the ground. "Nick, get the horses, will you?"

"Yes, sir." The Latin turned away from the brilliant light, catching Vladimir's elbow. His face was still in darkness. "Come on, Vlad, let's get packed up."

They crossed the Arno on a new military bridge. The triple arches carried a double-wide road paved with bricks. Vladimir trailed the others, loping along behind where the horses couldn't smell him. The nets were strapped to a packhorse, each sphere now padded with quilted wool and wrapped in soft hides. Care had been taken to hide the brilliant treasure. The horse did not mind; the spheres pressed up against the nets, making the load light as air.

"Are you sure my son will be safe?" Martina was riding alongside the prince, chewing on a tendril of hair curled around her forefinger. "I don't like the Empress . . . she's like a snake. Cold, with a quick, sharp tongue . . . she looks at me as if I were a fat mouse!"

"Helena?" Maxian mused, his attention on the city spreading out before them. He was smiling as well, but not at her words. The hot glow of distant fires warmed his face. "She's perfectly safe, just a little testy and sharp-tongued. She'll mellow toward you with time. Heracleonas and little Theodosius are the best-kept, safest, children in the world. You'll see; they'll be both spoilt rotten by the time we get back."

"Oh, I didn't mean that," Martina said, waving her hand dismissively. "His nurses took care of him before—he'll be fine in the Palace. He likes treats! It's *her*. I don't think she likes me."

Vladimir nostril's flattened closed as they passed through the gates of the city. High in the hills, with the wind out of the east, he couldn't smell the vast cesspool of humanity; hot metal and burning wood filling the valley. Now, as they rode through a vaulted tunnel thirty feet high, into the sprawling bustle of the city itself, the smell crushed in on him from all around.

Florentia had grown like a weed, sprawling across the vineyards and fields of the original *colonia*, pressing against the river, now lined with miles of stone and terra-cotta. Chimneys towered above red-tiled roofs, belching smoke and fumes. The street trembled with the echo of trip-hammers, forges, mill wheels, the racket of huge looms. Deep in the evening, the city was still bright—lit by hundreds of lamps, each giving forth its own hiss, its own sweet smell of oil. Men and women, faces streaked with soot, sweat, and fatigue hurried past on unknown errands. The river itself was barely a trickle, a muddy strip between high banks faced with brick, its strength stolen by a new dam in the hills.

They passed under a massive, four-tiered aqueduct. Two more waterways entered the city from the north and east, while the old two-tiered western aqueduct was covered with scaffolding and workers, even at night. Men labored by torchlight, reinforcing the pilings in preparation for another course and channel to run above the structure laid down at the founding of the city. Vladimir loped gingerly across a metal grating set at the crossroads of two streets. The sound of water gurgling was everywhere, both above and below. The prince and his party turned north, to the right. Steam billowed from a long brick building beside the avenue and the roar of crucibles reverberated in the heavy air.

Vladimir forced himself to continue, though the noise hurt his ears. At the prince's approach, a pair of huge doors swung open. Guardsmen appeared out of the darkness and a centurion with a plumed helmet raised a hand, squinting in lamplight. Nicholas leaned over, talking to the man. Then the guards parted and the gates rumbled back, big iron wheels squealing in greased metal tracks. The prince entered, head raised. Vladimir knew the young man was grinning in delight, pleased by the fruits of his labors.

Martina covered her ears and guardsmen ran to take her reins and help the Empress down. Nicholas dismounted, handing off his horse to a groom, quick brown eyes scanning the chaos in the foundry. Vladimir entered slowly—he hated the stifling heat and noise—and the massive doors rolled shut behind him. Dozens of sooty-faced men in leather aprons and metal-reinforced boots rammed the portal closed with a deep *thud*, then flooded past, returning to their tasks on the foundry floor.

The prince shouted above the din of hammers and the ringing sound of metal being shaped. Foremen hurried towards Maxian, appearing out of billowing smoke and steam, faces glistening with sweat. They carried padded wicker cages, fitted with long handles.

"Here are fresh hearts, newly caught!" Maxian called out, gesturing to the horse with the weighted nets. "Careful now! They're slippery and swift to fly!" Laughing, the prince peeled back the woolen quilts, letting light flood forth. Vladimir grimaced, holding up a hand to shade his eyes from the glare.

In the bright radiance, monstrous shapes appeared from close, smoky darkness in the long foundry hall. Massive, reptilian heads hung against the ceiling, suspended by linked chains. Empty eyes stared down, gaping in elongated wagon-sized skulls. Vladimir snarled up at the iron skeletons. His skin crawled, atavistic fear burning in his stomach. The wings were still bare of flesh, only arcing, skeletal struts of iron and copper. But even now men were laboring, sweat streaming from their bodies, muscles gleaming in the firelight, to fit sheets of iron scale to cavernous bodies. Cages of wood and iron that would, soon enough, hold the moon maids captive, carbuncle hearts bound in steel sinew.

"Come," Maxian shouted, gathering up Martina and Nicholas. He grinned at Vladimir. "Let's go inside, where we can think, hear and eat!"

"My lord," the Empress said, her face still flushed from the heat of the forges, "why do everything in such a remote location? It must be very expensive, building all this so far from the sea."

Vladimir pulled the heavy, padded door closed behind her. The roaring sound of molten iron spilling from the crucible shuttered down to a constant trembling in the floor. Martina sighed in relief, removing her cloak and tossing the heavy woolen garment on a low couch crowded with papyrus rolls, scraps of parchment and wooden-bound booklets. Carelessly, she cast aside her stole and sprawled in a canvas camp chair. Tables covered with more parchment, more papyrus, pots of ink, scattered goose quills and waxed tablets filled the room. For the past two weeks, the prince's entire attention had been devoted to the iron skeletons rising on the shop floor, while Martina immersed herself in every kind of ancient tome, searching relentlessly for any scrap of information that might identify their Persian enemy.

"I mean, you can't even barge all this iron and copper up the river now it's gone dry. The road down to the coast must be crowded day and night with wagons—and the teamsters will be drinking from golden cups!"

Maxian moved the length of the room, tapping a series of glass sconces set into the walls. At his touch, there was flickering, hurried life within each receptacle and then a steadily brightening glow. "I am not worried about the expense," the prince said in an offhand way. "If we want to survive, we have to pay! The Persians won't just go disappear."

He paused before a large, angled table. A heavy sheet of copper covered the entire surface. An intricate diagram was etched on the metal with a fine, neat hand. Vladimir studied the plan during his idle moments—the picture was something like a bat, breastbone folded back, entrails exposed, wings spread wide. But this was huge, with the head and jaw of a reptile. Six of its children grew, iron scale by iron scale, in the vast work halls outside.

"The workers I needed were already here. . . ." Maxian continued, running his hand across the smooth surface. Vladimir, watching the young man out of the corner of his eye, saw a pained look on the prince's face, a subtle tightening around his mouth. "The finest metalsmiths in the Empire, men and women skilled in making cunning devices, Lady Theodelinda's mills and metalworks, the jewelers and goldsmiths—everything we need. There is also a hidden benefit; we *are* far from the sea. Raiders cannot descend upon our workshops without warning."

"Raiders?" Martina fanned herself with a stiff sheet of parchment. Her face shone with sweat from only moments in the main hall. "We're in the heart of the Empire!"

Maxian looked over at the young woman, lips quirking into a cold half-smile. "These rebellious Greeks have a fleet . . . and their Persian allies have far-seeing eyes. Nothing is safe now, you know, with the bulwark of the East fallen. Even Rome herself might be attacked."

"Oh." Martina stared at the prince for a long moment, face reddening. He turned away, shaking his head at her foolishness. Her eyes brightened with tears. Vladimir turned away, touching Nicholas' shoulder. The Latin was stuffing his face with sausage rolls—laid out on one of the tables by the foundry cooks. Nick looked over his shoulder, nodded to the Walach and the two men quietly left. Vladimir scooped up a platter of roasted meat as he passed the table.

The Empress sat alone amid the mess, staring at the prince's back. He was bent over the diagram again. Fury sparked in narrowed moss-colored eyes. With a sharp movement, Martina stood up and snatched a scrap of dirty papyrus from between the pages of one of the books. Glancing down at the muddled diagram on the page, she wadded it up and tossed it behind the divan.

"Do you think I am a fool?" Martina said, picking up her stole and cloak. "Or your servant?"

"No," Maxian said, but his attention remained on the diagrams, brow furrowed in thought.

Martina's lip twitched into a scowl, and she pulled on the cloak. "Prince Maxian. *Prince Maxian!*"

"What?" He turned, surprised and irritated. One eyebrow raised questioningly, seeing her gather up a leather pouch of ink stone and quills and a small knife. "Where are you going?"

"I am going back to Rome," she said. The frosty tone in her voice finally seemed to touch the prince. "You've shown me some lovely things—I think I'll remember the softness of the oak gardener and the faerie lights in the stone ring for as long as I live—but you've no more need for me than for any tool you might find in your workshop!" She paused, glaring at Maxian. "When I started looking through these documents for you, it made me feel useful. I liked that . . ."

"Then stay!" The prince interrupted. "Nothing's changed about your work."

"True enough," she snapped. "I have been dutiful—I wade through oceans of rotting parchment and crumbling papyrus for you, searching for secrets that may not even exist—I serve as your lure for the wee folk, jeweled and ornamented—I keep track of the documents you forget, deal with the meetings you ignore. What better secretary could you have, than an Empress? Do you even realize I exist?"

"I do!" Maxian's distant, distracted air was gone. Now, for the first time, he seemed focused on Martina and he was troubled. "I could not have done what I've done, without you. I appreciate you, and am grateful for your help. What have I done to offend?"

"Offend?" Martina choked back a laugh. "A bloodless word. But you are bloodless—everything weighed in logic, carefully measured against need, time and the Empire's capacity to produce gears, wheels, tempered iron! Are all wizards like you, looking down upon men and women as if we were insects? Have you forgotten how to be human?"

The prince made to answer, a hot retort on his lips, then stopped. His mouth snapped closed. For a moment, he said nothing, then: "Lady Martina, I am sorry if I've ignored or slighted you. It was not my intent to make you a servant. I . . ." He fumbled for the proper words. "I need your help. If I've not said it before, I need you."

The Empress stepped back, wary, suspicion plain on her face. "You need . . . me."

"Yes," Maxian said. It seemed he would say more, but did not.

"You spoke slightingly to me," she said angrily, clutching the pouch to her chest. "As if I were a child who did not understand the Empire was at war. Don't you think I've noticed? My entire life has been spent in cities under siege, or Legion camps, or fleeing from treachery and defeat. My husband is dead, my stepsons missing. I can count leagues and ships and cohorts as well as you—perhaps better, for I've been in war, while you fly above the fray, safe on your iron mount!"

"Peace!" Maxian raised his hands. "I am sorry. Will you stay?"

"Perhaps." She glared at him, eyes narrowed to slits. "Will we walk in the woods for pleasure, under restful eaves, not hunting for more advantage? Will you listen, when I speak? Will you treat me as a friend, not a servant?"

"A friend," he said, making a little bow. "I swear it."

"Huh." Martina stepped to her table and pushed some of the pages around with the tip of her finger. "This morning, when you asked me if I wanted to go for a ride in the hills, I was very happy. I don't like sitting in this hot, smelly building for weeks on end. I wanted to go out, to see something new, to have a rest from this constant noise and vibration." She looked sideways at him, grimacing. "Do you even notice how foul this place is?"

Maxian shook his head, nonplussed. Martina sighed, shaking her head.

"Don't you see how drawn the workers are? They grow more haggard every day, their faces stretched thin, their eyes dull with fatigue . . ."

"But we have a schedule!" The prince's head jerked up in alarm. "I have to go down to Rome in a week and tell Galen when we'll be done. We *need* those fire drakes! The men can rest when they are done—soon enough, I think, only a few more weeks. It's hard work, but they must keep to the schedule!"

Martina raised a hand, pointing to the east. "Done? The road from the sea is still crowded with wagons—yet I know our warehouses are already filled with everything you need to complete these six drakes! I can read the foremen's schedules as well as anyone, lord prince!" Her voice rose crisply. "How many more times will you take me into the woods, dangling me as bait for the fey queen? How many more of the faerie do you expect to find?"

"None." Maxian pushed wearily away from the table, turning from her. "We've taken them all—all living hereabouts, anyway." He looked at the diagram, at some parchments held to the wall with pins, rubbing his chin in thought. "I've sent some letters—I hear the fey are still strong in parts of Gaul and Britain. We can get more. We *need* more."

"How many?" Martina struggled to keep her voice from rising further. "You've plans on your drawing table for another dozen iron drakes—and other grotesque devices of iron and steel. Do they need living hearts as well?"

"Some do." Maxian turned back, pensive, biting his lip nervously. "The drakes will give us control of the sky and the sea, but I'm sure the Persians will find a counter. The creatures I fought in Constantinople could fly. . . ." His voice trailed off and his head bent in thought.

"Prince Maxian!" The Empress shouted, her temper lost. The prince, startled, looked to her, eyes wide. "I asked you to listen to me. You seem incapable of this simple task. I'm not talking about your machines, or schedules, or the Empire. I was talking about having a chance to be alive, to talk as friends, to just . . . *be* . . . for even an hour."

The prince blinked, confused. He stared at her and Martina could tell he was truly puzzled. *What an onker*, she thought in despair.

"I could spare an hour," he said after a moment, "maybe tomorrow, or the day after."

"For what?" she said in a very dry voice.

Maxian tried to smile. "I have heard, from the foremen, there are still some woods uncut, undisturbed, up above the lake made by the dam. We could go there and sit for a little while, watching the sky."

"We could." Martina raised her nose imperiously. "I would like that."

"I," Maxian said, making a little bow again, "would like that too."

"Good," the Empress said, starting to remove her cloak. "We'll go at noon."

"Noon? Impossible, I have an iron pour—" Maxian fell silent, catching the fierce light in Martina's eyes. "Noon, then," he said.

The Empress shook her head in wonderment as she knelt beside the divan, one hand groping underneath for a wadded-up ball of papyrus. "Is he even trainable?" she muttered under her breath. Her fingertips touched the stiff shape of the scroll and she sat up, pleased.

"What's that?" Maxian leaned over, peering at the papyrus.

"Something you might get," she said in a smug voice, hiding it from him, "after we come back from the lake tomorrow."

"Oh." Maxian frowned. Martina, turned away, did not see that a cold and distant expression washed over his face. Then the prince grimaced, shaking his head at his own folly and he was an affable young man again. "Is it important?"

"Perhaps," Martina said, lifting her nose imperiously. "You will just have to wait and see."

ALEXANDRIA, ROMAN EGYPT

Shahin, noble brow covered by a wide-brimmed leather hat, waved cheerfully to an approaching customs boat. The Persian sat astride the portside railing of their coaster, one sun-bronzed leg dangling over the side. Like the Palmyrene crew, he wore only a short kilt-like cloth around his waist.

"Ho, the boat!" An Egyptian waved from the foredeck of the galley. The Roman ship was old, painted eyes peeling and the decking splintered and gray from the sun. Shahin kept a cheerful, open expression on his face, though he took a count of the men in the approaching boat. His own crew was substantially outnumbered. Despite their ship's age, the Egyptians turned deftly at their captain's command and slid to a stop alongside the Palmyrene ship.

The *Duchares* was equally decrepit, weather-beaten and sun-burnt, her rigging frayed, square sail mottled with patches. Shahin leaned down and grasped the Egyptian official's hand, swinging him up onto the higher deck. The man bowed in thanks, then looked around with an idle-seeming air. The big Persian noted the archers on the galley had arrows nocked. They seemed alert.

"Port of origin?"

"Ephesus," Shahin said, stretching his Greek to the limit. "By way of Rhodes."

"Huh. See any pirates, any Persians?"

Shahin shrugged and shook his head. The captain—a Palmyrene—hurried down the deck from the tiller, wringing his hands. The big Persian looked away, though he listened carefully to the discussion between the two men as he leaned on the railing. There was a matter of port taxes and entry fees and the Emperor's tithe for commerce.

Alexandria was impressive, he thought, squinting into the morning sun. Even from the sea, here at the edge of the grand sweep of the mercantile harbor, the city made itself felt upon the mind, the eye and the spirit. To his left, as the coaster rolled slowly up and down on the swell, a long, low island lay baking in the sun. Brightly colored buildings crowded along a sandy shore. Directly ahead, a sandstone causeway ran out from the city to the island, studded with square towers and lined by a crenellated battlement. Beyond the fortified mole, another island held a impossibly tall building surmounted by a lighthouse. Shahin felt envy, measuring the height of the edifice by eye. *Rome can build*, he thought, keeping a sneer from his face. He had never seen such a building—ones larger, perhaps, like the Great Hall of the palace in Ctesiphon—but none so high. On the summit, set on a tapering brick platform, a golden disk blazed in the sun.

The city sprawled along the shore from west to east, mile after mile of tan-and-white buildings baking in the sun, none more than two or three stories high. Shahin could hear, over the creak of the hull and the slap of the oily brown water, a vast, constant murmur. The city was filled with noise. *Crowded, hot and pestilential*, he realized. *How delightful.*

Then the wind shifted and a thick miasma rolled out across the water. Shahin staggered as the smell washed across him. *O lord of light! What a stench! How many people live here? How many pigs?* During his time in the desert, or at sea, he'd forgotten how foul a human city could become.

The Egyptian customs officer slapped him on a bare, powerfully muscled shoulder as the man passed. "Don't worry," he said in a cheerful voice. "You'll get used to it if you're here long. When the Nile floods, it gets better. All the refuse gets washed out to sea."

Shahin grunted, then helped the man—heavier by a substantial bribe—down into the galley. The Palmyrene captain leaned on the railing, waving good-bye. The desert man had a sick look on his face too. With the Egyptians gone, the Persian turned his attention back to the city. *How are we going to find the prince's agent in that morass?*

The noise was the worst. Shahin felt physically ill—not from the close, hot streets or the cloying smell of rotting vegetation—but from the constant assault upon his eyes and ears. Led by a Palmyrene sailor who had shipped to Alexandria before, Shahin and his men spent most of the day trudging through crowded streets, making their way from the port to the temple district. The press of humanity—dressed in a dizzying array of colors and hues, with brown, black, white and tan faces—surged past them in a constant flow. Shahin's arms were tired from holding his belongings aloft in a bundle while pushing through the chattering, shouting crowd. They passed streets of metalworkers, vigorously hammering away, through lanes filled with shrieking birds and animals, past block-long temples lifting a droning chant to the sky.

Out of the area immediately around the great harbor, the sailor turned left and they wound through smaller and smaller streets, swiftly leaving the broad avenues and regular streets of the Roman city. Shahin took solace only from the faces of the passing men and women. They looked familiar and Eastern; neither the angular faces of the Romans and their German allies nor the dark-eyed Egyptians. He raised his head, looking forward, and was rewarded by the sight of a temple portico faced with red stone, stair-stepped, and showing the blazon of the Lord of Light, Ahura-Madza.

"Is that where we're going?" He thumped the sailor on the shoulder, pointing at the Persian-style temple. The man glanced over his shoulder with a bemused expression.

"No . . ." The sailor stopped suddenly, causing Shahin and his men to crowd behind him like lost sheep. "That place is closed—the Romans are not fools!" He pointed and the big Persian saw the doors of the fire temple were boarded up. City militiamen sat on the steps, throwing dice on a blanket. The rest of the porch was filled with peddlers selling live parakeets and steamed shellfish from copper buckets.

"Where are we going?" Shahin leaned down, trying to keep his voice low. But in this constant noise, who would be able to tell what he said? The sailor paused, waiting for a dozen bearded men, round flat-topped hats on their heads, long black tunics flapping above their sandals, to walk past. The men were chanting, papyrus rolls held in their hands. They did not look up as they passed and Shahin frowned after them. The city was filled was strange sights.

"There is an inn, where we can find rooms. Not far now." The sailor slipped deftly into the flow of the crowd and Shahin, less used to such things, was forced to press after him, pushing aside three women carrying cane platters of bread on their heads. The bakers, insulted, shouted viciously at the Persians as they hurried past. Mihr, bringing up the rear, got a bruise on his shin from a sharp kick.

The street turned and turned again, and the crowd suddenly dissipated. Shahin felt a chill; they walked swiftly past crumbling houses with empty windows and doors. He realized, after they passed a tall raven-headed statue looming in an alcove on the left-hand side of the street, they had entered a burial district. A mangy dog lifted its head, yawning. It rose stiffly, back arched, watching them with cold eyes. Mihr walked backwards for a time, making sure it did not follow.

"Here it is!" The sailor sounded relieved. They entered a small plaza, thronged with people, surrounded on each of the four quarters by small, dilapidated temples. A confusing array of roads and narrow alleys opened onto the open space. Shahin felt relieved—he could see laundry hanging from balconies, housewives chatting from their windows, children playing. Young people talked while they filled their urns and pitchers from a cistern. The sailor climbed a flight of steps, ducking his head to enter a doorway. Shahin paused, puzzling out the letters cut into the white plaster beside the door. He failed, but traced an outline of spreading horns with his thumb. *Mithras, the Sun*, he realized. Then he did feel better. The Dying Bull was a Persian cult, but an old one, from his father's father's time.

"You *are* of the house of Suren! How delightful."

Shahin looked up in surprise, his mouth filled with porridge. A man of some age, his oval face defined by a short, neat beard and carefully combed white hair, stood beside the common-room table. The Persian swallowed, looking around suspiciously. None of his men were in sight. Most were sleeping on the roof, under spreading flower-heavy trellises, trying to escape the heat of the day.

"May I sit?" Without waiting for Shahin's leave, the man slid onto the facing bench.

"Who are you?" The Persian squinted at the stranger, examining his threadbare brown robe, mended tunic, proud nose and nimble, calloused fingers stained with ink. "Have we met before?"

"Not at all. My name is Artabanus." Casually, the fellow looked around. The common room was nearly empty at this hour, the usual tenants having departed for their day's labors. He produced a silver coin from his sleeve, presenting it to Shahin. "You've come on the king's business, I understand."

"The king? No." Shahin frowned suspiciously as he picked up the silver piece. A bearded man, notable for long mustaches, was stamped on the face. The minting was nearly fresh, barely worn at all. A bust of the king, large mustaches prominent, filled one side, while the reverse held a brief sketch of a fire altar and two attendants. "Prince Rustam sent me on this errand."

"I do not know the name." Artabanus seemed dubious. The man retrieved the coin, making the silver disk vanish from his fingers. He grinned at the trick, though Shahin did not find it amusing. "I am the king's man. Are you?"

"Yes," Shahin nodded, feeling a little odd to claim his old enemy with pride. But he *was* proud. The Boar was an honorable lord, far more trustworthy than the prince. . . . "The prince does the king's work in this. I am looking for an old device."

Artabanus nodded, scratching his ear. The coin, now gold, appeared in his hand. "The messenger, a very peculiar-looking fellow with jaundiced eyes, said you needed to get to Memphis, or perhaps further south, to Saqqara."

Shahin nodded minutely. The owner of the hostel clattered

down the stairs from the upper floor, his arms heavy with blankets. Nodding genially, he passed out onto the street. Shahin licked the last of his porridge from the spoon, then pushed the wooden bowl aside. "I have a drawing."

The mage nodded, raising an eyebrow when the papyrus was placed before him. For a time, the man examined the paper itself, then he muttered his way through the letters partially visible on the decaying sheet. Finally, he looked up again and sighed.

"This is very incomplete," he said, "I can only make out bits and pieces. Do you know anything more about this machine?" A well-trimmed thumb indicated the interlocking wheels and gears.

"A little." Shahin rubbed his nose. "It was named to me as the *duradarshan*. The device is made of bronze and gold and likely affixed to a block of jade the size of a chest." The Persian indicated the reputed size with his arms.

"Better . . ." Artabanus rolled the coin across his knuckles, back and forth, then made it disappear again. "In different times, I would go across the street, to the matron of the temple of Artemis. She is a font of old knowledge—a true Egyptian, I believe, not a half-Greek mongrel like the rest—but I don't think the king's purpose would be served by consulting her, do you?"

"No." Shahin growled, eyes narrowing. "You are friends with this Egyptian woman?"

"We've known each other for a long time, my lord." When he spoke, it was with long-held fondness. "Penelope is pleasant company and very well read. Also—rare for this fractious, theological city—she can see both sides, or more, of an argument. Besides, we are in the same business. Not so strange, not here, not in Alexandria."

"What *is* your business?" Shahin asked, sounding more suspicious than he intended.

"You mean," Artabanus said, looking around with a comically guilty expression, "beyond being a *spy*? I am the custodian of the fire temple—now closed, as you may have seen. Like Dame Penelope, I watch over a disused and mostly forgotten residence of the god. Sadly, there have been no riots, no protests by the common people over this outrageous act of the provincial government! And very little for me to do anymore. . . ."

Shahin gave the man a quelling, gimlet stare. "The prince felt you could lead me to the device. Can you?"

"Perhaps . . ." Artabanus considered the scrap of papyrus again. His brows narrowed and Shahin was relieved to see the man was concentrating on the matter at hand. "This is an ancient form of the Old Kingdom's writing. The name you mentioned—the *far-seeing-eye*—is in an equally ancient tongue. The writing shown in the sketch is older still. If memory serves, the oldest ruins are found at Memphis, where the Nile divides and enters the delta, and further upriver, at Saqqara." Artabanus frowned, pursing his mouth as if he tasted something foul. "Saqqara has a bad reputation—we should avoid the slumped pyramid, I think."

Artabanus examined the papyrus again, then sighed. "There is a scholar I know . . . his name is Hecataeus; he works in the Imperial Library. He knows *everything* about Old Egypt. He might have seen such a device mentioned."

The big Persian raised an eyebrow, glaring at the mage. Artabanus coughed.

"Not such a good idea, I suppose . . . he might mention our questions to the Roman authorities! I can take you to Memphis, if you desire, and we can see what might be found among the ruins of the old city."

Shahin rubbed his nose, thinking. *Such a faint track to follow . . . but what else do we have?* "I was told," he said, eyeing the mage suspiciously again, "you could lead me to this thing, and swiftly too. You do not seem sure of yourself."

Artabanus shrugged. "I am honored by the king's confidence and I am learned in these matters . . . but what have you brought me? Little more than the shadow of a memory out of ancient times. Yet Egypt is filled with old mysteries and some still live today. There are books I can consult, and friendly priests upriver with whom we can speak." The mage grinned. "Rome is not loved here and we will be welcomed in some houses with wine and honey, where Rome receives only millet."

"Very well," Shahin said. "We will leave as soon as you are ready."

Artabanus smiled, spreading five Roman coins, all alike, on the tabletop. "As I said, son of the house of Suren, I have little to do. We can leave today, if you like."

⊡)-0-)-0-)-0-)-0-)-0-)-0-)-0-)-0-)-0-)-0-)-0-)-0-)-0-)-0-)-0-)-0-)-0-(⊡

THE PALATINE HILL

))(

The Emperor pressed a short note into his tablet, reed stylus cutting into gray wax. His narrow face was smudged with exhaustion—dark circles under his eyes, a febrile quality to his skin. Anastasia thought he was falling ill. The others in the library were silent, waiting for him to finish. A muted scratching from the back of the room mixed with the tapping sound of fans rotating slowly overhead.

"How long until your flying machines are complete?" Galen put down the reed.

"Another four months." Prince Maxian, equally worn, young face made old by sleeplessness, slouched in a heavy chair opposite his brother. The table between them was strewn with fine Chin porcelain, half-empty cups of wine, bits and pieces of glazed duck, bread rounds, scraps of cheese and half-eaten apples. "But I have installed the fire heart in each steed. The foundry foremen in Florentia can complete the rest of the work without me—at least until my final invocations are required."

"And then?" Galen's expression was pinched. Despite considerable discussion, he was uneasy with these new weapons his brother promised. Mechanical devices—*toys*, he thought— were Aurelian's passion. The big redheaded horse should be *here* keeping an eye on Maxian, not in Egypt facing down the Persians. He would love this project: all gears, metal, *pneuma* and *spiritus*. "Each ... steed ... will need a thaumaturge to make it fly?"

"No." The prince sighed, knuckling his eyebrows. "That is what has taken so long. The fire-drake can accept the guidance of anyone—well, anyone the drake is *directed* to obey. These new ones will not be quite so fast, or so strong as the first one, but they will serve."

"Why aren't they as fast?" Galen squinted. The corner of his left eye was twitching. The Duchess hid a wry expression of compassion. A headache was stealing up on her as well.

Maxian breathed out in a long, irritated hiss. "Because, brother, when I built the first one, I was a student, following the direction of a master . . . and now, I can't remember everything old Abdmachus told me. At the time I was rushed. . . . I wasn't paying close enough attention." The prince bit angrily at his thumb. "But they are far beyond anything Persia has . . . these young drakes cannot reach Albania in two days of flight, but they will be able to reach Egypt in four."

"Can they fight? Are they worth two Legions of troops?" The Emperor stared at parchment sheets laid out on the table, obviously tabulating the ever-rising expense of Maxian's project. "We could fit out a dozen heavy galleys for this cost."

"A single fire-drake is worth a dozen galleys." The prince tried to keep his voice level. "A fire-drake can fly against the wind, over storms, even through hail! From such a height, a man can see hundreds of miles, spying the enemy at a great distance. A fire-drake can—"

"I've heard all of this before." Galen glared at his brother. "Very well, press ahead. You'll need more money, I suppose . . ." He pinched his nose, eyes squeezed shut. When they opened, everything was the same. The Emperor swallowed, tasting something bitter at the back of his throat. "Duchess?"

Anastasia stirred, sitting up straight. She was tired too. "We have done well with the telecast, my lord. The work is draining for the thaumaturges assisting us, but the results are spectacular." She made a wry smile, clasping her hands. "Though the visions do not always show us what we desire to see. Not all the time, at least. First—the *comes* Alexandros has advanced within sight of Constantinople—and it seems, if we count fire pits and tents aright, the armies of the Avar khagan have decamped. They are probably already back in Moesia by now."

"Really?" Galen sat up straighter himself. "How can you tell?"

Anastasia tried to maintain a neutral expression, but it was very difficult to keep a smirk from her lips. She inclined her head towards Gaius Julius, who was sitting quietly beside the prince, being unobtrusive. "A famous Roman historian once described the encampment practices of the barbarians, finding them as unique to a people—between, say, the noble Carnutes and the savage Belgae—as costume or language. In my experience this holds true for the camps of the Romans—unmistakably orderly when viewed from above—the Persians and even the Avars. A Persian army is encamped within the ruins of Constantinople and Alexandros' without. There are no Avar camps—distinguished, I must say, by admirable efficiency and professionalism, as well as a peculiar ringed shape—within a hundred miles."

The old Roman did not respond. He did not even blink at the gibe.

"And Egypt?" Galen leaned forward, his fingers toying with the reed stylus.

"Prince Aurelian's defenses are being tested," Anastasia said, pursing her full lips. Today they were lightly brushed with a dark madder hue. The powders and paints around her eyes were very light, barely disguising puffy skin and incipient wrinkles. Indeed, her clothing was very restrained, even somber. Yet she had discarded the cloak of mourning and a subtle gleam of fine gold shone at her neck and adorned her hair. "The Persians have advanced across the desert of Sinai with great speed. A fleet—actually, two fleets—accompany them. One flotilla of galleys stands offshore at a distance, watching for our own ships. A large number of barges or large rafts are drawn up on the beaches."

"Supplies?" Gaius Julius spoke for the first time. "Water?"

"Yes." The Duchess nodded. "Prince Aurelian built his line of defense to deny an attacker access to fresh water. The swamps, bogs and streams in front of his fortifications have been drained. Yet, the Persians foresaw this—they are shipping barrels of water down from Gazzah on their barges. They will be thirsty, but they will not perish."

Galen nodded, smoothing his hair back. "Unfortunately, they are professionals. Have you found the army that fought at Constantinople?"

"No." Anastasia shrugged. "The telecast can only see one thing at a time. The world is vast. Since we know it does not face Alexandros in Thrace, and cannot have fit on their fleet, I believe the 'missing' army is crossing Anatolia overland, heading back to Persia." She looked at the Emperor, who seemed as displeased as ever. "We think, from what we see, the army before Pelusium is mostly composed of the rebellious Greeks, their Arab allies and new contingents from the east. I think— and this is only a conjecture, my lord—the Persians have emptied their treasury, hiring large numbers of Turks, Sogdians and Indians to supplement their forces."

"Have you informed Aurelian of this?" The reed tapped rapidly on the tabletop.

"We have," Anastasia said, smiling at the absurdity of the situation, "dispatched a courier from Ostia with all this news. With good winds, the ship will be in Pelusium port in three weeks, more likely four. What we see today, he will know in a month. Unless, of course, he learns at spearpoint. . . ."

"Ahhh . . ." Galen snarled and the reed snapped in half in his fist. "Don't we have *any* faster way to send him this news?" The Emperor glared at Maxian. "Can a thaumaturge in Rome send a message to one in Pelusium, or Alexandria, today?"

"Yes . . ." Maxian smirked a little. "A fire-drake could carry the message swiftly!" The prince ducked as another stylus flipped past his head. "Peace, brother! Peace! I believe the Legion thaumaturges have a mechanism of their own, whereby two mages, each known to the other, with matching scrying bowls, can communicate."

"Like the telecast pairs?" Galen raised an eyebrow. "Could we *make* another telecast? Place one in Egypt with Aurelian? Speak with him as if he stood in this room?"

"That is impossible—" Anastasia began, teeth clenched.

"Wait," Maxian said, raising a hand to interrupt her. A faint smile played upon his lips. Anastasia was suddenly sure the prince had been waiting for this turn in the conversation. "There is something. . . . Gaius, hand me my bag."

The old Roman grunted, lifting up a battered old leather bag still marked with the caduceus of the Asclepion. The prince dug around inside, rustling papers and bits of metal. Then, with a triumphant smile, he drew out a torn, frayed section of papyrus. Part of a diagram was sketched on the paper in faded ink. Anastasia felt a chill steal over her, seeing the delicate way the prince held the ancient page. The design seemed familiar to her. *Oh goddess, curse these men with forgetfulness, strike sight from their eyes. . . .*

"Yes," Maxian said smugly, smoothing out the papyrus. "Martina found this in a collection of broken, incomplete scrolls sent back to Rome during the time of the Divine Augustus. I've had her going through everything about the ancients we could find, trying to find some mention of that Persian sorcerer. Something useful, you know . . ." The prince set the scrap of paper on the tabletop, squinting down at lines of ancient symbols. "This caught her eye, the design, the wheels within wheels. It's old Egyptian, almost unreadable, just the part of a page included in another scroll written by one of the notorious Kleopatra's secretaries."

Maxian looked up, grinning, and the exhaustion in his face was gone, swept away by a merry sparkle in his eyes. "But I know a trick." He pressed his palms together over the papyrus, closing his eyes. Then he opened his hands slowly, palm to palm. Wind tugged at Anastasia's hair and a cloud of dust hissed together over the tabletop. Sighing, dust and dirt, even one of the apple cores, leapt between the prince's hands. There was a soft flash and when Anastasia blinked tears away, the sheet of papyrus lay on the tabletop, crisp and new, complete, shining with black ink.

"There," Maxian said, lifting the roll by the corners. Perfectly clear in the center of the paper was an intricate drawing of a device, wheels within wheels, with gears and arcing sections. The Duchess felt very cold, looking upon a well-drawn picture of a telecast. She held her breath, wondering what disastrous secrets were written on the reborn page.

" 'In Nemathapi's name,' " the prince read, slowly, puzzling out the hieroglyphs. He squinted, though the symbols were very clear. " 'I, Menes, scribe of the—must be *kingdom*—write these words. Here I have drawn a—um—picture.'" Maxian paused, leaning back. For a moment, watching him, Anastasia was struck by an impression the prince was listening to something. "'A picture of the king's guardian,'" Maxian began again, and now his voice was assured and the translation swift. "'Uraeus, the eye of Horus the Avenger. Even as the god was hewn into pieces by his enemy, so is the eye divided into seven parts.'"

Anastasia controlled herself, keeping from flinching or gasping aloud only by digging her nails into her palm. Surely there would be a line of sharp bruises in the morning. Fragmentary thoughts flashed wildly through her mind, then she quelled them all. Without moving her head, she marked the places of each man in the room. *I could kill Galen*, she realized with a sick, helpless feeling. *But Gaius is already dead and Maxian beyond my power to harm. Then the Praetorians would rush in and my life spill out on the tile.*

Oblivious, Maxian continued reading. "'By the king's command, one eye has been sent to Abydos in the south, that his wisdom may oversee all lands under his sway. The other remains here, in Memphis, where all wisdom flows from the king and god and defender, Kha'sekhem, lord of the upper lands and the lower, protector of the earth.'"

The Duchess allowed herself to breathe. *Thank you, goddess! Only two!*

The prince laid down the papyrus, his head cocked to one side. "Hmm . . ."

"Too bad," Galen said, finding another stylus and turning back to his ledgers. "The other five are lost, then, and we have one, while the other was destroyed in Constantinople."

"No . . ." Maxian turned the papyrus over, looking at the design from another angle. "This diagram does not depict our telecast, nor, if memory serves, does it describe its lost companion. See—" His finger traced a line of spiky symbols on one of the outer rings of the device. "These are quite different." Maxian raised an eyebrow, smiling at his brother.

"Where did Emperor Heraclius find his? Where did we find ours?" Galen scowled at Anastasia, who blinked at him in surprise, then marshaled herself. Luckily, Helena had once told her—though the Emperor should have remembered for himself. *But he is tired and there are many other, far more pressing concerns to distract him, thank the fates!*

"Builders excavating a new foundation for the temple of Zeus Skyfather, in Pergamum, uncovered the device lost in Constantinople. Builders in . . . Spain, near the Pillars of Hercules, found the one we possess." Anastasia indicated the papyrus with an idle finger. "If the prince's memory serves, then there *was* at least one more, in the distant past."

"We can find it," Maxian stated, nodding to himself. "Even if the remains are broken or scattered."

"We can?" Gaius Julius said, raising a white eyebrow. "How?"

The prince grinned again. "I know another trick. . . . I can make a talisman, an . . . echo of the telecast we have here. Someone can go to Egypt with my amulet. If they are close to the sister device, the talisman will guide them. Time-consuming, but Martina believes at least one telecast was in the hands of the Ptolemies. If so, then the device was probably moved to Alexandria."

Anastasia looked to the Emperor, eyebrow raised. "Lord and God, if the prince can make such a talisman, it will be on our fastest ship within hours . . . a cohort of Praetorians aboard, with reliable guides."

"A ship?" Maxian rose in his chair, looking at the Duchess as if she were a simpleton. "For another telecast, I will go myself! Pegasus will have me in Egypt in two days. A ship, indeed!"

The Duchess's jaw tightened as she bit down on intemperate words. *He is the prince, fool girl!*

"Maxian, are you ready to fight the dark man?" Galen was watching them both, fist to his mouth, eyes narrowed. "If you go to Egypt on your steed of iron, he cannot help but know you are there."

"How?" Maxian turned on his brother, almost sneering. "We fly by night, we keep to the desert . . . the Persian army is trapped before Pelusium. They will not be able to interfere. He cannot fly over them!"

"Duchess," the Emperor said, watching Maxian with a cold expression. "Explain the situation in Egypt to my brother."

Anastasia bit the inside of her lip, tasted blood, then smiled formally. "Caesar Maxian, our situation in Egypt is precarious. The province has only recently come into Western hands. There is friction between the civil government—still Eastern—and our army. Caesar Aurelian's attention is wholly focused on holding the Persians out, and—to be blunt—there are factions within Egypt who would welcome Persian rule in the place of Rome. Also, these Greek rebels out of the Decapolis have many friends behind Aurelian's barrier. The cities of Petra and Palmyra had—*have*—enormous trading concerns in Egypt, substantial investments, agents in every port and town."

"She means," Gaius Julius said, leaning towards the prince, "once you enter Egypt, you will be noticed. The cities, the towns, are thick with Persian informants and sympathizers."

"We will not *enter* the cities," Maxian said, exasperated. "The ancient ruins are avoided by living men—and the telecast will be in a ruin, not the forum of Heliopolis! Gales, please, I can be to Egypt and back in a week, two at the most. I will find the telecast and deliver it to Aurelian. Think of the advantage we'll have then!" He turned to the Duchess, face eager. "Another eye to watch the enemy! We'll be able to converse instantly . . . if need be, I can mate the two as I did before, letting Aurelian step back across the Mare Internum as if he were in his apartments on the Palatine!"

Anastasia felt her face warm, her skin prickle, her heart race. The prince smiled, urging her to agree. Flustered, she closed her eyes, blocking out his limpid brown stare. "Wait," she said, raising a hand. She put the tips of her fingers to her forehead. A sense of vertigo ebbed and she felt her heart slow from a sprint to a walk.

Breathe, a voice echoed out of the past. *Center yourself, focus yourself. You are one, indivisible, infinite . . .* The Hunter's prayer filled her mind and she felt the strange sensation fade away. She opened her eyes, studiously looking only to the Emperor. Galen raised an eyebrow.

"Lord and God, what the prince says is true," the Duchess said, measuring her words. "His iron servant is swift and can carry him across many leagues. His powers are great and finding the telecast in Egypt—if one still exists—may be easy for him. But Egypt is vast and there are many ruins. I fear this search will take time, perhaps little, perhaps much."

"And in that time?" Galen met her eyes, shaking his head minutely.

"In that time, Lord and God, the Persians may discover the prince is in Egypt. They may even discover we possess a flying machine."

"So?" Maxian interjected, irritation plain in his voice. "What if they do?"

"Then, Caesar, they will try and capture or kill you." Anastasia did not meet the prince's gaze. "But you are very strong. I doubt they will be able to succeed."

The prince made a sharp *huh!* sound and looked to his brother again. "Gales?"

"You are not going," the Emperor said, giving Maxian a quelling look. "I do not think you are ready to fight this creature again, not one on one. When that day comes, I want every advantage to be in our hand. We must know this thing's name, its strength, its motive. We will fight on ground of our choosing and we will win."

"Madness—" Maxian stood up abruptly, though Gaius Julius made a fainthearted effort to catch his arm. "Then send your ship—which will take weeks to reach Egypt—and have your legionaries grub in the dirt—more weeks will pass—and then, then you·find the device and who can make it work? I can! And I will be here, in Rome, cooling my heels in the baths or at the races!"

"We have weeks," Galen said, expression hardening as the prince's voice grew more strident. "We have months. Armies—Persian or Roman—do not leap leagues in a day. Aurelian will hold Egypt until the Nile rises, and then where will the Persians be? Unable to advance for months more, while they wait for the river to fall. By then we will know where the main Persian army is, and how things stand in Thrace and Constantinople. These troubles in Britain will be resolved. Our new fleet will be gathered, the Gothic Legion ready to move by sea wherever we need. You . . ." Galen stabbed a finger at his brother, "will have finished your fire-drakes and if the gods favor us, we will know the intention and true strength of the enemy."

Maxian's eyes narrowed and he leaned forward, fists on the

tabletop. "What happens if the Persian sorcerer comes against Aurelian now, today, with full force? Will you hold me back then?"

"I will," Galen snapped, a flush rising in his face. "Aurelian can hold Egypt!"

"Like Constantinople held?" Maxian shouted. "You are a fool; you have no idea what powers are at play here!"

"Enough of this," Galen said, his voice very cold. "My decision is made."

The Emperor stared at Maxian, his face like granite, until— after a very long moment—the younger man looked away. "Securing another telecast is not critical, but it would be a boon. Duchess, send your ship and someone discreet and efficient. Maxian, you will make this talisman. I pray we find success, but this is a *diversion* from our real task."

The prince stared at the floor. Anastasia could see a vein pulse in his neck.

"Maxian?" Galen stood up, absently tugging his heavy tunic straight. "Aurelian will be fine. He is an able commander and well served by brave men."

Maxian did not answer. Galen watched him for a moment, then turned back to Anastasia and Gaius Julius. "You know what to do. Be quick about it."

"Yes, Lord and God," they said, bowing. The Emperor gathered up his notebooks. Maxian continued to stare at the floor, grinding one fist into the other. Galen waved the Duchess and Gaius out of the room. They left quickly, avoiding looking at the two brothers.

In the hallway, Anastasia motioned to the Praetorians to close the heavy, bronze embossed doors. The guardsmen did so, though no sound had issued from the room.

"Very wise," Gaius Julius said, sotto voce. He seemed pensive. "Do you need anything?"

"For what?" Anastasia's eyebrow arched in suspicion. She drew the cloak across her chest automatically. Just being this close to the ancient made her feel queasy.

"For this 'quiet' expedition to Egypt." He seemed very serious. "You've your own ships, I know, but if you need men, supplies, guides, money—let me know."

"Why would you help me?" Anastasia lifted the cowl of her

cloak, settling it over her hair. The high-piled, ornamented coiffure was striking, but also inconvenient and heavy.

"I think the boy is right," Gaius said, still speaking quietly, as if they were two friends at a dinner party, sharing some confidence. Anastasia realized, with a start, the old man was worried. "The Emperor is tired, stretched thin. We need the *speed* these devices offer. The speed to know, the speed to react. Such a thing could be the difference between victory and defeat."

"They may not be there anymore," the Duchess said, warming—against her better judgment—to the twinkling-eyed old man. "Thousands of years stand between Pharaoh Kha'sekhem and ourselves. Time for many misfortunes to befall such a device."

"I know." Gaius Julius managed a half-smile, still worried. He looked back at the closed door. "But such a prize . . ."

Yes, Anastasia thought, bowing politely and turning away. *But not one you will ever have!*

The Duchess frowned, stepping down from the litter, a brace of handsome young men kneeling on either side to help her descend. Her courtyard was crowded with two large, overly ornate litters, an even dozen bearers lounging in the shade of her vine-covered walls stuffing themselves with bread rolls and sausage and a clutch of Praetorian guardsmen drinking her wine. She dismissed her own litter with an irritated wave, then turned to enter the Villa of Swans.

"Mistress!" Betia was at her side, a quiet ghost suddenly made flesh. Anastasia glared down at her maid. The little blond girl was dressed in a too-short tunic with bare feet, and her face glowed with perspiration. "The—"

"Empress Helena is here," the Duchess said, disgusted to see the Praetorians eating a picnic lunch in her foyer—eating from her silver plates and cups! "With her usual circus troupe. . . ."

"Yes, mistress," Betia said, hiding behind the Duchess as Anastasia swept across the courtyard and into her home. "They arrived only a little while ago, with the two little princes."

"She's in the garden, I suppose." The Duchess paused, waiting for her servants to appear in the dimly-lit hallway. They did, taking her traveling cloak, her lace stole, the veil, removing her walking shoes. Betia knelt, fitting slippers to her feet. Anastasia felt a little better. The house was cool, where the streets of Rome in midday were swelteringly hot.

"No, mistress," Betia said. "The Empress is down in the gymnasium, watching Thyatis and Mithridates spar."

"What? Where are the boys?" Anastasia held out her arms, so Betia and another maid could dress her in a filmy, flower-embroidered silk half-jacket. "Aren't they a little young to be watching the gladiators?"

Betia smiled, her little oval face brightening. "They are in the garden, mistress, with the Empress's maid Koré to watch over them."

"Hmm." The Duchess waved away a young boy with a carafe of wine and a thin-shelled porcelain cup. "There is no rest for the wicked today."

Helena was eating grapes, reclining in a wicker chair among the pillars at the edge of the gymnasium floor. Like Anastasia, the Empress had shed most of her heavy, formal going-out wear, leaving the dark-haired woman in a gown the color of young aspen leaves, which set off the gold circling her wrists and throat.

"You're comfortable, I see." The Duchess lowered herself into a matching chair. Betia was already bringing another cup and more wine. It was cool and dim in the colonnade. No torches or lanterns were lit, the only illumination falling from high windows piercing the clerestory above the fighting floor. "Your men are well fed too."

Helena replied with a lazy smile, her cheeks bulging with grapes. *"Mmph!"*

"You look like a chipmunk," Anastasia said grumpily. She sipped the wine, then both eyebrows rose and she gave Betia a slit-eyed glare. "This is an excellent vintage! Are those thugs upstairs drinking the same?"

"No, mistress," Betia said, making herself very small and kneeling beside the chair. "Most of them wanted honey mead or wheaten beer."

"Huh. Barbarians!" Anastasia took another drink. She felt relieved to sit down.

A harsh, deep shout drew her attention to the sand. Thyatis, stripped down to breast-band and loincloth, was attacking, lean arms and legs flashing. The giant African, Mithridates, his wounded arm free of its bandages at last, was on the defense. The redheaded woman spun hard on her heel, leg lashing out. The African blocked, huge palm slapping aside the heel arrowing for his head. Thyatis bounced back, falling into a half-crouch. Mithridates advanced, bare feet sliding in the firm sand. He lunged, punching, massive fist blurring in the air. Thyatis weaved aside, flashed a kick at his stomach. He turned, catching the blow on rippling abdominals. A deep *thwap* sound hung in the air. The African snatched for the extended leg. Thyatis sprang up in the air, another ringing shout belling out, her heel snapping around at his head.

Mithridates threw himself back, rolling across the sand. Thyatis dropped lightly to the ground, landing on both feet and one hand. Her skin gleamed with sweat, but her breath was even and unhurried.

"Well done," Anastasia called out, clapping politely. Both of the fighters turned towards her, Thyatis brushing mid-length red-gold hair from her face. "Come and sit, I have business to discuss."

"Business?" Helena swallowed the last of the grapes and dabbed the side of her mouth with a cloth. "Should I go? Ooh . . . is it a secret?"

The Duchess made a point of ignoring the Empress, smiling at Thyatis as the younger woman sat down on the step between the colonnade and the sand. "You feel strong?"

"Yes," Thyatis said, running lean fingers over fresh scars along her stomach and side. "The arrow wound has knit clean."

"And you?" Anastasia lifted her chin to Mithridates. The African towered over all three women, but he seemed uneasy, standing a good distance away. "How is your leg?"

"Good," Mithridates rumbled, ducking his head. "That Gaul knew his business." He flexed his knee, muscles rippling under glossy mahogany skin. "Straight and true."

Anastasia nodded, pleased. She felt a brief glimmer of hope. "Something has come up, daughter. I need you, and Mithridates here—if you will help—to go to Egypt. You'll leave within the week, I think."

"Egypt?" Thyatis raised a pale gold eyebrow. She stood, shaking out her limbs. Nervous energy radiated from the young woman and she shifted her balance from foot to foot. The Duchess watched her expression change from interest to impatience to haunted memory in the space of two heartbeats. "The Caesar Aurelian is in trouble? Persian spies?" Thyatis tried to grin. She couldn't manage, settling for a grimace instead. "Someone needing to be made less . . . troublesome?"

"Sit down," Anastasia said softly. "You're making me dizzy. Mithridates, come over here where you can hear. I don't want to shout. Betia . . ."

The little blonde sprang up and darted off through the columns.

". . . make sure we're not disturbed!" the Duchess called after her. "Very well. Here is the matter in a nutshell—there is a device in the Imperial Library—a telecast. Mithridates, you've not seen the damnable thing, but it allows a thaumaturge to view things far away. It has other powers as well, but the point is this: another such device, perhaps even two of them, may lie hidden in Egypt. The Emperor directs me to recover these objects. To this end, I am sending you, Thyatis, to find the missing telecasts, and make sure they *do not* come into Imperial hands!"

Thyatis squinted at the Duchess. Helena screwed up her nose and put down an eggshell-thin wine cup. Mithridates showed no reaction, but then he was habitually impassive.

"Pardon?" Thyatis smoothed her short hair back in a nervous gesture. She shot a glance sideways at Helena, who was watching Anastasia with a sour expression. "The Emperor is sending *us*, but we're to make sure *he* does not get the . . . devices."

"I'm more concerned," the Duchess said, "in ensuring Prince Maxian and more to the point, a certain Gaius Julius, do not get their hands on these devices. I am not going to say anything more about the issue, save I wish to avoid true danger. The Empire does not *need* to have any telecasts. One is trouble enough."

"Oh." Thyatis raised an eyebrow. The young woman's attention was still focused on the Empress, who said nothing. "Are we the only hounds on the scent?"

"For the moment." The Duchess felt weary again, leaning back in the chair. "With the god's luck, the Emperor will let me handle this myself. However, the prince Maxian is very interested in recovering the objects. He is making an amulet that will lead you to a telecast if you get close enough. I hope he will just hand the amulet over . . . but he may not. You may have company on your trip."

"Who can I take?" Thyatis cracked her knuckles, canting her head at Mithridates. "We're shorthanded—I'll need more help than this colossus."

"True." Anastasia pressed her hands to her eyes. "We've lost so many men—"

"I want to go," Betia said in a small voice, barely audible. She was kneeling beside the Duchess's chair again, having quietly returned from her circuit of the gymnasium.

"—lately." The Duchess pouted, thinking. "Perhaps those Gauls have not left Italy yet; they might help. I have a feeling old Vitellix can handle himself in a pinch. Or . . . we can recruit among the Eastern expatriates—they are likely some able men to be found there. We can't trust anyone in Egypt, even the—"

"Mistress!" Betia managed to raise her voice, though Thyatis and Mithridates were watching her with amused expressions. The Duchess frowned at her maid.

"What is it, child?" Anastasia looked rather sour at being interrupted.

"I wish to go," Betia said, trying to look determined. "I can help."

"Hmm." The Duchess looked her up and down, seeing the girl's muscles were firm and lean, her wrists no longer spindly. The little German looked like she could run all day . . . *and she is discreet. Quiet. Unremarkable . . .* Anastasia considered the matter, tapping long-nailed fingers on the curve of the chair. *She's no older than Krista was, when I sent her after the prince.*

The memory brought a pang of loss to the Duchess, but she pushed the emotion aside. *The world is loss*, she thought. *Children age, go away, die. I cannot keep her safe and I need her eyes, hands, nimble fingers.* "Who would do my hair, paint my face?" she asked plaintively.

Betia bowed in place, forehead brushing against the slick, enameled tesserae on the floor. "You've other maids, mistress. Maximia and Constantia can brush your hair, set out your clothes, clean, fetch and carry as well as I."

"Perhaps," the Duchess thought aloud. *But they are not of the Order. You are my last ephebe.* "I will consider this." Anastasia beckoned to Thyatis, who rose, pearls of sweat shining on her face and arms. "Daugher, prepare for a swift departure. You will need help. If there are willing, discreet, trustworthy men you know, bring them to me."

"Trustworthy men? In Rome?" Thyatis managed a bitter chuckle. "I will do what I can."

"Good." Anastasia nodded, dismissing the young woman. Thyatis bowed, then jerked her head at Mithridates. Both fighters padded off through the columned hall, scooping up towels, their sandals and tunics from beside the fighting floor.

"Well," Helena said, breaking the silence. She sounded particularly wry. "You must think me blind and dumb, to ignore treason and intrigue against the Emperor's expressed wish. My guardsmen sit at your door. They would be pleased, I think, to arrest all within this house." The Empress brushed a long, straight tendril of hair from her face. She seemed amused, but there was a steely light in her eyes. "My husband does need more coin, to fuel this war . . . your estates are varied and rich."

Anastasia nodded. "This is true. Come, let's go to the garden."

"The garden?" Helena remained sitting while the Duchess rose. "Why there?"

"I am tired of sitting indoors," Anastasia said. She waited, Betia in her shadow, until the Empress rose as well. Helena made a face, but scooped up the basket of grapes and tucked the wine amphora under her arm. The Duchess glided out, Betia running ahead to open the doors.

* * *

The garden was filled with pale, diffuse light. Thin drapes hid the sky, breaking up the harsh summer sun. Anastasia sat delicately on a pink marble bench, screened from the main garden by a trellis covered with flowering vines. Subtle perfume hung in the air and the sound of water chuckling over stones added an air of peace and contemplation. Helena also sat, placing the bowl between them. Betia had disappeared, though the sounds of children laughing hung in the air. Anastasia parted green leaves, looking into the grassy bowl at the center of her house.

"A cheerful child," the Duchess said, face lighting with a smile. "His colic is gone?"

"Yes." Warmth seeped into Helena's voice. "Sometimes he even sleeps through the night."

A baby boy was crawling on the soft grass, head covered with dark, flat hair. Another little boy, blond, perhaps two years old, was rooting about in the stream. His arms and face were covered with mud. Watching over both of them was a young girl of five or six, amber colored eyes watching the infant's every move. There was an air of sharp attention around her. She was dressed in a pale gold tunic, indigo hair spilling over thin shoulders. In the afternoon glow, her tresses gleamed like spilled ink.

"They seem to get along well," Anastasia said, a catch in her voice. *There should be another little boy on the grass. . . .* "Who is the girl?"

"Koré," Helena said, sounding both pleased and possessive. "A refugee from the East. She served in the Bucoleon and escaped with Empress Martina. I found her on the Palatine, lost and crying. She is very diligent. They don't get away with anything!"

"I'm glad." The Duchess turned away, blinking to clear her eyes. "I'm glad you came today."

"Really?" Helena made a disbelieving face. "Were you going to tell me about this little plot of yours?"

"Yes," Anastasia said, nodding. "I need your help."

"Against my husband? I think not!" The Empress twitched her gown into line across her knees. "You had better have a good reason just for me to ignore what I heard today!"

"I do. Listen, Helena, I owe you a great deal, but I must ask another favor."

"I'm listening." An eyebrow rose skeptically. The Empress popped another grape into her mouth.

Anastasia fell quiet, clasping her hands. She stared off into the distance, across the garden, oblivious to the marble columns, the brilliant paintings on the walls, the unobtrusive servants waiting in the shadows, just out of earshot. Finally, she said, "My heart is troubled, Helena. I thought things were difficult enough, stepping back into this nest of snakes, taking up my old responsibilities." She shot a glance at the Empress, who had curled her feet up and was leaning back, stuffing grapes into her mouth. "You wanted me to cast aside the mourning cloak! You wanted me to bend my wiles upon the enemies of the Empire again! This is all *your* fault."

Helena made a muffled sound, and waved her hand in a get-on-with-it motion.

"Listen . . . you are a dear friend, and I am loath to keep secrets from you, particularly ones so involved with your husband's affairs. But . . . these telecasts are more than just a convenient window, more than just a toy. They are dangerous." Anastasia bit her thumb, worrying. *How much to tell?* "I wish . . . I wish we did not even have this one. By itself it is mostly harmless . . . but see how these men want another, and then another? There's the danger. In greed, and the desire for power . . . for a weapon to solve all their problems."

"So?" Helena wiped her mouth. She sounded vexed. "We need power, we need strength, we need an advantage! Persia presses us hard—you *know* how desperate our situation is. Aren't you loyal? The Empire needs every scrap of help it can get."

"I *am* loyal," Anastasia said mournfully. "To the Empire, to your husband—who *is* the Empire. To you, and your son. But . . . there are some things we should not disturb! There are—ah, I don't know what to say to convince you!"

"Huh. You're eloquent today." Helena curled a lock around her fingertip, closely examining each shining brown hair. "Let me try."

The Duchess gave the Empress a jaundiced look, but lifted her hands in surrender.

"Very well." Helena rubbed her nose. "First, there is more to you, my dear, than meets the eye, which is saying quite a bit since you are our master of spies and informers. Oh, don't look so shocked . . . anyone with half a wit can see the number of exceptionally fit young women passing through your house. No one believes they're your playthings—you are too partial to boys! I was watching Betia today, before you came. She and Thyatis were sparring. The little one is quick, very quick . . . where *do* they learn to fight like that?"

Helena laughed softly, watching the pained expression on Anastasia's face. "Don't tell me, silly. I don't need to know. But it is very beautiful, calming even, like watching water reeds bend in the wind. So, you are obviously mixed up in some kind of mystery cult, like half the women in Rome. . . ."

The Empress ticked off a finger. "Unlike those idlers, however, you are probably in charge, or close to being in charge." A second finger rose. "This brings you privy knowledge and your cult is ancient, isn't it . . . old and powerful, investing so much in these young women, over countless generations. Just watching Thyatis move opens such a vista of possibilities. . . ." A third finger rose.

"And because of this, you know secret things. Real secrets. Not gossip, not rumor, not stupid little lies about common, stupid people." Helena's face fell and sadness leaked into her eyes. Anastasia realized the Empress was speaking about herself and her correspondence.

"Helena . . ." The Duchess took her friend's hand. "I can't tell you these things . . ."

"I know." A bitter light flashed in Empress's eyes, but then softened. "Real secrets have to be kept, don't they? Not passed from hand to hand like an unwanted birthday present. So— there's something more to this telecast than just an ancient wizard's toy. Something dangerous. Dangerous to the Empire, or dangerous to your . . . friends?"

Anastasia's jaw stiffened and a bleak, exhausted look entered her face. "Dangerous to the world, Helena. Dangerous to everything that lives."

The Empress drew back a little. "Really?"

"Yes." Anastasia felt her stomach roil, even with such a sideways, oblique admission.

Helena took another grape—fat and juicy, red skin stretched taut over a ripe interior—and rolled it between her fingers. "You're not worried about Galen, are you? He has no time for these 'diversions' and 'toys.'" The Empress managed a reasonable imitation of her husband. "You're worried about Gaius Julius and his spidery old fingers."

No, Anastasia thought, *I'm worried about your little brother-in-law and his reckless, blind hubris.* But she said, "Do *you* want him to have even one atom more power and influence than he has today?"

"Not at all." Helena shook her head, drawing the stole around her shoulders as if the garden had grown cold. "I do not like the way he looks at me." The Empress stared out at the garden again, where little Theodosius and his baby-sitter were rolling on the grass, squealing with laughter. Her face was very still. "Each day, Anastasia, I pray Maxian remains without child."

The Duchess closed her eyes, turning pale. But Helena was looking the other way.

"If that day comes," Helena continued, voice cold as a German forest, "either the child or the prince will have to die. You may think me foolish—you may say Aurelian has a squalling brood—but the red-beard is not under the influence of *that man*." The Empress turned back to Anastasia. "I do not want to murder an innocent," she said, "but I will. So, I understand you and your fear."

Anastasia nodded. "My agents watch Gaius Julius every moment. His agents watch me and they watch you. So far, nothing untoward has happened, but it is a distraction. He is ambitious."

"My husband," the Empress said, voice lightening, "is very pleased with Gaius. He seems amused by the man, and impressed by his ability to solve problems, to deal with the minutae of the Imperial process. Galen needs such an aide, an ally."

"Has Galen told you who Gaius is?" Anastasia was curious.

"Yes." The Empress's mouth thinned to a hard line. "He was excited, happy even. He is *so* pleased. You'd think Maxian conjured him up as a name-day present!" Helena realized her hands were clenched to fists. She forced them open, staring down at thin, half-moon bruises on her palms. "He wants to discuss literature, the histories, all the politics of the old Republic. Every day I have to come up with a new excuse to keep the snake from my dinner table. I'm sure he'd try for my bed next."

"Oh." Anastasia felt a sinking sensation in her stomach. "How nice." *How Roman.*

The Empress looked at Anastasia with a calculating, appraising expression. "We need each other more than I thought, Duchess."

"Yes . . ." Anastasia met her gaze. "We do. Secrets for secrets, then."

The Empress nodded, watching her son again. The little dark-haired girl looked up, saw them and waved. Helena waved back, her fierce expression starting to fade.

"I will keep yours," the Empress said. "And you will help me get rid of a troublesome counselor. Agreed?"

"Agreed," Anastasia said, though she felt a little odd. The little girl was watching them. She seemed familiar. The Duchess narrowed her eyes. *Where have I seen her before?* The girl turned away, just in time to pluck young Heracleonas from the stream, where he was trying to be a fish and breathe water.

"Lord and God?"

Galen did not respond. He was sitting at his desk in the workroom on the second floor of the Tiberian Palace, staring out one of the high, rectangular windows. The day was passing, blue sky beginning to shade towards evening. The city was busy—he could hear the dull murmur of voices, hammers, lowing cattle, sacred geese honking—unmindful of his splitting headache. The Emperor refused to cry out, though he could barely stand up. A shimmering wash of sparkling lights clouded half his vision, pulsing in time to the throb of his pulse and the crushing pain behind his right eye.

"Master? Are you well?"

Galen closed his eyes, though the piercing light remained.

He licked his lips. They were dry. Maxian's anger had not abated, not even with Galen spending an hour—or two—in further, fruitless argument. *Our course is so clear.* At last the prince threw up his hands, shouting he "agreed" before storming out. Galen's headache split open then, like Zeus erupting from the groin of Chronos, and the Emperor was barely able to walk down the hall to his office.

Nilos and the other scribes, of course, were waiting, along with an endless supply of scrolls to review, edicts to sign, documents to approve. Barely able to see, the Emperor ordered them all out, producing a flurry of activity and then the too-loud trampling of many feet as his scribes and clerks vacated the office. The resulting quiet had not helped.

"Master?"

Galen opened his eyes, focusing on the worried, thin face of his head clerk. "What is it?" he whispered.

"My lord, perhaps you should go home. You seem . . . tired."

"That's very polite of you, Nilos." The Emperor exhaled with difficulty. "I have a headache with a name—the worst kind. Is there anything pressing?"

The Greek seemed uneasy and did not respond. Galen noticed the man had a stack of legal documents in his hands, wrapped with the dark red string the Palace staff used to denote manuscripts for the Emperor's attention. "What is this?"

"Nothing pressing, Lord and God," Nilos said, clutching the wooden folders to his chest. "You know . . . my cousin sometimes suffers from terrible headaches. He says it's like a vise crushing his temples."

"This feels that bad," Galen grated, squinting. "What does he do?"

"Goes to see a prostitute," Nilos said with a straight face. "Or eats Axumite beans."

"What is an Axumite bean?" Galen pointed at the documents. The motion made him feel queasy, but focusing on something other than his brother's pigheadedness was a welcome distraction. "That is a senatorial will, isn't it?"

"An Axumite bean," Nilos said, moving away and putting the stack of parchments on the far end of the marble-topped table, "is a little red bean from a green bush. If you chew them, many pains are banished. He says they help if you have a very bad headache."

Galen stood up and moved along the desk, supporting himself on the cool marble. "They help more than a prostitute? Do you have any?" He reached for the top folder.

"I know some," Nilos said, snatching the folders away from the Emperor. "But you should visit your beautiful wife. A most efficacious cure for many maladies! These things will wait until tomorrow. Or the day after."

"Give me the folder," Galen growled. "Or I will have you cut into tiny pieces by the guards. If this were Egypt, there would be crocodiles to clean up the mess, but I'm sure the circus is well stocked with hungry lions. . . ."

"Yes, master." Nilos said, relinquishing his hold on the documents. He looked a little ill himself. "Should I find you some Axumite beans?"

"Wait a moment," Galen said, opening the folder and squinting at the closely-set lines of handwritten text within. It *was* a will. He flipped through several pages of declarations and invocations to the gods for a just and swift disbursement of the inheritance. "This is the will of Gregorius Auricus."

"Yes, Lord and God." Nilos clasped both hands behind his back and focused on a point above the Emperor's shoulder.

Galen's brow furrowed and the pain behind his right eye abated, driven out by intense irritation. His finger paused on the signatures at the bottom of the last page. "This was prepared by the very Gaius Julius who is familiar to us?"

Nilos nodded, though his mouth puckered up like a quince.

The Emperor considered the date of preparation and announcement in the Forum. "This is a revised will, replacing an earlier draft?"

The Greek nodded again.

"Does a copy of the previous will exist?"

"Yes," Nilos said slowly, obviously hesitant. Galen raised an eyebrow.

"Have you seen the previous will?" Another nod. "The benefactor was—"

"Lord and God, there were several . . ." Nilos' voice trailed off, then—faced with growing anger in the Emperor's face—he rallied and was able to say, ". . . temples devoted to good works, master. The Vestals, the Asclepian hospital on the Isla Tiberis, the funeral clubs for soldiers without families . . ."

Galen looked down at the document again. His entire body became still and quiet. " 'All estates, lands, monies, investments, partnerships and shares previously owned by the senator,' " he read aloud, " 'are now the sole property of one Maxian Julius Atreus, son of Galen the elder, an adult Roman male without living father.' " The Emperor paused, then continued in a stiff voice. " 'To be administered and executed by his agent, Gaius Julius.' "

The clerk blanched a little at the tone, but nodded again. "Properly filed, master."

"Was it?" Galen closed the folder. "Yet all senatorial inheritances, particularly those without heirs of the body, must be approved by the Emperor. By *me*," he snapped. "Has my brother taken possession of this fortune, these estates?"

"Well . . . no, Lord and God." Nilos gained some heart. "But Master Gaius was already the senator's administrator and aide. He is already responsible for everything."

"Not now," Galen said with a sharp tone in his voice. "I deny this claim." He handed the folders back to Nilos, who was staring at the Emperor in surprise. "These properties are declared the property of the Imperial Household. All managers and foremen will be immediately replaced and an audit will be conducted to ensure the previous administrator has properly maintained the patrimony of the Emperor's beloved friend, Gregorius Auricus."

Nilos turned a little green.

"Do you understand?" The Emperor's poor humor disappeared, replaced by unsubtle anger.

"Yes, Lord and God." The clerk bowed, then crept out of the room. Galen did not notice his departure, for the Emperor was staring out the window again, across the massive buildings of the Forum. The city sprawled away to the edge of sight, a jumble of red-roofed apartments, shining temples and the imposing bulk of the Antonine Baths. He felt better, much better.

I am the Emperor of Rome, he thought, finding solace in the statement. *I am the Empire.*

NEAR IBLIS

Moisture brushed against Mohammed's face and he came awake. There was water, real water, cold and wet. Without thinking, he opened his lips. Something stiff pressed against his cheek, and water spilled into his mouth. He opened his eyes, startled. *Take nothing from this place*, he thought wildly. A shape knelt over him, blocking out the perfect blue sky, silhouetted by the round, motionless sun. He blinked, feeling his eyelids crack. "No . . ." he gasped out, trying to raise a hand. The motion was very slow, so weak his limbs had become.

"You need to drink," said a voice; a familiar, beloved voice. A woman's voice. "Or you will die."

"Zoë?" Mohammed tried to push himself up. Again, his muscles could not respond. Firm hands caught his shoulders and helped him lie back against the trunk of the fig. Mohammed smelled familiar perfume, felt comfortable fingers brush back his white hair. The shape moved out of the sun's path.

"Hello, husband." Khadijah knelt before him on one knee, head tilted to one side, a white scarf of Indian cotton binding back her graying hair. She smiled, the corners of her eyes wrinkling up. Mohammed grunted, speechless, the sight of her face—so familiar, as if they had never been parted, even for an hour—looking back at him, just as he imagined his long-delayed homecoming. "You must drink."

In her hands was a leaf, a fig leaf, brimming with clear silvery water.

"How . . ." Mohammed managed to raise his arm, holding the makeshift cup away from his lips. He felt a heavy pain in his chest, as if his heart were being ground in the wheels of an oil press. The kind, accepting expression on her face made everything worse. "You must be a phantom, a spirit of this place . . . leave me be."

"You are stubborn as ever," Khadijah said, fingers closing around his hand. Mohammed's eyes widened. Her arm was insubstantial, colorful yet transparent, like excellent glass. The fig leaf was startlingly solid, the water like mercury. "I am myself, but I am dead. Now, drink. The water is from this tree, which shelters you from the sun with its branches, which supports your weary head with its roots. I gathered dew from these same leaves."

"How can you be so real?" Mohammed tried to turn his head away, closing his eyes. "I know the master of this place—a creature of evil . . . I will not take anything from him."

Khadijah sighed and the trees echoed her, rustling and creaking in some unseen wind. Loom-calloused fingers tapped in annoyance on her pleated skirts. "You have always been a willful man . . . much like a mule! Listen, son of my uncle, if you do not drink, you will die. If you die, then no man will hear the voice from the clear air. How will the people find their way free from sin?"

Mohammed opened one eye a sliver, giving the apparition a look. She was scowling at him in such a well-remembered way, with such compassion and irritation bound in one, he opened the other eye in surpise. "How . . . oh, Khadi—I am so sorry!"

"You did not come home," she said, sitting back, face filling slowly with grief. "I waited. I became weak, finally I could not stand, or even raise a cup myself. Still, I waited."

"I am sorry." Mohammed tried to swallow, but his throat was too dry. "I came too late. Only two days late . . ."

Khadijah made a wry face, shaking her head slightly. Carefully, without spilling a drop, she set the leaf on the ground beside him. "My heart had strength enough to wait, but my body failed." An edge of anger glinted in her eyes and she frowned at him. "You sent the pots back, but *you* did not come home. You sent a letter—*my love, I am going to Damascus*—then nothing!

You didn't even get a good price for the cups and bowls. . . ."

A dry, hacking cough escaped Mohammed's chest. He was trying to laugh.

"You sound like a camel," Khadijah said, a slow, glowing smile breaking in her face. "Will you drink?"

Mohammed nodded, letting himself lie back against the tree. Khadijah moved beside him, lifting the leaf again and slowly, with great care, the Quraysh sipped the cool water. When the leaf was dry, Khadijah rose and reached up into the spreading boughs of the fig.

"Is this the land of the dead?" Still terribly thirsty, Mohammed managed to get the words out without coughing. "Am I dead?"

"No." Khadijah knelt beside him, a plump yellow-green fig in her shadowy hands. "This is a realm between life and death." She cut into the tough skin with the edge of her nail, then broke the fruit into sections. Black seeds glistened inside. "Here."

Mohammed let her put the pulpy fruit in his mouth, then began to chew. The sensation was painfully intense, each movement of his jaw a grinding, exhausting eternity. His lips stung, the cuts breaking open again. After a moment, he swallowed. "Why are you here? Why haven't you gone on to the fields of heaven?"

The Arab woman looked away, absently taking a long tress of hair between her fingers. She began to plait the strands into a braid. Mohammed watched in growing fear, as her expression fell into familiar lines. Hidden emotions glimmered in her face. *She is trying to decide something, something upsetting.* Khadijah said nothing, entirely focused on the avenues of the forest, on the perfect, evenly spaced trunks and the short-cropped grass.

"You cannot say? Or will not?"

Khadijah remained silent, still looking away. Her face assumed a stoic mask. She finished the braid, then began to unbind what she had just done. Mohammed reached out to touch her arm, but his fingers encountered only air, passing through the russet cloth of her shirt. "How did you gather the water? Does it rain here?"

"No," she said, finally looking back to him. Mohammed felt

her grief, now openly displayed, as a physical blow. Moisture glittered on her cheeks, beading on fine wrinkles. "There is no rain in this place." She lifted her chin, pointing behind him. "They water the tree with their tears. Their desolation forms the dew."

Mohammed turned, feeling bones creak and muscle stretch like old cord. The soil under his hands felt strange—glassy and smooth—not like real earth. A multitude stood in the forest, crouching among the trees and brush, staring at him with empty eyes. Their ranks stretched away as far as he could see. Most of those near him he recognized—his Sahaba, his friends—but their armor was dented and ripped. Faces turned towards him, but they bore terrible wounds. Mohammed felt ill, seeing ripped skin hanging in flaps, gouged eyes, the stumps of arrows festering in blackening flesh. Like Khadijah, they were faint, only transparent outlines against the hard, angular arrangement of the forest.

"Those men died on the field at Constantinople," Mohammed whispered, turning back to Khadijah in horror. "They died a martyr's death with the name of the lord upon their lips! Why are they here? Why are you here, who led a blameless life? You should be walking in green fields, beside a golden river."

Khadijah shook her head slowly. She turned towards the city, one hand holding back the edge of her veil. The blue sky seemed very bright behind her. "That door is closed to us," she said.

Mohammed looked and the city of delights was gone. Instead, there was the edge of desolation and a broken arch of stone lay scattered among thornbushes. Flinty hills rose up against a knife-edged horizon. "What did this?" He managed to croak out. "What has denied you peace?"

The woman smiled, reaching down to comb her fingers through his beard. Mohammed felt nothing, no pressure, no warmth, only the touch of tears falling on his naked, sunken chest. The sun was beginning to shine, a tiny, winking star peeking through her ghostly shadow.

"Khadi . . ." Mohammed tried to lift his hand, to clasp hers. His fingers passed through smoke.

She was gone.

The Quraysh fell back, eyes clenched tight, his fists trying to curl. His head fell among the stones with a rattling *clunk*, like a dry gourd dropped beside the river. "Ahhhhh . . ."

He could not weep, but he felt something well in his chest, pressing at his ribs, snatching away his breath. He tried to cry out, but something filled his throat, making his nostrils sting. *"Uuuhh!"* He lay on the ground, empty. The leaves of the fig were swaying, brushed by some unseen wind. Mohammed saw himself from above for an instant, a wrinkled bag of flesh wrapped around sticks and gnarled roots. Shadows drifted over him and he saw his men—the faithful who had fallen under his flag, expecting paradise—kneel around him.

Tears fell, faint and sparkling like grains of brilliant sand on a twilit shore. His dry flesh, spread across the ground, attenuated, exhausted, empty even of grief and loss, soaked up the moisture, a greedy rag. *No* . . . he tried to shout, but his lungs were empty, his throat cracked. The translucent shapes faded, each man's face becoming indistinct, his outline fading, blurring until it could not be distinguished from the stones and gravel beneath the tree. *Stop! You must not do this! I am not worth your sacrifice!*

The boughs of the fig suddenly shook, rattling as if a great wind rushed over them.

Mohammed, still so distant from his flesh, turned and saw a towering shape, wrapped in flame and darkness rushing up the slope from the wasteland. Something leapt towards him, wings spread from horizon to horizon, burning mouth wide in a shout. Mohammed heard nothing, but he saw the perfect sky convulse, ripped by lightning. Meteors fell, blazing with flames. The storm broke over the forest and the shapes of the dead quailed away. Thunder shook the ground, though Mohammed heard nothing, felt nothing. Acid sleeted from the sky, burning the flesh of the dead. Scourged with falling hail, with burning stones, with sizzling rain, the uneasy spirits turned away from the tree.

Mohammed fell, spinning, overcome by vertigo. He closed his eyes.

When he opened them again, Mōha was crouched over him, beautiful face split by a snarl. White teeth gleamed in the shadow of his face.

"Worry not, my lord!" Mōha said, chest heaving with exertion, limbs tense. "I have driven the wretched filth away! You will be safe. Quite safe."

Mohammed closed his eyes again, blotting out the man's face. He could still taste the fig in his mouth, the water on his lips. His heart felt light, as if a great weight had pressed against him for a long time. Now it was gone and he thought he was at peace.

⊡O•(O)•(O)•(O)•(O)•(O)•(O)•(O)•(O)•(O)•(O)•(O)•(O)•(O)•(O)•(O)•(O)•(O)⊡

IN THE ROMAN GARRISON AT PELUSIUM, LOWER EGYPT

)|(

Aurelian woke in darkness, skin crawling with alarm. The room was quiet, the lights low—barely a gleam against plastered walls. He could hear the steady footfall of a guard outside, pacing the hallway. The Roman kept still, heart racing with wild fear. He was certain a figure had stood over him, looking down with pale eyes. Trembling fingers grasped the hilt of a knife beside the cot. He listened. There was nothing—no sound of hushed breath, no half-felt vibration of hostile intent.

A dream, he thought, *but it fades . . .* A vision lingered; a vast city of cyclopean buildings, windows crowded with cheering people, flowers raining down on his face, the sun breaking through white, fluffy clouds, blazing on white-fronted temples. He remembered the smell of stallions, the creak of chariot under his feet as he rode through the crowded streets. A weight on his brow. Soldiers lined the avenue, holding back a boisterous, surging crowd with leveled spears. *Rome, my homecoming, but with a diadem of gold.*

The prince sat up, sweating despite a chill hanging in the air. He released the knife, shaking out his fingers. They cramped and bruised from gripping the hilt. His strength had compressed the wire wrapping into the iron tongue.

A thought came, unbidden. *If I returned home with these Legions under my command, I would be Emperor.* Aurelian snorted at the thought, shaking his head like a horse with flies tickling its ears.

"Madness!" He stood up, throwing aside the sheet. The Egyptian night was usually very warm here in the delta lowlands. The days were getting hotter too as summer dragged on. His tunic stuck to a broad, tanned chest, damp and clammy with night sweat. Aurelian paced to the door and pushed the panel open. The guard in the hallway started, swinging around in surprise, sword rasping free in his hand.

"Halt!" The boy was young, one of the new recruits. His face was pinched and beaded with sweat. The point of the blade aimed steadily at the prince's breastbone.

"Easy, lad," Aurelian said. He didn't feel so easy himself. The air in the hallway seemed stiflingly close. "Put your blade away."

The boy stared at him, teeth gritted, for a long moment. Then he squinted, seemed to recognize Aurelian, and returned the stabbing sword to its wooden sheath. "Something wrong, Caesar?"

"No." Aurelian shook his head. The momentary dream was gone, fading in the warm light of the oil lamps. "Just restless. Anyone been about? Hear anything?"

"No, my lord. Quiet as a tomb." The boy chuckled, straightening his helmet.

"Good." Aurelian considered returning to bed, but his stomach had woken up too. Familiar pangs drove the last of his dreams away. "I'm going to get a bite from the kettle."

The bottom floor of the old Ptolemaic palace was given over to kitchens and a mess hall filled with rough, wooden tables and long benches. A scattering of lamps provided faint illumination. Servants, kitchen slaves and thin, mangy dogs slept between the tables, filling the air with a groaning dissonant chorus. A low fire burned in the huge grate, enough to keep the night kettle warm and the porridge from solidifying into glue. Aurelian scooped grain and raisin mash into a wooden bowl. Crystallized honey from a nearby tub followed, ground in with a copper spoon. Stepping over the cooks, sprawled in rows near the fire, the Roman found an empty stone step against the wall.

"Who would believe me in the marketplace," a soft voice said from the shadows. "Caesar himself eating worker's gruel with a bent spoon? Impossible."

Aurelian swallowed, then licked the spoon clean. A cloaked, hooded figure leaned against the wall, back bent against the weathered feet of an enormous ibex-headed man. Cracked paintings crawled up into darkness, interleaved with old red-painted pillars and vertical columns of blocky hieroglyphs. "Men must eat," Aurelian said, pointing at the figure with his spoon. "Master Nephet."

A thin hand, burnished dark mahogany, drew back the hood, revealing a hawk-nosed silhouette and weary, piercing eyes. "Lord Caesar, I am flattered you recall my name, much less my voice."

"I have a good memory," the Roman said, scooping more porridge out of the bowl. The grain was barely milled, the raisins going sour, but he didn't care. The bowl was soon empty and the prince picked through his beard for crumbs. "You are up at an odd hour."

"The air is heavy tonight." The priest settled back against the wall again, face obscured, hands clasped on his chest, a staff held in the crook of his arm. "Do you feel the pressure?"

Aurelian nodded, putting down the empty bowl. He did not look at the priest. "I dreamed of Rome and a triumph. I was wearing a crown of gold. A king's crown."

"Rome has no king," Nephet said softly, bright eyes watching the prince. "The Senate and the people rule . . . isn't that what your banners say? No king, only an Emperor, the greatest of lordly men."

"Yes," Aurelian said, memory bright before his eyes again. He found it hard to look away. At the edge of vision, he caught a glimpse of his wife, their children . . . everyone was smiling and waving. "My brother is . . . Emperor." The Roman stopped, throat tight. A sense of loss welled up, reminding him of how far he was from home, how long it had been since he tousled the hair of his sons or kissed his wife. How strange and alien this flat, heat-baked land was.

"They will come against us soon," Nephet said. "Are the men ready?"

Aurelian took a deep breath. *The Persians*. He thought of the long walls, the dry rivers he had gouged from the mud and sand, the miles of rampart and barrier. His men were waiting, shields bright, banners standing proudly before each Legion. "We are ready," he said. The memories faded again, his mind rousing itself from something like sleep. "Do you foresee the day they will attack?"

Nephet laughed, but it was a soft sound, without malice, night wind rushing through palms. "Each day the pressure in the air will be worse, my lord. When we cannot endure it any longer, then they will attack."

Aurelian looked sideways at the old Egyptian. "They attack our will to fight," he stated. As the words left his lips, he knew they were true, felt something pressing at his mind, some taint in the air fouling his thoughts. "Are the other thaumaturges aware of this?"

Nephet nodded, eyes glinting in the shadow of his hood. "We can all feel this. Some of us, I'm sure, are afflicted with unquiet dreams. Those who are weak will hear the voices in the air more clearly." The Egyptian managed a grim smile. "Some will never hear the voices at all."

"That is fine for you to say," Aurelian growled. "What about my men? They cannot protect themselves. Can you drive these phantoms back? Strike at the magi plaguing us?"

"By myself?" Nephet shook his head. "No. This attack is subtle. The enemy is being cautious, even sly, taking his time. We would have to bind a pattern of resistance along the whole length of the defense!"

Aurelian stood, tossing the wooden bowl into the fire on the grate. He felt anger build, gnawing at his stomach like a fox. *This is my fault. I should have thought of this long ago.* "Yes, you will. Send messengers among the camps—the high priest of every temple will be here by noon. You have been idle, priest, but no longer!"

Nephet stiffened at the bitter tone in the Roman's voice. "What do you mean?"

"You *will* bind a 'pattern' into the ramparts, the walls, the gates. Every inch of stone, earth and wood from the sea to the marshes." Aurelian crushed the soft copper spoon in his hand, completely furious with himself. "We should have begun months ago!"

The Egyptian priest swallowed, shrinking back against the wall. *I suppose we should have*, he thought, a sick feeling creeping over him. *And why not? We knew what was coming. . . .* Nephet felt his skin grow clammy, the close damp air prickling. *Have we chosen to sleep—or been lulled there by quiet voices?*

THE IMPERIAL APARTMENTS, THE PALATINE HILL

)(

Pale yellow candles luffed, their flame bending in the draft of an opening door. Shadows fled across a painted wall, briefly illuminating a mottled shepherd leading his flock across a plastered Elysian hillside. The door creaked closed, the helmeted face of a guard disappearing behind the panel. Galen Atreus, Emperor of Rome, set a stack of parchment and papyrus sheets down on an iron table beside the entry. The candles settled and a steady, warm light returned. Marble and heavy drapes of muslin soaked up the pale glow.

"Galen?" A sleepy voice called from another room. The Emperor grimaced, pressing the back of his hand to a throbbing forehead. Beads of sweat shone behind his ear. "Husband?"

Helena stood in the further door, her hair unbound, falling long and straight beside her face, lapping across delicate collarbones. Galen tried to smile, but managed only a grimace. He started to undo the heavy brooch holding his cape at the shoulder. He was still fumbling with the catch when she took his hand.

"Let me." The Empress's nose wrinkled up as she concentrated and the clasp clicked open. "No," she said firmly when he tried to help, her voice soft. "Just stand still."

Helena put his cape aside, then the formal toga and a gem-studded belt. After just a moment, Galen was able to breathe deeply, constricting clothes gone, the insistent pounding in his head easing to a mild hammering. The Empress knelt, untying his sandals. "There," she said, taking his hand. "Now come and sit with me."

The night was warm enough to sit on the terrace and Helena led him to a couch piled high with quilts and pillows. Thin columns framed a balcony wound with ivy, looking to the south, over the high walls of the Circus. Torches burned around the obelisk at the center of the *spina*. More lamps illuminated the white portico of the temple of Victoria. Beyond the high walls, the southern districts of the city were sleeping. In the late hour, the houses and apartments were hidden in darkness, only faintly marked by scattered lights.

"You're writing?" Galen eased himself down onto the couch, feeling dizzy. A hooded lamp sat on a table, shedding a yellow glow on parchments, ink, quills, two half-opened scrolls. "Is Theo asleep?"

"Yes," Helena said, sliding down beside him. He lay back, resting the back of his head on the padded arm of the couch. Her thigh was very warm on his. Galen twitched when her thin-fingered hand brushed across his forehead. "He's right here."

Galen turned, though his head felt heavy, heavy as a lead ballast. His son was curled up among the quilts, thumb in his mouth, drool damp on the covers. A fleece was tucked around him, partially obscuring a round face mussed with dirt and grass stains. Gently, the Emperor caressed the boy's cheek with the back of his fingers. Theodosius squirmed away, burying his little face in the covers. Galen smiled, feeling the ache in his bones abate. "He's had a big day. . . ."

"Yes," Helena whispered, curling in beside him, her arm over his. Galen slumped back, resting his head on her shoulder. "Like his father. Have you eaten?"

"Something." Galen said wearily. "My guardsmen were sitting to supper when I left the offices."

The Empress leaned over, smelling his breath. Her nose wrinkled up again and she rubbed it smartly. "*Peh!* Sardines, elderly olives, rude cheese, all in a fish must. How fine . . ."

"Their wine was good," Galen said, turning his head to kiss her ear. She shivered. "And you?"

"Something," she said, chin raised imperiously. "Theo and young Heracleonas entertained me as their guest, in state and luxury as befits an Empress. We had bread and sweetened water and bits of sausage. Then they fell asleep and I fought hard to stay awake, to welcome my lord and husband at his homecoming."

Galen closed his eyes, his arm sliding under hers. He held her very tight, drawing a faint squeak. "A royal feast," he mumbled faintly, feeling sleep stealing over him. "Fit for a queen . . ."

"Husband . . ." Helena brushed hair out of his face again. "My arm will cramp if you fall asleep like that. Raise up a little." Grumbling, Galen lifted his head, letting her escape. She sat up, clapping her hands softly. A little girl padded out of the darkness, shining dark hair tied back in a silver ribbon. She was carrying a fluted glass pitcher, a pair of copper cups and a basket.

"Thank you, Koré, just put them there." Helena smiled at the girl, who dimpled, bowing.

"Shall I take the young master away to bed?" Koré's voice was soft and velvety.

"Not yet." Helena turned back a cloth laid over the basket. Steam rose up, carrying the smell of fresh bread. "Let his father see him for a moment."

The girl bowed, then disappeared back through the pillars on silent feet.

"What did you do today?" Galen's hands slid around Helena's waist and under her gown.

"Ah!" She said, giving him a look. "Your hands are cold."

"You're warm," he said, sleepy again. She tore bread from the loaf, dipped it in honey and stuffed the resulting gooey, sweet mess into his mouth. Obediently, he chewed.

"Eat, Lord and God," she said, pursing her lips at him. "I took the young princes about town, to the baths, to the Forum, to the gardens, to amuse and tire them out, so they'll sleep. Which they are, quite soundly. I saw and was seen. Gossip and rumor flowed over me, cascading from low to high. I wrote, I read, I wrote again. I was entertained by these young men."

"A good day," Galen said, throat tight. *Will I ever see my son*

*for more than brief moments? Will I look up from my desk some
day, years from now, and see him grown, bearded?*

"Yours?" She turned, drawing a quilt of red-and-green
squares over them. She ate a little bread herself. Galen took a
filled cup of wine, drained it, then another. Helena put the cups
away.

"Poor," he said, the headache throbbing up again behind a
smoky veil of alcohol. "A courier came from Britain. The situation there has grown worse. More Scandian raiders have come
in their long ships. There was a battle—a skirmish really—and
they defeated the regional militia. So, a Legion must be sent."
He squeezed his eyes hard, hoping to drive the grainy pressure
away. "I have no Legions to send. A message came from Augusta Vendelicorum too, on the Rhine. There is trouble across
the river. The king of the Franks has died and his sons are quar-
relling. The governor is worried the Frankish nobles in the Empire will get involved, on one side or the other. Gods! It never
ends. . . ."

"Shhh." Helena cradled his head to her chest. "Never mind.
Tell me later. Tell me later."

"No," he said, drawing away a little. "I want to send Aurelian a letter. A fast ship is leaving in the morning, a courier to
Egypt with the Duchess's men. Gaius' man Nicholas is with
them—he'll carry a message to Aurelian. Will you write it out
for me?"

"Me?" Helena took his pale, drawn face in her hands. "You
always write your own letters."

"I want you to write it out," Galen said. He was sweating.

Helena, disturbed, nodded. "Of course." She stepped carefully past their son, still asleep, and gathered up her writing
tablet and quill. "What do you want to say?"

"'Aurelian,'" he began, eyes shut tight. "'I hope you are
well, and not taken with the sun . . .'"

The Empress wrote, her hand steady, though she watched her
husband's face with growing apprehension. There was something desperate about him. She had never seen him this way before, not even during the civil war. Yet the letter was light, even
pleasant in tone, and filled with nothing of any importance.

*   *   *

The quill scratched a final line across fresh, cream-colored parchment, then stopped. A sharp, precise jab spiraled into a blocky *G* and *J*. Flicking ink from the end of the pen, Gaius Julius lifted the page and fluttered it gently. In this humid night, the ink was slow to dry. Whistling softly to himself, pleased with the way the draft edict had flowed into life from his pen, the old Roman laid the sheet out on the side table. Dozens of other letters were drying, arranged in neat rows.

Gaius rubbed his hands together and looked across his work table for the next item needing his attention. "Ah," he said, spying a lengthy request for tax relief. "The letter from Britain! Excellent." He was reaching for the top sheet when he heard a soft tapping at the door.

Gaius rose, motions smooth and assured. A long knife, mirror-edged, ostensibly for cutting quills, was conveniently placed at the end of the table. His gnarled fingers slid around the hilt, feeling welcome heft in his hand. "Enter," he called.

It was very late at night, past the third watch. Only a few lamps burned in his rooms, their thin smoke coiling away towards the ceiling. Very few men would be out on the streets at this hour. Even the inns and drinking shops were closed. By now, even the bordellos would be slowing down, the customers steeped in wine, exhausted, paying an extra denarius for the overnight.

The door opened and a thin, stooped figure entered, heavily cowled in a long robe. Expensive sandals peeked out from the bottom. Gaius set the knife down and turned away to a cupboard set against the wall. "Hello, Master Temrys. Would you like some wine? Or something stronger?"

Gaius' cheerful tone was met with a hiss as the man slumped into a chair. Gaius turned back, eyebrow raised, a pair of cups in one hand, and a dark blue glass bottle in the other. "Here's something from India, recently washed up in the Mercantile arcade . . . *soma*, I believe."

The visitor, his face already red with drink, stared at Gaius with open loathing. The man was well dressed under the heavy cloak and hood, his pockmarked face habitually sullen. "I heard something interesting today," he said.

"Of course." Gaius sat, the blue bottle on the table between them. Temrys' eyes flicked to the bottle, then away again. The old Roman smiled in a genial way. "Do you need some spending money? I can loan you as much as you'd like . . . no need to barter."

"This isn't about spending money," the Greek said, lips twisting into a sallow grin. Gaius Julius' eyes narrowed. The man was not drunk with despair. He actually seemed *happy*. That was very disturbing. The Palace chamberlain was notorious for his poor humor. Delight would require something particularly foul.

"What then?" Gaius affected disinterest, uncorking the bottle. A pungent, harsh odor wafted out. The old Roman poured a finger's worth of shining golden liquid into each cup. "Come now, tell! You're bursting to share, I see. It must be quite the most interesting thing I'll hear all day."

"It is," Temrys said, clasping his hands together under the tabletop. He blinked furiously. "A notice of audit came across my desk today, all wrapped in Tyrian twine, stamped and double-stamped with the Emperor's signet."

"Really?" Gaius Julius felt a little tickle. Something bad was in the offing. "Who is the lucky fellow?"

"To audit?" Temrys said, grinning, the tight flesh on his scalp wrinkling up, lips drawing back from yellowed teeth. "Or to be audited?"

The old Roman watched him over the lip of the cup. Golden fluid burned against his lips, but he knew better than to drink. Even the dead would find this vintage rough. "Either," he replied. "Does it matter?"

"There was a will attached," the chamberlain said, wiping his mouth. The cup in front of him shimmered in the light of the lamps. "It was a senator's will. It had been denied. By the Emperor himself."

Gaius set down his cup, looking sharply at his night visitor. "I see."

"Yes," Temrys said, picking up the cup. "I expect you do. Your name appeared in the will. But, strangely, your name was not on the auditing request. Now, why would that be?"

"I don't understand," Gaius said, thinking furiously. *What happened? How could the Emperor deny his brother . . . oh, curse that fool child! He's been arguing about the war again! And those stupid telecasts. . ... Galen slaps him on the wrist, reminding the boy who is Emperor.* The old Roman sighed. "I suppose the estate managers are being audited directly, one by one." *A process that might take years . . . while casting no overt blame on dear little brother, or myself. Very nice.*

"Oh yes," the chamberlain said, still grinning. He tipped the cup to his lips, then paused. "The estate of the late Senator Gregorius Auricus, of course, has been directly expropriated to the Imperial Household. I hear the Emperor was not pleased to see it go to his brother, who has other, more pressing, matters to attend to. Why burden our wise *custos* with matters of farm and field, of harvests and commerce?"

Gaius choked back a vulgar word. He felt his stomach churn, then settle. *My loans . . . everything I planned . . . wrecked! Damn that boy, damn him!*

"I thought you'd find this interesting," Temrys said, gloating, his throat pulsing with *soma* rush. His eyes dilated and he slumped back in his chair. "Very . . . interesting . . ."

Gaius Julius rose, looming over the chamberlain. The man was snoring already, struck numb by the powerful liqueur. He looked at the knife, gleaming in the lamplight, then shook his head. "No . . . that would be petty." The old Roman sighed, lips quirking into a wry smile. "And I am not petty. I forgive and I forget. Always." Gently, he lifted the chamberlain under the arms and carried him to the bed. Brown woolen covers covered him and Gaius peeled back an eyelid to make sure the man was still alive. He was.

"Well." Gaius Julius sat down again, picking up the letter from Britain. "Tax relief. Huh! I think not! We are all in dire straits, I think." He began penning a response, the quill scratching over smooth parchment in a clean, strong, swift hand.

The old Roman spent only the least thought on the letter; *no* was simple enough to relate. Instead, his thoughts worried and fretted about the damage the prince's recalcitrance had done to the delicate fabric of loans and bribes and gifts he had spun from the gold represented in Gregorius' estates. *Well, there's no more money for Alexandros' army, then, and the end of those plays and feasts I planned . . . stupid, stupid prince!*

)‑(

Wind kicked out of the south, throwing fine sheets of dust across the dune. Three figures paced along the crest of a long, wind-compacted ridge, desert cloaks ruffling around their legs. To their right, to the east, complete darkness lay on the land. The moon had not risen and there was nothing to break the mantle of night; no habitation, no campfire, not even the glint of a traveler's lantern. To the west, though, long twisting lines of lights burned in the night. Hundreds of torches and dozens of bonfires gleamed and flickered. Even at this late hour, there was a murmur in the air, the distant echo of hammers, mattocks, braying mules and shouting men.

"Do they sleep?" Shahr-Baraz stopped, boot toes on the lip of the dune, darkness below, only the bare light of the stars and far-off lanterns on his face. Sand spilled away, making a soft *ssssshh* sound. The King of Kings drew back a length of cloth covering his face. "They must sleep by turns . . . passing tools from hand to hand. Some will never see daylight, not with the exhausted rest they earn from such labor. Sorcerer, what do your secret eyes behold, in the camps of the enemy?"

The second figure was already watching the night, lean head turned to the west. In the darkness, a pale witch-light crept across his skin—invisible by daylight—heightening the cadaverous planes of his face and skull.

"I see a hive of bees," Dahak whispered, "swarming around a fat queen. Busy, always busy, coming and going, building, digging, setting stone and wood, bending the earth to their will. . . ."

"What are their numbers?" Shahr-Baraz pulled back the cowl, letting cold night air play in his hair. "How many Legions? Who is their master? How deep and wide is this wall of stone?"

The sorcerer hissed, displeased, and he looked at the King of Kings in anger. "You have eyes," he snapped. "Look for yourself!"

"I have," the shahanshah said, hooking both thumbs in his belt. The broad leather strap was heavy with scabbards and sheaths. A plain-hilted sword, two daggers and a mace hung against flat thighs. The king did not go unarmed into the desert night. "My scouts cannot see beyond the Roman lines—you can. Will you answer my questions?"

"I could," Dahak said, his full attention focused on the king. The air grew colder, the faint light around the sorcerer stronger. "Yet my attention is on many things . . . some are far away. Isn't your army strong enough?" A thin finger jabbed out at the lights in the west. "Do you need my help to pass this barrier?"

Shahr-Baraz frowned, a glint of anger in his eyes for the first time. "Our backs are to the desert, our enemies entrenched behind a wall of stone and earth the height of a goodly building. We must ship water from Gazzah, a hundred miles away, to share a cup among three men. The legionaries mock us from atop their wall and everywhere my scouts go, the Romans are waiting." The king waved a flat, broad hand, indicating the horizon from south to north. "Their wall runs from vast bogs of cane, mud and crocodiles to the sea . . . an enormous work. The Roman fleet is waiting on the blue water and I will not chance risking our fleet, or my men, on a sea attack behind the wall. We cannot go around to the south, for the footing is poor for our horses, the sand deeper, then the land a poisonous morass . . ."

"Then you do need my help," the sorcerer interrupted, smug. "You wish me to open a way forward, as I did at Constantinople?"

"Yes," Shahr-Baraz said in a level tone. "Can you summon the worms of G'harne to consume the Romans? Break down their rampart, shatter their gates?" The king's voice became contemplative, curious. He seemed to loom over the sorcerer. "Have you a second Axumite box? Holding pearls of an unusual hue?"

The Queen, standing quietly a few yards away, froze, barely

even breathing. She stilled her mind as well, thinking of things far away and long ago, pleasant and innocuous. Only in the faintest whisper, at the back of her mind, well disguised behind remembered chatter and gossip, did she shudder in fear. *What did he say? That was one of the forbidden names!* The words slipped away from her memory, bubbles of oil rising in dark water.

Dahak raised a hand, a muttered curse under his breath. The crawling, leprous radiance on his skin vanished, plunging them into complete darkness. Even the stars were faint and cast no light on the sand. "Be quiet!" The words were a low hiss. "Where did you hear that name?"

"From you." Even in low tones, the Boar's voice was a hoarse shout. "You were careless, I think, to tell me so much."

"I was." Dahak moved in the darkness and the Queen gained the impression he was drawing something, some figure or diagram, on the sand with his staff. "The old ones are not a toy to be brought out at a king's whim. Even I—and my power is great, O King—will not tempt them a second time."

Rumbling laughter answered and the clink and rattle of metal on metal. "A single throw of the bones, then? So be it. Are your dead men in the Roman camp?"

"No," Dahak said, grudgingly. Despite her best intent, the Queen's ears pricked up and she listened intently, eyes closed, barely breathing. "They cannot be everywhere . . . and the Roman magi are thick as flies, crawling about in their hive, long noses in everything. They are alert and fearful. I do not want to risk the Sixteen so openly."

"Can you send some in, even one alone? They will not mind death, or pain, if caught." Shahr-Baraz seemed ghoulishly pleased at the prospect. "I thought there were several in the delta already?"

"They are busy on other, more important, errands." The sorcerer sounded irritated. He was still concentrating on the lights in the west. "What is this? The Egyptian priests are binding a pattern into the stone and earth. They think they can keep out my dreams!"

Silence followed. The Queen could hear Shahr-Baraz breathing. Finally, the king stirred. "Do they know you are here?"

"No . . ." Dahak did not sound convinced. "Perhaps. They are not blind. They can feel me, as I feel them—buzzing gnats, a racket of crickets, the mindless chatter of the small . . . I can taste their fear."

"It is time to reveal yourself." Shahr-Baraz' voice was firm and the words a command.

The Queen heard a sharp intake of breath and two pale points of light gleamed in the darkness as the sorcerer turned towards the king. She clutched her cloak tighter, trying to keep out the chill seeping from the air. Frost began to form on the wool.

"You . . ." The sorcerer's voice was thick, barely intelligible. "You are not the master here!"

"We must break through the Roman lines," Shahr-Baraz said, ignoring the venom in the sorcerer's voice. "We cannot go around. We cannot remain here, slowly dying of thirst. Now, you have pressed me to strike against Rome. You were eager to go forward. If we do not attack within the next few days, I will turn around and return to Persia."

The Queen, heart beating like a drum, flattened herself onto the sand, quiet as a mouse.

"*Ssss!*" Dahak sputtered, then mastered himself. As the Queen watched, frost crystallized on the sand; tiny white flakes drifting from the sky. Her breath made a white haze in the air. "Where is the Boar's cunning now? You wish to charge ahead, to impale yourself on their spears? We must go around! Find a way!"

"We cannot," Shahr-Baraz said, perfectly calm. "Our fleet, though strong, does not have enough stowage for all of our men and horses. If we attack by sea, then we go ashore with a fraction of our strength . . . and the Romans will close upon us with all of theirs. I will not waste an army, even one composed of barbarians and mercenaries."

"The south, then. My powers will find us a path through the sand!"

The Queen quelled herself again, stilling a wild urge to cry out, or run. The sorcerer's tone verged on something like fear. *What horror could strike caution into that black heart?* Wild speculation churned in the Queen's mind, but thought was dangerous, and she focused, again, on inconsequential matters.

"Can your powers draw water from the sand?" Shahr-Baraz was curious again. "Each step we take from the sea and our barges means water, food, fodder must be carried for leagues across the desert . . . all exposed to Roman attack while we toil slowly through the wasteland." The King of Kings sighed, and the Queen felt his attention turn upon her for a moment. She remained still. It seemed, for a moment, as if he was going to speak to her. He turned back to the sorcerer. "Can you?"

Dahak did not answer. The cold grew. The Queen began to shiver uncontrollably. At last the sorcerer said, "I cannot. But I will *not* reveal myself to the enemy, not yet. It is too dangerous!"

"Why?" Even with such a short utterance, the Queen could hear the hint of a mocking smile in the king's voice. She began to wonder why he'd taken such a long walk, in darkness, with the two of them. She squeezed her eyes shut, expecting some brilliant flare of destruction to light the rolling dunes. "You have been very wary, sorcerer, since we captured Constantinople. Furtive, even."

"What do you mean?"

"I mean," Shahr-Baraz said in a musing tone, "you once feared to cross the narrow strait before Constantinople, demanding a bridge of saplings, layered with earth. Yet you later rushed to board a ship, the Queen's ship, to be carried across to Chalcedon—without a single precaution. I know full well you can summon powers and servants to carry you great distances in the blink of an eye—yet you hide in your wagon, surrounded by the army, moving at a snail's pace across the land. Indeed, you have abstained from your usual violence, your usual hunger." Shahr-Baraz paused and now the Queen *knew* he was laughing at the sorcerer. "Who are you hiding from, old snake?"

There was no answer, only a *crack* of frozen cloth as the sorcerer settled on his haunches, squatting on the ground like a common tailor. The Queen did not move—indeed, now she wondered if she *could* move, so cold had her limbs become. After a minute there was a muted, soft muttering. The Queen realized the sorcerer was arguing with himself.

Something touched her shoulder and she started. Shahr-

Baraz loomed over her. "You're freezing," he said quietly, mustache white with frost rime. The Queen could see the stars around his head, burning very cold and bright, like a crown. "Here . . ." He lifted her gently, powerful arms making light work of her thin frame. The Queen felt faint, her head throbbing. The king folded her in his cloak, and she swallowed a gasp, feeling the warmth of his body—hot as a furnace, it seemed—against her frigid hands. Curling herself up, the Queen pressed against his chest. The cloak folded around her.

"You are rash," Dahak said, rising up from the sand. His voice was brittle in the darkness, bottled fury straining against a tight leash. "Endless torments await those who have displeased me . . . your shell, stripped of will and thought, will serve as well as this living body! I thought you a wiser man, Baraz, a wiser man . . ."

"Huh." The king lifted his beard at the sorcerer. "I have listened to Khadames and his stories of your plans and plots, your secret fortress in the east, your ever-growing strength. You are strong, but I see you are afraid of *something*. Something you found, something you saw, in the Roman city. I will tell you now, sorcerer, I am *not* afraid. Of you, or what you fear." Shahr-Baraz stopped, waited a beat of his heart, then said, "We must attack or leave. You must choose."

"Sssshhhhh!" Lightning flickered in a clear sky, the stars rippling. The Queen heard a grinding sound. "We cannot go back." Anger, fear and defeat mixed in the sibilant voice. "We must go forward."

"Then *you* must reveal yourself, for we cannot advance without your strength to break the Roman wall!" The king's voice rose sharply.

"I *will not!*" hissed the sorcerer. Around the three figures, the sand was suddenly whipped by a fierce wind, swirling around them. The air blurred, filled with flying grit. "Not yet! I am not ready!"

"Then—" Shahr-Baraz stopped. Cold, frost-streaked fingers pressed against his lips. The Queen turned her head, barely able to draw breath in the chill air. She felt weak too, as if the power rising in the air drained her life out like a leech.

"There is a way," she croaked, rich contralto ruined by the

thin atmosphere. "Lord Prince, you could exert your power through another. You need not appear yourself, where men might see. They would see another face, and—being men— draw false theorems from poor evidence."

Dahak paused, eyes narrowing, and the pale radiance surging across his flesh brightened. Shahr-Baraz looked down, a slow smile growing in his face. His mustaches tickled her face and the Queen sneezed. Embarrassed, she wiped her nose.

"Can this be done?" The king sounded pleased.

"Perhaps . . ." the sorcerer growled, expression turning sour. "The jackal is biddable. . . . I can see through his eyes, move his limbs." A sardonic, foul smile grew on his face. "Oh, sweet Queen, you are filled with excellent advice. Yes—I can move dear Arad like a puppet—pour my will into his shell. He will be the very figure of power! Little Zoë and Odenathus can be at his side. . . ."

"Then," the king said, cutting off the sorcerer with a sharp tone. "We will attack in two days."

Dahak nodded, turning away. The night swallowed him up immediately, shadow on shadow.

The King of Kings climbed another dune, one of an endless succession stretching off to the south. A thin moon crept up the eastern sky, shedding a furtive, distorting light. The Queen was in his arms, carried as easily as a child, head leaning against a broad chest. The strange chill had fallen away and the desert night—cold by any other standard—seemed warm in comparison. The Boar's boots dug into the sand, which spilled away behind him in long trails. Ahead, the lights of the Persian encampments were beginning to sparkle.

"Why did you command our presence, my lord?" The Queen was still weak, but her voice was recovering. Feeling was beginning to creep back into her hands and feet.

Shahr-Baraz looked down, distant firelight glinting in his eyes. "I wanted to speak with you and with the sorcerer, in private, without witness or hungry ears at the door."

The Queen licked her lips. "We are . . . allies, my lord. You have but to ask."

He nodded. They reached the top of the dune and he paused,

rolling his shoulders. "Our other . . . ally . . . recently expressed his extreme displeasure with you, my lady. In my hearing."

The Queen tried to muster a laugh, though it came out more a rasping croak. "The lord Khalid does not love me today."

"No," Shahr-Baraz allowed. "This matter is none of my concern, save I am puzzled by your desire to send a troop of *his* horsemen to garrison a town previously held by *your* soldiers. I have not been king for very long, my lady! I would be loath to give up such a rich prize. . . ."

The Queen tried to laugh again, but this time nothing came out. Her thoughts crystallized like the dying air. *Could he guess? But how? He cannot read minds. . . .* For a moment, she couldn't think of anything to say. She was only conscious of the man's powerful arms and the heat of his body.

"I . . . saw trouble, my lord. There was bad blood between the two men—between Lord Khalid and the Ben-Sarid chieftain, Uri. I heard . . . rumors . . . Khalid would use the Ben-Sarid rashly in this campaign. So Uri would be killed by the Romans and Khalid's hands would be clean."

The Boar made a gruff, grunting sound of displeasure. The Queen's heart beat again. "This seemed wasteful and petty," she continued. "So I sent Uri and his men away, with a letter for the garrison commander, directing him to join us on the march in all haste. They are Greeks out of the Decapolis and will rejoice to fight beside their brothers."

Shahr-Baraz began walking again, half-sliding, half-stepping down the further slope of the dune. "The lord Ben-Sarid reached Aelia Capitolina safely, then."

"Yes," the Queen said, closing her eyes. "Later, Lord Khalid expressed his opinion to me. His words were heartfelt, if not temperate. He is not a reticent young man."

"No . . ." The Boar refrained from laughing, though the Queen could feel a powerful guffaw bubbling in his chest. "No, he is not. I saw the Greeks arrive—a strong garrison to leave in some hill town!"

The Queen made a tiny, shrugging motion. "The city has a large Roman colony. They are restive, needing a firm hand to keep them in line. Uri will do that, I think."

"Good." Shahr-Baraz entered the camp, striding swiftly now

across hard-packed earth littered with tiny stones. Guardsmen appeared out of the darkness, saw the King of Kings, then faded away again. It was very late and a rattle of snoring echoed among the tents. The Queen craned her head, looking about.

"I can walk, I think." She could see the tents of the Palmyrene contingent not far away. Shahr-Baraz halted, swinging her gently around to stand upright. She clutched his arm, nails digging into the heavy cloak, then stamped her feet. They were tingling fiercely. "Ow," she muttered.

"Have your slaves warm some water, then plunge your feet in," the King of Kings said, grinning. He held up his massive right hand. The last joint of his ring finger was missing. "I was trapped in ice, once, for just a little too long. Then we rode hard, killing two horses, before we could stop. I was lucky—could have lost my toes, even my leg. Good night."

The Queen watched the Boar stride off, unaffected by the long walk over the dunes, the dreadful cold, the sorcerer's anger, anything at all. She licked her lips, stomach tight. *The king is no fool. He might suspect*, she thought, turning remembered words over in her mind. *He might guess . . .*

Zoë shuffled off through the tents, thin shoulders hunched, thinking furiously.

THE PORT OF OLD OSTIA, LATIUM

T hyatis sprang up the gangplank of the *Paris* in three long steps, eager to be aboard the galley. The deck was crowded with oarsmen and sailors stowing their baggage, lowering barrels of water down into the storage space under the walkway between the oars or running fresh rope up into the rigging. The Roman woman had her armor slung over one shoulder in a tight bundle, with the long scabbard of her latest sword jutting lengthwise along her back.

"Where is the captain?" she called to a nearby sailor as she stepped aside, letting Mithridates and Betia come aboard. The African had a long spear over his shoulders, heavy with bundles of clothing, armor and other necessary items. Like Thyatis, he wore only a tunic tied at one shoulder, leaving the other bare. The blond girl slipped onto the ship, the top of her head—now protected by a straw hat—barely touching the underside of Mithridates' extended arm.

The sailor looked up, scowled at the interruption, then jerked his head towards the forward deck. Thyatis, fairly bubbling over with energy, strode off, the force of her passage making the pine-wood decking flex and groan. Mithridates looked down questioningly at Betia, who shrugged.

The *Paris* was sixty feet long, with a fore and after deck, two stepped masts and a shallow hull. The galley was built to maneuver, to land on shallow beaches and run up short-draft estuaries. The cantilevered oar benches were arranged in single-deck fashion, though Thyatis noted—as she reached the after deck and clattered down a flight of steps into the below-deck cabins—there were half again as many rowers as she would have expected. *A Thiran design*, she realized, then laughed softly, seeing a bow carved over the door lintel. *We are among friends, then, and why not? This is the Duchess's ship and her effort*. . . . The hallway under the deck was narrow and short, for the crew and passengers slept on deck under the open sky or a tarpaulin, rather than mewed up below. Thyatis pulled up, seeing the broad shoulders of a man blocking the door into the captain's cabin.

". . . are we waiting for?" A voice carried out into the hallway, sharp with a Northern accent around the Latin words. "You're missing good rowing water and a shore breeze!"

"Pardon, friend," Thyatis said, tapping the black-haired man on the shoulder. He turned, revealing a long, pale face dominated by luminous eyes and a glossy beard. Thyatis blinked, catching an odd shape to his jaw, his ears, even the line of his nose. Her fingertips brushed across metal-scale armor over powerful biceps.

"We're waiting," boomed a Greek-accented voice, "for the rest of our passengers."

"Passengers! We're not on a pleasure cruise up the Nile! I've messages for the Caesar Aurelian and . . ."

Thyatis stepped past the big man in the door, eyes narrowing in interest.

The captain of the *Paris*, a stocky, bald man with arms like tubs of lard and a chest straining against his spotted, stained tunic filled half the tiny cabin. Opposite him, a little taller but much lighter, a wiry Roman with a sharp mustache was waving an ivory message cylinder under the captain's nose. ". . . I've orders to get to Egypt with all speed. So you can just—"

"We can leave now," Thyatis said, her cold, level tone cutting across the lean man's rising voice. "We are all aboard."

"Who are you?" echoed back, from both the captain and the Roman.

"Thyatis Julia Clodia, an agent of the Imperium and representative of the House De' Orelio," she replied coolly. "Captain Pylos, feel free to leave harbor at the earliest opportunity." At the same time, she nodded to him, flashing her forearm—circled by an archer's wristband—for him to see. The captain nodded in response, relieved to turn things over to a superior officer, then pushed out of the cabin, muttering. A moment later, the ship trembled as he stomped up onto the deck, bull-voice shouting.

"You would be Nicholas," Thyatis continued, nodding to the shorter Roman, "and this would be Vladimir."

"I am," the man said, glowering up at her. "We also serve the Empire. We've been waiting for you, then, and your . . . baggage."

"My team," she said, suppressing a smile. Nicholas was standing on tiptoe now, which barely managed to bring him to her eye level. For a moment, she considered the man—he was finely muscled, with odd colored eyes, a dancer's waist and thick wrists. One eye was nearly obscured by a fierce, semicircular scar. *A swordsman*, she thought, looking him over. *Very quick, I think, with a temper and a sharp tongue and he's never even thought of working with a woman before. . . .* Thyatis looked around the cabin, saw a table built into the wall and sat. Now they were of a height and Nicholas visibly relaxed. "Have you been apprised of the mission?"

"I have," he said. "There is a device, hidden in some Egyptian tomb. We find the thing and bring it home."

Thyatis nodded, pursing her lips. She looked Vladimir over critically and the big, black-maned Walach stiffened, then almost blushed. "There might be more than one device—the *telecast*—and they are heavy. Vladimir, how much can you lift?"

"He can lift an ox," Nicholas snapped, stepping between the two of them. "He's with me, my partner and my friend. Can you lift so much?"

"No," Thyatis said, pointing past Vladimir with her chin. "But my friend Mithridates can."

Vladimir turned and his eyes widened. The big African was standing behind him, completely filling the passageway, head bent over almost sideways.

"Hello," Mithridates rumbled, smiling at the Walach.

Vladimir bared his teeth reflexively, then grinned tightly. "Kind of cramped down here, isn't it?"

"It is," the African answered, backing up. Stepping carefully, he eased back up the stairs. Vladimir followed and Thyatis was sure he was relieved to escape the tension between Nicholas and her.

"We'll need both of them to move such a weight," she mused, watching Nicholas back away to the other side of the cabin. "Nicholas—what kind of missions have you taken for the Empire?"

"Whatever they gave me," he said suspiciously. "Why?"

She spread her hands, taking a breath. "Have you dealt with anything odd? With wizards or sorcerers?"

"Yes." The Roman settled back against the wall. "Vladimir and I were bodyguarding a Legion thaumaturge the last year. We were in Judea, cleaning up some local trouble, before the revolt swept over us. Then we were in Constantinople . . ." Nicholas' voice went hollow and Thyatis raised an eyebrow in surprise. The man seemed shaken. "That was very bad."

"I heard," she said. "I know how you feel—I've been in some scrapes where it seemed the gods were far away." A vision of flames filling the sky beyond an iron doorway tugged at her memory, but she put the thoughts and the grief they brought away with a shake of her head. *Concentrate!*

"This one of those?" Nicholas' expression had softened and Thyatis breathed a little sigh of relief. The tension had faded from his voice and his shoulders relaxed from guard stance. "Wizards? The dead come to life—the sky shaking with infernal voices? A chill like Thule ice in the air?"

"I hope not!" Thyatis grinned, running the tip of her tongue against the back of her teeth. "These telecasts are sorcerous, though, and the Hill thinks the Persians would give left nut and right sword-hand to secure one."

"I heard." Nicholas ventured a tight little smile. "Master Gaius said he'd seen one—all ablaze with green fire and whirling light. He said the prince used one to . . ."

Thyatis felt the room grow distant, rushing away from her. The tone change in the Roman's voice was plain—Nicholas knew old Gaius, and the prince—he respected them. Her eye fixed on the man's collar, finding a silver medallion there, worked in the shape of a dolphin. *The crest of Caesar's house*, she remembered. The Duchess's voice followed—*The prince is charmed by the* duradarshan *and all it promises and dear Gaius Julius will bend heaven and earth to please our lord Maxian . . . So here is their agent, set before me as my second.*

She blinked and saw Nicholas looking at her with a quizzical expression. "I'm sorry," she said, focusing on him again. "I've seen one too. An unsettling experience." She made a sharp wave with one hand, pushing away ill memories of the prince. "We believe there might be *two* in Egypt, or rather, there were two *once* and we hope to find just one, or the parts of one."

Nicholas watched her intently with his odd eyes, but said nothing.

"Do you have a problem," she said after a moment of looking back at him, "working for me?"

"No," Nicholas replied, but his jaw was clenched tight. "I was told to follow your orders."

"Will you?" she said, pushing away from the table. He licked his lips, staring up at her. Thyatis noticed his fingers were clenched tight around the hilt of his sword and for an instant, she thought she heard a singing sound, like fine glass being rubbed wet.

"I will," he said, grudgingly. Then he swallowed, as if he

cleared his mouth of some poor taste, and said, "I've been the leader before, I know how it is. I—"

"Good." Thyatis said, cutting him off before he said something he would regret later. She swayed a little, as the ship shivered, pulling away from the dock. Thyatis leaned down, peering out a porthole and saw the narrow brickwork wall of the quay sliding past. Bronze rings, corroded and green, drifted past. "We're on our way, then."

She looked up, grinning, then frowned. Nicholas was already gone, leaving the cabin empty.

ALEXANDRIA, THE PORTUS MAGNUS

)H(

Shirin pressed herself against a colossal sandstone foot, cloak over her mouth against billowing dust and heat. A row of gods towered above her, hands on knees, facing the sea. Dead stone eyes watched a column of Roman legionaries tramping past, hobnail boots ringing on the paving, shields gleaming in the noonday sun. Every man's face was grim and sparkling with sweat. They filled the avenue, pressing beggars and priests alike aside. Dust settled out of the air, coating Shirin's dark hair. Ignoring the legionaries—she had lost sight of Florus and his maniple in the confusion of debarkation—she turned away from the port and padded down a narrow side street. Hot dimness folded around her and the Khazar woman moved forward confidently, her face covered by a heavy veil.

Mutilated beggars whined as she passed, pushing dirty, stained bowls against her feet. She ignored them, leaving the alley and entering a wider street. Off to her left, over the turbaned heads of the multitude—pressing and shouting, every face alive with the urgent fever peculiar to Alexandria—she could see a tall, white pillar rising above brick and plaster warehouses.

That is the clock tower at the base of the Heptastadion causeway, she thought, orienting herself. Her previous time in

Alexandria had been very short, though entertaining. Thyatis had led her through the warren of the city in haste and by night. Now daylight dazzled the eye, shining back from hundreds of copper pots hung on a storefront, glaring from enormous white buildings rising above the din and bustle of the street. *The merchant harbor and the theater are to the left, the Serapeum ahead.*

Without a pause, she darted into the crowd, slipping through a line of half-naked men carrying wicker baskets of owls. A line of obelisks marked the center of the great road, the base of each monument shining smooth—the ancient glyphs worn away by the passing shoulders and hands of the multitude. The Khazar paced herself, finding a rhythm in the current of the crowd and she followed the stream of humanity east towards the theater. If memory served, there were numerous shipping offices in the streets just north of the odeon and hopefully one of the agents could find her a ship to Pergamum and the Asian shore.

Fine-boned hands rested within her cloak, covering the hilt of her knife, touching the edge of the Eye and her pouch of coins. Dark eyes looked ahead, watching for eddies in the throng—a water-seller, a shouting priest, men arguing theology on the steps of a pillared building—watching for familiar signs. Within half a glass, a woman in the crowd—paused in the doorway of a baker's shop, her head shrouded in white cotton, silhouetted against the glow of ovens—drew her attention. Shirin slid aside, pressing herself against the nearest wall, watching the woman out of the corner of her eye.

She is of the Order. Shirin recognized something subtle in the way she walked. The Khazar woman froze, becoming entirely still, as she had learned to long ago in the stands of beech and oak at the fringe of the high prairie. The woman passed in the crowd, hands occupied with a basket of loaves, without a glance in her direction. Curious, Shirin eased away from the wall and followed, though she was amused with herself for tracking such an unwary quarry. *I fled their sanctuary*, she thought, watching the other woman's feet on the muddy stones of the street. *Would they take me in?* Shirin made a sour face, well hidden by her veil. *Would I want them to?*

* * *

Within a glass, the woman and her bread vanished through an inset door in a blank wall on an unremarkable side street. Shirin kept on, marking the turning into the blank-walled cul-de-sac. Her feet were tired and she was thirsty. The clinging humidity stole more moisture than it gave. A public fountain presented itself—no more than a marble trough set beside the street, warm silty water spilling from an ancient lion's broken jaws. She drank deeply, striving to keep track of children running past and the old men sitting before the doors of the houses. When she stood up, covering her face again, she realized the trail had led into a residential district.

The crowd on the street was sparse—nothing like the jostling, hot mob around the port or on one of the big avenues—and there were no official buildings, only a small temple with a stepped facade. Shirin frowned. *Did the woman just go home? Or is the Order's house a hidden one?* Then she remembered the Duchess's house in Rome—also on a street of houses, very quiet, unassuming. *No grand temple here. Just a domus beside a sun-dappled street.*

She thought of going to the blank door and knocking. Her stomach grumbled in response. *I am hungry.* She dabbed water from the edge of her mouth with her sleeve, then continued down the street, counting doorways. The little avenue turned and Shirin found herself at the edge of a small square. The graceful pillars of a small, neighborhood temple drew her attention for a moment, but then the smell of roasting meat made her lithe neck turn. A hostelry sat opposite the decrepit temple and men and women were eating under an arbor of vines and crosshatched slats.

Without thinking, Shirin entered the hostelry and sat, drawing back her hood, slumping in relief against the cool bricks of the ancient wall. Despite her weariness, she was careful to place her things close at hand, half-hidden under the cloak. The proprietor appeared as Shirin tucked in a fraying edge of cloth.

"Noble lady," the man said, brisk in manner, dark brown eyes flitting over her travel-stained cloak and well-made but threadbare clothing. She could feel him gauging her, finding her wanting. "Wine? There is roast mutton, some lentils . . ."

"That will be fine," she said, giving him a reserved look. She caught sight of an amulet hanging around his neck: horns and a bull's head. He bowed, waiting impatiently while Shirin pressed two coins into his hand. The innkeeper hurried off, sandals slapping sharply on the tiled floor. The Khazar woman relaxed again, wondering if there were private rooms to let, either above the taverna or nearby. From this place, she could see the entrance to the little street, but no more.

"Here you are." The innkeeper returned with a platter and slid wooden bowls of olives, shelled nuts, steaming hot lentils and a slab of mutton onto the table in front of her. "You've a knife?"

"Yes," Shirin said, her stomach stabbing with pangs of hunger. Despite an urgent desire to tear into the meat, she raised the wine cup and spilled a little on the floor. "For the bull and the sun," she whispered, just loud enough for the innkeeper to hear. The words woke a genuine smile and the man bowed in proper greeting. Shirin made a seated bow in return, waiting until he had bustled back inside before she slipped out her knife and cut a slab of spiced meat for herself.

A familiar accent roused Shirin from a warm doze. She was lying on a bench on the roof of the inn, under flower- and vine-heavy trellises, her cloak as a blanket, a borrowed basket as a pillow. Men clattered up the stairs, muttering in low tones. Shirin's eyes opened, then settled to bare slits. Two men appeared in the stairwell, bent under heavy burdens. Dust tickled her nose and she smelled the desert, camels, sweat and chipped limestone. *Laborers? Speaking Greek with Persian accents—not likely!*

"Ah, now," a man said, the harder, sharper Azeri accent clear in his voice. "Someone's taken my spot." Shirin forced herself to remain still, keeping her breathing even and measured, her lips slightly parted, as if in deep sleep.

"Shhh . . ." hissed the other man, groaning as he rolled the wrapped bundle from his shoulders onto the wooden floor. There was a clunking sound, from stone or metal. "Master Theon said a priestess was resting up here."

"Huh." Shirin heard the first man's tunic rustle, his boots scrape on the floor as he turned away. "She'll keep me warm tonight, then, if she's still here!"

The stairwell muffled the other man's response as he descended. Shirin waited a dozen heartbeats, then opened her eyes. The rooftop terrace was empty save for the benches and pallets on the floor—and two heavy, dusty bundles of cloth, bound with rope. Shirin rolled silently from the bench, gathering up her bag and cloak. She padded to the bundles, listening intently for any footstep on the stairs. Heavy, yellow dust trickled out of creases in the canvas wrapping. A soft nudge with her foot was rewarded with the clink of metal on metal. Kneeling beside the mysterious package, Shirin's nostrils flared. *Oiled metal*, she recognized, *hot from the sun, dusty and dirty*. Her fingers traced the outline of a boot print on the weathered boards of the floor. Black mud lay scattered at the head of the stairs. *The river*, she mused, then stood, drawing the cloak around her, covering her face. *But the packages are not damp— they came by boat?*

Shirin took a breath, settling her nerves, then stepped down the stairs, treading lightly. The upper floor of the inn was empty and she paused on the stairs before entering the common room.

The big main room was filled with noise—men were banging their boots by the door, tan-colored cloaks streaked with clinging yellow dust hung from hooks, the innkeeper— Theon?—was handing out heavy red-and-black cups of watered wine. Shirin fell into a hunter's quiet stance, paused at the doorway, ready to enter, yet still outside the immediate perception of the soldiers crowding the room. There was no doubt these men were soldiers—Persian soldiers—with their long ringlets cropped in Roman fashion, their calloused hands raising cups in celebration of journey's end.

"A wasted trip," she heard, ears pricking up in recognition. A cultured voice, a smooth, powerful baritone—*I know that voice*, Shirin realized with a start—growled close by. Two men—one tall, broad shouldered, narrow-waisted; the other short and graying, with a square head cocked in an attitude of listening. "A week digging in the dust—for nothing! Some chipped pieces of stone, a broken bowl . . ."

"My lord," answered the shorter man, his back to the stairs, "we know the weapon is no longer in Abydos. The tomb of Nemathapi was looted long ago. . . ." He sighed, shoulders rising in despair. "But I marked some scratching on the wall, inside the great chamber. Did you see the marks?"

"I saw dust and spiderwebs and crumbling plaster," answered the taller man. Again, Shirin felt a start, hearing long-familiar tones in the voice. *He sounds*, she realized with a chill, *like my husband.* "No more. What did you see, Artabanus?"

"Let me show you," the shorter man said, moving towards the window and an empty table. Paper rustled and Shirin, bending down a little to peer into the room, saw him unroll a scrap of paper covered with markings. Then the little man and the big Persian were between her and the scroll.

Cursing softly, Shirin backed up, arranged herself, the hood down over most of her face, the rest veiled, then stepped down into the room, head raised. The soldiers were drinking and peering out the windows at a bevy of maids drawing water from the public fountain. Shirin drifted across the room, as if looking for the innkeeper, until she could see between the hands and arms of the two men bending over the table by the window.

The papyrus was covered with angular letters, drawn in black charcoal.

"My lady?" The man with the bull amulet hurried up, wiping beer foam from his hands with a cloth. "You're not disturbed by the racket, are you?"

"No," she said, voice low, meeting his eyes with her own, crinkled in a smile. "I am greatly refreshed, sir. Thank you."

"You're welcome," he said, smiling back. "You bless my house with your presence."

Shirin made a half bow, her fingertips pressing his wrist. "You are very generous. Tell me, is there somewhere I might find a room for the night?"

"Oh, yes," the innkeeper nodded, turning and pointing across the square. "There is . . ."

Shirin took a step back, her head bent as if listening to the innkeeper. She caught a few words—the shorter, grayer man was speaking.

". . . protect us from . . . Kleopatra . . . snake . . ."

Then she stepped forward again, seeing the innkeeper turning toward her again. "Thank you."

The man nodded and she slipped out, turning left as soon as she passed through the door. Taking care not to walk between the soldiers and the fountain, Shirin disappeared into the streets, the corner of her jaw working as if she chewed a piece of heavy bread.

That was the great prince Shahin, she realized, chilled by the discovery, *and a Persian mage. Looking for a weapon . . . Kleopatra's weapon.* A block from the inn, where the road turned away, she stopped, sliding into a doorway. She looked back, able to see the front of the inn and its arbor and little tables. The tip of a pink tongue ran over her lips and she realized she was thirsty again.

Persian agents. She should inform the authorities. Immediately. Shirin's hand—hidden by the cloak—drifted to the jewel between her breasts. The smooth, cold touch of the stone steadied her, gave her hurrying thoughts focus, drew them into orderly fashion, halted their wild scrambling. *What do I owe Rome? How much trouble would I buy myself by approaching the city prefect with a story of Persian spies?* One dark eyebrow arched up and she glared at the inn. *Do I care what the Great Prince does? Rome is my enemy too!*

Resolved, the Khazar woman spun on her heel, flipped her hair over one shoulder and strode off into the city streets. She was sure a suitable hostelry or inn would present itself in due time. Then she could see about finding a ship to Cilicia and then home.

At the end of the street, she looked back over her shoulder, dark brown eyes troubled.

Kleopatra's weapon? Shirin shook her head, trying to dispel an uneasy feeling.

▨◊-[◊]-◊-[◊]-◊-[◊]-◊-[◊]-◊-[◊]-◊-[◊]-◊-[◊]-◊-[◊]-◊-[◊]-◊-[◊]-◊-[◊]-◊▨

NEAR IBLIS

⊒⊫⊏

B egone! You are no protector, no friend!" Mohammed, strength returning to his limbs, pushed Mōha away. The beautiful man leapt up, shocked, glorious eyes wide in surprise. The Quraysh drew himself up, leaning heavily against the trunk of the fig. The wood was rumpled and creased, coarse under his fingers. The sensation lifted his spirit.

"My lord! You wound me! I have watched over you while you slept, offered you food, drink, every hospitality . . . you are very weak, you should take your ease." Mōha gestured to the city, where lutes were singing and people danced in the streets. Another festival was underway and the citizens were carrying young women, wreathed in flowers, saffron and silk on their shoulders. The maidens' faces were bright with ecstatic joy.

"No," Mohammed said, standing at last. Now he could see the extent of the city, for the fig grew upon a height, and the metropolis was vast—sprawling away over rumpled hills, crowned with towers and minarets and domes. Enormous statues rose over the buildings—noble men, with long beards and wise faces—and everything shone with gold and silver. The Quraysh squinted, keen eyes reaching for the horizon. He realized there was no smoke, no fumes, no heat haze rising over all those close-packed buildings. There were no birds in flight over the rooftops. "You are a guardian set here, to trap me, to keep me imprisoned, like the poor spirits in the forest."

Mōha looked stricken. "My lord! Illness clouds your mind. The shades among the trees are the fearful; those men and women of the world who refuse to enter the city." The beautiful man knelt on the ground at Mohammed's feet, chiseled features slowly contorting, filling with despair. "Listen, my lord, do you remember how you came to be here?"

Mohammed blinked. He tried to reach back into memory, but could only grasp a fragment of sound—thunder rolling endlessly, booming and crashing over a plain. Before that moment, he could only barely remember standing in a tent with Zoë, eating a hasty breakfast. Everything else was shadow, fog, indeterminate. "No . . ." he said, grudgingly. The admission felt dangerous.

"I understand," Mōha said, in a soft, companionable voice. "Let me show you." He raised his hands, cupped, as if he caught water spilling from a pitcher. Color and light pooled between his fingers. "Observe, my lord . . ."

Mohammed tried not to look, but a horrible fascination came over him and he gazed down into the swirling bright color.

* * *

A towering figure clenched his fist, will pressing against the sky, the clouds, the earth. A rolling series of blasts shook the ground, a howling cauldron of fire and lightning and hail converging on a distant sphere of orange light. Abruptly, like a wick being pinched, the light went out. Across the distance, a struggling, fierce will suddenly failed. There was a wink of orange flame and then only rain and darkness. The fires burning across the field sizzled down to smoke and ash, drenched by towering thunderheads sweeping across the sky.

"You are finished!" roared a voice of thunder. "I will crush the last breath . . ."

A man shouted: "Now! He's done it!" A tall, powerful figure swung a leaded sap fiercely against the towering, flame-shrouded figure. The apparition staggered at the blow, then crumpled to the ground, blood seeping from a fierce purplish bruise behind his left ear. The attacker, a Persian, loomed over his body. A thinner, leaner man crouched over Mohammed, hands upon his face.

"Khalid and his bodyguard." Mohammed breathed, transported by the vision. Memories of pain, of rain sluicing across his face, of men crying out in grief, flooded into his waking mind. *They carried me upon their spears,* he remembered. *A hero's death.* Everything seemed to be very clear. "I was murdered. Betrayed."

"Yet you did not die!" Mōha leaned forward, face eager. His fingers clutched at the hem of Mohammed's robe. "You stand in the land between death and life! My lord, please, you must enter the city. You cannot remain here."

The Quraysh stared fiercely at the man's perfect face. "There is no city. I saw a wasteland of dark stones and a broken arch. You are keeping the dead from their peace! You are trying to lure them into the city, far from the voice of the lord and the paradise that awaits the faithful!"

Mōha drew back, eyes narrowing. "A broken arch? A wasteland?"

"Yes," Mohammed said, drawing strength from the living tree under his hand. "You do not belong here! Your master has distorted this place, keeping the dead from their proper rest. You are his guardian and my jailer. So, I will take nothing from you and I will not enter the trap of your city! You are false, an abomination and a lure!"

For the first time, a flash of anger occluded Mōha's beautiful face and Mohammed saw fear and pain and enormous, unbridled anger shining in the man's visage. Clenching a fist, tendons standing stiff in his arm, Mōha loomed over Mohammed, growing enormous. His head blocked out the sky and even the round, unwavering sun seemed to dim. "I—an abomination? You are a reckless, arrogant creature—no more than a lump of clay given flesh and breath! You think yourself mighty, having heard a whisper of the wind that blew across the void at the beginning of the world!"

A harsh shout pealed out from the giant figure and the evenly spaced trees of the forest shuddered, spilling limbs, branches, leaves in the roar of wind. "I have seen the face of the sky," Mōha boomed, "and knelt at a blazing hand, to take the manna that sustains life!"

The figure looked down and Mohammed was blinded by a burning radiance, brighter than the pale sun, a coruscating flare of dizzying intertwined shapes. The trees burst into flame and the short-cropped grass withered. The Quraysh raised a hand, blocking out the terrible glare.

"You are blind, blind and ignorant, O Man!" The flare of light abated, guttering down to a shining radiance, etching every wrinkle, every bone in Mohammed's hand like glass. "Your pride swallows all thought, all reason. This is my place— for the lord of the heavens and the world set me here—to guide lost spirits, to protect the land of the living from that of the dead. And the sleep of the dead from the troubles of the living."

Now Mohammed could make out, through the shining, half-blinding light, a winged figure towering over the plain. The city was gone, leaving only the wasteland he had glimpsed before, and the broken arch and the tumbled ruins of some greater city, now desolate. Eyes of fire filled the sky and Mohammed crumpled to the ground, nerveless, unable to stand.

"You served as I have served." The voice rumbled and rolled in the heavens. "And your time has ended. You must pass on, into the city of the dead. Only by restoring the gate will the restless, lost spirits find their way to peace."

"Why?" Mohammed tried to shout, to make his voice strong and powerful, but the words were weak and faint. "Why is the arch broken? Why is the golden city in ruins?"

"A door was opened," Mōha said, his brilliant flame wicking down to a standing, leaping bar of fire. Nothing of humanity remained, only a twisting, rippling sheet of light pulsing in time with Mohammed's beating heart. "One that should have remained forever closed. The dead are disturbed. Corpses go about in the living world. The living walk in the land of the dead. The stars shift in their courses, bringing a terrible constellation into view."

Mohammed felt a chill rush through his limbs, his heart. "I am still alive," he said in wonder. His thin, parched fingers gripped the trunk of the tree. "How did I come to this place? What sent me here?"

"You did," Mōha growled, the sheet of living flame shrinking again, outlining limbs, a noble head, a face, powerful arms. "You chose to cling to life, even when death opened before you. Already the gate and the city were shaken, cracked and splintered. You refused to die and with your *arrogance,* your *sin,* your *pride* the arch was cast down." The beautiful man, corporeal once more, stabbed a finger at the blackened, ashy woods. "You keep them from the land of peace. You are the abomination here, not I! You are the one who has brought ruin upon this world!"

Mohammed flinched. He remembered the sadness, the agony in Khadijah's eyes. The tears of the dead as they knelt over him, watering him with their tears. "I? *No* . . . You are the deceiver. I cannot trust you!"

Mōha shook his head, long hair spilling over broad shoulders. "Can you hear the voice of the lord of the world? The voice that speaks from the clear air? The voice singing in the courts of the morning?"

"No." Mohammed gathered himself, rising up, back pressed against the trunk of the tree. "I cannot. I am captive in some realm where his will cannot enter, where his voice cannot be heard!"

"There is no such place." Mōha's eyes were filled with grief. "Is he not the maker of all that is? How can he be shut out? He is already in your heart—do you deny this? If so, and you are here, then you can hear him, hear his beloved voice . . ."

"Can you hear him, then?" Mohammed stood, shaky on weak legs, but on his own two feet at last. "Does his voice sing in your heart?"

The beautiful man blanched and an expression of terrible loss cut into his face, graven deep in his eyes and the set of his mouth. "No. No, I cannot."

"What escaped from the land of the dead?" The Quraysh's expression was grim. "Was it you?"

"No!" Mōha said in disgust. "I am not mortal flesh, not clay! I am eternal, the first one, the dawn star in the firmament of heaven! Death does not touch me, not as it burrows in your flesh like maggots . . ."

"Who then? Was it the dark power that destroyed Palmyra?"

Another shout of laughter boomed across the plain, sending burned trees cascading to the ground in plumes of ash. Mōha wept quicksilver tears, which smoked and burned on the ground where they fell. "That is not dead," the beautiful man said, in a pitying tone, "which can eternal lie . . . You *are* a fool if you think such a power as the Lord of Ten Serpents could perish! No, *you* have escaped death, by refusing to enter the city. *You* have set the balance awry, leading to chaos in the heavens and the earth. *You* must set the balance right. Accept your fate! There is an end to all things."

"I will not abandon those who yet live, or those who have believed." Mohammed snapped, weary of the creature's prattle. "I will open this gate to the land of the dead and let the lost find their way home!"

Mōha grinned. "You have no strength to raise such a weight. You were only a vessel for the power in the tide, in the air, in the stars above. You can help neither the living nor the dead, save by entering the city." The perfect face grew pensive. "You must hurry. The dead are a multitude and their numbers grow with each beat of your heart."

The dead . . . The Quraysh's eyes widened and he turned sharply, looking back into the burned, blackened groves. The transparent, ephemeral figures had returned and without the strange trees to block his sight, he saw they covered the land for as far as he could see. "The dead cannot pass from life to death without entering the gate."

"You *are* swift of thought!" Mōha said in a mocking tone. "Are you deaf?"

Mohammed turned, eyes narrowed to bare slits, his face like iron. "The arch fell long before I entered this land. Khadijah was here, trapped like the others and she perished over a year ago. *I am trapped in the same way!* You are a deceiving, glib-tongued creature! You seek to lead the dead astray, to keep them from paradise, to turn their minds from the lord of the world! You are a false guide, a corrupt councilor!" The Quraysh raised a hand, his entire body suffused with righteous strength. "Be-gone, creature of sin! I cast you out, I deny you!"

"Sin?" Mōha changed again, burning light oozing from the pores of his flesh, opening foundry doors in his eyes, his breath hot. "You speak of sin? You, who have murdered, stolen, cheated? You who sought revenge, hate hot in your heart? There is no one who will stand beside you in judgment and speak in your favor! You are monstrous, a thing of bleeding clay, your hands running with innocent blood!"

"The world will speak for me!" Mohammed's tongue was quick with anger. "I have placed myself in the lord's care, ac-cepted his will, become his instrument! My soul will stand in the balance of judgment!"

"Will it?" Mōha's expression became grave. His hand pointed, stiff in accusation. "Here is the world, at your hand. It suffers for you, sacrifices for you, gives you life . . . do you praise it, offer it thanks? No, there is only dirt to grind beneath your feet, a crutch for feeble limbs. Dare you ask the world for judgment?"

Mohammed grew still. Someone was standing behind him. He could hear the rustle of cloth, the soft motion of breath. Stiff fingers touched his shoulder, and he could feel smooth, cool skin against his neck.

"You drank from me," a female voice sighed, like wind rustling in dry leaves. "Without care. You ate of me, without thanks. My soil is wet with rich red blood you spilt, without leave."

Mohammed staggered, falling to his knees. Harsh shadows fell on the ground, thrown by the steady brilliance shining forth from the figure of Mōha. His limbs grew heavy again.

"You sought glory in war, in the strife of men, abandoning your family, without forethought. You took up the path of vengeance, sending countless souls down to the house of the dead, without prayer to guide their path."

Mohammed struggled to rise, but his forehead cracked against the dry earth and his arms splintered, bones crushed by an ever-growing, terrible weight. He tried to cry out, but no sound escaped his dust-filled throat or passed his dry, crumbling lips.

"You spoke with the god's voice, without searching your heart. You strove in battle, without spying your enemy's banner or shield. Into an innocent's breast, you thrust your spear, blind in fury." A shadow fell across the Quraysh's face, but he could not see the slim, silver-gray figure leaning over him, harvest-gold hair shot with pale green, lambent umber eyes glistening with tears. "Illusion you took as a lover," he heard, as from a great distance. "Embraced as a dear friend. Pride killed you, son of the earth, who was born from clots of blood, mixed with clay."

The weight grew and grew, grinding Mohammed into the earth, skull fracturing under the pressure with a soft *pop*, thin, wasted shoulders flaking into dust.

⊡◖0◗◖0◗◖0◗◖0◗◖0◗◖0◗◖0◗◖0◗◖0◗◖0◗◖0◗◖0◗◖0◗◖0◗◖0◗◖0◗⊡

THE ROMAN CAMP AT PELUSIUM, LOWER EGYPT

)I(

"What was that?" Sextus raised his head, nostrils flaring. He stopped, reining in his mule, and held out a hand to bring Frontius up short. Both men were riding along the military road atop the interior wall of the Roman fortifications, heading for a mile-fort where—they were informed—the Caesar Aurelian was encamped. The fighting platform rose up directly to their right, reinforced with palm logs and slabs of looted stone. Men were sleeping along the rampart, wrapped in their field blankets, helmets and scabbarded swords close at hand. Pyramids of spears and javelins stood every dozen yards. At intervals, sentries leaned against the wall, watching the eastern darkness.

"I didn't hear anything." Frontius squinted around, raising his lantern. Butter-yellow light spilled across a roadway of planed logs. Off to his left, fields of stumps lay under a starry sky. A mile or more away, torches and bonfires outlined the square shape of a Legion camp. The moon had already set in the west, leaving nothing to dim the vast sweep of the river of milk. To the north, the engineer could make out a gleam of starlight flashing on the waters of the Inner Sea.

"I *smelled* something." Dismounting, Sextus scrambled up the fighting platform and climbed onto a wooden step behind the wall. Frontius, cursing mildly, followed. Peering over the embrasure, he saw more darkness—the dry river channel fronting the long earthwork, crisscrossed by lines of stakes—then the dim lights of the first wall and its garrison. Beyond that, there was nothing—only velvety darkness and the night.

"What time is it?" Sextus whispered. Frontius looked at the sky, searching for the gleam of Venus or Mars. They were low in the west, chasing the moon.

"Nearly dawn," he replied. His nose tickled. "Feh! What *is* that?"

Sextus thumped him on the shoulder. "The wind is turning from the east. That's an entire army awake and pissing out in the desert."

Frontius' eyebrows raised, then he sneezed. Disgusted, he wiped his nose. "We'd better hurry. His lordship needs to know about the dam."

The two engineers rode up to the gate of the mile-fort in haste, mules bleating in protest. The portal was open, torches blazing all around, an entire century of grizzled-looking veterans standing watch. Sextus slid from the mule, slapping away a customary bite, and saluted the centurion in charge. Runners were leaving the gate in a steady stream, each man holding a paper lantern at the end of a carry pole. The watch had weapons drawn and bare, their helmets cinched tight under stubbled jaws.

"I'm Sextus, First Minerva, a message from Scortius—to see the Caesar Aurelian."

The watch commander eyed him suspiciously and lifted his chin at a man—a priest—standing nearby. The Egyptian had his eyes half-closed, oblivious to the constant, quiet bustle all around him. "Menkauré? These two clean?"

After a moment, the priest nodded. At the same time, Sextus felt a tingling sensation, as if soft feathers brushed against his ears and neck. He shuddered, tossing his head. Frontius was scratching his nose furiously, scowling at everyone.

"Go on," the centurion said. His men parted, allowing the two engineers to hurry inside the fortress. Like its companions along the length of the fortifications, it was a hollow square, surrounded by a high, raised earthen wall and a palisade of palm logs, mud brick and—at the corners, where watchtowers loomed against the black sky—blocks of carefully hoarded stone. The lower delta was bereft of most building materials save mud and palms. Sextus squished across the muddy courtyard, weaving his way through groups of soldiers. The men were in full armor already, drinking from steaming cups, chewing on flat bread. Kitchen slaves moved among them, handing out cloth bags of bread and dried meat. The courtyard was poorly lit and it took Sextus a moment to find the Caesar's tents.

Within, a blaze of white light illuminated everything. The engineers halted, squinting, half-blinded by radiance spilling from crystalline globes hung from the ceiling in nets of bronze chain. When they could see again, Aurelian was waving them into the main room of the tent. The Caesar was surrounded by a phalanx of clerks and scribes, runners kneeling nearby, and two thin old Egyptian priests lurking behind his worktable.

"Sextus, Frontius—Mercury speeds you into the arms of Mars tonight!" Aurelian smiled, teeth white in the bushy thicket of his red beard. "The sun will be up soon and the Persians will be coming at us, I think."

Sextus nodded, saluting the prince. "You can smell them, my lord. The wind has turned from the east."

"I know." Aurelian rubbed his own nose. "The men on the first wall can hear them moving. Sound travels well over the desert." The prince motioned them closer, then said: "How stand things among the reeds?"

Sextus waggled a hand in the air. The huge project twenty miles up the arm of the Nile had been giving the Romans quite a time. "Well, my lord . . . things could be better."

Aurelian frowned, bending close. Even here, in a tent crawling with his own men, under the aegis of his own thaumaturges, the prince was minded to be circumspect. "What do you mean? Scortius sent no word of trouble."

Both engineers shrugged. "You know how poor this soil is, my lord, all bogs, quicksand and alluvial mud. No bone to this land, no stone, no spine! There was a subsidence yesterday; it collapsed part of the western dyke. The weight of the dam was too much for the ground to hold." Sextus shook his head, hands spread wide. "So do the gods will."

"How many feet of water did we lose?" The prince bit at his thumb, brow creased in concern.

"Only two or three," Frontius said, leaning in. His squint was worse in this brilliant light. "We rushed hods of fresh earth and stone to the breach and sank a barge filled with cane bundles in the gap."

"Scortius had us check the entire length of the dam for settling. . . ." Sextus continued, lips pursed. "The whole face is starting to crack. You know the project has been a rush from the beginning—well, we've never sealed the inner face of the dam—and now the levee itself is soaking up the river water, getting heavier and heavier. Without deep stone pilings, the entire structure is just too massive for the underlying silt to support."

"I understand." Aurelian's face cleared. The prince snapped his fingers, and a runner jumped up. "A message for Scortius, at the Reed Sea dam," he said to the boy. "The Persians are preparing to attack. The dam must hold for another day. He must stand by for a mirror signal. Hurry!"

The boy scrambled off through the crowd and was gone. Aurelian turned back to the two engineers. "Have there been any Persian raids on the area around the dam?"

Sextus shook his head. "In that morass? No, my lord. All quiet."

"Very well." The prince looked down at the parchment map on his table, thoughtfully stroking his beard with powerful fingers. The paper showed the environs of the town, with the Nile channel just to the west, then the four Legion camps arrayed between the outskirts of Pelusium and the secondary, inner wall of the fortifications. A dry canal between the secondary wall and the first, facing the Persians in the east. Another dry channel—an old irrigation canal—fronted the forward Roman position. Each half-mile along the outer works, a square bastion jutted back from the earthworks. The second wall was also provided with strong points, each offset from their companions in the forward wall.

"We expect a massive, sharp attack somewhere along the line today. There is no 'funnel' in the ground to the east, no natural avenue of advance. It's all open, rolling dunes, salt scrub and scrawny trees." The prince measured the map with his hand. "Their army is mixed, horse and foot alike. Were it mostly horse, I think they would attack along the axis of the old road—the footing is better. But now . . . I think they may attempt to strike at the southern end of the fortifications."

Sextus and Frontius examined the map. The Roman walls ran south into the huge extent of swamps and bogs making up the reed sea. Another five miles south of the last Roman bastion, the dam lay hidden among the sprawling wetlands. The junction of the marsh and the fortified walls was held by offsetting way forts, the two dry canals and—behind the entire defense—the camp of the First Minerva, their own veteran Legion.

"You think they'll try and break through, to swing south of the town," Frontius said. "Cutting us off from retreat, save over the Nile bridge. We'd be bottled up in Pelusium itself."

Aurelian nodded, but he did not seem convinced. "There's no reason to besiege the town—not if they can isolate us here and go around. Then we'd be forced to abandon the entire position, to fall back and defend the delta and Alexandria. The bridge is narrow—we'd take some time withdrawing across the span. So—I want the two of you at the southernmost mirror tower by daylight. If the Persians break across both ditches, I want the dam opened."

Sextus saluted, acknowledging the order. "Should we give the men in the forward works time to fall back across the second canal, if the first wall is breached?"

Aurelian's lips quirked into a grim smile. "Once the dam is opened, the canals will flood all the way to the sea within two hours. Time enough for the Persians to get their neck out of the trap. But I will not be there, Sextus. You will have to use your own judgment. Of course, when I send the signal—"

"—we will obey instantly, Caesar!" Frontius managed a chuckle, rubbing the back of his neck.

"Good. Now, go." Aurelian turned away. Servants were waiting with his armor, a single-piece breastplate of Indian steel, etched with the eagle and laurel crown of Rome and designed to fit over a mail shirt. Other slaves held his long single-edged cavalry sword, a plain, battered helmet, and a broad leather belt. Both engineers saluted, then hurried out. The southern mirror tower was five miles away, down roads sure to be crowded with men moving up to the fortifications.

In the east, the sky was still dark, without even a hint of the coming sun.

Zoë knelt on the rolled-up edge of her cloak, among a field of stumps, beside the old Roman road. Lines of men in armor tramped past along the raised highway, starlight glimmering on their helms, each man watching his file leader, following the bare gleam of hooded lanterns. The armies of Persia, the Decapolis and the Arab tribes had been in motion for more than two hours. Zoë shut the sound of boots and sandals on stone and sand out of her mind, fingertips pressed to her temples. She let her mind settle, let her thoughts calm.

One by one is one, she thought, *two by two is four. Three by three is nine. Five by five, twenty-five. Seven by seven . . .* The pattern steadied her, let the physical world fall away, a veil of silk unclasped. The so-familiar image of a dodecahedron spun in her thoughts, burning bright, brighter than the pale stars. Only a bitter taste in her mouth and a half-heard chirping of crickets sullied the vision. The presence of the lord Dahak was constantly upon her, a greasy tight film on her flesh, hidden iron in her mind.

The sorcerer crouched in the fallen orchard as well, though he wore the tall, powerfully muscled shape of his servant, Arad. The iron mask, the jackal snout, were bent as if in prayer. Zoë turned her attention away, banishing a familiar distraction.

He is well made, whispered a faint, thready voice in her mind. *My beloved.*

The dodecahedron swelled, split apart, fractured into dozens of similar geometries, then split again. A flood of shining motes darted away and Zoë looked upon the hidden world, blazing bright.

The columns of soldiers shone with ruddy light, the road a dull blue streak, the distant fortifications of the Romans a shining golden wall. Immediately to hand, the shape of the jackal was a black void, without the inner fire of a human soul or even the flickering pattern of an animal or bird. Behind the sorcerer, beside Zoë, Odenathus was also preparing himself, a steady forge-red pattern, all confidence and strength.

Auntie, be quiet, Zoë thought, only the barest fraction of attention upon her mind's companion. *I must prepare. There are Romans to kill.* Despite everything, the prospect roused a trickle of anticipation in her heart. The voice dimmed, though the Palmyrene girl could half-sense loss, sadness, and a flicker of electric blue eyes. *Our master is distracted, but he is not a fool.*

I understand. The Queen's voice receded into an inner, unmapped distance. *Dusares watch over you, child.*

Zoë grimaced, though her waking mind continued its plunge into the matrices of the hidden. A pattern of defense built around her, swirling with half-seen glyphs and words of power. She reached out to Odenathus, felt his familiar thoughts, then the shield of Athena was complete, a steadily burning blue-white sphere. One edge of the pattern enclosed the jackal, though the ebon power within the dead shape distorted the smooth surfaces, making them bend and dip like cloth pressed

down by a leaden weight. The Palmyrene woman concentrated
and the shield sluiced away, leaving the jackal alone and outside its aegis. The blue-white dome strengthened.

Ready? Zoë's thought brushed against her cousin.

Yes, he said and a warm sensation of eager confidence
washed over her. *Do you hear the horns?*

Zoë let her awareness recede a step, allowing her physical
senses to flood back into focus. Her skin tingled with the chill
of the night; her ears heard the soft wail of horns, the quickening steps of men on the highway, the snort of horses.

The attack is beginning. She rose gracefully, feeling the
mailed shirt bind against her chest, the weight of her helmet
tight upon her head. The jackal echoed her motion, though the
man Arad was nearly naked, only a loincloth of white cotton
around his hips. Odenathus stood as well. The two Palmyrenes
looked to the jackal, poised, ready to strike at the enemy.

We wait, came the powerful, crushing thought of the Lord of
the Ten Serpents. *Let the armies become locked in battle, all
fury and hate rising up, the sky filled with spears, arrows,
stones. Then the Roman wizards will be distracted and we will
move against them.*

His will gripped them like a vise, holding them powerless.
Zoë felt darkness flood into her, felt the Queen flee deeper into
the inner void, felt her limbs twitch with Dahak's intent, nerves
burning with fire. She hunched down, bowing at his side.

Yes, great lord! Zoë's and Odenathus' screams were indistinguishable.

Good. Good. The power turned away for an instant, focusing
on the rippling, incandescent wall of golden light. Zoë gasped
for breath, wild thoughts hurrying through her mind.

What happened? Tears spilled on the ground, her arms and
legs spasming. *He's not afraid! He was afraid before!*

She froze, breath coming in short, sharp gasps. Dismay rose
in her, icy water spilling into a shattered hull. *What if he was
only pretending fear? A ruse to snare treachery?*

With a tremendous effort, bringing to mind a calming meditation, she drove the thoughts of murder and insurrection from
her mind. A cold clarity settled over her.

* * *

Sextus jogged south, measuring his stride, conserving his breath. Frontius was lagging, still cursing under his breath, anger radiating from every pore.

"Dick-licking bastards! How could they steal our mules?"

Sextus ignored his friend, swerving around a wagon rumbling past. The road on the second wall was crowded with men; cohorts tramping past, torches held overhead, wagons filled with bundles of arrows, coffers of sling stones, more spears, healers in white cloaks, caduceus staves over their shoulders. The engineer pushed through a crowd of Blemmyenite archers, feathered plumes dancing over shaven heads. Sextus broke through into a clear section of the road. Furious himself, he glanced over his shoulder for Frontius. "Don't waste your . . ."

The eastern sky was glowing a pale pink. Tiny, crescent-shaped clouds caught the dawn as she climbed up over the rim of the world, burning like spilled, molten gold.

"Shit!" Sextus scrambled up the nearest steps to the fighting wall. A dim light spilled across the land, picking out the roofs of the watchtowers on the first wall, ignoring the deep cavity of the dry canal. Frontius clambered up, puffing, unable to speak, his breath spent. Sextus wiped his forehead, fingers brushing against chilled metal. He stared out across the sprawling fortifications.

The edge of the sun peeked over the horizon, a single burning golden dot.

Sextus swallowed. The world seemed very quiet, still, without motion or sound.

Distantly, attenuated by the cold air, a drum boomed out a solitary deep note.

Frontius leaned on his knees, gasping for breath.

The drum boomed again and the eastern sky was suddenly filled with a black cloud, winking with silver. Sextus watched the arrows rise—*so many! How could there be so many!*—and then plunge down into the forward works. The sound of metal rattling on metal, raining down on wood and stone, reached across the distance. An abrupt roaring sound followed and Sextus saw a mangonel set behind the Roman lines wind back, pause, then release with a thrumming *snap*. Flaming pitch flew up, arcing into the sky, trailing smoke in a spiral. Thousands of tiny figures, red cloaks black in the poor light, rose up along the forward fighting wall, javelins, spears, bows at the ready.

A great shout rang back from the heavens. Flights of arrows plunged down. All along the Roman lines, mangonels and scorpions bucked and heaved, flinging burning stones, red-hot pitch, spears into the killing zone within the outer canal. Tiny figures of men toppled back from the wall. At this distance, Sextus could not see their wounds, but his memory supplied the bloody, crushed faces, the sightless eyes.

"Come on," Frontius grabbed his shoulder. "We've got to get to the signal tower."

Dust began to puff up into the sky. The sun, huge and distorted, was over the horizon, blazing light slanting down, right into Sextus' eyes. Half-blinded, he turned away. They started jogging again.

Khalid slid down the side of the dry canal, dirt spilling away under his feet. Two dozen of his men crowded around him, shields raised. His boots sank into the soft, muddy soil at the bottom of the watercourse. He was in shadow, but the Roman fortification rising up a hundred feet away was bathed in lucidly clear morning sunlight. Thousands of Sahaba swarmed across the ditch. A huge shout belled out from every throat. Khalid joined them, slipping and sliding in the mud as he tried to run forward. His bodyguards struggled alongside.

Allau ak-bar! The men climbing the far slope struggled through bundles of thorny brush intertwined with sharpened stakes. In some places, the dried thorn was already on fire, belching white smoke into a perfectly clear sky. Arrows hissed past. Khalid heard a *thunk* and looked over to see the iron point of a Roman shaft sticking through the nearest shield.

"Forward!" he shouted, strong, clear voice ringing out over the canal. "Forward!"

He ran on, cursing the sticky black mud clinging to his boots. Bodies littered the canal, splayed in the surprise of death, feathered with arrows or pinned by javelin bolts. A huge burning stone plunged out of the sky, spitting flame and smoke. It crashed into three of the Sahaba running ahead of Khalid. He threw himself down, shouting in alarm. The stone bounced up, splintering into hissing chunks of green flame and flew past over his head. Khalid threw aside a flame-wrapped cloak and struggled up. Most of the men around him were dead, or afire, screaming.

Gasping, he plowed onward, coated with heavy mud. His shield was gone, lost in the mire, but his right hand still clenched the blade of night in a death grip. The slope loomed above him and he stared up, seeing his men still clawing their way up the incline. More arrows spiraled down out of the sky, but most of the shafts were falling behind him. He looked back, face smeared with mud and spattered with the blood of the dead. The sky was streaked with smoke. Burning stones shrieked past overhead, plunging into the masses of men swarming down the side of the canal.

Sahaban arrows whickered past, lofted up by Arab archers crouched at the edge of the watercourse. Khalid forced himself upright, joining the great shout lifting up from hoarse throats.

Allau ak-bar! He climbed past a sharpened stake, the tip splintered and smeared with blood.

More of his guardsmen climbed behind him. Two scrambled past, spears in hand, shields slung over their backs. Khalid hacked at thornbush, clearing the dry brown thicket out of his path. The Roman fighting wall was only yards away. Men in tan cloaks struggled along the wall, hacking up at legionaries stabbing down with spears and javelins. The young Arab paused, drawing a deep breath.

"Allau ak-bar!" he screamed, sprinting up the last few yards. The words filled him with wild strength. A dying Sáhaba fell back past him, throat torn out, blood spreading on his cloak. Khalid leapt onto a cockeyed siege ladder, then swarmed up the rungs, leading with the black-bladed sword. Spears jabbed at him, sliding between his legs. Frantic, he hacked down, the keen edge of the blade shearing through an oaken haft. The Roman soldier shouted in rage, flinging aside his ruined weapon.

Another spear slammed into his side and Khalid grunted as the metal rings of his armor took the blow. More Romans, faces obscured by plain iron helmets and cheek-guards, grabbed hold of the ladder and twisted sharply. Khalid shouted in dismay, then toppled back down the slope, crashing into four of his men climbing up behind him. All of them went down in a tangle, sliding into the thicket. Khalid's head smashed into the base of an angled stake and the world cartwheeled around. Stunned, he slid lower on the slope.

Men struggled above and more Sahaba fell, speared or shot at close range by Roman archers. Khalid blinked sweat and blood out of his eyes. The sun blazed down, blinding him. Nerveless, the young Arab groped for his sword. The blade of night was gone, lost somewhere on the slope. Groaning, Khalid rolled over, staring around wildly.

Hundreds of Arabs streamed back across the canal, their attack broken. Burning stones shrieked down out of the sky, crashing into the mud. Lakes of pitch burned furiously, filling the waterway with poisonous smoke. There were still knots of men fighting along the rampart, but they were dwindling in number. The legionaries concentrated their fire and rushed to shore up threatened parts of the wall.

"No," Khalid choked, barely able to speak. He felt sick, throat filled with bile. "No!"

Someone shouted above him. "There's a live one!"

Khalid froze, shoulder blades itching.

Out of the corner of his eye, something enormous moved in the sky.

"Hades!" Aurelian looked up in surprise, a wall of Praetorians in gleaming silver armor circling him. The priest Nephet was almost lost among their grim faces and muscle-bound arms, a thin, dry brown hawk in a plain robe. Black lightning flickered in a clear sky, reflecting in the prince's stunned eyes. The air above the forward wall shimmered and rippled with heat, revealing intermittent reflections of the earth below. The bulk of the bastion blocked Aurelian's view, but he could hear the sudden, strident din of battle. "Priest! What is happening?"

Nephet's thin old face grew grim, his eyes half-lidded. "The Persian magi, my lord, they are attacking the outer barrier." He leaned on his staff, attention far away. The prince saw the old man's arteries throb at the side of his throat. "Something is coming!"

Nephet's eyes flickered open, blazing with alarm. The hid-

den world was in upheaval, a vast, dark shape rushing towards
him from the east. "To arms, my lord! The enemy is here!"

Zoë swept through the air, a hundred feet above the canal. Below her feet, she caught a glimpse of archers arrayed in ranks
on the hard-packed earth. The Arabs were plucking arrows—
thrust point-first into the sand—and fitting them to the bow. In
the brief moment she perceived them, a thousand men fit fletching to thumb, lifted their bowstaves, then loosed. Iron-tipped,
gray-fletched shafts snapped out across the canal, lofting high
into the smoky, dust-filled air.

Before the Arabs could react to the apparition towering over
them, Zoë had to look away, searching for the enemy. Dahak's
will gripped her in steel fingers while she, Odenathus and Arad
rushed through the air in a tight triangle. The sensation of flight
was dizzying. Around them a dark haze swirled and shifted, a
formidable ward radiating out from the jackal. The Lord of the
Ten Serpents laughed to see their paltry shield of Athena.

You are my hounds, his thought crashed into hers. *I will defend, you will attack, bright teeth deep in the Roman neck!*

A vast shadow fell across the Roman fortification, mightier
than the towers, spilling across the rampart, the fighting step,
the crowds of legionaries staring up, eyes wide in fear, faces a
sea of white ovals. Ahead, the golden wall shimmered and rippled, sheets of ghostly light falling in a slow wave down the
face of the barrier. Zoë recognized the pattern—an interlocking
matrix of thaumaturgic will, dozens of layers deep, constantly
shifting, in endless motion to deny an enemy purchase—the
battle—projection of a Roman thaumaturgic cohort. She felt
the serpent's will move the colossal arm of the shadow and Zoë
answered, summoning the power in the earth, invoking the flat
blue shades of water, the living flame of reeds and trees. There
was no stone here, not save the cut blocks of the wall's foundation, but they had been leached of power long ago.

Lightning blossomed, stabbing out from her hand as she
moved her fingers in an old, old sign. The sky answered and
brilliant blue-white thundered against the golden wall, ripping
through gossamer, shattering delicate patterns, a sledge crash-

ing into new-blown glass. Zoë gasped in surprise—she had never thrown such power before! A dark current boiled in her mind, flooding her senses, threatening to burst free of the binding of flesh and will. An enormous pressure crushed against her and Zoë screamed in panic, feeling the might of the Lord of the Ten Serpents flow through her.

Another bolt flashed across the narrowing distance and the golden wall shuddered. Below, in the fight still raging along the wall, men screamed in despair, throwing themselves to the earth. Wooden towers wicked into flame, pitch exploded in its barrels, scattering smoke and living green fire everywhere. Zoë felt the Roman thaumaturges reel back, stunned. Of her own accord, she struck—fist twisting into a pattern to rip the earth, to sunder stone, crack wood.

The shadow arm moved in unison with her will and an ephemeral fist smote the earth.

Khalid, still on his hands and knees, flinched back. A huge, towering figure—*two hundred feet tall*, his mind gibbered—strode out of the desert, skin black as night, face that of an enormous jackal, white fangs a tall man's length, red lips hideous against the ebon flesh, eyes blazing crimson. Lightning flashed, rocking the air with a stupendous *boom* and splintered across the sky, flooding over some invisible wall rising up from the Roman fortifications. A long, ringing *tiiiiing* followed, as if a stupendous crystal shattered. The Arab threw himself down the slope, thorns ripping his flesh, his arm crunching against another stake.

Behind him, the actinic glare of lightning flashed along the wall, driving men back with terrible heat, incinerating those still struggling on the rampart. When Khalid stopped rolling, the entire slope of the earthwork was on fire, wooden stakes and thornbush alike billowing flame and smoke. The titanic jackal wavered, its edges dancing with heat haze. It smashed a fist down into the center of the Roman wall. Khalid flinched and the earth jumped with an enormous *crunch*. A huge blast of dust roared up, logs and clods of earth flying in all directions.

For an instant, Khalid saw the sky distort, burning sparks licking off in jagged paths through the air. Pressure beat against his ears and he gasped for breath. The air itself bent, throwing insane reflections of the sky, the ground, running men. The smoke-jackal bent a vast dark shoulder, pressing at the empty air, an enormous foot grinding across the earthen rampart, splintering wood and crushing soldiers already stunned by the blasts ringing in the air into a crimson smear.

Thunder boomed out of the west and Khalid—still cowering at the base of the slope—saw blue-white lightning leap down from the sky, flaring across the jackal's shoulder and chest. The thing howled, ebon flesh incandescent where the blast had lit, then smote the air with a fist, then again. Tongues of fire slashed out of the west, haloing the monstrous creature's head with smoke. Still the air bent and Khalid realized some kind of invisible barrier was deforming under the jackal's attack. He crawled away from the smoldering brush, then remembered the blade of night lay somewhere behind, lost among the flames.

"Curse it!" he growled, hurriedly wrapping the tail of his kaftan around his face, leaving only a slit for his eyes. The fires were still sputtering, flames licking up here and there, curling bitter white smoke from the ashy ground. The young Arab scrambled up the slope, casting about wildly, desperate to find the sword of the city. His skin flushed with sweat. *Where are my people?*

Together! roared Dahak and Zoë's mind submerged in a rushing black flood. The hidden world convulsed with stabbing white bolts of power. The Roman thaumaturges were weighing in, furious in their assault, bending the earth and sky to crush the shadow creature mired against the golden wall. Zoë felt the serpent curse in rage, then she, Arad and Odenathus moved as one, colossal arm swinging back as they bent their power against the tattered, deformed pattern. Dimly, though the helices of fire slamming into their own wards, she perceived a huge group of desperate minds—sixty? seventy?—hurling flame, lightning, every scrap of power against them.

The shadow's vast hands tore into gossamer gold, fingers wrapped in lightning, blazing with ultraviolet, and Dahak spoke a *word*. The sound reverberated in the smallest stone. Men fell dead for miles around, though others staggered and lived. The shining wall froze—constant motion stilled—and Zoë saw a vast overlapping matrix of geometric forms congeal from hurrying, inconstant, undefined motion. Dahak bellowed, forcing his strength through the shuddering form of Arad, and the golden ice shattered violently, breaking away in dizzying fragments from a pinpoint blast of will.

The opposing minds vanished from Zoë's perception, blown aside like leaves ripped from the trees by a titanic gale. The golden wall crumpled, breaking into brilliant shards, each one splintering into smoke, then nothing. The jackal strode forward, shadow long upon the land.

Khalid clung to the earth, feeling mud and brick buck under him like a wild horse. A log fell past, rolling down the slope. A huge ripping sound split the sky, then a shattering boom, followed by rushing, forge-hot wind. Khalid cowered, digging into the loose earth. A colossal footstep slammed down, followed by the screams of men. The Arab looked up and saw, not more than a yard away, a bronze-bound hilt gleaming in the wreckage.

"At last!" he croaked, crawling forward to seize the hilt with both hands. The blade of night sighed free from the earth and Khalid felt his heart soar with relief. The blade was unharmed! He rose to his feet, staring to the north. The head and shoulders of the jackal loomed up, wrapped in billowing smoke and dust. The thing's face was lit with flames. Stone splintered under its tread and Khalid saw a huge section of the Roman fortification was gone, cast down, only rubble and corpses remaining.

"Forward!" he screamed, pointing with the sword. "To me, Sahaba! To me!"

In the canal bottom, those men who still lived picked themselves up, caked with mud, streaked with crimson. Khalid ran along the slope, dodging fallen timbers, leaping across the dead. His men saw him, recognized the shining ebon blade in his hand, and they raised a tumultuous shout.

"The Eagle!" they cried, running forward, spears raised, catching the sun cutting down through the dust. "The Eagle!" Thousands of the Sahaba, shaking free of surprise and fear, flooded forward into the breach.

* * *

"That's torn it!" Sextus picked himself up from the road. An earth tremor had rippled the length of the wall and the military road, shaking open huge cracks in the earthwork, jumbling the logs laid down to provide a mud-resistant roadway. "Are you hurt?"

Frontius rolled over, unable to stand. His face was a tight mask of pain, gnarled hands wrapped around his ankle. "*Aiii* . . . I think it's broken." The engineer gasped. Sextus knelt down, fingers tugging at his friend's boot. Frontius turned a funny color, lips going white. "Don't . . ."

Sextus stopped messing with the laces, then slipped a knife from his belt. The heavy military leather resisted for a moment, then parted with a scraping sound. Sextus worked the remains of the hobnailed boot free, jaw clenching as he saw a purplish-black bruise around Frontius' ankle and shin. "It's bad," he bit out.

The earth quivered again and now a rolling series of crashing sounds, interspersed with thunderclaps, shook the air. Grunting, Sextus got a shoulder under Frontius, then staggered to his feet. The other engineer, hanging upside-down, croaked in alarm, then convulsed, vomiting. Sextus ignored the slick wet feeling on the back of his bare legs. He cast a look behind him, over his shoulder.

Smoke obscured the center of the Roman line. Black smoke billowed up from burning, damp wood. Clouds of dust were interspersed with the smoke and leaping flames intermittently lit the haze. Sextus blinked, unsure of his own eyes. Lightning jagged and ripped through the smoke, briefly illuminating something huge moving at the center of the conflagration. The engineer cursed, suddenly realizing what he was looking at. The distortion of scale was too vast to easily comprehend.

A colossal figure a hundred yards high plowed out of the smoke. Mangonel stones smashed against its chest, bursting with green fire. Clouds of arrows leapt up from the ground, clattering away from ebon-hued skin. A vast jackal head appeared from the smoke. Fire burst upon it like spring flowers—blossoming in a hundred radiant hues, then vanishing again. The *thing* chopped an enormous hand down and the earth shook. Sextus staggered, shifting his balance. A flare of unnamable color burst from the moving fist and siege engines blew apart in blue-black flame.

"Set is upon us," Sextus breathed, stunned. "The gods walk the earth!"

He turned, settling an unconscious Frontius upon his shoulders and staggered off down the road. The shape of the southern mirror tower loomed up ahead, only a half-mile away. It seemed intact, the morning sun gleaming on the polished shape of the disk in its cradle. Grim-faced Roman legionaries ran past, heading for the sound of battle.

Nephet groaned, pushing weakly at a smoking, charred timber pinning him among the dead. The old Egyptian's face was streaked with blood, his nose bleeding, thin fringe of hair plastered against a skull shining with sweat. His thin arm strained, then the square-cut timber lifted and clattered to the ground. Surprised, the priest looked up to see a powerful figure crouched over him.

"Lord Caesar!" Nephet turned his head and spit blood on the dusty ground.

"Get up," Aurelian growled, lifting the frail old man up with both hands. The Roman's eyes were narrow slits against bitter white smoke drifting through the ruins of the bastion. His armor was dented and scored with black streaks, his beard fouled with mud. "Can you stand? Can you fight?"

Nephet coughed, catching a fringe of the smoke hanging in the air. A sizzling *crack-crack-crack* roared overhead. The priest ducked, flinching away from the noise. Aurelian's fingers dug into his shoulders.

"Can you fight?" The Roman shook Nephet roughly. Memories flooded back, chilling the old priest's blood. He and the prince had rushed forward to the bastion, alarmed at the enormous noise and the flare of light. The old Egyptian had barely reached the wall in time to watch a conflagration unfold, then the earth heaved and something had smashed him to the ground.

"Yes." Nephet turned, leaning heavily on his staff. The side of one hand pressed against his brow. The skin felt hot, but touch served to focus his mind enough to descend once more into the maelstrom of the hidden world. *My brothers! To me!* The old priest sketched a glyph in the air, the mnemonic guiding his thought and will into the desired pattern. A pale, feeble radiance flickered into being around him—an incomplete, weak sphere of defense. Nephet reached out, his will winging across the battlefield, searching desperately for his fellow priests. *Sons of Horus, heed my call!*

Destruction lay all around, echoing between the physical and the ghost shapes of the hidden.

A hundred-foot-wide section of the forward rampart was gone, reduced to jagged heaps of brick and ash. The remains of an ancient triumphal arch listed drunkenly to one side—the old gate had been completely filled in, making a strong point in the wall. Now the sandstone slabs were cracked and splintered, scattered over a sixty-foot-wide swath from the gate. The bastion opposite, where Nephet had been standing, was cloaked with smoke, watchtowers burning fiercely, a massive gouge torn out of the sloping earthen berm. Glassy slag puddled, shimmering with heat, among the wreckage. The tents inside were blown down and dead and wounded men lay scattered like grain discarded on a threshing floor.

Hurrying lights—the shapes of men—poured through the breach, surging forward into battle with struggling knots of legionaries, regrouping after the blast. Nephet struggled to think—the wound on the side of his head burned with cold fire—and took some heart to see the Roman soldiers rallying around their Legion standards. Furious ghosts and vengeful spirits clustered thick around the ancient banners, driving back the whiplash of fear and despair radiating out from the enemy. The thin cries of the newly dead bolstered the hearts of the living. Older, stronger shades crowded around the legionaries fighting in the wreckage, turning aside burning motes of misfortune flooding the hidden world.

As Nephet watched, one young centurion—fighting alone against three robed Persians—blocked a stroke, then ducked nimbly aside, warned by the spirit-shape of another, older, stronger centurion—perhaps centuries dead—who shadowed his every movement. Other ghosts flickered in the air, knocking aside Arab arrows and sling stones falling from the sky.

A vast shape, anchored by three burning stars, swung forward towards the second wall. Nephet staggered, looking upon the shape of the enemy. Part of his mind yammered in fear, faced with the horror of a god loosed upon the earth. *Fool!* shouted his conscious will, *this is no god! They sleep, buried in the ice, imprisoned under the sea. This is illusion!*

Set looked down upon him with blazing wolf-eyes, the head grown so large it blocked out the sky. The sun was reduced to a pale red disk, wreathed in smoke and the fume of battle. An ebon hand reached down, splintering the earth. Nephet felt his physical body topple over, but the Caesar Aurelian caught him in a powerful grip. The priest's attention turned away, summoning up power from the soil, from the stones, from the lifeblood of the Nile at his back.

Sons of Horus, to me! Swift thought winged across the battlefield.

This brought a second shock—worse than the first. Only a half-dozen minds responded, some faint and weak, some strong, approaching rapidly from the west. *Are the others dead?* Nephet called into the dark void. Then, at the edge of perception, through storms of anger, fear and despair, he caught the faint scent of panic and flight. The priest blazed bright with fury. *They run? The mad fools! There is no escape now, not even in death.*

Nephet whirled, those few companions rushing forward to join him.

Too late, old man. A sly tickling brushed against his consciousness. Nephet froze, startled by a vaguely familiar touch.

Bow before me, like these others, it whispered, *and you will live.*

The old priest settled his mind; calming his heart, letting fear wash away, sand spilling into the desert, leaving only unblemished stone. *No*, he answered into the void, seeing the enemy loom over him, three burning eyes blotting out the sun. *I will not yield.*

* * *

Khalid clambered across fallen brick and square-cut timbers. He'd snatched up a round shield from one of the fallen. The breach in the rampart was wide, but with hundreds of his men, now joined by a few Persian *diquans* in heavy armor, swarming through the gap, he found himself among a crowd. The Sahaba chanted as they picked their way forward in a loose, disorganized line.

Ah-la-la-la-la! The long, ululating wail raised the hackles on Khalid's neck, though he had ridden to battle with the men of the desert many times. Thin curtains of smoke rolled across the field, obscuring the enemy. Khalid trotted forward, fearless, and found himself on a rubble-strewn road of planks, looking down into a second dry canal. Staked fences crisscrossed the canal bed.

"To me, Sahaba!" he screamed, turning, waving the ebon blade. "Bannermen, to me!"

A green flag appeared among streaks of white fog, sword and crescent moon plain on the simple fabric. Khalid felt his heart swell to see the banner of his people. "Over here!"

Deep shouts belled out, then the rush of booted feet. Khalid whirled, the sword licking across the face of a Roman soldier. The legionary ducked, shoving a heavy, rectangular shield at the Arab. Khalid skipped back, feeling the planks twist uneasily beneath his feet. The Roman stabbed underhand, the triangular tip of his short blade slamming into the edge of Khalid's shield. The Arab hacked overhand and the sable edge of the blade rang away from the iron rim of the big scutum. Gasping for breath, Khalid parried another stab, then slashed at the man's feet. The shield interposed again, sending the point of the blade belling away.

A line of Romans appeared out of the smoke, moving shoulder to shoulder, their shields a solid wall of laminated wood and iron. The Sahaba howled, rushing forward, swords and spears glittering. The legionaries answered with a hoarse bark of rage, standing their ground, and a sharp melee resulted—blades and spear points darting as each side tried to gain the advantage. Two burly Arab spearmen pushed past Khalid, slamming twelve-foot pikes into the Roman shields. One shield slipped, exposing the man behind, and he screamed, taking an iron spear point in his armpit. Blood smeared the leaf-shaped blade and the Arabs yelled wildly, trying to push into the opening. The Roman soldier fell away, vomiting blood, to be trampled underfoot. Legionaries filled the gap, jostling shoulder to shoulder.

Khalid wiped his brow, catching his breath. The battle eddied around him, leaving him alone and unmolested for an instant. The vast shape of the jackal towered across the canal, wreathed in lightning, staggering under bursts of fire. A constant *boom-boom-boom* shook the air, deafening everyone. Khalid barely noticed now, his attention focused on staying alive for just another grain. His Sahaba were locked in a fierce, stand-up melee in the rampart breach. Roman soldiers crowded in on the roadway from either side of the gap, trying to pinch off their position. More Arabs scrambled forward over the rubble, but now Roman archers on the shattered ends of the rampart shot down at them as they ran.

A basso *thwang* echoed in the air and a six-foot-long bolt snapped out of the smoke, ripping through the ranks of the Arabs fighting in the breach. Khalid spun, then cursed. The jackal was writhing in flame and lightning, leaving the Roman bastions across the canal free to fire their siege engines into the crowd of Sahaba. *We need more men,* Khalid realized, stomach going cold. *Or they'll crush us.*

Blade firmly in hand, he darted off into the drifting smoke, running back towards the Persian lines.

The jackal swung round, tripartite eye blazing, and the air convulsed. Something sped at Nephet, a whirling disk of blue-black fire. Desperate, his hands slashed into a complex pattern. The shield of Athena flared sun-bright, threads of green fire leaping into the shimmering globe from earth, stone and sky. The black disk collided, shattering into ravening lightning with a howl of sparks. Nephet was thrown down, stunned by the blast. His shield wavered, splintered, then collapsed in azure rain. Shaking off momentary weakness, the old Egyptian surged up, staff stabbing at the enemy.

The colossal shape of the jackal plowed into the second wall, grappling with the weaker, newer, matrix of battle wards.

Nephet wept to see how frail the anchors were, how weak the lattice vaulting up in the hidden world. He and the other priests had only worked on binding a ward of defense into the inner wall for a week. *Surely not enough time to withstand this thing's power. . . .* Spirit flames roared around black limbs, the jackal's mouth gaping wide, spilling dirty gray mist. The god ground into the defense, brawny chest streaked with clinging fire, splintering stakes underfoot, massive arms smashing through golden veils.

Muttering old words, passed down from priest to priest from the time of the Drowning, Nephet slammed his staff into the earth, fist jerking in the air, clutching at emptiness, then opening in a hard, sharp motion towards the shifting, immaterial titan. A jagged arc flashed in the air, arrowing into the thing's side. There was an efflorescence of rainbow color—blotting out the sun, casting wild shadows in all directions—and the jackal screamed, overcome. The shape toppled over, crashing against the failing pale gold wall. Cracks rippled across the ephemeral surface, then the wards closed, adapting to the blow, sliding together again.

Nephet gasped, feeling his old heart race, and found himself on all fours, sweat pouring from his thin body. *That was too much,* he thought vaguely. Mud under his fingers smoked and steamed. He was glowing, shedding a hot radiance from every pore. The pit of his stomach was cramping, his spine burning like a star. *I've got to rest. Just for a moment. . . .*

The jackal shuddered, splitting into three indistinct, wavering shapes for an instant, then rushed back together again. Those few Roman thaumaturges still alive attacked, whirling white sparks igniting in the jackal's shadow shape. Brilliant rays lanced out from each impact, eating away at the shadow. Again, the jackal convulsed, a broken mirror showing three distorted images. Nephet raised his head, snarling in delight. Clutching the staff, he forced himself to his feet, though the ancient, well-burnished wood charred at his touch. *Now we have it!* he exulted. *It's not one monster, but three magi!*

Nephet felt another priest of Horus strike, then beheld a rippling distortion blur across the field, sweeping around the faint patterns of watchtowers, walls, the hot spike of a scorpion winding back to hurl an iron bolt into the Persian ranks. Swiftly, seeing his chance, the old Egyptian slashed the air with his staff, glowing green traces shining in the void as he etched a sign of power. A viridian glyph formed, spinning out of infinity, a triangle broken into three, then into three, then into . . . Nephet wrenched his perception away from the abyss opening before him. He felt thin, attenuated, and realized the native power in the earth around him had guttered out, exhausted by the conflagration. *Oh, great god Horus, fill me with your strength! Strike down your old enemy, the father-murderer, the eater of the dead!*

The staff disintegrated, falling away from his hand as ash. His flesh withered, tightening to the bone.

Nephet forced his hands together and down, the triangular abyss compressing in an echo of his movement. Then, straining, his will fading, he shoved at the air, the blazing glyph leaping away, flashing across the field in an instant. Iridescent with power, the Eye of Horus slammed into the jackal, even as it rose, reformed, shadow shape solidifying into ebon muscle and sinew. The white sparks splashed away, unable to penetrate the revivified colossus.

Then the burning, lidless eye intersected with the dark god.

A half-sphere of darkness flared into existence as the glyph collided with a glassy surface. Then the glyph separated into three, then three again. In the blink of an eye, the sphere was engulfed in blazing green fire. Nephet held his breath, woozy, unable to stand. A shockwave ripped through the hidden world as the glyphs condensed with a ringing *bang!* Nephet was thrown back, crashing into a fragment of the battle ward. He slid to the ground, blinded by a blue-green flare.

The jackal was gone. The golden filaments of the battle ward scattered, driven by unseen winds. The old Egyptian blinked up at the sky, his eye drawn into the void behind the stars. Dizzy, his mind tried to grasp the totality revealed in the abyss, filled with whirling disks of glowing light, of great oblate spheres of fire, of endless darkness.

Fool—making a student's mistake! Part of his mind gibbering in fear, he wrenched his attention away. The chaos of stars faded and Nephet realized his face was wet. A ghostly, barely

visible, hand rose to touch his face and his fingers came away
slick with glistening blood. The shape of the Caesar Aurelian
loomed over him, a white outline against the jewel-bright sky.
A crown of translucent golden holly gleamed on the Roman's
head and shades hovered close around the prince, guarding him
from evil. They smiled down at Nephet, lambent eyes shining,
teeth white and sharp.

Why didn't I see you before? he wondered, raising a hand to
the mother wolf curling around Aurelian's insubstantial feet. A
prickly tongue licked his fingers clean, her breath hot on his
hand. Old grim-faced men, clean-shaven, hovered around the
prince, ghostly javelins and swords making a barrier of steel.
But the red-beard cannot see you, Nephet realized, his thoughts
becoming vague, his limbs heavy with sleep. *And I, only
now . . . .*

The priest's heart stuttered, then stopped. Blood moved
weakly in his body, but his mind was already falling into darkness. The shape of Aurelian pressed stout fingers against a frail,
old neck—then shook its head. Nephet's physicality began to
decay, even as he grew cold and still on the broken ground.

Across the ramparts, fires raged where the glyph had shattered through black glass. Even in the physical world, the dead
lay in windrows, the fighting wall toppled, bricks sizzling with
heat. Three bodies lay where one colossus had struggled. Arad
crumpled in a crater of vaporized brick and mud, his powerful
limbs splayed on the ground, Odenathus and Zoë cast aside,
faces slack in unconsciousness. Steam hissed from the earth,
silt and mud boiling.

The few remaining priests of Horus crept from the battlefield, wounded and exhausted, most barely able to move.
Some—blessed with servants—were borne away in litters. Others lay fallen, struck down in the struggle or stunned by the
tremendous blast. Only Zoë, sprawled on the slope of the rampart, head hanging over the lip of the canal, showed any sign of
life, her breast rising and falling, hand moving weakly, as she
tried to rise up.

•

Splinters dug into Sextus' hand, though the pain was barely noticeable against a rush of blood fire coursing through him.

Gasping for breath, he scrambled up the last section of ladder onto the mirror platform. The round, silvered disk was a man's height and blazed with a shimmering reflection of the noon sun. The metal surface was suspended in a wooden frame mounted on an iron wheel. Two Egyptian boys squatted on either side, faces wrapped with cloth, staring at him in surprise.

"You two," the engineer snapped, "swing the disk 'round to flash the dam!"

Stung by the fierce tone in his voice, the boys worked quickly, each working the arm of a screw mechanism to raise the disk. Sextus forced himself to lean back against the railing, out of the way, upper body hanging out over a dizzying sixty-foot drop. His knuckles turned white with strain while the boys rotated the screw, raising the disk a hand span. The metal ring at the base of the disk was freed from a locking pin on either side and one boy turned the disk—now rotating freely—toward the south. The other squinted across the muddy canals, over a huge, spreading swamp filled with glistening bogs, stands of green cane, acres of meandering waterway and drooping, thin-leaved trees.

Away through the mist rising from the wetland, Sextus caught a flash of light, a bright spark cutting through dirty gray haze. The lookout yelped at the same time, pointing, and both boys began making delicate adjustments to the orientation and incline of the disk.

A thudding boom echoed through the air and the engineer spun, heart thudding with fear, staring back to the north. From this southern elevation, even through trailing columns of smoke and dust, he could see both canals receding into the distance, straight as a plumb bob. The placement of the ramparts, their square-walled bastions, the even occurrence of watchtowers, the geometric efficiency of the fortifications was pleasingly regular.

A wave of flame billowed into the air—to Sextus' eye, an expanding sphere of overpressure as clear as the sun itself—blowing back smoke and dust with terrific force. Watchtowers swayed drunkenly in the hot gale, and secondary fires sparked as it passed. He saw something enormous and dark—*the god?*—stagger, then collapse toward the ground, vanishing like dew.

Within moments, while the boys sweated to adjust the disk, tremendous heat washed over the tower, making Sextus turn away, arm raised to shield his face. The mirror tower trembled, logs groaning, the disk rattling in its frame. Both Egyptians cried out, startled, and threw themselves onto the iron supports, clutching for dear life. The engineer hunkered down, letting the hot wind blow past, then looked again to the north.

Everything was in confusion. Even at this distance he could see tiny, still forms of the dead littering the ground. Sickened, his eyes darted to the breach in the first wall. A mass of Persians—their tan, yellow and brown cloaks clear to see—were forcing their way through the gap.

Oh gods! What do I do now? Sextus looked desperately to Aurelian's command post. The inner bastion was shrouded in smoke. Flames leapt up from hidden fires. *Are they dead? Has Caesar fallen?*

"Centurion?" One of the Egyptians clutched his arm. Sextus felt the world freeze, time sliding to a sickening halt. The boy's voice was hoarse with fear. "What message, Centurion? What message?"

Scorching wind roared against Khalid's face, blinding him. Shocked by the massive plume of light and heat rising over the Roman fortifications, the Arab hastily threw himself to the ground. A long, drawn out, rumbling crack of thunder echoed over the ramparts and canals, finally dying into a mutter over the desert. Cautious, Khalid looked up into silence and saw the smoke and fog gone, cleared away by the rush of wind. Less than twenty yards ahead, the Sahaba cowering in the rubble of the fallen wall stirred. Like Khalid, they had flattened with the explosion. The Roman legionaries peered back at them from the shelter of their shields. Even the Roman archers had fallen quiet and the air was free of whistling shafts.

"Men of Persia! With me!" Khalid bellowed into the silence, beating out the stentorian cry of a dozen Roman centurions by only heartbeats. The young Arab leapt up, shrugging the shield on his left arm into a secure grip, the ebon blade of the city whirling around his head. Hundreds of Persians and fresh Saha-ban fighters surged up from the canal with a great shout and to-gether they rushed into the breach. On the jagged ramparts to either side, more Persian *diquans* scrambled up the slope, a basso roar of "the Boar! the Boar!" ringing out.

Jalal loped alongside Khalid, his great bow strung. The young Arab stormed into the midst of the melee, where le-gionaries and Sahaban spearmen grappled in combat. A swift gray arrow, then another, whipped past Khalid as he ran, taking a legionary in the throat and eye only instants before the blade of night sheared through the man's guard and into his upper arm. Khalid shouted with glee, flashing a quick grin of thanks at the giant bowman, then the ebon edge of the sword flicked up, driving away a Roman's thrust.

The legionary overextended, his foot slipping on the broken ground, and Khalid turned sharply, arm lashing out, the keen edge of the sword cracking through a leather gorget and into the man's collarbone. Blood sprayed across the side of the soldier's face, then Khalid kicked him away. The Sahaba and the Per-sians pressed forward, driving back the stunned Romans. The young Arab saw the legionaries still suffering from the blast, which had struck them from behind, killing many and setting some afire.

A huge wedge of Shahr-Baraz' *pushtigbahn* crashed into the Romans along the northern roadway, their lamellar foot-to-crown iron armor proof against the legionary spears and swords. The Immortals chanted in unison, a hoarse, booming roar like the storm-tossed sea against a rocky shore. Khalid grinned again—the *pushtigbahn* swept the disordered legionar-ies back, capturing another hundred feet of roadway and ram-part. On his side of the breach, the Sahaba—now reinforced by Jalal and the more heavily armed and armored soldiers of the *qalb*—also gained ground.

With the smoke and fog blown back, Khalid could see across the second canal. The bastion whose siege engines had been hurling stones, burning pitch and iron bolts into their attack was afire. The jackal-god was gone, leaving a huge, blackened scar on the earthen rampart. The Roman mangonels and scorpions were burning, their watchtowers wrapped in flame. New smoke billowed up into the sky. Confusion, it seemed, reigned along the second line of defense as well.

He looked down, gauging the distance across the dry canal—another fifty feet of soft earth, spotted with muddy pools and wandering triangular fences of sharpened stakes—with a grimace. The Romans had planned well. He could lead his men across the canal, slopping through heavy mud and break down the obstructing fences, but this would take time. He squinted at the bastion and rampart opposite, then froze in alarm.

Roman troops appeared along the wall, looking about in stunned surprise, the sun glinting from their helmets. Already, men were working in the huge scar, piling up earth and broken beams, hastily building a barricade of ashy brick and wagons. Below them, below their archers and sharp-eyed centurions, a pair of figures lay on the slope, unmoving, unnoticed.

Zoë! Khalid thought, feeling his gut turn over with nausea, *and Odenathus. Are they dead?*

"Great Mars, how poorly we've served you today. . . ." Aurelian wiped soot from his eyes, hands black with ash. A small, bewildered group of Praetorians clustered around him, long cavalry swords drawn, faces and armor dusted dark gray. They were nervous—no Roman soldier was pleased to face magic and no one had never faced anything like this. Aurelian felt ill himself, off-balance and out of his depth. Watching the life drain from the priest of Horus had been wrenching. The hawk-faced man had seemed solid as old granite before the jackal stormed over the rampart, all smoke and fire and its single burning eye. "Runners! Where are my runners?"

One of the Praetorians turned, face white, his mouth tight with fear. "Dead, my lord."

Aurelian cursed, then took a breath to steady himself and scrambled up onto the remains of the fighting step running around the bastion. The explosion in the sky—whatever had struck down the jackal—had been devastating in the enclosed space below. Aurelian guessed he lived only due to luck and stout armor, but the crews on the siege engines, his couriers, and the priests had been without protection. Many now lay dead in heaps across the smoking, cracked earth.

Worse, the slope before him was stripped bare of stakes and entangling brush and a huge crevice split open the earthwork. The core of brick and wood had collapsed, the packed dirt falling away. Huge sections were fused into brittle, yellow-green glass. The fighting wall on the summit of the rampart was either on fire or blown down. Cautiously, Aurelian peered around the shoulder of a broken timber. Persian soldiers scrambled down into the dry canal, tan robes bright against the dark, muddy earth. The fighting in the breach on the first wall was dying down—the Persians driving back the legionaries on either side and pouring through the gap in a huge crowd.

"You'll have to do then," Aurelian barked, sliding back down the fighting step. "Manius, run to the seventh and eighth cohorts, they're waiting in reserve on the old road—get them here now. The enemy will try and rush the bastion, try to break through the broken section of the wall. Gnaeus, there are reserves on the first wall . . ." The prince pointed north, across the canal. The nearest forward bastion was already under attack from the inner road, robed figures climbing the sloping sides under a flitting cloud of arrows and javelins. ". . . in each strong point. Tell each bastion commander to detach one cohort and rush them to the breach. Titus—you go south of the attack—tell those commanders the same."

The three guardsmen sprinted off without a word. The other Praetorians leaned close, faces grim. The prince felt a strange disassociation between his thoughts—a swift torrent of considerations and decisions, his mind leaping ahead across hours, days, weeks—and the smoky air, the screams of the wounded, the peculiar brittle quality in the sky. He glanced over his shoulder again—the Persians were toiling across the canal in a mob. "The rest of you . . . gather up all the men you can find . . . shore up that wall; one of those scorpions is unharmed, get it working!"

Aurelian felt surety seize him, his confusion vanishing in a hard, bright instant of decision. His voice cleared, the hoarseness fading, ringing out. Everywhere within sight soldiers stiffened, looking towards him. The fear and confusion in their faces disappeared.

"Archers to the wall!" he boomed. "Don't let the Persians reach us in good order! Get the wounded back and hale men forward!"

Khalid gasped for breath, feet slipping in the loose, muddy earth. Persian *diquans* climbed past, the sun—slanting through clouds of dust and smoke—blazing from their swords and maces. The Arab took hold of a charred Roman stake and levered himself up another yard. A crowd of Sahaban fighters and *pushtigbahn* clambered past, silent and grim. A lone arrow snapped overhead. Behind Khalid, horns wailed in the heavy air. A glance over his shoulder revealed golden banners pouring through the break in the outer wall. Thousands of fresh Persian troops were coming up.

"Shields!" A cry echoed down from the top of the fortification. Metal and wood clashed, and a sudden wall of legionary shields appeared, horsetail helmet plumes dancing above the square-edged *scuta*. Khalid gathered himself, then sprinted up the slope, ash puffing up as he ran. The *pushtigbahn* and the Sahaba rushed forward as well, cloaks slapping against armor, breath loud and hoarse in the suddenly still air. The Romans tensed as well, the edges of their shields clanking one against the other.

"Throw!" a deep, bull-voice shouted and the Persians and Arabs threw themselves down, pressing against the earth, crouching behind their shields. Javelins flickered in the sky, falling among the attackers with a ringing clang. Immediately, the Arab soldiers rose and rushed forward again. Down on the floor of the canal, hundreds of their fellows raised a wild shout.

"Allau ak-bar!" the Sahaba screamed, charging up the last yards into the Roman lines.

Khalid scuttled sideways, ducking instinctively as a flight of arrows flashed up from the canal. The Arab archers were shooting blind, lofting their shafts high above the rampart, letting the arrows fall into the space behind the line of battle. Khalid ignored them and the men struggling along the crest of the wall—

everything but the shattered earth in front of him. He slipped over the lip of the crater, wincing at the heat radiating out of the burned, glassy earth.

Two bodies lay within the blackened circle. The jackal-headed man was curled up in the base of the hollow, while Odenathus—his face streaked with blood and soot—was crumpled only a few feet away. Suppressing a cry of despair, Khalid crawled down to his friend. His outstretched hand touched cold, clammy flesh and the young Arab felt his heart race. Odenathus' head rolled back, mouth slack, eyes sightless. Khalid crouched in the crater, ear pressed to his friend's chest. A faint flutter of breath rewarded him.

"You're alive, at least . . ." Khalid whispered to the unconscious Palmyrene. Still keeping his head low, the Arab slid down into the hollow, boots cracking through a brittle, glassy crust. Fresh steam rushed out, scalding his leg. Gasping with pain, Khalid rolled away from the sizzling vent. Biting his lip to keep from crying out, the Arab wrapped his cloak around both hands, then crawled up the far side of the crater. Zoë's leg lay within the ashy circle, but her body was exposed on the slope.

A sudden burst of shouts and the clatter of iron made Khalid turn. A javelin whipped past, thudding into the dirt beside Zoë's foot. The Arab yelped in surprise, then scrambled up out of the crater and threw himself onto the girl. Another javelin whipped past. Some Arab archers in the canal yelled, pointing. Khalid gave Zoë's body a heavy push with his boot—the girl slid down the slope, arms flopping. The archers began climbing up, eager to reach her. One of them rose up too far—another Roman javelin plunged down out of the sky and crunched into his chest. Surprised, the man toppled back, bow flying from his hand.

A deep roar echoed from the top of the rampart. Khalid spared a glance and saw a huge mob of *pushtigbahn* clatter up the slope and into the melee. The Romans staggered back, the *diquans* wading in among them, heavy maces flashing, long swords glittering crimson. Then a brawny, red-bearded legionary stormed into their midst, smashing his shield into the face of a Persian knight, knocking the man back down the slope. The *diquan* smashed into two of his fellows—still toiling up the incline—and all three fell in a huge bang of metal. Khalid wrenched his attention away, scuttling around the rim of the smoking crater. Odenathus' body felt light—he was wearing only a padded mail shirt under his tunic—and Khalid grunted, taking the man's weight across his shoulders.

Staggering, his boots cracking through shattered glass, Khalid weaved back to the edge of the canal. Zoë's body had slid down to the archers. Eager hands seized her armor and cloak, dragging her into a cluster of Sahaba.

"Run!" Khalid shouted, gesturing wildly. "Take her across!"

The archers looked up, surprised. Khalid bent, spilling Odenathus down the gravelly slope. The Palmyrene slid, picking up speed, rolling over and over. Two of the archers threw themselves under him, catching the wizard. Khalid swung over the lip of the crater, shoulder blades itching in warning. A sharp rattling sound split the air. Khalid ducked, pressing himself into the hot earth. A scream echoed back. One of the archers had taken a sling stone in the face. Blood spurted, the man clawing at a ruined eye.

The Arab pushed himself down the slope, dirt spilling away under him.

"The jackal!" a hoarse, sharp voice shouted. Khalid looked up as his feet hit the bottom of the rampart, sinking into thick mud. Zoë was struggling weakly among the men carrying her. Her white face was very plain against the dark earth, the soot-stained faces of the archers, the sky filled with smoke and dust. "Get the jackal!" A mail-clad finger stabbed back at the crater.

Khalid cursed vilely. Arrows fluttered out of the sky, falling like rain. One of the Sahaba, only yards away, rose up, loosed his own shaft at the Romans high above, then ducked down again. The Eagle pulled one boot free from the mire. He wiped his mouth, smearing blood across his cheek. Zoë was still struggling, though the men holding her were far stronger. "Get the jackal!" she wailed.

"Are you mad?" Khalid pressed himself close to the rampart, trying to hide from the missiles plunging down from above. He stared back at the girl, still struggling, then fearfully at the melee on the slope above. *Can't leave wizards just lying about! He might even be alive . . .*

The young Arab clawed at the earth, pulling himself back up the wall. Cautiously, he peered over the edge. The Persian attack had broken. The Immortals lay dead in drifts along the rampart, while the Sahaba were falling back in disarray. A huge crowd of legionaries formed up on the crest of the wall, faces exhausted, but obviously game for a second go. Khalid scrambled across the crater, pulse hammering in his ears. He grabbed the jackal's bare foot, fingers slipping from a layer of sweat. Khalid tugged violently, dragging the man towards him.

Someone shouted sharply in Latin. Khalid grabbed the ankle with both hands, digging his feet in and hauled for all he was worth. The jackal slid across the crater floor towards him, shoulders crunching through glass. A sling stone slapped into the mud, splashing Khalid's face. Biceps burning, he gave another huge heave. The jackal slipped free of the mire and fell into his arms.

An arrow leapt down out of the sky, slamming into the jackal's chest. Khalid grunted, stunned by the blow. The iron arrowhead pierced the body and grated against the iron links of his mail shirt. Sick with fear, Khalid rolled backwards, slipping over the lip of the crater. A roar of Roman laughter followed him, then jeering cries.

Unable to catch himself, Khalid fell heavily into the canal, then the jackal crashed down on top of him. The iron mask cracked sharply against his forehead and the young Arab cried out. Everything was spinning, the earth shaking, a growing roar rushing towards him. Dazed, Khalid struggled under the body, heavy black mud sliding up around his arms and legs, oozing into his armor.

"Release me!" Zoë punched one of the archers in the face, feeling his nose break under the iron rings of her glove. The man gasped, falling back, and she shrugged free of the others. She felt terribly weak—her sight in the hidden world came and went in disorienting flashes—but the crumpled shape of the jackal filled her vision. "We have to get him back," she hissed at the archers.

Without waiting for their response, she staggered forward, mud sucking at her boots. The Sahaba fell back from her in confusion as someone began shouting in alarm. Zoë ignored the noise, slogging through deeper mud to seize the jackal-headed man's belt. The leather was soft and slippery but she managed to get her fingers around the band. Grunting, she leaned away, levering the corpse against her thigh. With a greasy sound, the body slid away from Khalid. The young Arab thrashed weakly as he tried to stand up. Zoë heaved again, a hiss of breath escaping gritted teeth, and turned the jackal over. The corpse was heavy and cold, the eyes of the mask dark pits, exposed flesh puckered with small stones and a dark gash where an arrow pierced the chest.

"Wake up!" Zoë kicked the dead man viciously in the side. "Get up!"

A Roman slingstone snapped past, splashing into the mud. Khalid rose up, black with mud from head to toe. "Get down yourself!" he hissed at Zoë as he crouched, eyes flickering back and forth, watching for the next missile.

Zoë knelt and rapped her hand sharply on the jackal mask. It boomed hollow, red paint flaking away among carbonized metal and soot. "Make these limbs move," she shouted into a tall, blunt-pointed ear. "We have to get out of here!"

"Captain! Captain!" One of the archers splashed towards them, pointing upstream. "Look!"

Zoë turned, dark brown eyes narrowed in anger at the interruption. She froze, eyebrow rising in surprise. A rushing hiss reached her ears, and she could see a glistening brown wall rushing down the canal towards her. "Khalid," she said calmly. "Grab hold of the other arm."

"What?" Another slingstone snapped past his ear, making the Arab duck violently. "We've no time to—*urk!*"

Zoë twisted his head around, sharp fingernails digging into his ear. Khalid yelped, then shouted in alarm when he saw the onrushing water. "A flood!"

"You men—" Zoë cursed, seeing the backs of the archers climbing the far bank of the canal. Heedless of the water rumbling towards her in a slick green-brown wave, Zoë crouched, digging her arm into the muck, under the jackal's body. The corpse was sinking deeper. "Khalid, help me!"

The young Arab wrenched his attention away from the

slowly building wave. He was green himself, but shook free of his paralysis and grabbed hold of an arm and a leg. Together, they tugged at the body. It came free with agonizing slowness, black mud oozing away from pallid limbs. Without waiting for the legs to come completely free, they staggered together toward the eastern wall of the canal.

Distant laughter hooted in the air. The slingstones stopped falling. Zoë, forcing herself forward, foot by foot, mud sucking at her boots, had a wild, brief image of legionaries crouched on the rampart, calling bets on her, on Khalid, even on the corpse. The rushing water was close now, the hiss rising sharply to a roar. Zoë splashed on, boots filling with water. Khalid stumbled, dragging the corpse down as he fell. Zoë felt the slick, gelid dead arm slide over her shoulder. Desperately, she clutched at sinewy brown fingers. Her right foot sank deep into the mud. Khalid went down, the corpse slumping over on top of him. The oncoming water roared, drowning out all other sound.

A chill washed over Zoë, despite the close, humid air and sweat running from her temples and shoulders. Sick with fear, she dragged her left foot free, losing the boot. Khalid's arms clawed desperately at the mud, trying to keep his head above the muddy slurry rising in the canal. Zoë lunged forward, grabbed his hand, then set her legs, hauling back with all her strength. The jackal slipped sideways, falling into swiftly rising brown water. Khalid floundered up, splashing. Zoë spun him around, pushing towards the sloping wall of the canal. Brown water, thick with twigs and leaves, washed around her waist.

Tugged by rushing water, the jackal's corpse drifted sideways, head dragged down by the weight of the mask.

Zoë groped to catch the dead man, but the current snatched him away. Cursing again, she surged forward, splashing through chest-high water. The wave swept over her and the Palmyrene felt herself lifted up by rushing water. Biting her lip, she made one last grab for the jackal—caught his leg—then the wave slammed her into the side of the canal. Muddy water flooded into her mouth. Zoë choked, gasping, fingers digging into the cold flesh of the jackal's leg.

"Help!" she choked out. Hands reached down for her, filling her vision with writhing tan worms. Someone caught her hair, then her flailing arm. She slammed into the side of the canal again, breath punched from her chest. Still, she clung to the jackal with a death grip. A lasso settled around her shoulders, then the water began to fall and she was dragged free of the muddy roil by a dozen hands.

Khalid's face appeared, blocking out a blazing sun, and his teeth were very white in the dark silhouette of his face. "She looks angry," Zoë heard him say from a great distance. "She'll live!"

Zoë choked, coughed, spit nut-brown water and bits of leaves out on the ground. Gagging, she heaved, managing a thin stream of yellow bile. Her mouth was filled with fine grit, making her cough again. "Water . . ." she managed to say. The mouthpiece of a water skin banged her in the eye, then she managed to take a drink, spat, drank again, clearing her mouth. "Where is the jackal?"

"Here, my lady." Two of the Sahaba, tan-and-white robes stained brown to the chest, dragged the still-cold and unmoving shape of the man, Arad, to her. They dumped him on the ground, metal mask clanging dully on the logs of the rampart road.

Zoë crawled to the corpse, raising herself up on one arm. Brown water leaked from the mask, puddling under the man's head. Fingers trembling, Zoë touched his neck and throat. The flesh was cold and greasy. "Wake up," she growled. She coughed again, spitting up silt. "Wake up!"

There was a shuffling around her as the Sahaba drew away, muttering. Zoë's face contorted, a blue spark flaring in her eyes. Her hand, stiff with anger, slapped hard against the cold iron. The mask rang like a bell, ringing with tinny echoes. The girl's hand blazed blue-white for an instant and the iron mask split open. Grunting, Zoë wrenched aside the metal fragments, revealing a battered face, still and pale, without even the faintest motion of life.

"Oh, no . . ." The Queen's voice faltered, falling into a faint whisper.

"What is it?" Odenathus appeared, kneeling beside her. Half of his face was burned red, his cloak in tatters, tunic and armor charred. Khalid crouched at his side, noble young face stiff with worry. The Queen looked up, eyes bright with tears.

"I think he is dead," she managed, then covered her mouth with a mud-caked hand.

Odenathus leaned over the body, lips a thin, tight line. Gently, he removed the remaining pieces of the mask. The man on the ground was thin, cadaverous—a once-handsome face badly scarred by old wounds. The lips were black and stretched tight against jaw and teeth. The young Palmyrene pressed his hand against a hollow cheek, leaning close, listening.

"Nothing . . ." he started to say.

Black lips opened with a wet, rattling gasp. Odenathus jumped back in surprise, eyes wide in fear. The body twitched, fingers scrabbling on the muddy logs. Then the head rose, and sunken eyes blazed with sullen green flame. "There is still an edge on this knife," echoed a dreadful voice from a dead throat.

Khalid drew back, the blade of night halfway free from its sheath. Odenathus stared in horror, watching slow life rise in the corpse limbs, muscles swelling with strength, the skin flushing with warm color. The Queen stiffened, her face growing tight. A tic began at the corner of her jaw, then she turned away, covering her face with the charred corner of her cloak.

The dead man rose, joints creaking. The head swiveled, looking to the west, mouth stretching into a cruel grin. "Where are the busy bees now?" it coughed wetly. "Dead, dead in the hive . . ."

"Heave!" shouted a *diquan*, helmet slung on a strap over his shoulder, tightly curled beard shining with sweat. "Heave!"

Two hundred men, stripped to the waist, muscled backs gleaming with sweat, moved as one. A thunderous shout of *"ho!"* boomed out. Cables drew taut and then a plank roadbed rumbled forward. Palm logs splintered, rolling under the weight of the bridge section as the wooden truss edged over the lip of the canal. Persian soldiers splashed away from falling logs, then the section slid out, cables stiff, and ground into place atop the first wooden pier.

Shahr-Baraz stood atop the Roman wall, looking down on the outer canal. He smiled, a broad, feral grin shining through the sweep of his mustache. Delighted, he slapped his thigh with a gloved hand, turning to the men standing beside him. "Well done, captains! At this rate we'll have four bridges across the outer canal by nightfall."

"And then what?" Khalid squatted on the wooden platform, face lined with exhaustion. He pointed with his chin. "The Romans have cut down every man who managed to get across the ditch. The gaps in their wall are already repaired . . . their bastions on this wall by the sea still hold out. You expect us to attack across a flooded canal, up that spike-strewn slope and into the teeth of their javelins, spears, swords?"

The Boar nodded absently, pacing across the decking. The burned remains of a Legion mangonel listed to one side, half pushed from its base. The sun, swollen to an enormous orange disk by the smoke-heavy air, almost touched the western horizon. He paused at the edge of the platform, boot braced against the wooden sill, lean face painted with dying golden light. Already the canal was deep in gloom—dark purple water rolled slowly past—and beyond, the Roman wall was studded with lamps and torches. Two of his Immortals moved up, as quietly as their iron-shod boots allowed, big oval shields in hand and placed themselves between the king and his enemies.

"This is a narrow place," he said, rumbling voice quiet in rumination. "The barrier of the flooded canal is not so great—the water is shallow, the width only fifty feet. They cannot surprise us again with a flood. They have no bridges of their own—or none they will risk to our fire arrows. Tonight I will send fresh men forward and we will root the Romans from their nests on the first wall. They will not expect a night attack. Tomorrow, if we clear the forts at the canal mouth, we will strike again." A broad hand stabbed from north to south. "We will attack along the length of the wall, all at once. The Immortals will form a reserve, ready to leap into any breach."

The Persian captains shifted uneasily, but no one spoke out against the king. Shahr-Baraz turned, eyes gleaming under a golden circlet as he took their measure. Only Khalid showed his disapproval openly, with a black scowl. "We are not without means," the Boar said. "The power that threw down the Roman sorcerers today is still with us—unharmed! Our bridges will soon ford the first canal. There are light boats to be brought forward . . . our men will not struggle in the water."

Shahr-Baraz fought to suppress a grin of triumph as he spoke, but enthusiasm and confidence welled up in him, spilling out in vigorous gestures and a steadily rising voice. Slowly, the Persian captains began to nod, to agree. Some, like the prince of Balkh, Piruz, were desperately eager to attack. Despite the losses suffered in their foray across the second canal, the Immortals were set on proving themselves. The loss of nearly eight hundred of their number—trapped on the further rampart, pinned between the Legions and the flooded canal— had not dampened their appetite for glory.

Only the Arab, Khalid, remained unconvinced. The Boar watched the young man out of the corner of his eye. *He's thinking about today,* Shahr-Baraz realized. *He reckons the number of his dead—and does not like the tally! I will have to hold back his men from battle tomorrow . . .* The King of Kings suppressed a frown. The valor of the Arabs would be sorely missed. His Greeks and Persians were skilled soldiers, true, but they lacked the heedless bravery of the Arabs—the men from the south did not fear death, embracing a chance to join their Teacher in death's paradise. Their attack was like a thunderbolt . . . perfect to break open the orderly Roman line.

Shahr-Baraz put the thoughts aside. His men needed to see utter confidence from their captains, to forget the closeness of the day's struggle, to forget the rows of the dead or those swept away by the sudden flood. Nearly three thousand Persians, Arabs and Greeks had fallen today. Who knew how many Romans had died? Not quite so many, Shahr-Baraz guessed. But the enemy had lost their first line of defense, and they had not expected such an outcome. A feral grin welled on his lips. *Tomorrow will bring the same result . . .*

The Boar turned away from the riot of color in the western sky, from the Roman fortifications and the shadow-filled canal. He looked to the east, and his eyes—still keen despite advancing age—quickly picked out darkness against darkness. The Serpent, crouching fearfully among his Huns and iron wands. *Your great fear was unfounded, little snake,* he thought, smugly pleased. *Only the Legion thaumaturges faced your servants today. Your "great enemy" is not here!*

Shahr-Baraz was sure the Romans had suffered terrible losses among their magi. Tomorrow, the Serpent would reveal himself, his power unfettered by fear or caution. There would be a great slaughter and the Legions would break like glass.

"Come," the King of Kings boomed. "Come my friends. Let us go down to my tents, where a fine, rich feast is ready upon the table. Maidens are waiting, with wine in silver cups, with flowers in their long hair. You are hungry and tired. But victory is ours and your labors will be rewarded!" The king swept through the cluster of men, slapping some on the shoulder, meeting the eyes of others. They moved to follow him automatically, without a second thought, drawn in by his good humor, his confidence, the undimmed sun of his bravura. They descended the slope in a clatter of metal and tired, cheerful voices.

Only Khalid remained on the platform, sitting in shadow, exhausted, his face drawn and pale. His eyes were drawn to the west, to the Roman *limes*, where the legionaries were still at work by torchlight, digging and shoring, strengthening their walls of stone and earth and wood. Preparing for another day of battle.

A log creaked. Khalid woke with a start, disoriented. The sky had grown dark, the sun long down in the west, plunging the land into a close, warm darkness. A shape appeared out of the night, booted feet illuminated by a softly glowing paper lantern.

"Hello, Khalid." Zoë was limping a little, but she settled beside him on the logs with her usual deft grace, a covered basket in one hand. "I brought you some food." She folded back the cloth and Khalid felt dizzy—the smell of fresh bread and roasted lamb flooded up from the basket. Greedily, all good manners brushed aside by sudden hunger, he tore into the crispy loaf and dripping meat. After a moment, Zoë—nose wrinkled up at his haste—handed him a water flagon. Thirsty, he drank until the damp leather was dry and pinched. When he was done, he looked sideways at her, face stiff as a mask, suddenly embarrassed.

"Thank you," he managed, in a very formal tone. Zoë nodded slightly in response, hands clasped around her knees. She was looking out into the darkness, watching lines of torches wiggle among the Roman works. Like the young Arab, she seemed tired, exhausted by the day's struggle.

After a moment, Khalid shifted a little, growing nervous. He turned toward her, dark eyes narrowed in suspicion. "Why did you bring me the food?"

Zoë did not answer. She continued to watch the slow procession of yellow and orange lights across the canal. With the sun gone to his night bed, the surface of the canal reflected the Legion fires and lanterns, making shimmering warm constellations in the oily water.

Khalid, watching her now by the same dim, flickering light, realized she was overcome by sadness. Faint pearls of moisture gathered at the corner of her eyes and her bow-shaped lips were pressed tight against welling emotion. He drew back, unsure of what to say or do, and drew the cowl of his cape over his head. To his disgust, the linen was scored with charred holes. Shaking his head in dismay, he poked a finger through one of the larger openings, then snorted with laughter. "Roman moths."

"Hmmm." Zoë looked sideways at him, the faint ghost of a smile emerging from her desolate mood. "I don't think cedar shavings will keep them away from your cloak."

Khalid pulled the cloak onto his knees, then sighed in dismay to see soot blackening the fabric. Most of the cloth was burned away or reduced to a tangle of threads. He made an equally sad face. "Ruined."

Zoë stood. "You'll get another. The King of Kings would be pleased to gift you something rich—with golden thread and rich, soft silk. Far better than these scraps."

Khalid looked up, shaking his head. "I don't want a new one . . . the Teacher's aunt made this cloak for me, before we left Mekkah." He rolled the fabric between his fingers, watching flakes of charred thread pill away under his thumb and forefinger. "It was my favorite."

Zoë rose, making a sharp, dismissive motion with her hand. "It's just a cloak," she said. "A Persian one will fit you just as well."

Khalid stared after the Queen as she padded off down the slope. For a moment, she was a pale shape against the engulfing night, then she was gone. A peculiar sick feeling coiled in his stomach. He wondered how many of his men would be wearing Persian tunics, cloaks, armor when the sun rose again. *Too many,* he thought. *Too many.*

◽◾◽◾◽◾◽◾◽◾◽◾◽◾◽◾◽◾◽◾◽◾◽◾◽◾◽◾◽◾◽◾◽◾◽◾

THE MARE INTERNUM, EAST OF SICILY

⌖

"I don't know," Betia said slowly, biting her lip, looking from the imposing figure of Mithridates, late afternoon sun gleaming from smooth, glossy muscle, to Vladimir, bare-chested and peeling red. "They both look equally large. . . ." Her bright blue eyes traveled back to the African.

"Perhaps if you flexed them again, I could tell." Smiling, she kicked her heels against the boards of the foredeck anchor housing. A hundred feet of tarred rope lay coiled within, threaded through a cored-out marble bust. When they had last anchored, off the Sicilian shore, the head of Perseus had rested on a sandy bottom, where Betia could trace the taut line of the cable plunging through clear, sapphire water.

Grunting, the two men clenched their fists, biceps bulging. In truth, Betia was having a hard time determining which man's arms were larger, whose muscles were more tightly corded. She put her chin on her palm, paying close attention. The African grimaced at the Walach and Vladimir squinted back ferociously, baring long, white incisors.

"Hmmm . . ." Betia said, distracted again. "This is very difficult."

Thyatis settled onto the deck beside Nicholas, her long cavalry sword in one hand, a bundle of rags, a whetstone and oil in the other. With the sky still warm with summer, she had stripped down to a short linen kilt and a Persian-style shirt. Nicholas looked up, surprised—the woman's bare feet made no sound on the smooth deck—and his nostrils flared in response to her smile.

"Nice blade," she said, sitting cross-legged. Out of the corner of her eye, she caught his immediate frown and there was an abrupt click as he slid the steel back into a battered, worn leather sheath. An afterimage lingered for a moment—sunlight burning on a slick, oiled metal bar three fingers wide, a long series of squared-off glyphs flaring as they vanished into darkness. "True steel?"

"Yes," Nicholas said gruffly, averting his eyes.

Nodding companionably, Thyatis slid out her own blade, a heavy *spatha*-style sword, the surface mottled with the waterfall pattern typical of Eastern swordcraft. Pursing her lips, Thyatis hefted the sword, turning it this way and that in the sunlight, squinting at the surface. Then, with careful deliberation, she picked a clean cloth out of the bundle and began to oil the blade.

"This one's Rajput work," she said after a bit, when Nicholas' breathing had settled. "My second one. The first was . . . ah . . . lost in a bad fight. The Duchess was kind enough to find me a replacement."

"Good," Nicholas said, after sitting in silence, listening to the careful burr of the whetstone along the steel. "Hard to get a good blade these days . . . the Legions or the generals take them all."

"Expensive, you mean," Thyatis said, lifting the sword again and letting the sun slide slowly down the edge, eyes intent, watching for imperfections, scratches or oily fingerprints. Across the deck there was a sharp grunt and the Roman woman looked up. Mithridates had his arm out, stiff, and Betia, small, pale hands gripping his teak-dark forearm, was doing pull-ups. The Walach was watching, a huge grin on his face, and laughing. Thyatis froze for a moment, letting painful memories rise, then fade. *The past*, she thought sadly. *Not today*. Then she forced a smile. "Vladimir seems a good companion—you two been together long?"

"Three years, almost." Nicholas settled the battered sheath across his knees. Quick, nimble fingers rooted among his own gear, finding a bottle of heavy, dark oil. He began to treat the scabbard, working the oil in with his fingers. "I was working for the Eastern Office, doing cleanup work, odd jobs, you know the kind of thing . . . there was a sea attack on the city. We were on the same boat. I went overboard, to cut a tangled line free . . . he jumped in after me, the oaf!"

"Can he swim?" Thyatis turned her sword over and began to work on the reverse.

"He can now." Nicholas shook his head. "The big idiot was wearing scaled armor—like he is today!—must weigh sixty, seventy pounds; but he's strong, very strong. Between the two of us, we kept from drowning. He doesn't like the water, though . . . makes him nervous just to see a boat."

"Like a cat," she said, deadpan.

"Huh. Like a cat." Nicholas looked sideways at her. "You've met a Walach before?"

"I've heard some tales," she replied, keeping her voice light. "He get hungry much?"

"Sometimes . . ." Nicholas sighed, rubbing the back of his hand against his nose. "He counts us all as family, though . . . he won't think your maid a tasty snack or something."

Thyatis' lips twitched, then she looked back across the deck. Now Vladimir had his arm out level and Betia had drawn herself up, arms stiff on his forearm, body balanced over his fist and was slowly swinging her legs up over her head. The muscles of her back and shoulders were sharp as razors. Vladimir watched with open appreciation, stiff with the effort of holding her entire weight with one arm. "Betia's not a maid."

"Ah-huh. Why bring her, then?" Nicholas scratched his head and Thyatis realized he was truly puzzled. She hid a sigh, thinking, *but what do you expect? He has no idea what kind of training she's been through. . . .*

"She's our messenger, our spy in the marketplace, our quiet, hidden eyes in a crowded street." Thyatis pointed at the African and the Walach with the point of her blade. "Each tool to a purpose, my friend. Strength, size, speed, a deadly eye—not much use if you don't know where to go, who to kill, where to find a missing pouch of letters . . . our little Betia is worth her weight in gold, or more." She looked back at Nicholas, grinning. "You'll see."

"I suppose." Nicholas twisted the ends of his mustache in a nervous gesture. "You won't be worrying about her if things get hot, then? I would . . ."

"Are you going to worry about me?" Thyatis' voice settled into a professionally level tone. "Why would you worry about her and not about Vladimir? Or Mithridates?"

Nicholas made a face and raised a hand as if to deflect the question. "I see. We'll each take care of our own business."

"What we'll do," Thyatis said softly, eyes narrowed in a hard glare, "is trust each other. If any of us are in trouble, the others will help, but we won't assume Betia, or I, or you, require 'looking after.' Do you follow?"

"Yes," Nicholas said, rising from the deck. Thyatis could see he was irritated.

"Good," she said, rising as well. "Let's spar. I'm starting to feel rusty, sitting on this damp boat." She stepped back, clearing some space. The Indian steel blade gleamed in her hand, point drifting towards the deck, her grip light on the hilt.

Nicholas stared at her as though the seas had parted, revealing Typhon in all his awful glory. "What? You want to fight?"

"Yes," Thyatis said, letting her body relax into stance, shoulders level, rising up on the balls of her feet. It felt good, even to begin the proper exercise of form. The sword quivered, a seamless extension of her hand and will. "We need the practice—and the time will past the quicker for some honest sweat!"

Nicholas blinked, watching her, and he shook his head suddenly. "No—I won't. Not with bare steel! Let us take staves and spar with them instead." Thyatis saw his knuckles turning white on the hilt of the blade. *He's afraid*, she thought in amazement. *Afraid he'll hurt me. How strange!*

Chuckling, Thyatis sheathed her sword. Given the man's reaction, there was no point in pressing the matter. "Very well," she said. "The staff it is, then."

Relief flooded Nicholas' face and he tossed the scabbard to Vladimir, who had wandered over. The big Walach caught the weapon from the air with one hand. Mithridates was right behind him, Betia riding his shoulders, arms crossed on his bald head, pale legs tucked into his armpits. "Vlad—are there staves about?"

Thyatis rolled her neck, then deftly caught a length of oak tossed by the African. She spun the wooden staff in her hand, flipping it across her shoulders and into her other hand. Nicholas had his in hand as well and now his body relaxed into a fighting pose—not quite the same as Thyatis'. She saw he'd been trained by a master emphasizing power and the striking blow. She shifted her feet, turning a little away from him, hands sliding on the smooth wood. The hiss of bloodfire began to trickle through her and she grinned wide, feeling suddenly awake.

Nicholas began to circle, his feet very light on the deck.

⊡〔O〕·〔O〕·〔O〕·〔O〕·〔O〕·〔O〕·〔O〕·〔O〕·〔O〕·〔O〕·〔O〕·〔O〕·〔O〕·〔O〕·〔O〕⊡

THE VILLA OF SWANS, ROMA MATER

〕I〔

Anastasia stood at the edge of her garden, watching one of the serving girls hurry down the steps from the kitchen, platters of spiced eggs balanced in either hand, weaving through a thick crowd of citizens and freedmen. The guests were lively, talking loudly, drinking heavily, taking full advantage of the liberal feast provided by the Duchess. The girl turned sideways, up on tiptoe, and slid between the enormous bulk of a grain merchant, his coterie of henna-haired "nieces" and a cluster of grim-faced Legion officers. The soldiers were drinking heavily, sitting glum and quiet on benches lining the colonnade around the heart of the villa.

The maid breezed past, through columns glowing with copper Hispanian lamps and strings of cut glass and down into the garden. The arbor was heavy with lanterns and the wooden bridge crossing the stream was lit from below with the flickering glow of dozens of candle boats. Even with the evening well advanced, the center of the house was filled with laughter and light. Despite the festive atmosphere, Anastasia was content to stand in the shadow of rowan trees hanging over the garden's edge; pale, perfect face stippled with distant lamplight, watching the ebb and flow of her guests. Her invitations—each hand delivered by a phalanx of slaves—had incited a huge response. The porters and door guards had been turning away eager guests at the morning meal, and by noon the front gates were closed and barred against an expectant crowd. Eager guests flooded into the house at the earliest opportunity—even before the bakers and cooks finished the first course of the evening-long dinner. Anastasia allowed herself a small smile—she may have been in mourning a long time, but she remembered how to entertain and Rome's fickle social memory had not yet forgotten her.

Today, I am novelty! she thought. *Tomorrow? Day-old bread, a copper a loaf.*

Rising voices in the great hall, eager, nervous and excited caught her ear. *The Emperor?* Anastasia checked her hair—flowing loose, in dark, glossy waves, only barely restrained by threads of pearl and gold—then her gown and stole. The dress was new and modest, as befitted such troubled times. Still, the slick fabric clung eagerly to her breasts and flowed over hip and thigh in a cascade of ultramarine Chin silk. The spark in men's eyes was reward enough, even if she felt positively demure.

Across the garden, a crowd of people in the main hall parted, some bowing. Anastasia's violet eyes narrowed and then she frowned. *Not the Emperor. He's being fashionably late.* She was disappointed. *The so-current prince, and his . . .* The Duchess scowled. *. . . consort? Companion? Private secretary?*

Maxian entered, properly attired in a formal toga and tunic, only the traditional bare feet of the custos magicum departing from a patrician's ideal. Martina, hanging on his arm, hip pressed to his side, had not been limited by such social constraints. The Eastern Empress's usually plain brown hair was tightly curled and ornamented with brilliant jewels. Martina's gold-laced gown, silky transparent drape, her shoes—everything bespoke wealth and power. The Duchess grimaced, noting the possessive hand—studded with golden bracelets and glittering jewels—wrapped around Maxian's arm. The girl smiled brilliantly, and Anastasia's eyes narrowed. *Bleached teeth? Where did she find a wizard to—where else? Ah, child—what am I to do with you?*

Biting her thumb in annoyance, the Duchess strode out of the shadows and paused for a heartbeat at the top of the stairs. Not one head turned toward her. Everyone in the garden was focused on the prince and upon his too-brilliant companion. Schooling her face to genteel welcome, Anastasia descended to the grassy sward, the fingers of her left hand touching the edge of her scooped neckline.

"Lord Prince Maxian," she purred, gliding through the crowd of senators and their wives clogging the entrance to the main hall. "My lady, Empress Martina, welcome to my house." Anastasia caught the prince's eye, smiled warmly, then turned to the younger woman and bowed gracefully, taking her hand in greeting.

"Empress," she said, turning away from the prince and leading Martina forward, out of the clutch of sycophants crowding the girl, to the edge of the marble steps. "I hope my garden pleases you."

Martina answered her smile with a faint grimace of her own and Anastasia felt a sharp moment of satisfaction, seeing ill-disguised fear hiding behind the girl's kohl-ornamented eyes and lead-white face powders. "It's . . . beautiful," the Empress managed, trying to turn back, looking for Maxian. "The lamps are very pretty."

"They are," Anastasia said, squeezing Martina's hand and descending the steps. The Empress, unwilling to cast off her hostess' hand, followed. "Have you seen my stream before? A cistern above the house lets it flow and the water is recaptured below by a clever siphon." Anastasia leaned close to Martina as she spoke, as if they shared a confidence during temple services. Still unwilling to protest, though looking more and more startled with each moment, Martina found herself beside the stream, candlelight shining on her face.

Anastasia spared a sideways glance behind her and was pleased to see the prince entirely surrounded by a thick crowd of well-wishers and men in search of Imperial favor. *Good,* she thought, *I've a few moments, then.*

"The boats are very beautiful," Martina said, her fancy caught by the tiny manikins of boatmen and ladies placed around the paper cones holding the candles. Caught in the slow current of the stream, the little craft were slowly bumping and whirling as they passed down the stream. "What happens when they go out of the garden?"

"Shhh . . ." Anastasia bent close, finger to plum-colored lips, eyes twinkling. "We mustn't speak of such things or the illusion will be spoiled." Martina answered with her own faint smile. The Duchess squeezed her hand again, radiating warmth, the tilt of her head inviting secret confidence. "I hope you enjoy the party," she said softly. "I know you must be dying to dance or hear the musicians or do *anything* but toil through dusty scrolls . . ."

"You've no idea!" Martina said, surprised and pleased. For the first time, her face opened, losing the frightened mask. "Maxian is a dear—but he'll work until everyone is *dead* without notice or a care! I have to speak quite forcefully to him, sometimes."

"Good," Anastasia said in an approving voice. "Some young men need guidance or they'll ignore the house while it burns." She gestured to one of the maids, politely lurking just out of earshot. The girl hurried over with a pair of fluted, delicate glasses, half-filled with a sparkling golden draught. "Here, my dear," Anastasia said, deftly taking both glasses. "Try this—it will make you forget your cares! It's from Gaul."

Martina drank from hers, both small hands on the glass. She tasted, her nose wrinkled up, she sneezed, and then she laughed. "Oh dear! It has bubbles!" Embarrassed, the Empress covered her mouth.

"It does," Anastasia said, taking a sip. The liquor was sweet and sharp on her tongue. "There is a temple of Dionysos in Gallica Belgica, where the vines are blessed and the wine light and delightful. My late husband owned some shares. . . ." She raised the glass, tipping it against Martina's in a toast. ". . . and I have reaped the bounty of his investment for many years." The Duchess smiled again, leaning close to Martina. "But I do not share it with just *anyone*."

Martina smiled back, eyes twinkling. "Well, thank you for your confidence, Duchess. I am glad to be out of hot foundry rooms and in clean, breathable air!"

Anastasia was about to reply when a peal of bronze-throated

trumpets sounded, ringing back from the high, curved ceiling with a martial blast. Everyone froze, silent expectation settling over the crowd, then all turned as one. A brace of Praetorians, breastplates gleaming silver in the lamps, appeared in the main hall. The mob of senators and merchants and Legion officers parted.

Drat! fumed the Duchess, catching sight of Martina's open, happy face closing up, becoming suspicious and mask-like. *Just another few minutes and we'd have been best friends. . . .*

The Emperor appeared at the top of the steps, his son settled on one hip, his wife's hand raised shoulder height in his own. He was clad in pure white linen, a circlet of golden holly imprisoning his habitually lank hair and dark red boots. Beside him, the Empress of the West was appropriately subdued, in a dark, velvety brown, highlighted with old red gold at her neck, wrists and around her thin waist.

"The Augustus and God," bawled one of the Praetorians, his voice booming through the garden, "Galen Atreus, Emperor of the West, Protector of the East! The noble Empress, Helena, and their son and heir, Theodosius!"

The trumpets pealed again, echoes ringing through the halls, then falling away into silence. Galen, looking down into the garden, saw Anastasia and smiled, inclining his head. The Duchess knelt in response, making a flourish. Out of the corner of her eye, Anastasia saw Martina twitch nervously, then make a polite half-bow.

"Lord and God," the Duchess called, her clear voice cutting through quiet air. "We are graced and honored by your presence." Capturing Martina's hand again, she ascended the steps, taking care to match her pace to Martina's—who lagged, feet dragging, nervous and out of her depth. "Please, partake of my house, the entertainments, anything you might desire."

"Thank you, it is our pleasure." Galen said, managing a tired smile. Up close, Anastasia fought to keep down a frown. The Emperor's eyes were smudged with fatigue, his skin a poor color even disguised by powders and crushed rose dust. "Hello, Martina. Are you and your son well?"

"Yes, Lord Galen," Martina responded, her voice tight with nervousness. "And yours?"

Galen looked down at Theodosius, who was staring around with interest, most of one hand stuffed into his mouth. Anastasia felt a pang, seeing a flicker of happiness pass in the Emperor's face as he looked upon his son. "He is very well, thank you."

"Empress," the Duchess said, bowing to Helena, "welcome to my house."

"Thank you, Duchess. I see you've invited everyone I'd forgotten existed," the Empress replied, inclining her head to Anastasia. The Duchess stiffened, seeing her old friend was in a particularly sharp mood. The cutting tone in the woman's voice seemed to touch Martina as well, and the Duchess felt the Eastern Empress's grip tighten. Trying to reassure the girl, Anastasia gave an answering squeeze.

"My lord, my lady," Anastasia said quickly, before Martina had to respond, "will you be presiding this evening? Or simply private citizens, at the house of an old friend?" At the same time, the Duchess tried to catch Helena's eye, but the Western Empress was looking Martina over with a particularly calculating gaze.

"We are just private citizens," Helena said, before Galen could respond. "The party is for our dear brother-in-law, Prince Maxian, isn't it? We wouldn't want to spoil his chances for a good time by hovering, or making people bow every time we walked by. Besides, things are formal enough in the palace. Don't you think so, husband?"

"Of course." Galen nodded, seemingly relieved. Theodosius grabbed for a sweetmeat from a passing tray and the Emperor captured a grubby hand before it spilled the platter. Distracted by his son, Galen failed to notice the tense air between the three women. "Ah, good, there's Gaius Julius! Excuse me, ladies . . ."

"Helena," Martina said into the silence as the Emperor departed. "Good evening."

The Western Empress's eyes narrowed and Anastasia realized Martina had neither bowed nor used an honorific in addressing the older woman. *And why not,* the Duchess thought despairingly, *she's an Empress as well, and Helena's equal . . .*

"Good evening," Helena said, one long, dark eyebrow inching up. "Martina. A lovely dress." She tilted her head a little to one side. "Is this the fashion in Constantinople?"

The Duchess felt the girl flinch at the Western Empress's turned lip. Helena, in comparison, was very plainly dressed, even austere. The younger woman's gown exposed too much cream-colored breast and her jewels and gold now seemed over-done—even crass—when measured against Helena's restrained antiques. Anastasia glared at Helena, but the Empress just raised her head, looking back at her friend with a cool expression.

"Thank you," Martina managed to say, swallowing the beginnings of a stutter.

"You're welcome," Helena said, eyes glittering. "How is your son? Still healthy, I hope. Little Theodosius would miss playing with him. You know he is welcome to stay with us at any time."

"Heracleonas is a strong, healthy boy," Martina said, an edge of anger creeping into her voice. "Theo's colic has passed, has it?"

"Oh, yes," Helena said, making a dismissive wave with a pale white hand. "Did you come with anyone tonight? I worry you've no one of your own station to attend such events with."

Anastasia felt her heart sink into her stomach. *What has gotten into her tonight?* The Western Empress looked around, as if she searched for one of the great nobles of the East. *Why remind the girl her husband is dead?*

"I came," Martina bit out, "with the prince Maxian." Her fingers slipped from Anastasia's, balling into fists. The Duchess saw some of the senatorial wives lingering, eyes bright with interest, sharp ears pricked. Anastasia turned, shielding the two women from prying eyes, a hand on either Empress's arm.

"You did?" Helena smiled, though the motion did not reach her eyes. "That was kind of him. He is busy these days . . . everyone is, I suppose, with such dreadful things happening."

For a moment, Martina seemed to freeze solid, a flush rising at her throat. Then she mastered herself, essayed a brittle smile, and said, "We are busy, Helena, there are many projects under-way, all in the service of the Emperor and the State." Her green eyes narrowed. "We will need every advantage to destroy the Persians."

"Oh," Helena said, one tapered fingernail pressed to her chin in a pose of remembering. "I'd quite forgotten you work for the prince, collating the news of ancient days, searching for some fragment that might yield us victory." The Western Empress smiled, making a little bow. "This evening must be a welcome diversion, then."

Anastasia flinched inwardly and closed her eyes for the smallest moment. An image of Martina's face filling with fury at the word *work* remained. Then she took a deep breath and caught Helena's arm. "My dear, I must show you something new and marvelous in the glass hall. . . ." With a despairing look over her shoulder at Martina, who was almost shaking with rage, face white, barely restrained fury glittering in her eyes, Anastasia hauled the Western Empress away by main force.

Helena laughed as they passed into the portico leading from the inner garden to the outer.

"Oh, dear," the Empress said, chuckling, "did you see her face?"

"What has gotten into you?" Anastasia's tone was frigid. Helena stopped short, surprised.

"Oh, don't tell me you and the little lost princess are *friends* now? What a horror!"

"A horror?" The Duchess pushed Helena into a side chamber, thankfully empty and ornamented with enormous vases and ostrich-feather plumes. "She's young, inexperienced, bereft and desperately lonely. Why are you being so cruel?"

"I don't know." Helena leaned back against the smooth marble of the nearest urn, a sulky expression on her face. "She's such a fat little brown mouse, all weepy-eyed and pitiful. I don't like her."

Anastasia restrained a groan of despair, then marshaled herself. "You, of all people, should understand how she feels— weren't you lonely when you first came to Rome? Didn't you hate the proud matrons and their cutting tongues? I remember how unhappy you were—"

"Oh, please!" Helena stood away from the urn, eyes flashing.

"Galen had been Emperor only a month, with blood still on his boots! The little twit has been an Empress for nearly a decade. There's no reason she should mope about—so her husband is dead, her son still lives, and there is every chance Heracleonas will be restored to his throne. Galen certainly intends to see him there!" The Empress paused, a calculating look filling her face. "Though the young often die unexpectedly—"

"Be quiet!" Anastasia glared at Helena, fingers pressed against the Empress's lips. "Do not say such things—you've your own son—would you want others to wish him ill?"

"No, I suppose not." Helena batted away the Duchess's hand. "She grates on me and the way she looks at Maxian. . . . I'll not have her as a sister-in-law!"

Anastasia gave her an arch look. "How would you prevent such a match? The boy needs a wife, she needs a husband, and marrying Martina would ensure the loyalty of the Eastern nobility."

"No," Helena spat, lips twisting, "I will not make a rival to *my* son and his demesne."

"The East is our ally!" Anastasia was horrified and let it show, staring in amazement at Helena. "Heracleonas is not a rival!"

"No?" The Western Empress's expression grew grim, swift as night falling on some barren plain. "I know how the little mouse thinks. She's already clawed her way out of one dynastic wreck—her stepson lies dead in the ruins of Constantinople. The brother who hated her is struck down, taking with him all organized opposition." Helena raised a finger, forestalling another outburst from Anastasia. The Empress's voice became quiet and serious. "Listen to me, *Duchess*. Now she is here, among us, with her eye on my brother-in-law. He may be powerful, but he is not paying attention to the currents moving around him. If she captures his fancy, inveigles him to marry her, then her son's future is assured. Heracleonas *will* sit on the throne of the East—and more, he would be heir to the West as well. . . ."

"Only if something happens to Galen, and you, and Theodosius . . ." Anastasia looked over her shoulder, suddenly wary. "Why would that happen? Have you heard something?"

"I have." Helena's expression grew even colder. She stepped to the doorway, peering out. After a moment, she raised her hand. Anastasia drew back the edge of a draped tapestry, eyes following the Empress's pointing finger. "Who is the prince's wise councilor? His eyes, ears, mouth in the city?"

"Gaius Julius," Anastasia replied tiredly, seeing the man himself, standing tall among a crowd of the Palatine secretaries and officials, face beaming with a genial smile, his hands in sharp motion as he related some amusing story. The Duchess let the drape fall. She met Helena's eyes and found a mocking smile on the Empress's lips. "You're sure he—"

"Aren't you?" Helena shook her head in dismay. "Aren't you the master of intrigue? *He is Caesar*—the only sober man who ever tried to overthrow the Senate!"

Anastasia shrugged, checking her earrings. She felt tired and the night was still young. "I concede the point. There is, possibly, danger."

"And so?" Helena raised an eyebrow again. "What will you do about her?"

"Nothing violent!" Anastasia made a sign to avert evil fortune. "In any case, I was well on my way to making friends with her . . . before your heedless tongue spoiled everything."

"Huh." Helena looked out into the garden again, frowning. "She's hanging on him again, like . . . like a limpet, or a leech, or something equally slimy from some eastern bog."

"You are not helping." Anastasia stepped into the doorway, giving the Empress a sharp look. "If Martina is your friend, Gaius is denied a weapon, and the danger to your son all the less."

Helena made a sour face. Giving up for the moment, the Duchess hurried off. A hostess' work is never done.

"Hello, dear." Anastasia slipped up beside Martina, who had found refuge in the outside garden, at the edge of a maze of ivy hedges and stunted ornamental trees. The Eastern Empress barely looked up, her makeup smudged, her nose red. "I am sorry," the Duchess continued, settling onto the curving marble bench. "I've spoken sharply with the Empress Helena, minding her to keep a civil tongue in my house."

Martina laughed, a harsh bark, and turned, eyes filled with wounds. "It doesn't matter, Lady Anastasia. She'll hate me all the more, no matter what you might say. Don't place yourself in any danger on my account."

"Danger?" The Duchess brushed a blue-black curl away from her face. "Helena and I have known each other for a long time—we've quarreled before and I've come out none the worse." Anastasia sighed, making a polite show of despair. "But you and she . . . seem star-crossed, always at odds! Is there some history between you two, some old grudge?"

"No," Martina said, looking down at her feet. "She always yells at me and tells me I've done the wrong thing. She doesn't like my clothes, my jewels or the way I set my hair. I feel ugly when she looks at me."

"Dear, your hair is beautiful and your clothes exceptional." The Duchess moved closer, brushing wayward curls away from the girl's face. "The Emperor is your friend—and he will not forget you or your son. Look up, now." Anastasia raised Martina's chin, gently. The Duchess met a tearful gaze with a calm, determined expression. "You are still Empress of the East. You have no peer, save Helena, which—I think—is part of what sets her on edge. Go find the prince, stand with him, speak politely and with interest to anyone who speaks with you." Anastasia's lips quirked into a half-smile. "Stand straight and ignore the cold eyes and whispers. You are an *Empress!*"

"But I have no empire," Martina said mournfully, nervous fingers bunching up the train of her gown. The transparent drape was tangled in her jewelry. "I am in exile."

"You have powerful friends," the Duchess said, rescuing the silk and smoothing it back into proper shape with gentle fingers. "The prince Maxian not least of them. . . ."

Martina started to answer, then fell silent, though her eyes lit with relief. Anastasia turned, hearing a whisper of bare feet on the grass.

"Lord Prince," the Duchess said, rising from the bench, so she might kneel properly. "Welcome again."

"Hello." Maxian came to a halt, looking down at the two women. Anastasia, eyes demurely downcast, noticed his pale feet were grass-stained and had to suppress a laugh.

"Martina—are you all right?" The prince knelt, one knee on the bench. "Gaius Julius said you seemed unhappy."

The Eastern Empress rubbed her nose in embarrassment. "It's nothing."

"Nothing?" The Duchess rose. She caught Maxian's eye. "Your dear sister-in-law does not think Martina's hair or dress are suitable for my party. I have spoken to her—but Helena is in a particularly foul mood this evening."

"I see." Maxian nodded, avoiding Anastasia's eyes. He took Martina's hand, then drew her to her feet. "I've been on the wrong end of her sharp tongue myself." The prince grinned, and the exhaustion and fatigue clouding his face faded a little. The Duchess was struck by how alike Maxian and Galen seemed—a particular hollow look, filled with a brittle energy pressing them to nervous action. They both seemed to be stretched. "Martina—her bad humor will pass. It always does. The next time you see her, she'll be the sun to tonight's moon."

Anastasia started a little, reminded of an errand by the prince's turn of phrase. "Oh, Lord Prince, may I—as hostess—ask you—as a guest—for a small favor?"

"Of course," the prince said, finally meeting her eyes. "What can I do?"

The Duchess stared for a moment, disturbed by vivid memories, and she squinted in the dim light. The prince's eyes seemed a different color than she remembered. Had they changed—were they sharper? Did they gleam with an inner light in this half-darkness? Too, his face seemed thinner, more angular. Wrinkles had begun to appear where once the flesh of youth had been taut and smooth. With a start, she saw single white hairs threaded through his dark brown hair. *Where is the brash young man, so filled with the vigor of youth, who laughed in my bed? Swallowed, consumed, by the Empire and this endless war. . . .*

"Duchess?" Maxian canted his head to one side, concerned. "Do you feel faint?"

"No—no, I am fine. I was just thinking of how . . . old I feel, seeing you two. But no matter—later in the evening, there will be a performance. Acrobats, tumblers, that sort of thing—but I envision a fancy to make the entertainment special. Lord Prince, may I trouble you for a little magic?"

Maxian's face, which had grown still and quiet while she spoke—even suspicious—cleared and he laughed. "Of course, Duchess, I would be delighted to please your guests."

"Good. But later, my lord. Martina, please sit again, and I will send servants with wine and pastries. And I will make sure"— here the Duchess inclined her head, barely disguising a grin— "you are not disturbed by the sharp-tongued or the witless."

Martina nodded, clutching the prince's hand, but said nothing. Anastasia made to say more, seeing the girl's other hand knotting in her dress, but the prince clasped both his over Martina's. "Duchess, let me lend you my skill now—Martina, rest here a moment and I will be right back—and our evening may continue, uninterrupted."

"Thank you, my lord," Anastasia said, dimpling. "That is very kind."

The Duchess turned away and walked back toward the house. The prince followed, nervously tucking long straight hair behind his ears.

"This is a strange sight, an Empress alone amid such a splendid party."

Martina looked up into twinkling green eyes set in a noble face. "Master Gaius."

"May I sit with you for a moment?"

The Eastern Empress made a desultory gesture to the bench with her head, chin resting on both hands. "As you wish."

Gaius Julius sat, one thick-knuckled hand on his knee, the other gathering up his toga with the ease of long practice. In the light of so many candles, the pure white wool gleamed, and Martina thought the old man seemed younger, revitalized, far different from the serious, hard-working official attending the Emperor's council meetings.

"You do not seem happy tonight, my lady."

The Empress did not respond, continuing to stare at the ornamental trees and carefully pruned rosebushes. After waiting a moment, Gaius Julius nodded to himself, then sat quietly as well, eyes closed. The following silence dragged and at last the Empress turned her head, eyes narrowed to bare slits.

"I haven't given you proper thanks," she said, "for suggesting I help the prince with his research."

"You're welcome," Gaius Julius said, eyes still closed. "Is it interesting?"

"Hah!" Martina sat up straight. "The scraps of the past are interesting, in a dull numbers-and-lines sort of way. Too many documents reflecting the mundane, and too few filled with history. I have found almost nothing about our opponent—the old Greeks and Romans were more interested in themselves than in the doings of Persian and Parthian wizards."

Gaius Julius nodded in sympathy. "Have you found anything?"

"A hint," Martina said, scowling. "There is a letter, written by a Syrian merchant who traveled in old Parthia, before the rise of the house of Sassan. He relates a tale heard round a campfire in the north, while he was on the road from Roman Armenia to Ecbatana. He describes the rituals of priests dwelling in a great temple at a place called Gazaca. The merchant also describes the lord of light, Ahura-Madza, and his great enemy, Ahriman. He tells of an 'eternal' flame burning in the temple's heart and how this light holds back 'the night' and the might of Ahriman and his servants."

"Interesting," Gaius said. "I have always heard the Parthians and Persians followed a god of light—the more disturbing, now, as this enemy the prince fought is wholly of darkness."

"There is more," Martina said, gritting her teeth. "As you may know, I accompanied my husband on his campaign in Persia and Armenia three years ago. He wished to keep me close by, to ensure my safety from his enemies. During our journey, after the great victory at Kerenos River, he mentioned in passing the careful destruction of a Persian fire temple, a great one, at a town named Ganzak. He had sent his brother, the lamentable Theodore, to destroy the place—hoping to put the fear of Rome into the hearts of the Persians, to deny them the surety of faith and the comfort of their god's favor."

"Ah," Gaius said, running a hand over his balding pate. "The same town? The name distorted by time and changing dialect? In light of later events, you do not think that a wise decision."

"No." Martina bit her thumb, attention far away from the party and the glowing lanterns. "I think . . . I think the destruction of the temple let something enter the world. A dark spirit. A servant of Ahriman, perhaps . . ."

"But not the god itself?"

"Don't be a fool," Martina replied, giving the old Roman a quelling look. "If the Serpent Lord had burst into the world, we would all be dead, devoured by unquenchable hunger. No . . . I fear something less awesome escaped from the outer darkness. Some servant of the dark god—and the Persians have turned their faces from Ahura-Madza's light.

"You have not lived in the East, Master Gaius," she said, still chewing on a thumbnail. "The West is blessedly free of these dark spirits—but I know the Persians are aware of them, and believe. Their fortunes were abject after Ctesiphon and Chrosoes fell. I think they turned aside from the safe path, seeking victory and revenge at any cost. And look! Constantinople is theirs, Syria is theirs . . . Egypt besieged, our armies and fleets defeated."

Gaius Julius rubbed his temples, deep in thought. "Have you told the prince?"

"Yes," Martina said. "He agrees. He has redoubled his labors."

"Can he defeat a servant of Ahriman? A demigod?"

Martina managed a faint, weak smile. "He believes he can. He says victory will be a matter of 'arranging proper circumstance.' "

Gaius nodded approvingly. "Very wise. Has he told you what he intends?"

"No. He is being very secretive. I have not pressed him. I know he and Galen have argued about this matter, more than once. They are far from compromise on matters of sorcery. The Emperor refuses to believe such powers walk the earth."

"I know." The old Roman's face fell, revealing his own exhaustion and fear. "Things have changed—our Legions are no longer enough, our bravery and discipline are not enough—this has become a time of gods and monsters." Martina was startled to hear the weariness in the man's voice—ever before he had been calm and confident, always ready with a witty remark or a well-thought proposal.

The Empress realized, sitting on the bench beside the old man, she was not alone in her fear and uncertainty. She looked up and around, watching the faces of the nobles and courtesans and officers milling on the villa porch. *Is everyone afraid,* she wondered? *Do we all feel a dreadful weight in the air and taste bitter defeat when we eat and drink?*

Suddenly, she felt comfortable with the old man, and put her hand over his.

"Gaius, we have more than mortal soldiers to defend the Empire. We have have Maxian and his strength. Soon, the iron drakes will come forth from the forges of Florentina and Rome will rule the upper air. The world has changed, but Rome is changing too. Whatever comes from the east, we will match and overcome."

"Well spoken," Gaius said, looking up. A brilliant smile lit his face. "You cheer me, lady. So many troubles swirl around us, my confidence has been shaken. These intrigues and threats . . . they sap a man's strength, leave him morose, depressed, defeated before he even takes his place in the line of battle. There is no better antidote than swift, assured action."

"True enough." She paused, looking at him quizzically. "What intrigues depress you, Master Gaius?"

The old man snorted, looking around. His good humor sharpened and he pointed with his chin. "Rome is an old city, my dear, filled with all sorts of vipers. Our hostess, for example . . ."

"Anastasia? She has been kind to me, Master Gaius. Don't blacken her name!"

"She is kind," Gaius said, nodding sagely. He was quite cheerful now. "Don't you understand her role in all this? You've sat in the same councils I have . . . she is Galen's spymaster, his hunting hound, his judicious dagger. You mustn't trust her, Empress."

"Why not?"

"Because," he said, regarding her with an wistful expression, "she would have you murdered, and your son too, if Galen did not need you and little Heracleonas so badly. I am, I fear, in the same situation, as is the prince, whom we both love and serve."

Martina raised an eyebrow, but her color was improving as well. "*Do* you love the prince?"

"What recourse do I have?" Gaius laughed, the corners of his eyes crinkling up. "He is my patron and I his client. You may not know me well, my dear, but I am accounted generous and I do not forget my friends or those who have helped me. I am merciful to my enemies, open-handed to my allies and forgiving of those who do me wrong. Of all men, only young Maxian has won my unswerving, perfect, complete and unimpeachable loyalty. So—I do love him, as a man loves the finest friend of his heart."

The Empress clapped her hands together softly. "Well spoken, poet."

Gaius Julius blushed, running a broad hand over his bare crown, and looked away.

"Do you *think* the Duchess would have me and my son killed, or do you *know* this?"

The old Roman bit his lower lip, sighing. "It is what I would do, were our positions reversed. Indeed, she may be pressed to action by circumstance—or even ordered by the Emperor."

"The Emperor!" Shock flickered across Martina's face. "He has proved a good friend, Master Gaius. He has taken me in, afforded me every courtesy, shown me all respect. While I do not enjoy interminable meetings with him and his staff, he has not excluded me from anything touching upon my son's realm. I *know* him now, Gaius; he is the most honest and forthright of men."

"I know." Grief tinged the old Roman's soft words. "He is truly a *noble* Roman. Yet . . ."

"Yet, what?" Martina was becoming irritated.

". . . he lies each night in the bed of a woman who looks upon you with hatred, my lady. Who watches your son with gimlet eyes, gauging the length of his life with her own measure."

"*Sss* . . ." Martina hissed reflexively, face tightening in anger. "Helena."

"I watch her, my lady, very carefully." Gaius paused, allowing himself a small chuckle. "I fancy she thinks I dote on her or harbor some unvoiced devotion. I must admit she is a beautiful woman—elegant, restrained, as purely Roman as her husband—with a sharp wit, an agile mind and a volcanic temper." The old Roman glanced sideways at Martina, seeing the girl quail inwardly, biting her lip.

"As I observe, Empress, I see her watching you and Prince Maxian. I see her eyes darken with anger, I see her lips draw back from shining teeth, I see her hands clutch as if she crushed the life from a weakling throat."

"She hates me so much?" Martina said, panic rising in her voice.

"Oh, no," Gaius said, voice settling to a whisper. The Empress leaned close. "She cares nothing for *you*. It is your son she fears and hates. Or any child that might spring from your womb and the prince's loins."

"Our child?" Martina drew back, blinking, surprised. Gaius shook his head at her in concern.

"Dear lady, you can account the begetting of Imperial sons as well as any. A child from your union would be heir to East and West alike, should anything happen to the young masters Heracleonas and Theodosius. Helena is not a stupid woman—she knows how to ensure her son's patrimony. Wouldn't you fear the same thing, for your son?"

Martina nodded, remembering another bleak time. "I have. Theodore tried to use my stepson Constantius against me. But—Galen would not allow her to harm me. Anastasia would argue my case, Maxian would protect me! All I desire is my son on his rightful throne, in our proper city!"

"I know." Gaius Julius caught her agitated hand and settled it on his knee. "While the prince retains his brother's favor, while the Duchess is our friend, there is little to fear. Helena and her spite will be held in check by their good counsel. So do not worry, there is only the promise of danger."

The Empress nodded absently, nibbling on the skin around her thumb. "This is dangerous," she said in a worried tone. "We cannot afford strife among ourselves, not now. We must all work together, as one, to guide the Empire and overmaster Ahriman's servants. Doesn't Helena understand this?"

Gaius Julius hid a sharp, quick grin. "I hope so," he replied. "Otherwise, our defeat is certain."

Helena drifted through a crowd of olive merchants and provincial senators, expression tight and composed, avoiding eye contact, smiling politely for the room and ignoring anyone who attempted to speak to her. The rustics—Gauls, Britons and Africans—parted before her, some bowing, others pretending to ignore the Empress. She ignored them in turn—an acceptable exchange, she thought—and moved on. Ahead, the statue of Poseidon loomed above a sea of chattering people, deep in inconsequential conversations, wrapped in gossip, involved in their own small intrigues and plots.

The Empress caught sight of her son, head and shoulders above the crowd. Theodosius was sitting on his father's shoulders, chubby hands wrapped around Galen's forehead. Despite his burden, the Emperor was deep in conversation. The boy watched everything with wide eyes, following the passage of a troupe of dusky-skinned dancers and tambourine players with interest. Ostrich and peacock plumes danced over their heads, making a waving forest above the carefully combed hairstyles of the Romans.

"Husband." Helana reached Galen's side, touching his arm. Theodosius looked down, saw his mother and reached out small round arms to her. The Empress took her son, sliding him to her hip. Galen smiled in greeting, while pulling his laurel wreath from a pocket inside his toga and putting it back on his head.

"Hello, Helena. How is the party?"

"Dull," she said in an acid tone, ignoring the tribunes and legates around her husband. The officers' attention flicked between Emperor and Empress, then most began moving away, disappointed, with eyes averted. The unmarried officers lingered a moment, hoping to keep Galen's attention. One tried to speak, but caught Helena's icy glare and swallowed his words. "Walk on the terrace with me."

Galen frowned in surprise and tried to catch her hand. Helena was already moving away, her son clutched in her arms, head high. Grimacing, the Emperor hurried after her, irritation mounting at her rude behavior. They passed through a pair of double-wide mahogany doors fitted with small rectangular clear-glass windows.

The cool night air flooded over Galen and he sighed in relief. He hadn't realized how hot and close the hall had become. He stretched tired arms, feeling his mood improve. Helena turned, pacing down the long, covered porch looking out over the ornamental gardens behind the villa. Galen followed, steps slowing as he took in the tracery of lights and lamps hung along the walls. Beyond the high walls, rooftops and temple domes glittered in starlight. The Emperor felt memory tug, then sighed in remorse. The white buildings, shining with marble, reminded him of Alpine crags under the moon, though not so grand or vast as the Helvetian mountains.

He realized he missed the high meadows, the glare from hanging ice, the rush of water over glossy stones, the smell of heather and bluebells on the slopes, the tang of pine burning in a fire. The silhouette of an eagle turning against a brilliant cerulean sky. He remembered a year spent in the high country; a young, inexperienced centurion, tramping narrow trails and snowbound passes, watching for bandits, rustlers, raiding Goths and Germans. His chest tightened, compressed by the crowded city. *I miss the open air, sharp wind in my face, the creaking weight of my armor, the feel of sweat running down my back, even the food . . . gods, I hate this place!*

Helena stopped, parking herself in shadow between two windows. She turned Theodosius' head to her shoulder, where he immediately went to sleep, arms tight around her neck. Galen reached for her free hand, finding it cold and stiff.

"What troubles you, love?"

"Would . . ." Helena paused, unsure of what to say. Galen was surprised—when did she ever lack for words?—and looked closely at her face, seeing a reflection of his own weariness, mixed with barely hidden anger. "Gales, if I asked you for something, something political, would you do it for me?"

"What kind of thing?" He felt a jolt—the moment of glad emotion, drawn from old memories, was cast aside—replaced by wariness. Long ago they had struck an arrangement to order their lives, making a house with two rooms—one for matters of state, and one for themselves, where the business of the Empire should not enter. Something political would cross the threshold between the two. Galen felt his right eye twitch and the tickle of an oncoming headache stir.

"I am . . ." She paused again, shaking her head. Her fingers tightened on his, nails biting into the flesh of his palm. "I am worried and I want to protect my—our—son. This may seem strange, but you must listen and consider my request seriously."

As Helena spoke, she straightened up, looking him in the eye. Galen settled back a little, nodding for her to go on. The Empress visibly gathered herself.

"Your brother—Maxian—is becoming involved with the Empress Martina. Did you know this?"

"I have eyes," Galen said, but there was no rancor in his tone. "This worries you?"

"Yes," Helena nodded sharply. "Do you favor a match between them?"

Galen blinked, a little surprised. "Well, I hadn't really thought about it . . . but I see the *Emperor* must have an opinion." He sighed in understanding, shaking his head and looking out at the garden. "I have tried to stay out of my brother's personal life. Once, long ago, I promised our mother I would protect him—keep him out of trouble and out of Imperial service! Both Aurelian and I were already in the Legion then. She didn't want him to wind up like us, or our father. His talents had not yet revealed themselves. But now? He is our custos, by order of the Senate. My left hand, if Horse is my right." Galen looked at Helena, a sad half-smile barely touching his lips.

"I am distracted and busy, my love, but I think I see your fear. Should Martina and Maxian wed, their son would have a claim to the West, while ruling the East. It is an old dream—both here and in Constantinople—to reunite the Empire. Our current amity and alliance is newly born, barely six years old. Dreams might push a young man, new on his throne, flush with heady power, to grasp for both hanging fruit, rather than just the one."

Helena nodded, clutching her son tight to her chest. Theodosius made a happy, burbling sound.

"Maxian is his own man," Galen continued, musing softly, speaking almost to himself. "Our father is dead, making the three of us adults and heads of our own households. Martina is a suitable match—I cannot invoke some hoary old law, forbidding marriage by a patrician out of his class—and doing so would only insult the Eastern lords and cause an immediate rift between our two domains. Do you think they want to marry?"

"She will." Helena's voice was flat and emotionless. "She will think of her son."

"Two little boys," Galen said, trying to lighten the tone. "Rolling and playing in the mud at soldiers, as gladiators, the best of friends . . . you think they will grow to opposition, at each other's throat with bare steel?"

"I read," Helena replied, tears beginning to sparkle at the corners of her eyes. "I read of the past and see brother strangling brother, husbands drowning wives, children murdering their fathers, sending their mothers away into prison and exile. I read—and I see men reduced to pretending buffoonery so they might live amid slaughter, or prostituting their sisters, daughters and wives to win the favor of the Senate." The Empress's eyes grew brighter, but she fought back the tears and clear anger shone in her face instead. "Men will do *anything* to wear the laurel crown, don the red boots, lift the white rod."

"And women?" Helena looked so grief-stricken, disconsolate, her fingers digging into the child's arm. Galen felt his chest tighten again. "What would you do?"

"I will kill," Helena whispered, "to protect my son and see he lives."

The Emperor nodded, feeling a vast weight settle on his shoulders. He closed his eyes for a moment, taking refuge in soft darkness. "Very well. I will speak to Maxian, when next time and circumstance permit privacy. If he wishes to marry Martina, I will approve and applaud, but only on the condition he and his forswear their Latin patrimony."

Galen opened his eyes, brushing a hand over his son's thin hair. "Then I will claim Theodosius—even though he is but a child—as my official heir. Maxian's sons, if he is blessed with any, will rule only the East, not the West."

Helena made no response, pressing her lips to the boy's

head. Galen watched her, waiting. A long time passed and then the Empress said in a hoarse, ghastly voice: "We cannot cast the East aside? Or impress our own rule upon them? Send Martina into exile, blinded, tongue slit—her son rendered harmless?"

"No!" Galen shook himself, shocked. "We are too weak and hard-pressed by Persia. I have no Legions spare to garrison the East, even if we could subdue the Eastern lords. If either Empire is to survive, we must fight together, in common accord."

"Compromise," Helena said, "digs a shallow grave for more than one."

"It is all we have." Galen took his wife's hand, pressing her cold fingers to his cheek. "My love, your son will live and he will grow strong. In time he will sit on my throne. You have my word. Maxian is my brother—and our friendship, our love, is strong. We disagree of late over tactics, not our family. What you fear will not come to pass. He is my brother!"

Helena's eyes were pooled darkness. "So said Agamemnon as he drowned, throat crushed in Aegisthus' brawny hands. I do not fear *Maxian*, but his son, or his son's son."

"Anything can happen, Helena! Such a dreadful path you see before us. . . ."

"I watch your face while you sleep, husband," she replied, face drowned in shadow, only the pale hair of the boy revealed by the lamps. "Each day, your burden grows. These are dreadful times. Who is to say the future will be better?"

"I do." Galen stood straighter. "What other purpose do I have?" He gave Helena a sharp look. "Now—I will do as you ask, but you must do your part as well, for amity and goodwill. Regardless of what else happens, you must make peace with Martina—she is your sister empress—and our ally. Neither slight nor stifle her, but make her your friend, if you can."

Helena responded with a glare of her own, but Galen stood, waiting, until she—at last—nodded in agreement. He could tell she was *not* pleased and hid a sigh, knowing he would hear about this again, at length.

Bronze dolphin trumpets pealed, ringing bright and clear against the gilt satyrs and painted shepherdesses staring down from the domed ceilings. Quiet settled over the crowd, even

near the banquet tables where the boards groaned under the
weight of the Duchess's feast. A centurion, barrel-chested,
throat like an oak root, stepped up onto a bench near the inner
garden. "Citizens, guests, officers! Our hostess commands you
attend her in the garden and look upon the heavens above, filled
with wonder and delight!"

Obediently, everyone began to file into the center of the villa.
Maxian, looking very pleased with himself, pressed through the
crowd in the opposite direction. In the short hall between the
inner court and the outer garden, he found the Eastern Empress
and Gaius Julius. The young woman's face was grave and the
two were deep in conversation.

"Martina, excellent! Gaius, you too, come and see. The
Duchess has commanded a performance and I have done a small
bit to make it livelier than usual." The prince was grinning.

"It's not a dancing bear, is it?" Martina looked sourly at the
close, hot, crowd filling the hallway. Everyone in front of her
was markedly taller than the Empress. "I don't like bears."

"No, no," Maxian said, taking her hand and Gaius' arm.
"Come through here."

A drape slid aside at a wave of the prince's hand, starting the
hackles on Gaius' neck to life, revealing a servant's corridor. A
moment later Maxian pushed open a low ironbound door and
they stooped through, finding themselves at the back of the garden, behind a bower of rowans and white-barked elms. The
prince put a finger to his lips, urging silence, and the three
slipped through a cluster of quiet servants to a staircase leading
up into the kitchens.

"Stand here," Maxian whispered, picking up Martina and
setting her on the highest step. "Watch the sky."

Above the branches, framed by white pillars and terra-cotta
eaves on three sides, the vault of heaven stood in bright array.
The river of milk was a gossamer veil, here and there a star
shining through. Martina shifted, her hand on Maxian's shoulder, and started to speak. "What—"

The lamps suddenly died and the candles flickered out. Complete darkness filled the garden and the halls on either side. In
the unexpected gloom someone squealed and there was muted

laughter. Martina fell silent. Maxian put his hand over hers and she settled against him, arms on either shoulder.

A harp began to play, a light, shimmering sound. The low soft beat of one drum joined in, carrying the sound of the strings up and up, as if they rose to the glittering stars. Then a second drum, even deeper voiced than the first, woke to life. Maxian, still grinning in the dark, closed his left hand and mist rose. The drums rattled up, beat quickening, speeding like a runner on desert sands. Still darkness filled the courtyard and the halls of the house.

Just when the watching people below began to stir, impatient, there was a soft *twang* and fluting pipes skirled, drowning the steady drums for a moment. Above, three figures appeared against the night sky, softly glowing, arms outstretched. Two girls and a boy, bare skin shining silver, long colored ribbons wound through their hair. They ran across the sky, bare feet keeping close to some invisible track. The boy darted ahead, ribbons snapping behind as a comet's tail sweeps across the vault of night. Halfway across the courtyard, he sprang up, cartwheeling forward. The two girls followed close, only paces behind, and three whirling comets—shining silver, matching the stars, blazing ribbon flashing against sable firmament—rushed away into the darkness.

A gasp followed from below, as the crowd remembered to breathe.

The drums beat down to silence, the pipes falling to a breathy whisper. Everyone grew quiet. Again, the faint shivering *twang* fell from the air. The eastern sky brightened, flooding with a golden glow. Trumpets sounded, blaring a grand ovation. A man's head appeared, bent under an enormous, burning orb. He was muscled like a god and walked slowly on the air, toes splayed on either side of a barely visible cable. The sun rode on his back, a spherical lattice of fiercely blazing rods. The man strode across the sky, the orb shedding a cool, brilliant light upon the upturned faces below.

Behind the sun, as the bent man reached the halfway point, suddenly rushed the moon.

A pale sphere, glimmering, bouncing upon a lithe woman's

outstretched hands. She sped across the sky, faster than the slow sun, springing in long bounds—the cable catching her on each landing, then springing back, wire singing like a blade, propelling her skyward—and the disk brightened and waned as she passed the sun, even as Luna changes in her courses.

Again, the cold moon vanished into the west, into gathering mist. Old Sol stumped on.

Those watching below began to clap, then fell silent. The burning sun guttered down, growing dim, radiance failing, leaving only a dim spark at the center of the lattice rods. The powerfully muscled man stopped, swaying slowly back and forth, shoulders slumped in weariness, his outstretched arms making small adjustments to keep in balance. Maxian heard a hiss of dismay from the crowd and Martina's fingers dug into his shoulders. He lifted his hands, palms towards the sky, and the mist responded, billowing out to swallow the sun. Now the west brightened, but this time with a sullen red glow. Sparks shot up from the rooftop, accompanied by a chaotic, rattling clamor of drums and tambourines and pipes. Burning motes streaked heavenward.

Everyone in the house groaned and at least one man cried out in rage.

The distinctive shape of Vesuvius appeared, outlined in flame, rising over the roof. The drums roared, a heavy, furious beat. Black mist flowed from half-seen vents, red worms writhing down night-shrouded slopes. The man holding the sun swayed, the last light failing. Darkness swallowed the scene, save the fitful glow of the burning mountain.

Maxian heard people crying in the darkness, though he was unmoved by the phantasm. Silently, he turned his palms toward one another and pressed them against the contained air, as if something stiff resisted him. Beyond the eastern roof, a sudden light flared, a shining white beam striking through the curdling mist, driving back the abyss of darkness. The sun—dead, cold, rods black as slate—was revealed. The muscled man continued to balance the orb on his back, swaying little by little from side to side. White light played across him, casting his face in sharp relief, his tense muscles growing huge under such scrutiny.

Four men of diverse races appeared from the east, backs

arched, hands and toes gripping the cables. Bound to their backs was a four-square platform. With smooth grace, they scuttled forward, exemplary skill keeping the platform steady. Standing on their support, a man in white robes with a patrician face, bare ankles adorned by wings, wore a golden wreath on a high brow. He held aloft a crystal sphere, incandescent with white light. As he advanced, Maxian pushed his hands away from his chest and the mist and darkness boiled back. Vesuvius' refulgent glow dimmed, then vanished. The conical outline receded into mist and was gone.

The four crawling men scurried on until they came even with the sun. Now the muscled man rose, inch by inch, muscles straining, rolling the orb of the sun from his back and onto his hands. He stretched skyward, lifting the sphere of rods above his head. The noble Roman tossed the brilliant crystal into the air. The muscular man swayed, spinning the lattice and then deftly caught the flying crystal in a cup at the sphere's heart.

The sun blazed alight anew, flooding the courtyard and the sky with golden light. A cheer went up, torn from unwary throats, and everyone clapped furiously. No longer slow, the man bearing the sun ran off to the west along the cable, carrying the radiant orb away over the rooftop. Behind, the noble Roman bowed to the crowd gathered below, then the four bearers scuttled backward and in moments they too had vanished over the eastern roof.

Maxian snapped his fingers and every candle, lamp and torch in the house sprang alight.

A great clamor of glad voices rose, filling the air. The servants watching from the shadows of the arbor streamed away, chattering, their good humor restored. Even Gaius Julius was smiling.

"Nicely done," the old Roman said. "The winged feet were a good touch."

Maxian shrugged. "It was the Duchess's idea—I just added a little light."

"*Hmph.*" Martina made a face, but seemed content to lean against the prince, hands clasped across his chest, her chin resting on the crown of his head. "No one can accuse her of subtlety—Rome lights the world, indeed!"

Gaius Julius gestured at the people crowding back into the hall, appetites restored, faces bright with cheer. "They needed something to revive their spirits. The Duchess invited everyone of importance in Rome and Latium—if their will flags, then the Empire suffers. Now they see their Emperor, see his son, their bellies are full, their senses replete. They are inspired—and tomorrow they will set to their tasks with greater vigor, with a lighter heart. I say again—well done!"

"Thank you, Gaius." Maxian made a small bow in reply. "But I did little. How passes your evening?"

The old Roman tilted his head to the Empress. "We have been talking, Martina and I. I thought you'd been working too hard—but she tells me what she's found about our enemy—"

Maxian raised an eyebrow, face going still, his expression becoming cold and forbidding.

"—and I cannot fault you! Is there anything else I can do to aid your search? I have no desire to live in a world ruled by a three-headed dragon that lives only to consume and torment the living." He paused, a catlike smile on this face. "Cicero as consul was bad enough."

The prince relaxed, nodding. "We need more of everything, Master Gaius. More time, more skilled workers, a better grade of iron ore, more money to pay them and purchase materials. I would appreciate the effort if you kept such concerns fresh in Galen's mind while we are up in Florentia."

"Of course." Gaius Julius rubbed his chin, feigning thought. "I am reminded of a note that lately crossed my desk—a bequest was made to you, Lord Prince, and the Emperor remanded the property to the Imperial Exchequer. I will remind him of your good and loyal service, urging him to use the bequest—through his hands, of course—to fuel your enterprises."

"What bequest was this?" Martina leaned over Maxian's shoulder, interest perked.

"A small matter," Gaius Julius smiled faintly. "An old friend made Lord Maxian his sole heir—as he had gone down to the halls of the dead without male issue—a suitable, princely sum!"

"Who was this?" The Empress flicked her fingers, bidding Gaius hurry with his revelation.

"The esteemed senator, Gregorius Auricus," the old Roman

said, lowering his voice and making a sign to propitiate the gods. "Solely the richest man in Rome, save the Emperor himself. The master of vast estates, herds, flocks, wineries, oil presses, flour mills, merchant ship shares, bakeries—every possible source of wealth! All left for Maxian Atreus, without stipulation save 'to use for the good of Rome.' "

"Really?" Maxian was surprised and gratified. "How remarkable . . . but you say Galen refused to approve the inheritance?"

"Yes . . ." Gaius Julius made sort of a sickly smile. "The note—by the Emperor's hand—related the inheritance was being secured by the state, to finance the war and other . . . efforts."

Maxian laughed, with a little catch in his voice. Gaius Julius caught the change in tone, and hid another smile, though his eyes fairly gleamed. Martina, for her part, did not laugh at all.

"So," she said in an icy voice, "now the prince must petition for wealth rightly his? He must send polite notes, requesting his own revenues be released to himself? So he might continue his work, to strengthen the Empire and throw down these Persian monsters?"

"Yes—" Gaius started to say, but Maxian cut him off with a raised hand.

"This is within my brother's right—though I am puzzled by his decision. But, I will not argue the matter with him. That," the prince said with a smirk, "I leave to you, Gaius. Just get me the things I need." With that, the prince squeezed Martina's hand and stepped away. "I'm starving. Shall we eat?"

Martina did not answer. Instead, she gave Gaius Julius a look of such banked fury he stepped back in alarm. Ignoring them both, Maxian started off for the banquet tables.

"My lady?" the old Roman ventured quietly, as soon as the prince was out of earshot. She pursed her lips, obviously restraining a vigorous expression of disgust.

"Does the prince possess lands of his own, Master Gaius? His own livelihood?"

"Well . . ." Gaius Julius shrugged a little, clasping both hands behind his back. "Not to speak of—there are some small properties in his name; run-down apartment houses, a copper mine in Illyria; at one point he held a vinyard and estate on the slopes of unfortunate Vesuvius . . . nothing too large. Traditionally, the Emperor provides for his family—including any brothers or sisters."

"Does he?" The Eastern Empress's brown eyes narrowed. "Or rather, he keeps his brothers from accruing their own wealth, so as to protect his position." She paused, staring after the prince, who was following his nose to the food. "He doesn't care, does he?"

"Maxian? No—I don't think he does. It's not important to him."

Sympathy and anger warred in Martina's face for a moment, then her expression settled into a determined frown. "Then we will watch out for him," she said briskly. "To make sure he's not cheated again."

Anastasia was standing in an alcove just off the atrium of her house, when the water clock began to sound, signaling the seventh hour of the night. The party was winding down—more than half the guests had departed in small groups, escorted by link boys and armed slaves—and the chiming sound beat in her head like a hammer. Everyone else seemed determined to greet the rising sun over the ruins of her feast and many lesser lights were already asleep, curled up in corners or on the couches in the entertaining rooms.

The Duchess pressed the back of a thumb against her eyebrow, hoping to stave off an incipient and formidable migraine. In the brief instant, while her eyes were closed, she heard a murmur of voices and the clatter of boots and sandals on her tile floors. *Someone is leaving*, she thought, giddily. *Oh good!* Gathering herself, she stepped out into the hall and saw the departing guests were the prince, the Empress and the sly gray old shape of Master Gaius Julius.

"Lord Prince," Anastasia said, bowing slightly. "I am very pleased you came this evening. And thank you for your help. Without your 'additions,' I fear my little play would have fallen rather flat."

"My pleasure," Maxian said. He seemed very relaxed, his arm around Martina's waist, wine spots on his collar and sleeve. He smiled easily at her, as if they had always been old friends and never enemies. "Thank you, Duchess, for your hospitality. I'm glad our difference of opinion is in the past."

"Of course, my lord," she said, making a polite smile in return. With no desire to reopen old business—particularly with a happily drunk thaumaturge—she bowed to the Eastern Empress with a warm smile. "My lady Martina—I *do* hope your evening ended better than it began."

Martina, though she seemed quite content to lean her head on Maxian's chest, frowned at the Duchess. "You need," she said, in a slightly slurred voice, "to invite a better *class* of guests."

Anastasia felt her stomach—already brutalized by too much wine and too many salty olives—turn over queasily. *And she's a mean drunk*, the Duchess thought despairingly. At the same moment, she caught sight of Gaius Julius turning abruptly, looking behind him.

"My dear," Anastasia took Martina's hand. "I am so sorry—please, come again, when you are in Rome and we will sit together in private and have a wonderful, delightful time. I do not want your memory of my house to be distasteful."

"That would be nice," the Empress said, perking up. The Duchess saw her pupils were dilated and realized the young woman was half-asleep on her feet. "You have a nice house."

"Thank you." Stepping aside, Anastasia glanced over Martina's shoulder and saw, to her surprise, Gaius Julius deftly interposing himself between the prince, the Empress and an approaching Helena. The Western Empress was already clad in cloak and hood, her face tense. *Oh, dear.* "Come, I'll walk you out," she continued smoothly. "Your escort is waiting—alert and well-fed—I assure you!"

The porters were watching and the big door panels swung wide as they approached. The courtyard before the house was well-lit by torches and a bonfire. The warm night air flooded over them, carrying the sweet, heady smell of citrus and cooking smoke. Several Praetorians emerged, armor gleaming dully in the torchlight. They were alert, hands ready on the hilts of their swords, every other man carrying a lantern.

"My lord?" The centurion in charge of the detachment stepped up, saluting the prince. "Where bound tonight, Caesar?"

"Our house on the Cispian Hill," Maxian said, casting about for Gaius Julius. The older man appeared quickly, hurrying out of the house. As the old Roman passed Anastasia, he inclined his head and gave her a queer look, almost a wink or a nod. The Duchess did not respond, smiling politely, and kissed Martina on each cheek. The Empress smiled back, squeezing her hand.

"Good night," Anastasia said, watching them saunter out onto the street, surrounded by a moving wall of iron and bared steel. Despite the late hour and the prince's powers, his guardsmen were neither relaxed nor inattentive. The nighted streets of Rome were dangerous, even for members of the Imperial family.

"Well."

The Duchess turned, heart sinking, and found Helena waiting on the threshold, eyes glittering, watching the prince and his party disappearing down the street. "Helena, what—"

"What did I say to Gaius Julius or what did he say to me?"

Anastasia pursed her lips, registering the cold, even tone in her friend's voice. "What did you say?"

Helena drew up her hood. "I wished to speak with Empress Martina. I intended to apologize."

"And he said?" The Duchess looked down the street. Empty. Even the gleam of the torches on cobblestone was gone.

"He said the Empress was overtired and would be happy to speak with me at another time."

Anastasia closed her eyes again in relief, nodding to herself. Well done, old goat. *Well done.* "He was right, she was barely awake. Too much wine and food, I think."

"Really." The icy tone in the Empress's voice brought the Duchess around to face her again.

"Yes—I spoke with them both—she was barely intelligible." Anastasia stepped close to Helena, lowering her voice. "And she was drunk and irritable. Master Gaius did everyone a favor, I think, by keeping you apart."

Helena's lip twisted as she stepped away. "Should I send him a note in the morning, thanking him for insulting me?"

More Praetorians gathered inside and Anastasia heard the Emperor's voice raised in farewell.

"Listen to me," the Duchess hissed, drawing Helena into the

shadows at the edge of the door. "You must know how delicate things are. I know Gaius is at work—my informers and spies are watching him every minute—and he is doing many things in the prince's name, not all of them known to our dear Maxian. This business of the Empress and her affection is just one of his plans."

Helena screwed up her face in a gruesome scowl. "So you want to win her away from him—not the prince *him*, but Gaius Julius *him*. With your own game and your own plans."

Anastasia nodded, watching the Empress's face intently. "Yes. You have to be civil to her, at least, if you cannot be friends."

Helena's scowl did not recede. "You watch *him* closely then, with an eagle's eye."

"Every moment," the Duchess replied. Then the Emperor was in the doorway, his son asleep on his shoulder, and everyone was bidding one another good night.

NEAR IBLIS

)H(

Mohammed became aware of the sky rippling like glossy cloth. The branches of the fig tree were dark in relief against the unremitting brilliance of the heavens. He focused and the sky settled back into a perfectly unremarkable blue. The sun remained a bright disk, shedding only a cold clear radiance on white-limbed trees and emerald grass.

This world is illusion, Mohammed realized. The thought seemed to have emerged from a great depth, slowly ascending to his waking consciousness. *Did not Mōha change shape as I watched? Is not the city filled with phantoms and deceit? Is anything here real? Am I real?*

For an instant, Mohammed felt a plunging sense of vertigo. Everything seemed to whirl about him with tremendous winds—there was no earth beneath his back—no air to breath—not even the cold glare of the perfect sun on his face. Horrible, gut-wrenching fear clawed at his mind, urging him to scream or flee or strike out wildly. He could feel his hands and feet fray, dissolving in the storm.

I am real! he answered, trying to shout against the maelstrom. No sound issued from his mouth. Indeed, there was no sound around him, no rush or wail of the winds, no singing zephyrs, no blast upon his face. He forced his eyes open again. The sun remained overhead. The leaves of the fig silhouetted, perfectly motionless, against the blue sky. *I am real. The fig is real.*

Tentatively, he forced a hand to rise and brush against the mottled gray-and-white bark of the tree. *I can feel you . . . but where did you come from? From this sterile earth?* With an effort, for his muscles were stiff with disuse, Mohammed turned his head and looked into the forest. There were no fig trees. There were no trees with irregular bark, surrounded by a litter of fallen twigs. Not like the many-fingered leaves scattered around him at the base of his tree. Wait . . . He remembered putting something in his pocket, long ago, past an eternity of battle and driving rain and the god speaking in the sky with a voice of thunder. *I was eating a fig, as we sat waiting in darkness for the Persian horsemen to cross the stream. Zoë was at my side.*

Neck creaking, Mohammed looked down and found the tattered remains of his cloak still clinging to his body. Bloodstains on the cloth had turned dark brown and the leather greaves on his shins were cracked open. *I put the pit in my pocket, he remembered, the pocket of my cloak.*

Straining, his skeletal fingers groped in the crumbling fabric and found the pocket eroded away. Only the roots of the tree could be felt.

"A seed fell," Mohammed croaked, "on barren ground and yielded up this life. Where none had been before. Fruit to feed me, leaves to catch the tears of the dead, the conscience of the earth to remind me of the will of the lord of the world. As he made all things from darkness and men from clots of blood." He sat up.

As before, the city lay below him, beyond the grassy sward.

The creature Mōha was nowhere to be seen. Instead, the faint trill of pipes and the merry thump and clatter of drums touched his hearing, rising from the streets and houses below. The pungent smell of a dung fire pierced the air. The sound brought the promise of joy and the warm embrace of old friends in hospitable surroundings.

"What would I see . . ." he mused aloud, climbing to his feet, spindly arms clinging to the bole of the tree. His legs began to shake with fatigue. Mohammed gritted his teeth, tasting the sting of bitter alkali from eroded bone and enamel. "What would I see there, if I passed through the broken gate and into the city?"

"You would find rest and comfort," a voice said, "at the end of a long, hard road."

Mohammed pushed away from the tree to stand unsupported. A woman was walking up the hill towards him and for just an instant he thought Khadijah had returned from the forest of the dead. She was of middling height; her hair tied back, a long dress of soft, subtle colors falling to her feet. Her hands were unadorned with bracelets or rings and thin, almost translucent fabric clung to her breast and thigh.

Mohammed tensed, seeing now something of Zoë in her oval face, high cheekbones, dark eyes. Another spirit, he guessed. "Who are you?"

"I am Ráha," she answered in a warm, friendly voice. Streaks of white crept through obsidian hair. "The last of your guides."

Swallowing, Mohammed felt his dry throat crack. The voice was so familiar . . . but he could not put a name to her, no familiar face, nothing but a faint memory of singing—a lullaby—and a rocking sensation. *A camel? A ship at sea?* He felt his skin grow cold. *A crib? It was a crib. Mine.* "Where would you guide me? Into the city? Into death?"

"Yes," Ráha said, concerned. "Aren't you tired? You have traveled a long way, seeking solace for the emptiness in your heart." She lifted a hand, pointing to the gates and towers. "What you seek, what your heart desires, lies within the city. An end to your labors, deserved rest, your family, respect, honor. A white beard covering old knees as you cradle your grandson in your arms."

"And the dead trapped in the dark wood, what of them?" Mohammed tugged at the scrap of a cloak around his neck and the decayed wool fell to dust between his fingers. With the movement of his limbs, the rest of his garments sighed away, falling in a brown rain around his feet. "I will not abandon the innocent."

Ráha raised her chin, pointing into the wood. "They cannot enter, my lord, because you are here, balanced between life and death. While you remain, they cannot pass into the city and thereby to the land of the dead."

Mōha said the same thing, Mohammed remembered. *Is it true?*

"You must choose to pass on," Ráha continued. "You are endangering those who still live." She smiled and Mohammed felt her compassion like a physical blow, a balled fist in his gut. "Every spirit fears change—and yours is very strong! It clings tenaciously to the memory of life. These are not your arms and legs," she said, gesturing to the weak, spindly limbs holding him up. Ráha's forehead wrinkled in thought. "This is the flesh of a dead man, withering in the ground. You must let go of this illusion of life. Free the multitude trapped in this terrible balance. Don't you hear them wailing, frightened, each alone in the darkness?"

"I do," he said. "But I will not yield to your foul master! My work among the living is not complete. The great and merciful one has set me a task, which remains yet undone. So, I say to you, malign spirit, I will return to the living world. I will not enter the city. Yet, by my absence, the dead will be freed to pass on, and find peace."

"But," Ráha said, perplexed, "your work *is* done. The Emperor Heraclius, who betrayed the cities of the Decapolis, is dead, his corpse only one among thousands, nameless and unmarked. Your people have been freed, your enemies revenged. Even now they claim a great destiny in your name. Your teachings will live on, forever. The allotted span of your days has come to an end."

"The lord of the wasteland," Mohammed said sharply, "sets the beginning and the ending of each man's life—yes, he who made men from clots of blood, from clay—he sets the rising and the setting of the sun! Not you, not your master, not his slave Mōha or any other power! I was struck down by treachery, my efforts incomplete! The voice from the clear air guides me, showing a clear and righteous path against evil!"

Rāha stepped back from his vehemence, an expression of grave concern coming over her. "Evil? My lord, all things have an ending. There is no evil in death, only the wheel of change, of life, turning as it has always turned. The means of change do not matter, only its inevitability. *All things end!* Even you, even I."

Mohammed licked his lips, overcome by a sensation of nervousness. *She is speaking the truth.*

"O Man, observe," Rāha said, spreading her hands wide. A glittering circle opened in the air, through which Mohammed saw a thicket of pine and thistle. A stag crashed through the brush, followed by a swift, golden bolt of fur. The lion struck hard, massive jaws crunching into the stippled brown neck of the deer. Both animals went down in a cloud of dust and branches, the stag kicking, the lion's rear claws tearing bloody streaks across a heavy tan pelt. "Here is the engine of the world, of all creation! There is no permanence—only change—and in this world, men die. Women die. Everything passes with the turning of the wheel. New life springs from the old." Rāha looked up, her lambent dark eyes blazing. Mohammed felt a void open before him, saw scattered stars glitter on a field of sable. They grew, swelling enormous and dark, a doorway opening in the air before him. "Your time has come. Accept this."

A faint, ethereal wailing trembled in the air and Mohammed knew the dead were pleading with him, shouting in their faint voices, bending their will upon him for release. He felt the weariness of his bones, the fatigue settling in what muscle and sinew remained. Even his thoughts were slow, attenuated, stretched to the utmost. He heard temple bells and the chant for the dead, a slow, mournful dirge on a thousand voices. Drums rolled, echoing the tramp of sandals on a dusty plain. *A funeral procession,* he recognized. *It must be mine.*

"No," Mohammed managed to gasp. He was on his knees again, barely able to stand. "I will not abandon my purpose. The judge of judges will account the deeds of my life, when I stand before him. Until that day, when the lord of the world commands me lay down my purpose, I will not surrender."

"Are you the maker of all things?" Ráha knelt beside him, a pale hand on his shoulder. "Are you the judge of good and evil?"

"No!" Mohammed drew away from her. "I am only a man."

"How can you know your purpose continues? This *is* the end of your time. You must pass on!" A tone of urgent pleading crept into her voice.

"No—I will not! I will not be driven by thirst, by fear, by temptation, by the blandishments of the spirits here. I will endure. A great evil has entered the world—a serpent with countless heads, arms, bodies—I have seen the dark power walking under the sun, cloaked in the shape of a man. The voice from the clear air has spoken, setting me to strive against *shaitan* and all his spawn."

Ráha shook her head in despair. "Still you seek to name evil. I ask again, are you the judge of judges?"

"I am not," Mohammed snapped, "yet the voice of the empty places guides me to a righteous life! My heart sings to hear him, showing me a certain path. I will not let the whole world die, consumed by the serpent, crushed in leviathan coils! I will not step aside, while there is work yet undone!"

The woman rose, lips pursed. She cupped her hands and a spark appeared, fluttering like a butterfly. The flickering glow lit her face with warm light. "You are not *listening*. Certainty is oblivion. Immutability disaster. Only in the motion of change—in birth and death—is there life. The voice speaking to you is only one of many, only part of a great chorus. Everything, even what you name *evil* has a place in that choir."

"No—" Mohammed recoiled. "Not the abomination! The Lord of Serpents is a stain on the perfection of creation!"

A beneficent smile spread across Ráha's features. "Creation is imperfect. In all things a flaw—even in the wisdom of your guide, this voice from the clear air." She closed her hands over the light sputtering between her fingers. Darkness flooded the air around them, drowning sight of the grass, the city, even the swaying branches of the fig. "You claim the power in the desert as your patron, saying he raised the race of men from clay, from blood, from the very soil. So he did."

A vision burst over Mohammed, stunning his mind. *A vast city rose up around him, cyclopean towers piercing leaden clouds, titanic shapes moving in the chill air. In the distance, mountains of ice encroached upon the city, glittering blue-white walls looming over soapstone colored buildings. Abandoned doorways yawned on streets tenanted solely by cold whirlwinds. A singular slate-gray tower swelled into view, colossal, every surface covered with deeply incised glyphs and signs. A window filled his vision and he looked down upon a great chamber, filled with shining, dark machines. Glimmering lightning flared in the shadows and something huge bent over a slab of mirrored black stone. Glossy rust-colored wings shifted, one pair, then four rising and falling around a ridged circumference. A tiny creature squirmed and writhed on the gleaming table, screaming endlessly. Bright red blood smeared silky fur. Stubby-fingered hands groped mindlessly at the air. Delicate white cilia descended, adjusting minute jewel-like tools.*

Mohammed jerked back, horrified. Ráha was watching him from the darkness. The vision faded, the vast city falling away into dimness, buried by the relentless ice. The terrible cold lingered, pricking his skin as the tiny knives had worked in the living body of the furred creature.

"Did you think the birth of the race of men was pure? No— even in the beginning there was imperfection." Ráha drew close, her hands radiating a faint heat. The light between her palms glowed through her skin and Mohammed could see the outline of delicate finger bones. "From base flaw rose wonders unlooked for. The power, which presses the Sun and the Moon into its service, encompasses all things, men not least of all. Do not seek certainty, my lord. How can love grow, among such cold geometries?"

"Was—" Mohammed's horror choked the words in his throat. "Was this the face of the Wise One, who created men from dust, from a little germ . . ." He could not continue, stunned.

"Is the face of a newborn the face of a grown man?" The woman's voice was faint in the darkness. "Is the face of the grandson, the face of the grandfather? As the wheel turns, even the foulest act may plant a seed of joy. All things transform . . ."

Ráha opened her hands, letting stuttering, flaring light spill forth. Mohammed staggered back—in the flashing light, in the dark spaces between the warm golden flare, Ráha filled the world; enormous, blue-black arms like wheel spokes, reaching from earth to sky, myriad faces looking upon all directions and compasses. A thousand hands moved as one, a bending forest pressed by hurricane winds and delicate feet danced on the crown of the world, ringed with whirling, blazing suns. The man became aware of a tone, a singing single note, vibrating in the void. His eyes widened, and the last of his body cracked and crumbled into ash, rushing away in the wind from the abyss.

The woman closed her hands and the vision collapsed into a burning fire-encircled mote, then a shimmering cruciform letter, then into nothing. The golden light faded and the trembling tone faded away into the sighing branches of the fig tree. Even the sky snapped back into focus, a flat curtain of blue arcing overhead.

"Do you see?" Ráha said. "You must let go of this shell. You must go onward."

Mohammed could only feel the *thud-thud* of his heart. Even the woman's voice was very faint and far away. Glorious visions blinded him, and most of all, he heard a familiar, beloved sound, echoing in the spaces between his heartbeat, in the spaces between Ráha's words.

It is the sound of the morning of the world, he wondered, overcome with fierce emotion. *The wind blowing in empty spaces. The tide. The moon. The roar of the surf on a barren shore. It is the voice from the clear air.*

⊞-0-⊡-0-⊡-0-⊡-0-⊡-0-⊡-0-⊡-0-⊡-0-⊡-0-⊡-0-⊡-0-⊡-0-⊡-0-⊞

ABOVE THE HARBOR OF PHOSPHERION, CONSTANTINOPLE

)⊟(

Iron shoes clattered on stone paving, drowning the jangle and clank of armor and shields. Khadames jogged wearily up a sloping, narrow street, shoulder to shoulder with a mass of Persian *grivpani*. The soldiers were clad in lamellar mail from head to toe, vision reduced to a pair of reinforced eyeholes in a conical helm. For the moment, while the column rattled into an octagonal plaza overlooking the Golden Horn, Khadames' helmet bounced on a strap over one shoulder. Sweating heavily in the bulky armor, the general needed to see more than he needed protection—at least for the moment!

A steadily increasing din echoed back from the three- and four-story buildings; a sustained hoarse shouting and the ring of booted feet on stone. Khadames, though he was bone-weary, gathered himself and pushed ahead, jogging through the mass of his column. The other *diquans* tramped on, one foot in front of the other, but Khadames knew they were exhausted. The heavy overlapping armor and plated shoes of the Persian nobleman was not made for marching on foot. They were designed for fighting from a powerful horse. But here in the confines of the city, in these narrow, twisting streets and overhanging lanes, among the rubble, their chargers were of little use.

Khadames jogged into the plaza, a spiked mace already in hand, small round shield strapped to his left arm. A crowd of men ran towards him, shouting in alarm. They were a disordered, panicky mob of Armenian mercenaries with braided beards and fish-scale armor. Part of the motley army the King of Kings had left to defend the captured city. Khadames cursed tiredly to himself, resting his mace on one shoulder. *What did they see, a ghost?* His voice, pitched to carry, rang out. "Persia, to me! Bannermen, to me!"

Some of the fleeing men slowed, staring in apprehension at the column of armored *diquans* stomping up the street. Khadames clouted one of them on the shoulder, bringing him to a startled halt. "Why are you running?" the general shouted. The Armenian blinked, panic fading as he saw stalwart men filling the plaza, then turned and pointed.

"The Greeks are coming!" he blurted, eyes wide. "The spear wall is coming!"

One iron-sheathed hand grasping the man's leather collar, Khadames gestured in an arc with the mace. "Triple line," he bellowed, harsh voice reverberating from the scorched, soot-stained buildings. "Prepare to advance at a walk!"

Persian *grivpani* spilled out into the plaza, rattling and clanking, forming up around the tall, golden standards of the house of Sassan. The generals' own battle flag arrived—a deep crimson sunflower on a field of blue—and Khadames took comfort from the familiar banner's presence. His forefathers had fought for nine generations under the watchful eyes of the *tavgul*. The Persian knights began to form their line, small shields braced, maces, long swords and spears at the ready. The older, more experienced men pushed up to take the front rank. Khadames paced west to the end of the formation, dark eyes scanning the men, looking for loose buckles, untied straps, anything to fail in the shock of battle, fouling a man's arm. The front of a temple, painted columns cracked and splintered by terrible heat, formed an anchor for their flank. Khadames was pleased to see his men were still game for a fight.

"You—what did you see?" The general turned to the hapless mercenary, now in the hands of two of his bodyguards. "Where were you, and why did you run?"

The Armenian swallowed nervously, long neck bobbing like a crane dipping. His throat was chafed and red where iron armor rubbed against bare flesh. "Great lord," he stammered, "we were marching to the port from the Gate of Gold. By your command, we were told!"

Khadames nodded, gesturing for the man to continue. As he had feared when Shahr-Baraz departed, the army left under his command was too small—particularly without the feckless, cowardly Avars—to hold the massive length of Constantinople's walls. Had the city been a friendly one, with a citizen militia to watch for attacks and handle simple patrols, he could have managed. As it was, with the gate of Charisus and several hundred feet of the double outer wall smashed to rubble by Lord Dahak's invocation, his paltry force of horsemen and mercenaries were simply not up to the job.

The evacuation of the city had begun as the dawn wind rose, with the first ships slipping away from the Golden Horn, heading for the wharfs and quays of the eastern side of the strait. Khadames had hoped the Romans would fail to notice the withdrawal of the Persian regiments from the walls. The mercenaries had been informed a few hours later. Khadames hoped they would make a sufficient screen for the departure of his own men. *A faint hope*, he thought wearily, *and now crushed by circumstance*.

"We heard the Romans entered the city," the lancer hurried on, "so our captain bade us march—at double-time—back down the western road to the harbor." The man rubbed the back of a glove against his mustache. "When we entered the big plaza with the arch we saw the Greeks. Our captains made us form a line, spears forward, with other companies gathering there. But the Greeks rushed with their spear wall and broke through the line. All we could do was run."

Khadames nodded, though each word dropped into his stomach like a leaden weight. The "big plaza" must be the forum of the Bull, only a few blocks away to the south, nearly at the center of the city. If the Roman army and their thrice-damned "spear wall" were fighting there, most of his men remaining in the city were cut off. The evacuation was still underway down on the docks and time was running short.

"Very well," Khadames said, stirring himself to action. He glanced across the plaza; more Armenian and Persian stragglers were passing through the triple line, though their numbers had slowed to one and twos. He waved, drawing the attention of his lieutenant, who was busily moving among the men. "Kavilar! Stand ready to charge the Romans as they deploy." The general turned to the cluster of aides and runners gathered behind him.

"You men," he said, "quick to the harbor—tell the ship captains to debark as quickly as they fill their decks. The Romans are pressing hard—we want to get as many men away to Chalcedon as possible before they overrun the docks." Two of the runners nodded sharply, then sprinted off down the hill.

From this height, despite the smoke-blackened apartments surrounding the plaza, Khadames could make out the glittering blue waters of the Golden Horn and the white sails of his small fleet. The sight made the twisting in his stomach worse. Despite the King of King's assurances, the departure of the Arab fleet had left Khadames with too few hulls to carry his entire army to safety in one go. Years of soldiering the length and breadth of Persia had not prepared the elderly general for dealing with ships, currents and loading capacities. Worst of all, to his mind, there was no way the army could make the two-hour voyage across the Propontis to Chalcedon with their horses. Not without dozens of trips back and forth . . . not when a single warhorse took the space of five men . . . *Yet, what use is my army*, he thought bitterly, *without horses? We're not infantry, we'll have to walk back to Ctesiphon . . .*

"You and you," he barked, long-simmering anger spilling over into his voice. "Take five men each and run to the nearest cross streets, watch for other Roman columns! If they come, send a runner to me immediately!" Both sergeants jogged away, shouting for men from the rear ranks.

Beyond the impossibility of holding the lengthy fortifications, Khadames' army was scattered in a bewildering ruin. Constantinople was far larger than any Persian city and poorly laid out to boot. The streets wound and twisted like snakes, the plazas and squares seemed randomly placed, as if the gods cast them like dust or coins upon broken ground. The old general had heard there were hidden passages under the streets, covered cisterns and buried roads—but his scouts, crawling through the burned-out wreckage, had failed to find any of these secret places. *But the Romans will know their own city*, he worried, feeling bile rise in his throat. He looked down the hill again. Three merchantmen were pulling out of the harbor, long sweeps working, sails billowing taut with the sharp wind from the north. *We're too far from the docks*, he realized. *We need to fall back down the—*

"Here they come!" a dozen men in the front rank shouted as one.

Cursing, Khadames climbed the steps of the abandoned temple to get a better view.

The entire mass of Persians in the plaza stiffened to the right, men closing up ranks behind the shields of their fellows. The second line of men moved up, spears ready in both hands. The rear line milled in slight confusion—some of the fleeing Armenians had joined the Persian formation. Khadames took all this in with one swift glance, then his eyes flew to the mouth of the street leading from the forum of the Bull. Already, he could hear the booming *stamp-stamp-stamp* of marching men. Dust puffed from the buildings, hazing the air, then a thicket of glit-

tering iron appeared. The long spears of the Roman wall of battle suddenly filled the street, then the close-packed mass of legionaries emerged at a walk from the avenue.

The old general suppressed an atavistic shudder. *A phalanx*,
he thought in amazement, *in these late days! Four ranks with
sixteen-foot pikes. Who had the time and money to train them
this way?* To his knowledge, no one had fielded a phalanx in
battle since the rebel Indian king Soter Megas had been crushed
by the T'u-chüeh five hundred years ago. The Romans advanced in good order, their *sarissa* leveled in three overlapping
layers, with a fourth dancing in the air. Heavy, full-face helmets
made the Roman soldiers appear monstrous, without even a
hint of humanity.

"Steady! Hold. Hold!" screamed the Persian sergeants. Their
men started to back away, uneasily aware of the reach of the enemy weapons. "Charge!"

Khadames held his breath, waiting for the *diquans* to lunge
forward, blades and shields up, to crash into the Roman line.
The close-packed ranks of the enemy did not seem maneuver-
able and getting to sword strokes with them, inside the reach of
their spears, would be crucial.

"Charge!" The Persian sergeants ran forward, swords flashing. After a moment's hesitation, the front rank surged forward,
each man determined to keep honor, yet still grappling with
rising gut-twisting fear of the enemy's forest of bright steel.
Drawn by the same terrible compulsion, the *diquans* in the second rank also moved, a sudden shout bellowing from a hundred
throats. Khadames felt his heart leap at the brave sound.
"Shahr-Baraz! Persia!"

"Adorio!" the Romans boomed back, a colossal thundering
sound, and the spear wall leapt forward with a glad cry. In the
blink of an eye, the phalanx slammed into the Persian rush with
a cracking, sharp *clang*. Khadames stiffened, seeing the front
rank of his men stagger. The Roman pikes stabbed viciously,
knocking the heavily armored *diquans* down. The Persians
hacked madly at the ashwood spear hafts, trying to chop
through the lacquered wood. Mercilessly, the second and third
ranks of legionaries stabbed overhand. Heartsick, Khadames
saw a *diquan*, his flowing beard streaked with blood, fall,

pierced by two, then three, of the leaf-shaped blades. The man flailed wildly with his cavalry sword, but the enemy was still a dozen feet away, far outside his blows. Roman pikes ground the dying man into the street, then the blades licked back, bright with blood.

For an endless moment, the two masses of men struggled at the edge of the plaza, armor ringing with hammer blows, sergeants shouting hoarsely, the roar of men lost in the fury of combat welling up, reverberating from the walls of the empty houses. Then the Roman line took a step, then another, and the Persian front rank disintegrated. A carpet of dead men littered the octagonal stones of the plaza. The second and third lines of Persians shouted furiously and attacked again, surging forward. The legionary pikes fouled and some of the Armenians—eager to burnish tarnished honor—were among them, hacking wildly, shield to shield with the Romans. A pikeman went down, helmet caved in and the front rank of the phalanx began to erode into knots of struggling men.

"That's it," Khadames screamed, springing down the steps. He crammed the helmet onto his head, waving at the nearest men. "Forward, lads, into their flank!"

One of the runners, turning to see what the general wanted, shouted in alarm, pointing back behind Khadames. The general spun, suddenly off-balance, iron shoes skidding on paving worn smooth by centuries of pious traffic. Reflexively, his left arm came up, shield covering his face to his eyes. At the same time, he swung the mace back, ready to strike.

A big oval shield slammed into him, the reinforced iron boss smashing into his hip with a deep *crunch*. Khadames felt himself lifted from his feet, caught a brief glimpse of a blue-eyed man standing at least a head taller than him behind the Roman *scutum*, then the sky cartwheeled past and he crashed down on the paving. His helmet rang like a bell on stone, deafening him. Stunned and breathless, the old general gasped for air. A sharp, stabbing pain radiated out of his hip.

Wouldn't happen if I was on my horse, he thought blearily. *Got to . . . get up.*

Men with armored greaves on their legs ran past and the sharp ringing of steel on steel filled the air. Khadames pushed himself up on one arm. His mace was gone, wrenched from his hand by the blow. As he rolled over, the pain in his hip spiked and a gray haze washed across his vision. Numbly, he groped for the hilt of his sword. *Ormazd take this damned thing . . .*

The sword was trapped under his broken hip. Khadames, teeth gritted against a roaring pain in his head, rolled back, freeing the weapon. The sky blurred past again, partially obscured by rooftops and windows in a white-plastered wall. Heavy, clumsy fingers managed to curl around the wire-wrapped hilt of his blade. *There!*

A horsetail-plumed helmet obscured the buildings and the sky. Something heavy crunched down on Khadames' neck, metal scraping on metal, pinning him to the ground. Khadames tried to cry out, but only managed to force a gasp past the boot crushing his gorget. He dragged at the sword, feeling the yard length of steel slide free from the sheath. Sunlight flared from the head of a spiked axe, then the old general cried out as the blade whistled through the air. Steel rang on steel, and something crashed against his collarbone.

Bastard's just going to chop my head off! Khadames thought, trying to roll and knock the man from his feet. As he did, a sharp, stabbing pain crushed his chest. Choking, the Persian flailed with his sword. There was a curse and the boot disappeared from his throat. Khadames cut blindly with the sword again, but the edge caught only air. He tried to breathe, failed, and felt a gray tide wash over him. Wheezing, his head rattled back on the stones.

Battle swirled across him, the Persian knights counterattacking as the phalanx lost cohesion. One of the *grivpani* knelt beside Khadames, trying to help him rise. But the old general's eyes were dim and clouded, breath cold, his dutiful heart having failed at last.

One hand wrapped in Bucephalas' reins, Alexandros strode along the harborside. A broad Roman street lined the water, faced on one side by single-story warehouses—some now burning, others with doors hanging on broken hinges where the legionaries had broken them down to root out Persian stragglers—the other by the choppy, dark waters of the Golden

Horn. To the east, where the sun—slanting through dark gray clouds—glittered on the waters of the Propontis, he could see the triangular shapes of tan-colored sails.

"Chlothar, how many escaped?" The Macedonian pointed with his chin at the distant ships. At least two merchantmen were burning in the harbor, cordage and sail billowing smoke, hulls settling lower in the water with each passing grain.

"Our watchers on the Galatan hill," the big Frank replied, "counted sixty ships of various sizes. Maybe six, seven thousand men in all—packed on the decks like herring. They must have left their mounts, wagons and supplies behind."

"Good. We can use all those things." Alexandros grinned, teeth white in a face dark with sweat, soot and spattered, dried blood. The Macedonian felt light, invigorated. He still held a *spatha*-style cavalry sword bare in his hand. The fighting on the docks had ended only moments before and the prospect of a few Persians hiding out among the abandoned buildings was very real. "The Persians are fine horsemen—they will not have slaughtered them. Send the Eastern troops to quarter the city, block by block, calling for their fellows to come out, and find me those horses."

The Frank nodded, long pigtails bouncing on armored shoulders. Like Alexandros, Chlothar was stained and battered, with long creases bent in his armored breastplate and links missing from the mail covering his arms and legs. His face was grim and set. "I wonder, *comes*, if anyone lives in this death house. . . ."

"They do." Alexandros licked his lips—he felt thirst, which was rare in his current state—and looked up at the hills rising over the harbor. The sight of so many buildings, so closely packed together, filled him with amazement. This city rivaled Rome for the sheer mass of humanity once dwelling behind the gaping windows and blackened doors. "Even the windrows of dead we saw in the outer city cannot account for so many souls. More will be hiding, fearful, in cellars and hidden rooms or in the cisterns." He paused, remembering his father's men dragging prisoners in golden cloaks from secret chambers beneath the floors of a mighty palace. *Persepolis*, he thought, the scene as bright in his memory as if it had occurred yesterday. *They thought to avoid my justice for their regicide.* "They will have hidden from the Persians, thinking they would meet a horrific fate, but they will come out when they hear familiar voices calling."

The harbor district was battered, but the buildings still had roofs and walls and the courtyards were free of corpses and scattered bones. The outer wards of the city, between the great walls and the lesser, crumbling, ill-repaired old wall of Constantinople, were a different matter. The sights greeting his army once they entered the city proper had shaken even Alexandros, insulated as he was by the quirk of fate setting him beyond mortality. Entire districts along the Northern Road had been leveled, not a stone standing on stone, and the wizened corpses of the dead filled every space along the streets and byways. At one point, they had crossed a square where some colossal fire had raged out of control, shattering the paving stones, burning the lime from the buildings, leaving nothing but huge drifts of whitened bone and countless skulls.

Alexandros had never seen such devastation. *Did the gods struggle here, on earth? Surely only the bolts of Zeus Thundershielded could yield such destruction!*

"Where is the Khazar lord Dahvos?" The Macedonian turned back to Chlothar, wrenching his thoughts away from such a distressing conclusion. Unbidden, his eyes turned again to the east, squinting into the bright glare from the water at the distant shore of Chalcedon. "We must discuss our next campaign."

"Aye, *comes*." The Frank stepped away, calling for his household knights.

Alexandros climbed onto a low stone wall at the edge of the quay. Bucephalas bumped his leg with a heavy head, nose snuffling at the Macedonian's hand. "You'll eat soon, my friend," Alexandros laughed, rubbing the stallion's white forehead blaze. "Oats and apples, or a bit of carrot."

The eastern shoreline was obscured—the clouds over the strait were spilling dark wavering veils of rain—but he was sure he could pick out the glint of light reflecting from metal, from armor. *Asia*, he wondered, a sick hot feeling in his chest. *Again, my enemies are on the further shore.* He looked down and saw his right hand was shaking. Alexandros pressed the palm to his chest and found his heart racing like a hare.

"Not long," he promised himself, unable to repress a grin, "not long before I march on Persia again."

◙-[O]-[O]-[O]-[O]-[O]-[O]-[O]-[O]-[O]-[O]-[O]-[O]-[O]-[O]-[O]-[O]-[O]-[O]-◙

IN THE BRUCHION, ALEXANDRIA, ROMAN EGYPT

)-(

Is this how things usually turn out for you?" Thyatis hitched both thumbs into her girdle. She and Nicholas stood in a small, low-ceilinged office in the vast, confusing sprawl of the Bruchion—the consolidated governor's office, public park, royal palace and military headquarters of Rome in lower Egypt. The ancient complex filled nearly a quarter of the original city. This particular room was littered with scraps of papyrus and parchment, ratty-looking wooden desks and the faint, pervasive odor of scented balm. A shutter on the single high narrow window was jammed shut with old scroll cases and a scattering of lemon peels in one corner showed an impressive array of mold. Fruiting bodies sprouted from white fuzz, dark purple tips rising in tiny crenellated towers. The condition of the room indicated no one had actually worked in the chamber for weeks, perhaps months.

Nicholas' eyelid twitched at Thyatis' question and his scowl deepened. "Last year, when I was here, the tribune in charge of the Egyptian Office worked here." Angrily, he kicked a pile of discolored parchment aside with his foot.

"Just as well," Thyatis said, turning slowly in a circle. The humidity in the room was stifling. She squinted out into the hallway. There was another cubicle opposite—indeed, there were dozens of equally small, cramped offices packed into the warren of the old Ptolemaic palace—and Thyatis realized she could see the air in the passage as a faint haze. "We really don't have time to chase down the local authorities."

Nicholas grimaced, automatically smoothing the sleek points of his mustache. "You don't believe these rumors running wild in the streets? This is *Alexandria!* Someone sees a two-headed snake in their garden and they think the gods have returned! The Persians will never reach the city—Caesar Aurelian has *six* Legions with him! You have no idea how massive the fortifications at the eastern edge of the delta are."

"Hmm." Thyatis turned over some of the papers on the desk. The tan-colored parchment was covered with blackish-gray spots the size of her thumbnail. "Every official we've seen in this maze is either petrified with fear or smug as a cat thinking he'll move up when the Persians arrive. The soldiers in the port were the same way—the Romans grim and all-too-efficient, the Egyptians taking it easy, thinking they'll all have a body slave each and hands filled with the King of King's gold."

"They're fools." Nicholas shrugged. His confidence in the Empire was unshaken. "The authorities will remember who was loyal and who was not, afterward." He grinned at the prospect. "Some of the Eastern network must still be intact— I'll root around and see if I can find anyone to help us."

"A good idea," Thyatis said, stepping into the corridor. Two clerks hurried past, avoiding her eyes. When they were out of earshot, she said: "Come. It's dangerous to remain here. The Persians will have their own spies busy in the city. I'll get the others from the ship and find someplace quiet to stay on the edge of town. Meet me by sunset at the Nile Canal gate."

"Huh!" Nicholas perked up. Thyatis hid a smile—her *loyal ally* had grown increasingly impatient as the day progressed. He had a message pouch held inside his tunic with a leather cord. She'd considered lifting the packet, but thought—upon reflection—she preferred to see who merited such swift delivery. *Who do you need to report to, my friend? One of Gaius Julius' agents, doubtless, waiting with equal impatience for your delivery*.

"A good idea," Nicholas continued, looking relieved. "I've an idea of where to look. . . ."

Tossing off a Legion salute, though Thyatis doubted the man truly regarded her as his commanding officer, Nicholas strode off. Taking her time, the Roman woman followed. She was hot and sweaty under the properly demure *stola*, hooded cloak and undertunic of a Roman matron, but haste was never rewarded at times like these. The invisibility of the mundane and expected was her friend, a moving blind in the chaotic urban forest.

At the end of the hallway, she found one of the little offices occupied by an elderly Egyptian in priestly robes. He was carefully copying a papyrus scroll onto fresh parchment. A faint scratching sound followed the smooth, effortless motion of his quill. The squared, angular shapes of modern Egyptian appeared, glistening and dark on the cream-colored page.

"Holy father? May I have a moment?"

"Yes?" he said, looking up in irritation. "What do you want?"

"I am looking for my cousin," she said, making a small bow. "A Latin officer—he worked down the hall, wore too much hyacinth perfume, liked lemons?" She offered an engaging, commiserating smile. "Mother never liked the way he smelled."

The old priest snorted in laughter. "Your cousin is gone—I do not know where. He and the other Romans like him packed their bags a day or two ago and went off in wagons towards the port." A faint gleam of satisfaction surfaced in the man's dark eyes, then subsided again. "I believe," the priest continued, seeming to ponder, "they felt continuing to work here might become dangerous. . . ."

"Holy father, do you think the Persians will conquer Egypt?" Thyatis let her voice quaver a little when she said *Persians*.

"Many things could happen, child. But I am sorry—I do not know where Curtius and his friends went." He frowned and Thyatis felt a flash of irritation as she realized his thoughts were veering towards *a young woman abandoned by her male relations! How scandalous!*

"Thank you, father," she said, stepping out of the room before he started trying to help her. A bustling crowd of nervous men and women in the hallway swallowed her up. Thyatis let the traffic carry her through a wooded park filled with riotous wildflowers and into another, more public section of the complex. The tang of fear in the air tickled her nose and she listened to passing conversation with interest—an undercurrent of dread was in every voice.

I smell defeat, Thyatis realized, one eyebrow creeping up. *No one will speak the words aloud, but disaster looms*. Frowning now herself, she began to walk quickly, weaving through the clusters and knots of worried people in the passages. *A noose draws tight around our time, grains spilling from a hidden clock*. Thyatis took the steps out of the main building, down into a crowded, loud street two and three at a time. She felt a swift rush of elation, the air suddenly clear and sharp, the sun bright, the roar and mutter of the crowd exciting rather than depressing. *I'd forgotten how good the hunt feels!*

Standing in the shade of a winged granite ram twenty feet high, Nicholas watched Thyatis bound down the steps in front of the Bruchion and into the crowded avenue. For a moment she was still visible, cowled head bobbing above the crowd, then she turned a corner and was gone. He cleared his throat, and tried to shake away his anger with a twist of his shoulders.

"You're a fool," he muttered to himself, nervous fingers brushing the hilt jutting over his shoulder. Brunhilde was slung Legion-style on a cloth strap over his shoulder. Some calm returned with the touch, but he was still strangely on edge. The message pouch was safe and sound in his belt. "It's odd to have a woman centurion . . . but not that odd. Vladimir is odder. He's a panther in a man's shape. . . ."

The muttered statement failed to relieve his discomfort. He respected her skill—she was deft with a blade, strong, quick-witted, clear-headed, sometimes she was even funny!—but a nagging sense of disquiet refused to leave his thoughts. *I just don't trust her*, he thought angrily. *But we're on the same side, we both serve the Empire . . . does her skill offend me? Why shouldn't a trained woman approach my skill—and where was she trained?* The laconic centurion was a mystery. A tall, firm-breasted, long-legged, redheaded mystery.

"Bah!" he snapped, embarrassed by his thoughts. "Enough of this. There's work to be done, my lad."

Without looking around, he strode back into the palace, following the red cloak of a passing Legion officer towards the governor's offices. A few moments later he entered a cavernous room filled with hunched, busy clerks, furiously scribbling copies of orders, levies, manifests. Nicholas felt a great calm flow over him, smelling and hearing the machine of the Empire in motion. Standing quietly beside the doorway, Nicholas let his gaze wander across the bent heads. *He has to be somewhere . . . there!*

Near the further door, one clerk had a tall stack of leather pouches beside his desk. Each pouch was dark with wear and closed with a winged silver clasp. Two Legion officers were talking quietly to the man. The Greek nodded briskly to the Romans, then accepted a set of parchments. Nicholas touched the packet in his belt again, then pushed away from the wall and walked quickly up to the dispatch master.

"You've charge of the cursus publicus?" Nicholas stopped beside the slave's desk, left arm on the wooden surface, cloak bunched to hide his belt.

"Yes," the Greek said, attention focused on the newly delivered letters. "Just put your messages there in the pile."

Nicholas reached down and seized an exposed ear. With irresistible gentleness, he turned the man to face him. "I have a privy message," he said softly, "from the Emperor, for his brother."

The clerk stared at him in amazement, rubbing his ear. "Fool! I'm the governor's secretary. I'll have you thrown into the street!"

"Will you?" Nicholas drew the message pouch out of his belt, turning the packet to show the dark Tyrian purple seal of the Augustus and God Galen, pressed with the Emperor's own signet, and bound in crimson twine. The Greek's expression congealed into white-lipped fear.

Nicholas' ill humor vanished; replaced by smug satisfaction to see the Greek quail at his words, lean face paling, nimble hands beginning to tremble. "I am the voice of the Emperor, carrying his word, from his own hand. Are you listening now?"

"Yes," whispered the clerk. His eyes focused on Nicholas with gratifying intensity.

"Good." The Latin straightened up, letting the packet drop casually. "I'm on another Imperial errand, my friend, so I leave this matter to you. I've heard the Caesar Aurelian is busy in the eastern delta. You see this reaches him with *all* speed. I've come straightaway from Rome, and neither the prince nor his brother will be pleased if you delay their correspondence."

"Of course not," the Greek managed to say. He picked up the letter with only the tips of his fingers. "A courier is leaving in a few hours. He'll take it."

Nicholas leaned down abruptly, bared teeth white in a sun-browned face. The clerk drew back, the corners of his eyes tightening in fear. "I'll come back later, to make sure the letter sped to Caesar on swift, sure wings. Mercury could do no better, I'm sure, than you will."

The man nodded eagerly, sliding the letter under a small stack of similar packets. "Yes, my lord. The prince will have it tomorrow morning."

Tomorrow? That's too soon. It's two or three days to Pelusium.... Nicholas frowned, right hand knuckled against his side. "Where is Aurelian now? Is the prince on his way back to the city?"

The Greek stiffened again, but this time his eyes flitted around the room, particularly to the door leading deeper into the governor's domain. "Things aren't going well," the clerk whispered. "The Legions are trying to hold a line at Bousiris."

"On the Nile? The Persians are on the Nile?" Nicholas swallowed, throat suddenly dry. *Half of Egypt fallen since we left Rome?*

He was outside the palace, in the street, pushing his way through porters bent under wooden crates and leather-bound trunks before he was aware of moving. There was a man he had to see. Nicholas started to run, though muttering crowds pressed him on every side. The sun, already swollen orange from its descent into the smoke-haze over the city, was only a hand above the buildings to the west.

"Seven by seven," Betia chanted softly to herself, "makes forty and nine."

The little Gaul drifted along a side street in a quiet, residential neighborhood. A raw wool chlamys hid most of her petite figure and she carried a heavy wicker basket. Behind her, at the junction of the street and a small plaza, the corner of an old, crumbling temple was just visible. Seven streets and alleys fed into the plaza and Betia had taken her time while circling the crossroads. From the decrepit temple of Artemis, with its half-seen sanctuary and dusty stone goddess draped in bull testicles, she had chosen the seventh opening. The girl thought the placement of the goddess' temple particularly apt, as the smoke-stained, decaying facade of a Mithraic sanctuary squatted across the plaza. The seventh passage was little more than an alley, but Betia had passed into the fetid dimness without hesitation.

Now she counted doorways, measuring her paces against the Huntress's tread. At the ninth doorway she smiled—her count measured forty steps—and paused, setting the basket down and stretching in apparent weariness. Before her, a worn, curved set of steps led down into deep-set alcove. The dark stone of the door arch did not match the buildings on either side.

Bending down to lift up her basket, Betia looked up and down the passage, saw no one, and slipped down the stairs. The soiled gray wood of the door thudded hollowly under her small fist, but she was careful to knock only thirteen times.

The sun was wallowing down into the west, filling the sky with violent orange threads of cloud, by the time Nicholas managed to reach the Nile Canal gate. Thyatis was sitting, hands on her knees, upon a massive sandstone foot attached to a section of round, weatherworn leg. The rest of Pharaoh's body was gone, shorn off at the ankles by some ancient catastrophe. A matching statue across the canal was in better shape, retaining both legs and part of a pleated kilt. A crowd of local children in shapeless white-and-brown tunics sat on the ground, watching her feet intently.

"Hullo, Nicholas." Thyatis did not look up.

The Latin slowed to a halt, sweating. The perfect stillness of the crowd of boys drew him up short and he closed his mouth, swallowing a tired-sounding "hello yourself."

A wooden box lay between Thyatis' legs, top knocked askew. Something gray-green rose from the opening, swaying from side to side, a glistening black tongue flicking in the air. Nicholas stiffened as a scaled hood unfolded, revealing a chilling pattern of gray-and-white spots. The cobra's body was the thickness of his forearm. Tasting the air, the snake's flat head drifted from side to side.

Nicholas looked down, saw something on the sand and realized there was a nervous white mouse sitting between Thyatis' bare feet. A bit of twine made a collar and a lead running to the Roman woman's ankle. The little creature lifted its paws, brushing a tiny, pink nose. The cobra's mouth opened in a silent hiss, sensing the motion, then uncoiled in a fantastically quick burst of gleaming scales and thick, corded muscle. Nicholas grunted, a flat-bladed knife flicking from his hand. The metal spun once, then the leather hilt smacked into Thyatis' reaching palm. With the same motion, she reversed the blade and flipped it lazily back to Nicholas.

The Latin caught the blade from the air, mouth open in surprise. There was a strangled hissing, and the box rattled violently as the cobra writhed, head caught between Thyatis' feet. The quivering throat of the snake was firmly clasped in the space beside each big toe. Unconcerned, the albino mouse continued to clean its face, twine drawn almost taut by the movement of the woman's ankle.

"Enough games for today, my friends," Thyatis said. The children scrambled up, speaking in whispers. Most of them were staring with equal fascination at the mouse, the snake, and Thyatis' smooth ankles. One boy approached the cobra, slipped a noose on the end of a stick around the head, then unceremoniously stuffed the reptile back into the box. The snake hissed furiously, body lashing back and forth, but could do nothing. Another child retrieved the mouse, slipping the little fellow into her grubby shirt. Thyatis stood up, rolling from one foot to the other, then bowed gravely to the assembled audience.

The children bowed back, then the eldest—his face twisted into a terrible, tortured grimace—pressed a collection of silver coins into the Roman woman's palm.

"Not a bad day's work," Thyatis said, grinning at Nicholas as she counted the coins into a pocket of her tunic.

Nicholas swallowed, sucked on his teeth, then said: "You're fast with that trick. Do it before, somewhere?"

"The knife, the snake, or the betting?" Thyatis gathered up her sandals, carry bag and sheathed longsword.

"Either—no, the snake. I've never seen one so . . . large."

"I have." Thyatis' good humor faltered, the corners of her mouth tightening. "There was only one this time." She grinned again. "The game is much easier when you can see them. The *naga* are from Taprobane, I think. Have any luck finding your friend?"

"Some." Nicholas grimaced, feeling queasy again at the news from the governor's palace. "Have you found a house for us?"

Thyatis nodded, noting his circumspection. Twilight filled the recesses of the gate and lamps were beginning to sparkle in the heavy, dark water of the canal. Soon the massive portals would be closed for the night, but while a smudge of light remained in the western sky a constant stream of dusty laborers, shopkeepers, priests and slaves flowed past, only inches away. She tilted her head, indicating the road leading out into the suburbs of the city. "I have. It's not far."

Beyond the gate, a flat plain stretched away to the south, crowded with gardens and single-story houses. An encompassing tropical gloom quickly engulfed them as they walked, barely disturbed by the intermittent lights of outlying buildings. Only a steady stream of workers trudging homeward into the city lit the road—every fourth or fifth man carried a pitch torch or lamp. No one else was heading out from the gate.

After ten grains, Thyatis turned into a side lane. Ahead, Nicholas saw the glitter of water and smelled the pungent, rancid aroma of cooling mud, rotting cane and birds.

"I found a place on the lakeshore," Thyatis said, voice smiling in the darkness. "Not very popular in the summer, I gather. Too many mosquitoes and flies. But there is a place to tie up a shallow-draft boat and a high wall with plenty of trees."

"Sounds private." Nicholas nodded in appreciation. He slowed his pace a little—the road was rapidly devolving into a muddy track. "I found two of my . . . ah . . . *friends*. One of them told me the Persians have broken through the defenses at Pelusium. The Caesar Aurelian is trying to stop them at Bousiris, on the main channel of the Nile."

He paused, waiting for Thyatis to comment, but she did not. "The other says there is a man at the Museum who knows everything about the Egypt of the old Pharaohs. Particularly those who ruled before the Greeks came. His name is Hecataeus, a Cypriot. I'm told he's a poet, but I find that hard to believe. . . ."

"Hmm. The Museum holds the greatest library in the world." Thyatis' voice was soft in the darkness. She stopped. Nicholas could make out the bare outline of an arched whitewashed gate. "The others are already inside. Does this poet know any of the ancient languages?"

"Supposedly he's the best. Even with really old carvings." Nicholas shrugged, thinking of the restored parchment and the indecipherable glyphs ringing the wheels within wheels of the telecast. "Do you want to show him the . . . ah . . . the device?"

"No!" Thyatis chuckled, reaching over the gate to lift the locking bar. "We show no one what we're looking for." Her voice turned wry. "We probably shouldn't know what it looks like ourselves."

Keeping her fingers from shaking by an act of complete concentration, Betia unfolded the paper. The room hidden under the temple of Artemis was very old. Blackened stones matched the cutwork of the obscure entrance and the arch over the door only a pair of tilted slabs. She was sweating, moisture beading in tiny, shining drops on her neck, though the air in the room was cool, almost chill.

"This, my lady," Betia said, keeping her eyes focused on the parchment, "is what we have been sent to secure." The drawing of the telecast was stark in the lamplight, resting in a pool of light surrounded by darkness. " 'The Emperor Galen, Augustus of the West, has determined one, perhaps two of these devices once dwelt in Egypt, possessed by the pharaoh . . . ' "

" ' . . . Nemathapi, long may his name be cursed.' " The words were clipped, each one given full weight by exacting pronunciation. A withered hand, heavy with rings of lapis and garnet, moved at the edge of the light and one of the sisters of the temple moved the parchment to the far edge of the stone table. The light, spilling from a hooded lantern, moved to keep the diagram illuminated. "A vapid little man, like all his kind, who wished only to live forever. And he will, for *we* will not soon forget him or his treachery."

Betia remained silent, kneeling on the cold floor, head bent. The time spent in service with the Duchess now seemed very pleasant, her training on the Island a fondly remembered idyll. Her cheek stung from where a brawny sister had clubbed her to the floor of the atrium. Apparently the daughters of the Huntress in Alexandria were no friends of Rome. The cold, forbidding voice in the darkness filled her with dread, for this was *Egypt* and some things here, she heard, had learned to walk, when they should rightly crawl.

"But you do not serve the Emperor Galen, do you child? Not if you bring me this foul news."

"No, my lady," Betia squeaked. "The task of finding the telecasts was entrusted to my mistress, the Duchess De' Orelio and she has sent her agent, Lady Thyatis, to see the device does not fall into the hands of the Emperor."

Dry, papery laughter echoed in the darkness. "De' Orelio? How droll. Yet you said *sent to secure*—your mistress Thyatis owns two masters? Has she come in the company of the Emperor's men, a guide, an advisor, a bed companion for their captain?"

"No." Betia stiffened and almost looked up. A powerful, calloused hand caught her neck and shoved her down. The girl bit her lip, mastering her anger and let herself breathe in, then out. A strange odor tickled her nose, but she ignored the slow pricking of gooseflesh on her arms. "She leads the Emperor's company—we are five: Thyatis, myself, an African, an Eastern soldier and a Walach. We arrived today, aboard the *Paris*, straightaway from Ostia port."

A lengthy silence followed her words and Betia became uncomfortably aware of silvery trails of sweat purling down her arms as she knelt.

At last the voice resumed, though a thread of anger suffused the clipped voice with growing heat. "The *Duchess* intends a game of shells, then, where your precious Thyatis vigorously searches, yet never finds. Or, perhaps, you expect us to conjure up some likely-seeming bits and pieces, a token for the Emperor, so the *Duchess* may claim success in her so-dutiful task?"

Swallowing to clear a dry throat, Betia said, "My lady, all my mistress bids me say is this: you should know what Lady Thyatis seeks, and do whatever is necessary to ensure she does not find the device! She does not wish to know where it might truly lie! A false trail could be laid, leading Lady Thyatis astray. . . ."

Again, the silence dragged. Betia felt her calves begin to cramp, and shifted her weight subtly, pressing her heels against the smooth, glassy stone floor until the spasm passed.

"There is slight merit in such a suggestion," the voice said, simmering with anger. "What she does not know, she cannot reveal. Still, by my memory both Eyes are intact and well hidden." A whispering sigh followed. "Yet, where is the honor of noble Khem? Lost—corrupted long ago by foreign blood, by *men* seeking power and ancient secrets—and nothing built by human hands can remain hidden forever."

Cloth rustled and from the corner of her eye, Betia saw a withered hand enter the pool of lamplight and lift up the parchment. In the darkness beyond, the voice was only a dark, indistinct shape. "Child, listen. I wish, as do the old in their dotage, the *duradarshan* had been destroyed long ago or cast into the sea or shattered in Ptah's forge. Yet, they were not. Both Eyes are intact, whole, unmarked, unblemished. Nemathapi was not the only ruler to desire them—even though men had forgotten their true use and power—for even in his degenerate age they were, they are, a sign and symbol of the first kingdom."

The hand shifted, turning the parchment. Rubies and cabochons blazed on ancient fingers. "There are those in the city, even today, who might know where the Eyes came to rest. Tell your mistress—this formidable Thyatis you love so much—we shall send a swift party to move the Eyes to a place of greater safety. Too, my daughters will set a watch on those who *might* know the provenance of old Egypt's treasures."

The dim coal of anger grew stronger with each word. "This much," the dry voice said, almost spitting, "we will do for the Queen of Day."

Betia remained kneeling while the priestesses filed out of the room, carrying a litter and the woman hidden within. Some time after they were gone, she dared raise her head. The parchment remained on the table, glowing softly in the light of the single lamp. Tentatively, she picked it up. Across one corner, where a nail might lie while reading, there was a sharp new cut as if a swordblade had been drawn across the parchment.

The chill in the air did not abate and Betia left as quickly as she could.

A fragment of half-familiar sound caught Shirin's attention; some tone of voice or remembered trick of phrasing reaching her ear through the din and racket of the street. Cautiously, she looked up from her hamper, one hand checking the lace veil across her nose. The Khazar woman was sitting on the top step of a triumphal entryway into the Museion, a long, rectangular building within the greater royal district of the Bruchion. Dozens of other people loitered on the staircase, reading scrolls, eating their lunch, declaiming about religion and politics. Among them, she was happily anonymous, just another woman of the city with a bag of fresh vegetables, watching the constant parade of humanity passing in the avenue below. The top step allowed her to sit half in shadow, her feet in the hot sun.

Two figures were climbing the worn sandstone steps in haste, voices low.

Shirin expected to see the big Persian and his smaller, older accomplice. By luck, she had caught sight of the two men three days previous as they entered the Museion. Unhappily, they had vanished into the sprawling complex before she could follow. Her vigil since then, in as wide a variety of clothing and appearance as she could manage, had been fruitless. Unwilling to openly question the clerks and scribes working inside, she had settled in to wait and watch, hoping they would return.

She had *not* expected to look up, attention drawn by a carrying voice and see Thyatis almost in arm's reach. Shirin froze in surprise, hand still covering half of her face, eyes flitting away from the tall, broad-shouldered woman in traditional garments. The man at her side was shorter, whipcord lean, his tanned face distinguished by a pair of particularly sharp mustaches. Still muttering to one another, they swept past. As they did, Shirin heard a soft *clink* of metal and leather from beneath Thyatis' cloak and stole.

A *sword or other blade*, part of Shirin's mind commented casually. The Khazar woman turned, watching the two Romans disappear into the dim vault of the atrium. Colossal columns rose up on either side, framing the entrance into the outer court-yard. Shirin shook her head, blinking away surprise. "Get up, brainless fool!"

Gathering up her basket and tucking the veil behind one ear, she hurried into the dim corridor. Ahead, she caught sight of Thyatis' red-gold hair gleaming in the sunlight as she and her companion crossed a wide, marble-paved court where the booksellers plied a busy trade. The Romans weaved their way through hundreds of stalls and rugs, piled with all variety of ar-tifacts and musty age-worn tomes. Determined to keep them in sight, Shirin matched her pace to theirs, though she cursed Thy-atis' long stride and not for the first time.

"Well, my lord, perhaps we can do some business." Smiling broadly, the Cypriot stepped around his worktable, bowing po-litely to Nicholas. Despite the stifling heat, the scholar was dressed in a heavy Greek-style *himation* and tunic. The perva-sive smell of mold and rotting papyrus throughout the Museion was held at bay by incense and a sluggish breeze from two tall, open windows. Citrus trees crowded the openings and glossy leaves brushed against the sill. "I am familiar with the name of Nemathapi," the reputed poet continued. "Do you have a . . . picture . . . of what you seek?"

"Perhaps," Nicholas said, eyes narrowing in suspicion. "You've studied him, then?"

"Of course." Hecataeus' smile crystallized into a predatory grin. "I am accounted an expert in the old dynasties. I have learned to read the old forms of the traditional glyphs. You have *something*, don't you? I cannot conjure knowledge from the thin air! There is also the matter of compensation. . . ."

Thyatis could feel the tension in Nicholas' back like heat from a fire. As before, she was dressed conservatively, pretend-ing to be his wife or servant. Ignoring their bickering over money for a moment, she let her eyes drift over honeycombed racks—each square niche filled with a papyrus or parchment scroll. The shelves covered each wall from floor to ceiling and the table was piled high with more documents, unrolled for easy perusal, held down by a variety of statuettes. Quietly, she drifted away from the low argument between the two men, hands clasped inside her cloak.

Each scroll was labeled in Greek with a neat hand. Thyatis raised an eyebrow, seeing the vigorous slant of the letters and the careful precision of each parchment tag. She turned at the corner of the room, looking over the desk again. There were day-old, ring-shaped stains on the unfinished wood and a plate with moldy crumbs. A glossy surfaced cup sat beside the remains of breakfast, half filled with wine. Badly trimmed quills and goose feathers littered the floor. Nicholas had produced a paper while her back was turned, filled with a transcription of the glyphs and markings shown in the original depiction of Nemathapi's device. He and Hecataeus bent over the writing.

". . . ah, only a fragment, I'm afraid. Still, I should be able to make some sense of this . . ." The poet's voice was very smug and Thyatis frowned. Something in the room was out of place—the dissonance bothered her, setting her teeth on edge. She continued her slow circuit, attention drawn again to the table. There were some fresh parchments laid out, the ink still newly dark. Hecataeus moved them aside as she watched, clearing a space to examine Nicholas' paper. Her nostrils flared a little, seeing the set of his hands, and ink smudged on his right index finger.

"Ah, now," the poet said, settling into his chair. "Some of these symbols are familiar to me. . . ."

Thyatis stepped out of the room. The hallway was high-ceilinged and dark, spaced with unadorned pillars. Scroll racks filled every possible space, rising two and three times the height of a man. More small offices opened out between each pair of columns, though most of the doorways were crowded with hemp baskets filled with tightly rolled scrolls. An inordinate number of cats lazed about, sleeping on the papers or cleaning themselves on the windowsills. Humming tunelessly, Thyatis began to poke through the books, finding some of the papers so old they were glued together by the humidity. She rattled a basket experimentally, then extracted one particularly decrepit looking manuscript. Dust scattered, making Thyatis sneeze.

"What are you doing? Put that down!" A small hand seized

Thyatis' wrist and the Roman woman looked down with interest at a tiny, dark-skinned woman hanging on her arm. "Guests are not allowed to touch the books!"

"I think," Thyatis said, lifting the little woman from the ground with one hand, feeling a flush of satisfaction at the smooth, powerful movement of her muscles, "this particular book is long gone. My name is Diana. What is yours?"

The little brown woman kicked Thyatis in the thigh with a sandaled foot. More dust puffed from her shoe. The Roman woman suppressed a smile. "Here," Thyatis said in a placating tone. "I've put the book back. And I'll set you down. Now, tell me your name."

Scowling furiously, the woman bounced back, then darted in to check the placement of the manuscript. Satisfied the document was back in its proper place, she squinted up at Thyatis, her hair a tangle of russet curls around a sharp, triangular face. "I am Sheshet, a curator of the Museum! Who let you in? What are you doing here?"

"Let me see your fingers," Thyatis said in reply, catching the woman's left hand with a quick movement. Sheshet yelped in surprise, but the Roman woman released her hand as quickly as it had been seized. "You labeled the scrolls in Master Hecataeus' office?"

"Yes . . ." The quick anger in the little woman's expression faded, replaced by a penetrating, considering stare. "You've come to see the Cypriot, then? An ode for your lover, I suppose." Sheshet sniffed insultingly. "He can be amusing, sometimes."

"No," Thyatis said, listening with half an ear to the poet droning on about *high kingdom bas-reliefs*. "My friend has a document he wants translated. A very old document, from Pharaoh Nemathapi's time. . . ." Sheshet's expression froze and Thyatis caught a flicker of calculation in the woman's eyes. *Well, well*, she thought, *they are surely a close family, here, all loving and trusting*. "Ah, you've heard the name before."

"I have." Sheshet pursed her lips, drawing out the words. "Maybe." She rubbed two fingers together. Thyatis considered the woman's sandals—worn, patched—and her garments, no more than a threadbare tunic and *stola* with a frayed belt. Her only jewelry was a tarnished silver ring showing a star cradled in the arms of a crescent moon, her nails chipped and dark with ink stains.

"Let's talk quietly," Thyatis said, lifting Sheshet up and striding away down the passage. They passed more openings into crowded rooms, then at the end of the hall she found a quiet corridor leading off to the right. Miraculously, the passage was not completely filled with baskets and boxes, so she set the little woman down on a crate, where they could see eye to eye.

"You are very strong," Sheshet said, straightening her tunic. For the first time, the Egyptian woman seemed to *see* Thyatis and the Roman felt a chill under the penetrating gaze. "You're a soldier." She reached out and turned Thyatis' right wrist over. Her cracked fingernails slid over glassy scars. "Are you an *archer?*"

"Sometimes, when need drives," Thyatis said, evading the question. "Your dear Hecataeus knew Nemathapi's name already—you've heard it too—has someone else been to see him, asking about a *device?*"

The curator's eyes glinted in amusement. "How much will you pay?"

"Tell me," Thyatis replied, "and you'll have enough for more than parchment, papyrus, ink, quills . . ."

The little woman laughed softly, looking down at her grubby clothing. "You mean, buy fewer books? Spend something on myself?" Sheshet shook her head. "There's not enough money for such luxuries, not in this world."

"Gold, then," Thyatis said, producing a double-weight aureus from her belt. "Who came to see Hecataeus about the old pharaoh?"

Ink-stained fingers snatched the coin from Thyatis' hand and the Egyptian woman weighed the gold in her hand. "Unclipped. Very thoughtful of you. A Western coin." Sheshet flipped it over, running a thumb across the stamped image. "A commemorative of Emperor Galen's triumph over Persia—very fresh, unworn." The woman licked her lips, thinking. "You've come recently from Rome then, drawn pay from the Imperial Treasury. You are *official*, aren't you?"

"Yes," Thyatis said, leaning close. Sheshet did not flinch

away, meeting her eyes with an amused expression. "Who came to see Hecataeus?"

"Persians," Sheshet said carelessly, pocketing the coin. "Two of them—a big man, bigger than you, with a horseman's waist and dangerous eyes. The other, though, he's been in the city so long he speaks like a Rhakotis native . . . they had a rubbing; charcoal on thin parchment. They were looking for a tomb." The curator paused, wiggling her fingers.

"How many books do you want to buy?" Thyatis said, both eyebrows raised in amusement. She produced another gold coin.

"How many books are in the world?" Sheshet laughed quietly. "The poet said he needed to consult a *geographica*, but they wouldn't leave. So he came into my office and asked me to find some references while they waited."

Thyatis nodded, remembering the stains on the old table. "They had wine, from unfired cups."

Sheshet nodded, shrugging her shoulders. "Hecataeus is cheap, he won't buy good cups for his guests."

"What did the rubbing show? Was there a picture, wheels set within wheels?"

"No." Sheshet's interested perked. "Just some old graffiti. Scratchings from a wall—the stones were large and well cut— you could see the pattern of the chisel strokes reflected in the rubbing." The woman brushed curls out of her eyes, squinting into an unseen, internal distance. "A bronze chisel . . . even in the course of one block, you could see the strokes shallowing as the blade dulled . . . Nemathapi lived long ago, when iron was scarce. His tomb perhaps, or a funerary temple." She paused. "But there were no chips of paint shown in the rubbing—I doubt some *Persians* would clean the surface first. A tomb entry chamber then, unpainted."

"What," Thyatis said grimly, "did it say?"

"Oh, that." Sheshet grinned, dark brown eyes lighting up. When she smiled, her sharp cheekbones and narrow chin transformed into something almost inhuman. "The tomb had been plundered and the thieves left a message for those who might come after, both to mock any rival finding an empty hole and to deflect the anger of the gods. They were clever, the men work-

ing in candlelit darkness, chipping away at stone laid down a
thousand years before. . . ."

The echo of voices, not far away, brought Shirin up short. Stepping quietly, she turned the corner of a hallway filled with
rough-hewn wooden crates. Not more than a dozen yards away,
she could see the tall figure of Thyatis speaking to a short, dark-
haired woman. Gold glinted for an instant, then vanished into
the Egyptian woman's hand.

So, Shirin sniffed, *we're back to work, are we?* Irritated, the
Khazar woman scratched her nose, ink-dark eyebrows narrowed in calculation. *But who are you working for? The Order?
The Duchess? The Emperor . . . your handyman is a Roman
soldier—that much is clear from his boots, his hair, the long-
shanked stride. So, the Imperial government again. But how?*

A momentary vision of Thyatis, her wild, ecstatic face
streaked with blood and sweat, standing on glittering, hot sand
filled Shirin's memory. Her stomach turned queasily, thinking
of the slaughter and the delight so plain in her lover's eyes.

You won out, Shirin thought, half-remembering things she
had heard about the Romans and their customs. *You killed all
those men and the Emperor set you free. He must have taken
you back into his service.* The unsettled, greasy feeling in her
stomach began to gel like meat fat cooling on a skillet. *Now
you're hunting again and this time you're here, searching for
the same thing the Persians want. Kleopatra's weapon.* A calm
sense of certainty entered her. Fragments slid together; the grim
look on the Persian faces, the dust on their cloaks, their long
journey down the Nile fitting into a recognizable pattern. Shirin
squinted at the woman in the ragged dress. *A clerk or scribe,
working here, cataloging the books. Hmm. A race to find
Kleopatra's . . . treasure? Tomb? Hiding place? Those Persians
thought it was downriver, but it wasn't, so they came to the Library, following an ancient trail. I should tell Thyatis what I
heard in the inn. . . .*

Relieved and satisfied with her reasoning, Shirin started to
step out into the corridor. Then she stopped, eyes lingering on
the set of her friend's shoulders, her head, an escaped curl of
brassy hair peeking from under the woolen hood of the cloak.

Her chest felt tight and a rush of emotion made it impossible to breathe. *Strong arms to hold me, a dear head in my lap, a laughing freckled face, sparkling sea-gray eyes . . . not a mad, contorted face, so like my husband's. My friend, my beloved . . .*

Suddenly weak, Shirin put her hand out against the gritty, sandstone wall. Memories of her children running on a sandy beach welled up, Thyatis sprinting after them, roaring like a lion. Everyone sitting under a piece of sail, sunburned, eating red-backed crabs caught in the shallows. Thyatis dancing beside a bonfire, a sea of ebony faces laughing and clapping in time to thundering drums. The sky dark with flamingos as countless flocks burst up from a marsh. Thyatis holding Avrahan and Sahul each under a scarred, sun-browned arm, face tense, waiting, listening for the lionesses creeping in the high yellow grass. *Oh, lord of my fathers, she won't know my babies are dead!*

Shirin put a hand over her mouth for a moment, tears squeezing out between tight eyelids. Sometimes this life was too much for her to bear. When she opened her eyes again, Thyatis had moved aside, one hand raised to the Egyptian woman's face.

Thyatis produced a knife, and laid the shining, oiled tip just below the curator's eyelid. "I'm getting impatient."

Sheshet bared her teeth, showing glittering white incisors. "You are hasty. They proclaimed their pharaoh, said they worked in her name, by her command. So she would take the ill-luck from their desecration and they would be spared."

"Her?" Thyatis' nostrils flared and the tip of the knife slid sideways, away from the curator's unblinking eye.

Shirin jerked back, feeling the sharp, angry motion of Thyatis' shoulders as a physical blow. The blade of a knife glittered in the dim light for a moment, then disappeared. Distressed, Shirin stepped back, into deeper shadows. Thyatis' stance radiated repressed anger and impatience. The Khazar woman drew the corner of her cloak across the bridge of her nose, leaving only the pale gleam of her eyes visible. *Careless violence? A blade set to an innocent eye? You've made no friend in this one.*

Foolish Roman! The Egyptian woman's face, half seen over Thyatis' shoulder, was a blank, tight mask.

Is this truly you? Shirin felt sick. *Not the friend, the gentle lover I thought you were?*

The Khazar woman was no stranger to violence—she had killed, to protect herself—but this casual willingness to maim, or kill, turned her blood cold. *I should turn away, and leave all of this behind—Persians and Romans alike* . . . But she did not and continued to watch from the darkness.

"Kleopatra, seventh of that name." Sheshet's lips compressed and she began to radiate an encompassing sense of delighted satisfaction. "I knew immediately, as soon as I read the beginning of the invocation. Half-Greek, half-Egyptian, with the truncated spelling favored by the Ptolemies. Yes, the notorious, beloved Queen of the Two Lands broke into old Nemathapi's tomb and took away this *device* you're searching for. I've heard she liked trinkets. The older, the better."

Thyatis blinked. "But the Persians had already found *his* tomb . . . they were looking for *hers?*"

Sheshet nodded. Thyatis returned the knife to a sheath strapped to the inside of her arm. A tense knot swelled in her stomach. "Do you know . . ."

". . . where Kleopatra's tomb is?" The curator shook her head slowly. "One of the great mysteries of Egypt, archer. Many men have looked, but no one has ever found her resting place."

"What about him?" Thyatis nodded towards Hecataeus' office. "What did he tell the Persians?"

"Him?" Sheshet whistled derisively. "He couldn't tell them anything. He can *read* the old languages, but he spends his time looking for naughty stories or poetry to pass off as his own, not for anything useful!"

"Good . . ." Thyatis produced another coin. "If the Persians come back, we were never here. Agreed?"

"Of course." Sheshet accepted the coin. "Three volumes in one day—the end of a long drought for me."

"Thank you," Thyatis said in a heartfelt tone. Out of the corner of her eye, she could see Nicholas standing in the hallway, looking for her. "Good day, Mistress Sheshet."

"Good day." The Egyptian woman watched, curls clouding her face again, as Thyatis strode away down the corridor. "Good riddance," she whispered, rubbing her eyelid where the point of the knife had left a small indentation in her skin. "Stupid barbarian!"

Then she considered the heavy gold in her hand and a perplexed expression flitted across her face. "That Persian didn't pay me so much before . . . but he might now!" Cheerful at the thought of more books of her own, the little librarian slipped off into the shadows between the pillars.

"We'll need camels," Nicholas said in a soft voice, as they walked causally down a long, granite ramp leading onto one of the triumphal avenues bisecting the city. "Workers, shovels, picks, levers. Maybe a sled if it's too heavy to carry on a single camel."

"The poet had something?" Thyatis kept a pace behind and to one side, as a proper wife should. At the same time, she was ghoulishly amused; the position gave her a clear strike at the man's neck simply by lifting her arm.

"A fragment of a traveler's account—a lonely tomb in the desert, revealed by a passing sandstorm. The sealed door bore the stamp of the Ptolemies—and all the other tombs are accounted for—all save one . . . the last one."

"The notoriously famous Kleopatra," Thyatis said, pretending mild surprise. "How romantic. You think the account is real? Hecataeus didn't strike me as being reliable . . ."

"He isn't." Nicholas grinned over his shoulder at her. "He's careless. Someone else had gotten to him first, asking the same questions. Guess who?"

"The Persians," Thyatis replied, feeling her neck prickle. She kept walking, listening with half her attention to Nicholas. *Someone watching us?* The feeling was very strong. *Someone I know?* It was an effort to keep from turning abruptly and staring. The avenue was crowded, with shrill chanting peddlers standing on the elevated bases of obelisks marching down the

center of the thoroughfare. Wagons rumbled past, dogs barked
furiously in the alleys, merchants were shouting from the store-
fronts. Every scrap of pavement was covered with rugs laden
with trinkets, little statues, gewgaws, "real rubies from Serica,"
pens of chickens and goats. Thyatis let her eyes lose focus, her
breathing slow to match her pace.

"The Persians," Nicholas continued with grim humor, barely
audible above the din. "They braced him about Nemathapi before, but he couldn't help. This time they brought some scratchings from a tomb they found down in Saqqara. Now they were
looking for Kleopatra's treasure, thinking something 'like a
wheel' would be hidden there. Well, he had no idea where the
tomb might be and he told them so. They weren't pleased, but
went on to the next antiquarian on their list."

A familiar silhouette darting through the crowd drew her attention and Thyatis blinked, focusing, and saw the little librarian moving swiftly through traffic on the other side of the
boulevard. The little woman dodged behind a phalanx of chanting monks wreathed in incense from swinging censers and carrying a bored-looking calico cat on a golden pillow. Thyatis
squinted, rising up on tiptoe, but Sheshet had vanished behind a
moving wall of silk umbrellas. When the procession passed,
there was no sign of the little Egyptian.

Off to buy those books already, Thyatis thought, shaking her
head in amusement. The feeling of being watched lingered.

"Fortunately for us, the poet had a nose for profit," Nicholas
continued, unaware of Thyatis bobbing up and down behind
him like a giraffe in a tall stand of acanthus. "He started to ap-
ply himself, rummaging through the books and histories.
Wanted to find the tomb himself, I'd wager, though he only had
a hazy idea of what might be hidden there. I'd swear from the
way he acted it was the first time he'd ever found anything in
that mausoleum! He showed me the account—crabbed on the
back of a lading document." The Latin patted his belt and Thyatis heard stiff paper rustle.

"How much did Hecataeus want for his fabulous discovery?"

Nicholas glanced sideways at the woman, a smirk dancing
on his thin lips. "Not much," he said.

"What do you mean?" Thyatis picked up her pace. "How much did you give him to keep his mouth shut?"

Nicholas laughed sharply and the Roman woman raised an eyebrow at the ugly sound.

"He gave me his back," he said softly, "and I paid him in steel—five inches tempered—right at the base of the skull."

Thyatis felt a peculiar sense of dislocation, as if she walked beside the Latin soldier and also looked down upon him from a height. She felt dizzy for a moment, then the sensation passed. "What did you do with the body?" her mouth asked automatically.

"Wrapped in a robe and out the window into the garden behind a hedge." The corners of Nicholas' eyes crinkled up as if he laughed, or smiled, but nothing humorous shone in his face. "Anyone who happens to see him will think he's asleep. At least, until he starts to smell."

"We'll have the money for your camels and workers, then." The queer double vision passed and Thyatis felt herself whole and chilled by the man's careless, offhand murder. His action reminded her too much of her own threat to the little librarian and she felt a little ill. Her thoughts spun for a moment, then settled. *The poet can't have found the real sepulcher. Can he?* The prospect seemed remote. "Good. How far away is the tomb?"

"Not far," Nicholas said, sounding eager. "The merchant was traveling on the western shore of Lake Mareotis, on his way to the coast with a string of camels. When the storm had passed, he walked for a day northeast to reach the village of Taposiris, which is only a day's ride west of the city. But we can reach the area faster by crossing the lake with a barge."

Thyatis nodded, suppressing an urge to finger the amulet around her neck. The prince's bauble was cold and still and she prayed to the Hunter it would remain so. *Otherwise*, she thought, *Nicholas will have to be paid, just as he paid poor Hecataeus.*

Thunderheads grumbled in the east and the air had acquired a heavy pearlescent quality as afternoon progressed. Yellow cone-shaped flowers spilled over the garden walls, filling the heavy air with a pungent, cloying aroma. Two figures turned into the lane, walking quickly, heads bent in conversation. At the end of the lane, the muddy track vanished into the flat, glassy water of Lake Mareotis. In the green shadows under the reeds fringing the lake, a quiet, hooded figure watched the man and woman stop at a wooden gate. The man—thin, nervous face radiating impatience even at this distance—rapped sharply on the wood. A moment passed and the woman squared her shoulders and looked around curiously.

The watcher hidden in the reeds froze, lowering her head. Midges and gnats crawled on brown arms and the *zzzing* of patrolling mosquitoes was very loud. Time dragged, measured by the tiny, prickling movements of the gnats as they crept across smooth, tanned flesh.

Creaking hinges signaled the gate swinging wide. Nicholas and Thyatis disappeared through the archway and the sound of brisk commands and sudden, unexpected activity filtered through the humid air. In the reeds, the watcher ventured to lift her head enough to see the gate again. The tall, redheaded woman was standing inside the arch, the portal nearly closed, watching the lane. Again, the watcher grew entirely still, slowing her breathing.

A grain passed, then two, then—after fifteen grains had slipped through the glass of life—Thyatis shook her head in disgust, and closed the wooden door.

In the reeds, Shirin breathed out a long, slow gasp of relief. Her arms were trembling, on the verge of cramping, and her shoulders rippled with disgust. *I hate mosquitoes*, she thought viciously. *Lord of my fathers, strike them all down!* Shuddering again, the Khazar woman crushed the carpet of midges and gnats on her arms with her palms, leaving a smeared, greasy, red-streaked paste. For the moment, she ignored the bugs rustling in her hair and slipped through the forest of reeds to the edge of the lake. A tiny trail of flattened mud led off along the shore.

Keeping a wary eye out for crocodiles and snapping turtles, Shirin padded towards the next break in the reeds. Something had happened and she suspected the Romans would be moving soon. *Where are you going?* Shirin wondered, the image of the redheaded woman clear as crystal in her memory; Thyatis' face framed by the half-closed gate, a curl of red-gold hair fallen over gray eyes. *Did the Egyptian woman tell you something useful?* Her full lips twisted into a frown. *What was the sleek, dangerous man doing while you were talking to her?* Perhaps the other Roman had found something in the archives. Still moving cautiously, she turned onto another path between the huge, softly trembling reeds and moved inland. *I think I'll need a horse . . . no—a camel for heavy sand or sharp stones.*

Veils of falling rain swept across the surface of the lake, alternately revealing and obscuring whitewashed houses along the shoreline. The growl and crack of thunder rolled among the clouds, though the storm itself had moved away to the north. Squatting in the bottom of a long canal boat, Patik waited quietly, water streaming from the brim of his leather hat. Artabanus crouched behind him, coughing softly in the damp, wrapped in a woolen cloak and a conical hat made of straw. Two more of the Persian soldiers were behind him, asleep, or nearly so, under their cloaks.

A hundred yards away, the edge of a stone wall reached down to the water's edge. Patik was watching the opening, waiting patiently in cover. Somewhere to the west, the clouds parted, letting the sun blaze down across the rainy sky. The Persian commander blinked, dipping the brim of his hat to shield his eyes from the sudden brightness. Coruscating rainbows shimmered across the falling rain, gilding the reeds and the brassy surface of the lake.

"There!" The little Egyptian woman in the prow of the boat pointed with a thin, bird-like hand. A blunt-nosed boat edged out from behind the crumbling wall. Parik tensed, one hand sliding along the haft of his oar. The curator turned, grinning brightly at him. Her glossy, water-charged hair was plastered to a narrow skull. As far as the Persian could tell, the woman hadn't even noticed the torrential downpour. "Do you see her?"

Patik nodded, eyes narrowing. One of the figures poling the heavy barge was a woman, bright hair bound up behind her head. She and a huge African were pushing the boat away from the shore. Six or seven Egyptians in straw hats and dun-colored robes helped with paddles. A pair of camels stood uneasily in the center of the barge, hemmed in by piled supplies. "I see her. She's a Roman agent?"

Eyes glinting mischievously, Sheshet nodded. "They know where the tomb is. Follow them and you'll have your prize. Now—give me the rest of my money."

The corner of the big Persian's left eye gained a slight tic at the avaricious expression in the little Egyptian's face, but he drew a purse from his belt and scrupulously counted out five heavy silver coins. The curator examined each one, turning the disks over in her hands, holding them up to the light—fading now as the clouds rolled on, obscuring the sun. Artabanus' fingers moved to a knife at his side, but Patik shook his head slightly and the mage subsided. "Satisfied?"

Sheshet nodded, looking up at the Persian with a queer, knowing expression. "You're an honorable man, aren't you?" Her voice was very soft, almost drowned by the renewed patter of rain on the water and the sides of the boat. Patik did not respond, though the line of his mouth tightened a fraction. "You are. A hard-won lesson, I think."

Shaking her head in compassion, she caught his hand, squeezed it gently, then scrambled the length of the boat, hopping over Asha and Mihr, and then to shore. Both of the soldiers lifted the brims of their hats, peering curiously at Patik.

"Let's go," he said, ignoring the questioning expression on Artabanus' face.

All four bent to their oars and the long skiff slipped out from the reeds, surging across the open water. Ahead, nearly obscured by mists rising from the blood-warm water of the lake, the Roman barge plowed steadily west. A moment later, a second boat, this one holding Tishtrya, Amur and their own supplies, followed, gliding out from the reed forest like a ghost.

A door panel shuddered under a powerful blow. Hinges creaked and a stout wooden bar twisted in its braces. Outside, a harsh voice spoke sharply. The door slammed open, bar shattered, hinges torn from the mud-brick wall. With a loud *bang*, the panel flew across the room and crashed into a wicker screen. A tall, powerfully built figure ducked under the lintel. Features obscured by a deep hood, the intruder strode noiselessly through the house. The room darkened as it passed. A long cavalry blade, etched with spidery runes, gleamed in one hand. A second figure, much like the first, followed. Neither spoke as they quartered the dwelling, finding the remains of a hasty meal and evidence of a recent departure.

A rear door, standing open, led them out onto a grassy sward leading down to the lakeshore. The taller of the two bent beside the muddy verge, examining trampled turf and boot prints. An aura of anger radiated from the creature as it stood, face still in shadow. The rain had tapered off, though the dark woolen cloaks of the two figures were glossy with lanolin, easily shedding what moisture dripped from the leaden sky.

"They go upon the waters," the taller figure said in a hollow, cold voice.

The other nodded, turning to reenter the house. "We shall go around," it said. "But swiftly."

"As the spirits quarter the land," answered the first, anger curdling in its terrible voice. "Beyond the light of the sun."

THE SUMMER HOUSE, AT CUMAE

)l(

Galen, Emperor of the West, stood beneath an arbor trellis, the light from hanging lanterns glinting in his hair. Not far away, the rippling shake of tambourines and lilting flutes lent a merry sound to the night air. People were dancing on a lawn of fresh-cut turf, under barren, ghostly trees. Beyond them, the roofs of the villa rose above a bleak landscape. Drifts of ash and pumice covered the hills. A forest of pine and cedar surrounding the house had been stripped down to bare trunks, the skin of the trees burned white or dark by fiery circumstance.

The sea below the cliffs was dark, waves silent on a windless night, and the sound of the musicians carried a great distance, echoing in the desolation beneath Vesuvius. The arbor vaulting above the Emperor's head, the green lawn, and the fragrant rosebushes were all newly planted—only days ago—for the prince's celebration. Luckily, a low ridge rose between the scattered buildings and the crumpled cone of Vesuvius. The lee of the ridge had protected the villa from the explosion's initial shockwave, but did nothing to prevent a cloud of fire from consuming the house, blackening the plaster and setting the roof timbers alight.

Like the other revelers, the Emperor was dressed in his finest tunic, toga, boots, and a length of Tyrian purple cloth plunging almost to his feet. Nervously, he measured the length of the cloth with his fingers, over and over. He was nervous, being even three days' swift ride from Rome. Yet, he could not gainsay his brother the Emperor's presence and blessing.

"Gales?" Maxian's voice carried easily from the edge of the lawn. There were no leaves, no brush, no foliage to absorb the sound.

"Here," Galen said. His brother approached, silhouetted against the bright windows of the villa, which blazed with crystalline lamps. The radiance of the thaumaturgic devices was like the sun, though without King Sol's beneficent heat. "How do you feel? Nervous?"

Maxian laughed and Galen could hear bone-deep weariness in his brother's voice.

"I'm too tired to feel nervous. I'm glad you let us use this place—a ceremony in Rome would be overwhelming. There are more guests *here* than I know!"

Galen nodded, avoiding his brother's eyes, and sat down on the marble bench under the arbor. The stone felt odd under his hands; freshly cut, still grainy from the carving saw. *Brand new*, Galen thought, distracted. *Like everything else here. How strange . . . the villa seems so hollow without the patina of ages on the stone and wood.*

"Is something wrong?" Maxian sat as well, peering curiously at the Emperor. "Do . . . do you approve of this match?"

Suppressing a wry grimace, Galen looked at his brother. "There are difficulties associated," he said, trying to keep his own weariness from showing. "Tell me the truth, piglet, are you sure of this course?" Before Maxian could answer, the Emperor raised a hand. "Wait a moment. Let me say on."

The prince nodded dubiously, a hint of anger gleaming in his eyes.

"Two men sit before you; your brother and your Emperor. Each is troubled tonight, yet each holds a different council. Your *brother* wishes you only happiness, for you to follow your heart, to find peace, to live a long, untroubled life. Your *brother* looks upon the lady Martina and sees a quiet soul, used to books, to pursuits of the mind. Your *brother* thinks she is a likely match! Her family is beyond rebuke, her lineage old and honorable. Your *brother* sees her look upon you and sees love." Galen smiled, forcing his hands to lie still on his knees. His palms were sweating.

"Your *Emperor* . . . well, he is a cranky fellow, filled with suspicions and fears. He worries, this Emperor, and he frets about the state and the people." Galen laughed hollowly at himself. The prince's eyes narrowed, thinking his brother was laughing at him. "There is some humor here, piglet. The *Emperor* is not worried about *you*, he is worried about *Martina*."

Maxian sat up straighter, surprised. Galen smiled mischievously at him, then brushed back the fall of thin hair from his forehead. "What a look you give me! Listen, men and women in Rome are minded to treat marriage lightly—they may join and un-join by common consent, without permission, without trial. For anyone else, if this match should fail—then set it aside! If you cannot live with her, or she with you, then you may amicably part, each retaining the properties and wealth of your personal estate. In *Rome*, the patricians and nobles swirl in a constant dance of alliance and arrangement." The Emperor paused, looking out over the lawn, keen eyes searching among the dancers and revelers drinking and feasting at long tables.

"See there?" he pointed. Maxian's eyes followed, though a shade of incipient anger still haunted his face. "There is the Senator Pertinax. He has been married and divorced seven times." Galen smiled genially, thin lips quirked in amusement. "Each time he swore the marriage would be his last . . . yet each pairing ended and in a confusing variety of ways." The Emperor looked to his brother again and frowned.

"Not so in the East. They take such matters seriously among the grandees of the Eastern Empire. If you marry Martina, her cousins, her people, the great lords will presume you do so for life, in a binding of man to woman, forever. Is this your intent?"

Maxian's poor humor had not improved. For a moment, he said nothing, then: "Oh, I've leave to speak now? Are you finished lecturing? You expect me to cast her aside then, when my fancy *inevitably* passes to another?"

"It does not matter," Galen said quietly, ignoring Maxian's sarcasm, "what you intend. The future is uncertain and many things may happen. Can you see what will come now, with your power?"

"No," Maxian said, biting back harsher words. "I cannot. I will take the days as they come."

"Very wise!" Galen said, rubbing the back of his head sheepishly. "I had no idea what trouble I was getting into when I married Helena! Lovely, dear trouble. But I would not change my mind, if given the chance again. Do you love her?"

Maxian started to answer, then paused, staring at his brother. A perplexed expression flitted across his face, then settled into a rueful grimace. "I . . . don't know. It seems . . . proper . . . we should be together. Her son needs a father. I . . . I don't want to be alone. Must I love her, to marry her? I am following my heart, if you must know. Why are you so concerned?"

Gritting his teeth, Galen suppressed a sigh of despair. *Why can't Father be alive to deal with this sort of thing? I must have angered the gods somehow* . . . "Your brother wishes you only happiness. Your Emperor suffers an ulcer thinking of what might happen if you and she part in anger."

"Oh." Maxian made a face like he'd bitten into a rotten lemon. "Cold-blooded, aren't you?"

"The *Emperor* must be," Galen answered ruefully. "Your happy marriage seals the alliance between East and West in your conjoined bodies. A divorce . . . splits us when we cannot afford any division." The Emperor grimaced, grinding his teeth. "There is another matter . . ."

The prince's face fell, hearing the tension in his brother's

voice. However, before Galen could speak, a great clamor rose
from the house and a troop of Legion officers clattered out onto
the portico lining the seaward side of the villa. Galen could see
their faces shining with sweat, boldly illuminated by flaring,
sputtering brands held high. Voices loud in rough, drunken harmony, they shouted:

> *Inspired by this joyful day*
> *Sing wedding songs*
> *With your glad voices*
> *And shake the ground with your dancing,*
> *And in your hand brandish a pine torch!*

The dancers on the lawn and the people among the tables
laughed and rose—if they had been sitting—to respond. Maxian also stood, though Galen tried to hold him back with a hand
on the hem of his toga. Those on the lawn, equally drunken,
gathered, arm in arm, and made the proper, traditional reply:

> *For—as Venus*
> *Once approached Paris*
> *Now Martina approaches*
> *Maxian; a good maiden*
> *Will marry with good omens*

The soldiers, breath restored by the pause, turned to the
house, now joined by a crowd of men and women and children
who had been inside. They parted, the officers' hands on each
man's shoulder, making a corridor before the main doors of the
villa.

> *Come forward, new bride!*
> *Don't be afraid. Hear our glad words.*
> *See! Our torches*
> *Burn like golden hair.*
> *Come forward new bride!*

Gaius Julius appeared in the doorway and bowed to the assembled crowd. He raised his head, looking out across the

lawn. Galen finally rose, feeling duty settle on him with a heavy weight. The Empress Martina's father was long dead, her male relatives lost in the destruction of Constantinople. There was no one else of proper rank to present the bride. He raised his hand, catching Gaius Julius' eye. Maxian also waved, but before he could stride away across the lawn, Galen caught his hand.

"Wait, there is one more thing we must discuss. It's about Heracleonas."

"What about him?" Maxian turned back, a quizzical expression on his face.

Galen took a deep breath, suddenly changing his mind. Abrupt, honest words were set aside. His brother looked so young, as a man should be—nearly innocent—on his wedding day. *There is no need to trouble him with the dire thoughts tonight,* Galen decided. *I will strike a temperate course.* "His birthday approaches, as does Theodosius', and I thought to make a proclamation on the happy day, declaring to the people of Rome and to the world, Theo my heir and Caesar-presumptive to the Western throne. At the same time, Heracleonas will be proclaimed the heir to the East, under my protection, and yours, as his new father."

"Very well," Maxian said, shrugging his shoulders. "It matters little, with so many years to pass before they may take the red boots and white rod."

"True," Galen said, hiding a breath of relief at the prince's easy acceptance. "But the people will be pleased, I think, and such statements will set the minds of many lords at ease." *The people should be pleased! Games, donatives, corn tokens cast to the crowd . . . and the restive dukes and governors will be set on notice the Emperor has not forgotten the matter of succession!*

Maxian nodded in agreement, then turned away. Gaius Julius approached, bearing the glossy white raiment of the groom. Inside, Galen saw the women gathering in a great crowd. Martina would be there, her hair bound up in six locks, parted by a bent spear, anointed and oiled, prepared for the *sponsalia.* Swallowing rising disquiet at his own evasion and dissembling, the Emperor followed his brother into the house. Despite his best efforts and the glad day, he found a bitter taste lingering in his mouth. *A poor omen*, he thought bitterly, *if I cannot speak openly with my own brother*.

The main courtyard of the villa had been transformed—the smoke blackening scoured away, the shattered roof tiles replaced, dead shrubs and flowers rooted out and replaced with new, fresh plantings. Galen took his place at one side, standing on marble tiling. Pine torches sputtered and blazed around him in a great circle and the bride and groom stood before him, as yet apart.

Some fathers might make a long speech, but Galen was already tired and the night promised to be long. He raised his hands to the crowd filling the courtyard and the colonnade. Everyone fell quiet, even the servants perched on the roof, who gained a better view with their daring than many of the patricians below.

"Here stand before you Maxian Atreus, son of Galen the Elder, and Martina, daughter of Martinus. They are from good families and of noble blood. As princeps of the State, I speak for Martina as paterfamilias, her guide and defense against the trials of the world."

Galen, face composed in a stern and commanding mein, turned to Maxian. The prince was trying not to grin broadly. Despite his obvious good humor, Maxian managed to speak in a suitably respectful voice. "Do you promise Martina, your daughter, to be given to me as a wife?"

"May the gods smile upon us," Galen answered formally. "I promise her to you."

"May the gods smile upon us." Maxian said, making a slight bow.

The Emperor smiled warmly at Martina, who was sweating a little in a heavy woolen gown. The night had grown warm. Fine, pure white cloth was pleated and cinched at her waist with a silken band, tied in an ornate knot. A flame-colored veil shrouded her shoulders. As Galen had expected, the girl's hair was done up in six plaits and crowned with fragrant blooms.

"Martina, daughter, have you set aside your child's dress?"

Martina smiled back and the Emperor was gladdened to see a

spark of happiness in her eyes. The petulant, depressed young woman who had fled the destruction of her city seemed to be a fragment of the past. The Eastern Empress had gained confidence in the passing months. *Perhaps this is worth it, then,* Galen thought, grasping for some beneficent omen.

"I have, Father," she answered. "I have put my toys aside."

"So," Galen said, raising his voice so all might here, "go forth, as one, and stand fast together the length of your days." He lowered his hands.

Maxian, grinning like a loon, took Martina in his arms and kissed her soundly. The Empress squeaked, hand clutching the floral wreath, then pressed herself against him. Galen watched, filled with unexpected sadness. His own wedding day seemed very long ago. Then he turned away, leaving the circle of torches. Well-wishers converged on the bride and groom from all sides, laughing and shouting. Gaius Julius was among them, though his eyes followed the Emperor with interest.

"Ho! See the bride, see the groom!" A great shout rose from the men in the crowd and they hoisted Maxian on their shoulders, then Martina as well. Someone began to sing and the whole group congealed into a procession winding around the garden and out into the dining hall. Torches bobbed above the heads of the revelers. Laughing, the young Empress flung her crown of flowers out into a thicket of grasping hands.

Again, Galen stood in quiet darkness, face shrouded by the folds of his toga, watching men and women dancing in the great hall of the villa. He felt unaccountably cold, though the summer night was close and almost hot. Maxian and Martina had taken three turns on the freshly tiled floor, swirling past his vantage to the lively rattle of drums and the wail of pipes and horns. At the moment, the prince was dancing with a young girl—one of the senatorial daughters, whose head barely reached his waist, her hair bound up with ribbons and posies. Empress Martina sat at the edge of the floor, face flushed, laughing in delight. A heavy golden cup wavered in her hand. Galen tensed, then breathed out in relief as Gaius Julius—sitting beside the Empress— caught the goblet as it tipped.

"Husband?"

Galen turned, startled and pleased. Helena approached, walking quickly down the pillared hall. She was dressed plainly, a heavy scarf around her neck, pulling gloves from her hands. A courier's satchel was slung across her chest, riding under her breast like a suckling child. Two Praetorians hung back behind her, then faded into the shadows when they caught sight of the Emperor. Galen thought they were wearing riding leathers, but couldn't be sure.

"Helena! I thought you weren't coming." His mood lifted, buoyed by her simple presence.

"There is news," she said in a clipped, emotionless tone. Galen felt an almost physical shock, seeing her face in the light. More than simple fatigue, or a hard ride up from the port, lit her eyes with such a grim flame. "From Egypt," she continued.

Galen looked around, shedding the ceremonial drape with a shrug. There was no one within earshot. The cloth, forgotten, fell to the floor in an untidy tangle. "Tell me."

Helena breathed deep and the Emperor saw she had ridden swiftly, her hair tangled, high cheeks flushed with effort. Even her accustomed makeup was sketchy and old. "The thaumaturges watching the telecast sent me word the day before yesterday. They had turned their attentions to Egypt. They found the defenses at Pelusium abandoned, the Persian army and fleet decamped."

"What?" Galen rocked back on his heels. "Where is Aurelian?"

"At Bousiris," Helena said, opening the satchel. She tried to smile grimly, but failed. "Anastasia has always warned our all-seeing eye can only look one place at a time . . . it took the thaumaturges an hour of casting about to find the Legions. They are digging furiously on the western bank of the main Nile channel, building a rampart from Bousiris north. The Persians are busy across the river too." Helena drew a sheaf of papers from the pouch, then knelt on the floor. Galen knelt as well, watching in growing cold nausea as she spread out hasty drawings—maps—on hexagonal tile.

"We looked for signs of the Persian advance." Her slender fingers shifted two of the pages, and a crude diagram of the Nile delta became recognizable. "Their foraging parties have struck as far south as Boubastis. This much we see from the smoke clouding the sky and roads clogged with fleeing peasants."

"Where is their fleet?" Galen bit out, furious with himself. *Of course*, he raged silently, *there is nothing to be done, not by me, not now . . . not when we are so far away, and our arm so slow to reach the enemy.* "Can they cross the Nile?"

Helena looked across at him, over the scattered papers, in the dim hallway. The music from the dancing echoed faintly from the ceiling, coupled with the laughter of the guests. "Yes," she said quietly. "They have a great fleet of barges. They are moored along the Boutikos canal, in a long array."

The Emperor closed his eyes, marshalling his thoughts. The Boutikos sliced across the delta from Pelusium in the east to the main Nile channel just north of Bousiris, then jogged west to reach the second channel, the Kanobikos, above Alexandria. In better days, the broad canal flowed with commerce, carrying the lifeblood of Egypt and the Empire across the endless paddies and fields of lower Egypt. He bit his thumb, considering. Now the waterway was a lunging spear, aimed right at the heart of the Roman province. Galen felt a familiar pricking begin behind his left eye.

"They were ready to fight on the water, in the swamps and mire." His voice was level, contemplative. "Supplies, water, arms, wounded men—all can be swiftly moved on the canal." He took a breath, feeling certainty congeal his thoughts into a discrete pattern. *What must be done, must be done.* "Do you have a writing tablet?"

"Yes." Helena settled into a tailor's crouch, drawing a wooden tablet from the courier bag. Individual sheets of thin wood, faced with wax, were bound together with copper wire. The Empress looked up, a stylus poised in one hand. Galen tried to smile, but the bleak look in her eyes matched his own temper. He looked down at the maps, disheartened.

"Have we heard from Aurelian directly?"

The Empress nodded, scrabbling in the papers and producing a sheet of papyrus. "This came while we were trying to find the army. Aurelian sent a dispatch three weeks ago—he had been attacked at Pelusium by the Persian army and a 'burning giant.' His thaumaturges were unable to hold back the enemy. . . ."

Galen's palm hit the floor with a sharp *crack!* "The sorcerer."

Helena nodded again, offering the letter. Galen shook his head sharply in refusal, running both hands through his thin hair.

"He's put everything in this one throw . . . But why Egypt . . ." He bit his lip, thinking again.

"Grain? Wealth?" Helena looked at him quizzically. "Does it really matter?"

"It matters. Something drives the enemy to his current path . . ." Galen looked out through the pillars, into the dining hall. Maxian and Martina were dancing again, this time to a gentle, melodic tune. The guests were stamping their feet in slow, measured time. "What of the situation in Thrace? Constantinople?"

"Good news," Helena said, lip curling at the sight of the young couple moving in unison. "The *comes* Alexandros has retaken the city and the Persians are in flight across the strait. We observed Khazar horsemen crossing the Propontis on ferry barges. Groups of riders—perhaps the Persians, or their mercenaries—are scattering east into Anatolia."

Galen drew a relieved breath. *Something . . . something positive in this wreckage. But what does this sorcerer want in Egypt?* For the first time, the Emperor felt himself lost, groping in darkness for some fragile light of truth. He knew why Shahr-Baraz would desire Egypt—taxes, wealth, abundant grain and denying Rome these same things—but the same could be said for Constantinople and the rich fields of Thrace. But a sorcerer? Why abandon one prize and strike at the other? Tantalizing fragments taunted him, but he could not make them gel into a reasoned whole. He shook his head angrily.

"Very well, we will send the fleet—now regrouped at Ostia-port and reinforced with our squadrons from Hispania and Britannia—to Constantinople in all haste. Whatever thaumaturges can be spared are to be aboard, with these mirrored bowls Maxian spoke of—we may need immediate speech with their admiral! Let them take Alexandros' army aboard and straightaway to Egypt. Together, Alexandros and Aurelian can crush these Persians before the walls of Alexandria."

Helena had begun to write, but now she stopped, staring at

her husband. "And Maxian? You'll be sending him, won't you?"

The Emperor stared through the pillars again, stricken with gut-wrenching despair. He started to speak, then stopped. Helena waited, stylus tapping impatiently on the edge of the tablet.

"He must go," Helena said, when she could keep her peace no longer. "If the Perisan *monster* is striving against Aurelian, he will not be able to hold Egypt! Maxian will have to go, if we hope to hold Alexandria and the delta."

Still the Emperor said nothing. In the dining hall, men raised their cups in a toast to the young couple and the prince's face glowed with delight. Galen remembered times now lost, when they were all children, brawling in the kitchen, running in the grassy fields above Narbo, Aurelian daring Maxian to cross the aqueduct vaulting the swift-flowing Atax. His mother silhouetted in the doorway of their room, watching the boys sleeping by firelight. *Does it come to this?* he thought, mournful again. *A young man sent out to war on his wedding night? What about my promise?*

"Husband?"

A thought occurred to him, whispered by some unseen messenger and Galen let relief hiss out in a long breath. "No, not yet. Iron Pegasus can carry him to Egypt in the space of a week. The fleet will take . . ." He paused, calculating distances and time. ". . . two weeks to gather and reach Constantinople. Another five days to load Alexandros' army aboard, then a week to reach Alexandria." A very faint smile creased his lips and he felt lighter, relieved. "Time enough for him to enjoy a taste of marriage, I think. We will wait until Alexandros is in position, then send him forth. By then, his flight of iron drakes may be hatched and ready to wing—that will give Persia pause, I think!"

He looked back to his wife and saw she had gone deathly still.

"What is it?" Galen was afraid to ask, but felt compelled. Tears sparkled at the corner of Helena's eyes, creeping through kohl already smudged by her nighttime ride. Swallowing, she wiped them away, leaving trailing black streaks on her cheeks.

"I always loved that big horse," she said in a choked voice. "It's not right."

The Emperor nodded, understanding her reaction all too well. There was a tight constriction around his heart. "He's a soldier, Helena. Always has been, always will be. Aurelian will understand."

"Will Famia? What about his boys? They're so worried already. . . ."

Galen could think of nothing to say. What came to pass, would come to pass.

Waves hissed against across empty sand, foam glittering in faint moonlight. Luna, a thin sliver, rose over the mountains in the east, shedding barely enough light to challenge the jewel-bright stars. Maxian, his toga and tunic a pale flare of white against the dark shore, splashed into the surf. The water rushing past his ankles was still warm from the day's heat.

"Where are we going?" Martina said sleepily, arms curled around his neck, tousled head nestled against his chest. The Empress's elaborate gown was rumpled and sweat-stained from a long night of dancing, feasting and drinking. Maxian waded deeper into the bay, bare feet sinking into heavy, soft sand. Waves lapped around him, rising to his waist. Foam touched Martina's bare feet and she squeaked in surprise. "That's wet! Where are . . ."

Maxian raised his chin, pointing, and the Empress turned, eyes widening in surprise.

A boat rode at anchor, not more than a dozen yards away. Long-prowed, with gilded figureheads of rampant gods at fore and aft and shallow sides chased with gold. An awning of muslin suspended from wooden arches sheltered the deck, barely visible in the moonlight.

"Oh," Martina said, then she hissed as the warm water rose up around her. Maxian smiled in the darkness, feeling her cling tight to him. "Are there sharks?" she whispered, still half-asleep.

"Not in this cove," he said. "A barrier net closes the entrance and nothing enters that might spoil an Empress's wedding night."

"That's comfort—*eek!* That's cold!" Maxian waded to a ladder hanging from the rear deck, water swirling around his chest. Martina, her head still above the waves, was completely immersed.

"Hold tight now," he said, letting her legs fall free in the water. Her grip tightened on his neck like a vise. With his free hand Maxian grasped the rope, setting one bare foot to the lowest rung of the ladder. Then he swung himself and Martina out of the water in a smooth motion onto the deck. Water sluiced from their sodden clothes, spilling away on polished teak planks. In the moonlight, a very pale, indistinct radiance touched the awning ropes, the railings, even the piled cushions and quilts on the deck. The deck rolled softly under their feet, the motion barely noticeable, yet giving the impression of yielding, infinite depth.

"I'm freezing," Martina said in the darkness. The heavy, saturated wool of her gown sent streams of water spilling down her legs. Maxian let his own garment fall to the deck. "Why is it so dark?"

"Here," Maxian said. "Let me show you." He drew her close, hands peeling the sodden gown away. The Empress shuddered, then let out a gasp as he caressed the skin of her shoulders, her upper arms. Warmth spilled from his touch. His palms slid over the curve of her breasts, her round stomach, her flanks. The gown fell away and then she was dry. Martina pressed herself against the prince, finding his smooth chest bare under her fingertips.

"You're so warm," she breathed, her body conforming greedily to his. She turned up her face, lips parted. Maxian smiled down and above his head, the tracery of wires suspending the translucent awning began to wink to life, fluttering with pale blue, yellow and carnelian. Unnoticed by the Empress, the ship had begun to move, the ladder lifted from the sea by invisible hands. Now the tiller shifted and the sea hissed past under the prow. In darkness, the ghost-barque turned to the cove's entrance, passing between towering black pinnacles. Ahead, the open sea waited.

"Are . . . are they the fey?" Martina turned, feeling delightfully smooth skin sliding against her back, the Prince's arm curled between her breasts, his fingers against the side of her neck. Looking forward, she saw pale lights trace the length of the ship, throwing a soft, intimate light over couches, bedding, silken pillows. "It's so beautiful. . . ."

"All of this," the prince whispered, his breath hot on her neck, "is for you."

Jewels blazed in the awning and the deck shone like molten gold. A comfortable, encompassing warmth folded around her, made all the more delicious by the sea's cool grasp, so recently released. Maxian picked her up, then settled among the cushions, deep quilts yielding to his knees. Laughing softly, he dropped Martina to the deck, then smiled as she bounced— startled—on the deep pile.

"Ah, this feels wonderful. . . ." She stretched, luxuriating in the glassy sensation of Chin silk. "You are very . . . *ah!* . . . naughty!" Maxian slid his knees inside hers, parting her legs. Martina's eyes grew large in the dim light, seeing him bend over her. Long, dark hair trailed on either side of his face, spilling across her white breasts. Seeing him in this glamour, Martina realized how beautiful he had become, his face lean with high cheekbones, his body trim and muscled like an acrobat, long, powerful legs illuminated by the subtle light.

He bent to kiss her, but she suddenly stiffened, turning away.

"What is wrong?" he said softly, moving to look at her face. She was biting her lip, eyes squeezed shut. "Martina?"

"Don't look at me," she hissed, tears pearling from her eyes. "Please make the lights go out."

Maxian sat up, head tilted to one side, sun-browned hands on her waist. "You don't like the lights?"

"They are very nice," she said tightly, curling away from him, drawing her legs up to her stomach. "Please put them out."

"Why? I want to see you. . . ."

"Don't!" The Empress compressed herself to a tight ball, hiding her face in her arms. "You don't want to see me—I'm *fat* and *round*—not beautiful like you and your family. Please, make it dark again."

"Oh." Maxian knelt beside her, trying to stroke her hair. Martina flinched away. "You're not happy with your body?"

"No!" The Empress raised her head, tears streaming through caked kohl. "Are you *stupid?* I'm short and round and I have a fat stomach—not like cold Helena, who is so *perfect* and *slim* and *elegant!* Or even Anastasia, though she's nice to me at least, but she's got so much beautiful hair, and striking eyes and her breasts don't point down because she hasn't had any babies and she can wear fashionable clothes and if I try them they look horrible or cheap and everyone laughs behind their hands when they think I'm not looking!"

She punched him, tears streaming freely. He barely felt the blow against the hard, flat muscle of his chest. Maxian caught the fist, then spread her fingers against his breast. "Shhh . . ." he whispered. "Hush. I've gift, a groom's gift—and not scissors or a paring knife—for a bride on her wedding night. Let me take these cares away. . . ." Again, he bent to kiss her, but Martina buried her face in the pleated quilts, sobbing.

Maxian drew back, letting her lie shuddering in exhaustion. A troubled look crossed his face, followed by an attitude of listening, then a slow, broad smile. He nodded thanks to the air, then settled his hands on the crown of Martina's head.

"Don't touch me!" she hissed, trying to strike his hands away.

"Shhh . . ." he said, closing his eyes. "Behold."

Martina started to struggle, but a warm, liquid glow spilled from his hands and her eyes rolled up. Mouth parted in a soft *aaah,* her back arched as she stiffened, caught in the glamour. Sweat beaded on bare skin and her fingers dug into the quilts. Slowly, with infinite care, Maxian drew his hands through her hair, which thickened, grew, spilling into soft, chestnut waves. Spreading her tresses across the pillows he lay alongside her, hands firm upon her face and neck, cupping her breasts, smoothing the skin of her stomach, circling her thighs, fingers running down to her toes in gentle, irresistible progress. The shimmering glow seeped into skin, rendering her flesh pliable, adding muscle, stealing fat, lengthening bone.

As he worked, face shining with soft, rippling blue white light—like the sea gleaming from a shield or a grotto roof—she moaned and squirmed, unable to speak, transported by his touch. When, at last he was done, he rose to his knees, looking down upon her. A certain expression filled his face, an amalgam of pride, delight and satisfaction. *Well done!*

Martina lay among the silken sheets, languid eyes barely

open, heart-shaped lips parted, glorious dark brown hair spilling to her waist, breasts now high and firm, velvety stomach curving irresistibly to the sweet cradle of her thighs, legs long and tapering. The sight of her struck him in the stomach, a heavy blow of desire.

"Could Pygmalion have done better?" Maxian's eyes sparkled. "Martina?"

"Yes, husband?" The Empress's eyes fluttered open and looked upon him with joy. Her fear, self-doubt and exhaustion were gone—wiped away by his power. "Where is my bridal bed and bower?"

"Here," he said, standing, silhouetted against the star-filled sky. He raised a hand and the sea foam blazed with deep green light as if the sun rose in the depths, filling the sky with pillars and columns of twisting cold flame. "On a sea of dreams."

The prince knelt between her legs and now Martina accepted his caress with wanton delight, rising to meet him. He gasped at the hot breath of her kiss. Then she cried out, surrendering to him.

The ship bore into the west, glittering spray falling back from a high prow and the ghosts of men kept watch in the rigging, spying the deeps for reefs and hidden rocks. Sails of starlight caught invisible zephyrs, carrying the lovers on, into warm, close darkness.

THE DESERT BEYOND LAKE MAREOTIS, LOWER EGYPT

T here!" Nicholas pointed, eyes shaded against the blazing white sky by his burnoose. "A worked edge."

Sandals crunching in loose pea sand, Thyatis climbed a low dune to stand beside the Latin. Pillars and knobs of crumbling russet-colored stone rose from the desolation, stretching to the horizon in either direction. Beneath the eroded towers, dark red sand moved slowly south, driven by a constant gusty wind. The Roman woman had never seen a more inhospitable place. All signs of life were absent—no short grass, no lichen, no birds—nothing but keening wind and the rattling sound of sand blowing against rock.

Ahead, beyond Nicholas' pointing finger, she saw a larger pinnacle jutting from the wayward dunes, burnished sandstone striated with dark streaks. The lowering sun threw a long shadow to the east, but her eyes found a dissonant angle on the face of the worn, curved rock.

"Not a door," she said, voice muffled by the heavy linen covering her mouth and nose. "But something made by man."

Nicholas nodded and they advanced cautiously. Thyatis drifted to the left and the Latin to the right. A hundred yards behind, the camels and workers waited patiently in the lee of another knob of fluted stone. Thyatis kept a sharp eye on the avenues of sand and barren rock between the pillars, watching for any movement. Disquiet had plagued her since they'd entered the wasteland—she was sure someone was watching them as they picked their way across the broken, rough ground. Nicholas darted ahead, reaching the side of the pinnacle. His hands searched over grainy, pebbled stone. Up close, the sharp edge that had seemed so clear from a distance vanished, lost in wind-carved surfaces.

Thyatis continued to watch their backs, crouching against the base of the rock, letting her tan-and-brown silhouette merge with the land. The sense of unease grew and her fingers tightened on the hilt of her sword. "Anything?"

"No." Nicholas stepped back, looking up. "But I'm sure . . ."

Thyatis froze, feeling a strange trembling against her breastbone. Without looking down, she slid one hand into her tunic, groping for the prince's amulet. The copper disk, warm from the heat of her body, was vibrating. Gritting her teeth, she clamped down—though the device made no audible noise—and felt the metal humming.

Curse this Roman and his mysterious friends! Thyatis felt a brief spike of fury, then quashed the emotion. She twitched her shoulders, trying to keep from tensing up. *Curse the Persians too for inspiring a lax, slovenly Cypriot to find something valuable in the morass of that library for once in his wretched, short life!* She looked sideways at Nicholas, who was crouching on the sand, looking up at the stone face from an odd angle.

"See anything?" Thyatis startled herself with a wry laugh. Upside down, he looked like a monkey.

"Maybe . . ." Nicholas began digging in the sand blown against the base of the pinnacle.

Thyatis watched him, weighing her options. If the prince's talisman told true, there was a telecast nearby. She couldn't let it be found, either by Nicholas or anyone else. *Should I kill him now?* she wondered, glancing back to the rest of the caravan. Mithridates and Betia were watching her, while the others kept an eye on the camels or the wasteland. The pinnacles and spires broke up the horizon, making everything a jumble. It would be easy for someone to approach, hiding among the broken rock. *Murder Vladimir and the workers . . . tell the Emperor the Persians ambushed us . . .*

The thought made her feel ill and cold. She didn't know how she felt about Nicholas, but Vladimir was a gregarious, outgoing fellow and this mess was none of his making. *What is so important about these cursed devices anyway?* The Duchess's fears seemed remote and insubstantial under the desert sun, with a hot wind tugging at her robe. Thyatis felt irritated too. She had never been troubled by the thought of striking down an enemy of the state before—but was Nicholas an enemy? Cursing under her breath, she kicked sand away. *My dear mother has to make everything so complicated. . . .*

"Here!" Nicholas turned, grinning. His hole in the sand had gone down a foot or more and the worn, smoothed stones had changed, revealing a sharper, clearly man-made cut in the rock face. "Hallo!" He sprang up, waving at the others. "There is something here!"

Thyatis whistled softly, a warbling trill, and Betia—standing watch over the camels fifty feet away—turned to face her. The little Gaul was wrapped from head to toe in desert robes, a mottled brown and tan and white, only pale blue eyes peering from a thin slit in the cloth. Thyatis had been circling the pinnacle, watching for anyone or anything, and now stood out of sight of the excavation busily underway at the base of the rock face.

The fellaheen had been digging industriously for over an hour, their mattocks and spades burrowing into the firmly packed sand. Nicholas' discovery had proved to be the side of a frieze. Only the legs and feet of three figures remained, protected by the packed sand. Everything exposed above the ground level had been obliterated by seven hundred years of ceaseless, gnawing wind. Thyatis felt a steadily rising tension in her gut, mirroring the slow appearance of a stone door covered with hieroglyphs and animal figures. Nicholas squatted at the top of the pit, watching with excited interest.

Ignoring Betia for the moment, Thyatis let her eyes unfocus, turning slightly and surveying the surrounding landscape. There was no movement, nothing out of the ordinary, no suddenly familiar silhouette against the organic shapes of rock and sky. Vladimir and Mithridates—muscles gleaming with sweat—were hauling bags of sand out of the pit, daring each other to carry heavier and heavier weights.

Circle, Thyatis signed at Betia, when she was sure no one was watching. *Look for tracks or signs. Stay out of sight.*

The little blonde nodded, then her hands moved sharply. *Archers?*

Thyatis signed *I hope so,* then resumed her drifting movement between the pinnacles and jagged stones. She hoped the Daughters were somewhere nearby. Any hope of them having come and gone remained faint—the amulet around her neck continued to shiver, the hum vibrating through her breastbone.

Torches guttered, whipped by the dying sundown wind. Thyatis stood at the top of the pit, now grown to a dozen paces wide and twice as long. The excavation revealed a pair of fluted, acanthus-topped pillars and a step buried long ago by the sand. Nervous, she bit her lower lip, watching men strain against stone. A massive granite slab closed the entrance to the tomb, but Mithridates and Vladimir leaned on a pair of iron pry bars, gleaming mu..les tense with effort. The fellaheen made a crowd on the ramp, watching with trepidation. At least one was chanting nervously, making signs against ill fortune. Nicholas seemed terribly pleased with himself, caught in the excitement of opening something hidden for hundreds of years.

Mithridates grunted, a deep basso noise, and the bar in his hands began to bend, torqued beyond the ability of the iron to withstand. Vladimir braced his feet again and shoved, flat muscles rippling under a thick pelt of fur covering his back and upper arms. His effort was rewarded with a grating sound, then dust puffed from the edges of the stone door. Thyatis held her breath, fingers white on the hilt of her sword.

The slab groaned again, scraping, and then an opening appeared—dark and fathomless in the wavering light of the torches—on one side of the slab.

"That's it!" Nicholas shouted, scrambling down into the pit. He snatched up another pry bar and squeezed in, thrusting the iron into the crevice. Several of the fellaheen—seeing none of the Romans had perished so far—crept up and lent their own wiry muscle to widening the opening. After a long moment of grunting and sweat streaming from matted hair, the door rumbled to one side. All five men stepped back, grimacing. The tomb exhaled a draft of dull, dead air. Nicholas thrust a torch into the doorway.

Broad, crisply cut steps led down into darkness. Ruddy orange light revealed wall paintings in brilliant azure, umber, crimson and white—cranes and kings and delta fields thick with game birds and peasants working pumps, scythes, bellows. Nicholas stepped into the passage, reaching out with a tentative hand. His touch barely brushed the painted colors and they crumbled away to rose-colored dust, leaving only a faint memory on the smooth stone.

"Come," the Latin barked, gesturing for the fellaheen. "Bring the torches and the sled."

Mithridates and Vladimir climbed out of the pit. Thyatis caught the African's eye as he bent to lift the wooden platform with its greased rails.

"Betia?" he whispered, casting about for the little Gaul. Thyatis flashed him a quick smile, indicating the encompassing darkness with a momentary tilt of her head.

"I'll follow," Thyatis called down to Nicholas, "and watch our backs."

"Good." The Latin singled out two the fellaheen. "You and you, guard the camels."

Grinning in relief, teeth white against sun-darkened faces, the two Egyptians scrambled out of the excavation. Thyatis followed Vladimir and Mithridates down into the pit, blade now bare in her hand. The tunnel was already filled with flickering light as Nicholas and a crowd of fellaheen descended, torches and lanterns held high. She turned in the doorway, casting a wary eye at the desert, but could see nothing—not even the stars, or the late moon—beyond the torches thrust into the sandy ground. Some distance away, the camels honked and grumbled at the approach of the two men.

Frowning, the Roman woman turned and stepped lightly down into the tomb. Her neck was prickling again. *There is someone out there* . . . She hoped Betia would be careful.

Quiet and patient, Patik stood in the shadow of a nearby crag. A dozen yards away, torches guttered in the wind, illuminating the pit. The Persian watched with interest, a faint gleam of light sparkling in his eyes. He never failed to be intrigued by the ability of men—even experienced soldiers—to be blinded by the simple division of light and darkness. The torches were visible for miles across the desert plain, winking between the standing stones. He and his men had approached cautiously, but even the Roman watchers had remained within the circle of light, blinding themselves. Patik had no cause for complaint.

Two of the Egyptian workers approached the camels and gear piled in the lee of one of the stone pinnacles. Both of the animals were nervous, but the men—tired from a long afternoon and evening's labor—ignored their warning grunts. Amur, his armor and face blackened with soot, rose quietly from the ground as the two fellaheen passed and his scarred hand was over one mouth, his knife sawing in one neck before anyone could do anything. The other Egyptian walked two paces, then turned, curious, missing the sound of his friend's footsteps. The Persian thrust hard, driving his dagger into the man's throat. A choking, gargled cry was drowned by blood flooding from the wound and Mihr caught the body before it could fall to the ground.

"Move," Patik hissed, padding forward silently across the loose sand. Despite his size and bulk, he showed a feral gracefulness in motion. The big Persian paused at the top of the excavation. No one was in sight, not even in the tunnel mouth. Tishtrya and Asha slid down the slope at the Persian's signal, then crept into the tunnel.

"Are you ready?" Patik kept his voice low, even doubting there were any Romans within earshot. Artabanus nodded, looking a little sickly in the poor, wavering light. Patik doubted the mage had ever seen a man killed before, at least not at such close range.

"Good." The big Persian descended into the pit, finally drawing his own sword. Asha was visible, ahead, crouched in the tunnel at some kind of turning.

Allowing herself a breath of relief, Shirin raised her head from the sand. The edge of the pit was only two strides away. Echoing, the soft voices of the Persians receded into the earth. As she watched, two more Persians slipped out of the darkness, one man wiping blood from a knife on his tunic and disappeared into the excavation.

"Lovely," the Khazar woman breathed out slowly, then carefully backed away into the darkness. Beyond the circle of light thrown by the torches, only starlight picked out the tumbled stones and massive pinnacles. But this was enough for a daughter of the house of Asena. Padding softly on bare feet, Shirin circled away from the lights and the buried door. She had hoped to follow Thyatis into the tomb, but had waited—unaccountably nervous—and the sudden appearance of the Persians had almost stopped her heart with surprise.

Who else is creeping around in the darkness? she wondered, drifting behind another towering column of sandstone. Disturbed by the thought, Shirin looked to the east, hoping for the moon to rise, but Orion was still low on the horizon and when Luna did rise, she would be thin and pale. The land among the pillars was very dark and the intermittent, wayward wind obscured as many sounds as it carried. *I have to do something*, she decided, turning back towards the tomb. *I should warn Thyatis.*

A faint sparkle caught her eye as she moved back around the wall of stone. Off to her right, starlight shifted on disturbed sand. Shirin paused, looking towards the circle of torches, then back to the pale, gleaming avenue between the stones. Gritting her teeth, she darted forward, iron knife bare in her hand. Stooping over the sand, she saw the faint outline of footprints arcing away from the Roman camp. The unsettled feeling in her stomach worsened. *There is someone else out here.*

Head raised, eyes straining to pierce the night, Shirin followed the tracks in a half-crouch, one hand drifting over the sand, finding the shallow wells of someone moving lightly on the earth. After a few moments she reached another towering sandstone pinnacle. Gingerly, she picked her way around the scalloped, eroded wall. The breeze fluttered, disturbing her hair, then died.

She froze. A tremendous silence filled the night, without even the whisper of the night wind to disturb the sand. Counting thudding, enormously loud heartbeats, Shirin waited. Nothing moved in the darkness. Cautiously, she resumed creeping along the stone face. Twenty steps later, she froze again. A breath of air brushed her cheek, ruffling a wayward curl.

Anticipation mounting, Shirin's fingers explored the rock, finding a narrow vertical crack. Air hissed softly from the opening. *A cave,* she realized, remembering her uncles' tales around a winter fire, very long ago. *A big one.* She pressed against the rock, fingers pressing and poking in the hollowed stone. A sharp-edged groove revealed itself to her searching fingers, then another. Frowning in the darkness, Shirin traced a half-familiar pattern. *A bow? Newly scratched in the stone?*

Without thinking, she traced the sign of the Archer in the air, nodding to herself. *The Daughters must have been here recently.* Putting her shoulder against the rock, the Khazar pushed, feet slipping on the sand. There was a scraping sound, then the stone face slid away and she fell, startled, into the greater darkness beyond. A rumbling creak followed as she scrambled up from a smooth floor and the counterweighted block rotated back into place, cutting off even the faint ghost-light of the stars.

Time passed, the eroded face of the pinnacle remaining stolid and unmoving despite the faint sound of metal banging on stone. Eventually the faint noise stopped and silence settled on the sand and rock.

Some time later, the curved arm of the moon lifted above the eastern horizon, casting a pale, silvery light over the wasteland and the rocky knobs. The shadows grew deeper, though the sand glittered faintly. A figure, hunched and bent over the rippled sand, appeared in the dim radiance, creeping along Shirin's trail. After casting back and forth across the marks of her sandals, it reached the rocky face. Thick fingers, clad in burnished dark mail, examined the worn surface, poking and prodding.

A hiss of anger broke the silence. The figure drew away from the hidden door and moved back along the footsteps in the hard sand. Another shape, also cowled and shrouded, met the searcher and together they loped off towards the Roman excavation. The torches had burned down to glowing ash, which did nothing to prevent the entrance of the two wights into the tomb.

"Another dead end!" Nicholas cursed, backing up. Behind him, two of the fellaheen scrambled backwards up a sloping ramp. Their torches flared along the low ceiling, leaving washes of soot on the bare stone. Nicholas glowered at the rough-hewn stone wall closing off the end of the passage.

"Let's try the other way," Thyatis said. She was trying to hide a smile. Nicholas was covered with dust and grime from head to toe. Squinting with his bad eye, he crawled out of the square-cut opening into the larger tunnel. "There are plenty of passages to search."

"Funny," he growled. The entrance ramp had led down into a high-ceilinged gallery lined with plastered columns. Despite the excited shouts of the fellaheen, they had found nothing in the entryway but broken pottery and desiccated bits of bone and skin. Thyatis didn't think the remains were human, but she'd steered clear of the detritus anyway. "Does anyone *see anything?*"

The workers, squatting on the floor of the passage, shook their heads. Most of the men had lost their initial fear—no vengeful spirits had emerged from the painted walls to threaten them and the tomb was proving a dull succession of debris-filled rooms, rubble-strewn corridors and dead-end passages like this one. Thyatis did not respond. As before, she remained at the rear of the group, watching the passage behind them, squinting into the darkness beyond the light of their torches and listening. Sound echoed strangely in the contorted tunnels. A little while ago, there had been a clattering sound—like metal falling on stone—behind them.

"Vlad? Do you hear, see, *smell* anything?" Nicholas sounded worried and impatient.

The Walach looked up, eyes glittering in the torchlight. His beard and long hair were streaked with white dust and he looked miserable. "I smell you," he growled, "and these pitch torches. Not much else."

"All right," Nicholas sighed. "Let go back to the last junction. Vlad, you lead."

Thyatis waited, pressed against the corridor wall, while everyone reversed direction and crowded past. Mithridates brought up the rear, dragging the sled easily behind him. As he passed, Thyatis grinned at the Numidian. The wide-shouldered African smiled back, though he had to crouch to keep from striking his head on the ceiling.

Clanking and rustling, the group trooped back down the tunnel and into a junction of sloping, ramped corridors. One led up, back to the first gallery, the others went off in every direction. Over the heads of her companions, Thyatis could see Vladimir crouched in the octagonal room, casting about, nostrils flared. Nicholas, his long blade bare in his hand, was watching from the tunnel mouth. After canvassing the chamber, Vladimir paused at the bottom of a ramp trending upward.

"Someone's been this way," the Walach called, his voice echoing in the domed ceiling. "I can smell garlic, maybe, and some kind of metallic-tasting oil." Turning, he tasted the air in the other openings. "Someone passed this way too with incense, myrrh, beeswax, coriander . . ." He squinted down the passage. "A lamp with scented oil. Sweet."

Just in front of Thyatis, Mithridates turned, looking over his shoulder, one eyebrow raised skeptically. The Roman woman shrugged, stepping up beside the African.

"We're the first people in this tomb in hundreds of years," she whispered. "All those smells are just sitting here, undisturbed." At the same time, she felt a cold prickling, wondering just how good the Walach's eyesight was, if his sense of smell was so sharp. Sparring to pass the time on the *Paris* had already proven the barbarian was fantastically quick and strong. He didn't have the hard-won skill owned by Nicholas or Thyatis, but he could wield his long-bladed axe tirelessly.

"Are there any tracks?" Nicholas thrust his torch into the doorway of the downward ramp.

"No," Vladimir said, padding down the tunnel in a half-crouch. "The smell is getting stronger."

"Right." Nicholas followed, beckoning for the others. Most of the fellaheen followed, though two of them were peering up the other passage. Thaytis, following at the back of the group, scowled at them as she crossed the octagonal room.

"You two," she hissed, "this way!"

At the same moment, one of the Egyptians—head wrapped in an elaborate turban—pointed, whistling in surprise. "Look, my lady, something's there!"

Thyatis was at his side in an instant. The ramp sloped up and turned onto a platform. At the bend, there was some kind of debris glittering bright and golden in the torchlight. In the poor light, it was impossible to tell what it was.

"Leave it," she growled, feeling her hackles rise. There were white shapes in the rubble too, like bones. "We can check it later."

The other fellaheen, making a hasty sign against spirits, hastened to catch up with the others. Thyatis followed, smirking. *Someone has an atom of good sense*, she thought. Then she stopped, frowning. *Where was the first man . . .* Thyatis spun, leaping back towards the ramp. She caught sight of a pair of sandals disappearing up the tunnel and skidded to a halt.

The Egyptian snatched up the shining object—a funerary

vase, fluted and golden, footed with lions' paws—and turned it over in his hand. The debris, disturbed, rattled and bits and pieces of wood bounced down the ramp.

"Get down here!" Thyatis kicked a small wooden jackal head away with her sandal.

Her head snapped up—the rattling sound becoming a shockingly loud rumbling—and in the flaring light of a falling torch, she saw the Egyptian turn towards her, then the tomb wall at the top of the ramp came loose. Thyatis leapt back, startled. A rectangular plug of stone rotated down with an enormous dull *boom*. The Egyptian's scream was cut short as the entire structure slid greasily to a halt. A massive *thud* punched the air as the stone plug rammed into the lintel of the doorway. Dust cascaded from the ceiling, making Thyatis sneeze. Stunned, she scuttled backwards.

The block shuddered for a moment, then became still. The Roman woman sneezed again, wiping a thick patina of white dust from her face. There was no sign of the man or his golden prize. The newly exposed slab filling the doorway was carved with a relief showing kilted men bowing before the Judges of the Underworld.

"That's very nice," Thyatis muttered to herself. Nicholas and Mithridates appeared at her side, staring in surprise into the dust-filled chamber.

"What happened?" Nicholas' voice was very tense and sharp. Mithridates had a spear-like pry bar in his hands. "Where's Fenuku?"

"Under there." Thyatis turned away, digging grit out of her eye with a thumb. "Let's go."

Vladimir's trail of incense led down into another pillared hall, this one crowded with crumbling wooden crates and wicker hampers filled with rotting, desiccated goods. On edge, the fellaheen and the Romans picked their way through the chamber to an entrance sealed with a heavy slab of raw, unworked stone. The Walach pressed himself against the barrier, snuffling along the join between the floor and the door. After a moment, eyes closed, nose twitching, he rose, nodding. "Through here."

"Huh," Nicholas said, glaring at the unremarkable slab. "How did they get it into the doorway?"

A lip of stone ran around the entire opening, hiding the edges of the stone block. There was nowhere to drive a pry bar into a crevice. The Latin knelt, running his fingers along the edges. The fit between the block and the frame was snug and tight. He looked back at Thyatis, grimacing. "Are we going to have to chip our way through? Do we have chisels and hammers?"

"We do. But I don't think we have a week," she replied, looking around the hall. The plastered walls were covered with decaying paintings—most of them cracked and shattered, leaving piles of untidy plaster chips on the floor and gaping holes in the long, panoramic scenes. "They must have sealed the chamber from the other side. Perhaps there is another entrance in some other passage."

Nicholas' face contorted into a scowl and the man turned back to the door, glaring at the mute stone. "Everyone start looking!"

For himself, he bent to examine the door frame again. The fellaheen, huddled together, began poking dubiously at the piles of debris on the floor. Mithridates stood the sled on end and leaned it against one wall. The weight of the wood broke through a thin plaster crust, causing another cloud of dust to rise and images of men and women bowing down before a beardless pharaoh to collapse into dust and paint-tainted chips.

Thyatis remained alert, keeping an eye on the Walach prowling among the scattered junk. Despite her heart's misgivings, she was beginning to think the barbarian would have to be killed first. Thyatis was confident of her ability to overmaster Nicholas in a duel of arms . . . but the Walach? A moment later, the barbarian paused sharply and reached down into a clutch of spiderwebbed wicker baskets.

"Nicholas! Look at this. There are two of them." Vladimir held a stout cedar post in his hands, one end recessed, the other carved to make a point. He smelled it carefully. "There was a rope tied around this and the ends were coated with grease." The Walach's forehead crinkled up in thought. "Fat. Pig fat."

Nicholas took the length of lumber and looked from it to the door, and back again. "A post?"

Thinking, he ran a hand over the recessed cavity. Crushed fragments of wood, dark with ancient oil, bent all in one direction. "How did they close the door . . . men had to enter the tomb, then leave again, sealing it up behind?" Nicholas turned to Thyatis, nodding to himself, imagining the ancient scene. "They tilted a slab up, just inside the door, balanced by these posts. When the last man departed, they jerked the posts away, letting the slab fall into the doorway, perfectly cut and aligned."

"Could be," Thyatis replied. She took the post from him, examining the ancient wood with pursed lips. "The slab had two cone-shaped bumps, to match holes cut in the floor. So the posts were secure while the block was balanced, and now you can't push the slab back, because bump and cavity make a key in the floor. There might even be a brace cut from the floor at the back end of the slab."

"Curse these builders. . . ." Nicholas bit his thumb. "Clever . . . using a balance like that . . . we have to make the slab go back as it came down." Certainty filled his face. "Look, they can't have put anything in the path of the block falling, so we can push it back the *same way*."

"I suppose." Thyatis raised an eyebrow. "How?"

Nicholas stepped to the door frame again. "This," he said, pointing down at the stone lip around the entrance. "This edge gives us a little leverage. We can chisel slots at the base of the slab for the pry bars, then hammer them in, tip up from the bottom and push on the top at the same time."

Begrudgingly, Thyatis nodded in agreement. The fellaheen were already digging mallets and chisels out of their leather carrying bags and Vladimir and Mithridates gathered up their long iron bars, ready to set muscle against stone. Nicholas looked very pleased with himself, but the Roman woman noticed he stood well back from the slab as the Egyptians crouched down to begin chipping away at the sandstone.

Shirin came to a halt at the base of a ramp and hurriedly pinched out her candle stub. Smoke curled towards the triangular apse of the tunnel roof, vanishing into encompassing darkness. A narrow hall opened out before her, filled with double rows of fluted, acanthus-topped pillars. To her right, fire-yellow lights danced among massive stone sarcophagi, to her left was a wall faced with stone steps depicting a procession of gods and demons, carrying gifts and funerary goods. Halfway down the wall, a shadowy recess led into some other, as yet unseen, room.

Muffled whispers ghosted in the air as the Khazar woman stepped into the chamber.

The motion around the coffins ceased, and Shirin felt a prickling sensation. A cluster of figures draped in desert robes turned towards her, swinging round their lanterns. Shirin was suddenly, horribly, aware of her recklessness—these people didn't know her. She didn't know them! They might not even be the Daughters of the Archer she thought to follow through the tunnels and corridors. Covered by her cloak, she grasped the hilt of the long knife in her belt, letting the point slide free of the sheath.

"Who are you?" a sharp, female voice whispered in the gloom. Two of the figures glided towards her, metal glinting in hand, swift-assured violence pregnant in their movements.

"Peace, friends," Shirin said softly, backing up the steps. She made the sign of the Archer with her free hand. *The hunt to the swift*, she realized. *Starvation to the slow! Time for judicious truth.* "I've come from the Roman temple, following those tomb robbers."

The lead figure paused, tugging a fold of her burnoose down, revealing a hawk-nosed, pox-scarred visage. Dark eyes blazed in the lantern light. "Show me your face."

Shirin matched the woman's movement, drawing aside her veil. The Egyptian sneered, one thin hand darting out to drag the rest of Shirin's scarf aside. Suppressing a sharp desire to strike the invasive hand away, the Khazar woman remained still, gaze adamant and unflinching.

"You're a pretty spy," the woman said after a moment of scrutiny, her jaw tightening. Shirin thought she saw weighed calculation in the glittering eyes. "You followed us?"

"I saw your tracks in the sand," Shirin responded, shaking her head. "They led me to the hidden door. . . ."

"What is your name, *Roman*?" the Egyptian woman snapped, a grim light in her eyes. "Was the Hunter's door open? I'll flay someone alive if it was!"

"No," Shirin said, uneasy with the woman's careless threat. "It opened for me. Listen, a party of Romans has entered the tomb. I saw them break through the main door. Can they find these chambers by another path? And there are—"

The Egyptian interrupted with a harsh chuckle. She raised a short-bladed sword, hilt up and grinned at Shirin with a mocking smile. "Your Roman looters won't find this chamber. They might not even live to find the false tomb!"

Irritated by the woman's bravado, Shirin recovered her scarf, draping it around her shoulders. "I'm not a Roman," she said in a controlled, even tone. "My name is Shirin. What are you called?"

"Penelope," the woman said dismissively. "Stay out of the way. We have to find this device they seek. Be ready to leave."

Before Shirin could respond, the Egyptian spun on her heel and hurried back to the massive, bulky shapes of the coffins. Her eyes now adjusted to the torchlight, Shirin saw the other Daughters were busily levering slab lids from the sarcophagi, grunting and straining. A faded, three-part mural covered the entire rear wall, showing a sun disk framed by hawk wings and dozens of protective gods.

Suddenly, as Shirin paced along the facing wall, trying to grasp the size and shape of the chamber, the stones under her feet jumped with a thud. Eyes wide, the Khazar woman shrank against the wall, groping for support. Dust trickled down around her in thin, corkscrew streams. The shock in the earth did not repeat and the Daughters—now sliding one of the coffin lids aside with great care—did not appear to have noticed.

That wasn't an earthquake! It was behind me. Shirin turned, hurried along the ledge, looking for a door, an alcove, anything at all. A dozen steps down, she came to the recessed opening and found, to her surprise, a pinhole of glowing light within deeper shadow. Looking over her shoulder, Shirin saw the Egyptian woman Penelope barking orders for her followers to break into the second coffin. From the puzzled, angry look on the woman's face, Shirin guessed there'd been no "device" in the sarcophagus.

Muffled noise came to her ears and she turned back to the point of light, suddenly worried. Inside the recess, there was a curved wall and a stone ledge. Kneeling down, Shirin put her eye to the tiny opening and found herself looking—through delicately painted gauze—into another funeral chamber. This space too was filled with painted round columns, wall mosaics and two stone coffins.

Sparking orange torchlight flared, momentarily blinding her. Shirin drew back. This close to the wall, she could hear sharp voices calling in the room beyond the spy hole. Roman voices. Feeling a chill on her neck, she swallowed and looked again.

Fellaheen in tan-and-white robes swarmed into the chamber, followed by an enormous Numidian and a familiar-looking Latin soldier. The Romans were busy poking and prodding in every crevice and container in the other tomb. Shirin froze. A shape moved across the pinhole, cutting off the light. From only a foot away, she heard a familiar voice.

"This wall is solid," Thyatis called out, rapping her knuckles across the surface of a drum column protruding from the wall of the tomb chamber. Clouds of painted, sparkling dust fell away from each blow. The air in the room grew hazy as the fellaheen, Mithridates and Vladimir made a rough sweep of the chamber. The dais holding the two coffins was raised on a series of steps, with pillars crowding close on either side. Nicholas stood beside the doorway, examining the triangular shape of the door barrier. As the Latin had posited, the slab was keyed to holes in the floor.

There was nothing in the chamber matching their description of the "device."

"How large is this thing?" Vladimir's accent seemed almost humorous in the thick air. He was crouched atop one of the coffins, long fingers tracing the chiseled outline of a king buried in stone. "Could it be inside one of these *jenazah*?"

Nicholas turned towards his friend, scratching the line of his jaw as he thought. "Well, the one in Rome is as tall as a man, but the bronze disks might be folded up, or packed together. . . ."

Thyatis paused in her examination of the wall, nose twitching. Her sense of smell might not be a match for the Walach, but there was *something* in the air. A sweet, warm scent like drying roses. She stiffened, memory tugging at the hem of her cloak. *Wait! I remember . . .*

"Here!" one of the fellaheen shouted, distracting her. "Master, I've found a hidden door!"

Thyatis leapt down from the ledge, reaching the man's side in an instant. The Egyptian pointed fearfully. Like the column Thyatis had checked, the roundel seemed to be part and parcel of the stone, but some ancient tremor in the earth had split cunning plaster and paint away, revealing a cavity.

"Stand back," Thyatis barked, as the fellaheen crowded up. Mithridates and Vladimir pushed through the men, each man holding an iron-headed sledge. The Roman woman drew her blade, letting the mirror-bright metal rasp from the sheath. Nicholas took up a position on her left, his blade bare, and—for an instant, in the dim light of the torches—the length of metal seemed to gleam with an inner fire.

Thyatis nodded to Mithridates. "Clear the opening."

The African set his shoulders, muscles bulging under his tunic and the sledge whipped into the plaster lathes, shattering the ancient wood. More dust billowed forth, but Mithridates narrowed his eyes and the opening was entirely clear in three more blows.

Thyatis fanned the air with her straw hat. The light of the torches revealed a short passage and a startlingly normal-looking door. Surprised, she felt a breath of cold air brush her face.

"I'll go first," Nicholas said, eagerly shouldering Thyatis aside.

A loud *crash* echoed through the hidden tomb and Shirin scrambled out of the watch post. The Daughters had frozen in shock at the sound. They were staring in horror toward a second opening to the Khazar woman's left. Another crash followed, then a third. Shirin raised an eyebrow. *Well*, she thought, *I guess the Romans did live to find us!*

"Out!" Penelope hissed, harsh voice cutting through the silence and surprise. "Everyone out through the tunnel. Now!" The older woman drew back, her shortsword aimed at the sound.

The women around the second sarcophagus abandoned their tools and ran for the passage, cloaks flying out behind them. Shirin darted across the chamber to the opened coffins. Penelope was in the tunnel mouth, her face a furious glare, beckoning for the Khazar woman to hurry. Behind Shirin, she heard the clatter of men forcing a door open. Faint streaks of light painted the wall above the sarcophagi, thrown by Roman torches. In the poor light, Shirin paused, gazing curiously down upon the centuries-dead figures in the two coffins.

At her left hand, a woman of medium height was fully wrapped in traditional bandages, her hands crossed on her chest, holding a crook and an ankh. A golden mask covered her face and a jeweled, golden sun disk holding a layered eight-rayed star lay on her breast. The Khazar woman frowned, seeing the star, old memories intruding. *How odd . . .* she thought. *Why does she bear a crest from old Persepolis?* The death masque showed a personage of no great beauty, but even across the centuries Shirin felt a palpable chill to look upon the likeness of Kleopatra, Lord of the Two Lands, Queen and Empress. Small ceramic jars lined the stone bier, wrapped in gold and silver vestments, accompanied by goods of all kinds.

Another crash reverberated through the dusty air. Shirin wrenched her hand away from the star jewel. *No time for souvenirs!* she thought guiltily. The second coffin held a man—tall, proud, with broad shoulders—though his silver masque revealed a petulant lip and his strength of personality paled in comparison to the Queen. For him, the Khazar woman felt only pity before dismissing him from her mind.

Orange light flared bright against the wall and Shirin faded into deeper shadow. Penelope was already gone, the sound of running feet fading in the tunnel. Halfway up the steps, Shirin paused, looking back into the tomb, wondering if a familiar figure would appear, silhouetted in the light. Instead, a man appeared in the broken door, leading with a long straight sword. The metal flared bright in the darkness and Shirin drew back again.

At her breast, the ruby became suddenly warm and she clasped a hand over the jewel, hiding an unexpected pale red glow. Entirely surprised, Shirin ducked down behind a fallen column, wondering what could possibly have excited such a response in the jewel. *Where did Thyatis get this thing?*

The Roman soldier crept forward, torch sputtering in one hand. "There are two coffins here," he shouted, "and they've been disturbed!"

The scrape of a sandal on stone registered in the periphery of Thyatis' attention and she spun left, blade rising into guard, even as a hurled spear flashed past. One of the fellaheen staggered, the iron head driven between his shoulder blades with a slapping sound. The man barely had time to cry out in pain before blood flooded his mouth and he was on his hands and knees, shuddering with death tremors.

"Ware!" Thyatis shouted, the tip of her sword flickering in the air. Another spear point lunged out of shadow and was deftly knocked aside. "To me, Romans! To me!" She bounded forward, snatching a dagger from its sheath on her belt with her free hand.

Men rushed around the toppled slab, curly beards gleaming in the light of fallen torches. One of them, towering a head above the others, leapt into Thyatis' path. For a single, frozen second she thought dead Chrosoes had returned to life—so closely did the bareheaded man swinging a spiked mace at her face resemble the King of Kings. She leaned aside, the mace blurring past, and lunged. The tip of her sword sparked from the man's breastplate, then skittered to one side. He jumped back, slapping her thrust aside with his own blade. They circled, the world narrowing down to the scrape and rustle of feet on stone, mirror-bright metal cutting the air, harsh breathing filling their ears.

Beyond the Persian's shoulder, Thyatis caught a glimpse of Mithridates swinging his pry bar over his head like a stave, a wild, hoarse shout roaring from his lips. The fellaheen, pinned against the tomb wall, were wailing in fear, and another hurled spear cut one down.

The Persian lord attacked, mace smashing overhand as he led with his right foot. Thyatis bobbed aside, evading the blow, then slashed her blade at the man's face. His own sword snapped up and sparks shivered in the air. A furious passage followed, blade on blade, the Persian stamping on the attack, Thyatis nimbly evading his powerful strokes. She blocked a sharp cut with the dagger, letting the blades bind, going hilt to hilt with the man. He grunted, feeling the strength in her arm, then shoved.

Thyatis spun aside, letting his motion carry him off-balance, then let her own momentum slam her left elbow into the side of his head. The iron vambrace on her arm cracked against his ear, drawing a shout of pain and spattering blood. She cut viciously with the sword, though the Persian rolled away. The Roman blade scored a long gash across his thigh, just above the knee. He went down.

Another Persian shouted wildly, charging at Thyatis. She whirled, blocking his spear down and away with her sword and dagger *en crosse*, then snap-kicked him in the face. The Persian staggered, stunned, and Thyatis' wrist flicked over, driving the point of her spatha into his jugular. Choking, the man fell backwards, fingers groping wildly at his throat.

In the same moment, Mithridates bellowed, catching two of the Persian soldiers across the chest with his pry bar, lifting them bodily from the floor. Massive muscles straining, the Numidian slammed them into the nearest pillar with a ringing *clang!* Breathless, the Persians were flung to the floor, armor creased by the blow. Grinning wildly, Mithridates sprang forward through the gap. Another Persian soldier threw himself at the Numidian, cutting sideways with both hands on his long sword. Mithridates parried with one end of his iron staff, smashing the blade from the man's hand, then lashed the bar across the Persian's face. Metal met metal with a ringing *bang!* and the side of the Persian's helmet caved in, spraying blood across a nearby statue. The stricken man crumpled like an empty sack.

Thyatis wrenched her attention away, wildly parrying an overhand blow from the big Persian's sword. In her brief moment of inattention, he had regained his feet. Now he attacked furiously and Thyatis met him blade for blade in a whirl of strike and parry and counterstroke. They lunged back and forth across the stone floor, barely cognizant of the melee swirling around them.

Her arms burning with fatigue, Thyatis slowed a fraction as she tried to evade another blow. The haft of the mace slammed down on her right arm, knocking the dagger loose. The blade spun away across the floor. Bloodfire surged, driving her limbs to new speed. She slammed the Persian's blade away, then rotated smartly, hewing down with the spatha in both hands. The man tried to wrench the mace away, but the keen edge of the Roman sword struck the wooden haft and squealed through dense oak.

Casting the stub away with a grimace, the Persian circled, panting, both hands on the hilts of his blade.

Thyatis did not pause, rushing the man, her blade singing in a deadly figure eight. The Persian parried, then blocked, grunting as the Roman woman put her shoulder into the blow. They locked hilts, sandals sliding on the bloody floor. Her vision narrowed to a shimmering gray-ringed tunnel, Thyatis realized the man hadn't used the point of his blade at all, relying instead on a blizzard of cuts and slashes. Blade shirring on his, she flicked the tip of her spatha up. Eyes wide, the man flung his head back, narrowly avoiding losing his lower jaw to the bright metal.

Taking the opening, Thyatis slammed his breastplate with a lightning-quick kick, sending him to the floor in a clatter of metal. Regaining her balance, she danced in, stabbing viciously as he scrambled away, sword lost, across the stone floor.

An upflung hand took one of her blows, the spatha biting into splinted mail on the Persian's forearm. Thyatis wrenched the blade back, then sprang away as the man kicked at her legs.

Relieved of immediate engagement, the scene around Thyatis sprang back into focus. Frenzied words, spoken in some unknown tongue, reverberated in the air, sending a wild chill washing over Thyatis' arms. Out of the corner of her eye, she saw Mithridates charge a portly, middle-aged man in desert robes, the iron bar whirling above his head like a scythe. The Persian made a stabbing motion in the air, his voice rolling like thunder. Vladimir loped forward, a gore-streaked axe in his hands. Nicholas was looking up from a dying Persian, surprised, the brilliant ruby glow of his longsword shining in his eyes. Dead and wounded men littered the floor.

"Sorcerer!" Thyatis shouted, hurling herself behind the nearest pillar. A violent alizarin flare followed hard on her shout, coupled with an enormous, ringing *crack!* Tremendous heat billowed past and Thyatis ground her face into the column, eyes squeezed shut. Even through her lids, she caught a glimpse of the room blazing with witch light and felt her armor swell with sudden heat.

The echo of the blast rang and rang, reverberating from the walls. Plaster caught fire, ignited by the flames. Thyatis scuttled out, low to the floor, and saw the Persian wizard stagger to his feet, haloed by a wheel of fire. Mithridates' corpse toppled to the ground, torn in half by the blast. Droplets of molten iron hissed and sizzled on the stones. Face contorted in hate, Thyatis snatched up a discarded hammer and overhanded it at the Persian.

The metal head struck the air with a tinny, ringing sound and then the wooden handle burst into flame. Stunned, the Persian wizard flinched back and the corona of near-invisible fire around him flickered out of existence. Before Thyatis could react, a huge groaning sound filled the room. Feeling the floor tremble under her feet, the Roman woman jumped back, groping for the shelter of her column.

To her right, one of the pillars—shattered by the sorcerous blast—cracked, splitting lengthwise. Stone and debris cascaded down. The entire room shivered, stone grinding on stone. As Thyatis looked up, a queasy feeling roiling in her stomach, the ceiling spiderwebbed with cracks, jetting dust, rippling like a lake disturbed by a fallen stone.

"Go, go, go!" Penelope, seamed face twisted into a rictus of commingled fear and blazing anger, wrenched Shirin along the corridor, flinging the younger woman forward. Ears still ringing from the mysterious blast, the Khazar woman picked up her robe and sprinted up the tunnel. The entire tomb seemed to sway, the ground still trembling with motion.

Ducking under the lintel of a corridor junction, Shirin turned, staring back down the tunnel. The Egyptian woman came up limping, coughing in a cloud of billowing white dust. "Go." She shoved Shirin out of the way, falling heavily into the rough-hewn room. "Turn right and climb the ramp!"

Penelope fell to her knees, tangled in the loose cloth of her robes, a harsh gasp wrenched from thin lips as her left foot touched the ground. The ceiling groaned in counterpoint, countless tons of rock shifting minutely. Gritting her teeth against the choking cloud, Shirin hooked an arm under the older woman's shoulder and dragged her up. "We're both getting out," she hissed, hoisting Penelope onto her shoulders. Despite her imposing personality, the Egyptian felt spindly and bird-like, light on Shirin's back.

Without waiting for another tremor, the Khazar woman sprinted up the right-hand tunnel.

At the top of the ramp, the corridor split again and the other Daughters were waiting, eyes wide in fear. Shirin staggered to a halt, Penelope's forearm tight around her neck.

"Run," the old Egyptian woman barked at her followers. "Make sure no one's watching the Hunter's door!" Shirin made to follow, but Penelope slapped her breast hard. "There . . . the statue."

Shirin ran to an alcove holding a cat-headed statue girded with spears and banded armor. Favoring her ankle, Penelope swung down and leaned against the wall. Grimacing, the old Egyptian slammed the pommel of her knife against the god's chest. Pottery cracked, then broke under a second blow. Shirin, pushing aside curiosity, lent her own weight to the effort, shattering chipped edges, revealing a cavity inside the statue.

"Grasp hold of the loop," Penelope gasped, one hand—now streaked with blood from lacerated knuckles—groping inside the opening. Shirin thrust her own hand in, found a waxed, slippery length of rope and pulled. There was a distant ratcheting sound and she felt a heavy resistance on the cord. Penelope grabbed hold of the ancient black rope as it emerged from the broken statue. Pulling together, both women strained against the line, bracing their feet against the statue pediment.

The clanking sound rose to a sharp pitch, then suddenly tension released on the line. Shirin fell heavily, cracking her hip on the floor. A dull, thundering *boom* sounded in the distance and grit puffed from the broken statue. Penelope rose wearily, favoring her leg. She grinned ferociously in the light of a sputtering, broken lamp.

"Sleep well, old Queen," she barked, laughing like a hyena. "Rest in the earth, forever undisturbed by the sons of Herakles the defiler!" A claw-like hand gripped Shirin's shoulder, sharpened nails digging through the cloth of her tunic. "Come, child, we've only moments to escape."

"Get up!" Thyatis shouted as grit rained down from the groaning ceiling. She kicked Vladimir over, saw he was breathing— though stunned—and grasped his wrist. The Walach was surprisingly heavy, all corded muscle and bone, but she brooked no resistance and dragged him to his feet. Pushing him ahead of her, Thyatis scuttled towards the entrance. The floor rippled under her feet, shuddering in response to a new creaking in the walls. The big Persian shouted in alarm.

Ignoring the enemy and the trembling walls, Thyatis shoved Vladimir through the half-opening beside the toppled slab, then jumped through herself. Nicholas scrambled after and Thyatis didn't wait, bolting across the outer chamber for the ramp leading up to the surface. A rolling series of thunderous cracks followed, slamming down behind them. Thyatis vaulted a wooden casket of tiny statues, skidded on an uneasy floor and slammed into the wall beside the tunnel entrance.

Vladimir, eyes wide in fear, scuttled past on all fours and up the ramp.

"Come on!" Thyatis shouted at Nicholas. The Roman ran towards her, his footing poor as the floor rippled and buckled, slabs canting up at strange angles. He leapt towards her, catching her outstretched hand. A massive block of stone plunged from the ceiling behind Nicholas, smashing on the floor, sending flakes of sandstone whistling through the air. Thyatis ducked, feeling splinters ring from her armor. Then they were both scrambling up the ramp.

Another block broke free with a roar and slammed down near the entrance to the tunnel. Dust and smoke from burning plaster billowed into the room, obscuring two figures as they stumbled and staggered out of the tomb chamber. A feeble spark of light flared from an upraised hand and the wizard appeared out of the murk, half-carried by the big Persian.

At the top of the ramp, Vladimir sprang to his feet in the octagonal chamber. Thyatis saw him start back in surprise, then the domed roof splintered, raining chunks of stone and wooden supports into the room.

"Go," she screamed, grasping hold of Nicholas' collar. Choking, the Latin scrabbled at the stone and Thyatis threw him into the chamber. At the same moment, the roof of the tunnel buckled, and came sliding down with a roar.

Flinging herself forward, Thyatis rolled out of the opening just before a granite slab crashed down, blocking the passage. Half-blinded by dust, now plunged into complete darkness, Thyatis scrambled across the chamber, working from hazy memory. Three steps on, she crashed into a dazed Nicholas. "Vladimir! Where are you?"

"Here," came a hoarse shout from the gloom. Thyatis shuffled forward, one arm under his, her right foot now bare on the rubble-strewn floor. Cursing the fickle, ungracious gods, she led with a groping hand, feeling rock splinters under an unexpectedly bare foot, then suddenly found Vladimir's shoulder. "Follow me!" the Walach barked, relieved.

Together, the three Romans fled up the ramp, Vladimir in the lead.

Behind them, the tomb rippled and shook as ancient balances and weights released, each corridor and chamber roof collapsing in violent sequence. A choking, smoke-stained wind rushed past Thyatis, the tomb's breath exhaled in final death. The walls groaned again, but the Walach gave a glad cry. "I can see the sky!"

Thyatis looked up, eyes smarting with tears, and saw a faint rectangular outline ahead filled with the cold gleam of starlight.

A dull series of *booms* rattled the ground, then tapered off into silence. In the pale moonlight, Thyatis could barely make out the slow, rolling cloud of dust and smoke issuing from the tomb door. When complete silence returned, the Roman woman turned away and trudged back across the drifting sand to the others and their camels. Nicholas was waiting, a few paces from Vladimir and Betia, who stared at the ground, each lost in their own thoughts.

"Anything?" The Latin's voice was still hoarse from smoke.

Thyatis shook her head. "No, no one came out."

"Good riddance," Nicholas said bitterly, sheathed blade held against his chest in an oddly intimate pose. "Did the amulet ever react?"

"No." Thyatis kept her voice level. She hadn't spared a thought for the prince's talisman, though it was still tucked safely between her tunic and armor. Aside from its first trembling when they approached, she didn't remember any odd sensation. In the struggle in the tomb, she'd had no moment to spare for any warning or sign the amulet might have given. "If a telecast was in there, we didn't get close enough."

Nicholas spit on the ground, silently furious. "What a waste."

"True enough." Thyatis nodded, feeling a cold, empty sensation at the thought of Mithridate's easy smile. Bending her head, she said a short prayer for the departed dead. *But you will not go into the darkness alone, comrade,* she thought. *The Aryan lords will bear you golden cups, filled with new wine. Their sorcerer will be your servant in high-ceilinged halls, overlooking fields of golden wheat.* She tilted her head towards the camels. "Let's move—the Persians may have friends about."

The Latin nodded sharply and turned away. Thyatis walked up to Betia and Vladimir, shrugging the scabbard of her own sword to a more comfortable position on her shoulder. "Vladimir, thank you," she said softly. "We wouldn't have gotten out without you and your nose." The barbarian gave her a blank, exhausted look in return, then nodded sadly.

"There's blood debt aplenty," he said, then coughed. Betia helped him stand up. The Walach managed a wry grimace in the place of a smile. "We can't pay Mithridates back . . . but another grain for that wizard to do his work and we'd have all been roasted on a spit."

Thyatis nodded in agreement, clasping wrists with the barbarian. "But we live," she said.

"We live." Vladimir limped away towards the pile of baggage. Nicholas was already loading the camels with bags of water and bundles of clothing and tools.

Thyatis looked down at Betia, her own weariness and grief undisguised. "Did you see anything?"

Betia nodded, her eyes smudged pits of darkness in the moonlight. Her small face seemed carved from ivory. "I saw the Persians come," the little Gaul said softly, "but before I could creep down into the tunnel, two more . . . men came."

"Two?" Thyatis tensed, feeling the darkness—which had seemed almost comforting, a dark cloak laid across the land, hiding them from any prying eyes—fill with malice. "What kind of men? Persians?"

Betia shook her head minutely. "I don't think so. I could not see their faces and all their garb and armor was black as pitch. They . . . crept along the ground like Vladimir when he hunts. They were following our tracks."

"Where did they go?"

The little Gaul pointed off into the night, towards the jumble of pillars and wind-carved spires rising from the desert to the north. "That way. They didn't come back." She shivered. "I think they were ghosts."

"Why?"

Betia's face remained impassive, though Thyatis regretted the disbelief in her voice. The girl deserved better—she was no apprentice, not any more!

"When they were well gone, I went down onto the sand," the Gaul said sharply. "They left no tracks. No trace at all. There was a strange feeling in the air."

Thyatis nodded. "If the Persians have allied themselves with infernal powers, they will receive aid from unexpected

sources." She shook out her shoulders. "The more distance between us and this place, the better."

Betia said nothing. Thyatis made to take her hand, but the little Gaul flinched away.

"Keep watch behind," Thyatis said, pretending nothing had
happened. The girl would deal with these matters in her own
way. There was little time for anything but flight now.
"Nicholas, let's move. There are *lamiae* abroad tonight!"

The camels made a low, grumbling sound, but the Latin had
bound their mouths closed to prevent the ungainly creatures
from bellowing. Vladimir moved downwind, a bundle heavy on
his back. Thyatis cast an eye around, making sure they'd left
nothing behind. Nicholas rapped the lead camel on the haunch
with his switch and the animal shuffled to motion, broad three-
toed feet splaying on the sand.

"What did she see?" Nicholas strode up, the hood of his
cloak cast back on broad shoulders.

"Two figures," Thyatis answered, settling her feet in a new
pair of boots. They were too big for her feet, but Mithridates
didn't need them anymore, did he? "Betia didn't think they were
human. The only other players in this game are the Persians, so
I think they summoned *special* help—but it didn't quite arrive
in time. They must have gotten something from our poet too."

"Huh. Doesn't matter now, does it? Not with the tomb buried
under countless tons of sand and rock." Nicholas' voice was
very sour in the darkness. Thyatis couldn't see his face in the
moonlight, but knew the man was grinding his teeth. "We
didn't cover our tracks very well. They could have followed us
out here."

"Into a dead end," she said with a certain wry tone. They began to descend from the ridge, down into one of the long, stony
valleys running east and west, parallel to the prevailing winds.
The footing was poor, but they could make better time than on
the soft slopes of the dunes. "Now the question is . . . did the
Persians know where the 'device' really is? I think they
didn't—not if they followed us out here."

"True," Nicholas said, his mood lifting. "The Cypriot was
telling the truth, then! He hadn't time to contact them between

finding his blessed lading document and our arrival." He stopped, though the camel kept ambling along. "Should we go back?"

Thyatis bit her lip, considering the situation. She wished the Duchess were here. Then the conniving old woman could clean up her own mess! *The needs of the moment are more pressing,* she realized. *If the prince's toy spoke true, there is a telecast in there. Is it safe to leave behind, buried in the sand? The Persians might dig it out.* Thyatis realized she was fingering the amulet in kind of a nervous tic. Nicholas was staring at her, hands on his hips, head canted to one side.

"No," Thyatis started to say, then stopped. She suddenly recognized the scent she had tasted in the tomb air. Unbidden memories rose, lifting her head with a start.

"What in Hel are you smiling about?" Nicholas growled, picking at the scab around his eye. "Do we go back or not?"

"No." Thyatis shook her head, schooling her lips to a grim, thoughtful line. But her heart was singing, though a corner of her mind cautioned vigorously against disappointment. *The coffins were disturbed,* she remembered. *Someone else was in the tomb with us. She was in the tomb. I smelled her perfume. That's why this toy didn't react—the telecast had already been taken away!*

Near giddy with relief, Thyatis let herself breathe, feeling a vast weight lift from her.

"No," she said again, suppressing a wild grin, "there's nothing there. Just coffins and broken stone and dead men. Let them dig all they like." Then gladness fled sickeningly and she almost turned around, to run back towards the buried tomb, to dig wildly in the collapsed rubble. Gritting her teeth, Thyatis started walking east again. *There is another entrance,* she reminded herself, *another way out. The telecast was not there! They—she—escaped, they carried the device away in time. Betia's warning was heeded. Please, goddess, let it be so.*

"What about the other one, then?" Nicholas sounded surly again. Thyatis barely heard him.

"That one," she heard herself say, distantly, "we'll find without them finding us."

* * *

Fallen stone creaked and grumbled, slowly settling. The sandstone pinnacle above the tomb adjusted itself, squeaking and shifting, to the abused fracture lines running through its stony heart. In one of the tunnels—only partially filled with fallen debris—the dust settled in thin, veil-like sheets. At the end of the corridor two black shapes knelt amid haphazard slabs and jammed, splintered sandstone blocks.

Without the hiss of strained breath, in silence save for the scraping grind of stone on stone, they lifted a massive plinth. One figure held the slab upright, while the other crawled beneath—heedless of the mass teetering above—and dug into the looser shale below. After a moment, someone coughed and a hand waved weakly from the rubble. Obsidian fingers seized the collar of the man's armor and dragged him forth. Another body was recovered in a similar manner, then all four clambered back up the sloping tunnel and out under the night sky.

The two dark shapes dropped their burdens on the sand, letting Patik and Artabanus sprawl on the cooling ground. The wizard coughed weakly, his face streaked with blood, a purpling bruise spreading on the side of his face and shoulder. Despite his wounds, the middle-aged Persian clutched a tangled leather sandal to his chest.

"You breathe," one of the dark shapes said in a cold voice. "Speak." It rolled the big man over with the point of an armored shoe.

Patik gasped, blood leaking from the corner of his mouth and his eyes wavered open. The looming figure was only darkness against darkness, vaguely outlined by missing stars. "The . . . *cough* . . . Romans found nothing. The tomb was . . . *wheeze* . . . empty."

The dark shape considered this for a moment, attention turned away from the Persian noble. Patik let himself slump back into the rocky sand, laboring to breathe. His entire body was gripped by twisting, muscle-deep pain. Like the wizard, he was badly bruised, his ear still bleeding.

"The Accursed were here," the figure said, dead voice ringing hollow in the close-fitting helmet. "They would not have come, were the sepulcher truly empty."

Cloth rustled, then metal sang on metal. Patik managed to

open his eyes and saw the shape raise something—*a curved blade?*—against the night sky. Frigid blue-white light played along the *athame,* sparking and sputtering.

"*Uttish'tha,*" commanded the voice, harsh syllables echoing back from the standing stones. "*Ash'hrrada!*"

Patik felt Artabanus flinch and the wizard moaned, one trembling hand trying to block out the sight of the sky. The big Persian narrowed his eyes—crawling blue light played across his face—briefly illuminating the sandstone wall towering above them. The light burned his skin and he turned away, suddenly afraid he might be blinded by the witch light.

"*Uttish'THA!*" The sound boomed in the air, making the sand jump and quiver. Sharp, cold wind played in the avenues between the pinnacles, tugging at Patik's hair, swirling the cloaks of the dark shapes. Again, the earth groaned and shifted, then settled.

The dreadful bluish light died and slowly the stars reemerged from the encompassing dark. Patik shuddered, realizing something vast had obscured the winking, faint lights during the strange interlude. He was aware of darkness withdrawing into the sky, folding in upon itself.

Only the Shanzdah remained and the Captain turned to look upon Patik again, two faint points of radiance burning in the cowl of his hood. "We will follow the Romans. They will lead us to the prize, the *duradarshan,* the Gate unopened and unrevealed." An ironbound hand reached down and dragged the Persian to his feet, as effortlessly as a man might lift a child.

"You will run ahead, Great Prince, our hound." Something like laughter issued from cracked, withered lips. "And we will course behind, hunting with bright spears."

Thunder growled in the distance, though no flare of lightning lit the night. Shirin, laboriously climbing the slope of a dune at the edge of the plain of stones, turned. Penelope, still riding on her back, thin hands clutched at her breast, lifted her head. Both women looked back, seeing nothing but darkness in the shallow valley. The other Daughters continued on, climbing the dune ridge, keeping themselves below the unseen, night-shrouded summit.

"What was that?" Shirin whispered, though she was sure they had left the Romans and Persians miles behind. Gusts of night wind lapped around her ankles, sending individual grains of sand stinging against her skin.

"Keep moving," croaked the old woman. "Something foul is abroad on the plain. We should not wait for it to find us."

Shirin resumed her steady pace. The slope of the dune was long and there were many miles to cover before dawn. Haste in such soft sand would not be rewarded, save with useless weariness.

After a time, as they approached the crest, Shirin turned her head questioningly. "Mother," she said, using a term often heard on the Island during her abortive training, "in the tomb—the dead Queen bore a blazon—an eight-rayed star set in gold. Was that her personal crest?"

Soft, breathy laughter answered and the Khazar woman frowned, thinking the old Egyptian would not reply. But then Penelope said, in a sly voice: "Her family held the star of Vergina in high regard. From the first days of their house, the sunburst rode on their shields and banners."

"I've seen it before—the same star or rayed sun—in . . ." Shirin paused, swallowing the words . . . *in Ctesiphon, in the house of my husband, King of Kings, Khusro Anushirwan, or on the ruined buildings of old Babylon* . . . ". . . in the east."

"Many kings ape the guise of the Lord of Men," the old woman said. Shirin could feel Penelope's thin body shaking with laughter through her back. "Yet, Great Egypt had better claim than most to the Temeniad crest."

"What do you mean?" Shirin frowned, plowing step-by-step up over the dune crest and down the opposite slope. The moon was riding high in the sky, illuminating the long, rippled face of the ridge with gleaming silver. Ahead, the shapes of the other Daughters cast long shadows across pure, unblemished sand. "The sons of Temenos are the house of Royal Macedon. Why does—"

A spidery hand closed over Shirin's lips and she stopped.

"Hush," Penelope said, whispery old voice soft in the Khazar's ear. "Some things should not be said under such a baleful sky, certainly not aloud. Let us say not all roots were cut that black day in Amphipolis when Cassander hewed down the last saplings of the Agead oak. One seedling escaped, and found new, royal soil in Egypt where he grew and thrived under the Saviour Ptolemy's name. Our buried Queen was the last of a noble line . . ." Penelope's voice trailed away, lost in sadness.

Shirin made a face, shaking her head. The thin hand withdrew and she tramped on, under the thin moon, into the desert. Far ahead, the sky was hazed with mist and fog, for the delta sweltered in the summer heat, even at night. Shirin thought she could make out the waters of Mareotis, sparkling under the moon.

Encompassing pitchy darkness drew back, broken by green fire licking among gauze-wrapped limbs and fallen chunks of stone. The lip of the stone coffin holding Kleopatra had held back the falling slabs and shattered blocks. She lay, buried deep under the ruined ceiling, her golden mask undisturbed and the rayed sun on her breast hummed with emerald fire. Viridian tongues flickered and coursed around half-hidden rings and intersections of ancient bronze.

Far above, a booming voice died and a black knife lowered. The sky shuddered, darkness receding. Greenish flame wicked down, pooling into ancient glyphs etched in bronze, then faded into night's embrace.

The Queen slept, her treasures deeply buried, safe again from the grasping hands of men.

NEAR IBLIS

Mohammed sat under the fig, legs crossed, deep in thought. Ráha's visions had passed, leaving him with an unexpected clarity of vision and thought. The thirst once burning in his throat now seemed negligible, the weakness in his limbs a passing memory. The cerulean sky and white-barked trees revealed a queer flatness, as though they were painted on air. His own hands, scarred and weathered with age, stood proof of his own solidity. He looked within, seeking the singing note once perceived among the dizzying splendor of the world.

Assailed by sensation on all side, deafened by the beat of his heart, the whistle of air into his lungs, Mohammed groped for concentration. A frail voice emerged from unsure memory: *He causes the night to pass into day, and the day to pass into night . . .* He felt his mind settle, turning inward.

For a long time, he found nothing but violent, chaotic emptiness. At last, banishing all attention to the outer world, ignoring even the smooth sensation of the fig bark against his back, he found a delicate whisper of the glorious sound. Strangely, at first the trembling note was distant and faint, but as he focused and beheld, it grew in strength, a long, wavering tone, rising and falling, louder and fainter, drawn from a single source, yet infinite in its variety.

A great yearning to yield himself to dissolution came over him. *Why not join with the heavenly chorus,* wayward thoughts urged. *There is perfect harmony and peace within the celestial gate. Enter!*

"Master?" A voice spoke, penetrating his consciousness. Mohammed opened his eyes and saw before him the creature Mōha. Perfect lips moved, saying: "You are emaciated, pale, near death. Please, you must pass on from this place. You must choose to go forward. Abandon this useless striving—"

"I will not," Mohammed said, his voice strong once more. Looking upon Mōha's face, he was struck by the pitiful nature of the creature's disguise. How could anything so false seem beautiful after looking upon the heart of the world? When he had seen the burning stone and the glory of the unbounded universe revealed? The guardian seemed small and weak, an ivory doll, doomed to wander in half-life, among these dead things, for all time. "Only the Great and Merciful Lord may set the length of my days. When he wills they end, then they will end. Until the day he summons me into his presence, to judge the deeds of my life and dispense perfect, immutable justice, I will never abandon the straight and righteous path."

Mōha's face contorted in frustration. "My lord, did you see nothing in glorious Ráha's eyes? You looked upon the heart of the world—such things leave no man unchanged! You cannot lie or dissemble to me—how can you cling to pitiful life, to this decaying shell and scrap of rotting flesh, in the face of such glories? Let go, yield the illusion of mortality and pass onward!"

Mohammed shook his head. "I will not abandon striving. I will endure."

The creature flinched away from Mohammed's commanding tone.

"Please . . ." Mōha begged. "You will suffer endless torments, you will grow old and die, weak and finally alone. How can the fleeting pleasures of a mortal life compare to what you have seen?" He stopped, groping for some convincing word.

Mohammed shook his head. Certainty burned in his heart and the sound of wind in the trees swelled, filling his limbs with strength. Hunger and thirst no longer touched him and his wizened arms and legs felt strong. "All you say is true, guardian, but I will *not* step aside from the straight and righteous path. I choose to live, even if I must suffer the torments of those doomed to the fiery pit."

"Foolish man!" Mōha shouted in anguish. "If you must choose slow corruption, then set aside your impossible task, cease this useless struggle. Live a meritorious life in quiet! Return to your home, set your grandchildren upon your knees, speak wisely in the city council, do no evil to men, weigh honestly and in full measure in all your dealings. But do not inflict these agonies upon yourself!"

The Quraysh started to speak, but paused. Something in Mōha's voice had changed and the creature now seemed smaller, wizened, reduced. The glamour of towering strength, of an undimmed flame, faded and Mohammed found his heart filled with pity for the creature trapped between life and death.

"The world," he said slowly, considering his words, "contrives against men who would follow the path of righteousness. On every side, enemies tempt and distract men from the blessing offered by the Compassionate One." Mōha started to speak again, but Mohammed raised his hand, quelling the outburst.

"Lust," Mohammed said, "is the first enemy; the second a

dislike for higher life; the third is hunger and thirst; the fourth is craving; the fifth is torpor and sloth; the sixth doubt; the seventh falsehood; the eighth glory; the ninth exalting oneself and despising others, the last—the last is the fear of death."

Mōha flinched away from the ringing words, crouching against the ground and moaning softly

"These are my enemies," Mohammed boomed. "No feeble man or woman can conquer them, yet only by overcoming them does one win bliss. Shame upon me if I am defeated! Better for me to die striving in battle than to live quietly in defeat!"

"You do not know the burden of such a life," Mōha whispered, unable to raise his head.

"I do," Mohammed said, sharp eyes glinting. "I choose to live. Regardless of what may come."

THE SQUARE OF FOUR TEMPLES, ALEXANDRIA

Pressing through a sullen, listless crowd, Thyatis turned into a narrow, shadowed alley. Even here between a pair of crumbling apartment buildings, ragged men, women and children squatted on the ground, watching bitterly as she passed. The Roman woman had not bothered to assume a pleasing guise or hide her armor beneath a matron's gown. Instead, she walked quickly, left hand riding on the hilt of her sword, grimy cloak fluttering behind her in the steaming air. The half-hidden fear percolating through the streets and offices of Alexandria had blossomed into open panic.

Thyatis tasted a heady, stomach-churning mixture of despair and anticipation in the air. No official news was posted in the city agora or on the walls of the temples, but the steady stream of families entering the city through the Nile Gate revealed the course of battle. Somewhere in the east, beyond the massive rampart and moat under construction at the edge of the suburbs, the Roman Legions were fighting a delaying action, hoping to buy time for the city. Their failure to halt the Persian advance burned in Thyatis' stomach like acid, making every grain precious, the relentless passage of the sun a goad lashing her impatience.

Heedless of who might see, Thyatis stomped down a flight of ancient steps and into a dark-walled alcove. Her fist, gloved in leather and iron chain, slammed on an age-blackened door. The portal rang hollowly, once, then twice. There was no answer.

Thyatis squinted from beneath the cowl of her hood, noting with interest the absence of anyone sleeping or sitting in the alcove. She smiled grimly. *The Hunter watches over all places, both the low and the high.*

Time was short and the Roman woman turned back to the door. Her fist slammed against the ancient wood again, making a dull booming sound in the room beyond. She began to consider how to break down the portal.

"What are you doing here? You should leave!" Penelope, old wrinkled face twisted into a ferocious grimace, leaned on a reed cane in the doorway of the dining hall. Shirin rose from a bench, laying down a jeweled clasp on a neat bundle of her clothing. The pin was bent and she had been examining the fragile copper to see if the tip of her hand knife would do for repairs. The low-ceilinged hallway outside the hall was filled with women hurrying to and fro. Everyone was packing in great haste, loading wicker baskets and wooden trunks with the contents of the Temple.

"I wish to speak with the Priestess," Shirin said, a sharp tone in her voice. "Is she still in the temple?"

Penelope laughed, limping into the room. The Temple healer had poked and prodded the swollen, purplish bruises, eliciting a hissing gasp from the old woman. Shirin guessed the ankle was broken, though she refrained from comment. She doubted Penelope would accept any advice.

"You'll see no one, now, dearie." Penelope pointed with her sharp chin to the east. "An old enemy rushes closer—and we'll soon be gone." The Egyptian woman laughed, deep-set wrinkles crinkling up around her eyes. "Like ghosts, into the sand and sea."

Shirin's lips thinned in anger. "What about the *duradarshan*? Will you leave the weapon for the Persians to find? To use against Rome?"

Penelope stared at her for a moment, then sat gingerly on the edge of the table. "You've not been long in the Order, have you?" The old woman eyed her suspiciously. "The Daughters of the Hunter care little for the empires of *men* . . . we are not Roman slaves! I do not know," she said in a haughty voice, "how things are done in the house of the Queen of Day, but here, here you are in *Egypt* and our kingdom is ancient, far older than these Roman upstarts! They are only flowers on the desert—come and gone in a season."

"You will be Persian slaves soon," Shirin replied testily. "Their priests are not fond of other faiths, not like openhanded Rome. You will find life under their sway far less pleasing! But I care nothing for Rome either—what of the device? You looked in the tomb and found nothing—does it lie somewhere else?"

"I don't know," Penelope said, shrugging thin shoulders. "The annals of the Old Time say two of the *duradarshan* were brought into Khem—which is Egypt—after the Drowning. Legend and rumor say Kleopatra the Betrayer found one, carrying it to her grave. Yet you and I both stood in her funeral chamber and saw nothing—only withered bone and bandages." The old woman spread her hands. "Perhaps the rumors were lies, the legends baseless . . ."

"And the other?" Shirin stood over the own woman, her smooth forehead wrinkled in irritation. "Where does it lie?"

"Bah!" Penelope stood abruptly, then staggered, forgetting her weak ankle. Shirin caught her by the shoulders and helped her take up her cane. Penelope's expression grew sour and she pushed the Khazar woman away. "I do not need your help, *Roman*. Why should I tell you such a thing?"

Shirin stepped away, reining in growing anger. "I oppose these Persians, even if you do not. They serve a dangerous priest, allied with the enemy of all which lives! I will see their plans and stratagems confused and set to naught, with or without your help."

Penelope grunted, raising an eyebrow at her bravado. "There is no one here who can help you. Our mistress has already departed for a place of safety and soon we will join her. *You* may do as you wish." Again the bitter laugh. "If you can do anything at all."

Shirin stared at the old woman, restraining bitter words. The desire to strike the obdurate Egyptian swelled in her breast. *Violence wins nothing here*, she reminded herself, struggling to control her temper. Shirin decided to try a different trail in the prickly grass. "Tell me one thing, Penelope. You said Kleopatra was the last of the Temenid kings of Macedon—how did this happen? I thought . . ."

The question drew a guffaw of mocking laughter from the old woman. She grinned evilly at Shirin, wagging a wrinkled bony finger. "A pretty piece of gossip, child. Why should I say anything at all?"

Shirin's hand darted out and snatched the woman's cane away. Penelope goggled, shocked by such rude behavior and Shirin caught her as she fell. The Khazar glared at the Egyptian, teeth gritted, incisors bared. "I saved your life in the tomb. Now tell me."

"So you did." Penelope groped for the cane, sweat beading on her seamed old face. "Great Alexander had a son—a posthumous son—by the Empress Roxane. Young Alexandros was sent to Macedon to rule as king on his father's throne. But his grandmother Olympias, who proved a veritable tyrant, seized the boy's regency. One of her enemies was Cassander, who raised rebellion against her and overthrew Olympias' regime."

The old Egyptian smirked, making a ripping motion with her hands. "The mob beset Olympias and tore her to bits—limb from limb." Penelope laughed hollowly, enjoying her ghoulish tale. "A Bacchanalian end for her. Her wiles could not deliver her from the rage of the commons. Poor Roxane was strangled, dying far from home and her family, without friends, amid so many enemies. The boy Alexandros? He was thought dead as well, drowned or left with his throat cut."

"But he did not die," Shirin snapped. "He came to Egypt? Saved by who? By the Daughters?"

"Hah! Never." A feral light gleamed in Penelope's eyes and she made a crushing motion with her hand. "Wily Ptolemy stole the boy away, while Cassander slaughtered Olympias' supporters and stole her armies. Young Alexandros was brought to Egypt in the company of Ptolemy's new queen, Eurydice. The court was told the child had been born on Cos . . . his old name was never spoken and the young boy took his new father's name, Ptolemy the Second. In this way, the blood of Zeus and Herakles flowed down into Pharaoh."

"I see." Shirin released the woman and put the cane in her hands. "Now, tell me—"

A loud crash interrupted, causing both women to turn in surprise. Out in the hallway the Daughters carrying baggage stood frozen, staring in surprise down the passage. One of them hurried into the dining hall, sweating and wide-eyed.

"Mistress Penelope! There's a Roman soldier here—she broke down the outer door with her bare hands. She demands the priestess attend her immediately!"

"What?" The old Egyptian woman spat on the floor. "Throw her out!"

"We tried," the messenger said, rubbing a violent bruise on her cheek. "She's a Daughter, from the Roman temple."

"Two in a day?" Penelope turned to Shirin, but the Khazar woman was gone, making the old woman blink in surprise.

Thyatis growled, storming down a narrow passage, head tilted to one side so avoid the low, triangular ceiling. She had her *spatha* in both hands, blade partially drawn. A clutch of women fell back as she advanced, hampers and baskets held before them in a wicker barrier. "Where is the priestess in charge of this pestilential hole?" Thyatis felt no qualm at shouting in the sacred precincts.

The acolytes cowered behind their baggage, but an arched opening appeared on her right. In the room beyond an elderly Egyptian woman was sitting at a table, a perplexed expression on her face, chin resting on her hands, curled around the head of a cane.

"Are you the Hunter's Daughter?" Thyatis stabbed the sheathed sword at the old woman.

"And you would be?" Yellow teeth bared in a cheerless grin.

"Thyatis Julia Clodia," the Roman woman said briskly, stepping into the room. She swept back her hood, revealing a grim, suntanned face. "Agent of the Duchess De'Orelio. I need your help."

"Do you?" the woman grunted. "My name is Penelope. You sent a messenger before—the little snip of a Gaul?"

Thyatis nodded, snapping the *spatha* back into the sheath. "Yes. You sent agents to remove the telecast from the tomb in the wasteland of spires?"

"We were there," Penelope allowed, looking the Roman woman up and down with ill-disguised curiosity. "Come to check on our work, have you?"

"I don't care about your *work*," Thyatis said, pacing up and down the chamber. She felt nervous, on edge, filled with restless energy. A score of acolytes peered into the door from the hall, so she bared her teeth at them, making a rumbling growl low in her throat. The women fled, letting a drape fall over the opening. Thyatis laughed. Two other passages opened into the chamber, but they too were closed with heavy, dark-green hangings. "As long as the device is out of Roman and Persian hands, I'm happy."

Penelope snorted in laughter, her upper lip curling in disdain. "Why are you here, then?"

"There is another telecast," Thyatis said, feeling the air thicken with pressure. She was getting a headache from all this. *Things used to be so much simpler*, she groused to herself, feeling old. "At Sîwa, in the west."

The old woman stiffened in surprise. "Who told you that?"

"A little bird," Thyatis replied, feeling her stomach clench at the Egyptian's sudden alarm. *It's true then*, she realized with dismal certainty. "She sang very sweetly once my companions put her in a cage with iron bars."

An expression of disgust flickered in the Roman woman's face. Nicholas had kidnapped the little librarian without consulting her. Another rash act, leaping to the last lap of the race without forethought. He hoped to win the crown and please his masters in Rome, with or without Thyatis' consent. "Time is very short, Priestess. I've been told the trek to Sîwa takes twelve days. How fast can you and yours be there?"

"In the same time," Penelope bit out. "We are not gods to fly across the land."

"You'd best run then," Thyatis said, taking another turn around the room, restless hands examining cups, dishes, the bronze sconces for lamps lining the walls. "We will leave at first light by ship—the Duchess's own *Paris*—for Paraetonium on the Libyan coast. The governor's approved our port passes with goodly speed, which is amazing. With the current winds, we'll be ashore in the port in two days. My lieutenant is impatient. By camel, I'd guess we should take ten days to reach the oasis."

"Huh." Penelope sagged back against the table, bitter exhaustion lining her face. "We couldn't reach there any faster ourselves." A gleam entered her eye. "But there's no need . . . we *can* be in Paraetonium before you, if we take oar tonight and once you and your men are in the desert, riding south, we'll beset your party and slaughter everyone." The old woman sat up, rapping the cane sharply on the floor. "Easy work, with your help."

Thyatis stiffened, coming to a halt beside a bench laden with someone's baggage. Her nostrils flared and she turned to Penelope, an outraged expression on her face. "Murder?"

"Yes!" Penelope jabbed at her with the cane. "Your loyalty to the Order surpasses your service to the Emperor. If these men threaten to find the *duradarshan* then they must be slain." The Egyptian frowned, eyes narrowing as she considered Thyatis' conflicted expression. "The Queen of Day would have no qualm about such an act—didn't she send you out specifically to prevent the Emperor from gaining such powerful, dangerous tools? Well, now, here's a perfect answer to your puzzle! There are bandits and brigands aplenty who prey on the pilgrim routes to the temple of Amon-Ra. No one will be surprised if your party is attacked."

Thyatis felt her throat constrict. *Murder Nicholas and Vladimir? Strike them down while they sleep, or are at sword strokes with the foe?* The tight, twisted feeling in her gut grew worse. *I can't kill them—they're not friends, no, but they are comrades in arms. Without Vlad, I'd have died in that, tomb, crushed under rubble or suffocated. Nicholas . . .* There were times she'd be glad to strangle the man or chop him into tiny bits, but he was a fellow soldier and a good one. He shouldn't be used up, betrayed by these schemes. *But what else can I do?*

Heartsick, she sat down, bending her forehead against the blessedly cool boss of the sword hilt. "Mother, I can't use them so callously. They don't deserve to be discarded—"

"Bah!" Penelope rose, leaning heavily on the cane, face stiff in disapproval. "Foolish child. They are only *men,* only soldiers. They will not be missed. Have they told anyone else of their discovery?"

"Perhaps." Thyatis put her head in her hands. "I learned less than an hour ago."

"I will send a galley to Paraetonium tonight," Penelope said, voice filling with authority. "With those Daughters who know the use of weapons. One of our agents can supply us with camels and supplies. If any *man* has learned of the treasure buried under Sîwa, we must remove it with all speed."

Thyatis felt relief and a sudden desire to let the old woman handle matters. *Would your hands be so clean,* answered a mocking voice in her thoughts, *if Vladimir and Nicholas died by another's hand, when you knew what fate awaited them?* The illusion of surety vanished. Thyatis found a jeweled brooch in her fingers. Pressing the sharp edge of the clasp into the edge of her thumb felt good. The pain focused her thoughts, slowing the spinning sensation in her chest.

"I can delay us," Thyatis said, thinking aloud. "Make sure we reach the oasis late . . . then we will search and find nothing. Disappointed, we return to Rome with empty hands."

"Hah!" Penelope laughed softly at her naïveté. "Just kill them and have done."

Thyatis stood, still rubbing the edge of the clasp against her thumb. She felt calmer. The Egyptian's bloody answer had raised another concern. "No. We can't just kill them. My companions are agents of a rival lord. If they find nothing at Sîwa and are satisfied with their efforts, there will be no further search. Everyone will assume the devices were lost in the distant past, destroyed or stolen."

The Egyptian woman made a face, then a sharp cutting motion with her hand. "Why risk?"

"My mistress' enemies are already suspicious—and what about the Persians? We've fought them once and only won through because the men you revile stood at my side." Thyatis pinned the brooch to her cloak, feeling oddly lighthearted. The pressure of events seemed negligible now, bearable. Time, however, was fleeting and she had a great deal to do before they departed for the west.

"Get to Sîwa first," Thyatis ordered the old woman, her confidence returning. "Take the telecast away. If things go awry, don't wait for me!"

"We wouldn't anyway." Penelope sniffed, looking down her nose at the Roman. "You've no need to know where the Eye may go." A ghoulish smile crept into her wrinkled face. "You might be captured and tortured by the enemy."

Thyatis ignored the old woman's cackle, stepping out into the hallway. In the doorway, she paused, squinting at the bundle of clothing. Something was naggingly familiar. The drapery behind the bench had fallen away from the wall. A slender olive hand was partially visible, ringed with gold and silver bracelets. Thyatis felt the world spin to a halt, every grain of dust in the air perfectly clear, the motion of the old woman limping across the floor towards her dragging slow. Her hand rose, touching the brooch, remembering the ornament at last.

Shirin?

The drape billowed, driven by some current in the air, and the hand vanished.

Thyatis blinked.

"Well," Penelope said in a waspish voice. "You've so much time to wait about?"

"No," Thyatis said, licking her lips nervously. The drape remained closed. "I have to go. Nicholas will become suspicious if I'm gone too long. We have . . . a lot to do."

"Then go!" The old woman rapped the Roman sharply on the wrist with her cane. Thyatis blinked at the pain, baring her teeth in a snarl. Penelope glared up at her, dark eyes flashing with irritation. "I don't want to see you again, do you hear?"

"Yes," Thyatis said, turning away, though her feet felt like lead. She didn't look back, and was running by the time she reached the end of the hallway.

Once more, Patik waited in a cold, gray dawn. The heavy, damp air seemed particularly chill. Glistening clouds of fog filled the twisting, winding streets of Alexandria. The rising sun was still below the eastern horizon, but the sky swelled with pearl-sheened pink and steadily lightening blue. Artabanus crouched at his side, hands tucked into his armpits, gaze fixed on the crumpled leather shape of a sandal on the ground before him. A block away, the civilian port stirred to life, the docks crowded with ships preparing to depart. The big Persian allowed himself faint amusement. The Romans were fleeing the city in droves in anything that floated. He had heard no recent news from the east, but the fear and panic running riot in the city were satisfying enough.

The King of Kings comes, Patik mused smugly, *driving the Legions before him with whips of steel and fiery brands.* The irony of the thought almost drew a chuckle. Once he had held the boar-mustached Shahr-Baraz in contempt, looking down upon the lower-born man from a height of pride and arrogance. Events had shown him the fallacy of such attitudes. The *diquan* rubbed his nose, looking back on lost years in his memory. He had flown high, carried by a noble lineage and relentless ambition. Yet now, standing in the shadows of a crumbling temple in the city of the enemy, stripped of titles and lands, he found himself almost content. *Here I stand by means of virtue and strength, not the deeds of my ancestors.*

Satisfied with the state of the world, the Persian checked over his arms and armor, making sure no straps had come lose and nothing had been forgotten. The portico of the dilapidated temple was a poor place to prepare, but they dared not lose their quarry, not when they were so close.

Artabanus stiffened. "They move," he whispered. The sandal made a soft noise as it hopped up and down, mimicking a long, vigorous stride. Patik looked back into the shadows. Two darker blots of night were waiting, endlessly patient and barely distinguishable from the gloom between the columns. A sense of watchful anticipation heightened with the mage's words. Patik turned back to the view of the docks, squinting in the gray light.

"There," he pointed after a moment. The tall woman was hard to miss standing a head above the shorter, darker Egyptians. The Romans hurried up the gangplank onto a lean two-masted coaster. "They are going aboard. I think the ship is called *Paris.*"

A faint hiss answered the observation. Patik raised an eyebrow to Artabanus, but the mage was far too nervous to find any humor in the displeasure of their immediate masters. After a moment, there was a shifting sensation and the shape of one of the Shanzdah—the one who spoke most—emerged from the shadows.

"You will follow by sea," the creature said, thin, chill voice matching the fog-streaked air. "We will follow on land."

The big Persian nodded, gathering up his carry bag. Artabanus rose, clutching the twitching sandal to his chest. The mage had lost weight in the last week and a sunken, wasted look haunted his face. Frowning, Patik turned back. "How will . . ."

The shadows within shadows were gone, leaving the temple porch cold and empty.

"They will know," Artabanus whispered, refusing to look up. "Their master's reach is long."

Patik shrugged in agreement, then looked both ways before sauntering down onto the street.

⌨〔○〕•〔○〕•〔○〕•〔○〕•〔○〕•〔○〕•〔○〕•〔○〕•〔○〕•〔○〕•〔○〕•〔○〕•〔○〕•〔○〕•〔○〕⌨

SOMEWHERE IN THE NILE DELTA, WEST OF BOUSIRIS

〕」〔

Horns blew wildly in the dawn, followed by the shouts of men and the wail of *bucinas*. Aurelian jerked awake, eyes burning with fatigue. Without waiting for his servants, he snatched up a well-worn leather scabbard leaning against his field cot and ducked out into a thin, gray morning. Two of his Praetorians stood tensely outside the tent, armor pitted with rust and scored from a dozen affrays. Their beards were matted and foul—even Aurelian's clung greasily to his face. Both men were wounded, but they stared down the road with glittering eyes, blades drawn and ready. The fighting will of the Roman army might be bent, but it had not yet broken. The prince looked east, seeing the edge of the rising sun shimmering through heavy, mist-streaked air.

Fire bloomed beyond a line of palms and olives, billowing up into the dark morning sky. A flat *crump* followed; the sharp, explosive sound muddied by the air. Aurelian could see the mist blow back, pressed by an invisible hand. All around the prince, weary legionaries woke from nightmare-haunted sleep. The army lay sprawled across stubbled fields, sleeping in culverts or huddled under dirty, stained tents. Men rose in the low-lying mist, blinking, hands on weapons even before they were fully awake.

"They're attacking at the main crossing," one of the Praetorians said, shading his eyes against the pink glare of the rising sun. The man slapped the side of his face, crushing a dozen feathery mosquitoes drinking along the edge of a half-healed scar. A bright smear of blood trailed into his beard as he wiped the dead insects away.

"Stand ready!" Aurelian called to bannermen and signalers still rubbing sleep from their eyes. He took care to speak clearly. His voice had been reduced to a hoarse rasp. The usual crowd of aides, messengers, standard-bearers and aquilifermen had dwindled to two or three walking wounded. The rest were dead, missing or detached to other cohorts as replacements. "Signal the ready reserve to move up on the far left."

Aurelian's servants emerged from the tent, carrying his baggage and armor. Without orders, they began breaking down the pavilion. The army would retreat again today and they wasted no time in packing up and moving west along the rutted farm road. The prince held his arms out, letting his remaining aide slide a grimy, rust-stained cuirass over his tunic. He buckled the straps himself, listening to the slowly mounting sound of battle in the east. Another sharp *boom* rippled across the fields, coupled with a column of flame and oily black smoke.

"Bring something I can stand on," he called, the armor tight across his chest. The last servant handed him a dented cavalry helmet and he pulled the strap snug under his chin. By now the dozen Praetorians and guardsmen remaining in the camp stood nearby, bundles of carefully hoarded javelins over their shoulders. The servants were gone, trudging west under heavy loads.

Two of the Germans grunted, pushing a farm cart up the track, boots slipping in thin, silty mud. Aurelian climbed aboard, then onto a rickety, worm-eaten wooden seat. He peered east, bleary eyes searching the sky for the telltale ripple of a thaumaturgic blow. For the moment, though roiling columns of flame and smoke obscured the view, he saw nothing out of the ordinary. No phantoms, no colossal beasts spitting fire.

Through the trees, he could make out the edge of the river. The water was beginning to shine as the sun rose. Persians—recognizable at this distance by their sunflower banners and tall helmets—advanced in a loose line towards the edge of the orchard. Aurelian could see legionaries crouched among the trees, waiting for the enemy to come into javelin range. Beyond them, the prince saw the barricade at the old bridge crossing burning furiously.

Just like yesterday and the day before yesterday, he thought grimly, shifting his attention to the left. The Persians had developed a frustratingly efficient means of advancing against the Legion opposition. Aurelian's troops would deploy behind a natural barrier—in these swampy lowlands a canal, tributary arm of the Nile or marsh—and dig in with spade and mattock, throwing up a rampart faced with stakes. The Persians would advance, encounter the barrier, then fell back. The next day, or perhaps the day after, the excrement-faced *mobehedan* sorcerers would savage the Roman fortifications with fire and lightning and ghastly phantoms. While the legionaries suffered and died, unable to strike back, a heavy flanking attack would be launched to the left or right, wherever the ground was more suitable. After a sharp engagement, the Romans would be forced to retreat.

Aurelian could count the number of Legion thaumaturges still alive on the fingers of both hands. The levies from the Egyptian temples had been slaughtered in the debacle at Pelusium. Those priests still living had been sent back to Alexandria a week ago, most of them wounded, in mule-drawn carts. The prince fought this hellish, vermin-infested delaying action without sorcerous support. He'd never seen such casualties. Those burned by the foul green flame were the worst—many lived through the blow, but there was no way the Legion healers could tend to them all. More than once, Aurelian had ordered the wounded slain as a mercy. In this dank air, filled with swarming clouds of gnats and flies, men's wounds suppurated in a day and gangrene set in within two.

Choking back rising nausea, Aurelian tried to focus on the

line of battle. There, where the orchard ended and some open fields ran alongside the shallow river, a sharp melee raged across the open ground. Two cohorts of Romans, fighting shoulder to shoulder, mixed it up with a crowd of men in brown-and-tan robes. A shrill wailing touched the prince's ears. *Arabs,* he thought glumly. *Fanatics.* The desert tribesmen expressed no fear of death, hurling themselves into the fray with reckless abandon. Aurelian had no idea where the rebellious Greek city-states had found the mercenaries, but he doubted they were being paid in any mortal coin. Luckily, not many of the religious zealots seemed to be with this wing of the Persian army.

After breaking through at Pelusium, the Persians had split their army into two columns. One advanced along the northerly axis of the Boutikos canal, a waterway running across the Nile delta from east to west. This force, as far as Aurelian had seen, seemed to be composed mostly of the Persians and the infantry contingents of their allies. A second force—the main body of the Greek rebels and the Persian horse—had swung south, taking the Roman military road sweeping along the southern edge of the delta. The hard-surfaced road was the long way 'round, but passable for cavalry. Both canal and highway led, inevitably, to the gates of Alexandria.

"Runner!" Aurelian called, swinging down from the wagon. A legionary turned toward him, bare head swathed in bandages. One eye watched the prince, the other obscured by a ruined flap of skin. The prince looked him over, feeling the constant sick churning in his stomach spike. He recognized the man—one of the young patricians who had joined his expedition to learn how to be an officer.

"Caius, get over to the left and tell whoever's in charge to disperse his men." Bitter anger was plain in the prince's voice. This campaign forced a harsh new reality even on the tradition-bound legionaries. Standing in steady lines, shoulder to shoulder, was sure death if one of the Persian sorcerers was nearby. "When the reserves come up, they must advance in loose order! No bunching up!"

The legionary jogged off, disappearing into a stand of willows. Aurelian waved his bodyguards and aides over. "Where's the next place we can dig in?"

"Fifteen miles west, lord Caesar," grunted Scortius, his head of engineers, waving toward the water. "This canal we've been falling back along crosses the Bolbinitis channel beyond the town of Bouto." Aurelian saw a flash of despair in the older man's expression.

"How far to Alexandria from there?" the prince asked softly.

"Less than fifty miles." Scortius looked lost, his craggy old face slack with exhaustion. Only decades of strictly-held Legion discipline kept the veteran from weeping. The prince clenched his own jaw, measuring distances in his mind. Scortius took a breath and continued. "From the crossing over the Bolbinitis, the canal runs straight southwest into the Kanobikos channel at Hierakonpolis and meets up with the military highway from the south. That's the next place to make a stand." Scortius swallowed. "Unless Fourth Scythia has been flanked down south . . . then the pus-eating Persians could be behind us already."

Aurelian put his hand on the upright of the wagon to keep from swaying. His stomach turned over again, a hot coal of pain burning down in his gut. Nothing impressed Aurelian about the Persian preparations for this campaign more than their provision of shallow-draft boats. Poled by skilled river men—from Mesopotamia, doubtless—the King of King's river flotilla let the invaders use any canal or arm of the Nile as a swift means of advance. Aurelian and his officers struggled to keep from thinking of water as a defensive barrier. Against this enemy, a river was a broad road. "Can we block the canal?"

Scortius shook his head, gray hair hanging lank beside his face. "We can fill the canal with mud or bricks or block it with sunken boats—but they've the men to clear most any obstruction we can put in. And if we're forced back to the main channel of the Nile? The river's a quarter-mile wide! We don't have the men, material or time to make a dam."

"Very well," Aurelian replied, forcing confidence into his voice. *Can't spook the men with my own fear.* "We fall back to the Bolbinitis as we've done the past week, cohorts alternating. All wounded into boats and back to Alexandria at best speed. Scortius, get your engineers back to Hierakonpolis as fast as you can. If the gods smile even a little bit, the Fourth Scythia has kept the Arabs at bay and they won't be blocking our retreat."

The engineer nodded wearily, knuckling sweat from his eyes.

"At Hierakonpolis . . ." the prince continued, trying to marshal fatigue-addled memories, "the military highway comes up from the south, goes over the Boutikos canal, then makes a turn west and vaults the Nile channel. Both crossings are arched bridges. Use the stone—I remember enormous granite pilings and a heavy roadbed—to block the canal. We'll make a stand at Hiera on the eastern bank. If we have to retreat again, we'll use the Nile bridge, then destroy the main span." Aurelian summoned up a feeble grin. "That should make a fair barrier for their damned boats."

"Yes, my lord." Scortius nodded. "We'll do what we can."

A column of legionaries tramped past, heads bent in exhaustion, the setting sun throwing a hot glare in their faces. The air was so muggy their passage didn't even raise a pall of dust from the road. Instead, their hobnailed sandals squelched wetly in a slurry of watery mud. Aurelian squatted in the shade of a farmhouse gate, a courier's pouch opened on the ground in front of him. His guardsmen were sound asleep under the eaves of an abandoned stable, their boots lying out on a bricked patio, drying in the last remnant of the day.

The prince brushed flies away from face, reading the dispatches with a steadily sinking heart. The governor of Lower Egypt was in a panic, urgently requesting troops from Aurelian to police the port and streets of Alexandria. So many citizens had fled, crowding any ship sailing west or north, that refugees flooding in from the countryside had begun looting the abandoned shops and houses. Squatting and larceny was the order of the day. Civil order, in the opinion of the governor, was close to collapse. Crushing the papyrus sheet into a crumpled ball, Aurelian pitched the letter aside. *There will be order aplenty, when we're forced back to the city*, he thought savagely. *I'll deal with this fool of a governor then, if he's still there. And any looters.*

The other dispatches revealed more by their lack than their words—no fresh Legions to bolster his shrinking, battered army. The Imperial fleet was nowhere to be found. Civilian shipping left the Portus Magnus in a constant stream but did not return. He rubbed his face, looking at the straw pallets with longing. There was only one dispatch left—a crumpled, stained packet bound with red twine. He picked it up with thumb and forefinger, feeling a chill steal over him.

A letter from my brother, he realized. *What now?* Aurelian leaned back against the wall and cut the binding away with a sharp slash of his hand knife. Despite the poor condition of the missive, the wax seal was intact and the prince doubted anyone had dared read the contents. Unfolding the parchment, he frowned—this wasn't his brother's neat, economical printing. Instead, the letter was penned in a graceful, flowing hand, though there were abrupt amendments and several struck-out words.

"Why did Helena write this?" he grumbled, scanning the closely set lines. As he read, his frown deepened. The letter, rambling and obviously dictated in haste, contained no orders, no privy news, in fact nothing of a military nature. Aurelian flicked a green-blue bottle fly away from his nose, puzzled. This read like the correspondence of two patrician landowners with absolutely nothing to say to one another. Even the opening was odd—beginning with their boyhood nickname rather than a formal salutation. *Horse*, he read, starting over. *The weather is very fine, with rains and sun and clear* . . . A strikeout interrupted the sentence.

A wagon rumbled past—portions of the farm road were footed with brick, making them passable even during the wet season. The prince looked up, raising a hand in salute to the latest detachment of soldiers passing by. These men were covered with mud, spades canted over their shoulders. They stumbled past, barely raising their heads to greet the prince. At the end of the column, two weary figures trailed behind a huge-wheeled wagon, dozens of empty dirt hods hanging from leather straps on a pole between them. One of the men squinted at Aurelian as he passed.

The prince saluted the two engineers, but his mind was so dulled he couldn't muster the breath to speak their names aloud. Neither Frontius nor Sextus answered, though they did nod in response. Aurelian looked back to the paper. Something—a memory? A clear thought?—was trying to force its way into his consciousness. Thoughts of sleep and a hot bath battled for his attention, but there was no chance of rest, or leisure, not while the Persians harried his army so closely.

Tomorrow, there would be another—not a battle, but a running skirmish—as the Persian vanguard tried to overwhelm his rear guard. The easterners were tenacious and their generals were taking far too much delight in the slow, methodical destruction of the Roman army. Like boys torturing a fly, or a spider caught in a loft, or a lame dog that couldn't run away.

The elusive memory surfaced, buoyed up by a brief vision of a very young Galen painstakingly writing out a school lesson, sitting at the big, wide table in their mother's kitchen. Aurelian picked up the letter again, feeling the warmth of fond memory fade away. *Hawk made a secret language for us,* the prince remembered. *The first letter of each word making a new word. A strikeout or correction making a space between . . .*

He squinted at the page, trying to formulate the hidden sentence in his mind. After a moment, he gave up and began scratching the translation in the dirt of the farmyard. Grains dribbled past and Aurelian found himself staring at the ground, a dead sense of despair rising from his brother's terse, hasty message: *Eque, tres menses mihi eme. Nullus post te est. Accipiter.*

" 'Horse,' " he read aloud, " 'buy me three months. There is no one behind you. Hawk.' "

Aurelian put his head in his hands, closing his eyes. The stabbing pain in his stomach grew worse and he thought he would throw up. Helena, in her meticulous way, had dated the letter. A month had passed between the packet leaving Rome and reaching him here, in this abandoned farmyard. *Two months . . . we'll be forced back into the city in another week, or no more than two. And no reinforcements.*

The prince considered the effort he had invested in the massive, expensive fortifications at Pelusium and across the peninsula holding Alexandria. Sixty thousand men had moved heaven and earth to erect the barriers—the greatest set of field-works the Roman army had ever created. A harsh laugh escaped Aurelian, driven from his gut. *Caesar himself could not have done better,* he thought bitterly. *All useless. The Persians have changed the geometry of war.*

Dreadful experience had taught him how to survive where sorcerers rained death upon from the sky, or shattered stone and brick and wood with a thought. *Hide. Maneuver constantly.*

Fight in loose order. Close quickly with the enemy, to deny their magi a clear target. Ambush them in confined spaces. Counterattack whenever possible. Aurelian realized all too well his own penchant for monuments and clever engineering had thrown away those advantages, leaving his soldiers to bear the result of his folly. *I let them scout and prepare unhindered and then stood up and took the axe in the neck, just like a Roman pig. . . . Two months! How can I hold Alexandria for two more months?*

He needed thaumaturges far more powerful than Rome had ever produced to meet the Persian and Arab priests on even terms. *I need the gods, or ancient heroes, at my side. But I will get nothing.*

The prince looked around. There were no gods in evidence, only a rambling farmhouse filled with men sleeping like the dead, worn down past endurance by an endless succession of losing battles. His mind was still grappling with the enormity of his brother's decision. Aurelian had never expected Galen to make the "Emperor's choice" with *his* life! The roiling pain in his stomach faded, overshadowed by a vast emptiness in his chest.

"Two months, then." Aurelian pushed himself upright. He felt dizzy. The road was empty, the last of the First Minerva's cohorts having marched past to take up positions down the road. "Sixty days."

His mouth was dry, but Aurelian went looking for the cooks to see if they'd managed to get a fire going in the kitchen grate. The prospect of hot food—even only barley gruel—was enough to keep him awake and moving and alive.

[◨]-[0]-[0]-[0]-[0]-[0]-[0]-[0]-[0]-[0]-[0]-[0]-[0]-[0]-[0]-[0]-[0]-[0]-[0]-[0]-[◨]

THE OASIS OF SÎWA, WEST OF ALEXANDRIA

))[(

Under a twilit sky, a lone pillar rose from the sand, three faces worn smooth by the wind. The fourth side, facing the north, retained shallow outlines of hawk-headed men and cranes and kilted servants bowing down before a sun-crowned king. Thyatis roused herself as her camel ambled past, dragging the corner of her kaffiyeh away from a parched mouth. Her lips were dry and cracked, mouth foul with the taste of salt and week-old grime. At least the sun had set, releasing them from the torment of its blazing furnace. The night wind was rising and cooler air pricked her to alertness.

"Quietly now," she called to the others riding behind her. The camels snorted in reponse, but the rest of the Roman party was too thirsty and exhausted to speak. Thyatis slipped a leather cord from the crossbar of her spatha freeing the long blade for a swift draw. Her armor was tied in a bundle to the high-cantled saddle behind her. Riding without close-fitting mail heavy on her shoulders and chest felt strange, but the heat in the open desert was only bearable in loose robes.

The camel plodded on. The string of riders approached a thick line of palms and scrubby, dark brush. Thyatis' head rose in surprise as she smelled open water. Everything under the palms was dark—the light of the moon, an arc of dusky red high in the sky, failed to penetrate the foliage—but she swung down, heedless of any possible danger. Her legs were stiff and sore, but the Roman woman pushed through the branches and stumbled into a shallow pond.

Thyatis slid to a halt, the water unexpectedly cold against her legs. Mud oozed into her sandals.

"Wait," she hissed, furious at herself for rushing ahead, as Vladimir slid through the hanging branches. The Walach froze at the edge of the pond, hand halfway dipped to the quicksilver surface. "Smell first, my friend. We don't know who might have been here before us."

Thyatis drew her sword slowly, oiled metal sliding free without a sound. She could feel Betia and Nicholas and the others waiting in the darkness. Everyone's discipline had broken at the heady, irresistible smell. Vladimir withdrew his hand slowly, watching her with huge eyes, then audibly tasted the air, canting his head to one side. He bent low over the water, then dipped his hand again, long tongue flicking over the back of his hand.

"Water," he whispered. "Mud. Dates. Camels. Men. Women."

"Poison?" Thyatis coughed quietly, clearing a dry, dusty throat.

Vladimir shook his head.

"Drink then," she said, "but take your time." She forced herself to stand, alert to any disturbance in the night, while he drank. When the Walach had finished, he slipped back into the brush and Thyatis waded quietly to the edge of the pond. Betia came next, gliding between the palms like a ghost. The Roman woman continued to listen, nerves on edge, suppressing a start every time one of the camels honked or grumbled.

"Why is it so still?" Nicholas squatted beside her, wiping his face with a damp rag. Thyatis sipped slowly from one of the waterbags. She had washed her face, hands and arms in the pond, but longed for a real bath. *Everything sticks together in this heat. . . .* The pilgrim road from the coast south to Sîwa crossed nearly a hundred miles of lifeless, sun-blasted desert. Endless miles of rocky flats interspersed with acres of gravely lowlands. Thyatis had expected a desert filled with sand, like the lands around Lake Mareotis. But here in the western reach, there were no springs, no water and no shelter to speak of. Only wells built a day's march apart along the trail allowed passage from the coast. The last of those cisterns, cut into a shallow canyon twenty miles north of the oasis, had been bone dry.

"I don't know," Thyatis said, keeping her voice low. Stands of palms and scrawny trees stretched away to the south, forming the main body of the oasis. In the fading sun, as they had descended the flank of a flattened, rocky ridge, Thyatis had seen whitewashed houses and sand-colored temples at the center of the depression. The glittering expanse of a dry lake blazed beyond the green fields. People—priests, shepherds, artisans—were supposed to live here, drawing life from the bubbling pools and the fields the springs allowed. Flat-topped mesas surrounded the valley of Sîwa, though they were nothing more than barren white stone and chalky gravel. "There must be someone here."

She pointed into the darkness. "There is a hill at the center—you saw it from the ridge? The temple of Amon-Ra is there, and the Oracle, and the quarters of the priests."

"I saw." Nicholas shifted in the moonlight, nodding. Thyatis felt Vladimir and Betia stir. The others were resting farther back in the grove. Everyone was worn down by the punishing heat. They had pushed hard from the coast. Thyatis' thighs and back simmered with dull, constant pain. Camels had a strange, loping gait and she'd felt nauseated for five days while they ambled south. She longed not just to be clean again—preferably via hours spent soaking in blisteringly hot water—but a masseuse afterwards, iron-hard hands kneading her tortured muscles into welcome oblivion.

"What did your bird say? Where do we go now?"

Nicholas rose, grimacing as abused muscles complained. Thyatis didn't think he was used to riding so much either. *He was happy at sea,* she remembered. *A Roman sailor, how funny!* He cracked his knuckles.

"She said—if we can believe her more than we could our poetic Cypriot—to enter the Mystery itself, the nave. The god looks down on a pit, from which bitter fumes rise. If we descend the pit, there is a stair and a chamber below." Thyatis could see the Latin's teeth shine in dappled moonlight. "The priests of the Oracle store the offerings there."

"And among those gifts, offered up so long ago, is one of Nemathapi's legendary telecasts?" Thyatis forced disbelief into her voice, though she prayed silently for the Daughters to have been and away with their prize. She had watched carefully as they came south, looking for the signs of another party on camels coming and then going. She had seen nothing.

"She had good reason to speak true," Nicholas answered. "I saw the papyrus myself—the signs and devices—one clearly described a telecast, given as tribute to the Oracle by the pharaoh Djoser in thanks 'for his salvation.' And if the librarian lied?" He laughed. "She'll still be in our cage when we return."

Thyatis stood as well, breathing deeply, forcing her tension out in a sharp *huh*. Bird-like Sheshet was tucked away in a prison cell beneath the governor's palace. She wondered if Nicholas would really put burning irons to the woman if they found nothing in the temple. She wondered how the librarian had known the truth. *The matron Penelope seemed sure there was an Eye here . . . shouldn't such a thing be a closely held secret? But then—the priests of Amon-Ra would know and they*

might tell another, and then another . . . who would care for old
bronze and rusting gears?

"Doesn't matter," Thyatis said aloud, flexing a cramp from
her calves. They complained, but she ignored the soreness.
"We'll check and see." She smiled tightly at Nicholas, fist over
the prince's amulet. "If there's nothing here, we'll know soon
enough. If there is, we'll find the telecast one way or another
and take it home. Everyone have enough to drink? Are the waterbags full?"

The legionaries with the camels whistled in acknowledgement and Vladimir rose up, shaking out his shoulders, long axe
swinging in his right hand. Scaled armor rattled softly. The barbarian grew more lively and awake as the night deepened and
the air cooled.

"Vlad, you lead." Thyatis said, flipping her cloak free of both
arms. Betia had helped her squeeze into the mailed armor. The
metal was almost hot from riding on the back of a camel all day.
In the damper, chillier air of the oasis, the warmth felt good.
"Nicholas, you're on the right. I'll take the left. Florus . . ."

One of the shapes in the darkness raised his head attentively.
Nicholas had tried to commandeer an entire cohort from the
city garrison for their expedition, but had only managed to
wrinkle free a handful of men—four recruits fresh from the
Italian provinces and a veteran centurion to watch out for them.
Thyatis didn't mind—they had borne up well in the dash from
the coast—and they were willing to take orders. She hid a
smile. Better yet, they were too exhausted to ask questions.

". . . you cover the camels and the gear. Betia will follow
along behind. Remember, people get lost in the dark. If you get
separated, meet us back at the pillar we passed by the edge of
the oasis."

Everyone nodded, a motion more felt or sensed than seen.
Thyatis tucked her braids behind both ears, then padded off
through the palms. The long blade was back in its sheath, but
her hand was poised to draw at an instant's notice.

The night remained entirely still, without so much as the
squeaking passage of bats to break the silence. Thyatis began to
get a queer feeling between her shoulder blades. *This just isn't*
right. . . . Even in the desolation out beyond the ridge, the

desert came alive after sunset, filled with scurrying lizards or scorpions, the hushed passage of hunting owls, sand moving in the night wind. The night under these close, humid palms felt watchful and oppressive.

A narrow road climbed the temple hill, rising up from a crowded little mud-brick town filled with twisting streets. Stumpy obelisks and eroded sphinxes lined the outer edge of the avenue. The rusty moon had begun a slow descent towards the western horizon. Nicholas darted from turn to turn, rushing forward in sharp bursts. Thyatis followed, keeping her sandals soft on the irregular slabs of fitted sandstone.

A dozen yards behind, the others crept forward, hugging the inner wall where deeper shadows covered them with a black cloak. Below, the town was abandoned and silent. No dogs barked, no lantern or candle flared in a window.

At the top of the hill, the road passed through a squat gate of brick. Thyatis stepped around the corner, through a pale section of moonlight and into deeper shadow. Nicholas was already crouching across the road, his outline obscured against the crude shape of a lion in bas-relief. She exhaled slowly, testing the air, and saw fog condense from her breath. The night had grown steadily colder.

Pillars rose up against the starry sky, huge and round, tapering towards the heavens. If they had ever supported a roof, the vault had collapsed long ago. Thyatis snapped her fingers softly—Nicholas' head turned sharply towards her—she pointed off along the main path through the colonnade. "Lead," she whispered.

Nicholas glided away into darkness. Thyatis stepped back to the edge of the gate, feeling her flesh crawl with uneasiness. *Too quiet . . . what's going on?* There had been no sign of pursuit on the trail. *Has this place been abandoned?*

She flashed her hand in the pale slat of moonlight, beckoning to the others. A moment later, she heard the *thump-thump* of camel paws on the ground, then Betia was crouching beside her. The legionaries loomed over the girl, smelling of rust, fish sauce and sweat-stained leather.

"Where's Vladi—?" Thyatis turned sharply in alarm, staring

into the darkness among the columns. There was nothing, only more shadow and the vague outlines of crumbling brick walls and more pillars. The shrine and temple had fallen on bad times. Her hand twitched to the hilt of her sword, but she repressed the urge to draw the blade. "—mir."

"Here," the Walach said, deep voice rumbling despite an effort to keep quiet.

"We're switching off," Thyatis whispered, turning back. "Nicholas is ahead. You back him up. Florus, the camels will have to go around—they won't fit through these columns. Betia, you've the rear guard."

"What about you?" The little Gaul's voice was so faint Thyatis almost missed her question.

The Roman woman bent close, close enough to smell lavender oil and juniper in Betia's hair. "I'll flank."

Vladimir padded off, armor lying quiet against his heavy, felted shirt. The legionaries crept after, each man leading a camel by a shortened rein. Thyatis caught Betia's shoulder as the girl moved past.

"Well behind," Thyatis breathed, her hand trembling against the urge to draw her blade and whirl with a shout. "Something is watching us. If anything happens, get away." The girl touched her fingers, then vanished into the gloom, drawing up the hood of her cloak. Thyatis squinted into the darkness, but the little Gaul had already vanished without a sound.

Be safe, Thyatis thought, putting everything but soundlessness from her mind. Knuckles white on the hilt of her blade, hand gripping the scabbard, she drifted off to the right, circling around the columns. *I should take my sandals off*, she thought after a moment, hearing a faint *scuff-scuff* of leather on stone. A thin layer of sand covered the floor and she felt each grain as it rolled under her tread like a gong ringing from the Capitoline.

She passed through two, then three ranks of pillars. They were old and worn, lacking the smooth plaster facings of younger temples. There was no marble here, not so far from the sea, only crumbling brick, streaked with salt crystals. The moonlight faded and she looked up. A single chimney-like tower loomed against the stars, obscuring Luna's faded crescent. Without hesitation, she slipped forward, blade inching from the scabbard. The sensation of watchfulness was fading and she swiveled her head from side to side, staring down the dim corridors between the columns as she ran forward.

Where are the priests? Where are my sisters? Have they fled? she thought. Suddenly, the maze of pillars ended. There was a courtyard, bounded on four sides by columns and an ancient, crumbling pediment. Before her, the round tower rose from a blocky foundation. A doorway gaped, twice the height of a man, three times as broad. Thyatis turned, thinking *what was that?* There had been a noise, half-heard, at the edge of perception.

HERE, something spoke in the darkness, COME TO ME.

Thyatis' eyes widened, light blooming on her face like the rising sun. Her mouth opened in a shout but no sound emerged, drowned in surging waves of color. Silence continued to grip the night.

COME, I HAVE BEEN WAITING, the voice boomed, though no sound reverberated in the air.

Brilliant white light blazed in the courtyard and Thyatis crumpled to her knees, eyes squeezed shut against the blinding glare, one hand thrown up to block out the brilliance flooding from the doorway. Tears streamed down her cheeks and the sword fallen on the ground began to smoke.

ENTER, MY CHILD. ENTER.

Where is everyone? Nicholas paused, hand against grainy, eroded brick. He looked back along the avenue. One of the camels ambled towards him, a wash of moonlight gleaming on a legionary's iron lorica. Here on the summit of the hill, the curved horns of the moon were clear in the sky. The Latin felt a flash of relief to see the others, then stiffened. Still sheathed, Brunhilde suddenly began to hum, sending a piercing vibration through his hand and arm.

"Ware!" Nicholas shouted in alarm, leaping away from the column. The dwarf-blade sang free from her sheath in a glittering arc. A pale, bluish light gleamed in watery steel, silhouetting the columns and fallen blocks of stone. Behind him, he heard the rush of feet and half-sensed Vladimir at his side.

A deep, cold voice boomed in the darkness, then three hulking figures were revealed by the wavering blue light. Two were clad from head to toe in dark cloaks and mailed armor, not even the glitter of an eye shining in the slit of their helmets. The other was a stocky, muscular Persian, blue highlights shining in his curly beard. Nicholas motioned Vladimir aside to clear fighting room, eyes fixed on the Persian captain.

He didn't die in the tomb, Nicholas thought, licking his lips, weighing the situation in his mind. *What about the mage? Did he live too? Is he in the darkness, waiting to strike?* The image of Mithridates—such a big man, corded with muscle, effortlessly powerful—convulsing in the blast of witch flame haunted the Latin's dreams. But Brunhilde's presence in his grasp steeled his resolve, for she had never betrayed him, never failed in battle, not matter what foe they faced.

No one spoke, the Persians spreading out themselves. Big beard wielded both a curl-crowned mace and cavalry sword, while the other two bore only swords of some dark metal. Nicholas blinked—they were hard to make out, even in the simmering glare of the rune blade—no more than dark outlines against an indistinct background. White breath curled from his lips. Brunhilde trembled eagerly in his hand, her desire sending a hot shock of bloodfire coursing through his limbs. He could hear the legionaries' hobnailed sandals rattle on stone behind him.

More Persians appeared from the shadows, gripping axes and long, straight swords. Nicholas settled into balance, briefly wishing he had a shield. *Even numbers, then, unless Thyatis hears . . . where is she?*

Steel rang on steel with a high, singing note, then an echoing rasp of disengagement. Betia did not wait, turning away from behind the camels. She sprinted off between the pillars, sandals slapping on the cobblestones, chill air cutting her throat. Almost immediately, her foot smashed into the edge of a broken block of masonry. Biting her palm to keep from crying out, the girl hopped away, tears streaming down her face. *Fool girl! You can't run around blind!*

"Thyatis?" she croaked, trying not to shout wildly. "Thyatis!"

Limping, her toe sparking with pain every time she put weight down, Betia pressed ahead, groping among the dark columns. She wished desperately for a light, but the candles and lanterns were slung in a woven basket on one of the camels.

A grumbling *crack* smote the air, making her start forward in surprise. Lurid yellow light shone forth for a moment, throwing long shadows down the aisles between the columns. Betia spun, staring back towards the road in horror, then the light faded and the sound of men shouting in battle echoed.

"Thyatis!" Betia shouted, caution discarded, stumbling forward. "Where are you?"

Nicholas rolled aside wildly, blocking desperately with Brunhilde. The air was still ringing with the blast of light. Camels shrieked, enveloped in flame as they charged down the road. Two of the legionaries sprawled on the ground, armor popping and sizzling, iron glowing cherry red. One of the cloaked men hewed down with his ebon blade and dwarf steel rang like a bell, turning the stroke. Nicholas felt the blow rock his arm back to the shoulder socket, then scrambled to his feet.

The Persian wight circled, blade held high over the shadowed helmet. Nicholas took hold of Brunhilde with both hands, blinking sparks from his eyes. A jagged after-image of the sorcerous blast lingered, making blind patches in his vision. The creature attacked, chopping hard at Nicholas' head. The Latin skipped back, the triangular end of the Persian blade hissing past. Out of the corner of his eye, he caught a glimpse of Vladimir attacking, long axe whirling, driving back Curly Beard.

The clang and rattle of iron on iron was harsh in his ears, the legionnaires at sword strokes, big rectangular shields up, with the Persian soldiers. Men grunted, rushing and darting in the terrible light. Brunhilde's radiance was barely enough to let Nicholas pick out details on the armor of the shape attacking him. He parried again, arm still stunned from the previous blow. He was forced to give ground.

The wight pressed the attack, chopping at his leg, then slapping Brunhilde aside with a monstrously powerful, wrenching blow. Nicholas gasped, still stunned by the strength in the black-clad arm. He scuttled back again and his hip slammed into one of the obelisks lining the road. He felt a chill, realizing there was nothing behind him but cliff and the steep, rocky hillside.

Brunhilde trembled a little as he raised her in guard. The dark shape slid sideways, cutting off his retreat down the avenue. Nicholas gathered himself, settling his grip two-handed on Brunhilde's hilt.

"Into the columns!" He shouted and rushed the black shape, stabbing for the thing's invisible face. The Persian met him head-on, throwing a shoulder into the Latin's rush. Nicholas, jaw tight in a snarl, whipped Brunhilde down, letting her take the ebon sword edge on edge. The stroke jarred his shoulder, rocking him back. Metal squealed—a high-pitched scream Nicholas felt as a crushing physical pain behind his right eye. A cold laugh issued from the heavy cowl, only inches away. Nicholas wrenched Brunhilde aside, slamming his hip into the Persian's groin. "Let's go!"

The ebon blade shattered, metal parting in a tortured groan. The wight staggered, then hissed in fury. Nicholas whipped Brunhilde sideways, a blur of smoking azure light. An up-flung arm caught her stroke on a wrist guard, but the dwarf steel trembled like a struck bell, shearing through the softer iron. Something brittle snapped and Nicholas bounded past, leaving the Persian sprawled on the ground.

"Go go go!" He bolted past Vladimir, taking a wild cut at the bearded Persian's head. The legionnaries were running too, though at least one of them was a still shape on the ground. The Walach gave a skirling howl, then leapt into the darkness. Nicholas didn't look back, darting around the first column he passed.

"Thyatis!" *Where was the woman*? His arms felt like lead already, sweat streaming from his neck into his armor. Steam curled away from his exposed skin. Vladimir charged past and Nicholas grasped wildly for him, catching the man's cloak. "Get over here," he snarled.

Light sparked high above, a sudden flood of greenish refulgence. Nicholas looked away, half-blinded. Something hissed in the sky, floating above the broken crowns of the pillars, shedding a hot, spitting light. "Thrice-cursed sorcerer! Come on."

The enormous voice rang, shaking the ground. Whirling rainbow light etched the crevices between the stone slabs into perfect clarity. Thyatis caught a glimpse of enormous stone feet, pitted and scored by centuries of exposure to the sky and wind. Her entire body shuddered, pulsing in time to the sound filling the world. Blinded, she crawled on the floor, screaming soundlessly, groping for some kind of shelter. Smeared blood glowed ruby alongside her nose, picked out in the brilliant glare.

THE CIRCLE BEGINS TO CLOSE. THE SHELTER OF THE STARS FAILS, RIVEN BY INEXORABLE TIDES.

Thyatis clawed at the edge of a slab, dragging herself forward.

A viper unfolded a glossy, pearl-colored hood. Tiny black eyes glittered above a hissing mouth. A dark green tongue darted. A dusky hand grasped the viper swiftly, just behind the mottled, scaled, head. The snake's jaws yawned, revealing a pink mouth and pale white fangs. The hand moved swiftly, each motion assured, squeezing the poison sac behind the muscular jaw with deft fingers. A milky drop oozed out, dropping into a pink palm. The venom hissed, bubbling the skin, then the hand lifted to Thyatis' mouth. Her tongue dipped, tasting the burning liquid. For a moment, it seemed there would be no pain, only a spreading numbness. Then the muscles in her chest contracted violently and she could feel her heart being crushed by a series of jolting spasms. She fell backward, stiffening, and her last sight was of the great doors crashing aside, revealing a crowd of grim-faced men in iron helmets.

Gasping, tears streaming from blind eyes, Thyatis turned her face from the coruscating light.

A PAEAN OF JOY RISES FROM THE CAMPFIRE, VANISHING INTO THE RISING DISK OF HOLY FATHER SUN.

A crowd of men pressed close around her, white robes shining with midday heat. Their faces, puffed with fat, glistening with sweat, smiled genially at her. Tired, head throbbing from the noise, Thyatis sat on a stone bench—one among hundreds—waving off pressing hands on either side. A man approached, freshly-shaven chin gleaming red. His mouth moved, but Thyatis could hear nothing over the roaring sound of the colossal voice. He too, she waved away, but he refused to leave. His hands grasped her shoulders, pinning her to the seat. Thyatis brushed the hands away, her voice raised in a sharp rebuke.

A blow rocked her back and she looked up to see a black-eyed man with a grim, seamed face draw back a bloody dagger for a second stroke. Limpid fire lit in her limbs, one hand snatching a freshly-cut stylus from the pocket of her robe. Before the man could react, she grasped his wrist and slammed the point of the stylus into his bicep. He screamed—though the noise was lost in the rolling boom of the voice speaking again. She leapt back, crashing into the bodies of many senators crowding close on all sides. Another blow stunned her, and she looked down, seeing a Corsican-styled hilt jutting from her chest. Cold welled in her breast, filling her throat. A ring of men surrounded her, faces drawn and tense, eyes wild in fear. Every one held a drawn knife.

Thyatis swayed, feeling blood sluice down her side, but did not fall. Instead, she tore her gown with trembling fingers, letting half fall decently over her midriff and legs. The other section, perfect white linen spotted with bright red blood, she raised over her face. She closed her eyes.

Another blow slammed into her side, then another, and another . . .

Drooling, Thyatis collapsed onto the stone floor, fingernails still clawing to drag her forward.

LEAVES FALL INTO A RUSHING STREAM, GOLDEN-RED, SWIRLING AMONG GRAY STONES.

Her eyes were partially open, only bare slits fringed with long eyelashes. Above, she could make out a flat ceiling, chased with gold, ornamented with blocky geometric diagrams. The sun was shining in—bright, very bright—through cross-shaped windows. She could smell myrrh, coriander, roses, lavender, sweet scented oil. Figures moved into her field of view—men in red cloaks and bronzed armor were shouting, their faces flushed with emotion. They were all so familiar. . . . Perdiccas struck one of the other captains a heavy blow with a fist glittering with golden rings. Another appeared, this man with a heavy beard and quick, knowing eyes. Alone of the angry men in the room, his eyes showed true grief.

WIND SIGHS AMONG TREES BLOSSOMING IN THE COURTS OF THE MORNING.

Pain lanced along her arms, burning like a fire. She stag-

gered, nerveless fingers letting fall a cloak of golden leaves. Discolored streaks appeared on massively muscled forearms, then the poison rushed up across her biceps. Gasping for breath, she fell heavily on a floor of carefully fitted slate. A chair of stone stood on a raised dais. A plastered wall stood behind the throne, painted a dusky red, with curling lines of geometric waves running just below the ceiling. Dolphins sported in a stylized ocean. A gray-haired woman stood over her, tears streaming down a seamed, lined face, wrinkled hands pressed against her ears. Someone was screaming endlessly, like a gelded bull.

How did Deianira grow so old, Thyatis wondered, before searing pain ripped all thought from her mind.

HANDS TOUCH IN THE DARKNESS AND THERE IS HOPE.

Scarred, furred fingers reached out—barely lit by intermittent flares of sullen yellow light—and grasped a gleaming, golden tablet. Spindly legs braced against a surface of glistening dark metal. She tugged furiously, chipped nails bleeding. Then the tablet came free. Clutching the glowing stone to her chest, she scuttled down into darkness, slipping and sliding over oil-black surfaces. The light burned against her chest, filling her with warmth, driving back the endless, eternal chill.

THIS IS YOUR TIME.

Betia froze, startled by a greenish white light blooming in the sky. She set down her injured foot gingerly, then realized with a shock she was surrounded. A wicked-looking knife—plainly illuminated by the strange radiance—pressed against the side of her throat. Eyes wide, she turned her head slowly. She blinked. Four women crouched in the shadow of a massive column. One of them, dark eyes glittering over a dirty veil, held the point to her throat.

"I'm—" Her gasped words stilled, blade pressing into her flesh. A finger rose to the woman's lips, hidden behind tattered linen. Betia closed her mouth. Fingers shaking, she raised a hand, sketching a quick bow sign in the air. ". . . please, I'm no enemy."

The knife withdrew slowly. A rattling *boom* sounded through the forest of stone. The hissing light in the sky fell slowly among the pillars, shadows dancing wildly in the avenues between the colu..ns.

"Move," hissed the woman with the knife. All four of the Daughters darted out into a plaza of fitted stone. Betia sprinted after them, ignoring the sharp pain in her foot. There was a huge doorway under a wall of brick, then they were inside, in darkness. Betia stopped hard, panting. Someone drew back a leather cover from an oil lantern, letting a warm yellow glow spill into the vast chamber.

Directly ahead, a mammoth statue rose towards a ceiling hidden in darkness. Huge, square-fingered hands rested on round knees and a stone beard was visible at the edge of the lantern light. Betia's arms rippled with goose bumps, looking up at dead, staring eyes. The light flickered and glowed on disks of mother-of-pearl set in the sockets and she felt sudden, overwhelming dread. Then she looked down, unwilling to face the god in his sanctuary and yelped in surprise.

A figure lay sprawled on the floor at the edge of a pit.

"Thyatis!" The tallest of the cloaked Daughters bolted forward, knife forgotten, and knelt beside the Roman soldier. Betia hurried forward as well, her mind moving again, and together they rolled the supine form over. Tapering olive fingers peeled back one of the Roman woman's eyelids, and pressed against a powerful, scarred throat. "She lives . . ." said the Daughter in an emotion-choked voice.

Betia felt paralyzing fear recede. She bit her thumb nervously. Thyatis seemed cold and dead to her, face pale under a wash of freckles and old sunburn. A flutter of breath barely moved her lips. "What did this? Can we wake her up?"

"There's no time for acquaintances," barked one of the other Daughters, before the dark-eyed woman could answer. The old woman's veil had fallen away, revealing a wrinkled, angry face. "We've got to go!"

Shouts echoed outside on the plaza, followed by the sound of running feet. Betia jerked around, pulling back the sleeves of her cloak. Bloodfire ticked in her throat, making a rushing sound in her ears, and she jacked back the lever on the spring gun at her wrist. The spring closed with a snap. Outside, she saw figures rush from the columns. Another sparking, hissing light flashed in the sky,

"Help me," the olive-skinned woman snapped. Betia turned,

meeting fierce dark eyes and together they lifted Thyatis up. The Roman was heavy, her limbs slack in unconsciousness. Betia gasped, pushing on a muscular thigh with all her strength. The Daughter shifted, getting her shoulder under Thyatis' breastbone, then took the larger woman on her back with a grunt. "Follow."

Staggering under the weight, the olive-skinned woman placed a foot on the top step. Betia stared giddily down into the pit, brickwork walls illuminated by unsteady lanterns in the hands of the Daughters. The stairs corkscrewed down and beyond the flaring, intermittent light there was only darkness. A cold, sharp-smelling wind blew up in the girl's face and she swayed at the lip, then caught herself.

Steel rang on steel outside and a man screamed in pain. Betia darted down the steps. Barely twenty feet down the pit—though the stairs continued on, winding into the depths of the hill—a section of the wall had folded away. Betia ducked into the opening, following Thyatis' disappearing foot—one sandal strap dangling—and the receding light of the lantern. A tunnel with a triangular roof slanted down at a steep angle and the Gaul found the shallow, worn steps difficult to navigate.

Behind Betia, the wizened old Egyptian woman braced her feet against the floor and pressed on a stone counterweight with all her strength. Ancient cables groaned, squeaking with dust, and then delicately balanced stone plugs rumbled and the wall swung closed with a dull thud. Grit drifted from the ceiling, making the woman cough. Then she too hurried down the slope, feeling her way along the wall in the darkness.

With a shout, Nicholas leapt into the midst of the Persians as they charged out of the forest of pillars. The dwarf-steel blade flashed overhead as he cut at the lead man. The Persian—not the big bearded one, but one of his confederates—shouted in alarm, throwing up a block with his broadsword. Brunhilde clove through the weapon with a ringing spark and Nicholas felt a solid jolt in both arms. The man's helmet splintered, cloven through by the blow and steel grated on bone. Twisting his wrists, Nicholas wrenched the blade free, a wash of blood darkening the metal.

More Persians swarmed out from the columns, two attacking him as he backed up. Vladimir had started to chant a high, wailing war cry and the Walach threw a long, twisting shadow in the glare of a fresh witch light sputtering overhead. Nicholas slapped aside a swinging mace with the flat of his blade, then bulled in, smashing the nearest Persian in the face with his fist. Mailed knuckles banged on the noseguard of the man's helmet, but the soldier rocked back, stunned. Grimacing, Nicholas grasped the protruding iron, digging his thumb into the man's eye.

The other Persian soldier charged, hewing wildly overhand with his cavalry sword. Nicholas surged back, swinging the broken-nosed Persian into the path of his fellow's blade. The overhand blow sank deep into the man's back, drawing a hoarse grunt and a fountain of black fluid from the dying Persian's mouth. Nicholas lunged, jamming Brunhilde under the collapsing man's arm. The chisel-shaped tip of the runeblade cracked against the attacker's breastplate, ripping through close-set links of chain and sank into his chest with a flat, slapping sound.

A queer, shivering cry sounded and Nicholas swung round, chilled by the sound.

One of the black-cloaked men waded into the fray, head and shoulders above the Persians and Romans struggling back and forth across the little plaza. The creature bounded forward, flat black blades in either hand. In a blink, the thing hewed the head clean from a set of Roman shoulders, then smashed Florus to the ground with a blow of his fist. Nicholas' eyes widened, seeing the plates of the centurion's lorica crumpled and splintered.

In his hand, Brunhilde suddenly woke to life, flaring blue-white like the sun shining through sea ice. Nicholas felt her scream in defiance and crabbed forward, his veins roaring with bloodfire. The shape turned, the blue glare shining in empty eye slits. There was a cold *hiss*, and the wight rushed forward, cloak streaming back.

Nicholas parried high, slapping away the point of the sword cutting at his head. The second point stabbed in, flickering in and out of sight as the illumination in the sky faded. Nicholas blocked, hilt to hilt, driving the creature's blade into the ground. He stamped down, trying to catch the thing's instep. His hobnailed sandal ground on an armored foot, but found no purchase. The thing smashed an elbow into his chest, throwing Nicholas back, breathless, through an archway.

Vladimir leapt in, axe-blade glittering in a swift arc. The blow glanced from the Persian's breastplate, tearing the cloak away, sending sparks flashing and chunks of iron spalling away. Nicholas rolled up to his feet, then darted in from the flank. For a moment, there was a blur of metal, blades licking back and forth as they fought in the doorway. The Persian parried effortlessly, weaving a double-bladed barrier of steel in front of him. Vladimir hacked at his legs and the creature leapt up, slashing at Nicholas' head.

The Roman panted, sweat streaming down his arms and legs. Everything narrowed to a swirling gray tunnel, focused solely on dancing black metal and the void of enameled armor shifting in and out of sight. He lunged again, trying to catch the thing's elbow joint. Brunhilde was slapped away and Nicholas had to leap back, arms windmilling for balance to escape losing his head to a powerful sideways cut.

His back foot, sliding on the floor, suddenly found a raised lip of stone.

Beyond the thing's huge shoulder, he caught a glimpse of Florus twitching into oblivion, blood spilling from his slack mouth in a thin stream. The other legionaries lay scattered on the plaza, arms and legs twisted in death. The big curly-bearded Persian loped through the arch, shaking gore from his mace.

"Run!" Nicholas shouted at Vlad, gasping as he weakly blocked another cut. He strained, muscle against muscle, hilts locked, Brunhilde's point driven down to the floor. The Walach scuttled past and vanished below Nicholas' line of sight. The Latin kicked, catching the black-cloaked thing on its hip. The blow knocked the Persian back and Nicholas skidded sideways. An open, stone-sided shaft yawned beside his foot.

Black-cloak fell back a step, adjusting its grip on one blade, flipping the other in its hand. Nicholas gasped for breath, crouched, Brunhilde's tip wavering in the air. Curly-beard circled to his left and the two Persians adjusted their spacing. Nicholas swallowed, keeping both opponents in view. His arms burned with fatigue.

* * *

Vladimir leapt down the curving steps, two and three at a time. The intermittent glare from outside barely illuminated the pit, but gave the Walach's huge, dark eyes enough to see by. The stairs circled away into the depths and he could feel a cold, steady wind blowing up past him.

Deep, part of his mind gibbered, one hand sliding along the rough brickwork. *Can we get out?*

"No choice," he growled, hearing Nicholas panting harshly above and the slippery, ringing clash of metal. "Got to be better below than above!" Vladimir spun, bounding back up the steps. As he did, flared nostrils caught a fragment of scent in the roiling air. *Thyatis?*

He stopped, limbs tensed, bending to the crumbling old stone steps. *Yes!* The Roman woman's particular blend of leather and soap and sweat was suddenly everywhere. "Not alone—Betia too!" The little girl's heady aroma of lavender and juniper was very clear.

Vladimir crabbed sideways down the steps, nose close to the curving surface. *Her hand brushed along the wall . . .*

Then the trail stopped abruptly and he frowned, puzzled. Nothing but a wall faced him, lines of thin, splintery brick and fragments of old plaster. Long-splayed fingers tested the masonry. *Something smooth?* One of the bricks was not brick—a cunningly cut piece of marble among the course. Hissing in effort, he jammed his hand against the glassy surface, feeling it give.

"Nicholas!" he screamed, putting his shoulder against the wall. There was an answering rumble and brick screeched on brick. "Nicholas! This way!"

Brunhilde whirled in a blur; fat hot sparks leaping from her edge as Nicholas waded in, throwing a blizzard of cuts and thrusts at the wight. Startled, the black shape gave ground, parrying deftly. Nicholas jumped past the shape, driving down one ebon blade—extended in a block—and then flicking the dwarf-steel blade back. The creature didn't flinch, interposing the haft of the other blade, but Brunhilde struck square with a ringing *clang* and shrieking—a piercing high wail of audible sound—shattered the glossy dark metal. The ebon blade splintered with a crash and the wight staggered back, stunned. Nicholas, teeth gritted in a feral snarl, bulled in, smashing aside the other blade, slashing Brunhilde down across the front of the black helmet.

Metal squealed, iron flashed hot and the dwarf steel burned through. A hoarse, gargling cry went up; a black, mailed hand clawing at the still-unseen face. Nicholas slammed his shoulder into the creature, sending it crashing to the floor.

The big curly-bearded Persian shouted hoarsely, leaping in, mace swinging at Nicholas' face. The Roman ducked, then sprinted past. His boot hit the lip of stone at the edge of the pit, then he kicked off, plunging down into the darkness.

Wind whipped past for an instant, then Nicholas crashed into the steps beside Vladimir. The Walach's eyes were wide in surprise, his mouth a round *O*. His long-fingered hands grabbed for the Latin, who swayed wildly on the edge of the steps. Vladimir seized the front of his shirt, giving a great heave. Both men toppled back into the dark opening yawning in the side of the pit.

Nicholas, breathless, his legs smarting with the blow of his landing, gasped for air.

Vladimir scrambled up, eyes wide, searching the walls. Above, at the top of stairs, a terrible voice boomed in anger. Boots clattered on brick. Light flared in the shaft, a sullen red glow. In the glare, the Walach caught sight of a glistening smear of sweat on a stone jutting from the wall of the passage. Heedless of the consequences, he grabbed hold of the rock and pushed, muscles bunching under his armor. A grinding sound issued from the walls and he felt the stone give slowly.

Outside, the light flared brighter. There was more shouting.

Vladimir snarled, long teeth white in the hurrying flare of torchlight. The stone scraped and ground and suddenly sank flush with the tunnel wall. A slab of stone faced with brick rolled out of a recess, powered by hidden counterweights, and slammed closed. The Walach caught a glimpse of armored men in the opening before he was plunged into darkness.

"Forward," he hissed, scooping up Nicholas from the ground. Brunhilde's gleam had faded to a dull watery blue, but there was still enough radiance in the passage for the Walach to find their way down, deeper into the earth. After a moment, the

Latin managed to get his legs under him and they ran as fast as they could, leaping from step to step.

A heavy *boom* echoed in the passage behind him, then another. Dust sifted from the ceiling. An indistinct voice shouted words of power and the floor trembled violently. Vladimir stumbled, picked himself up and ran on.

<hr>

THE GATES OF IBLIS

Mohammed stood at the gates of the city, a newly carved staff of fig wood resting against his shoulder. Sounds and smells washed over him—the clash of cymbals, voices raised in raucous song, lamb covered with ground spices and pepper and salt roasting on a spit; the stamp of dancing feet; the skirling sound of pipes and the hoarse twang of a zither; water falling; children laughing; the beat of hammers on molten iron; wind sighing in the rigging of a ship under sail; the call of an imam as the sun rises, summoning the faithful to prayer; the racketing of looms, the *clack-clack* of a shuttle; dust and wind rushing before a summer storm out upon the desert; breathy poems hurried under a moonlit sky—and he felt all his certainty fail.

Within the gates of the city, on the narrow street, ablaze with color and light, he saw Zoë on a balcony, looking down into the avenue, her hair a dark cloud shot with shining pearls. Khadijah was standing beside her. They were laughing, standing hand in hand. Below them, among the throng, a wizened old monkey with scarred hands was dancing in a circle of light, while drums pounded and men clapped a heady beat.

Both women turned towards him in welcome, one old, one young. Their glance was a blow, driving him to his knees. Seamed knuckles whitened on the staff and Mohammed felt his heart race, hammering in his chest. He could hear them calling, their voices all but drowned out by the cacophony of the city.

"This gate," he gasped, driving all thoughts of the flesh from his mind, forcing himself to his feet, "is closed."

Again, he stood erect, the staff grinding into the earth, before the gate.

"This gate is closed," he declaimed, voice growing stronger. His vision of the city wavered, distorting in a heat haze. The glad sounds died, growing faint and tinny, then ceasing altogether. "This gate," he repeated, "is closed!"

He raised the staff, striking the air. "Let the gate open!"

The clear air rippled away from his blow, walls and towers and houses contorting, growing large, then small in turns. Beyond the minarets, the sky darkened, a storm boiling out from the horizon. Lightning stabbed among seething gray-green clouds. Winds howled, rushing over the city. The ripples faded, clarity restored. Mohammed saw every face turn towards him, even the tiny old monkey. There was nothing in those eyes, not even the grief of the dead.

"Let the gate open!" he commanded, striking again with the staff.

Clear air splintered like a fractured plate. Mohammed heard a great sigh rise up from the forest behind him, the exhalation of countless voices. Wind tugged at his robe with ghostly fingers. He struck downward with the staff. Hanging fragments of sight and sound rushed away, scattered, driven by the winds howling around the Quraysh. Thunderheads rushed across the sky, flashing with lightning glare, plunging the plain into darkness.

Out of the corner of his eye, Mohammed saw shapes fly past, rushing forward in multitudes. The glassy air fell away into an infinite distance. Every fragment of the city receded with tremendous speed, then vanished. Only darkness remained, intermittently broken by flaring, jagged lightning. Beneath his feet, the grass shriveled and died, becoming crushed, black, glassy stone. Irregular pillars and monoliths were revealed in the howling wind and cloud. Harsh, metallic air bit at his lungs. Smoking hail pelted down from the sky, shattering on the towering rocks.

Mohammed stood at the edge of desolation, trembling with cold. He turned slowly, keen eyes tracing the horizon. His heart raced.

The massed dead were gone. So too were the white-barked trees, the hill, even the remains of the young fig that had sheltered him. There was no sign of the creature Mōha. *All was illusion*, he thought, starting to wrap a length of cloth across his mouth and nose. Then he stopped. *Is this any different?*

"Be still," he commanded, refusing to raise his voice above the raging storm. "Be still."

Wind whipped his robe back and forth, shrieking among the tumbled glassy stones. Mohammed felt his skin abrade, flayed by flying sand. His breath grew short, stolen by the poisonous air.

"I am still," he said to himself, closing his eyes. He shut out the sound of roaring wind, concentrating on the beat of his heart. It began to slow. He counted heartbeats, settling his breathing. "I am still."

The wind whimpered down to nothing, a bare gust eddying around his feet. Then it stopped. Everything became very quiet. Mohammed continued to count, stretching out the interval between breaths, between the trip-hammer blow of his heart. At last, it beat normally, his breathing steady and even. "I am still."

He opened his eyes. The storm was gone.

A flat black sky shimmered overhead, perfect as a starless night. There was no sun. He whistled softly in dismay and turned, surveying the plain. Crumbling, ruined boulders littered the earth. Splintered green-and-black glass covered the ground, twisted into fantastic shapes. A queer directionless light filled the air. Broken, cone-shaped spires delimiting the horizon cast no shadows.

In the silence, the sound of someone gasping for breath was very loud.

Mohammed turned towards the noise, seeing nothing but tumbled debris. The sound came again, a whimpering cry followed by unintelligible words. Raising an eyebrow—the sound, for no reason he could name, sounded *real*—he began climbing across the flinty slope, using the staff for support. There was no trail or path, but he managed to pick his way past the shattered translucent cones and across fields of splintered, gleaming obsidian.

He ducked through a wildly twisted curlicue of half-melted

metal, pierced with dozens of shattered bubbles, and found himself looking down upon a hollow in the earth. A man lay on the ground, back to an eroded, pockmarked slab of rust-streaked basalt. He was gasping for breath; a long, lean body savaged with scars and open wounds, his face seared with glassy burns. Crippled hands spasmed into fists. Mohammed stood at the edge of the hollow for a long time, watching the naked man shuddering on the black sand, crying out to himself in hideous pain.

At last, face graven with compassion, the Quraysh slid down into the pit and put his hand upon one withered shoulder. The man's eyes snapped open, staring wildly up at the sky. Slowly, as if he came back into himself from a vast distance, the man focused upon Mohammed's face. He blinked, trying to see, then stared in incomprehension.

"Hello, Ahmet," Mohammed said, leaning over his friend. "Do you remember me?"

The dead man blinked, then slow recognition bloomed in his broken face.

BENEATH THE TEMPLE OF AMON-RA, AT SÎWA
IN THE WESTERN DESERT

))I((

Groaning, Thyatis jerked awake, a hand flinching across her eyes. A pulsing hum filled her chest. Woozily, she stared around, expecting to find a courtyard flooded with unendurable brilliance. Instead, the soft light of oil lanterns bathed her face, illuminating bits and pieces of a huge, vaulted chamber. The Roman woman worked her jaw, fingers coming away damp with blood from her nose. Blinking tears away, she rose to her knees. The amulet between her breasts trembled with constant vibration.

Twenty feet away, three women in desert robes were straining atop a sandstone platform, iron pry bars in their hands. The

little blond Gaul, Betia, bent her shoulder among them, teeth
gritted in effort. Iron wedges scraped between the stone and a
ring of bronze. Under their feet, Thyatis could make out familiar interlocking gears and sweeping metallic arcs. This telecast
seemed ancient—not clean and polished like the one in
Rome—but corroded with age and ill-use.

Spitting to clear her mouth, Thyatis stood, shaking away a
pulsing sensation of vertigo. *What happened to me?* she wondered, checking her skull for a wound or a lump. *I must have
passed out.* The dizzy sensation was passing and she bent to
lift a wooden lantern sitting beside her. Warm yellow light
spilled across a floor of alternating blue-and-red hexagonal
tiles. Thyatis raised the lantern high, staring in wonder around
the chamber.

Fat-bellied pillars rose on either side, tapering towards a ceiling shrouded in darkness. Intertwined wave patterns ringed
each column. Beyond them, only partially illuminated by the
lantern, she saw soaring walls covered with massive, intricate
murals—blue waves crashed on rocky shores; men plied nets
from sharp-prowed boats; dolphins leapt and dove in the azure
sea; rocky islands thrust from the waves, peaks crowned with
brilliantly colored temples; long-necked dragons swam beneath
copper-colored waves, chasing eel-like fish; huge-winged birds
filled the sky, metallic wings shining under a glorious, warm
sun. Thyatis stared, mouth agape. She had never seen such
beauty in paint before. Without thinking, she stepped between
the pillars, swinging the lantern from side to side. The vibrant
colors seemed fresh, though instinctively she knew they must
be older than Rome or even Egypt.

The wall curved off to the left and right. The murals rose
thirty feet, or more, interrupted every ten or twelve paces by
fluted column roundels. She saw a great island covered with
rich fields and forests; a massive city formed of three ringed
canals dominated a flat plain beside the cerulean sea. Leaning
close, Thyatis could pick out delicately painted stadiums, gym-
nasiums, temples, plazas, gardens filled with glorious flowers,
villas, every kind of shop and foundry. At the center, a massive
palace complex filled a circular island, dominated in turn by a
golden-roofed temple.

What is this place? It's marvelous! Thyatis turned back to the central chamber, sandals slapping on marble tile. The Daughters were still struggling with the bronze disks.

"Let me help," she said, startled by the hoarseness of her voice. Betia looked up, relief plain in her oval face.

"Quickly," the Gaul said, sweat streaming down her pale neck. "We haven't any time!"

Thyatis nodded briskly, the last of the fog clouding her mind falling away. She sprang up a flight of steps onto the platform, barely noticing an enormous stone shape rising above them in the darkness—a kelp-bearded king, grim visage staring down out of the shadows, seated on a throne of stone, frozen marble waves crashing at his feet. The dais at his feet was sixteen feet wide, and the bronze disc sat in a circular depression bordered with dark green marble. The Roman woman accepted an iron pry bar, testing the weight in her hands, eyes narrowing as she surveyed the placement of the disc.

Flush on all sides, she saw with disgust. *But why not? At a sorcerer's command they will fly up, wrapped in flame . . .* She knelt, swift fingers running along the edges. The metal lay flush with the stone, though in some places the Daughters had already scored the marble with deep gashes, trying to find a point of leverage.

"This won't work," Thyatis muttered, shifting her attention to the center of the overlapping discs. "We need to—"

The sound of running feet interrupted her. Thyatis' head rose, squinting across the circle of lanterns. Another of the Daughters ran into the chamber, cloak billowing behind her.

"They're coming!" a familiar voice called, the woman sliding to a halt at the base of the dais. "The Romans are right behind me!"

Thyatis rose, staring down in mingled surprise and fear at Shirin's face. The Khazar woman stepped back, startled at the sight of a tall, broad-shouldered Roman above her, then smiled brilliantly in greeting. The Roman woman felt a sharp tension in her breast ease, her own smiling flickering in response.

"You're—"

A hoarse shout echoed from the unseen ceiling. Everyone turned. A flickering blue radiance danced in the entrance tunnel, shining on half-hidden statues of rearing bulls and bare-breasted goddesses.

"Go!" Thyatis snatched up her pry bar, waving the Daughters away. Her gaze locked with Shirin's for a fleeting instant. "Go, now!"

Two men stumbled out of the tunnel mouth, a blade filled with cold light raised above their heads. Thyatis recognized their outlines and the tread of their feet even before they emerged into lantern light.

"Quick," she called to Nicholas and Vladimir, "help me! I've found the cursed thing!"

Without waiting, she knelt on one knee, sliding the pry bar into the innermost bronze gear. Grimacing with effort, she wedged the iron into an eye-shaped opening, and then backed up, keeping tension on the bar. Both men scrambled up onto the platform, Nicholas staring at her in rage, Vladimir's eyes wide to see the pattern of arcs and gears set into the floor.

"Where were you?" Nicholas lunged at Thyatis, teeth bare. "My men were slaughtered up there!"

Thyatis caught his fist, feeling furious strength in his arm. Tensing, she pushed it aside with an open palm. "I heard you fighting," she said, swallowing a sick feeling at the lie, "but the way was open. I rushed ahead and found our prize."

Nicholas stared at her, the corner of his jaw twitching with muscle spasms. Thyatis' gaze did not waver.

"Our duty," she said softly, "is to find this device. Here it is. Now, we must be quick if we've any chance of getting away."

"How?" Vladimir looked up, sharp nails scratching at the junction of metal and stone. "There's no gap . . ."

"Like this," Thyatis said, turning away from Nicholas. He continued to stare at her with a fixed, unblinking expression. She threw her weight on the end of the pry bar, shoulders flexing as she pressed down. A metallic creaking answered her motion and the center disc groaned in protest. "Nicholas, help me. Vladimir, you stand ready to get your shoulder underneath. . . ." Bracing her legs, the Roman woman bore down again.

Nicholas dithered for an instant, eyes flicking back and forth between the bronze disc and the tunnel mouth and Thyatis. His nostrils flared, but Thyatis saw him take himself in hand with an effort of will. "Put your weight on this, with me," she ordered, beckoning with a tilt of her head.

The sound of a distant crash rippled through the air and the floor trembled a little under their feet. Snarling, Nicholas leapt to her side and together they dragged on the end of the iron bar. Squealing metal answered, then the entire bronze disc tilted up. Vladimir, poised and ready, ducked underneath, putting his own broad shoulders under the weight of metal.

"Vlad," Thyatis gasped, feeling her forearms burning with effort. "Can you lift this?"

A hollow grunt answered, then the Walach squared his legs, the tendons in his neck straining. Each of his hands curled back, groping across ancient gears until they found the edge, then long fingers curled around the beveled surface. Thyatis plucked the pry bar out of the eye-shaped opening—now twisted by the lever's pressure—and stepped back. Nicholas did the same, on the opposite side of the disc. Vladimir swayed a little, then found his footing.

"I can," he grunted. "But it will be slow."

"Good. Nicholas, you go with—"

Greenish-white light flared in the chamber, blinding Thyatis, casting long-reaching shadows from the pillars. She turned, automatically dropping into a guard stance. Nicholas was in motion as well, springing down onto the open floor, the runeblade glittering in his hands. The tunnel mouth flared with light, then the shadows of running men grew large on the walls.

Wheezing, Vladimir stumped down the flight of steps. Without stopping to consider, he followed the faint smudges of footprints on the age-old floor and the delicate traces of juniper and lavender in the air. A half-hidden passage yawned before him, slanting gently upwards.

Thyatis stared after the Walach with a sinking heart—*the Daughters fled that way, but how else will he get out?*—then groped at her waist for the hilt of her spatha. The weapon was gone, lost somewhere in a dream of blazing rainbow light. Swallowing, she stepped down onto the hexagon-tiled floor, taking the iron bar in both hands. *Your weapon is the mind*, ran a training chant in her memory, summoning up memories of sweat and clashing hardwood on the training floors of Thira.

Calmness settled over Thyatis as her body responded, shifting into line with the tunnel mouth, left hand leading, right high, cold iron nestled in her palms. Thyatis looked sideways at Nicholas. The Latin was watching her, though he'd fallen into a crouch, one hand run forward against the crossguard of his sword, the other almost on the pommel.

"You're not going?" Thyatis frowned.

Nicholas shook his head, and she could see a glint of barely repressed fury in his eyes. "What about our *duty*?" he snarled. "Two more lives for some rusted bronze . . ."

She nodded stiffly, acknowledging their dispute. Her own anger was beginning to spark in reaction to his. "Later, then."

Armored boots rang on stone and the black shapes of the Persians spilled from the tunnel mouth, spreading out across the floor. Instinctively, Thyatis and Nicholas drew apart, the woman drifting left, he to the right. As she moved, feet light on the floor, the Roman woman felt the air begin to cool. Watching the enemy, her eyes widened in surprise.

Though the curly-bearded Persian had stepped down onto the main floor, she was surprised to see him stand aside for another shape—a tall, hulking figure, enameled black armor gleaming in the lazy greenish white light hissing near the ceiling—this one flexing a cavalry blade of flat, dark metal. The thing's helmet was gone, revealing a withered skull and dark pits for eyes. The skin had contracted against the bone, revealing long incisors and jagged, dry scars.

The thing's head turned and Thyatis felt a physical shock—a rolling wave of frigid air chilled the sweat beaded on her arms and cheeks—and a growing, horrible sensation of something *other* curdled in her stomach.

"If you yield," the creature said, voice grating and echoing in a dead throat, "our master will give you new life and you will escape oblivion."

"Never!" Nicholas barked, spitting in the Persian's direction. Thyatis didn't waste her breath. Her attention was not focused on the horrific creature or the big Persian cavalryman but on the sorcerer she could see hiding in the shadows of the tunnel mouth, face drawn and gray, hands trembling. She dismissed two wounded Persians—mortal men by the sweat sheening their faces and the blood leaking from beneath mail hauberks—from her consideration, gaze flicking back to the dark captain.

"Resist and you will perish without hope of rebirth." The rattling-bone voice continued, as if the Latin's outburst had been inconsequential.

Thyatis let her body relax, each muscle falling into a long-accustomed pattern of motion. She advanced, the iron bar held loosely in her hands. Specificity faded from her vision, sharp-edged clarity fading into patterns of motion and intent. Nicholas was also moving, the glittering tip of Brunhilde dancing in the air. Her senses released from grasping consciousness, Thyatis felt a new shock, making her heart race in fear.

A dim yellow glow flared in the dead thing's eyes and a mind-crushing sense of vast oppression flooded the chamber. The dark captain stiffened, one claw-like hand convulsing. The lights dimmed, oil lanterns hissing out, the sputtering light dancing at the ceiling dimming abruptly. Only the blue-white flare of Nicholas' longsword remained and Brunhilde flared bright, though the shadows had grown pitch-black at the edges of the chamber.

You waste time, whispered a terrible voice, issuing more from the trembling air than the creature's throat. A chorus of crickets and squirming, rattling sounds fluttered at the edge of hearing. *Find the Eye!*

"*Haiii!*" Thyatis tore herself free of a drowning, choking sensation, leaping forward with a mighty bound. The iron bar lashed out, crunching across the face of the corpse-thing. Bone shattered, white fragments spinning away in the air and the head flew back. A blur of motion, Thyatis whipped the butt of the bar back, ramming the circular end into the withered cheekbone. The jawbone shattered, black dust jetting from empty eye sockets. The bar burst through the skull with a crackling sound.

The air condensed in terrific cold and Thyatis cursed, leaping aside, the iron bar lodged in the corpse's head. Mist boiled from the falling body and she felt the sweat on her face and hands and arms freeze, then shatter with a brittle sound as she moved.

A sodium glow flared bright in hollow eye sockets, then died. The crushing atmosphere lifted in a dizzying rush.

Chaos erupted in the chamber, the Persians charging Nicholas, Curly-beard dragging a singled-edged knife from his belt. Thyatis sprang back, cartwheeling towards the platform. The knife flashed past between her legs, clattering away from a pillar. She snatched up another pry bar.

She looked back, catching a frozen instant of time: Nicholas met the two Persians with his own rush and one man toppled, right arm sheared away. The Latin's blade keened with a high note, blood wicking away from watery metal. Curly-beard spun away from Thyatis, his mace swinging in a tight arc at Nicholas' back.

"Look out!" Thyatis shouted, springing forward.

Nicholas blocked a thrust by the other soldier, then swung back, his sword a blue flare in the darkness. The mace slammed into his crossguard with a ringing *tang*! The Latin cried out, blade flying from his grasp. Directly in front of Thyatis, the corpse-thing rose from the floor, one mailed hand grasping the iron bar. She skidded to a halt, stunned to see the creature still live and the dark captain wrenched the pry bar free from his ruined skull. A powerful wrist flicked and Thyatis threw herself to the side, still goggling in horror. Jagged iron slashed past, clanking from the side of the platform, then bouncing across the floor.

Gathering herself, Thyatis dodged in, swinging her iron stave in short, controlled arcs.

Nicholas scuttled backwards, gasping for breath. Curly-beard advanced swinging to his left, while the other Persian soldier dodged in from the right. The Latin had managed to claw a long knife from his belt, but the loss of Brunhilde left him feeling naked and powerless. She had never been far from his grasp in nine years and his left hand continued to grope reflexively for her familiar, wire-wrapped hilt.

The big Persian grinned, lunging in, cavalry sword darting in a sharp cut at Nicholas' head. The Latin sprang to the side, slashing automatically at Curly-beard's exposed arm. The knife cut empty air, nearly a foot short of the enemy. Sparks flew from a column as the Persian sword rang away from ancient stone. Nicholas gave ground, scrabbling backwards up a pair of steps and into the side gallery.

Out of the corner of his eye, Nicholas glimpsed movement and flinched away. The other Persian's sword blurred past, glancing from his arm. The legion armor clanked, but held, turning the blow. Nicholas spun, wrenching his arm from harm's way. The Persian soldier dragged his sword back into guard, but the Latin jumped in, kicking, and caught his thigh with a hobnailed sole. Cursing, the Persian scuttled back. Nicholas suppressed a wild urge to charge the man with only a knife, ducking away among the pillars instead.

Curly-beard leapt after him, shouting, and then the other Persian gave chase as well.

Thyatis pivoted, swinging the iron bar with the entire force of her upper body. The corpse-thing blocked with a forearm encased in overlapping black scales. Her blow clanged against heavy armor and bounced back. Struggling to keep hold of the vibrating bar, Thyatis kicked at the thing's knee. Her boot hit iron plate guarding the joint and glanced away.

Ignoring the blow, the corpse charged, throwing a gauntleted, spiked fist at her head. Thyatis blocked high, feeling incredible power in the undead arm, then rolled away. Breathless, she bounded up, smashing aside another punch with the iron bar. Sparks popped from the violent intersection of metal and metal. Thyatis gave ground, parrying desperately as the corpse stormed in, fists slamming at her face and body. The bar rang and rang again.

Gods, this thing is strong! Thyatis ran out of room, her back forced against the platform. Snarling, she gave a short rush, batting aside a swinging fist, hearing wire crack under the force of her blow, then jammed the bar shorthanded into the remains of the withered skull. More bone shattered, skittering across the floor. The other massive arm slammed across the front of the body, but Thyatis was inside its reach. She dropped to the floor, rolling out and up in a single, fluid motion.

Headless, the corpse swung towards her, metal scales bouncing away across sandstone.

Thyatis circled, tensed for the next attack. It came with a rush, corpse legs propelling the black shape towards her, arms spread wide for a grappling crush. The Roman woman's feet flashed on the floor, the iron bar swinging over her shoulder. She swung into a crouch as the dark shape slammed into her back, breastplate cracking against the iron bar. A smooth, effortless motion followed as she rotated shoulders, body, and a gracefully sinking leg into a fluid arc. The corpse-thing flew head over heels and slammed into the stone floor with a resounding crash.

Thyatis bounced up, exultant and immediately caught sight of a middle-aged Persian man with a neat beard and haunted, deep-set eyes. His fist punched towards her, haloed by whirling light and guttering flame. A roaring shriek filled the chamber, reverberating from the domed ceiling. The Roman woman threw herself forward, but she knew the reflex came just a grain too late.

Artabanus staggered, the hilt of a throwing blade jutting from his throat. He tried to cry out, but choked, blood flooding from his mouth, fouling in his beard. The power he'd summoned to hand ignited, blasting wildly across the chamber in a series of burning blue-white rings. Flame lashed across fat-bellied pillars, superheating the limestone. Smoke boiled away from stone and the plaster of the wall behind the row of columns burst alight. Almost invisible tongues of blue fire rippled across frozen waves, blackening cedar-crowned islands and masted ships.

Shirin bolted from the shelter of a hidden doorway, vaulting over a stone bench. She seized the hilt of her blade, then kicked the dying man free. Blood spattered on her robes, but the man's arm and hair were already burning, ignited by his own blast. Ignoring the hoarse gasps and drumming feet, she snatched up the long sword flickering dimly in the shadows.

"Roman! Catch!" Nicholas heard a strangely accented voice shout and darted out from behind a pillar. The wounded Persian soldier was dead ahead, startled and turning to look over his shoulder. A bar of dim blue-white flew overhead. Eyes wide in surprise and exaltation, the Latin leapt up, eager fingers seizing

Brunhilde from the air. He came down hard, then skipped aside, cursing in alarm.

Curly-beard's mace smashed on stone. Nicholas backpedaled, settling his grip.

Behind the Persian cavalryman, the Latin saw the wounded soldier topple, neck twisted at a strange angle. A woman in desert robes, long, glossy black hair whirling around her face, dropped to the ground, recovering from a spinning kick. Nicholas caught only a glimpse of her face, but the image burned in his memory—glorious brown eyes, a straight, noble nose, bow-shaped lips, a feral snarl of victory.

A reflexive block—nerve and muscle responding before conscious thought could interfere—saved him from losing his head and snapped attention back to the matter at hand. Curly-beard's cavalry sword licked back, but the big Persian shouldered in with his other hand, the flanged mace swinging hard at Nicholas' cross-guard. The Latin danced back, weaving Brunhilde in a figure eight. The Persian grinned, teeth white in a thick, black beard, advancing in a sideways scuttle.

Nicholas lunged in counter, sword tip flicking at the man's inner arm. The mace blocked with a ringing *clang* and then there was a flurry of blows, each man lunging and striking in turn, boots scuffling on tile, the ring and clash of steel harsh in the air.

Thyatis looked up from the floor, amazed to still feel life in her limbs, and groaned to see the glorious wall paintings rippling behind a sheet of flame. Smoke boiled into the air, filling the apse of the ceiling. A dull roar grew, coupled with a staccato cracking sound as ancient stone expanded in the heat. Plaster shivered, splitting along ancient foundation lines, millennia-old dust mixing furiously with burning paint. She scrambled to her feet, groping on the hex tiles for a weapon.

Only yards away, the shape of the dark captain shuddered on the floor, then rose, spilling black dust, fragments of bone and broken iron scales. The head was entirely gone and one arm hung limply at its side. Thyatis swallowed, backing up, mouth dry in fear. The shape stood, leaning a little to one side, then lurched toward her. The crushing pressure was building in the air again.

"Let's go!" Shirin seized her arm, dragging Thyatis back. "Look later, you dumb ox!"

Thyatis tried to speak, but the dreadful vision of the undead thing reaching for her held her captive, a cobra's prey hypnotized by the swaying hood. Shirin slapped her hard on the side of the head. Blazing pain in her ear snapped Thyatis out of her daze and she skipped back, shouting in fear, from clutching iron fingers.

Together, they sprinted out of the chamber, away from the shambling corpse-thing and into the shadowed side tunnel. Behind them, Artabanus convulsed on the floor in the final throes of death, the gradient of his evocation rushing to violent release, lightning leaking from his mouth and eyes, flaring ruby red through vaporizing blood. A stunning *crack* rolled and boomed in the chamber, coterminous with an incandescent flare of white light.

Nicholas stumbled backwards, blinded by a stuttering roar, and tripped over the body of one of the Persian soldiers. His head smashed against tile and he felt the room spin, then vanish in a billowing cloud of gray-black smoke. He coughed weakly, unable to rise. Someone ran past him, but he couldn't see who it was. Smoke burned in his throat and pinched a flood of tears from his eyes. Flames roared closer, the heat beating at his face like a hammer.

The sight of Thyatis fleeing the hall, hand in hand with the desert woman, abandoning him, was all too clear in his memory. He wept in frustration, rolling over, head throbbing with dull, thudding pain. He'd dropped Brunhilde again. Blinded, he groped wildly on the floor, searching for her.

D ahvos mounted a broad flight of steps with a swift pace,
noon sun gilding his wheat-colored hair. Full summer
rendered the day hot and bright, hazing with steadily rising humidity. He did not pause on the threshold of the high doorway,
though a moment passed before his eyes adjusted to the dimness within. Guardsmen—attired in full Legion armor and
bearing the sunburst flash of the comes Alexandros—drew
back, seeing a grim, fixed expression on the Khazar's face. The
easterner's riding boots rang sharply on dimpled marble floor-
ing as he entered, drawing the attention of nearly everyone in
the vast hall.

Clerks and captains alike looked up and a frustrated looking
priest started towards Jusuf, hand raised in admonition, then
halted, seeing the glitter in the khagan's eyes. Like the lesser
temples in the city, the house of Zeus was a long rectangle, but
it beggared all others for sheer size. The central nave was
nearly five hundred feet from end to end, and each aisle of pillars was of gargantuan size, for they supported two decks of
galleries overlooking the main floor.

High above, a series of vast circular windows piercing the
walls, once filled with colored glass, had been reduced to spiderwebs of copper and iron—allowing thick, dust-sparkling
beams of sunlight to fall in brilliant pools on the floor below. In
the harsh light, much of the temple interior was in deep shadow
and the domed ceilings—ornamented with lavish golden mosaics—were hidden from the casual eye.

At the far end of the nave, in a circle of sunlight, the comes
Alexandros hunched over a trestle table covered with papers,
maps, cups and wooden ledgers. A block of heavy, plain stone
rose behind the Macedonian, draped with irregular dark cloth.
Dahvos approached, alone, without his customary escort or the

constant shadow of his half-brother. Alexandros did not look up, an expression of complete concentration on his shadowed face.

One of the Goths arrayed around the table turned at the unexpected noise, squinting out of the pool of sunlight. Dahvos brushed past him without a word and the northerner darkened in rage at the affront. "Here now," he growled, beard bristling out.

He reached to lay a meaty hand on the Khazar's shoulder. Dahvos turned, fixing the man with a basilisk stare. His face was a mask of light and dark, but the Goth saw something in glittering blue eyes and lowered his hand. "Pardon, my lord . . ." he stammered.

Dahvos' nostrils flared minutely, then he turned to the shorter, lither man still standing, staring at the maps and charts laid out before him on the table. "Lord Alexandros."

"Kagan Dahvos," the Macedonian replied without looking up.

The Khazar expressed no obvious reaction at the slight, though the angry gleam in his eyes deepened. Instead, he drew a parchment packet from his belt and laid the cream-colored paper on the table. "These . . . orders . . . arrived in my encampment last night. You sent them?"

Alexandros glanced up, raised an eyebrow, then returned his attention to the maps. "Yes."

A faint, wintry smile glanced across Dahvos' lips, then vanished again. "The Roman army has completed preparations for a campaign across the Propontis? You have sufficient supplies? Enough shipping, wagons, pack animals, servants?"

Alexandros nodded, finally looking up from the letter he had been reading, eyes flickering around the circle of men waiting at the edge of the light. "So the orders said, kagan."

Dahvos folded back the first page of the packet with his finger. " 'You command my . . . *auxillia* . . . to cross in advance of your main body,' " he read, " 'to secure the opposite shore and disperse any Persian resistance in the neighborhood of Chalcedon. The Roman army will follow the subsequent day.' " The Khazar looked up, lips thinning in a humorless smile.

Alexandros nodded in agreement. "That is correct."

"Ships are mentioned—merchant ships and barges—which will provide transport for the crossing. Many are named, as are their captains." Dahvos' forefinger transfixed a second sheet in the packet.

"Yes." Alexandros stood up straight, his face filled with weary resignation. "They were."

Dahvos met his eyes and Alexandros blinked, all too aware of the furious anger boiling behind the Khazar's bland, controlled expression. The kagan bared his teeth in a tight smile. "These ships you mention, *comes*, are in my direct employ. They were—they *are*—hired to provide my army with supplies, hospital and transport." Dahvos' voice began to rise, a sharp tone coloring his words. "My men, my cataphracts, lancers, bowmen, scouts, sutlers, blacksmiths . . . they are *my* men. Under my command."

Alexandros raised a hand in a sharp motion. "Kagan Dahvos, I under—"

"My *nation*," Dahvos snapped, overriding the Macedonian, "is a Roman ally, not a subject." He looked around at the officers and captains watching with wide eyes, then back to Alexandros with a long-toothed grin. "We are not sworn to the Emperor, we are not *feodus*. We came to fight beside our *friends*, against the Persians." The Khazar picked up the packet with the tips of his thumb and forefinger, dangling the papers in the air. "Allies are *consulted*, not ordered. Allies are equals, not servants."

The packet fell, clattering on the tabletop, papers spilling awry among the cups and inkstones.

Alexandros stiffened, hand brushing a wayward lock of hair from his high forehead, eyes narrowing. His jaw tightened for a moment, then anger receded, driven down by an almost visible effort of will. "Then I will ask, Kagan Dahvos—will you cross the Propontis, to clear the way into Asia?"

Dahvos said nothing, watching the Macedonian from shadowed eyes. Alexandros stared back, at perfect ease. The moment stretched, grains tumbling from an invisible clock. At last, Dahvos stirred, saying: "I will cross the strait with my fleet and my army. If there are Persians lurking among the summer houses and villas, we will drive them out. This much, we will do for the memory of Heraclius, who was my uncle's friend."

Pursing his lips, Alexandros considered the kagan. He

waited, but there were no further words. "Your . . . fleet . . . will not return?"

Dahvos shook his head slowly; face mask-like in the slanting sunlight. "On the second day and after, we will press on, into the east. The army of Khazaria will make its way home along the shore of the Sea of Darkness, through Paphlagonia and Colchis. If the Persians or their servants bar our way, we will strike them down." He paused, looking around the circle. "But we will not do your bidding. You can find your own way across the Propontis."

With a barely polite nod, Dahvos turned away and strode away across the vast floor. He did not look back, though his keen ears heard a scuffle, men muttering and a sharp, commanding voice call for quiet. At the doorway, Dahvos paused, running a hand along the marble frame. Panels of tiny figures surrounded the portal, showing men and women at daily tasks, marvelous in their diverse array. He bit his lip, took a heavy breath and then went out, clattering down the steps with a steadily lifting mood. He wiped soot-blackened fingers on his riding trousers.

By the time he reached the plaza he was smiling. Jusuf was waiting astride a slate-colored mare, her mane twined with ribbons and feathers, holding Dahvos' own mount. A troop of his own lancers stood ready, their gear and armor packed, lances polished, bows securely cased in painted leather cases, quivers packed with newly fletched arrows.

"We're going home," the kagan said, swinging up onto his horse. The dappled gray snorted, pawing the ground. She wanted grass and raw earth under her hooves, not streets of painful cobblestones and cracked marble. "To the camps, then to the port."

The city sprawled untidily around them as they rode west, towards the shattered towers of the Charisian Gate, mile after mile of blackened, brick-faced buildings crowding the avenue. In many places, the buildings had been completely consumed by fire, reduced to shattered piles of rubble. Solitary arches of an aqueduct loomed against the sky, the watercourse fallen in ruin. The sound of hooves on stone rang and echoed from empty doorways and gaping windows. They trotted past work gangs digging in the destruction, clearing the entrances to the baths and public cisterns.

Life was returning the city, in fits and starts. The arrival of Alexandros' army had drawn some survivors from their hiding places, but not all. Strange rumors circulated in the camps—mysterious cook fires had been found, littered with cracked bone—haggard shapes glimpsed at night by patrols, flitting from shadow to shadow, or eyes gleaming from the darkness beyond the watch fires. Dahvos would be glad to leave this place.

"No," Alexandros said, shaking his head at Chlothar's angry suggestion. "Let him go."

"But, my lord! The Persians have scattered, we can—"

The Macedonian raised an eyebrow at the Frank's outburst and the big man closed his mouth with a snap. Alexandros looked down at the table again, allowing himself a heartfelt sigh. A letter—delivered only the hour before—lay unfolded atop a map of the city and the strait, new parchment covered with a swift, sure hand in blue-black ink. He read the terse directive again, then set the paper aside. The maps of Asia taunted him, showing a monstrous network of roads—*good roads too*, he thought, *well-drained and surfaced, which do not mire with mud or rain, or become impassible with the winter snow*—and thriving cities. Rome had been busy all the long centuries while he slept.

Once, he had led an army across these lands—through wilderness and trackless ways, on paths marked by no more than piled stones—and even then his advance had been a bolt of lightning, a thunderstoke . . . He traced a path on the map with his fingertips, reading tiny names inked beside carefully drawn cities. *Nicomedia*, he read. *Germa, Tyana, Antioch* . . . then the door to Persia and Babylon. *An empire . . . my empire*.

Longing stabbed in his gut, a tight fist twisting his entrails. Alexandros bit the inside of his lip and closed his eyes. After a moment, the spasm passed. "Chlothar . . ."

"My lord?" The Frank was watching him, worry etched on his long face.

"We have received new orders," Alexandros said, tasting bile at the back of his mouth. "Let the Khazars go—they will do us no harm and they will keep the Persians across the water occupied." He gestured for his officers to gather around the table. "The trouble in Egypt has grown worse. The King of Kings Shahr-Baraz is there, with a powerful army. The Caesar Aurelian is hard-pressed. By now, he may be besieged in Alexandria itself."

The officers, Goth and Roman alike, blanched at the Macedonian's even, emotionless words.

"The Emperor Galen bids us take ship for Egypt with all speed, with every man we can put aboard." Alexandros flashed the men a cheerful smile. "Of course, there is no fleet to take us to Egypt. Not yet. My latest report relates the Western fleet is at Tarentum in southern Italia, refitting and being reinforced by squadrons from Gaul and Britannia." The smile shaded into a half-grin and the Macedonian tugged ruefully at his chin. "The quartermasters will be pleased, I'm sure, to learn our hard-won levy of wagons and draft animals and fodder will now go for naught."

Another sharp pain, this one of raw disgust, throbbed in Alexandros' chest. He had prepared meticulously, for months, for a land campaign in Asia and Syria. His own Legion had swollen to nearly twenty-five thousand men—more Goths, more barbarians from over the border, expatriate Huns, Germans and even a smattering of Avars cut loose from their defeated army—and nearly every man had a horse to ride, or a mule to carry his baggage. Six thousand wagons had been secured or made. A hundred thousand arrows, countless spears, horseshoes, rope by the mile, barrels and baskets, sword flats and iron plate. The one Western Legion he had held back from the Egyptian campaign, the veteran Third Augusta—*Faithful Pegasus*—was once more at full strength. Hundreds of deserters from the Legions shattered before Constantinople had filtered back out of the hills. Shamed men had begged to serve again, regaining their honor. One in ten had paid the price for cowardice, while the others were carefully scattered among reliable units. Those men fought under the eagle again, but each started afresh, no more than the lowliest legionary, no matter if they had been officers before.

The standards of two Eastern Legions had been recovered

from the Persian camp in the old palace. Beneath them, Alexandros had organized the motley collection of Eastern cataphracts and individual soldiers who had survived the siege and the destruction of the city. Fourth Parthica—*Capricornus*—and Sixth Ferrata—*Old Ironclad*—were each nearly at full roster and eager to prove themselves, though the Macedonian did not trust them to the crucible of battle, not quite yet. Soon, though.

"We will not be crossing into Asia," he said. The words had a bitter, bitter taste. "Demetrios, I will leave you the Fourth and the Sixth with these orders: to hold Constantinople and these lands around, to restore order in Thrace and Macedon. Be cautious, but do not hide in the city. Ensure the people can return to their homes, that the aqueducts are repaired, the cisterns opened. The strait is open and trade will resume, as it always does. You must clear the harbor and the docks of wreck and ruin. Commerce must find a home here again. The city will live, though she has been sorely wounded." Alexandros caught the man's eyes and held them fiercely. "You hold this place in trust for the young Emperor. Know he will return to judge your stewardship! I hold you to the same measure."

Demetrios swallowed, then nodded sharply. The nobleman's prickly anger and pride had worn away during their campaign to reclaim the city. He had seen the skill and bravery of the Goths and the Western legionaries. In the beginning, his own men had not fared so well, but now they had heart. They had tasted victory again and served under their own standards and banners. Such things gave men a sense of place and surety.

"I will, Lord Alexandros." Demetrios bowed to the Macedonian. Alexandros could see the man's thoughts turn to the mighty task set before him and smiled as the Greek's face became somber. *There is hope for one of them, at least. While he is willing to think, and to listen.*

"Chlothar . . ." Alexandros stopped himself from sighing again. There was work to be done and no time for laments. "Prepare our men, and the Third Augusta, for transport by sea. Lord Demetrios will win custody of our wagons and horse. Tarentum is . . . two weeks away, by sea? We will have no more time than that, I'm sure."

The Frank's face screwed up like a puckered quince and

Alexandros felt the same disgust. Months of heavy labor cast
aside . . . their swift-mounted army would now ride, crammed
like goats into a stinking hold, then walk to battle, wherever the
wind had taken them.

Horses neighed angrily, struggling in their hoods. Grooms and
cataphracts alike crowded around the lading ramp of the barge,
hands seizing cables and ropes, others pressed against heavy,
sweaty brown flanks. The first of the Khazar chargers kicked,
splintering a wooden stay, knocking a man into the water. Spray
fountained up and the plainsman struggled out, drenched, water
lilies in his hair. Jusuf, watching from the shore, jogged down,
bare feet squelching on the muddy beach.

The barge had been acquired the previous year in Chersonessos on the northern shore of the Sea of Darkness. Months of
travel around the verge of the brackish sea had seen Khazar
shipwrights cut away the bow to install a levered bridge that
winched down on a beach or sloping shore, letting the horses
carried within trot safely to land. Splashing out into the muddy
water, he reached the end of the ramp. On this section of shoreline, the sea had proved shallower than expected.

For two miles in either direction, here opposite the great
city, the Khazar army was unloading in a confused, riotous
mass of men, ships, barges, boats, horses and wagons. Somewhere to the north, Kagan Dahvos and the main body were unloading at the port of Damalis, in a proper harbor, with lading
cranes and winches. Here, two men pitched to and fro on the
ramp, trying to hold it down by main strength. The horses
could smell water in front of them and bucked, neighing in
fear. Jusuf waded up, just as a fine-looking gelding clattered
forward, long mane flying.

"Watch out!" shouted one of the men, a dark-haired Greek
with shoulders like Atlas. Jusuf nimbly avoided a flying hoof,
swinging up onto the ramp. With his added weight, the wood
settled into the water and he caught a flying rein, pulling the
horse's big square head close to his own. Hot breath whuffed in
his face, and Jusuf grinned in delight.

"Easy, easy there." The gelding shied away, pulling at the
rein, but the Greek had climbed up as well and laid gentle hands

on the horse's shoulder. Between the two men, they managed to coax the gelding into the water and then to dry land. Smelling one of their own safely ashore and hearing him chomp noisily on carrots and apples proffered by Jusuf from a leather sack at his waist, the rest of the horses followed in better humor.

The troop of cavalry—a *jegun*, as the T'u-chüeh would say—gathered under a copse of trees an arrow's flight from the shore. Jusuf and his guardsmen had tethered their own horses in the shade. He passed among the cavalrymen, taking their measure, speaking to some he knew from the markets of Itil. They were southern Khazars, from Samandar the White beside the Salt Sea. Jusuf was pleased with their spirit—everyone was cheerful and eager to be home again. Some of the men cast covetous eyes on the rich, loamy soil and the hillsides covered with orchards and gardens. The plains of Khazaria were neither so rich nor so plentiful in their yield. Jusuf did not think any would stay in the warm south, though he allowed he could be mistaken. He missed the open sky and endless, rolling vistas of the steppe. This land was too hot, too close and too crowded.

Reaching his horse, the tarkhan's heart lifted to see a heavy enameled bow case still slung on the saddle. Two of his guardsmen had remained with their mounts while Jusuf had gone down to the shore. Horseflesh was highly prized, even among the dirt farmers. He ran a proprietary hand over the black case. The bow within was nestled in Roman cloth as soft as a woman's hair. Nervous to see the weapon so exposed, he turned a corner of the riding blanket over the painted wood.

"Ready, tarkhan?" His guardsmen were mounted and ready, each man on a different mount than he'd brought ashore in the morning. The army was preparing for a long march; soon they would be alternating walking and riding to spare the horses. Jusuf nodded absently, taking a last look around the grove of trees, measuring the faces of the men and the health of the horses in the jegun. As he did, his eye lit on the same dark-haired Greek cinching the bellyband of a Khazar horse, a scab-barded gladius and axe swinging from a strap over his shoulder. *What is this? A Greek among us?*

"Wait a moment." Jusuf ran his hand gently across the bow case before striding off through the high grass. His guardsmen sighed, then settled in to wait. Who knew what these officers were doing? The kagan had declared the army would land and then march east along the main highway until they reached the town of Kosilaos, all in a single day. Twenty miles from the Chalcedonian shore, more or less. A late night's camp, they grumbled.

"What is your name, soldier?"

The Greek looked up and Jusuf slowed to a halt, struck by the man's odd dark eyes. This close, the Khazar was impressed by the scars—old and new—making a tracery on his exposed arms and neck. The broad shoulders were no illusion either, feeding powerful arms and wrists like tree roots. A *legionary*, Jusuf guessed. *How odd*.

"Ruf—no, call me Hippolytus, my lord," the man answered. As he did, a peculiar expression of relief filled his face. "Hippolytus," he said again, taking his time with the word.

"You're a Roman soldier," Jusuf said. "Why do you ride with Bulan's *jegun?*"

The Greek offered a slight smile, causing a deep scar at the corner of his mouth to twist like a snake. "I was a soldier for the old Emperor," he said in a deep voice. "Heraclius is dead, and his son taken into the west." Hippolytus shrugged, making his mailed breastplate shimmer. "There is nothing for me in the Empire anymore. I wish to go to a new land and begin a new life, far from Rome and Achaea and everything here."

Jusuf nodded slowly, searching the man's face. It was weathered and old, graven by many misfortunes and mischance. *How old is this man?* The black eyes seemed fathomless, barely reflecting the dappled sunlight. A sense of enormous, long-held grief radiated from him. Grief and terrible loss. There was something familiar about him too. . . . The Khazar felt a chill raise the hackles on his arms and neck but then the moment passed. Just another elderly Greek soldier with too many memories.

"You've sworn fealty to the kagan, then? Accepted his bread, placed your hand on his stirrup?"

"Yes," the Greek said, placing a broad palm over his heart.

"Then," Jusuf said, striking upon a thought and finding it pleasing. "You will ride with me, and my guardsmen—your Turkic is not so good, I'd imagine?"

"No," laughed the Greek, "but I find languages easy."

"Good. Ride with me, then, and I will teach you the ways of our people, Hippolytus."

"Very well." The Greek turned to Bulan, who had ridden up to see what transpired. "Captain—this man wishes me to go with him—is this meet?"

"Thief of a prince," Bulan growled at Jusuf, making the tarkhan smile. "Recruiting your own war band, are you? I'll trade him to you, my lord, for a brace of your Thessalian mares."

Jusuf raised an eyebrow at Bulan's bold words. "You've grown avaricious down among these Greeks! I'll gift you a wagon instead, with sprung wheels and a tarp."

"Done." The beki jegun grinned as well, showing gappy yellow teeth. The Khazar spat on the ground, then clasped wrists with Jusuf. "And done."

"Come then." Jusuf waved the Greek towards his guardsmen, who had taken the opportunity to lie down in the grass under the trees. Two men remained on watch, while the others napped. "We've a hard ride, before night falls. The kagan wishes to be gone from Roman lands with all haste."

Hippolytus nodded in agreement, swinging up onto his horse. For a moment, he looked back, across the broad, sparkling waters of the Propontis, at the domes and towers of the city shining in the afternoon sun. A bleak look crossed his face, but then he turned away, idly scratching at a still-healing scar on his breast. The wound was itching under the breastplate, but he knew the angry, reddish flesh would knit soon, leaving only one scar among many.

)=(

Vladimir crouched in a thicket of low-lying shrubs, thick, waxy leaves tickling his face. The gray plants, mixed with stands of ragweed and nightshade, covered a low hill south of the promontory holding the temple of Amun-Ra. From the rise, Vlad could peer down through drooping palms at the road descending into the village. Behind him, the vast expanse of a shallow lake gleaming silver in the moonlight stretched out into the desert. The red moon was nearly touching the western horizon and the Walach could smell dawn coming.

He was panting, exhausted from carrying the heavy bronze disc out through the long, narrow tunnel. At the end of the passage, a ladder leading up into the floor of a house on the outskirts of the abandoned town had nearly stymied him. The muscles in his back and legs cramped painfully, reminding him of the enormous effort required to hoist the metal contraption up through the trap-door.

Smoke billowed silently into the night sky, obscuring the forest of pillars and single round tower crowning the hill. Intermittently, flashes of reddish and orange light washed over the walls of the ancient buildings. Vladimir felt his throat tighten each time. Nicholas and Thyatis were inside, somewhere. *They are probably dead*, he thought mournfully. *And I can't find Betia!*

The little blond girl's trail had vanished in the town, lost among the stink of human habitation and rotting flesh. The exit house of the tunnel had been filled with corpses. The dead were well preserved in this dry, salt-tinged air, but the slow business of corruption was taking its inevitable hold. Vladimir grinned cheerlessly in the dark. *I know why the stone houses are so silent*. Soon the ants and beetles would find the drying flesh and reduce the corpses to a carpet of white bone.

Motion on the road caught his eye and he stiffened, wide

dark eyes drinking in the faint moonlight. Three figures descended the sloping ramp in haste, flitting between the obelisks and sphinxes. A deep, angry growl rumbled in his throat. *Persians*. Even at this distance, the Walach recognized the striding gait of the curl-bearded horse rider. The other two shapes, dark on dark, sent a shiver down his spine and triangular nails dug sharply into the ground. *Curse it! The corpse walkers survived*.

Vladimir swallowed, distraught. These Persian creatures were not the *surâpa* of his homeland—they did not go abroad in the guise of living men—they were something worse, something made, cobbled together from corpses and venom and old, dry-smelling evil. He had felt their tremendous strength, traded blows with their tireless arms, seen the snake-quickness of their movements. There was no way he could face all three of them and win—not this young, still green Walach! One of the old ones . . . they might know a chant to strike down this enemy, but he did not.

Despite a trembling urge to flee, to lope away across the desert, to run until he was in green forest and meadowed glade again, Vladimir remained crouched on the hill, watching, while the three Persians disappeared among the crumbling walls of the town. Some time later, while he watched and waited, he saw them emerge from the date palm orchards beside the lake. Then he flashed a white grin in the darkness, for they stooped over a trail he had laid himself. A little later, he saw them again, spread out to cover more ground, entering the desert east of the oasis.

"Now," he growled to himself, rising up, shaking sand and prickly leaves from his back and thighs. "There's a little time." Patting the telecast lying half-buried in the sand beside him, he crept down the hill, then ran swiftly through the streets of the town and began to climb the long ramp to the temple.

Hoarse coughing, like a bellows rasping at a forge, lent speed to Vladimir's sore legs and he jogged into the little courtyard at the top of the hill. Ahead, the great doorway into the sanctuary was limned with leaping flame. Dirty white smoke poured out of the temple from windows and doors, twisting away into the night. A hammerhead cloud of smoke and vapor built in the otherwise clear sky, lit from below by a sullen orange glare. Vladimir tore off his tunic, wrapping the grimy linen around his face, then—squinting—he plunged into the smoke, keeping low to the floor.

The great statue loomed ominously, red flame beating at sandstone legs, stern face staring down through coiling fumes. The pit at the god's feet hissed and roared, jetting fire. Vladimir crawled to the edge of the stone shaft, ears back flat against his head. Something moved on the stairs—a huddled shape, wracked with terrible, hollow coughing—wrapped desperately in a blood-stained cloak.

"Nicholas!" the Walach shouted, cry muffled by the cloth over his mouth. A stiff wind gusted out of the pit, feeding the fire roaring in the tunnel mouth. Heedless of the heat, Vladimir plunged down the stair. Nicholas grasped feebly at the step above him. The Walach snatched him up, batting at tiny flames leaping on the man's clothes, then staggered back up the steps.

The effort of dragging the telecast out into the desert came back, his calves and thighs trembling with the effort of each step. Barely able to breathe, Vladimir went down on both hands, Nicholas clinging to his back like a cub and scuttled for the door. Moments later, the Walach rolled on his back, gasping, sucking clean, cold air into his lungs. His eyes streamed with tears and the choking, bitter smell of smoke clogged his nostrils.

Beside him, Nicholas heaved weakly, barely able to move. His cloak and tunic smoldered, littered with glowing embers.

"There. They got out." Thyatis breathed a sigh of relief. She rose, biceps and back aching with fatigue. She could still feel the impact of the corpse-thing's blows vibrating in her forearms. Keeping her head low, Thyatis slid down the dune to where the others were waiting. Three of the women, shrouded from head to foot in long robes and heavy veils, turned away as they clucked at the pack camels. One of the beasts groaned in protest and drew a slap across the snout for his trouble. A bulky package was strapped to the creature's back, tied down with cords and wrapped in woolen blankets.

A smaller shape—Betia—watched Thyatis for a moment, a

dim outline against the predawn sky, then she too turned away to slog down the long reverse face of the dune, sand slipping and sliding under her feet. The Roman woman swayed a little, feeling exhaustion cramping her legs, stealing their strength. The last figure, cloaked like the others, her breath a faint white puff in the deep cold of the desert night, stood watching Thyatis in silence. One camel remained, kneeling on the slope, reins clutched in the figure's hand.

Thyatis felt like a fool, at a loss for words after envisioning this moment for so long.

"You look wretched," the woman said at last, her voice tinged with a smoky rasp.

"I . . ." Thyatis stumbled into silence again, her thoughts a wild jumble. She felt dizzy again, fear churning in her stomach. Unable to stand, she squatted on the sand, one hand out to support herself. "I should go back . . . with them."

"To Rome?" Shirin settled beside her. Her voice was soft. "To the Emperor?"

"They are my men," Thyatis said, head down. She was having trouble breathing. "They'll think I've—"

"Betrayed them," the Khazar woman said, stretching her hand out, a black shadow creeping across faintly gleaming sand. "Penelope told me about the device. You've done your duty by the Order, keeping the telecast from those men. From your Emperor."

Thyatis coughed hoarsely. Smoke bit at her lungs. "Those two are my responsibility. They are *my* command. I can't abandon them in this wasteland." Dizziness whirled away, leaving her head feeling empty and drained.

Shirin caught her shoulders, easing Thyatis back onto the sand. Gentle fingers pressed against the Roman woman's forehead, her throat, her hands. "You're far too cold! You've been hurt," Shirin said. "Are you bleeding?"

Thyatis shook her head weakly, staring up at the stars. In the chill air, she could smell Shirin very clearly—a subtle mix of sweat and crisp linen and roses. She was very tired and a cold sea of sleep lapped around her legs. "I . . . I don't think so. There's just so much . . ."

Grunting, Shirin hooked her fingers into the leather straps holding the clamshell halves of the Roman lorica together. Digging her feet into the sand, the Khazar woman dragged Thyatis to the kneeling camel. Grimacing, her own muscles complaining at the heavy weight, Shirin rolled the Roman onto the camel's back, drawing a honk of outrage. Disgusted, the beast rose on ungainly legs. Shirin danced around the splayed feet, avoiding a kick, keeping Thyatis from falling.

The Roman woman *oofed* in pain, the high-cantled saddle digging into her stomach. A moment later, the camel began ambling down the slope in a swaying gait. Shirin ran alongside, one hand wrapped in the lead. Thyatis squirmed weakly, then fell still in exhaustion.

Later, the ground leveled out. Shirin could see the others far ahead, a sparse line of humped silhouettes against a slowly brightening eastern horizon. Wind ruffled her cloak, drawing the veil away from the Khazar's face. They passed scattered black stones, pitted and scored with dimpled cavities.

"You cannot go back to his service," Shirin said gently, seeing Thyatis had woken from her daze. "You balanced two masters for a long time, but in the end, you must choose between the Empire and the Island."

The Roman woman groaned, then pushed herself up, swinging one leg forward over the saddle. Her face was flushed with blood from hanging upside down, tangled hair in disarray, her armor dented and stained with smoke. Shirin laughed, watching her rub grime away from bloodshot eyes.

"What?" Thyatis tried to glare, but lacked the energy for more than a befuddled stare.

"I missed you." Shirin put her hand on Thyatis' sandal, slim fingers wrapping around her toes. "All smelly and disheveled, stinking of iron and blood." The Khazar woman smiled up at her friend.

"Like old times," Thyatis croaked. If anything, she was looking worse, staring at Shirin with empty, hollow eyes. "Shi— you should know—your children . . . your children are—"

"They are dead," Shirin said, squeezing Thyatis' foot. "I know. I found their bodies."

"You . . . you did?" Thyatis' eyes widened, a pale streak of tears oozing down her cheek. "How? I looked and looked in the ruins . . ."

Shirin nodded, leaning her head against the camel's flank. The creature was warm, gut rumbling with digestion, hide smelling of tamarisk and broken shale. "The cook . . . the Duchess's cook told me where to find them. But everything was gone, all burned houses and naked trees and ash. I had to . . . dig. But I did and laid them to rest afterwards." She looked up at the sky, starlight gleaming on her face. "They are with the sky-father now, in peace and plenty."

"Shi—I . . ." Thyatis stopped, coughing, then cleared her throat. She switched the camel on the top of its head, making the creature grumble and slow to a halt. The Roman woman slid down, landing heavily. Shirin caught Thyatis with a hand on her elbow, keeping her from falling on her face.

"You should stay on the camel," Shirin said with asperity. "You might not have been cut, but you're certainly bruised within an inch of your life."

"No," Thyatis said, standing away from the Khazar woman. She squared her shoulders, chin rising. "There's more. I . . . I was responsible for them, for the blast. We fought on the mountaintop . . ." Thyatis' voice trailed away, then she rallied. "I was too slow, Shirin, and all those people were killed. Your children were killed, because I looked away at the wrong moment."

Shirin stared at the Roman, lips twisting into a surprised grimace, then settling into a tight, hard line. "What are you talking about?" Her eyes glittered, even in the encompassing darkness. Thyatis took an involuntary step back, licking her lips.

"The Duchess sent me—sent us—to murder Prince Maxian. He was hiding out in a villa on the slopes of Vesuvius. I nearly had him in the crater—my knife was at his throat!" Thyatis' voice slewed into a harsh growl. "But it wasn't enough. The mountain erupted. I think . . . I think he did something, disturbed something, and Vesuvius just . . . blew apart."

Shirin stood silent and Thyatis waited. After awhile, she sat down, still waiting, but too tired to stand. The eastern sky brightened steadily, shading from deep blue to pink and then a pearl white. Finally, Shirin stirred, shaking the cowl of her djellabah back. She faced the sun, long hair a wavy cloud behind her head, and she breathed deep, holding her arms wide. The dawn wind was dropping, reduced to gusts and zephyrs scudding across the barren plain.

"This prince . . . what was his name?"

Thyatis looked up, startled at the grim determination in the woman's voice. "Maxian Atreus, the younger brother of Emperor Galen."

Shirin nodded to herself, fine white teeth biting her lower lip. "A wizard? A sorcerer?"

"Yes." Thyatis watched her friend with growing puzzlement. "Shi—I'm sorry."

The Khazar woman stepped to the Roman and held out her hands, an expression of deep and abiding grief making her cheeks hollow and her eyes dark pits smudged with pain. Thyatis took them and stood, leaning heavily on the slighter woman. Shirin held her close, face pressed against leather and iron, raven-dark hair tickling Thyatis' nose. The Roman woman sighed, overcome by enormous relief, and then staggered, barely able to stand. Again, Shirin caught her and put Thyatis' hands against the camel for support.

"Tell me one thing," Shirin said, voice suddenly cold. "Did you have any idea what would happen on the mountaintop?"

Thyatis looked sideways, meeting the Khazar woman's eyes, shaking her head. "We all thought *we* would die at the prince's hands, or those of his servants. I didn't think he . . ." Her voice failed, her attention focused on something very far away. She resumed, voice faint. "No one knew how powerful he was or what he would do to live."

The sun was a hot pink spark on the eastern horizon as Vladimir and Nicholas wearily climbed the low hill, pushing their way through prickly scrub. Sand dragged at their feet, making every step an effort. Reaching the hollow, Vladimir collapsed to his knees and laid down, panting. A cold mist rose from the lake, making the air damp and chill. The Walach luxuriated in the temperature, knowing too well the sun would soon be full in the sky, burning away the fog and hammering the land with unrelenting heat.

"Where . . ." Nicholas started coughing again, a raw rasping sound. After the spasm passed, he managed to croak, "where is the telecast?"

"There—" Vladimir rolled over, outflung arm indicating the section of sand where he'd buried the bronze disc. He stopped, staring. "—it is."

Hastily excavated sand made an untidy pile around an empty hole. Vladimir closed his eyes, feeling the earth tilt under him. When he opened them again the hole remained. Nicholas knelt beside him, face white with fury as he examined the ground.

"I've not your nose," he muttered, rising to pace through the brush. "But people were here—more than one." The Latin paused, fingers gently working a scrap of beige cloth free from a thorn branch. "Here—does this smell familiar?"

Vladimir took the scrap of cloth, eyes narrowing, and drank deep of the faint aroma clinging to the loose-weave fabric. The smell was tantalizing, then he remembered and a deep growl issued from the back of his throat. At the same time, the Walach rocked back on his heels, gritting his teeth against a sudden, hollow feeling. Nicholas watched his friend with dead eyes, quick mind having leapt ahead to the same inevitable conclusion.

"Thyatis," Vladimir said dully, staring at the hole as if the woman were there herself, laughing at their slow, dull minds. His fingernails shredded the fabric, letting the threads drift away in the dawn breeze. "She was here. With the others."

"Which others? The Persians?" Nicholas squatted down, realizing he was silhouetted against the skyline. His face had grown very still, lips a harsh slash, eyes dark slits in a tanned face. "How many?"

The Walach did not answer immediately, but crawled slowly around the hole, head low to the ground. Then he crept off into the brush and did not return for some time. When he did, a ghastly expression haunted his face. Nicholas was waiting, Brunhilde across his knees, chin in his hands.

"What did you find?"

Vladimir squatted beside the hole, digging his long fingers into the sand. "Betia was here too, and three or four other women. There were camels hidden down there." He pointed at the deserted, quiet village. "They put the telecast on a camel and went away into the desert to the northeast."

"On the pilgrim road?" Nicholas did not meet his friend's eyes, focusing on rubbing soot from the scabbard with his tunic sleeve.

"No. There is another trail following the line of ridges."

Nicholas looked up, pale mauve eyes glittering in reflection of the spreading cloak of dawn. "Our camels and water?"

Vladimir shook his head. "Gone." The beasts had fled wildly from the ambush on the temple mount and though he'd seen their tracks, they were long gone. "We have nothing," he said, biting his knuckles.

Nicholas rose into a crouch, fixing the Walach with a furious glance. "Don't be a fool! We are alive and there is water in the oasis pools. These houses will be filled with food, water bags, everything we need."

Vladimir nodded, but he looked to the north. Flat-topped mesas dotted the horizon, flattened as by the blows of giants, their sides crumbling and rocky with shale and chalk. Beyond them lay the open desert, wind-blown plains of rock and stone, and endless rolling sand beyond. "How . . ."

"We walk," Nicholas said, moving down the hill, still keeping low. "First to Praetonium and then a ship to Cyrenaicea or Rome herself."

Vladimir stared after him for a moment, then shook himself from head to toe, like a wet dog, and followed.

THE NILE CANAL GATE, ALEXANDRIA

I t's your turn." Frontius sat with his back against pitted old sandstone, squinting sideways at his friend. Both men were in a scrap of shade thrown by a merlon rising from the tower wall. The sun was a huge, brassy disk in the morning sky, his heat magnified by sodden delta air.

"I think not!" Sextus replied, between gulps of tepid brown water from a cup. A bucket sat beside him, wedged into the corner of a stone embrasure. Two more buckets filled with river sand completed the fire-brigade station. "Who was cutting the cables on the Heliokonpolis bridge while the Jackal came on at us, thundering like the gods and spitting fire?"

"You," Frontius allowed, closing his weak eye. Sweat oozed in a steady, slow stream down the side of his nose. "And handily done too. But I took the last look-see. It's your turn now."

Groaning, Sextus peered over the edge of the embrasure, helmet crammed down tight on his head, a sweat-dark leather strap biting into his stubbled chin. The sky growled and rumbled with muted, distant thunder, but there were no clouds on the horizon. Instead, a heavy grayish haze hung over the fields and canals facing the city. The engineer's armor clamped tight against his chest and upper arms, the metal burning with sweat. He blinked a trail of salt out of his eyes, searching the irregular, rumpled landscape for the enemy.

The irregular wind out of the north fluttered to a stop. A suffocating pressure began to build in the humid air.

All along the Roman lines, a sloping, packed earthen berm two miles long, faced with slabs of scavenged stone and brick, riddled with sharpened stakes, topped by a fighting platform reinforced with palm logs, mud-brick and irregularly placed towers, the Legions tensed. Every man crouched down, pressing himself into the muddy corduroy walkway. Sextus counted himself lucky, on one hand, for their position stood at the Nile Canal gate—a proper fortification of sandstone and cement, long predating the earthworks—and on the other, he was shivering with fear, for the exposed bastion of the gate towers were sure to draw the full attention of the enemy.

The engineer had seen the strength of the Persian sorcerers— more than once—and the rush of blood in his veins was loud in his ears. A half-mile of lumpy ground, denuded of vegetation, buildings and every scrap of brick, stone and wood faced the wall. Flocks of white birds pecked among the waving, knee-high grass. Sextus wiped sweat from his eyes, searching for the Persian lines, for the glint of watery sunlight on spears and helms. . . .

There!

The air twisted, a monstrous shape winging towards the Roman lines. The heat-haze rippled, bunching and roiling around a swift sparkling mote speeding like Apollo's arrow towards the gate. The birds spurted up from the ground in a panicked cloud of white feathers. Screeching in alarm, they darted away across the bobbing grass.

"Down!" Sextus screamed, kissing the stone. Every man in the tower did the same, eyes screwed shut against the expected flare of brilliance. A wild rushing sound ripped overhead, then a colossal *thwang* reverberated through stone and air. Sextus' eyes flew open in surprise, staring up, and his mind—normally quick, even in exhaustion—took a moment to grasp what he saw.

A furious black spark whirled and sputtered in the air. Curlicues of lightning danced around the edges, illuminating—just for a fraction of a grain—a queer distortion in the air. The shuddering pocket of flame flared, leaping across some invisible surface and the engineer gaped to see the ravening destruction unfold, spilling away from him, lighting the sky, the tower and the rampart for thousands of yards in either direction, but held in the air like a stone distending a taut cloth. A rumbling, deafening *crack-crack-crack* rocked the engineer, throwing him to his knees, but the hissing, spitting destruction he expected to rip across the top of the tower, incinerating the defenders, cracking stone, scorching their scorpions and ballistae, stalled in the wavering air. Flame roared away, flooding down into the ground, into the foundations of the tower, like water spilling from a millrace.

In the blink of an eye, the blast was gone, leaving only sizzling earth and clouds of steam boiling up from damp fields. Sextus shook his head, trying to clear his mind, then he saw the previously empty plain surging with the enemy. The northerly wind resumed, stirring turgid air.

"Here they come!" The engineers leapt to their ballista. Frontius scrambled up on the far side of the machine, grasping hold of a metal-faced plate set in the firing port of the wall. Sextus took hold of a smooth wooden handle with his left hand, then seized hold of the firing lever with the other. Frontius, ducking, dragged the metal plate aide, revealing the fields and the road below.

Thousands of Persians and Greeks swarmed forward, shrieking war cries, running across the rumpled field towards the wall. Nearly every man, Sextus saw in the brief instant he spared to survey the attack, bore a shield and they came on in two distinct waves. The first ranks were men with climbing ladders, shields, axes, long spears—then the second were archers, already advancing in staggered line, some men lofting arrows towards the defense, the others drawing shaft to string as they jogged forward. The sky darkened with flights of shafts.

On the road itself, a three-story-high tower rumbled forward on massive wooden wheels. A huge crowd of Persians packed the road behind the siege engine, pushing for all they were worth. On the fighting top, a dozen men in glittering, head-to-toe armor crouched behind wicker and hide shields. Sextus cursed, dragging the heavy ballista up and around. A four-foot-long wooden shaft lay in the aiming groove, tipped by six inches of triangular iron. Wooden slats flared from the butt-end of the bolt.

"Aiming!" Sextus cried, narrowing his left eye as he sighted against a curved iron brace set above the bolt. Regularly spaced marks were etched in the metal. His right hand tightened on the lever. Frontius and one of the boys assigned to the engine scuttled aside, taking up positions behind and beside each torsion arm, hands light on matching wheels. Another legionnaire was ready at the engineer's shoulder with a second bolt.

The top of the fighting tower clanked into sight through the iron loop. Sextus slammed the lever down. Oiled metal squealed in release and the big triple-corded cable snapped with a sharp *thwack* against rope-padded stays. The entire ballista rocked violently forward. The bolt flicked away, faster than Sextus' eye could follow. He stayed focused on the Persian siege tower, ignoring the frenzied activity of his crew as they reloaded.

The bolt smashed through a wicker screen and into a Persian soldier's breastplate. The man sprang backward, as if by surprise, jerked by the massive blow. The soldier behind him tried to duck aside, but the bolt tore through the *diquan's* chest, out through his right shoulder and punched into the second man's mailed chest with a ringing *tonk!*

"Range one hundred yards!" Sextus barked. "Three-quarters tension!"

Frontius and the other soldier at the iron wheels immediately began cranking them 'round as fast as they could. Sextus waited, watching the siege tower rumble closer, listening to the thunderous boom of Persian drums, the splintering rattle of arrows hitting the parapet, sweating more from fear now than heat. His eye caught another shining mote speeding through the air towards the tower, leaving a coiling tail of disturbed air behind. He clenched his teeth, willing his bladder to hold firm. The *clank-clank-clank* of the winch jumping back with each turn of the iron wheels filled his ears.

Somewhere out on the plain, Old Snake's voice raged, summoning hellish powers to ripple the air, draw thunder from a clear sky, sending destruction upon his enemies. Sextus had never seen the face of his enemy—few living Romans had seen *any* of the Persian magi—but every legionary, from the lowest servant to the Caesar himself, knew the sound of their voices. Every soldier had drawn their own mental picture of the tormenting sorcerers, fueled by the shock of battle and the grudging, exhausted respect earned by both sides. The disaster at Pelusium had nearly broken the Romans, but they had rallied to duty and honor and a bedrock faith in the Eternal Empire.

The brilliant mote slammed into some invisible barrier in the murky air and again Sextus saw the sky twist and deform. Azure tongues of flame lapped out in a twisting cone and the mote blossomed into a blinding flash. A wave of heat rolled over the top of the tower, but the furnace blast was attenuated and weak, barely a fraction of its full power. Again, the unleashed power wicked down into the earth, spilling like molten iron across the face of the old towers.

"Hah!" Sextus raised a fist against the malefic power hidden out in the haze-shrouded fields. "Rome builds to last, serpent!"

Old Snake was their most implacable foe—a cruel, hateful voice filling the heavens with abominable sounds, sending fire and choking smoke, or crawling death, or simple annihilation in a curdling green blast—but the Crow was little better, a furious apparition, a woman's voice shrieking in hate, her actions shrike-swift. There was no mercy in her, though the legionaries dying in the mud, or fighting hand-to-hand with the Arab and Greek fanatics wearing her colors, swore she was the beauty of the night, rather than the day. There were other lesser lights, the sly Hawk who wrapped the Persians in smoke and mist, hiding their movements from all but the most discerning eyes, and the formidable Jackal, whose blunt, irresistible attack had smashed the Fourth Scythica into oblivion at Heliokonpolis, coming within a hair of seizing the great bridge before the span had plunged, foaming, into the Nile channel.

Sextus could not say why he knew the face of the enemy—save their will was so strong, their awesome presence so widely felt, every man agreed upon their name and number.

"Loaded!" barked the soldier at his side, snapping Sextus' attention back to the moment at hand. A fresh bolt lay in the channel, the twin windlasses drawn back, Frontius shouting at him, stepping aside. Sextus sighted, saw the siege tower eighty yards away, swung the aiming handle a fraction, then slammed the release lever down again.

The ballista rocked forward, cable slammed into padded rope, another bolt flashed toward the enemy. Frontius leapt back to his wheel, cranking for all he was worth. Tanned muscles worked under a linen tunic and Sextus watched the jerking progress of the windlass bar with eager eyes.

The screams and shouts below the tower changed timbre and the first Persians scrambled up the sloping embankment, weaving their way through a forest of sharpened stakes and tangling brush. Legionnaires on the fighting platform began to hurl stones and javelins, or shoot at point-blank range with bows. Turbaned men toppled and fell, sliding on the greasy, soft slope. More scrambled past, their war cry ringing against the heavens.

Allau ak-bar!

The siege tower rumbled on, face studded with arrows. Flames licked among the hides and wicker shields. A corpse fell from the fighting top, limbs loose in death, to plunge into the mass of soldiery crowding forward below. Sextus' hand danced impatiently on the firing lever, waiting for the bolt to slide home.

A third and fourth wave of Persians, Greeks and Arabs swarmed out of the fields, loping forward past the corpses of their fellows, a waving forest of steel spear points and wild, mad faces. A corner of Sextus' mind measured the roaring wall of sound, the mass of the enemy and realized their main weight had fallen here, on the old gate.

Right in the thick of it, aren't we?

"Loaded!" shouted the legionary. Again, Sextus adjusted his aim, squinting, sweat streaming into his eyes. His hand slammed down on the lever.

Caesar Aurelian, his dented, chipped armor streaked with rust, jogged up a log-paved ramp. His Praetorians paced him in a rough square, their gear equally worn, faces blank with fatigue. Hard experience had taught them to set aside their crimson cloaks and distinctive horsetail helmets. Like Aurelian, they wore only the simple armor of a legionary, without signs or flashes of rank. The aquilifer ran alongside, his golden eagle wrapped in cloth and held at his shoulder. No Roman would fight without the sign and sigil of the city behind him, but raising the aquila on this battlefield would only invite dangerous attention.

The top of the battlement was crowded with armed men, both those struggling on the fighting platform, stabbing or shooting at the Persians swarming up the slope below, and wounded men lying or sitting on the plank road behind. Medical orderlies trotted down the ramp, canvas stretchers in hand. Aurelian forced himself to look away, catching a glimpse of a young man—no more than a boy—being carried past, one hand clutched desperately over the stump of his arm, blood oozing through dirty brown fingers. A wooden dowel was slowly splintering between his teeth.

A ripping sound smote the air and everyone not actually locked in hand-to-hand combat on the wall ducked. Aurelian crouched down, watching with narrowed eyes as the sky quivered and flashed, streaked with carnelian flame. Heavy clouds of smoke drifted across the battlement, making vision difficult.

Some of the clouds were tinged yellow or green. As they passed, men choked and fell to their knees. A few died, vomiting black fluid, a steady wind out of the north holding back the latest Persian deviltry.

"It's Old Snake for sure," one of the Praetorians hissed, rising from the ground. Aurelian nodded.

Shielded on both sides by men with heavy, laminated shields, the Caesar climbed up onto the fighting platform. Two legionaries moved aside automatically as he grasped one of the support poles and squeezed between them. Below, the Praetorians glanced around nervously, sweating with fear at the exposure their commander risked. Aurelian kept his head below the top of the rampart, glancing quickly to the north.

The fortification stretched towards the sea, curving slightly to follow the line of the ancient Ptolemaic wall. Smoke boiled from burning buildings behind the line and he could see men fighting here and there. Arrows slashed through the air in both directions, but in comparison to the conflagration around the Nile Gate towers, the rest of the front was quiet.

To the south, Aurelian saw much the same—the line of the wall studded with smoke and activity, then the glittering waters of Lake Mareotis on their flank. Again, he cursed the Persians and their fleet of river barges. Against another enemy, the lake would be a broad moat protecting the southern side of the city. Now, he was forced to keep nearly an entire Legion back, deployed along the shore to prevent landings behind the main wall.

A brilliant flare of light cracked overhead and men screamed in fear. Aurelian's head whipped around and he saw a section of the nearer tower burning furiously. Some kind of clinging flame dripped down battered, scored stone, heavy black smoke rolling up in oily waves. A siege catapult atop the tower burned as well. A man, wrapped in flame, plunged from the height, mouth open in a soundless, flame-encompassed scream. The prince blanched, eyes swinging to the sky, but then he realized the catapult itself had broken a torsion arm, spilling naphtha across the stone platform.

Bless the gods, the prince thought wildly, *it was only a fire arrow!*

A frail shield protected the legionaries fighting on the battlements and towers. A thin, gossamer veil standing in the hidden world between mortal men and the full might of the Persian sorcerers. Those few remaining Roman thaumaturges were cloistered back in the heart of the city, sweating with effort to sustain the pattern of wards and defenses lining the rampart. By sheer luck, Aurelian had made two critical, seemingly unrelated decisions regarding the defense of the city.

First, he had ordered his new fortifications built atop the foundation of an ancient wall. Unbeknownst to him, the intricate patterns of defense laid down during the time of Ptolemy the Savior, the first Macedonian king of Egypt, remained intact, though weakened by the theft of the wall stones themselves. Still, like begat like, and the new Roman wall inherited a measure of the ancient strength.

Second, the disaster at Pelusium had laid low so many thaumaturges and priests, Aurelian had shipped them all back to convalesce in Alexandria. The horrendous retreat across the delta, despite the horrific casualties suffered by his legionaries, had not cost him a single thaumaturge. Stunned by the strength of their enemy at Pelusium, the priests had labored furiously to strengthen the ancient ward line ringing the city.

Still holding, Aurelian prayed, watching the queer distortion in the sky.

A basso roar of anticipation boomed beyond the wall as the Persians reacted. Aurelian popped his head up, face grim. The old highway was littered with wreckage. Two siege towers had come within a dozen paces of the walls and both were still burning furiously. Thousands of Persians swarmed below, sending up flight after flight of arrows. As Aurelian watched, one of the burning towers toppled away from the road, pushed by a forest of hands. In its place, a heavy ram rolled forward on a wooden frame, pushed by lines of men in full armor, silver battle masks down.

The sharp *twang* of a ballista bolt cut through the din, firing from the remaining tower. A Persian pushing the ram toppled, struck through. Stones and burning pitch rained down in sheets of flame. The dead carpeted the ground and the wounded crawled among corpses, desperate to escape the rain of destruc-

tion. Persian orderlies dragged away those who might live, or
cut the throats of men wounded beyond succor.

Aurelian ducked back down, then slid from the fighting step.
"They've a ram," he barked to his guardsmen. He waved
sharply for his aide. "Phranes, get down from here and find the
tribune commanding those two cohorts of the First on reserve
in this sector. Get him up and into the gatehouse immediately.
You lot, with me!"

Ignoring the anxious expressions of his guardsmen, Aurelian
jogged along the rampart, heading for the rising iron-kettle din
of battle around the smoke-shrouded towers. As he ran, the
prince loosened the *spatha* bouncing at his waist and settled the
grip on his shield. It was clear to him the Persians were throwing their full weight at the gate and by the gods, he intended to
stand with his men, not hide in some tomb down in the city.
Left behind, Phranes cursed wearily, long face twisted into a
grimace and then ran off down the ramp past a constant stream
of wounded descending towards the hospital.

The sky groaned, tormented by hidden forces, rising
columns of smoke splintering into mirror fragments.

The *Paris* pitched up a long, rolling swell, sails taut with a
quartering wind. The courier ship scudded northwest from the
merchant harbor of Alexandria, the long low island of the
Pharos falling away to starboard. Thin sheets of smoke hung
over the water, fragments of an enormous black cloud building
over the port. On the foredeck, Thyatis leaned against a guy-
line, hip pressed against the railing, staring back at the embattled city.

Night was falling, a warm orange glow lingering in the western sky and only the distant light of burning buildings illuminated her face. Footsteps padded on the deck, soft and faint, but
Thyatis heard and turned. Shirin approached, her oval face
framed by a dark cloak, smudges of fatigue darkening her glorious eyes.

"There's food," Shirin said, sitting on the deck. Her legs dangled over the lip of the rowing gallery. Below her, the off-watch
crew was already asleep, curled up among the benches in an
untidy mass of blankets and pillow rolls. The Khazar woman

unwrapped a loaf—fresh this morning from a bakery near the port—and broke it in half. Thyatis settled in next to her, the meal between them on the deck. Shirin moved her leg, sliding her bare foot over Thyatis' toes.

"Thank you." Thyatis cut a hunk of bread from the heavy oval. She smeared oil and garlic paste and soft cheese across the spongy surface.

They ate in silence for a few grains, listening to the creak of the rigging and water hissing past under the bow, watching the southern horizon flicker and blaze with fire. Occasionally, bright sparks lofted above the city, then guttered out. Thunder rolled continuously, though the sound grew faint as they drew steadily away. Thyatis felt grainy, drained, her thoughts—if not harshly driven back on course—turning always to the city and the Legions fighting there. A tiny voice muttered in the back of her mind, urging her to return, to take up sword, spear, bow and climb the walls to fight beside her brothers.

"I want to ask you a question," Shirin said in a low voice. Thyatis looked over. The Khazar woman was methodically paring slivers of cheese from the round with her knife. They made a little pile on the deck. "Once you promised to stand beside me, to share my life. Do you still?"

"I do." Thyatis moved to take Shirin's hand, but stopped, the gesture quelled by a fierce expression on the Khazar woman's face.

"Do not take me lightly, Roman," Shirin warned sharply. "I am of the house of Asena, and my fathers ruled from distant Chin to the Roman border, from the ice to the mountains of Persia. Our numbers are like the grass, limitless, and our hearts stronger than your steel." She paused, full lips drawn in a tight line. "You say this Prince Maxian caused the eruption that destroyed Baiae? Which laid waste to so many towns and villages? Which strangled my children while they slept, burning the flesh from their bones, wrapping their skeletons in ash?"

Thyatis nodded grimly, understanding the venom in Shirin's voice all too well.

"Then I give you leave to separate yourself from our handfasting." The Khazar dug a hand into her gown and drew out a thumb-sized jewel on a heavy chain. The cabochon blazed as it emerged from hiding, catching the last gleam of the fires raging around Alexandria. Thyatis' lips pursed in surprise and she shook her head automatically.

"Shi—the Eye of Ormazd is *yours*. Given freely, not a token of binding."

Shirin pressed the jewel firmly into Thyatis' palm. "You gave this to me when we parted on Thira, against our time of meeting again. That day has come and I wish you to choose again, without doubt. I know where I am going, but you do not have to ride beside me."

"What do you mean?" Thyatis understood, even as the words flew from her mouth.

"I laid my children in the ground without grave gifts," Shirin said. "I believed accident took them, sky-father gathering them up with gentle hands, as he does those who die before their naming. But if this *prince* is the cause, if he *sacrificed* them so he might live, if he *murdered* them, then they do not rest easy. They *do not* run in green fields, golden flowers in their hair, rejoicing in the light of the sun through the trees." The Khazar woman lifted her knife, turning the mirror-bright blade to catch the last feeble gleam of the southern horizon. Deep and abiding anger flared in her harsh voice. "They are lost in darkness, shades without sustenance, helpless without weapons, forced to walk without mount or bridle, lacking even the grave gifts to buy entrance into the house of the dead."

"No," Thyatis said firmly, mustering her thoughts. "Not so. Not so. This much I have done, Shirin, I have laved the earth with blood to feed the uneasy dead, to lighten their burden in the sightless world. Thirty warriors I've sent to join them, an honorable guard to bear their cups, to carry their burdens. A dozen ferocious beasts I've offered up, hot blood spilled in fair contest on the sand!"

Shirin's dark eyes widened, understanding dawning in her face. "The arena! I watched you fight—your face was wild, mad, transported . . . is this the Roman way, to honor the dead with living men's blood, spilled in combat?"

Thyatis nodded, feeling suddenly weak, emptied again. Memories crowded around, thick as Nile mosquitoes, faces emerging from darkness, mouths wide in anger or fear. *My men. Our children. Nikos.* "Yes, this is the Roman way."

Shirin clasped her hand over Thyatis, enclosing the jewel. "I would put a dog of a slave at my children's feet, my gift to lighten their burden in the world of shades. This is how things were done in my grandfather's time. Will you help me?"

The Roman woman shook herself, feeling a spark flare in her breast. "Shi—you don't know how dangerous this—"

"Yes, I do." The Khazar woman nodded, eyes glittering again, but now her fury was banked, glowing hot behind a shield of purpose. Hidden in their hands, the jewel gleamed with an inner fire. "I swear I will kill this prince of Rome."

Gape-mouthed horns blew mournfully, sending a long, ululating wail out across the fields before the city. Exhausted soldiers raised their heads at the sound, looking up from beside the raised highway, their faces painted with the ruddy, red light of a vast, smoke-bloated sun. Fires continued to burn among a long swathe of grass and drifts of fly-infested corpses. A bitter white haze drifted over the Roman wall, swirling around shattered towers and obscuring the forest of stakes sprouting from the disordered earth.

The horns winded again and men began to limp away from the fortifications, retreating by ones and twos across the fields. Night came winging out of the east, swallowing the land in a black throat and none of the Persians cared to remain among the dead after sunset. All along the wall, points of light began to flare as the legionnaires cast pine torches down upon the slope.

The squat shapes of the two gate towers were lit from below by the smoking remains of the great ram, glowing coal-red from the fires that had consumed the wooden frame. The ancient sandstone blocks were burned dark by countless blows. The jagged, gappy parapet of one tower stood black against a sullen orange sky.

Shahr-Baraz, King of Kings, turned away from the doleful view. His army fell back, bloodied and beaten, from the Roman fortifications. On this depressingly flat plain he could not see the full sweep of the disaster, but what lay within sight was enough. A full day had passed in relentless, repeated assault. Four times, the *pushtigbahn* had stormed forward against the gate. Four times, the legionnaires had thrown them back in disarray. Though other attacks had gained the rampart on more than one occasion, sharp Roman counterattacks had driven them back each time. His heart heavy, the Boar paced into the loose collection of tents forming his headquarters.

Bastard Romans . . . they've denied us even a roof over our heads. Despite the inconvenience, Shahr-Baraz was impressed. The enemy had not wasted any time in recovering from the disastrous retreat across the delta. The approaches to Alexandria had been stripped bare; every house, gyre, barn, temple and chicken coop had been demolished and hauled away. Stone and brick had gone into the massive wall, everything else into the bellies of the Roman soldiers or hidden in the vast city just out of sight. The Boar ducked into his tent, idly twisting the ends of his mustache to even sharper points. He sat in a canvas field chair, hearing the old walnut legs creak with his weight and sighed, rubbing his face with both hands.

A distinctive chill mist crept into the tent, flowing across the damp floor in eddying waves. Shahr-Baraz looked up, weary anger simmering in his eyes. The dark, angular shape of Prince Rustam appeared in the entrance, flanked by the gaunt shapes of his two apprentices.

"Come in, then." Shahr-Baraz gestured to the cots and camp chairs his servants had dumped under the canvas. He tapped an oil lamp with a thick, scarred finger. The wick had dimmed to a pinpoint with the sorcerer's approach. Shahr-Baraz breathed softly, letting the flame catch again and spread a slow, yellow light across table and chairs.

Hiding a mirthless grin, the King of Kings cocked an eyebrow at the sorcerer. "You look well."

Rustam bared his teeth in response, dark lips wrinkling up from long, white incisors. A dry hiss issued from the creature as he sprawled in a canvas seat, but he hadn't the energy for anything more.

Shahr-Baraz nodded to the other two figures, tilting his head to indicate the other chairs.

Pale oval face drawn with fatigue, Zenobia limped stiffly to one of the cots, her jaw pinched as she lay down on the hard boards. The Queen's robes were caked with mud, her hands bruised and streaked with blood. She turned her face towards the King of Kings, brilliant eyes dulled to fractured jewels, barely able to move. Her hands folded on her breast, withered doves lost in the dark, ragged pleats of her gown. "My lord," she whispered, though even so much seemed to drain her.

The jackal-headed man said nothing, squatting on the ground inside the door, his iron mask scored and dented. One ear, never properly repaired after the conflagration at Pelusium, was now entirely torn away, leaving a gaping hole in the metal, showing matted black hair and a pale scalp covered with scars.

"Have we failed?" Rustam managed to lift his head enough to speak. The king observed him closely, seeing the usual glamour fading, leaving the mottled, reptilian skin of the creature exposed. Inwardly, Shahr-Baraz sighed in despair, seeing the truth of his ally laid bare by such great exhaustion. The familiar princely face was no more than a comforting shell around something dark and lean, all spidery muscle and long, tapering ears flat against an inhuman skull. Something abhorrent, which should be cut down and cast into cleansing fire. The Boar's lips twisted into disgust, then settled—driven by implacable will—into a tight, flat line. *Khadames was right about our dear prince. But I've made my choice.*

"No," Shahr-Baraz said after a moment, "but today was costly, very costly."

He cleared his throat, realizing he was tremendously thirsty. "Bring wine and food," he called to the servants hiding in the darkness outside the tent. The rustling sound of running feet answered him and he turned his attention back to the sorcerer. "What happened?"

Rustam stirred again, nictating membranes rippling back from dark eyes. His voice was thready and weak. "We should not have kept attacking."

"I know that." Shahr-Baraz felt his temper stir. "You assured me the 'ward' was frail and easily destroyed. *Just once more*, you declared, and the towers would crack, the rampart split and we would be within the city."

A thin-fingered hand raised in protest, then fell wearily away again. "The Romans . . . no, the *Egyptians* are clever. We should have taken more time . . . divined their purpose, examined their defenses! I would have seen what they prepared, with just a day . . ."

Shahr-Baraz snarled, waving away the protest. "Useless words. We all agreed to strike with speed, to try and over-whelm them before they had more time to prepare. We were overconfident and have paid for our hubris! Tell me what happened today. Tell me what we can do to avoid such a debacle again!"

The sorcerer started to speak, then stopped and took a breath. He settled deeper in his chair and the Boar realized the creature was trying to muddle through his memories. The king leaned back for a moment himself. Despite his admonition to the others, his own thoughts turned unerringly to what he might have done, should have done . . .

The Persian army had rushed down the Nile with all speed, trying to catch the retreating Legions before they found shelter in Alexandria itself. Unfortunately, despite destroying nearly an entire Legion in a pitched battle at Hierakonpolis, they had failed to seize the crossing. Roman engineers had collapsed the causeway, blocking the river channel to Shahr-Baraz' flotilla. For their part, the bargemen brought in from Mesopotamia had reacted swiftly, building a pontoon bridge across the arm of the Nile. The king had thrown his army across, then raced down the highway into Alexandria's suburbs.

His wild lunge had fallen short. The surviving Roman Legions entered the city in time to occupy a freshly built ring of fortifications. Shahr-Baraz was impressed, again, at the speed and efficiency of the Romans in siege work. Very early this morning, he had felt a pang of regret as well—all that work, he thought, would soon be rendered useless—shattered by the power of the Lord of the Ten Serpents. Even with his army weary from the forced march down the Nile, Shahr-Baraz had elected to attempt an immediate, full-scale assault. Pressing hard had broken the Romans before, why not here too?

"I was deceived," Rustam said, rousing himself from thought. "I looked upon their battlements and saw only newly turned earth, freshly raised stone. So similar to that we faced at Pelusium . . ." His voice trailed off in a weary hiss, razor-edged nails making a clicking sound on the arm of his chair. Rustam's thin face contorted in disgust. "There must be an older wall or foundation beneath the new construction. Something built by the ancients . . . deep with strength. These crawling, pus-drinking, shit-eating Egyptians must have known! They have made a new pattern atop the old—the very likeness of a battle ward—but they are keeping well back. I can barely feel them, hiding in the city . . ." He began to mutter and hiss, voice fading into unintelligible curses.

Shahr-Baraz sighed openly now, turning his attention to the Queen. Slitted blue eyes met his.

"They *are* clever," Zenobia said in a husky, exhausted voice. "We strike and the force of our blow bleeds into the earth. We press and the shield bends. Flame is swallowed, lightning grounded. We can feel them at a distance. They are wary and careful, working only through tokens set in the earth." The Queen's eyes crinkled slightly in amusement. "They will not face us in the open field or pit might against might. They are not fools."

"No, they are cowards!" Rustam straightened, the tip of his black tongue flicking between needle-like teeth. He stared hollowly at the king. "We must sleep and regain our strength."

"How long?" Shahr-Baraz knuckled a heavy fist against his chin, meeting the sorcerer's gaze.

"Days, at least." The prince's expression tightened. "Dare nothing while we recover!"

Shahr-Baraz raised an eyebrow at the brusque order. "This shield, does it hold out my men's spears and arrows?"

"No." Rustam's face contorted into a foul grimace, reminded again of his failure.

"Then we will take the city regardless, if we have sufficient men and time."

The sorcerer's eyes narrowed reflexively, shoulders hunching up. The king hid a spark of interest at the reaction and he waited, patient as a hunter lying beside a mountain trail.

"We do not have . . . time or men." Rustam's eyes flickered with a sullen glow. "We must press them, before they receive . . ." His voice changed tone subtly. ". . . reinforcements. The Emperor is sure to send more men to hold the city—they cannot afford to lose Egypt!"

"Really?" Shahr-Baraz leaned closer, watching the sorcerer with open curiosity. "Why is that?"

Rustam stiffened again, lip twitching into the beginning of a sneer. "Don't be a fool—Rome is drunk on foreign grain! You've seen the great ships—there will be riots in the Forum if the bread dole is reduced!"

Shahr-Baraz blinked slowly, like a lion waking from full-bellied sleep. He watched the sorcerer intently, exhaustion forgotten. "You're speaking of Constantinople," the king said softly, mouth thinning in well-contained anger. "Where so many citizens now lie dead, they will not riot for lack of grain or wine. Rome draws her bread and meal from Africa, from Sicily, even from Spain." He made a sharp, dismissive gesture with his hand. "The Romans fight for Egypt because it is *theirs*. They fight to deny us. But the Empire will survive without the province."

Rustam scowled, glaring at Shahr-Baraz. "The longer we wait, the stronger they become."

"Certainly." The king nodded in agreement, putting both hands on his knees. "We need more soldiers. We need time to prepare for a proper attack along the entire length of the wall." His face twisted, but no one could have called the resulting expression a smile. "Khalid needs time to clear away the barrier at Hierakonpolis. I need those riverboats. And of course, you must recover your strength. You will need every ounce." The king bared blunt yellow teeth.

The sorcerer eyed him warily, still struggling against bone-deep fatigue. "I won't be able to just brush aside their barrier," he rasped. "And you've not the soldiers to attack the whole length of the wall. Nor are you likely to get them—we're eight hundred miles from Ctesiphon! There are no more soldiers coming, nowhere to levy fresh troops . . ."

Shahr-Baraz' cold humor did not abate. "Not so. There are reinforcements in plenty, all around us."

Rustam blinked, staring at the king in surprise. "What do you mean?"

"You are tired," the king replied, waving his servants into the tent. The women entered, eyes downcast. With trembling hands, they set platters of cold meat, hard-crusted way bread and flagons of sour wine on the table. "Sleep, lord prince and when you wake look about you. You will find allies in plenty, I think."

At the edge of the tent, Zenobia's eyes flickered open in alarm. She stared at the king, watching him in profile as he drank deep. A sick expression crawled across her fine-boned face, then she closed her eyes with a shudder. She understood his meaning all too well. *How low have the lords of Persia fallen? Where is their fabled purity and devotion to Ahura-Madza?*

"Allies, here among the enemy?" the sorcerer said in a querulous, weary voice.

Shahr-Baraz nodded again, amused. "All around. You will see."

THE HOUSE OF GREGORIUS AURICUS, ROMA MATER

L ate afternoon sun slanted across a broad desktop of close-grained wood. The entire surface was covered with neatly arranged piles of parchment, separated by wooden dividers and interspersed with jars of colored ink. Gaius Julius bent over a marble writing surface, quill busy in his hand, while he listened to an elderly Greek reading a dispatch from Gothica.

"' . . . our forces have pursued the Gepids into remote fast-nesses where our horse cannot go and our columns are disor-dered if they advance. Because of this, the enemy continues to resist, though any attacks made by them are repulsed at high cost and with few casualties to our own soldiers.' "

The Greek paused, raising a neatly plucked white eyebrow at the back of the old Roman's head. Gaius, continuing to write, nodded impatiently for the man to continue. The secretary sighed, wishing for the days when he served the elderly Grego-rius—who did not keep such long hours!—and took a breath to resume his recitation.

The door to the study banged open and a tall, dark-haired woman swept into the room. Gaius Julius looked up in irrita-tion. "There'd better be—" The old Roman stuttered, caught by

complete surprise. "Kri—" He paused again, gathering his
wits, eyes narrowing in recognition. "My lady Martina, I had
no idea you and the prince had returned to the city. Has something happened?"

"No, Master Gaius, not at all." The Empress Martina glided
up to the table and perched herself on the corner, daintily setting aside the papers lying there. She smiled down at the old
man, a dazzling display of perfect white teeth and bit her lower
lip, dimpling at him.

Gaius Julius set down his quill, careful to keep ink from
spilling on the letter, and shook out the sleeves of his toga.
Then, watching the Empress from under half-lidded eyes, he
bowed graciously. A chill wash of fear and surprise trembled in
his arms and legs, but he had faced worse before and he showed
nothing of his consternation in face or attitude.

"My lady, you look well," he said in a very dry voice. "Marriage must agree with you."

Martina laughed, a gay, ringing sound, and stretched luxuri-
ously. Firm, full breasts pressed against cream-colored silk and
a wavy cascade of dark, auburn hair spilled down her arched
back. A slow, hot smile burned in a classic face. She stepped
away from the desk. "Do you think so?"

The Empress raised her arms, turning, letting the heavy silk
cling to her thighs and flat stomach as she twirled. Golden
bracelets fit snugly on round, white arms and silver rings
flashed on slim, tapering fingers. Laughing again, a full merry
sound, she came to a halt, faintly flushed.

Gaius remained impassive, watching the woman's face,
searching her dark brown eyes with a faint frown.

"You don't like my new look?" Martina pouted. "I do."

"The prince's . . . wedding gift?" Gaius Julius hazarded,
driving his tumultuous thoughts to ordered, quiet calm. He
stepped around the desk, looking the Empress of the East up
and down with a critical eye. Martina preened, enjoying his attention.

She looks like Krista, the old Roman thought, stomach
clenching with troubled memories, *but . . . improved.* He struggled to suppress his frown, to keep clear disgust from his face.
A boy's dream—larger breasts, more perfect features, longer

hair, more . . . everything. Gaius smiled, summoning cheer into his seamed old face. Resentment flickered at the back of his thoughts, but this too he drove away without mercy. *The prince favors who he will . . .*

"Are you happy?" Gaius asked, returning to his seat. He felt better with the wide desk between the two of them. "Is this what you wanted?"

"Yes!" Martina stared at him in open astonishment. "Of course! I hated my old body and now the loathsome fat thing is gone, cast away like a snake's skin, and I am . . . new!"

She giggled again, taking two gliding, dancing steps to the windows. The garden at the center of the prince's town house was not large, but old Gregorius' gardeners were both dedicated and patient. Cherry and lemon trees shaded a pool filled with delicate golden fish. She put her hands on the window frame, breathing deep of the scented air.

"I cannot wait to see Helena's face," she said, looking over her shoulder with a mischievous expression. "She'll wrinkle up like a prune!"

"She will not be pleased, no." Gaius considered saying more, but held his tongue. *Would this transformed creature even care? The old Martina might have . . . but now? I think not.* "Did you enjoy Capri? The island is very beautiful."

"Is it?" Martina turned to face him, leaning back against the window. A dreamy, distracted expression filled her face. "I didn't notice." She bit her lip, grinning, eyes sparkling with remembered delight. Her hands smoothed pleated fabric down over her stomach. "We were very busy, you know. But I remember smelling hyacinths and roses and jasmine outside the windows." She made a slight moue. "I didn't want to leave."

"Why *did* you come back?" Gaius rearranged his papers idly.

"Oh, he was troubled by bad dreams." Martina made a disparaging gesture. "He had to come back, quick as can be . . ." A thought came to her, and the Empress's expression brightened. "He's gone off to bother the Emperor, which means I'm free to entertain myself in the shops." She gave Gaius Julius a calculating look, then shook her head, making tiny silver beads set among her curls chime softly. "You'll never do! You're old, and have so much *important* work to do."

Gaius Julius could not help but scowl. The Empress's eyes glittered in response, and she clapped her hands together.

"Ah! You are still a little vain, aren't you? Even being so old." She came closer with little dancing steps. The mischievous twinkle was back in her eyes. Laughter bubbled in her voice. "Do you want to know a secret?"

"What would that be?" Gaius Julius held his ground, though instinct urged him to back away or run. The Empress took his hand, sliding his long fingers over the rich, luxurious fabric covering her hip. The old Roman's nostrils flared, involuntarily taking in a cloud of soft perfume—a dozen dizzying scents wrapped around a spicy core—and he became very still. Martina pursed her lips, fingers tracing his cheeks, the wrinkles under his eyes, passing over the thinning fringe of hair clinging stubbornly around his ears. She leaned close, resting her forehead against his cheek.

"Haven't you guessed," she whispered and the sound of her laughter made another cold chill trickle along his spine. "You've known the prince longer than I! You see what he can do with me, with *nothing*." Martina pulled away, holding both of Gaius' hands. A look of triumph wreathed her perfect face, and her eyes glittered with a cold, victorious light.

"The prince will never die," she said softly. "Nor will I, or you, or Alexandros, or any of his favorites. Look at me! I will be this way, forever!"

Gaius Julius' jaw clenched and he forced down a choking sensation. His body held no bile to flood the back of his throat, for which he was grateful. "Yes," he said after a pause. "While the prince lives, he may heal all our hurts, tend all our diseases. We will live while he endures."

"Endures?" Martina made a face, the pink tip of her tongue flashing between snowy teeth. "We will not *endure*, we will rejoice in limitless days! We will be free from death, disease, age . . . every plague and plight of men. Forever."

The old Roman said nothing, watching her preen and laugh, filled with the prospect of endless joy. The Empress's face glowed with a vast, consuming delight and he felt old, very old. At the same time, he suppressed a shudder of atavistic fear.

Why did our prince fashion a new Alaïs from the clay of shy Martina?

Galen, Emperor of the West, protector of the East, ran both hands through lank, dark hair. His usually sharp brown eyes were dull with fatigue. Tiny flames reflected in each pupil and his skin shone a sickly green in the radiance of the telecast. He leaned on a narrow table, staring into the depths of the whirling device, attention wholly upon flickering, shrike-quick visions passing before him.

Two scribeswomen watched by his side, one sketching the revealed scene on papyrus sheets with a hard stick of charcoal, the other scribbling notes as fast as she could.

"There." Galen coughed, pressing the back of a hand across his lips. He gestured to a pair of thaumaturges sitting beside the telecast, faces tense with effort. "There beside the road, there is a bivouac . . . magnify those tents."

The disk of fire flared, point of view swinging wildly from on high—where the outline of a great city was revealed on a peninsula dappled with shadow and the failing light of the sun—down past towering clouds of smoke, over battlements and ramparts strewn with the dead and wounded, past a sandstone tower blackened by fire and across trampled pastures. Tents swelled in the gleaming disk, and Galen looked down upon cohorts of men sprawled in exhaustion across stubbled fields and farmyards. Cook fires shone against encroaching night, cooks busy filling kettles of grain mash. Then tents appeared, glowing softly by lamplight. Banners stood limp in humid night air, but the Emperor saw a brace of black chargers pawing the earth, eager for grain.

"Yes," Galen hissed in satisfaction. "The largest tent, show me inside!"

"My lord! We dare not!" Beside the massive block of stone holding the telecast, one of the thaumaturges guiding the device looked up, long old face white with strain. "*He* is nearby."

Galen looked back to the disc, frowning, then saw the faint outlines of men crouched outside the tent, nearly invisible in the falling twilight. Their long pigtails and flat, sharp cheekbones could still be made out. "Huns." The Emperor cursed. "The sorcerer's bodyguards. Very well, draw back and show me the army camps instead."

Again, the vision changed, rushing back into the darkening air. A vast array of tents, campfires, wagons, men marching along muddy roads filled his vision. "Steady there," Galen said, turning to the clerks at his side. "Can you make a count of the campfires and tents, while light remains?"

The women nodded, though their faces were puffy with fatigue and dark circles smudged their eyes. "Yes, Lord and God."

"Thank you." He squeezed the gray-haired one's shoulder. "When does your relief—"

The double doors to the old library swung wide, hinges groaning in protest. Galen looked up, surprised, his heart sinking in anticipation of dreadful news—*was there any other kind?*—then he breathed a sigh of relief. "Maxian!" He stepped towards his brother. "How was Capri?"

"What has happened?" The prince's face was taut with fear as he brushed his brother's welcoming hand aside. Maxian stared into the wavering vision burning inside the ring of the telecast. "Is this Egypt? Why is it so dark?"

Galen turned, caught short by Maxian's angry demands. "Yes, this is Egypt," he said in a measured voice. "The sun is setting."

The prince did not look at his brother, all attention focused on pinpoints of light scattered in deep shadow. Sunlight still gleamed on a few spires rising from the smoke-fogged warren of Alexandria. The Nile channels gleamed pewter, beginning to catch starlight in their waters.

"Show me Caesar Aurelian," Maxian commanded, raising a hand. A faint sound, like a ringing bell, hung in the air. The two thaumaturges yelped in alarm, starting wild-eyed from their couches. The disk blazed blue-white, flooding the room, forcing Galen to turn his head, gritting his teeth in pain. Both of the scribes cried out in surprise.

The Emperor blinked, then opened his eyes to a suddenly darkened room. He whistled in surprise. The telecast looked upon Aurelian, his red beard tangled and shining with sweat, mouth moving soundlessly. The stocky prince was in a tent hung with lamps, new wrinkles around his eyes, hands moving in sharp gestures. A crowd of Roman officers stood around a campaign table littered with maps. Aurelian turned, fist clenched, his face blazing with purpose.

"He lives," Maxian said, relief plain in his voice. He brushed sweat from his brow.

"He does." Galen waved the clerks out of the room. Both women tiptoed away. The thaumaturges looked to the Emperor for guidance and he tilted his head towards the door. They fled. "Maxian, our Horse is fine. There was a battle today, but—all things considered—it went well. Very well."

Maxian turned to his brother, a ghastly expression on his face. "I dreamed . . . I dreamed he was dead. His face was pale, blood streaked the water, lapping over him . . ."

"Nothing has happened to our Horse," Galen said frimly, taking Maxian's shoulders in hand. "Nothing."

Shoulders slumping in relief, Maxian sat heavily on the table. Behind him, the vision of his brother continued to declaim, now indicating the maps with a stubby finger. The officers leaned close, faces intent on the diagrams.

"I couldn't sleep," Maxian said softly, avoiding Galen's eyes. His right hand batted at the air beside his ear. "Voices were whispering, telling me things—they said Horse was dead, cut down, lungs filling with water—and I could do nothing. Everything was in ruins. . . ."

"It's not true," Galen said, managing a very tired smile. "But I have the same dreams, when I try to sleep, filled with disaster and calamity." He rubbed his eyes. "In truth, this battle today was the first good news in weeks."

"I should be there," Maxian said, sitting up straighter. He glared at his brother. "The Persian sorcerer is there, isn't he?" The prince turned to the telecast, taking obvious comfort from the sight of Aurelian in good health. "Show me the enemy," he said in a commanding voice.

"No!" Galen lunged forward, then pulled himself up short. *I can't control the cursed thing with my fists. . . .* "Maxian—if we can see him, he can see us!"

The scene shifted with dizzying speed, flashing over flat-roofed buildings—a towering wall—men marching along a rampart studded with stakes and towers, winging over trampled grass and boggy ground. Maxian grimaced, looking pained. Galen made a halfhearted gesture at the disc. The Persian camp swelled into view, tired, curly-bearded faces flashing past.

"Please, Max, they don't know we can watch them!"

Growling in disgust, Maxian sketched a sign in the air and the disk abruptly went dark. A whining hum skittered down, then bronze clattered on stone as the sphere of fire hissed into silence. A low, ringing tone bounced and jangled from the ceiling as the last, innermost gear rattled from side to side, then lay still.

"Your secret is safe." Maxian's voice was surly and the prince drew himself up, lips curled in almost a snarl. "And I am safe too, trapped here in Rome, while our soldiers bleed in some Egyptian field, and *my brother* tries to hold back sorcery with nothing but mortal bone and muscle!"

"Maxian." Galen's voice was cold and held a quelling edge. He matched angry glares with his brother. This time, Maxian did not relent or look away. Instead, Galen did. The Emperor sat down on the edge of the table, bone-deep exhaustion flooding back, stealing the last fragment of hope he'd clawed from the ruin of the Persian attack. "Listen. Today the Persian army made four full-scale assaults on the defenses of Alexandria. They did not stint themselves—I watched your Persian sorcerer rage for the better part of a day, trying to throw down the rampart and those towers—and they failed."

The Emperor opened his eyes, giving his brother a frank and appraising look. "You were not there. Our best guess is Aurelian managed to save a few thaumaturges from the wreck of Pelusium, and they are holding on, working only to defend, not to attack. The Persians were forced to strike directly into our fortifications, man-to-man, steel against steel. Our old Horse and his men held and made the Persians—and their Greek and Arab allies—pay dearly."

Maxian's tight, angry expression softened a little. "But . . ."

"Listen to me, just for a moment. Then you'll have your say." Galen paused, struggling to arrange his thoughts, to remember everything he held in play. His memory was beginning to fail, battered by too little sleep and too much to do.

The prince almost spoke, then gestured sharply for the Emperor to continue.

"The Persians are far from home," Galen managed to say, after two deep breaths. "Their numbers are limited and by our count, only half-again Aurelian's strength. But we hold a strong position. The harbor remains open, for they are loath to commit their fleet for fear of ours, so Alexandria will not starve. I have sent letters to the *comes* Alexandros in Constantinople. In another week, perhaps two, the remains of our fleet will be able to shift his army to Egypt. Then we will outnumber the Persians by two to one."

Maxian's eyes blazed. "I can be in Egypt in three days," he cried.

Galen did not respond and the prince flushed, stung by his brother's icy demeanor, then sat down again.

"When our fleet approaches the Nile mouth," the Emperor said in an even, steady voice, "the Persians will sortie to destroy them. On another day, I would gladly accept a sea battle—our fleet would be packed to the railings with legionnaires—and victory would be likely. But on *this* day . . . We have been watching the battle closely and you should know the Persian sorcerer is no longer alone."

"I know," Maxian said sharply, "a dog-headed man fought beside him at Constantinople, though I thought it destroyed . . ."

Galen's lips twitched into a wintry smile. "The Jackal lives. There are two others, apparently equal in strength."

"Two more?" Maxian stared in surprise.

Galen nodded, rubbing the back of a knuckle against his eyebrows. He squeezed his left eye shut, trying to quell the *tap-tap-tap* chipping away at his concentration. "Yes. A man and a woman. Their faces are shadowed and indistinct, but we think they are Greeks." The Emperor shook his head, sighing. "The city of Palmyra had a great school and many learned sons and daughters. I wonder . . . no matter. No matter."

"There are four of them?" Maxian sounded ill. He sat down.

"Four." Galen's face was grim. "Can you defeat four sorcerers?"

"I . . . Perhaps." The prince swallowed, rubbing his temples. "How many Legion thaumaturges can accompany me?"

Galen did not answer for a moment. His eyes narrowed in calculation. "Tell me this, brother. Can you protect our fleet against them, if you stand one against four?"

"Of course—" Maxian paused, then turned his head to listen. His expression twisted into frustrated anger. "No, no, I cannot. Not if the Serpent engages my attention—then the others will savage our fleet. Each ship will require a thaumaturge aboard, to see to its defense."

"We account barely twenty Legion thaumaturges still in the West." Galen's voice was heavy.

"Only twenty?" Maxian's eyes widened in shock and a taint of despair crept into his voice.

"Twenty. Aurelian had a round dozen with him and they are dead or pressed to the limit in Alexandria. More died before Constantinople and Alexandros' Gothic Legion, for all his valor and their skill, accounts *none* among their number." Galen spread his hands. "The Eastern Empire's wizards are scattered, slain or fled. So . . . I have you, and these twenty."

"How many ships are in the fleet?" Maxian bit his thumb, staring into an unguessable distance.

"Two hundred, large and small, and they will be stretched to the limit to carry Alexandros' army."

The prince took on a pickled look, grinding his fist against his teeth. After a moment, he gave his brother a sick, exhausted look. "I can't protect so many. If these Persians can handle fire, they will wreck half the fleet, or more, before we can make harbor."

Galen nodded. "I thought as much." He essayed a smile, but knew the expression was no better than a death's head. "I am not a wizard, yet I can listen and learn and count as well as any man. This is not easy to say, but . . ." Then he stopped, grimacing at a bitter taste in his mouth. "We are outmatched for the moment. We need to buy time."

"Time for what?" Maxian's voice rose, frustrated and angry. "What difference will a week make, save the Persians may find a way into Alexandria and our *brother* and thousands of Roman soldiers will be dead?"

"Be quiet and listen!" Galen snapped back, his patience eroding. "I have been following the reports from your workshops in Florentia very closely. In three weeks, the first of your flying machines will be complete. In four, they will all be ready to fly." He raised a finger sharply. "When they are ready, you will take them to Egypt. The fleet will arrive at roughly the same time. With the long eyes of your iron drakes, we will be able to spy the Persian fleet long before they can see us—I hope to reinforce the city before the enemy can respond. And when he does . . ."

"I will be waiting, in the sky." Maxian's lips stretched in a feral grin. "Their fleet will be helpless against an attack from above."

"Even so," Galen said, showing a little of his own satisfaction. "The odds will shift in our favor, I think."

Maxian's exhaustion faded, bunching his fists eagerly. His spirits revived, then worry clouded his face again. "Four weeks . . ." He stared at the quiet, still telecast, then back at Galen. "What if our Horse can't hold the city that long? What then?"

Galen shook his head sadly. "He has to hold on, piglet. We don't have another option."

"That's not good enough!" Maxian's anger flared again. "Let me go! I can land Iron Pegasus on sand or sea and snatch him away if things go poorly."

"No," Galen said, stiffening. "*He* must stay. If he leaves, the defense will collapse. You saw those faces in the telecast—the men are weary, driven to the edge, but they *believe* in him—his confidence holds them together. Aurelian must stay in Alexandria until we can relieve him." A finger stabbed at the prince. "And *you* must make ready. You have to be in Florentia in three weeks to complete the sorcery binding the iron drakes. Without them, we've no chance to salvaging the situation in Egypt."

"But—"

"Are you ready to face this monster?" Galen's voice cracked like a whip, making Maxian flinch. The Emperor advanced on his younger brother, eyes glittering. "You'll only get one throw in this game, one toss, one set of bones rattling in the cup. The next time you face the Serpent, you *must win*."

Maxian snarled back, a guttural, unintelligible sound. He raised a hand, naked fury in the choppy motion. "I will be ready!" he shouted. "I am ready now!"

"I don't think you are," Galen barked in a cold, cutting voice. "Rested, yes. Focused, no! I've given you all the time I can, but your idle youth is now past. Now you must fight and win and there is no margin for failure!"

"Idle youth?" Maxian goggled at his brother. "Idle youth! I've not been idle, you arrogant bastard! I've been working without a pause for—" His mouth snapped shut. With obvious effort, Maxian mastered himself. "I will be ready," he snarled.

Galen held up four fingers in response. Maxian's jaw clenched, but he said nothing, turning on his heel and stalking out. The doors groaned as he passed, then slammed shut, driven by invisible hands.

In the quiet, deserted room, the Emperor slumped back against the table, palms pressed against burning eyes, a sick, queasy feeling roiling in his stomach. After a moment, he sighed again and pushed away from the table. He was very tired.

He'll be ready now, the Emperor thought, *a very terror, raging to crash into the midst of the enemy and savage them.* Galen made a weighing motion with his hands, then shook his head at the bargain he'd made with his heart and the Empire. *I hate this. I have two brothers . . . but the Empire needs victory more than one general, or even a Legion.*

Gaius Julius released the Empress's hands, stepping to the windows himself. He did not look down upon the shady trees and cool green lawn below, but out over the red-tile roof and white walls of the villa. He lifted his chin, pointing at the Palatine Hill sweltering in summer heat. "Do you think Helena will let you live so long?"

The old Roman turned, amusement gleaming in his eyes. Martina's face was a frozen mask.

"She is not a jealous woman," he continued, "but she has eyes to see and a mind quick enough to grasp the implications of your new . . . body. Oh, the prince could cast a glamour upon you, making you seem your old, familiar self. But would wearing such a guise please you, my lady, when you have such fine new plumage to show?"

"It would not!" Martina made a striking motion with one hand; her firm, muscular arm cutting the air. "I want to see shock in her face and envy and raw jealousy! I want every head to turn to me and leave her standing alone and ignored at the edge of the room, while the great lords and ladies fawn at *my* feet. I want—"

"You want to be the *Empress*," Gaius said, deftly interrupting her tirade. "You wish to *rule*."

Martina's nostrils flared and she fell silent, rosebud lips moving, silently tasting the words. Gaius Julius watched and considered while the girl thought. Nervous tension made his right hand tremble, but he stilled the offending limb, forcing quiet upon muscle and bone by sheer will. He had prepared for this moment for some time, laying plans, making friends among his enemies, assuring himself of a means of retreat and advance alike, securing his flanks, sending out emissaries to neighboring nations to measure their interest and enmity. Yet despite all this—a patient, measured approached learned at the foot of Mars through long years of war—there was still a tight, brittle tension in the moment before action broke, in the quiet space before spears clashed against shields and men roared their war cries, rushing forward onto the field.

So Gaius Julius waited, watching the woman think, seeing a flush rise in her breast, seeing her eyes brighten, her features draw tight with predatory sharpness. The old general remembered another woman, one with coal-dark hair, alabaster skin, piercing eyes like the sea in morning light, and he felt a pang in his heart, realizing he missed Kleopatra terribly.

You are not her, child, he thought sadly. *Though your physical charms surpass hers, you will never have her wit or quicksilver mind, a hawk soaring on summer air . . . will I ever see such a light in human flesh again?*

A memory tugged at his thought and Gaius' quick mind focused for an instant. *Who have I seen who struck me in just such a way . . . there was someone, a girl with gray eyes . . .*

"Yes," Martina pronounced, straightening, lifting her head. "I want to be the first woman in Rome, without equal or rival."

Gaius forced himself to concentrate on the moment at hand. "And your son? What do you wish for him?"

"An empire," Martina answered sharply. "A single, undivided empire."

The old Roman flashed a tight little smile, feeling his pulse quicken. The distracting memory was set aside. "What of your benefactor, your protector, the Emperor Galen? He has made many honorable pledges to you. . . ."

"Oh." Sorrow and guilt flared in Martina's face, but she shook the shadow away in a cascade of shining curls. "He is weary—let him retire, as Emperors have done before and live out his waning days in a garden by the sea, tending his cabbages."

Gaius Julius laughed softly, raising an eyebrow in appreciation. "Do you think he will agree as readily as Diocletian did?"

Annoyance and irritation replaced the sorrow in the woman's face. "He should! Even he must see how the world has changed. And if not . . . then wiser heads may prevail and save everyone such grief."

"And his son?" The old Roman tucked his hands into the folds of his toga, leaning back against the cool stone of the wall. "Will your Heracleonas miss his playmate?"

"I will not miss him or his mother!" Martina said, sharp delight spreading across her face. "Let her go into retirement as well, and the boy—he may suffer any sickness of the young—as she has pointed out herself!"

Gaius' gaze lingered on the woman's breasts, taut against the silk gown, and the curve of her shoulders, shining now with a faint sheen of sweat. He met her eyes with a cool glance and they were glistening dark, pupils swollen into the iris. *So quickly is the mild, bookish girl overthrown by a heady taste* . . . he thought sadly. Gaius stepped to her, holding out a broad, flat hand.

"We are agreed, then, my lady?"

Her soft, damp hand settled over his and she nodded fiercely. "We are agreed."

"Then," Gaius said, recovering his hand and bowing deeply to her. "I suggest we leave our common master, the prince, out of any deliberations or discussion." The old Roman essayed a thin smile. "He has much on his mind, for the war in Egypt goes poorly. Soon, I fear, he will be forced to take the field against the Persian mage. The gods of Rome give him strength for that contest!"

"He will win." Martina's confidence shone in her eyes like sun blazing from a raised shield.

"I pray so," Gaius said, keeping his own counsel in the matter. He pressed dry lips against the inside of her wrist, drawing a breathy giggle. "Then you shall have your heart's desire."

Martina laughed again and sat up on the windowsill, looking out upon the city with greedy eyes. Gaius Julius turned politely away, returning to his desk while the woman began talking softly to herself, white arm raised to indicate this temple or palace on the further hills.

". . . there will be a garden, filled with statues of all the great poets . . ."

The letter lay on his blotter, lacking only a signature. Gaius Julius read it over carefully, then—scowling at the lost effort— set it aside in a pile marked for speedy destruction in fire. He drew a freshly-cut sheet from a waiting stack and settled himself on the curule chair to write.

Dear Alexandros, he began, quill scratching across smooth lambskin, *as you have doubtless learned from the Emperor's courier, the Imperial fleet is almost ready to carry you to battle. Do not wait for their white sails, but march your army west by the Via Egnatia to Dyrrachium on the Epirote coast, where ships will be waiting for you. . . .*

Maxian heard singing and gay laughter. Disturbed from meditation, his thoughts rose from a still pool, breaching invisible waters. He sat, legs crossed in the Persian style, at the center of a small room adjoining the bedroom he shared with Martina in the house of Gregorius Auricus. Once, the chamber had held the old senator's desk and bookcases and personal items. Such things had been quietly removed by the servants and Maxian was content with a bare, polished floor and empty walls. A chatter of jays rose in the outer rooms as Martina's maids entered.

She is up to something, whispered a patrician voice in the prince's ear. *Listen to her tone, like a wolf speaking sweetly to the lamb!*

"Be quiet," Maxian said, lips barely moving. The sensation of a man—an old, white-haired gentleman with ink-stained fingers—faded. The prince bent a tiny fraction of his will against wood and metal. The door between the two rooms swung closed, bolts sliding into iron hasps with a sharp clunk. "I need to think."

The chamber grew dim, the light from the windows fading. Slowly, one by one, faint lights sprang into visibility in the air around the prince. Each varied in color and hue and speed, a restless cloud of sparks swinging around the seated man, each in their own orbit. Many were barely visible, only the faintest drifting streak of light, while others blazed bright, almost a candle flame in the darkness. They cast a wavering, golden glow across Maxian's sharp features.

He closed his eyes, letting thoughts settle, letting his mind grow calm and clear, his hands at rest upon muscular thighs, palms open.

I need more strength, he thought, considering his enemy. *The Oath is weak in Egypt. The Dark Queen will not be at my side. My enemy has gained allies, while I have none.*

Impressions of the Persian sorcerer unfolded in his memory, coming to life for his inner eye. Again, he relived the battle in the streets of Constantinople and his fear was far away, confined and controlled. Maxian watched carefully, gauging the strength of his opponent. This time he paid close attention to the jackal-headed man, watching the creature crawl from shattered icy stone, iron mask smoking dull-red with heat. When the opponents parted, each retiring undefeated, Maxian let the vision begin again. This time, he focused upon the powers roiling and shuddering in the hidden world, flowing around the prince, the sorcerer, the Dark Queen and the Jackal, like a storm-driven tide.

The Jackal, Maxian thought deliberately, *is a slave, held by a noose of power. The creature wields its own power—not inconsiderable!—yet is a pawn, an extension of the Serpent's will.*

Intrigued, the prince studied the shining matrices shifting and distorting around the two Persians. Maxian had placed a mark of servitude on a man before—he had even roughly grasped control of Alexandros once, when the need pressed him—but those efforts were crude in comparison to the chains binding the jackal to its inhuman master. Maxian felt fear of his enemies' skill eddy up again, but repressed the emotion.

You are powerful and skilled, the prince thought, holding an image of the Persian in his thoughts, *yet so am I. You are ancient and steeped in lost knowledge, but I learn swiftly. Per-*

haps . . . Maxian shook his head, wishing yet again he'd kept his temper and the Nabatean wizard Abdmachus were still alive to guide him. *I miss the old fool*, he thought ruefully. *I need his skills—hard-won through years of effort—I've no time to spend in diligent study to gain them. . . .*

A thought occurred to the prince and he turned to the glowing air spinning around him.

"Columella!" Maxian commanded, "show yourself!"

One spark, brighter than the rest, dipped and dodged among their multitude, speeding to rest before the prince. Maxian moved a finger and the mote blazed with light, swelling rapidly into the half-transparent shape of a man. An old man, with a fine Latin nose, hunched shoulders and thinning white hair. Behind the image, another spark—a sullen green—slowed to a halt, hanging behind the ghostly shoulder, light dimming into near invisibility.

"Old man," Maxian said curiously, "you whisper advice in my ear, lend me your knowledge of ancient tongues, watch over me while I sleep. Why?"

Columella's seamed and wrinkled face twisted into a rueful grin, hands raised in a shrug.

I live in you, Maxian heard as a faint whisper, *though you murdered me while I sat reading.*

Maxian flinched a little, but his brother's acid voice echoed in memory and he knew there was no time for guilt or second thoughts about the past. Only the future remained, clouded by onrushing disaster. "What did you do in life?"

I was a scholar, the old man answered dreamily. *I read, I wrote . . . I plundered the past for poetry, for stories, for anecdotes to make my patron laugh at dinner parties. Some accounted me an expert in matters of the vine. I never guessed learning the signs of the ancients would prove such a fruitful business!*

"You have helped me," Maxian said, considering the cloud of light spinning around him. "You have skills I lack . . . What of these others? What do they know?"

Faint, thready laughter answered him. Columella's ghost shook its head. *What do you wish? There are entire cities here, lord prince! Bakers, fishermen, soldiers, prostitutes . . . who do you think guided your hands, your lips, when you lay with the Empress? They are eager, you know, eager to taste a little life again, through you.*

"Are they?" Maxian smiled in amusement, holding up his hands. Swarms of sparks crowded around his fingers, and now he could hear individual voices, pleading, praising, begging for an instant of his attention. He started to feel dizzy, then scowled furiously, closing his hands. "Enough! There is no time for this."

The sparks fled from his anger, whirling away in the air. He felt great relief as their voices fell silent. "Better," Maxian allowed, turning his attention again to the old scholar. Columella had grown faint in the passing moment, but now his image strengthened, becoming almost solid.

"Are there any among your number," the prince asked, keeping a firm tone in his voice, "who know aught of thaumaturgy or the matter of wizards?"

The cloud of light stirred, drifting this way and that, then parted. A feeble spark limped into view, barely a smudge of pearl against the dark air. Maxian focused upon the mote, willing it to spring to fullness before him. Radiance swelled, filling a withered, hunched frame and dull, nearly lifeless eyes.

"Who is this?" Maxian turned to Columella again.

This is Quintus Metelus Pius, the scholar answered. *He served in the Legions as a thaumaturge for much of his life. He was retired to Oplontis with his pension, living in a little villa by the sea, with hyacinths in the—*

"Enough." Maxian focused upon the dim spark, willing it to flare with life, with fullness, to show him the old man's face. He sent a thread of power into the failing, weak consciousness. "Let him speak for himself."

A flare of dull copper lit the room and the mote rushed into a man's shape. Maxian stared in surprise—*this was no old man!*—this was a Legion officer in full health. . . .

Quintus struck, ghostly face transformed by rage, will brilliant with desire. A ghostly fist slammed against the prince's face. Maxian staggered, rolling back on the floor, blood flying from a suddenly broken nose. Power flickered in the air, accompanied by a grumbling, low rumble. Maxian's hair stirred, driven by an unseen wind.

Now! screamed thousands of voices. *Smash him! Crush him! Set us free!*

The legionary leapt forward, fire blazing from his hands. Maxian shouted in fear, fingers leaping into a sign of defense. A glittering, blue-white shield sprang into the air. Quintus struck with both fists, a coruscating dodecahedron pattern crashing into the prince's ward. Angles intersected, clashing violently and Maxian's pattern splintered. Glassy blue-white fragments smoked in the air. The prince struck the wall, feeling bones creak. Quintus swelled in size as countless sparks flooded to him, guttering out in headlong sacrifice. Lightning rippled along the ceiling, burning the stones black with soot. The legionary slashed his hand down, eyes alive with fire, and Maxian staggered, a long, red wound lashed open in his neck and chest. Stabbing pain flooded his mind and the pattern binding self to self began to fray. A chorus of exalted screams rocked the air.

Tasting bitter iron in his mouth, Maxian groped to raise his shield again. A multitude of sparks swarmed around him, each tiny, angry will beating at his consciousness. The prince's face stilled as he concentrated, ignoring the frenzy around him. The Oath was waiting, surging around the room, vast and implacable, the combined will and thought and memory of millions of loyal Romans. Maxian seized hold, letting the black tide roar through him. The room seemed to compress and he looked down from a great height, seeing the entire city spread out below him like a mosaic. He reached down, finger stabbing at a single, shining spark.

Quintus' shape wavered and a vast wailing shrieked in the air. The legionnaire shattered, the frail, weak pattern of his ghost-mind smashed aside by Maxian's unleashed power. There was a flare and the prince felt screaming despair flood into his bones. Half-consciously, he sensed the ghost trying to flee and reached out, seizing the man's guttering, nearly exhausted will in a icy pattern of interlocking diamonds.

"Treachery earns destruction," Maxian grated, staggering away from the wall. He closed his fist and felt the Legion thaumaturge's will shatter, pinned between irresistible forces. "But you are not yet discharged from my service."

His face a cold mask, the prince enveloped the fragments,

drinking them into his consciousness. Memories flooded into his thoughts, memories and smells and sensations and skill like a draught of crisp Caucinian taken from a freshly broached amphora. Remorseless, his pride and honor stung by the thaumaturge's ambush, Maxian winnowed out the man's training from the freshet of other memories and emotions. *Shields and wards,* he saw, *patterns and tricks, every kind of subtle skill . . .*

The prince opened his eyes and saw the world through sharper eyes. The ghost of Columella remained, one eye burning green, though the radiant cloud had dimmed tremendously. Maxian felt a little sick, though the exercise of such power no longer wore against him, but elevated his mind.

You should not be surprised, my lord, Columella said, shaking his head sadly. *There are many among your attendants who wished you ill. They were young, still in love with life, and they resented such abrupt cessation.*

"But you do not?" Maxian strode to the center of the room, translucent armor glittering around him in the hidden world, his power licking along the floor like a burning red sea. The ghost bowed, shaking his head.

As I said before, even this half-life is better than oblivion.

Maxian laughed hoarsely. "You do not believe in Elysium?"

I see only darkness, my lord.

"Very well," the prince said, turning his attention to the slowly shifting cloud of sparks. "My mind is upon you now, little spirits, and you must choose." Maxian's face drew intent, eyes darkening, an odd, bluish light flickering around him in a gossamer shroud. "The loyal will remain, the treacherous will find true oblivion waiting for them. I have no time and no patience to coddle you. . . ."

Rippling ultraviolet shaded through the room as the prince bent to his task, face a grim mask. The wailing roared up again, though no human ear could perceive the shrieks and moans of the tortured spirits. Columella turned away, his face against the wall. He could not bear to see such a judgement, though his withered old heart exalted to find another crumb of existence on his plate. The greenish light in his eye dimmed, flickering down to nothing, no more than the faintest spark of hate. Waiting patiently, hidden among the ghostly pattern of the old scholar.

Caesar! Caesar! A ship is entering the port! It's one of ours!"

Aurelian turned away from a high, narrow window, brow furrowed in unease. *Why have the dogs stopped barking?* Following his usual custom, the prince was wearing the full armor of a common legionnaire, heavy, red hair hanging greasily around his shoulders. The last of his servants had been sent away as medical orderlies, leaving Aurelian to see to his own kit and toilet.

One of the local boys swerved between rows of tables crowded into the big room, brown face slick with moisture. Aurelian held up a hand, making the lad skid to a halt. The prince was uneasy; he had been peering at the sky, which was turning an odd green color with the onset of late afternoon. The street outside the building was empty too, which was strange. Usually a constant, noisy throng trampled every square foot of ground inside the walls, particularly with the city population swollen by men and women fleeing the fighting in the countryside.

"What did you see?"

The boy wiped his face, catching his breath. A light rain was falling outside, presaging the usual grumble of afternoon thunderstorms. Grayish haze lay over the city, discharging a tepid, oily drizzle. As summer advanced in the delta, the weather grew more and more oppressive. Even sunset brought no relief, the city sweltering throughout the night in a bath of its own heat and sweat. Aurelian mopped the base of his neck with a damp rag. He really hated this place.

"A grain hauler, master! Four decks of sails, as tall as the Lighthouse!"

Aurelian squinted through the window at the sky again. "Which direction?"

"From the west," the boy answered, flashing a smile. "A Roman ship!"

"Is it?" Aurelian swallowed, feeling a cloying thickness in his throat. He turned, glowering at the men laboring over the desks. The flight of the civil government from the city had left him with only a few dozen competent clerks, who labored in the headquarters occupying the harbormaster's offices near the junction of the Heptastadion causeway and the city. The vast complex of the Bruchion—the usual governor's residence— was crowded to the rafters with refugees from the delta and upriver.

"Phranes!" One of the clerks turned to face him, leathery old face drawn tight with fatigue. "Hasn't the grain fleet been rerouted to Africa?"

Phranes nodded. "Aye, my lord. We're expecting nothing from Rome."

Aurelian's face twisted into a sour grin at the dry cynicism in the man's voice. Not a single ship had arrived in port for the past eleven days—not so much as a fishing barque or a courier boat. The prince guessed the Roman fleet was being held back—*At Syracuse? Or Lepcis Magna?*—while the Emperor prepared a counterblow. *But relief will not come for another . . . week. If then.*

"Lad, were there flags or banners of any kind?" Aurelian's fingers curled around the pommel of his gladius, a habitual, unthinking action. The heavy weight of metal on his shoulders and chest was comforting.

"Just the usual ones, Caesar." The boy shrugged, spreading his hands.

Aurelian looked out the window again. The queer copper coloring was spreading through the clouds like ink spilling into a murky pool. His lips tightened. The city had fallen silent.

"Runners!" The prince spun on his heel, sharp voice booming across the quiet room. Scribes and clerks jerked around, staring at him in surprise. "Phranes—gather everyone up and issue spears, knives, whatever is to hand! Barricade the windows and doors. You boys, get to the wall commanders instantly—the Persians are about to attack. You, my lad, tell the commander of my Praetorians in the atrium they're down to the docks at a run, to keep your grain hauler from landing, or to capture the vessel if naught else."

Everyone was frozen for a moment, then Aurelian snatched up his helmet and bolted from the room at a dead run, weapons and armor jangling.

"To arms!" he shouted, jogging down the steps onto the broad dockside avenue. Messenger boys sprinted past; a dozen brown whippets unleashed. "Romans to arms!"

His guardsmen leapt up from their pallets, weapons in hand. They immediately poured down the steps behind him, a mob of men in stained, battered iron armor. Every man—whether he had been sleeping, gambling or complaining—was ready to fight; spears, axes, swords already in hand. Aurelian flashed a grin, seeing their grim faces intent upon him.

"A ship filled with the enemy is closing upon the docks. Take her if you can, else burn her to the water. If she's truly ours, hie back here to me as fast as you can. I'll need your strong arms! There will be bloody work today. Sound the alarm as you go, and go swiftly!"

Aurelian slid the helmet on, tightening the strap under his chin. The Praetorians flooded past, shaking out into column as they scrambled out of the building. Their boots rang loudly on the paving stones. High above, on the roof, someone began ringing an alarm bar, a clashing, tinny sound that fell flat in the leaden air. The prince strode out into the avenue, staring up at the sky.

The green stain continued to crawl across the heavens and its shadow was dark on the rooftops.

Where shall I go? he wondered, limbs trembling with blood-fire, a nervous, grainy edge to his thoughts. He yearned to rush down one of the deserted streets, screaming a battle cry. Instead, to his disgust, he realized there was nothing to do but go back inside and wait for messengers to come to him.

With a last, furious look around, Aurelian stomped back inside.

Khalid al'Walid splashed through the surf, feeling stones and gravel roll under his boots. A low island lay before him, the highest prominence a golden roof rising above a brood of accompanying temples. The beach was crowded with men in green-and-tan, clambering out of long boats and barges and skiffs. More boats filled with dark-bearded men maneuvered offshore, sails white against a brassy sea. The young Arab grinned in delight, feeling warm water slosh against his calves. The strand was empty, without so much as a fisherman in sight.

"Forward!" he shouted, clear young voice rising above the slap of the water and the shouts of the Sahaba as they disembarked. Threads of fog rolled overhead, hiding the sun and obscuring the flat, green sea behind them. Khalid trudged up through golden sand, aiming for an opening between the buildings ahead. Arab skirmishers scattered across the beach, bows in hand, heads high and alert.

"Form on your banners," the *qalb* section commanders yelled at their men. "Form up! Form up!"

Horns and trumpets wailed, adding to the racket. Arab and Greek soldiers milled on the beach, searching for their tentmates and rallying standards. More boats ran in to the shore and men leapt down into the water with abandon. The barges in the first wave backed oars, trying to clear the beach. Most of the soldiers clinging to the railings were pale-faced, but they splashed into the water, desperately eager to reach steady ground. All possibility of organization had been lost as soon as the flotilla had put to sea from Canopus, seven miles away at the mouth of the Boutikos channel. "Forward! Forward!"

Blank walls etched by the wind and sea rose up at the crest of the beach. Khalid jogged up, now surrounded by a mass of Sahaban fighters in heavy Persian-style armor. The young general's sharp beard and flowing green-and-gold robes were easy to recognize, even in the confusion of the landing. Men gathered around him, seeing his eagle banner snapping in the landward breeze. Between the ancient tombs, an alley led off into a maze of buildings.

Khalid slowed, reaching the entrance to the lane. Sea grass crept to the foot of the walls and scraps of plaster clung to bare stone. The young Arab squinted down the twisting passage, surprised by the heavy quiet pervading the island.

"An island of tombs," he said aloud. "Is anyone alive here, save ourselves?"

Shaking his head, Khalid looked about, spying the hulking figures of Jalal and Shadin among the men climbing up from the beach.

"Generals!" The Eagle stepped out of the phalanx of his guardsmen. The two older Arabs looked up at him with tight, closed expressions. "Jalal—take charge of the landing. Get everyone ashore and formed up. Shadin—you take half the men around that way . . ." Khalid pointed towards the gleaming red roof and terraces of a massive temple rising at the eastern end of the island. Statues lined the rooftop, most of them gleaming white where their colorful paint had been stripped away by the sea wind. "Capture the lighthouse and the harbor entrance. I'll strike across the island for the causeway."

Both men nodded silently, eyes invisible in the shadow of their helmets. The young Arab could feel their disapproval of his command, but they said nothing. Khalid stared after them as the older men turned away, gesturing for their own aides, messengers and guardsmen. For a moment, he considered calling them back, but put the thought aside. *They are Sahaba*, he reckoned, *and they will fight for the memory of the Teacher, if not for me*.

"Forward," Khalid shouted, striding into the lane. With a rasp, he drew the ebon blade once carried by Mohammed from its jeweled sheath. In the diffuse, limpid sunlight the weapon gleamed with a twisting inner flame. A cheer went up at the sight of the blade of the city, and Khalid felt his heart soar at the sound. "With me, lads," he cried, grinning, feeling a wild, unrestrained joy rise in his breast.

At the head of his thousands, the young general strode down the deserted street between ancient, crumbling tombs. What remained of the day's strange quiet immediately dissolved into the commotion of running men in armor, sandals and boots slapping on the paving stones.

"Hold up a moment." Sextus stood, wiping sweat from a suntanned brow. He stared out to sea, across the flat, placid waters of the Great Harbor. The engineer held a large sledge in his hands, but the hammer was forgotten for the moment as he bit his lip in concentration. Frontius paused, sitting up, hands on his knees. Both men had been squatting near the edge of a great arched vault, examining the stonework around a keystone supporting the central section of the massive Heptastation causeway.

A crowd of local workers—fellaheen in white breechclouts and turbans—watched the two Romans suspiciously. The locals were laden with a profusion of iron bars, hammers, mallets, buckets of water and wooden splitting wedges. A handful of Roman citizens in mismatched armor stood near by, watching both the Legion officers and the fellaheen with jaundiced expressions. The citizens had been drafted from their businesses, homes and offices to provide a city militia. Despite the continuing siege, most of the locals seemed content to let the Legionnaires fight.

"Something is happening." Sextus' voice was flat and Frontius started in alarm, then stared out to sea, following the sharp angle of his friend's pointing arm. Almost two thousand feet away, across the open waters of the harbor, he could barely make out the dark smudge of the sea—intermittent flashes of white from crashing waves outlining the long rubble-filled breakwater.

"I don't see anything . . ." Frontius stood up as well, squinting ferociously. Off to the left of the breakwater, the towering shape of the Lighthouse—the famous Pharos—made a gleaming white outline against the lead-colored sky. A brilliant disk on the summit of the forty-story building flashed in the dimming sun. The engineer cursed the fickle stars who had burdened him with poor sight. "What is it?"

"Fog," Sextus said in the same flat voice. The older engineer shook himself, then bent down and began jamming his tools and books into a leather shoulder bag. "Rising fast too, all along the breakwater."

"It's afternoon," Frontius said in a disbelieving voice. "There's never any . . ."

Sextus looked up, eyes narrowed against the afternoon sun glittering from the water. "Sorcery, my friend."

Frontius blanched. He had seen enough horrors in the last four weeks. Still, he was a legionary and if something was happening on the breakwater . . . Frontius turned, squinting at the low, green shape of the Pharos island lying at the outer end of the causeway. "You don't suppose—"

"You men!" Sextus bellowed, startling the citizens and fellahin alike into wide-eyed attention. "With me, all of you! Double-time!" The engineer began running north along the Heptastadion towards the palace-crowded island. Frontius caught up with him in a moment, wiry legs easily meeting the pace.

"What do you—" One of the citizens, a baker by trade, was left with his mouth hanging open.

The other Latins stared after the two engineers, then hurried to pick up their jumble of weapons and tools from the ground. A moment later, they too jogged off into the haze rising from the harbor. Watching the Romans disappear into the fog, the fellahin looked warily at one another, then turned and scuttled towards the city as fast as they could.

Khalid burst from the avenue at a run, shield snug against his left arm, a dim, mist-veiled sun gleaming in the curving blade of his sword. A guttural roar boomed from his men as they saw the enemy. The road wound out between low buildings and onto a broad causeway flanked by a retaining wall on either side and stout pillars carved with dolphins and cranes. The entrance to the Heptastadion was blocked by overturned carts and building materials. Khalid caught sight of Romans crouched behind the barrier, some in armor, some not. Their faces were only blurs as he ran forward, shouting, "at them!"

The Sahaba rushed forward, more and more men spilling out of the alleyways and down the street. Khalid leapt forward at an easy run, seeing the barricade loom before him. Then, only ten paces or so away, the Romans stood up and Khalid shouted a warning.

"Javelins!" He swung up his shield, turning his body away from the flying spears and stones.

Something heavy smashed into the laminated hide and cedar of his shield. Khalid staggered, startled by the strength in the cast, then rushed ahead again. He leapt over the body of an Arab youth choking on his own blood, a short-hafted spear jutting from his chest. The triangular tip had punched clear through the boy's scaled breastplate, leaving thin streams of crimson crawling across polished metal.

Khalid felt his shield drag and cursed—a javelin was stuck in the hides, head twisted, wooden shaft banging against his knees—pausing to knock the missile away with his sword. Arabs and Nabateans pushed past, surging against the barricade. Shouts and screams tore the air and the clanging racket of iron on iron beat at Khalid's ears. The javelin clattered to the ground and the young general tried to push forward through the press of sweating, close-packed men.

Khalid's effort failed. Too many armored backs crowded in front of him. The Romans met the charge with a brisk play of blades and spears on the barrier, throwing the Sahaba back, leaving scattered bodies trapped in the jumble of carts and logs and blocks of stone. Khalid cursed again, this time at himself and wormed his way back towards the rear ranks.

"Shields!" he screamed, trying to be heard above the din. The Romans were shouting insults now and flinging amphorae into the crowd of Arabs. The crash of breaking pottery and the sting of vinegar filled the air. Khalid's throat was already hoarse and the day's battle was only minutes old. "Form shield wall!"

He broke free of the crowd and immediately began dragging men back by their belts and helmet straps. "Everyone back! Form a line!"

More Sahaba pressed toward the barrier, running up out of the confusing maze of tombs and temples covering the island. On their barricade, the Romans were laughing. Some men with bows now shot from between the wagons, knocking down Arabs trapped in the press of the crowd.

"Everyone back a pace!" Khalid shouted again and now his banner leaders began to repeat his command, beating on their soldier's helmets and shoulders with the flat of their swords. Slowly, the mass of Arabs, Nabateans and Greeks fell back, letting their shields come into play. More dead littered the ground before the barricade. The dusty ground clotted with blood and wine.

The Jackal stepped forth from the remains of a farmhouse a hundred yards from the Roman rampart. Before him loomed the doubled towers of the Gate of the Sun, a pair of granite and sandstone monsters rising four and five stories above the plain. On either side, the sloping berm of the fortification ran off into cloudy, humid air. The ancient stone was scored with jagged black streaks and glassy, star-shaped craters. Thickets of stakes and tangled brush—most burned and withered from terrible fires—covered the slope on either side of the gate.

Not a single man could be seen on the wall, for the Romans had finally learned prudence.

The Jackal's mask had been repaired and repainted, chalky eyes bright, the lolling tongue fresh as blood. Even the shattered ear had been reforged and replaced. His body, twisted with scars and puckered wounds, was filled with new life— strong, muscular, shining with sweat in the dreadful heat. A clean white kilt fell from a belt of dark leather. His bare feet dug into the rich, loamy black soil of the delta.

The Jackal raised his hand and the sullen green sky rippled with slow waves. Distantly, a long, drawn-out rumble of thunder answered his motion. The presence within the mask felt the air pressure change and shift, saw gradients of power surge in the land—dark blue leaching up from hidden waters—bricks crumbled in the ruined building and grass withered as the Jackal summoned power to his rising hand.

Fists clenched, then pointed towards the looming wall.

A week and a day had passed since the failure of the first Persian assault. The Jackal's master had regained his power, gathered his wits, seen the wisdom of the Boar's plan and labored a long time beneath dark and moonless skies among the tombs and fields surrounding the city. Undisturbed by the Roman thaumaturges hiding in the city, the Lord of the Ten Serpents had hidden his foul work with night and distance.

A dry rustling chattered in the air and the Jackal leapt lightly up onto the top of a broken, splintered brick wall. Immediately, figures shambled forward below him, first one—groping sightlessly forward, eyes black pits, fingers skeletal twigs—then another, and another.

Within moments, a vast crowd of dry brown shapes crawled and shuffled out of the fields, emerging from the mist, their outlines indistinct in the steadily fading light. A dull green haze advanced in the upper air, roiling across the sky, tendrils rushing forward, then curling around some unseen obstacle before oozing onward again. A clacking murmur began to rise from the host shuffling towards the wall.

The Jackal turned, looking south. A mile away, at the Nile Gate, a figure in radiant white turned as well and she raised pale cream arms, wrapped tight with gold and silver. The Raven answered his unspoken thought. Their power moved in the hidden world, motivating desiccated limbs to jerking, fumbling motion. The two figures turned to the city, looking out over the advancing host of the uneasy dead.

On the wall, motion stirred, then feeble sunlight glanced from a helmet. The day grew dark as the oily clouds advanced. Shadows deepened in the ruins and under the eaves of the buildings.

On the plain below, the dead began to shamble forward, almost at a run, and their dry limbs rubbed and scraped, a forest of winter-bare twigs and branches shaken by an invisible, irresistible wind. The first of the dead began to climb the slope. One drove itself, unthinking, unheeding, upon a sharpened stake. The wood tore through ancient, withered skin, then jabbed from the corpses' back. Black dust puffed from the wound. Undaunted, the shape clawed forward, leathery body tearing in half with a dry, ripping sound. Relentless, the head and torso crawled up the slope. Severed legs beat violently in the dirt.

A long, wailing cry sounded, ringing back from the towers and ramparts. On a fighting platform atop the wall, a torsion arm snapped against a hide-wrapped wooden bar. With a loud *twang*, a wicker ball caked with pitch arced into the air, crackling and burning, trailing black smoke. The missile plunged into the vast, jostling crowd advancing across the field. Pale green-and-orange fire blossomed, consuming a dozen, two dozen of the dead. Without a sound, they marched on, dry flesh making ready tinder, puffy white smoke rising to join the dark oily effluvia of naphtha. More corpses staggered, heedless, into the bonfire.

A brownish-gray tide rose against the wall, scrambling and crawling up the slope. Where one corpse fell, tangled in thorns or pierced by a stake, twenty crawled on, grinding the fallen into dust beneath skeletal feet. A *clack-clack-clack* of splintering bone rose, swelling into the heavy air.

Distantly, the Jackal heard men shouting in fear. More scorpions *thwanged* and more missiles lofted into the afternoon sky. Bombs fell, billowing into flame with a snap and rush of igniting air. Figures on the wall began hurling stones that crashed and bounced among the silent, advancing mob. At the Gate of the Sun, burning oil fell in sheets of flame onto corpses and withered skeletons crowding at the portals themselves. Huge clouds of smoke boiled up and the dry rattling jerked into a cacophony of burning skin and cracking bone.

Still, the dead continued to swarm across the fields.

Atop his wall, the Jackal trembled, power rushing through him like water in a mining sluice, eroding his tattered soul. A mile away to the south, the Queen shuddered as well, her still-living body suffering the piercing, red-hot pain of the sorcerer's working. Sweat blinded her, yet she did not fall. Instead, she stood alone atop a half-burned siege tower, a golden diadem shining in her dark hair, plainly visible from the walls.

This she did by choice, for she would not turn her face from the destruction of such a fair city.

"Loose!" Khalid screamed, trying to make himself heard above the din. His archers perched on the temple roofs shot, bows singing with a flat *twang-twang*. The Romans on the barricade ducked, black shafts flashing past. The young Eagle glanced left and right, gauging his men—they tensed in the shield wall, eyes glittering beneath shadowed helms—then slashed his saber down. "Charge!"

Shrieking, the Sahaba stormed forward down the road. More arrows flicked past overhead, and the Roman archers in the jumble of carts and crates loosed as well. Khalid heard something hiss past his ear as he ran forward. He picked up speed, howling a war cry, then sprang up onto the barricade.

A Roman stabbed at his legs and Khalid blocked the stroke deftly with his shield. Laminated pine splintered with the blow as Khalid hacked down at the man's head. The Roman ducked away and Khalid jumped into the midst of the enemy, saber whirling in a flashing, black streak. One of the militiamen jerked around in surprise, just in time to take the blade across the bridge of his unprotected nose. Bone shattered, a fine spray of blood-and-white fragments splashing across the faces of his fellows. Khalid slammed the shield into the Roman's broken face with a wet crunch. More Sahaba scrambled over the barricade.

The Romans stabbed back fiercely with spears and javelins. Men toppled, guts spilling out in shiny coils of gray and white.

Khalid took two blows on his shield in succession—a legionary in full armor pressed him, short sword flickering like a snake's tongue—then drove the man back with a sharp rush. The black blade keened in the air, cutting at the Roman's elbow. The man, squinting furiously, gave a step. Finding no room to maneuver in such close quarters, Khalid abandoned any pretense at skill, slamming in with his shield. The Roman took the blow with a grunt, then smashed his own rectangular scuta against Khalid's smaller, round buckler. The young Eagle's boot skidded in something wet and he went down with a clatter.

Stunned, Khalid tried to scramble up. Someone stepped on his chest, pinning him under a heavy wet boot. Robes billowed around his face, blinding him. Frantic, Khalid slammed the pommel of his sword into an obscuring leg, heard a bellow of fear, then the offending Sahaba toppled aside, one eye a bloody ruin. The squinting Roman's gladius whipped back, streaked with blood.

Shouting in fury, Khalid scrambled up, leading with the point of his blade. He thrust, catching the Roman on the shoulder-plate. The saber bent on impact, skittering across curving iron. Shouting in alarm, the legionary blocked sideways with his short sword. The point of the Arab blade bounced away, leaving a deep scratch in the metal. Khalid recovered, whipping his sword into a figure-eight parry. For an instant, he locked furious gazes with the Roman, then the entire enemy line of battle was retreating.

Somewhere, a horn blew wildly amid the drone of deep-throated tubas. The Romans—legionaries and militia alike—fell back onto the causeway. Khalid caught his breath, slumping to his knees. Droplets of crimson oozed from the edge of his blade, joining a thick paste of urine, feces and blood on the ground.

"Press on!" Khalid croaked, fighting for breath. He was winded. Two of his men grasped his shoulders and dragged him to his feet. The young Eagle called for his standard bearer, seeing the man a dozen yards away, a stained cloth against the side of his face. "Bannerman! We must move—"

A deep *whump!* caused Khalid to swing round. The Romans, falling back along the causeway, had set fire to a wagonload of oil. The wooden cart spilled sideways as Khalid watched, lips thinning in dismay. Hundreds of amphorae cascaded to the ground, already wreathed in pale yellow flame. A huge cloud of heavy black smoke surged up into the hazy air. Sheets of fire rushed forward on the paving stones.

"Spears!" Khalid shouted, skipping back. The vanguard of the Sahaba fell back, shields and cloaks raised to protect their faces from the roaring flames. "Sand and wagons and spears!"

Some of his men ran off to gather tools. The young Eagle looked away, terrific heat beating against his lean face. Both harbors were nearly empty. Off to his right, the only ship in sight was a huge Roman grain hauler near the merchant docks. Khalid fingered his beard, keen eyes trying to pierce the haze between himself and the distant vessel. *Another daring ploy*, he thought, *but did it gain us anything? Has Usama seized the warehouse district? Or does he lie dead?*

Men returned with long poles torn from the ornamental facade of a funeral temple. Khalid roused himself, wiping sweat from his face. The *qalb* filled the causeway from railing to railing, every man's face eager to press ahead.

"There," the young Arab pointed, "push the wagon away!"

With a cadenced shout, a hundred men advanced, long poles held by five or six men each. In an instant, the pikes plunged across the roaring flames, thumping against the charring wood of the cart. The soldiers strained, digging in their feet. The cart creaked and groaned, spilling oil onto the ground. Fresh flames jetted up. Amphorae shattered in the heat, consumed by flame, flinging red-hot fragments of pottery into the faces of the Arabs. Everyone ducked, still pushing for all they were worth.

"Heave!" Khalid shouted. His men answered with a basso roar. "Ho!"

The cart squealed aside, crunching into the low stone wall lining the edge of the causeway. Boys ran forward with heavy baskets, flinging sand onto the pools of burning oil.

"Heave!" Khalid shouted. The men on the poles, faces glowing with effort, sweat streaming into their armor, gave a groan of effort. The cart tipped, boards shattering. One of the wheels spun away across the causeway. "Heave!" Another massive effort and the cart teetered on the wall, then plunged over the side in a billowing rush of smoke. A great splash fountained up. Oil and smoke spread on the waters.

An arrow fluttered down out of the sky, shattering on the paving stones near Khalid.

"Archers, forward!" The young Eagle pointed with his saber. Nabateans ran up, their long bows taut, shafts to the string. More men handed baskets of sand and dirt from hand to hand, and the oil began to flicker and die, smothered by the advancing fire crew. Arab bows began to sing, flinging arrows into the half-seen line of the Romans beyond the roiling smoke.

"*Qalb*-men to me!" Khalid strode forward. Fighters appeared out of the man of soldiers on the causeway, each man in heavy armor, with longer, oval shields. These men were armed with maces, heavy swords, stabbing spears. "Prepare to rush!"

Khalid fell back a step, letting the Sahaba run past and form up in a line of three ranks.

Arrows continued to snap back and forth between the opposing lines. The smoke was beginning to blow away, carried in a desultory afternoon breeze. Khalid felt sweat pooling in his shirt and against his spine. *Hot work out here, even with the water so close . . .*

"Charge!" Horns and trumpets echoed his scream and the *qalb* rushed to the attack, iron-shod boots trampling through the flames still licking on stone. There was a breathless, still moment as they stormed forward. Then the Roman line appeared out of the murk and there was a massive *crash!* as iron met iron, shield against shield. Men began to shout, a deep, angry roar, and a din of blades and spears and shields drowned all other noise.

Khalid waved more men forward. Now they would see whose arm was the stronger, whose heart the steadier.

"What is happening on the outer wall?" Aurelian's voice snapped in the dimly-lit room.

One of the runners stared at him with wide eyes, gasping for breath. The Egyptian had just run the length of the city, from the commandery at the Gate of the Sun. Everyone in the headquarters grew silent, waiting for him to speak.

"There are too many," the boy panted. "They're attacking everywhere, along the entire length of the wall, from the lake to the sea."

"Impossible!" Aurelian's angry response was instant. "They don't have the men to—"

"My lord!" The boy was on his knees, hands clasped. "It's true! It's true! I saw fighting everywhere. . . ."

Aurelian snarled, grinding a fist into his thigh. "How can there be so many?" he shouted, glaring at his aides and clerks. "The wall is three miles long!"

A commotion in the entrance distracted him and the prince's eye lit up to see one of his Praetorians push into the room. The big German's helmet was missing, his lank blond hair matted with sweat and an ugly cut oozed yellow serum from the side of his neck.

"Carus! What happened at the ship?" Aurelian leaned forward eagerly.

"Greek pirates," shouted the man in answer, "but we were ready. They are all dead. The ship is ours. But there—"

"Excellent." Aurelian grinned. Then he heard a strange sound rising outside. "What is that?"

Everyone turned to the windows, staring out into an unnaturally dark afternoon. The entire sky was a sickly, corroded-copper green. Strange thread-like clouds writhed in the sky. Aurelian squeezed to the nearest window, head canted as he listened.

Far away, a dull, roaring sound boomed down empty avenues. A moment later, the prince could feel the floor under his feet begin to shake. "Sorcery?" He turned, eyes searching for Phranes. "Where are our thaumaturges?" Aurelian barked, a sudden queasy feeling turning his stomach. The clerk started in alarm, then pushed off through the crowd.

"Carus, where are my guardsmen?"

"At the causeway," the German shouted, waving his arm. "There is fighting on the causeway!"

"Look out!" Sextus yelled desperately. Frontius glanced over his shoulder, cursing, and staggered as an Arab axe slammed into his turning back. Metal plates splintered and wires snapped. The engineer was driven to his feet, blood oozing between the metal plates of his lorica. Sextus fell back himself, fending off a questing spear jabbing at his groin. A confused melee spilled around the base of the white pillar standing at the junction of the Heptastadion and the city proper, swirling knots of men struggling across the circular plaza. One of the enemy, dark brown face split by a mad grin, lunged at Sextus again.

The engineer banged the spear aside with his shield. Wildly, he searched for Frontius among flashing blades and rushing men. The Arab stabbed overhand, triangular iron point flashing at the Roman's eyes. Sextus slewed his shield into the path of the spearpoint, catching it square. Metal ground on wood and Sextus—grimacing furiously—lunged in, stabbing with his gladius. The Arab danced back, the shorter blade missing cleanly.

The clatter of boots on stone rose up behind the engineer, but he was fully occupied trying to keep the spear from slashing open his knee or the inside of his thigh. A huge *crash* sounded and burly men with red cloaks suddenly rushed past the engineer. Sextus gasped with relief, staggering back out of the line of battle. A cohort of Praetorians tore into the Arabs and the spearman was hacked down by a long, heavy blade wielded two-handed by one of the Germans.

"Frontius!" Sextus scrambled sideways, towards the water's edge, rolling bodies over, searching for his friend. Rumpled corpses lay in clots on the plaza, Roman and Arab alike. The roar of men and the clash of arms was very loud, but the engineer ignored the stiffening melee around the base of the pillar. His hands, black with grime and sweat, searched among tormented bodies. Many groaned as he moved them, blood spilling from slack mouths, eyes rolling wildly, but he could not find Frontius.

Fighting shoulder to shoulder, the Praetorians drove the Arabs back. Many of the more lightly armed and armored desert men found their shields splintered, helms driven in, arms beaten down by the massive Germans. Horns wailed and the attackers fell back. The Praetorians halted their advance, dressing their line. Militiamen dragged the wounded back from the line and into the shelter of the buildings fronting the plaza.

Sextus reached the water's edge—the dockside ended in a

smooth marble wall overlooking turgid, dark water—and cursed sadly. His squint-eyed friend, the veteran of so many campaigns and scrapes, was nowhere to be found. Mastering himself, Sextus turned back to the plaza, surprised to find a chipped gladius still clutched in his hand. His arm began to shake as the rush of bloodfire dwindled. He hadn't had a moment to think since they'd run to the end of the Heptastadion and found the road filling with rebel mercenaries. . . .

A steady stream of Arabs in green-and-tan jogged down the causeway, swelling their numbers on the far side of the plaza. Sextus looked around, feeling sick. A line of Praetorians blocked the main part of the road junction, but they were swiftly becoming outnumbered. The engineer stared back towards the main docks and the building where the prince made his headquarters. *We need reinforcements*, he thought wildly. *But who . . .*

A crowd of men in tunics was running up the docks towards him, a tall, redheaded figure in the lead. *The clerks? And Caesar Aurelian?* Sextus felt unaccountable relief, even at the odd sight of such a motley band coming to their aid. Taking heart, he groped for a shield among the dead, finding one still intact, and quickly slipped his arm into the loops.

"Allau ak-bar!"

The dreaded cry roared from hundreds of throats. Sextus looked up in alarm in time to see the mass of the Arabs surge forward, every man screaming defiance of Rome. The line of Praetorians tensed, then rocked back with the charge. The Germans began their own hoarse, bellowing chant, stabbing and hacking with abandon as the enemy came to grips with them. The legionnaires gave three paces, then stood firm. A brutal hammering smote the air and men fought and died locked shoulder to shoulder with their fellows. Men from the second and third ranks stepped up as those in the first fell, faces grim and filled with terrible purpose.

Aurelian ran up, long hair streaming. A ragged band of clerks and scribes followed at his heels. Sextus moved to join the prince, who threw himself into the fray around the white pillar, when he caught a strange sound—no, *two* strange sounds. The engineer slowed, turning, and saw one of the avenues leading into the plaza fill with running people.

They were citizens, not soldiers, and they were screaming, a mad, wild sound filled with utter fear. Sextus froze, goggling at the huge mass of men, women and children packed into the street. They came on like the tide, every face mad with panic. In the brief instant he watched, a dozen or more fell and were trampled beneath relentless, hammering feet.

"Sextus!" A gasping voice caught his ear and the engineer crouched, eyes searching the littered dead. A hand waved weakly, a body trapped under the corpses of two Arabs. Sextus leapt to his friend, grasping a bloodstained arm and dragging him into the sickly gray light. Frontius choked, coughing, and spit hair and torn bits of bloody flesh from his mouth. "Help me . . . up."

"I've got you," Sextus grunted, rolling a body away with his boot. Frontius was heavy, one arm hanging limp, a thin red stream spilling from his leather sleeve. "Can you stand?"

Frontius nodded weakly. One eye was half-closed by a massive purple bruise and his helmet was gone. Sextus got a shoulder under the man, then stood. Frontius gasped, head rolling back, eyes bulging, but did not cry out. Without waiting, Sextus began dragging the other engineer towards headquarters and the *medikus*, all thoughts of standing and fighting gone.

The mob swarmed into the plaza moments later as the two engineers trudged west along the docks. A hopeless screaming mass of people flooded around them. Half-naked men leapt into the harbor waters. Some began swimming for the island offshore, others simply disappeared under the dirty brown water. Sextus staggered, slammed in the side by a woman in a patrician gown. She shrieked, clawing at his face. Frontius groaned weakly as the engineer swung him out of the way. Sextus' bunched fist cracked across the woman's nose, throwing her to the ground. She vanished under a pressing, pushing mob. The air stank of fear and sweat and a dry, musty odor like the dust in a long abandoned room.

Grimly, Sextus struggled west along the dock, forcing his way through the steadily worsening crowd. The citizens had seen *something*, but the engineer didn't have the time to discover what had driven them into flight. *Something bad*, he hazarded, knocking aside an elderly man in a bathing towel. *A phantasm or terror sent by the enemy, no doubt.*

His whole attention focused on gaining another yard towards the dubious sanctuary of the headquarters, Sextus ignored the stabbing yellow heat lightning rumbling and cracking in the low clouds, as well as the drumming roar echoing down the streets from the east.

The Gate of the Sun shuddered, heavy iron-bossed cedar panels shaking with the blow of a ram. The roadway below the looming towers was crowded with thousands of Persians in heavy armor. Sunflower banners danced above their heads and golden masks gleamed in the pale sun. Once more, the *pushtigbahn* threw their shoulders into the ropes guiding an iron-sheathed ram.

"Swing!" chanted a bull-voiced sergeant. The ram swung back, then slammed into the gate with a *crash!* Wood splintered and ancient hinges groaned. Crouched along smoke-darkened walls, swordsmen tensed, waiting for the panel to shatter. "Swing!"

Dahak leapt from the roof of his rune-carved wagon, dark cloak trailing, flying above massed ranks of *diquans* and spearmen and sappers with shovels and picks. A shining gradient buoyed him up, cutting the tether of the earth and he landed, bare feet slapping down on soot-blackened stone, atop the northern gatehouse tower. The air around him shimmered and flexed with the faint remains of the Roman ward, but the prince's lips stretched back over chisel-sharp teeth. Feet covered with fine ebony scales stepped down among crushed, mangled bodies. Not a single legionnaire remained alive atop the tower. The shattered, twisted remains of a siege engine littered the wooden roof.

"All things fail," he growled, then muttered words in a tongue lost before the Drowning swallowed the glory of the antediluvian world. A whirling sign formed in the air around him, rotating counterclockwise, blazing with subtle, iridescent light. The sign expanded, twisting and distorting the air. The Roman pattern shattered, crumbling into flickers of light and slowly falling rain. The Lord of the Ten Serpents raised both hands, his will pressing on stone and timber and the invisible bindings of the ancients. Geometric forms splintered, power draining away into the silty earth and a flash of sullen green light lit the entire length of the rampart. "The work of men not least."

The floor under the sorcerer shook again with the blow of the ram and his flattened ears caught the sound of splintering wood, then a roar of victory from the living men crowded into the road below. The panels squealed open, pushed by hundreds of hands, and the Persian army poured into the city. Dahak smiled, lifting his head to look upon Alexandria the Golden.

So, hated child, your handiwork is cast down again . . . I told you I would triumph in the end!

Already, the restless dead overwhelmed the wall at a dozen points. Against their limitless numbers, the Romans lacked the men to repel every assault. Columns of shambling figures crawled over the rampart as far as the eye could see. A few of the Roman towers continued to hold out, flame spilling down sandstone, men struggling on the parapet, stabbing and hacking at the ghoulish horde surging up from below. Yet, even as Dahak watched, he saw a wall topple, borne down by the weight of so many animate corpses and the dead flood into the breach, a seething carpet of brown ants, withered hands and rotted teeth dragging down the legionnaires fighting within.

Dahak laughed in delight, seeing living men torn apart by the grasping talons of the *gaatasuun*.

The city spread out before him, a rumpled carpet of terracotta roofs, temples and marble spires. Smoke billowed up from scattered points—fires set in fear or caught by accident— sending up towering pillars of black and gray to mix with the uneasy green sky. Off to his left, Dahak could see the arcades of a Roman theatre rising above clustered apartments, to his right a dense agglomeration of three- and four-story buildings, richly painted, with flat white roofs. One of the buildings was burning fiercely, flames jetting from tall, narrow windows, flinging tiny white specks into the sky. The roof tiles glowed cherry-red with heat from some tremendous inner conflagration. The sorcerer squinted, bending his attention upon the roaring fire, and suddenly barked a foul curse.

Thousands of sheets of papyrus and parchment were being born up on columns of flame.

Pages? The Library? My Library! Dahak turned towards the distant port, seeing more smoke rising, and very distantly, the sparkle of spears and armor on the long causeway connecting the island of the Pharos to the middle of the city. *Khalid and his men are still fighting to enter,* he realized, eyes swinging sickly back to the burning Library buildings. *I need those books . . .*

Voice speaking like thunder, the sorcerer leapt into the air again, invisible servants swarming to him, a glistening flight of loathsome birds to hold him up. He sped north with unseemly speed, his will reaching out heedlessly in the hidden world to damp the flames and hold back the roaring conflagration from the library stacks.

Behind him, the Gate of the Sun echoed with the tramp of marching boots and the cheers of the Persian soldiery as they entered the city.

Confusion reigned in the plaza around the white pillar. Mobs of frightened citizens continued to pour out of the city, throwing the Roman line into disorder. The Praetorians dissolved into knots of individual soldiers fighting to keep together. The Sahaba fared no better, pressed back by screaming, weeping women. Khalid bounced from foot to foot, shouting commands to his men. The roar of the crowd, a vast, frightened baying, drowned his voice. The mob pushed the Arabs back, forcing them to lock shields and dig in their feet to hold back the human tide.

"They're getting away," Khalid shouted, pointing with his sword. A mass of legionaries were fighting their way west along the docks. The young Arab could see a tall Roman— the man had to be an officer with his commanding presence— rallying the legionnaires to him. "Follow me!"

Khalid darted off to the right, hacking around him with the blade of the city. The shining dark edge sheared through a scrawny neck, then into the arm of a fat woman cradling a baby. The child flew off into the crowd, the woman wailing, pudgy fingers clamped over a spurting wound. The Sahaba hesitated, many of the men unwilling to strike down the innocents sobbing around them, but then rushed forward, following their general. In a grain, their faces were tight, unfeeling masks as they stabbed and chopped their way forward. With the main body of the Sahaba leaving the causeway, the citizens flooded past towards the island.

Blade dripping crimson, Khalid broke out of the mob, loping forward among the fallen. Ahead, the legionnaires had resorted to pushing their way through the mob by brute force. They had locked spears into a wedge and advanced step-by-step, forcing aside the crowd by main strength. The harbor was white with foam, dozens of people plunging into the water.

The red-bearded officer was in the middle of the rear rank, a commanding voice shouting to his men; an outstretched arm holding a Roman cavalry sword out to mark their line as they backed up. Khalid sprinted up, suddenly filled with perfect, icy determination. He did not recognize the man's face, but every instinct screamed *general!* to him. The Sahaba rushed soundlessly after him, lean wolves hot on the scent.

Khalid leapt a sprawled body, the blade of night darting out, just as the Roman turned his head.

The man blocked, spatha whipping up to smash Khalid's stroke aside. The Arab was stunned, obsidian blade nearly torn from his fingers, and skipped back wildly. The Roman blade clove the air where he'd stood, powering through a tight arc. One of the Sahaba, charging up to help his commander, met the blur of steel with a lunging spear. The Roman turned sideways, the spear point slashing past, and the return stroke clove the Arab's head from his shoulders.

Khalid goggled, lean, dark face spotted with blood. The Sahaban fighter's head bounced away, gargling, and crunched into the retaining wall beside the dock.

"Form up," bellowed the Roman, warning his men. Khalid dodged in, trying to circle, finding himself hemmed on three sides by the crowd and the line of soldiers, the other by the harbor waters. *Where's Patik when I need him?* he wailed inwardly, blocking an overhand cut. The ebon blade sang with a shrill note, taking the blow, and Khalid nearly lost his grip again. Fear sparked in his heart, draining strength from his limbs, and he fell back, parrying wildly. The Roman laughed, trading blows with another of the Sahaba. Almost contemptuously, the red-beard knocked the man's mace aside, then transfixed his throat with a sharp jab. Six inches of steel sprouted from the back of his neck, then withdrew in a blur.

The fear curdling in Khalid's heart disappeared in a blaze of fury. *No man laughs at me!*

He leapt at the enemy, flinging his shield aside. Taking the blade of the city in both hands, he powered in, the full strength of his wiry shoulders in an arcing cut. The Roman blocked, matching strength for strength, and the Arab's stroke cracked against an immobile barrier. Wincing, Khalid parried weakly, and the Roman drove his sword into the ground, steel springing back from marble paving.

The Sahaba surged around the two captains, stabbing overhand, and were met by massed shields and the grim faces of the legionnaires. Again, a brisk play of long cavalry blades, maces, axes and spears sparked on the docks. Khalid hung back a half-step, watching his enemy. The Roman did not abandon the front rank, wielding his hand-and-a-half blade with aplomb. Another Arab was struck down, helmet crushed in, neck severed from behind by a looping, sideways strike.

Gods, Khalid breathed, *what a champion! Even Patik might find his match!*

The Sahaba fell back, leaving a handful of bodies on the pavement. The Roman line stood unshaken. Khalid felt the air change, momentum shifting around him. The panicked crowds had thinned, through the ground still jumped with an enormous, drumming beat. *The dead are coming*, Khalid realized.

Someone started shouting behind the Roman lines and Red-beard turned, falling back a step. Khalid cursed as another legionary stepped smoothly into his place. Some kind of courier ran up, gabbling at the general.

Khalid glanced around at his own men, seeing weary faces, though they were still game for another go. He licked his lips. *He'll know he's trapped . . . the dead will be upon us soon and there's no way out. Perhaps . . . perhaps he will surrender!* The young Arab's heart leapt at the thought, for the honor and unsurpassed bravery of the Roman general touched even him.

"Roman!" he shouted, stepping out of the wary line of Sahaba. "Roman, listen!"

Red-beard turned towards him, wiping sweat out of his eyes. "What do you want, rebel?"

"Your city is lost," Khalid called into sudden, encompassing silence. Everyone fell quiet, the men on both sides staring at him in speculation. A few citizens ran past, faces haunted, but they spared no attention for the two opposing lines of soldiers. The young Arab pointed to the east. "Great Persia enters the city—his armies swollen by the risen dead—and you have no hope but honorable surrender. Yield your swords to me, and I will protect you!"

The red-beard gave him a considering glance, then leaned down, speaking softly to the messenger. The man nodded sharply, then bolted off down the docks. The Roman smiled, a grim, wintry expression without humor or malice. "Romans do not surrender," he called, voice ringing in the air. "If you wish our swords, you'll take them from the dead, as the ghouls you are!"

A laughing shout rose from the legionaries and many of the Germans clashed their swords and axes on their shields, raising a drumming, raucous noise. In response, the Sahaba growled and Khalid's face set, graven stone showing no mercy or remorse.

"Allau ak-bar!" the Sahaba roared, taking a step forward in unison. Fresh reinforcements joined them from the causeway. Khalid caught sight of Jalal and Shadin from the corner of his eye, and felt fresh hope jolt through him. The Romans matched the shout with their own: "The City! The City!"

A wordless cry ripped from Khalid's lips and he bounded forward. His men followed a breath later and a ringing crash echoed from the buildings and the water. Again, a fierce melee raised a vicious din on the docks, as Roman and Sahaban sodliers grappled, trading blows. Men toppled from the line of battle, slicking the ground with their fresh blood.

A pack of *gaatasuun* were feeding in the entry hall of the Sema as Dahak entered. The sorcerer's face darkened with rage, pale eyes passing swiftly across the scattered bodies of priests and attendants. The prince's tunic was scorched and riddled with ash-burned holes. His usual poor humor deepened into simmering rage as he took in the carnage filling the tomb hall. There was dark, drying blood everywhere and the floor was slick with greasy-white entrails and offal. One of the corpse-men squatted on the floor, desiccated flesh peeling from a mottled black-and-gray back, as it pounded a newly dismembered head against the tile paving. The skull made a sharp, cracking sound as the blow split open the cranium. The *gaatasuun's* withered fingers pried aside bone, letting a long black tongue dip into the opening. A thick slurping sound followed.

Dahak made a sharp motion, no more than the effort of a man brushing aside a fly and the dozen or more corpses feeding in the chamber stiffened—motive force denied—and then crumbled to dust. The skull—suddenly released—clattered across the floor and came to rest at the prince's feet.

The Lord of the Ten Serpents bent down, face twisted in a grimace—half amused, half irritated. Black fingernails bit into bone and he lifted the skull. Once, a man with a neatly trimmed beard and a powerful nose had worn this ragged, bloody scrap of flesh and glistening white. There was a gelatinous sloshing sound as the head rolled between Dahak's fingers.

"Where is the Sarcophagus?" A snap of command, echoing with a trembling hum, filled the prince's voice. His high brow creased in mild concentration.

The skull stiffened in his hands, a leprous white glow sparking in empty eye sockets—no more than red-rimmed holes, where dusty fingers had lately gouged—and the jaw twitched and spasmed. The tongue, at least, remained whole and a gargling sound issued from the broken head. Dahak grunted, finding the words unintelligible.

"Speak clearly!" the prince commanded, and sinews crawled like worms under torn flesh, muscle knitting to bone, arteries swelling with a thick, dark gray humor—not blood, no, but close enough to serve. Watery charcoal-colored fluid spilled from the mouth and Dahak held the thing at arm's reach, so as to keep his long pantaloons free of such offal. "Where is the body?"

"Not . . ." croaked the priest's dead tongue. ". . . here . . . taken."

"What?" A hiss of rage followed and black talons squeaked through fibrous bone. "Who has taken the Pretender's body? When?"

"Persia . . ." The head sighed, more fluid spilling from the mouth and staining the prince's hands. "Shapur the Young took him . . . away."

"Shapur?" Dahak stared at the leaking head in dismay. "Shapur the Manichean?"

The head tried to nod, but could not. The leprous radiance dimmed in the eye sockets and Dahak's face contorted into unbridled rage. His fist closed with a convulsive jerk and the skull shattered into fragments. Spitting furiously, the prince cast the bits and pieces away. As they flew, black flame enveloped them and only dust sifted to the ground.

"Curse him, curse the child and all his debased house!" Dahak turned slowly, blazing eyes sweeping across the dumb stone faces of ancient kings and gods. They did not amuse him, these stiff Ptolemies and weak-faced animals grafted to human bodies. The prince stalked among the rumpled shapes of the dead priests, searching for another whose cranium was intact enough to question.

After a moment, he sighed in despair. The *gaatasuun* had been swift to satisfy their hunger.

"All this effort, for nothing . . ." Dahak leaned against a wall, suddenly weary. The vast effort of revivifying the tomb-lost dead and drawing them forth from the ground, sending them in crashing, endless waves against the Roman walls, imbuing each dead husk with enough of a spark to motivate hands and legs, began to tell. The prince stared around, feeling defeat leech the strength from his body. "We have taken an empty coffin—only dust and worms and vermin hiding in the walls."

He pressed a hand across his eyes. They burned with fatigue and even the thin, greenish sunlight slanting down from high, close-set windows hurt. *So much time wasted. The Sema empty and my agents will have to search the length and breadth of Persia for the Pretender* . . . An old, half-heard voice emerged from black, turgid memory. *Shapur raised a great edifice at Taq-I-Bustam—perhaps he hid the body there—I will send the Shanzdah to shatter mountains and cast down cliffs to find out!*

Dahak rose, face set, the moment of weariness past. His will asserted itself, banishing weariness and despair alike. Eyes narrowing to burning slits, he turned his attention outward, sending his thoughts winging across the leagues to the west.

Where are my faithful ones, he asked the void. *Have they found our other prize?*

Faintly, the Shanzdah replied, feeling his will searching for them. *We are here*, they called.

Dahak frowned again. He caught a sense of limitless emptiness, of heat, of fist-sized black stones lining a narrow track winding between desolate hills. The first of the Shanzdah was walking, leather boots sliding in fine sand. *Where are you? Where is the* duradarshan? *Where is Lord Shahin?*

We failed, came the cold reply. Dahak snarled silently, feeling nothing but truth reaching across the leagues to him. *The Romans were here—and the witches helped them—they stole the device. This shape* . . . A sensation of chill humor echoed . . . *was almost destroyed.*

"Enough!" Dahak released the connection violently, mocking laughter ringing in his thoughts. The prince stared around the old temple with a sick, conflicted expression. "Lost in the desert . . . witches interfering again! Why didn't I crush them all long ago . . ." He realized he was muttering and closed his mouth with a snap. Fixing his attention on the nearest wall, Dahak breathed slowly until his racing heart slowed to a walk. The wall was painted with scenes of men giving sacrifice to the sun, whose golden disc encompassed them in beneficent rays, carrying Amon's blessing. All the races of the earth were represented, from the pale hair of the northmen to the shining blue-black of the southern tribes.

His reptilian face twisting in despair, Dahak pressed his fingers against the fresco, slowly tracing yellow-painted lines, a round solar disk flanked by spreading hawk wings, rich fields of corn and wheat. A strange sound echoed in the chamber, throbbing among the roof arches. Dahak started, staring around, one hand raised in the beginnings of a pattern sign.

There was no one in the funerary temple. He was alone.

What was that? The prince's eyes slid closed, one transparent lid sliding over another. Even in the hidden world, there was nothing around him, no invisible adversary, no spy, no secret watcher. *Was that someone crying?*

The prince looked back to the painting and his jaw tightened. The sun in the middle of the composition mocked him, so perfectly round, fulfilling and sustaining the world of men. Dahak turned his face toward the ceiling, letting his sight peel away the stone arches, the tiled roof, then a sea of air, the thin white clouds so far above the curve of the earth, then an abyss of distant fire and the cold, dead moon.

I do not need to see this, Dahak thought, wrenching his attention away from the void. *The Hyades have not risen and Al-Debaran still hides behind the world. There is still time.* His hand, still resting upon the wall, convulsed, iron-hard nails digging through plaster into the stone below. *But not much, no . . . not much. Not even as men measure the hours.*

"Row!" A Praetorian, long blond hair wild around his head, screamed at a dozen soldiers. The men shied away from the barbarian, but their hands already wrapped around the long, polished pine handle of a huge oar. Sextus caught a glimpse of the men straining, faces red with effort, as he staggered up the gangway. Frontius flopped on his back like a marlin, drooling vomit on his shoulder. The wounded engineer was not doing well.

Two legionaries at the top of the gangway seized both of them with rough hands and threw them bodily onto the boarding deck of the grain hauler. Moments later, axes thudded into hawsers and the entire wooden ramp plunged into dirty brown water. Sextus rolled over, groaning, his hip twinging with sharp, stabbing pain. "What . . ."

Four enormous oars bit into the water and the grain hauler—despite her mass—jerked away from the dockside. Her holds were empty, making her surprisingly light on the water. The engineer bounded up, panic driving away the throbbing in his hip. "What are you doing?" Sextus threw himself to the railing, staring down at the dock. The two legionaries were busy lashing a wooden panel across the opening, closing off the space where the gangplank had laid.

Two men splashed in the water below, hands groping against the smooth marble facing of the harbor wall. A crowd pressed against a stone balustrade above them, staring at the ship with wild, wide eyes. Everyone ignored the men—stonemasons by the colored cords twisted into their tunics—as they struggled helplessly in the water. A guttural moan of despair rose from the mob, though no single person seemed to have raised their voice in a shout.

Sextus grabbed the nearest legionary's shoulder. "We can't leave," he hissed, pointing down the harborside. The crowd was beginning to mill, disturbed by some commotion. Light flashed on metal, though the sun had grown very dim, shrinking to a pale disc hidden in heavy viridian clouds. "There are still Romans trapped ashore!"

"Get away from me." The legionary turned on Sextus, shoving his hand away. He looked sick, face sallow behind a stiff black beard. He clutched the axe with both hands, knuckles white against the close-grained wood.

"Those are *our* tent mates," Sextus said, voice rising in horror. "We don't leave them behind!"

"Get away!" The man shouted, pushing Sextus back with the axe handle.

On the deck, Frontius stared up, lips nearly white with pain. "Sextus . . ."

"Look at them," the engineer shouted, turning on the other soldiers standing by the railing. He waved at a band of men in armor pushing through the mob. Other men pursued, swords and spears hacking and stabbing, striking down men and women packed so closely together they could not flee. "They need us! Stop rowing! Turn the ship!"

The sweeps continued to dip into the harbor and the massive ship inched away from the dock a yard at a time. A good twenty feet of open water now separated the hull from the marble facing. One of the stonemasons had vanished under the slowly roiling brown surface. The other managed to dig his fingers into a mossy crevice between two stones. He was shouting weakly, begging for help.

The crowd ignored him, staring at the grain hauler. Aboard, the legionnaires at the railing stared back. No one spoke, and the oars dipped again, opening the distance another yard.

"Ho, the ship!"

A strong, familiar voice rang out. A tall man with a singular red beard shoved through the crowd to the retaining wall. Barely a half-dozen men still fought at his side, several of them sorely wounded. Only yards away, through the mob, Sextus saw the Arabs pressing, blades rising and falling in fierce, brutal cuts. People were screaming now and the entire mob seemed to wake with a start. It moved, a herd surging, spooked by sum-mer thunder. Twenty or thirty people—those jammed closest to the water—were shoved into the harbor with a mighty splash. Sextus jerked as if struck with a whip.

"Throw them ropes," he shouted, turning again to the other legionnaires. They stared back, faces blank. "Fools!" the engi-neer snarled at them, then ran along the railing. He found a heavy rope knotted at intervals and snatched up the coil. He ran back, screaming curses at the other men on the ship.

He reached the gangway and knelt, hands quick as they wound the rope into a heavy bolt stapled to the deck. Sextus braced his foot, standing, and hurled the coil into the water. On the dock, the legionnaires turned at bay, forming a too-small circle with their shields. The engineer leaned out, screaming at the top of his lungs—"Here! Here! Swim to the ship!"

The red-bearded man looked back over his shoulder, a spatha bare in his hand. Sextus recognized him at last. "Lord Aurelian! Here, Lord Prince, here!"

Shrieking, the mob parted, men and women trampling those too slow to flee. The Arabs pushed through behind a thicket of spears. The legionnaires on the wharf locked shields and the ring and clatter of steel on steel drifted across the water. Sextus bit his thumb, silently begging the prince to leap into the water. Instead, his powerful head was clearly visible among the others, his long blade flashing, driving back the first rush of the enemy.

Oars rose, shedding brown, silty water, and the ship crabbed out into the harbor. Two burly legionnaires bent to the steering oars on the rear deck, trying to turn the grain hauler to catch the wind. The sails—huge squares of stitched canvas—luffed as the ship turned. For a moment, forward motion ceased, though all four oars dug deep into brown water, the crews on the sweeps groaning with effort.

"Here, my lord," Sextus screamed again, beckoning.

A towering Arab clashed with the prince and the two men—each head and shoulders above his companions—exchanged a fierce series of cuts and slashes. The ringing *clang* of blade on blade was clear even on shipboard. The prince held his own, then advanced, whirling the spatha in a driving attack. The Arabs fell back, stabbing at his feet and head with their spears. A clear space emerged, though in the brief interlude, two more of the legionnaires—already wounded—had been stricken down.

More green turbans pushed through the crowd and the engineer realized the avenues leading down to the docks were now filling with a rustling, shuffling mob far different from the panicked citizens who had first rushed down to the shore.

"My lord," Sextus wailed, hand hanging in the air. "Please!"

The Arabs rushed forward, shouting a sharp, high cry. Aurelian met their attack head-on, smashing one man to the ground, then slashing his blade back, catching another behind the head. The Arab toppled, helmet smashed down over his eyes, spine bared white to the sky. The others jostled, trying to get at the prince. Spinning, Aurelian took two, long racing steps and leapt over the retaining wall. His trim, powerful body speared into the water with a sharp splash.

Sextus shouted in relief, leaning over the side to grasp the knotted rope, flipping it out towards the shore. The Arabs rushed forward, the last legionnaire slumping back against the marble wall, four or five spears grinding into his chest, his neck, his armpit. Blood splashed across white stone. A young man with a sharp face and neat, coal-black beard leapt atop the wall.

The engineer threw the rope again, though he could not see Aurelian beneath the turgid surface, not yet.

A forest of green-and-tan crowded at the wall. The young Arab shouted, pointing. Aurelian's head burst from the waters, more than halfway between the ship and shore. He took his bearings, then struck out for the hull, swimming strongly. Sextus felt a chill, realizing the prince was still in full armor. *The strength of ten!* his mind gibbered, calculating the weight of metal and leather. "Here, a rope!"

The knotted line flew out again, splashing into the water only yards from the prince. Aurelian caught sight of the rope and turned, muscular arms cleaving through the low waves.

On the retaining wall, the young Arab was arguing with his soldiers, gesturing violently toward the man swimming in the water. Two of them—older men with heavy beards—shouted back. The sound of defiance in their voices drew Sextus' attention. One, a tall, hook-nosed man carrying a long, curved bow shook his head sharply in refusal. The young Arab turned away, face twisted in fury, and snatched a spear from one of his fellows.

"Dive, my lord!" Sextus screamed at the prince, seeing the Arab take a hurling stance, shoulder sliding back, the iron head of the spear poised at his chin. "Dive!"

Aurelian doubled his pace, surging through the water. The rope was only feet away. The Arab whipped around, spear leaping from his fingers, arcing into the sky. Aurelian grasped the rope and slid under the waves, the weight of his armor dragging him down. Sextus hauled, feeling the line stiffen and spring out of the water. Other hands grasped hold, a whole crowd of men around him, and they pulled for all they were worth.

The prince's head shot from the water, his arm tangled in the line, and a wake foamed around his shoulders. Glittering, the spear flashed down. Sextus shouted again, though there were no comprehensible words. Aurelian twisted, flinging himself away from the missile. The spear plunged into the water, only a hand span away. On the ship, a hundred legionnaires cheered lustily in relief. Sextus continued to haul, rope burning between his fingers. A moment later, as more spears plunged into the water, Aurelian was dragged against the side of the ship. Arrows flashed past the prince's head, burying themselves in the oaken planks of the ship with a meaty *thack!*

A dozen hands reached down, dragging Aurelian up to the railing. The knotted rope wound tight around his arm and shoulder, biting deep into bruised flesh. Sextus grasped hold of the prince's shoulder strap, hauling him—clanking, water spilling from his armor—over the side. Everyone collapsed to the deck in a sodden heap, Aurelian's pale, drained face framed by wet iron and glistening leather.

"My lord," Sextus cried, tears streaming down his grimy face. "You live!"

Aurelian grimaced, bluish lips drawing back from clenched teeth. His fingers clutched Sextus' hair. "Do I?" the prince gasped, shuddering, and Sextus looked down. Blood flooded from Aurelian's side. A long gash tore open his lower stomach, some unseen blow severing the prince's armored skirt. His belt was missing and the lower edge of the lorica was twisted and bent.

"No!" Sextus pressed desperately against the wound, feeling gelatinous, coiled tubes squirm away under his fingers. "No! We saved you, my lord, we saved you!"

Aurelian's face drained of color, though someone was trying to force the nipple of a wineskin into his mouth and his body shook with a racking cough. Blood covered Sextus' forearms and the prince died, there on the deck of the ship as she wallowed out into the harbor, away from the fallen city.

"Oh no." Frontius leaned over the prince, his face gone ashy white. The other men drew back, and a mutter of despair coursed from dozens of lips. Sextus, his arms washed red, laid the prince down, taking care his head did not crack against the planks. Still kneeling, the engineer turned to stare back at the docks. The hosts of the enemy crowded the wharfs, and even at this distance Sextus could see the young captain and the two older men.

They raised their spears and swords in salute, a bright forest of flashing steel. A great basso shout rang out over the turgid waters and a thousand naked blades thrust to the sky in a single, sharp movement. Frontius stepped to the railing, staring in incomprehension. Again the blades flashed, and the roar of sound rolled out. The sound seemed to fill the air, driving back the heavy pressure that had grown over the city. Then again, as the Roman ship reached the long sandstone breakwater.

"What are they doing?" Frontius looked back at Sextus. The engineer stood, thin streams of blood spilling from his arms.

"They praise a brave man," Sextus said, though his voice was nearly unrecognizable. "As we will praise him. As he deserves." The engineer turned to the crowd of legionaries crowding the deck. Every man seemed as one dead—eyes hollow, faces caked with soot and sweat, armor dotted with blood—yet their gaze turned to him as he raised a hand.

"Bring a priest—if any survives among us—and a winding shroud. We will not burn our lord Aurelian at sea, but upon our homecoming. For him, we will spill the blood of beasts, of men. For him we will spill wine, and send a great smoke to the heavens. He will not go into the dark alone, without servants, without grain, without wine. *He* will not suffer in darkness, for we—the Legion—will always remember him!"

There was a stir among the crowd and the men parted, letting
a white-haired centurion approach. Sextus was greatly relieved.
Here was a priest of Mars Ultor, come to give a soldier a soldier's rites. Frontius gripped his shoulder. "Father Wolf," Sextus called, kneeling again beside the prince. "Give our comrade
a blessing grace, to carry him across the Dark River. You men—
where are the eagle standards, the golden plaque, where is the
name of the city? Here is a son of Rome—it's bravest son—and
he needs know we pray for him, the city prays for him, that he
is not alone in the cold darkness."

Again the crowd on the deck parted and the banners and sigils of the Legion approached, passed hand to hand among the
soldiers. The ship was beginning to roll, buffeted by northerly
waves and the sails filled with wind, driving them west at a
steady pace. Someone in the mass of men packed onto the deck
began to beat a drum. Father Wolf bent down, seamed face
pinched tight in grief. The priest of Mars reached down, as the
legionaries began to chant the "passage of the fallen" and
closed Aurelian's eyes for the last time.

∎━O━O━O━O━O━O━O━O━O━O━O━O━O━O━O━O━O━O━O━O━O━∎

THE VIA CAMPANA, JUST WEST OF ROME

)I(

Golden light slanted through a stand of willows surrounding the way station. Gaius Julius, carefully dressed as a
patrician on holiday, tipped back his wide-brimmed straw hat
and squinted with interest against the glow of late afternoon.
Two men were riding hard towards him along the horse path
paralleling the highway, cloaks billowing behind them, faces
half-masked by scarves. Despite the dust and grime of travel,
he recognized them immediately.

"Ho!" he shouted, stepping out of the shady trellis in front of
the cistern. His guardsmen stood up as well, a round-dozen
men in bulky tunics and ill-disguised weapons. "Master
Nicholas! Hie too, my friends."

The two horsemen reined in, the thin, dark haired-man in the lead staring at Gaius in surprise. The old Roman saw both the Latin and the Walach had ridden hard—hair lank and greasy, clothes caked not only with good Roman dust but also salt and tar—and he forced a welcoming smile.

"Here," the old Roman said, lifting a wineskin. "Something to drink. And there is food inside, hot from the brazier."

Nicholas blinked, finally recognizing his employer and tension drained from him, leaving the young man slump-shouldered with weariness. Vladimir was no better, though he was quick to slide from the nervous horse. The Walach staggering into the shade of the arbor, barely able to walk.

Gaius Julius helped Nicholas down, then waited patiently while the man drank deep from the skin. A brisk, crunching sound filtered from inside the way station and when Gaius and Nicholas entered, they found Vladimir busily devouring a huge section of roasted mutton.

"Eat first," the old Roman said, guiding Nicholas to a stone bench. "Then we'll talk."

The last tinge of gold faded from the sky as servants moved through the vine-covered arbor, lighting copper lamps from long, smoking tapers. Gaius' guardsmen were outside, sitting with the horses, making sure no wayward travelers disturbed their master's conversation.

". . . so the *Urbes Brigantium* landed at Portus today and we made haste up to the city." Nicholas stared at the old Roman with a hollow-eyed look. "How did you know to meet us?"

"There is a messenger relay from the port," Gaius said, lifting his head slightly to indicate the distant coast. "The captain of the *Brigantium* sent a note ahead to the Palatine, which came to my hands from a friend. I left immediately, of course. But you did well to make such a fast passage from Africa."

"Bad news travels swiftly," Vladimir said, his head bent. The Walach refused to meet the old Roman's eyes. Nicholas seemed similarly despondent. "Have you heard anything of our . . . companions?"

"The traitors, you mean!" Nicholas roused himself, anger glittering in his pale eyes. "Curse Thyatis, her maid and her mistress! We had the telecast in our very hands and then we had nothing. . . ."

Gaius Julius nodded, his quick mind burning with rage, anger, envy—*deftly done*, he allowed—and Nicholas' singular hatred of the Duchess's agent loomed large in his thoughts. "This Thyatis Julia Clodia . . . describe her more fully."

"Tall," Nicholas muttered, his face twisting with mingled distaste and admiration. "Gray-eyed, strong, quick—very quick—with a blade. A deadly opponent. A whirlwind of steel. I've never seen such a woman before."

"Because you were not in the City the last year," Gaius Julius said, feeling an unexpected, jarring rush of emotion, of relief and delight. *She is alive! Diana is alive!* "There were a series of games in the arena, and champion of these contests was a woman named 'Diana' who must be—cannot be anyone—but your 'Thyatis.' She is a marvel, indeed." His voice trailed off, as memories of their too-brief encounters surged up, fresh and sharp as if not a single day had passed between now and then.

"A marvel? More like a harpy!" Nicholas spat on the dusty ground. "A faithless friend . . ."

"No so," Vladimir said, very softly. "She saved our lives and we hers. There is a debt—"

"There is *no debt!*" Nicholas' voice rose sharply. "She betrayed us!"

Gaius turned away from the two men as they fell into a muttered, fierce argument. His disappointment at failing to secure the prince's toy faded, replaced by a strange lightness in his heart. *Thyatis Julia Clodia . . . an odd name. Why would the Clodians name a daughter Julia? We were rarely friends when I was alive. Rivals, yes—sometimes allies if the wind turned from the proper quarter in the Senate—yet not even enemies. Marc Antony now, he kept a Clodian wife for a time . . . did he have a son by her?* Gaius shook his head in amusement. His old head was filled with a marvelous array of useless facts. *But things change, even in Rome, with all these centuries passed.* The old Roman was pleased to learn his "Diana" was a daughter of Rome, even if she sprang from such dissolute remnants. Silently, he congratulated the Duchess on her choice of agent. *Would I had her in my own quiver,* he thought ruefully, watching the two younger men out of the corner of his eye. *But these fellows, and others like them, must suffice.*

"Come, my friends," Gaius said, gathering up his hat. "Do not quarrel. The heat of the day has passed and we've refreshed ourselves. Your news is welcome, for these 'friends' are revealed as our enemies. We may take a more leisurely pace as we return to the city."

Everyone clattered out of the way station, grooms and guardsmen milling about to bring up the horses. Gaius stood to one side, his thoughts still plagued by inconsequential questions.

"Who were her parents?" he wondered under his breath. "How did she come to serve the Duchess? And a Legion centurion! Unheard of . . . just unheard of." Gaius' old face was lit by a half-hidden smile. "Ah, I would like to see her again." Then he frowned, the thought leading to an inevitable conclusion. *But there will be no glad meeting of friends long parted . . . not now.*

⬛〔0〕-〔0〕-〔0〕-〔0〕-〔0〕-〔0〕-〔0〕-〔0〕-〔0〕-〔0〕-〔0〕-〔0〕-〔0〕-〔0〕-〔0〕-〔0〕⬛

THE PALATINE HILL

)H(

Galen slumped back with a groan, covering his face with both hands. The flickering, watery light of the telecast washed over him, throwing odd shadows into the corners of the chamber. No one spoke, leaving only the hissing buzz of the device to fill leaden silence. Grains passed, threatening to drag into a glass and the two ladies sitting at the writing table exchanged a slow, mute glance. They made no sound, but the Emperor stirred, absently brushing lank, dark hair from his high forehead.

"Turn it off." His voice was emotionless, thin face a flat mask. Even his eyes were shuttered and dim.

The thaumaturges on duty bent their heads, muttering softly, and the whirling fire dulled, wicking down to a faint radiance and then to nothing. The bronze disks spun out of the air—this time their descent was gentle—settling quietly into flattened rings. Their task done, both men rose, faces averted from the Emperor's grief and padded out of the room. A moment later, the two ladies followed, their quills and inks and stores of parchment tucked away in wicker baskets ornamented with colored ribbon.

The Emperor remained, staring straight ahead, hands on his knees. He said nothing. His eyes looked upon nothing save a bare, plastered wall.

Galen waited grimly while the members of his privy council entered the room. A pair of oil lamps hissed quietly, providing mellow illumination. Outside the open windows, a warm, windless summer night lay over the city. The hour was very late, deep into the third watch. Everyone was tense—even the usually unflappable Gaius Julius seemed on edge, darting a sideways look at the Emperor as he took a chair—and they were unexpectedly quiet.

The lady Anastasia entered last, sweeping through the doorway in a long, gray gown, her neck ablaze with pearls and glittering white stones. She bowed formally to the Emperor, then to Martina—who lounged beside an irritated Maxian, her hand tucked in his—and claimed a seat between Galen and Gaius Julius. She made no mention of the late hour or the abrupt summons received in the midst of a play. A pleasing scent of coriander and myrrh reached the Emperor's nostrils, but the sensation barely registered.

Galen stood, face impassive, hands flat on the table. "We have lost Egypt," he said in a quiet voice.

Everyone became very still and Maxian's head turned away from his wife to fall upon his brother with a palpable intensity.

"Alexandria has fallen," the Emperor continued, his eyes fixed on some point in the air above Martina's head. Galen took a breath, though his voice did not alter in tone or inflection. "Six full Legions have been destroyed. The entire province now lies open to the enemy. There are small garrisons at Elephantine and Luxor, but they will not be able to resist the Persians. I expect they will surrender and seek repatriation to Cyrenaicea, or employment in the ranks of the conquerors."

He fell silent. Gaius Julius and Anastasia eyed one another, wondering who would pose the first question and break the leaden, dead silence gripping the room. Only Maxian moved, slowly clenching his hand into a fist.

"The lord Aurelian." Galen stopped, nostrils flaring. Something flickered in his eyes, the first time they had shown any emotion at all. "My brother Aurelian, Caesar of the Western Empire, is dead. He suffered grievous wounds in the defense of the harbor and breathed his last while escaping the city aboard an Imperial grain transport."

Maxian started to speak, then stopped, staring at the Emperor with an accusing, anguished expression. The air between the two men seemed to tremble. Martina placed her hand on the prince's arm, speaking softly, and the young man's face closed tight, a shuttered house, with neither lights in the windows nor smoke curling from the chimney.

"We will soon know," Galen said, continuing as if nothing had happened, "what the Persians intend. There are some forces left to us—the army at Constantinople, the fleet, the iron drakes now reaching completion in Florentia. Despite this blow, we still stand. We will yet prevail."

Silence filled the room again and Galen picked up a wooden booklet. Out of long engrained habit, he opened the notebook, stared sightlessly at the page within, then closed the cover again. "That is all. We shall meet again tomorrow and discuss what must be done."

Anastasia rose, swaying slightly, and the others followed. She bowed to the Emperor, searching his face for some sign of life, finding nothing. Galen turned away without a word and walked slowly through the door. Helena—her face hidden by a deep hood, yet recognizable by jeweled bracelets on her thin arms—was waiting to take his hand. A cordon of Praetorians closed up behind them and the Imperial couple was gone.

The Duchess bent her head for a moment, taking a breath and saying a prayer. The others rustled, gathering up their cloaks and—in Gaius' case—a lantern of the type used by the night watch. He had come in haste from a villa on the outskirts of the city.

"My lord—my lady." Anastasia looked up at Maxian and Martina passed. The woman's face was very calm, her huge eyes sliding to meet the Duchess with a tranquil, untroubled gaze. Anastasia—who had not personally seen the Empress since her return from Capri—repressed a shudder. Her spies had reported the girl's transformation, but the languid, predatory gleam in her eyes was new and unexpected. Nothing seemed to remain of the shy, insecure woman glad of the Duchess's friendship. The prince looked at Anastasia, lips tight on bared teeth.

"What do you want?"

"I am sorry, my lord." Anastasia bowed again, looking away. Maxian's eyes were liquid with fury and grief in equal measure and the Duchess felt a chill steal over her, remembering the powers he held at his command. "If there is anything . . ."

Maxian brushed past and Martina laughed softly, looking back at the Duchess with a sly, pitying smile. Anastasia watched them depart with a heavy heart. Gaius Julius had already slipped out, leaving her alone in the room. Even the guardsmen were gone.

"Well," she said aloud, straightening the neckline of her gown. "What a delightful evening."

Gaius Julius ended his report and set aside a waxed tablet. The old Roman looked to the Emperor, who had been listening with a fist planted firmly against his chin, eyes closed. A dreadful pall hung over the room despite strong, bright sunlight streaming through the windows. Late summer in Rome now afflicted them with stupefying heat during the day and bathwater-warm nights. Blessedly, Gaius' new existence seemed to exempt him from these extremes in the same manner he escaped hunger, exhaustion, even the need to drink.

The Emperor opened his eyes and Gaius almost sighed to see the desolation lurking there. Galen controlled his face and attitude well, adopting a rigid, controlled manner. His voice did not quaver, but the old Roman knew heartbreak when he saw such dead eyes. *I . . . we . . . should wait,* he thought with unexpected compassion. *There is still plenty of time for our plot to flourish. Years, in truth.*

Twin weapons had placed themselves in Gaius' hands and every instinct urged him to strike now, while the iron blazed hot and the hammer rode high. The collapse of Egypt had wrenched the very heart from the Emperor, leaving him distracted and vulnerable. The unexpected arrival of young Nicholas and the Walach Vladimir two days previous had provided another sledge, not so great as the first, perhaps, but more suitable for delicate, precise work. Gaius wrestled with the problem as he sat down, weighing both options and finding neither entirely satisfactory.

This Emperor is a vexing creature, Gaius mused. *I admire him and respect his keen mind. He is a brilliant administrator and an able leader—is there any Roman virtue he does not possess? Is there any reason not to serve him, and him alone, with vigor and piety? Yet . . .*

His eyes drifted sideways, across the calm and composed face of the Duchess, sitting at the Emperor's left hand with her own notes, to the Empress Martina. A demure gown and stole failed to disguise her lush new body, but Martina was showing an unexpected talent for subtlety. She did not flaunt her charms, but hid them beneath expensive silk and linen, leaving her clean, raptor-like face unadorned by paint or powder. Instead, she let striking eyes and flawless skin carry her to victory over any observer. Gaius was sure no artful waxes made her rosebud lips so moist and soft—she had no need, now, or ever, of petty cosmetics. *Not with our custos on the job,* Gaius thought grimly, *ever watchful for blemishes or sagging skin. . . .*

Yet, Maxian still overshadowed her with a lean, intense aura. Abiding anger suffused his movements, charging the sharp tilt of his head, the measured way he spoke and the fierce, hateful gaze he turned constantly upon his brother.

Gaius watched them both and here too his heart was heavy with bitter knowledge. *Two brothers estranged over the third, he mused, when Rome needs them to stand together. Does my ambition reach too high? How dangerous are these Persians?* The old Roman had been surprised by the loss of Egypt. His estimation—one shared by the Emperor, he knew—had been for Aurelian and his veterans to hold Alexandria almost indefinitely. The Legions were good at siegecraft and the Persians notoriously poor. Indeed, he—like the Emperor—had planned on the siege dragging on for months.

Now the other African provinces were in peril. Shahr-Baraz and his lancers could strike due west, rushing along the desert coast. There were no natural barriers to hold them back from reaching as far west as Carthage. More provinces lost, more revenues denied, more strength flowing to the enemy . . . Gaius quelled the wayward thoughts. *They have reached the end of their tether*, he reminded himself firmly. *They may have taken the city by sorcery and a daring ruse, but they are still very far from home, without fresh armies or fleets. They have to stop! They must stop.*

Galen had related the destruction of the Legions in the city in short, clipped sentences. Pressed, Maxian had responded, saying the manipulation of so many animate dead was dreadfully taxing. The enemy could not march them against Rome, not without exhausting himself utterly. *Like a berserker's rush*, Gaius took some faint hope from the thought. *We will not have to fight a legion of the dead day upon day, only once in awhile, when the Persians have the time to prepare.*

Everyone agreed the true stroke of genius had been to land an army on the island of the Pharos, splitting the defense. Even with his dead tone, Gaius had been able to see the anguish in the Emperor's heart as he spoke. His brother had been taken unawares, again, by the Persian general's reckless disregard for water barriers. The old Roman was impressed—he had led his own armies on the sea—but like most Imperial generals he saw a fleet as a means to go from port to port, not to flank a prepared position—not to wield with such élan!

Gaius Julius dithered—and was vastly annoyed to find himself in such a state. *I am decisive! Bold! I act with considered, informed recklessness!* He looked across the table, irritated, and met Martina's eyes. She looked back, a hidden smile playing on perfect bow-shaped lips and one sharp, ink-dark eyebrow rose in open challenge. Gaius felt blood surge in his loins and looked away to the Emperor, trying not to blush. *No*, he reminded himself, *she is the impatient one, though her son cannot take his throne for decades!* The old Roman decided to take a middle course and build, slowly, for the future. *But*, he realized, *I can take one small step forward.*

"Then, we are agreed," Galen said, beginning to gather his

notes. The movement of his hands was sure and steady, but slow and lacking his usual brisk efficiency.

"Lord and God," Gaius heard himself say, "there is one more matter."

Galen's hands stopped and he set down an ivory stylus. "Yes?"

The old Roman straightened his shoulders and met the Emperor's eyes directly. *The speed of our onset*, Gaius recited to himself, drawing confidence from old, old memories, *unnerved them suddenly and completely. There was time neither to plan, nor to take up arms, and they were too confused to know if they should stand or flee.*

"My lord, our privy expedition has returned from Egypt."

Of the men and women seated at the table, only Martina did not start in surprise and she turned her head, looking out the nearest window in apparent boredom, letting Gaius' gaze linger on her fine neck and rising curve of her breast. Maxian's eyes, in particular, blazed with anticipation and a certain avaricious delight.

"Did they find at least one telecast?" The prince's voice was hoarse with anticipation.

"Yes, my lord, they did. One of our loyal soldiers bore it on his back to safety." Gaius turned to face the Emperor, straightening formally in his seat. "But the device was then lost and my agents have returned empty-handed. Lord and God," the old Roman inclined his head to the Emperor, "they beg your forgiveness for failure."

"What happened?" Galen stirred, frowning. Another dram of wretched news did not seem to tip his cup. His gaze was flat and cold, without amity or emotion of any kind, matching his brother's expression almost exactly. Gaius turned his head very slightly—just enough to catch a sense of the Duchess, who sat watching the discussion with intense interest.

"Our agents, Lord and God, both those supplied by the Duchess Anastasia and by myself, did find by diverse means a tomb of some repute, far out in the desert waste. Persian agents had also found the place and a struggle followed. Many perished and the Persians were driven away. One telecast—in form and shape much like our own—was recovered and moved to safety in nearby hills. Unfortunately . . ." Gaius' eyes slid sideways to the Duchess. She observed him with a cold, composed expression. The old Roman suppressed a smile. ". . . someone was watching and, when our man left the device to succor a friend trapped in a burning building, stole the telecast away."

The Emperor's lip twitched and he blinked slowly. "The Persians?"

"No, my lord," Gaius said with a relieved voice. He raised a hand in sign against ill luck. "Not the Persians! We can give thanks to the gods for that, at least. The only bright star in an otherwise dark firmament. No—the man who bore the telecast from the tomb is a Walach in Imperial employ."

The old Roman glanced around the table, nodding in a friendly way. Almost grinning, he laid a forefinger alongside his long nose. "For those who have not made their acquaintance, these Walachi are a swift, brutal people, more beast than man, given to transports of rage and excesses of bloody vengeance. Yet this one . . . while he has learned Roman virtue and drunk deep of our nobility and civilization . . . he retains—with his strength and speed—*nares leves*."

"What do you mean?" Galen made an impatient motion, a sharp, irritated anger beginning to prick in his face. "A fickle nose?"

"A discerning nose, I should say," Gaius replied. "He knew who took the device by their smell and taste in the dry air. Our expedition suffered many unexpected setbacks and maladies and on a cold desert night this man—this *loyal* Roman—divined the provenance of the thieves."

Gaius turned to look at Anastasia, raising one bristly gray eyebrow. The Duchess did not react, regarding him coolly, her hands entirely still on the tabletop.

"My lord, two members of our expedition did not return and I do not believe they perished in the desert, by fire, or sword, or the action of the enemy." Gaius Julius' voice took on a formal timbre, as though he stood before the Curia, speaking knowledgeably upon a matter of the law. "They are Thyatis Julia Clodia, a centurion in the Imperial service, and Betia, a maid in the household of Anastasia d'Orelio, Duchess of Parma. I believe they took the telecast and fled into the desert, seeking their own gain therefrom."

Anastasia blinked slowly, but her expression did not change by so much as an atom. Gaius Julius felt a warm glow of respect suffuse his cold, dead heart. *Look at her! Caught in her own ploy and fairly exposed, yet she does not show fear, remorse, even panic. Ah . . . the world is filled with wonders!*

"Duchess?" The Emperor stared at her in open dismay, brows furrowed. "What do you say to this?"

"I can say nothing, Lord and God," she replied quietly, challenge plain in her pale violet eyes. "This claim is as new to me as it is to you. Master Gaius, if only your own men have returned, who is to say they did not lead their companions to some unfortunate pass and contrive a tale to make them heroes and the unfortunate dead, villains?" A grim smile played on her lips. "Give me leave to speak with these men and we shall ascertain the truth."

"Of course," Gaius Julius said in an expansive tone. "They wait in the antechamber even now. Let us bring them in and you may put these questions to them yourself!"

"Do they?" Anastasia raised an eyebrow and Gaius thought he caught a flicker of surprise. *Interesting*, he purred to himself, *she thought I was lying? But why? The women were her own agents . . . perhaps . . . perhaps they did steal the device for their own game, betraying the Empire and her, both*. He started to frown, then caught himself.

"Enough of this." Galen spoke up, rising from his chair. He glared at the Duchess and Gaius Julius alike. "Another failure of our aims." He pointed abruptly at the Duchess. "These men will stay in Imperial custody and a truthsayer will be summoned. Then I will question them." He turned a forbidding expression on Gaius as well. "I will not countenance any dissent or distrust—particularly between the two of you—not in this dark hour. If I find *either* of you have been playing your own game, putting us all at risk, you'll find yourselves taking the view from the Tarpetian Rock!"

The Duchess stiffened, one white hand fluttering up from the tabletop, then forced down again. Gaius Julius made himself to nod in acquiescence, though the basilisk stare the Emperor turned upon him made his blood run colder still. "Of course, my lord."

The old Roman nodded politely to the Duchess. "My lady, perhaps I was hasty. My apologies."

She inclined her head, showing polite acceptance of his contrition, but Gaius was sure she would not forget his accusation. He hid a predatory smile—the look on the Emperor's face had been enough reward for today—if even the slightest seed of distrust grew between them. . . .

Galen watched the Duchess and Master Gaius bristle at each other and forced down a sense of rising hopelessness. The "revelation" of the mission's failure had not taken him by surprise—the captain of the *Urbes Brigantium* had sent him a warning as soon as the Imperial galley docked at Portus. He was not surprised his two spymasters were at odds either— plotting and scheming against one another should be like breathing—but watching their faces and seeing their mutual animosity there was one more blow than his stomach could handle today. *Why did I ever think two spies were better than one?*

"Then we know where we stand," he said aloud, drawing everyone's attention. "It seems unlikely—given their overextension—the Persians will continue to attack into our territory for the rest of the year. They will have to digest their fat new conquest and they have wounded soldiers who must heal and recuperate." Galen did not bother to disguise the bitter tone in his voice.

"What we must decide," he continued, though Maxian's expression was growing darker by the word, "is if we will attempt a counterattack in the next month or two, before winter makes the seas too dangerous to essay with the fleet. The *comes* Alexandros and his Goths could be landed at one of the small ports on the Cyrenaicean coast, allowing them to march east to attack Egypt." Galen nodded to his brother. "Our new fleet of the air is almost ready—"

"Ha!" Maxian's laugh was a sharp, abrupt bark. Galen fell silent, surprised. The prince rose, lean face a pale streak against the dark colors of his cloak and tunic. "Would that be wise? Brother—you are my sworn Emperor and blood of my blood—but you are becoming witless in advanced age!"

Galen flinched from the cutting tone, then his face settled into granite. "What do you mean?"

"Egypt is lost!" Maxian's hand cut the air in a ferocious blow. "Consider the Persian sorcerer's skill—he cannot send his army of the dead a great distance—but nothing stops him from giving them life again if our army marches into his hands! You are counting living men, thinking we might muster equal numbers, but *we cannot!*" The prince's face twisted into such an expression of rage and disgust even old Gaius drew back. "You sacrificed fifty thousand men to buy a month's time—yet if we strike against Egypt—we will fight those *same six Legions!* Every fallen man is now a Persian soldier, one who does not need pay, food, wine, oil or even a centurion's boot up his backside to fight." Maxian stared around the table, contempt and grief mixing in equal measure on his young face. "We have entered a terrible new world and you will be lost if you try a familiar guide or map to find your way."

The Emperor grasped the back of the chair next to him, exhausted mind awhirl with hideous visions. "I . . . I had not thought of that." Galen's voice was a barely audible whisper.

"No," Maxian said, casting a pitying glare at his brother. "You had not. No one did."

"What . . . what do we do, then?" Anastasia managed to speak, though she too had grown pale. Only Martina remained unmoved, watching her husband with a sly smile on her face, long fingers playing in russet curls.

"The Persian sorcerer and his servants," Maxian said frankly, "must be destroyed as soon as possible. Without them, the Persian army will be only living men again and they our soldiers can defeat." He flashed a grim smile, holding his brother's eyes. "Our old Horse could not match them, save in the strength of his heart and indomitable will, but I will make good his sacrifice. We will watch the enemy with our hidden Eye and when the sorcerer moves away from Egypt—and he will, I am sure—I will be waiting."

"No . . ." Galen started to speak, but Maxian gave him such a quelling look the Emperor fell silent.

"I will find him and destroy him." The prince's voice cut like a flensing knife stripping meat from the fat. "I know what must be done. I have an idea of *how* it might be done. This is the business of the *custos magus imperium* and you all would do well to leave these matters to those who have some comprehension of the powers at work."

No one looked up as Galen entered his offices on the northern side of the Palatine. The Emperor paused inside the doorway, surveying rows of writing tables and clerks hunched industriously over them. A soft, pervasive scratching sound lent a familiar, comfortable air. Even Nilos pretended ignorance of his presence, though Galen was sure the first secretary had not missed the sound of boots marching in the hall or the heavy wooden panel creaking open. The Greek was concentrating furiously on some letter on his copying stand, keeping his eyes averted from the door and his master's face.

Galen could not manage a smile at their painful circumspection. *Am I a ghost, then? Reduced to transparency, even in my own home? Ah, but I must look like a spirit—drawn, lifeless, haggard—with only torment hiding behind my poor mask of a face.*

The Emperor crossed the room, finding the effort of walking almost too much to manage. Every muscle felt sore, as if he'd ridden for days over bad ground. He squeezed Nilos' shoulder in passing, then closed the inner doors behind him.

Two walls pierced by broad windows let in a flood of cool northern light. A marble-topped desk made an *L*-shape, though the smooth gray Cosian slab was invisible beneath such a confusion of parchments, scrolls, inkstands and quills Galen wondered if the stone retained any of its subtle color. Back creaking, he lifted a fresh set of letters and edicts from his seat, dumping them among their disorderly fellows. Galen slumped in the camp chair, leaning his forehead—which seemed so hot, like the air simmering over the forum—against the back of his hand.

Maxian's voice rang harsh in his memories. Galen was not blind enough to deny the truth of his brother's words, though their disparaging tone cut him to the quick. *I am lost*, he thought, mood darkening as a shrill voice in his head recounted a litany of missteps and disasters. *I do not grasp the abilities or strengths of our enemy—not well enough to overcome them.* A loathing smile twitched on his lips. *And dear old Gaius Julius does no better. We are both artifacts, out of our depth, passed by in the rush of time and events.*

He missed Aurelian—not just for his solid, cheerful presence—but for the surety the big red beard gave Galen's world. A pillar, a mountain, a sure strength at his hand, someone to trust, someone to confide in . . . Maxian's sunny complement. *But now only we two remain*, he thought morosely, *two brothers too much alike to keep their quick tongues to themselves, without the moderating influence of . . .*

Galen pressed the palms of his hands over both eyes, trying to blot out beloved memories. The splitting pain of his headaches, at least, had receded, but now he was left with an enormous emptiness that captured every spare thought. "Enough of this," he said aloud, trying to force his mind onto a useful path. The Emperor squinted at the piles of papers.

"What to do?" Galen rubbed his jaw, realizing the muscles were tight as a drum. "Let us say my dear brother does have a way to defeat the Persian monster . . . then we will still have to fight Shahr-Baraz and his Immortals and these damned Arabs and Greeks." The Emperor looked at the southern wall of his office, where a stitched parchment sheet held a carefully drawn map of the Empire. His eye was drawn to Constantinople. A sense of neglected business tickled. "Ah—Alexandros had best not sail down to Egypt now! He'll put his head in the noose for sure. Nilos! Get in here!"

The door opened slowly, the Greek peeking with a wary expression on his face. Seeing a familiar, irritated expression on the Emperor's face, the secretary ventured a faint smile. "Yes, Lord and God."

Galen glared at the mess, scratching his head. "Help me find the latest reports from the fleet, and from *comes* Alexandros and his Legion."

"Here, sir." Nilos closed the door softly, then rummaged through the debris around the edge of the desk. After a moment, he excavated a packet of letters stamped with the seal of the cursus publicus and bound in dark green-and-red twine. The Greek dragged over a chair, setting a hamper filled with tax receipts on the floor. "This one—" he passed over a single sheet "—is from Alexandros, arrived just two days ago. And these—" A heavier packet, stained with some dark sauce, filled Galen's outstretched hand. "—arrived today from Tarentum."

"You've read them?" The Emperor raised an eyebrow, untying the fleet dispatch.

"No, Lord and God." Nilos managed a wry smile. "We've just been trying to keep things sorted."

Galen nodded absently, scanning through the listings of ships and men and supplies. He flipped to the last page, where a scrawled note occupied the bottom of the sheet. As he did, the Emperor's brow furrowed and he looked up at Nilos. "The fleet has moved to Dyrrachium in Epirus? Why?"

Nilos' eyebrows raised, and he shook his head. "I don't know, Lord and God. Who ordered them there?"

Galen looked back down at the page, brow darkening. "As per 'your orders,' this says. I sent no order . . . did you, or one of the tribunes?"

"No, my lord." Nilos looked perplexed. "Shall I find out who did?"

"Yes," Galen said slowly, setting the dispatch aside. He split the seal on the single sheet with the edge of his thumb. "But they've already set sail, so the best we can do is dispatch a courier to Dyrrachium and send them on to . . ." His eyes settled on the terse message, then widened in surprise. Galen flipped the paper over, nostrils flaring as he read the quickly scrawled destination on the front. The ink had smeared a little, obscuring the first line, leaving 'The Palatine' still readable. ". . . Constantinople."

"Master?" Nilos leaned forward in concern. Galen closed the letter abruptly and tucked the sheet into the pocket of his toga. "Is something wrong?"

"No," Galen looked up, an affable smile on his face. A hard glint was visible in his eyes. "Send round for two Legion couriers—strong riders both!—and write them up priority passes for the dispatch inns from here to Augusta Vendelicorum and Londonium."

Nilos nodded, though he expressed no comment at the need to send a message by all speed to Germania and Britannia. The secretary went out, leaving Galen alone in the office.

So. The Emperor pushed the fleet dispatch away with the tip of one finger. *The Goths are already on the road to Dyrrachium and the Imperial fleet will be there waiting when they arrive.* A bead of sweat slowly formed on his forehead, trickling into the sharp line of his brow. *A swift passage to Italia, then, for thirty thousand men.* Galen leaned back in his chair, wood and canvas creaking as he settled. *A fast march up the Via Appia and they will be in Rome in a month's time.*

The Emperor nodded to himself, remembering the shocked expression on old Gaius' face when he heard of the disaster in Egypt. *We both agreed, didn't we? Aurelian could hold out for another month, perhaps two, or even longer. Long enough to let these Goths place their foot on my neck.*

Galen could see the logic, though his heart twisted at the ramifications. *Then the new Emperor turns to deal with the Persians, armed with the fleet of the air and all our remaining strength.* A snarl transformed his face. *He thinks himself so great a general then, to do what Aurelian could not?* The bitter thought brought the Emperor up short, and a cold sense of revelation came over him. *Why not? Old Gaius is an exemplary general and Alexandros even greater. Why shouldn't they risk all, to gain all? They have never been defeated—and my rule has proved of only marginal worth. . . .*

A terrible weight pressed down on Galen, forcing his head into his hands. He felt pinned, trapped by circumstance and fate, ground fine by the millstone of events. *Oh, gods of Rome, why not let them rule? Then I will be free of all this. . . .*

The door creaked and Nilos entered, carrying two leather-bound packets. "Here are—my lord?"

The Emperor forced himself to raise his head. Bitter gall choked his throat and every motion was exhausting. "I will write a letter for each," he managed to croak. "These men must leave today."

Nilos bobbed his head and fled through the doorway. Galen fumbled for a quill, then spilled more than a little ink on the papers before he could force his hand to begin writing. There was still nearly a Legion's worth of troops in Britannia, scattered here and there, who could be wholly withdrawn to Germania. He hoped they would be enough to let three, perhaps four, of the Rhine Legions march south. *Britannia can fend for herself,* he thought bleakly, *and I pray the Franks-Beyond-The-River continue their kinstrife over Guntram's inheritance and keep their eyes from Gaul and Noricum. Or I will lose more than just Rome and this office and this cursed, heavy crown of laurel. I need troops who will remember I am the Emperor!*

"Ah, luxury!" Vladimir brushed aside a heavy curtain and looked with joy upon his own bed. The sheets and quilts were neatly pressed and tucked in—the house maids in the prince's home were nothing if not efficient—and he dumped his kit bag and stinking armor on the floor with a crash and clatter fit to wake the dead. "Ahhhh . . ." The Walach sprawled on the cot, feeling leather straps creak under the pallet. Goose-down pillows cradled his head and Vladimir felt the weariness of the road ease from his bones. He stretched, luxuriating.

"Aren't you barbarians supposed to take strength from sleeping on the cold ground?" Nicholas stepped into the room with less exuberance, his fine-boned face showing its own relief at coming home. "Living without restraint or habitation breeds a gigantic race . . ."

Vladimir made a rude gesture in response, then bent to dump his boots on the floor.

Nicholas laughed and set down his bags. As he did, he spied a letter on the table set against one wall. "Vlad," he said curiously, picking up the brown parchment, "you corresponding with some noble lady behind my back?"

The Walach made a quizzical, snuffling sound. "Nick, you know I can't read or write. Must be for you."

"No," Nicholas said, sitting down on the edge of his cot, "this is addressed to you from the Office of the Legions."

"Huh?" Vladimir shrugged, scratching behind his ear. "What does it say?"

Nicholas opened the page and screwed up his face, reading the tightly spaced lines with a frown. He owned some knowledge of letters, but not much, and the terse official language was hard to follow. After a moment, though, as Vladimir watched, his frown faded, replaced by a sigh of regret.

"What?" The Walach felt the thick dark hairs on his arms stir.

Nicholas looked up, shaking his head sadly. "Our missing lad is dead, Vlad. They found his body in the ruins of Constantinople, gaffed like a trout."

"No!" Vladimir sat up, horrified. "Not Dwyrin!"

"Yes," Nicholas said, handing across the parchment sheet. "They identified his body from the Legion brand and his *signaculum*. I'm sorry, Vlad."

"Poor cub." The Walach wiped a moist eye. "We should have stuck close to him, Nick, like herd dogs on a lame ewe. It's not right, a young lad like him accepting the crow-queen's embrace without even knowing a girl's kiss."

The Latin shook his head. He'd assumed the boy was dead long ago—the Empire would not let such a powerful wizard go astray—but held his tongue, seeing his friend's open grief. "No, I guess not. But death is never fair, though the *walkure* are always quick to stoop over the fallen."

Vladimir dragged his boots back out from under the cot. "I have to go out," he said gruffly.

Nicholas nodded in understanding, but did not follow. He had his own bitter thoughts to fill the time between weary consciousness and blessed, forgetful sleep.

THE SERAPEUM, ALEXANDRIA

T he floor jumped in echo of a resounding crash. Paving stones the size of a man creaked and dust clouded the air, shining brilliantly where thin slats of sunlight broke through the high roof. A broad-shouldered man, his long beard waxed and curled, mustache flaring beside and away from ruddy cheeks, turned his head slightly in question.

"They are tearing down the statues of the ancient gods, my lord," said the woman walking at his side. While the powerfully-built man was clad in cunning, articulated armor from neck to foot, she was dressed in soft, gleaming white, with golden necklaces heavy on her breast. Raven-dark hair framed her face, now done up with pins and rods into an elaborate headdress.

Shahr-Baraz frowned, fist caressing the hilt of his sword. "By whose order?"

"His," Zenobia answered, bowing towards shadows filling one end of the ancient hall. "The sight of so many 'false gods' displeases him."

"Do they?" The King of Kings strode forward, then slowed. Tall iron stakes barred his path, driven into the stone floor without regard for ancient propriety. A palpable chill pervaded the air and the Persian's breath began to frost in his mustache. Indistinct shapes stirred in the darkness and the Boar felt hostile eyes settle upon him. "I would speak with Prince Rustam," he called, stopping just short of the outmost ward.

There was no answer. Shahr-Baraz scowled at the Queen standing by his side. She said nothing, face impassive. In that moment, while they waited, the sound of boots on stone rang around them and the young Eagle, Khalid al'Walid appeared, dark hair shining in the intermittent sunlight. Odenathus was with him, the two men laughing in conversation.

"We are all here, then," the king said suspiciously, turning back to the shadowed hall. He raised a bushy eyebrow—the iron wands had gathered soundlessly to one side—leaving a passage open into the inner chamber of the temple. Suppressing instinctive dread, Shahr-Baraz strode through the opening and into the room beyond. The Queen followed silently and even the two garrulous young men found their speech faltering in such forbidding air.

Once, the central nave of the temple had held a great statue of the god, surrounded by stone and ceramic attendants. Now the altar was bare, the statuary broken and scattered. A carved pair of sandaled feet rose in the darkness, but the body of pink marble was gone. The sorcerer stood among the detritus of recent violence—a smooth head lacking a body, part of an arm, the splintered remains of incense burners and lamps—his outline swallowed by encompassing gloom.

A faint, gray light shone down from drifting specks in the air. Dahak turned as the king entered, his eyes pale flames in the darkness.

"Pharaoh," the sorcerer said, ignoring the Boar, "does the common herd bow down in fear before our jackal-headed god?"

A spasm flitted across Zenobia's face, but she maintained her composure, making a shallow bow. "Yes, my lord, they do. They look upon your servant in his might and glory and they are filled with despair, thinking Set has burst the chains of the sun and now walks among them, as the gods did in days of old, before man first struck fire from flint."

"They are nearly right," Dahak whispered, climbing the steps to the ruined altar. "Do they labor at my tasks? Do they sweat under the whip, dreading each night as a coming death, as a plague?"

"Yes." Zenobia's gaze hardened, her rich lips thinning to a cold line. "Every ship of seagoing size is on the beach, hulls being patched, tarred, careened. Messengers have been sent to every port, summoning the merchants of Palmyra to attend your will."

"I am pleased." Dahak found a cracked piece of rose-colored sandstone on the dais and took the fragment in his hands. He peered at the stone, then let it fall. "And you, Pharaoh, do they prostrate themselves when you pass; do they call your name, begging your favor, your protection, your intercession?"

The Queen said nothing.

"Do they?" The sorcerer glanced at her, lip curling. Zenobia staggered, her skin rippling as though worms crawled beneath the flesh, gnawing at muscle and nerve. She cried out—a short, breathy cry of agony—and fell to her knees. Dahak smiled, showing gleaming white teeth. "I think they do. What name do they give you?"

Another spasm shook the woman and Zenobia let open fury and hatred flare in her face for an instant. Then the calm mask composed her features again. "They call . . ." she gasped, fighting to speak. "They call me Kleopatra Returned and weep with joy, hoping I will save them, save their husbands, save their children from the mines, the pits, the labor gangs. . . ."

A gleam of delight flared in Dahak's limpid, pale eyes. Zenobia collapsed against the stones, breathing ragged, but the pain lifted from her white limbs.

"Well done," the sorcerer said, turning at last to the King of Kings. "You are displeased, old Boar. You do not like what has happened while you've been away upriver."

"No, I do not." Shahr-Baraz' voice was hard and commanding. "There is no need for these charades and shadow games. Our hand is strong upon the neck of Egypt. There is no need to slaughter the fellahin—they will work for us as readily as they worked for Rome. The Nile is rising and everyone must wait for the river to fall before the planting begins. This is a time of rest for these people. . . ."

Dahak nodded, eyes glittering in suffuse gray light. "I do not care about the harvest."

"Then we will all starve," Shahr-Baraz replied in a sharp tone. "And we've no need of a fleet—"

"We have every need of a fleet!" The sorcerer's voice cracked like a whip, shocking the king into silence. "We are not waiting for the sacred river to flood the land! We are not waiting for a *harvest!*" A thin, dark finger stabbed at Odenathus, making the young wizard flinch and turn pale. "When will the fleet be ready to sail?"

The Palmyrene blinked in surprise, looked sideways at Khalid, who shrugged, then back to Dahak. "My lord prince . . . our crews are working night and day by your command, and wearily too, after fighting for so many months without respite—but they are willing men and loyal. They will not disappoint! Four weeks, I would say, before we complete the refitting."

Dahak snarled, a ripping, taut sound and his fingers curled into a fist. Odenathus stared in shock for a moment, then suddenly howled in agony. Blood clouded his eyes and flickering, black lightning raced across his face and breast. Mouth wide in a pitiful scream, the young man collapsed to the ground, body jerking with muscular spasms, spine bent into a harsh bow.

"I've no margin for weeks to pass in idleness," hissed the sorcerer, opening his hand. Odenathus crumpled like a broken dove, sprawling on the floor, limbs twitching and loose. Khalid almost bent to take his shoulder, but caught sight of Dahak's furious visage and stepped back.

Shahr-Baraz had no such patience and took two swinging steps up onto the platform.

"Fool!" A heavy fist smashed across the sorcerer's cheek, rocking Dahak back on his heels. The Boar loomed over him, face glowing with fury. "These are our allies! Not our servants, not our playthings!"

"Aren't they?" Dahak scrambled to his feet, mouth wide in a feral grin. The blow—strong enough to have toppled a wrestler—did not seem to have affected him at all. The two men faced off, tension crackling in the air, a mad look in the sorcerer's eyes. "They are *my servants*, O King! Do not dispute my commands, for you may find your own neck bent beneath my foot!"

"Dispute?" Shahr-Baraz's voice settled into a precise, cold tone. Metal rasped on metal as the Boar drew the heavy sword at his side. "You are my sworn man, sorcerer, and you will obey your king!"

"Obey? A king?" Dahak laughed softly and his outline shifted, distorting, and he grew, suddenly towering above the Boar. A shocking chill flooded the room and the chittering of insects and crickets and bats roared loud at the edge of hearing. "I am not your *man*, old fool. I am not human at all!"

A cone of frigid gray illuminated the altar, pinning the king in its pitiless glare. Dahak emerged into the light, head lengthening, incisors jutting from black, withered jaws. Deep-set eyes burned red and Shahr-Baraz stifled a groan, stepping back. The sorcerer's hand—taloned and dark, rippling with scales—clutched at the air. The heavy hand-and-a-half sword sprang from the Boar's fingers, then metal shrieked as the blade twisted and tore. A heavy, crumpled ball of steel clattered away into darkness.

"Bow," roared an inhuman voice. The Boar staggered, gripped by invisible claws. Dark streaks of red scored his face and creases *pinged* into the laminated metal protecting his shoulders and arms. A great shout leapt from the king's throat and he strained, tendons bulging in his neck, sweat beading on ruddy skin. Dahak pointed his hand to the floor and Shahr-

Baraz was thrown down, forehead grinding against frost-rimed stone. "You are my servant, old Boar, since the moment you sat upon my brother's throne. So are the great snared, with power and glory and honor!"

The sorcerer glared at the others, gaze settling upon the Queen, who stood once more, hands clasped at her waist, blue eyes defiant.

"You wish to taste the lash again?" Dahak dragged the king back by his hair, exposing a bull-like neck. A long talon came to rest beside a beating vein, pressing against the skin. "Shall I bleed this boar out, before I let him hang under my eaves, curing for the feast?"

"You may," Zenobia said in a clear, ringing voice. "But you will cast aside a great general if you do."

Dahak barked laughter, a baying, ringing sound. "I will make another, even as you serve, and dear Arad serves, so will the King of Kings dance to my fluting pipe!"

"Will you?" Zenobia took a step forward, oval face intent and calm. "Then you will have to struggle each day to bind his great heart—for he will accept no collar, even one of the mind—and then you will have to watch me as well, and Arad and Odenathus and Khalid—and all the captains of your host." Each name, each word, she pronounced with perfect clarity. "Can even your cold mind cover such great distances? What of your Sixteen? Do they serve with a willing heart? Can you even trust such a creature as C'hu-lo, who will never rest until he looks upon the Rampart of Heaven with a king's eyes?"

"I will!" Dahak's hand lashed out in a flat, chopping motion. To his surprise, Zenobia did not topple, screaming with pain, her body contorted by fiendish punishments. Instead, she staggered, and a flickering pale glow shimmered in the air between them. Half-seen geometric patterns roiled in the air, flashing in and out of sight. The sorcerer bared his teeth, snarling in thwarted rage. His will roared forth, compressing the room to a tiny mote of illumination suspended into infinite darkness. With an effort, he crushed her shields and laid bare her mind to his control once more.

"You see," Zenobia whispered, her body pinned to the floor by Dahak's raging thought. She ceased resisting, letting him flood into her. "Every moment will be like this. A struggle, a contest of wills, until you snuff the last spark of life in this body."

Dahak gasped, sweating with effort, withdrawing his power. The cold grew worse, but Odenathus had recovered himself and muttered soft words. A arc of golden light circled himself, Zenobia and Khalid. The young Arab had been watching with wide eyes, hand firmly on the scabbard and hilts of his saber, though he had not dared draw the weapon. "You could only resist me for an instant . . ."

"You are stretched thin," Zenobia replied as she rose to her feet again. "The king has recovered, even in this brief moment of relief." Her hand lifted, arm white against the darkness, and Dahak became aware of the Boar crouched behind him, a long knife shining quicksilver in his massive hand. "Strike him down and you cleave away your right arm, your iron fist on the field of battle. Strike me down and your precious Kleopatra is gone. Each of us you crush, your power is reduced by equal measure." A flinty, cold smile flirted with her mouth.

"Even Arad will prove troublesome, if I am gone. Then you will face the Romans alone."

A dry hiss answered her and Dahak rose up, shadow boiling and writhing around him. For a grain there was a colossal form pressing against the walls, the floor and the roof. Stone splintered and flaked. The scattered marble limbs ground to dust. Odenathus' shield wavered, compressed by seething coils and then the apparition passed.

Dahak once more confined only to the shape of a lean, hungry-looking man, stared at the Queen. "Do you think you've drawn me to a stalemate?"

"If so much," she replied gravely, "then I've found victory."

A spasm flickered across the sorcerer's face and Zenobia drew back in surprise. Something like a human countenance shone through for a moment, then the seeming faded, leaving only cold, inhuman features close beneath a shell of flesh. "Victory," the thing said, the word falling away into a low, rumbling hiss. "An ant clinging to a stem of grass in a field of stones should claim so much."

Endless weariness pervaded the air and the Queen felt a chill—not from the icy air—but in the secret place in her heart where two women struggled to survive in the face of constant, unspeakable horror. "What do you mean? We are not . . . ants."

"Less, then, less than a grain of sand on an endless beach." A queer, unexpected tone of grief entered the sorcerer's voice. "Only Khadames guessed—only he saw—and he is dead."

Zenobia felt the trickling chill double, flooding her tiny sanctuary, drowning her and Zoë and their fragile hope in swiftly rising black water. She knew the thread in his voice all too well. *We struggle each day with the same blighting acid. . . .*

"You are afraid," she said, shocking herself with audible words. "You."

Dahak's grimace transformed—rage, loathing, a death-like grin—and settled into sullen fury.

"Yes," he spat out. "I fear oblivion, even I who have reached across the abyss and stolen life from death, who command the air, the earth, all the powers that crawl and walk and ride upon the wing!" The sorcerer's hands fluttered open, groping in the darkness. His voice changed again, swelling with agony and despair. "I see the sun rise and some dead part of me begins to live! I walk in the green hills and I rejoice to feel cool air upon my face! I see the multitude and see their arts, hear their songs, feel the rushing, flowing life in their breast and I am . . . afraid."

A tapering nail stabbed in the air, splitting darkness from darkness. Stars rushed out of the void so revealed and Zenobia swallowed a shout of amazement. A blue-green world whirled past in sable night, a pale moon winging at her shoulder.

"Here is such a small thing," Dahak groaned, framing chaos with his hands. "Yet so precious! I cut out my heart, killed my soul, bled away every human feeling—yet they remain! This tiny, frail pocket remains. . . ." He turned, face ghastly with fear and incipient horror. "You do not understand, you *cannot* understand. How could you, for you have not looked upon the abyss and seen the dread chaos yawn before you, blotting out stars, suns, entire worlds?"

Struggling to master her astonishment, Zenobia groped for words. "No . . . we have not. Can any human look upon the abyss and survive, or keep mind enough to tell another?"

"No." Dahak shook his head. While she spoke, he had mastered himself. The cut sealed, the green world vanished, the stars swallowed up once more. Only his voice remained, a dry, whispering echo in the encompassing darkness. "Know this, rebellious Queen. There is a door of stone hidden far from here. Hidden and sealed with signs and powers beyond your grasp to bind or loose. While that door is closed, the green world you love so much lives. Should it open—and it stands closed now only by my will!—then this frail refuge will be annihilated, swallowed, consumed in the blink of an eye."

Zenobia said nothing, though her heart quailed before such a vision.

"We are a fluke," the sorcerer's voice whispered. "An aberration. Random chance casting up a bubble shining in golden sunlight. Now, you will do my bidding and follow my will, and *serve freely*, or all this will be lost."

"You will destroy the world, if your desire is thwarted?" The Queen's voice trembled slightly.

"Not I," Dahak answered in a hoarse, exhausted voice. "Not I."

"Then . . ." The Queen struggled with a clenching pain in her gut. *He is telling the truth!*

"I baited annihilation," the sorcerer said mournfully. "I opened the door just a hair, just a thin crack, and snatched power and glory and knowledge from dread chaos' domain. But I drew attention in the briefest of moments—in a slice of time so small no human mind could catch, or follow, or measure, its passing—and now the door is closed, but it is known, and watched relentlessly." A hollow laugh echoed. "The watchers at the threshold do not tire or wander or sleep. They have eternity at their beck and call and they are very hungry."

"But while you exist, the door is closed," Zoë said tensely, pushing the Queen aside. "You are holding it closed against them."

"Yes," echoed out of the darkness. A few faint gray sparks began to drift among the pillars, shedding a corpse-light upon stone faces. "I disturbed a delicate balance and what once remained closed of its own nature yearns to open fully."

"Can the door be truly closed again?" Zoë regretted the question as soon as the words escaped her lips.

A mocking silence was her only answer. The Queen looked down, unwilling to venture further words.

"You can die, then?" The Boar's voice rumbled out of the dim shadows. Shahr-Baraz had quietly taken a seat on the floor beside Khalid—who sat clutching scabbard to breast, barely breathing, eyes screwed shut—and Odenathus, who watched the Queen with a queer, troubled expression. "You are afraid not only of your own oblivion, but what will come after."

The silence shifted, charging with malice and anger. The Boar pursed his lips, thinking. After a moment, he smiled faintly. "You are a canny old snake," the king said, "but secrets are hard to keep. Shall you tell these children, or shall I?"

"Tell them what?" snapped a cold voice. Twin points of pale light gleamed in the shadows.

"Tell them about the Roman. The Roman and the sea."

The pale gleams blinked once, then twice. Shahr-Baraz laughed softly.

"Our Lord of the Serpents," the Boar began, voice rumbling with ill-disguised humor, "does not like the water. If memory serves, he dreads even to ride in a ship. He asked me to build a bridge of earth and saplings just cross the Propontis. He took to the upper air—on a mount I've had the misfortune to ride myself—rather than cross the sea on a fine, swift boat. Once, once he was forced to swim in the salt sea for a dozen heartbeats—he still bears those scars on face and body like the gouges of a burning iron. No, he does not like the deep waters."

The twin points of light flared, glittering like the edge of a blade catching the moonlight.

"Shall I say on?" Shahr-Baraz matched gazes with the thing in the shadows. "I shall, I think. If you are outraged by the truth, you can surely destroy us all."

The Boar gave the others a calm, almost amused look. The Queen marveled at his equanimity and in the crystalline moment while their eyes met, she realized he was entirely free from fear. *Has he ever been touched by fear?* she wondered. *Does he even know how it feels, how it tastes?*

"There is a Roman wizard," Shahr-Baraz continued, nose wrinkling like his namesake. "And he is very strong. By my eyes, as strong as our old snake here. They met, they fought, during the fall of Constantinople." The king flashed a smirk at the darkness. "A draw. We have not met him yet on this campaign. They are holding him back, waiting, I think, for the right moment to strike us unawares."

The Boar lifted his chin questioningly at the shadows. "Is he alone?"

"No." The twin points of light thinned to narrow slits. "There was a witch at his side."

"A witch?" The Queen's eyebrows rose in surprise. *What kind of witch? One like us?*

"Yes," hissed the sorcerer. "But Arad was by *my* side. Still we drew even."

Shahr-Baraz nodded, pleased to have learned so much. "Now Arad is not your only servant—Odenathus and the Queen are your allies—there will be four against two. Will this suffice if you meet again?"

The sorcerer did not answer and the King of Kings nodded to himself again. "I am not a wizard," he said in a contemplative tone. "But I think I understand the matter of this door of stone. By its nature, a door is intended to *open*, and any wayward, wind, or current of the air, may shift such a fragile balance."

Both the Queen and the king looked to the shadows and found the gleaming eyes dulled nearly to invisibility. Shahr-Baraz hid another mirthless smile, giving the Queen a challenging look.

"This Roman," she hazarded, watching the kings eyes, "his powers are much like yours, Lord of the Ten Serpents?"

"Yesss . . ." A hissing trill spiraled away into silence. "I feel him in the hidden world, a storm around which all currents twist and run awry."

"Do they touch the door?" Shahr-Baraz' voice was keen and sharp.

"They will," Dahak whispered, something of his hidden fear surfacing again. "If he lives."

"He is growing stronger?" Zenobia forced herself to voice the question. *Father Sun crush this serpent and free my soul from helping him!* "What will happen if he finds the door of stone?"

A cough of laughter answered. "Men are curious creatures, far worse than cats. What ape has ever failed to plunge his hand into a dark hole, scratching for something sweet?"

The Queen looked at Shahr-Baraz questioningly. "Could we tell this Roman the truth?"

"We will not!" Dahak surged out of the shadows, sending a cloud of gray sparks rushing away from his advance. Wild shadows flared on the walls. "The moment he perceives the door, the watchers beyond the threshold will become aware of *him* and their thoughts will crowd his mind with visions and enticing dreams. Even a moment's desire or hesitation or wayward intent on his childish, reckless part and the seals will fail."

The sorcerer stood over them, sullen black flame licking around his outline. He seemed ready to strike them both down where they sat. Shahr-Baraz raised a quieting hand.

"We will not tell him," the king said. "Despite all this, I have no love for Rome."

The Boar stood, holding out a hand for the Queen. Tentatively, she accepted, finding his palm warm and dry and immensely comforting. Shahr-Baraz glared at the sorcerer. "You should have told me this before. We have wasted time. . . ." The king paused, canting his head to one side. "Wait a moment. You urged me to attack Egypt—what were you seeking here? A tool? A weapon?"

Dahak's lip curled into a sneer. "Nothing. A dry well."

Shahr-Baraz gave the sorcerer a level stare in return. "Are we stronger for all this?"

"No," Dahak allowed, sneer fading into a scowl. "No, I am beginning to tire."

"Can we wait," the Queen said, hating each movement of her lips, "until you regain your strength?"

The sorcerer shook his head, a look of equal disgust playing across sharp, inhuman features.

"Then we must press them hard while we can," Shahr-Baraz said, pursing his lips. "Why do you need the fleet? Why this army? You could summon one of your horrors to fly you to the enemy. End this with a single, swift blow."

"He will not be alone," Dahak growled. "I recognized him when we fought. He will be well protected, surrounded by fanatical Legions, mewed up in their strongest fortress."

"Why?" The Boar made a grunting sound. "Who is he?"

"Their Emperor's brother," Dahak replied sourly. "And he

has . . . clever toys. Things we lack and have no time to make."

Toys? The Queen searched her memory, remembering something. . . . *Yes, a disk of gears and interlocking wheels; he called it a* duradarshan, *but not a toy* . . . In that moment, Zenobia remembered something else, something the sorcerer had said and she felt a faint gleam of hope flare in her secret heart. She almost looked to see if there were a window opening into the chamber, then caught herself and fixed her attention on the King of Kings.

"Prince Maxian?" The Boar sounded surprised and thoughtful. "Isn't he a priest of the temple of Asklepios the Healer? Hmm . . . if his powers turn towards yours, he would be a puissant foe. And he *will* be guarded by armies."

Dahak grimaced, but said nothing.

"Well," Shahr-Baraz turned to Odenathus and Khalid, who were listening with wide eyes. "We *do* need the fleet then and quickly too. And we must freight an army, one strong enough to fight through to Rome if we must." The king's eyes twinkled. "I've a thought about that . . ."

Zenobia turned away from the discussion, sick and consumed with loathing. *Our freedom was only moments away and now we choose to place the collar on our own neck?*

We must, Zoë answered, though her helpless anger was even greater than her aunt's. *What choice do we have, if the world is to live?*

The Queen's humor did not improve. The truth tasted of ashes.

<hr />

THE CHAMBER OF SIGHT, PALATINE HILL

N ext window." Galen slumped sideways in his chair, face puffy with fatigue. "Next window."

The telecast shuddered and hummed, the rushing sound of spinning gears and wheels filling the room. The Emperor watched listlessly, forcing his mind to comprehend and classify each image as the device jumped and flickered. "Next . . ."

The scene suspended in the burning disk flashed and another section of sandstone wall came into view. Square windows bisected by iron bars drifted by. Galen could see people moving about within, sitting at low writing tables or shuffling baskets of scrolls from place to place. *Business is business in Egypt*, he thought glumly. *Regardless of who sits on the throne of the Two Lands.*

"Wait!" The Emperor squinted—this window was larger than most. A woman stood framed by a windowsill, swinging open a pair of wooden shutters. For an instant, it seemed she met the Emperor's eyes through the burning lens, but then she turned away. Galen frowned in surprise, seeing she wore an elegant, yet archaic costume, more reminiscent of old Egyptian statuary than any recent fashion he knew of. "Who is this?"

The two thaumaturges seated beside the device shook their heads slightly.

"Can you show me the room? Do you feel the Serpent close by?" The Emperor continued to watch the woman speaking—there was another figure, perhaps two, in the room—he could see an elbow and someone's hand gesticulating.

"He is not . . ." The elder of the two Roman thaumaturges concentrated. "Not that I can sense."

Galen bit his thumb, considering the Egyptian woman's striking profile. *A Queen? Where did the Persians find a Queen of old Egypt? Hmm . . . is that the jeweled hilt of a Persian cavalry sword on a man's belt?*

"Look inside," the Emperor decided. "Let us take a small risk."

"A risk of what?" A husky, tired voice intruded. Galen looked over his shoulder. Maxian stood in the doorway of the library, draped in gray and black, his hair unkempt and stringy.

"Max, come sit." Galen rose, shaking a cramp out of his leg. He took his brother's hand and led him to a couch against the wall. In the telecast, the mysterious woman continued her discussion, entirely ignorant of the distant, spying eye looking over her smooth white shoulder. Maxian sat with a sigh, leaning his head back against the wall and closing his eyes.

"Bring food," Galen said to one of the servants hovering outside the door. The Emperor turned to the thaumaturges and scribes. "Rest for a moment. Go down to the kitchens and get something to eat; cheese, kippers or oiled bread. There may be some minted goose or flamingo left."

Maxian seemed to have fallen asleep by the time everyone had shuffled out and Galen could turn to him again. The Emperor smiled faintly, feeling a great sense of compassion for his younger brother—who seemed so old, narrow face lined with fatigue, his hair a tumbled mass of oily strands, hands stained with rust and oil and countless tiny scratches. Galen sat thinking, forehead resting in his hands, trying to remember if he had ever been so exhausted in the Legion. There had been a time in Pannonia . . . *I think not*, he grumbled to himself. *Marching and fighting was easy, compared to this slow death by tiny, pecking bites.*

"What were you looking at?" Maxian spoke, eyes still closed.

"The palace of the governor of Egypt," Galen said, leaning back himself. The wall was blessedly cool against his back. "I believe the Persian commander has taken up residence there. We're peering in the windows to see if we can spy out what they intend to do next."

The prince laughed, an honest sound, filled with weary mirth. "Momma would whip your behind with a strap for such rude behavior, if she were alive to catch you."

"She would." Galen snorted. "How are you?"

Maxian grunted, raising a hand and making a dismissive motion. "I live. The work in Florentia is complete. Only interior fittings remain—chairs, windows, floors. There are three-dozen men eager to try their hand at flight." He opened his eyes, fixing Galen with a fierce stare. "We are almost ready."

"Good." The Emperor looked away, unable to meet the accusation in his brother's smudged brown eyes. "Good. The fleet is ready, Lord Alexandros is ready . . . there are other Legions coming, but I've not heard—yet—when they will reach Rome."

"Do we know which way the enemy will move?" Maxian rubbed a fine-boned hand across his face and the stubbled, patchy beard vanished. He smoothed back his hair and the grease and oil faded. Exhaustion dropped away, leaving him bright-eyed and alert. "What have you found?"

Galen watched his brother with open disgust as the younger man stepped lightly to the telecast. The prince did not bother to mutter or make an arcane sign—the disks and gears shuddered, blazing with hissing flame as the device sprang to life. "Show me the Bruchion," Maxian commanded, "and what we looked upon before."

The Emperor suppressed a start of surprise—the difference in clarity and acuity between Maxian's command of the device and the Legion thaumaturges was no less than night and day—staring into the distant room at a shallow angle. The Queen now sat in a swan-backed chair, legs curled under her, brilliant blue eyes sparkling as she watched a handful of men argue over a map.

"Sicilia!" Galen blurted, coming to his brother's side.

"Yes," Maxian agreed, shifting his hands. The telecast focused, showing a crumbling papyrus sheet marked with brown ink. The outline of the great island was plain to see, and a heavy, thick finger stabbed at icons of towns and villages sprinkled along the eastern coastline. "What are they looking at?"

"The bay of Catania," Galen growled, his grim face fluttering with broken sunlight streaming through from the Egyptian room. "They are arguing about landing their fleet at Syracuse—there to the south, where the island turns in a jagged horn—or at Catania, where the bay is broad and wide, and there are long, shallow beaches."

"Why there?" Maxian turned, frowning. "Won't they need a harbor to unload their ships?"

Galen shrugged. "Syracuse is strongly fortified, the harbors closed by a causeway and chain. Look!"

The finger jabbed at an inlet beneath the sketched sign of a great mountain, then moved inland and south, crossing into the mountains above the representation of Syracuse. A fist thumped on the table as a young, hawk-faced man in oddly-cut robes made a violent gesture. Galen watched their faces, lips pursed, frowning in concentration. Maxian, in turn, watched his brother in amusement.

"The young one thinks they should land close to the city," the

Emperor said after a moment. "The others—the veterans—disagree. They think no one will resist the landing so far away, letting them unload in peace." Galen rubbed his chin. "Rash youth will be—ah!"

The man owning the thick fingers moved into the scene, a fierce beard curling from a jutting chin, deep-set eyes flashing as he spoke. The Emperor watched him greedily, drinking in details of his garments—a simple tunic over a mail shirt, with the hilts of a heavy sword and mace riding on his hip—and the movement of his lips.

"The King of Kings," Galen breathed, flashing his brother a wan smile. "Shahr-Baraz the Boar, greatest of the Persian generals. Not our most formidable enemy, but close, very close. Even without the sorcerer's help, he would test us fiercely." The Emperor pointed at the young, dark-complected man. "This must be the commander of the Arab mercenaries—he seems very reckless—the shahanshah will overrule his suggestion to land directly at Syracuse."

A moment later, the King of Kings shook his head, curls bouncing, and made a firm, final indication on the map.

"Catania, then," Maxian said slowly, thinking, his eyes comparing the ground shown on the map to a trove of memories from time spent at his sister-in-law's estate. "Under Aetna. Is their fleet ready to sail?" The prince's eyelid twitched and the scene dimmed, the view springing back over the rooftops of a city, which dwindled until only the blue-green orb of the earth swam in the fiery circle. A long wing of white cloud covered most of the Middle Sea.

"Soon enough," Galen said, biting his thumb. "We've been watching them work. It's odd, they've torn out all the rowing benches in their galleys to clear space. Every galley stepping a sail is being refitted and the civilian merchantmen are being stripped down. No comfortable journey for those men, by Poseidon! I'd say they can put ten thousand men ashore with the usual complement of supplies and gear." He flashed a grim smile. "Barring storms."

Maxian considered his brother, then said, "what if they brought nothing? No supplies, no horses, no tents, nothing but soldiers packed tight as cordwood?"

The Emperor made a disgusted face. "By the gods, Max, it's a full week's sail from Alexandria to Syracuse—half those men would be dead from heat and . . ." Galen's voice trailed off.

"Corpses packed below decks," Maxian said, a forbidding expression darkening his face, "do not feel the heat or cry out for water or even foul themselves in rough seas. Corpses can be efficiently stacked, laid one upon another in honeycombed rows and now they have so many fresh bodies to use . . ." A glint of something like hatred flared in the prince's eyes and the Emperor felt his flesh crawl, feeling the brunt of his brother's fury.

"Ah—that is foul." Galen grimaced. "But you're right again—and this means a good forty thousand dead men will swarm from those ships." He turned pale. "And every graveyard and tomb they pass . . .

"Will be filled with fresh recruits!" Maxian looked closely at his brother, as if for the first time. "You've been too long without sleep, Gales. You look terrible."

"Thanks—" The Emperor hissed in surprise as the prince caught his hand, pressing flat-tipped fingers against the inside of the Imperial wrist. A soft green light glowed, shining through flesh and blood and bone. *"Yiiii!"*

"Better?" Maxian's eyes crinkled up in amusement, though the dark core of each pupil seemed cold and remote. Galen shook himself, feeling a tingling rush from the bottoms of his feet to the crown of his head. The grainy, deep-set weariness he had been struggling through was gone. Even the room seemed brighter and the Emperor stared around in surprise. Details on the further walls were clear and sharp and he could pick out birds chirping in the trees outside the windows.

"Ay, my sight's been failing!" Galen rubbed his eyes, then looked again in wonder. "Well, bless me." He smiled at his brother, making a little bow. "Thank you."

"Huh." Maxian seemed embarrassed by the gratitude. "I wondered why your mind's become so slow of late." The prince shrugged. "I should have realized sooner."

"Better late . . ." Galen started to say, but stopped, thinking of Aurelian. "What do we do about Sicilia? Our fleet is at Dyrrachium, loading the *comes* Alexandros' Goths—but there are only thirty thousand of them and *not* prepared to fight the dead. Will the flying machines make enough of a difference?"

"Perhaps." Maxian's instant of good humor vanished and Galen could tell thoughts of Aurelian tormented him as well. Grief shadowed the prince's face, making him seem much older. "If we can catch their fleet at sea we will have a good chance. But I cannot guarantee anything—not against this foe."

"We must stack the odds, then," Galen said. "Our only advantage is knowing where they will come ashore. I will put every man in arms on the road to Sicilia. The fleet can ferry them across the strait at Messina. If the gods smile and old soldiers answer their Emperor's call, we can meet them with forty thousand legionnaires."

Maxian started, then gave his brother a queer, measuring look. "I am going south tomorrow," he said abruptly. "A thought occurs to me and will take time to play out." He put his hand on Galen's shoulder, then wrapped his brother in a tight hug. "I hope to see you again."

"You too, piglet," Galen said, fighting to keep his eyes dry. "What do you intend?"

The prince ducked his head, avoiding the Emperor's searching gaze. "Nothing you would approve of," Maxian mumbled, walking quickly to the door. "But these things must be done, for victory."

"What did you say?" Galen reached the door only a step behind, but Maxian was already gone. The Emperor frowned, looking back at the disk. The green earth turned slowly in the shimmering orb of light. The sight made Galen raise an eyebrow in surprise. He had never seen the device operate by itself before. "Well, well . . . show me the bay of Catania."

Gaius Julius leaned against the wall of a small *caupona* at the foot of the Caelian hill, seamed old face plastered with a pleasant expression, a cup of wine in his hand. Like most of the other men crowded into the dim, smelly room he was clad in a tunic and long stonemason's apron. Everyone was glad to be out of the sun and done with another day's work on the restoration of the temple of the Divine Claudians. The old Roman was watching the door and narrow steps leading down from the street out of the corner of his eye.

While he waited, Gaius paged through a set of crumbling parchment sheets. He had not pillaged the Senatorial records in a long time—not since he'd been writing *Praises of Hercules* as a boy seeking to link the god's lineage to his own. The smell of decaying paper brought back fond memories and the sight of so many books had filled him with familiar avarice. These old rags, though, they held only part of what he had been seeking.

When he had walked the earth as a breathing man, the Clodians *gens* had been only one of a dozen rivals. The braggart Clodius Pulcher had employed gangs of thugs to terrorize the Senate, had cast aside his noble birth to be elected as a plebian, had used his delectable sister Clodia as a bribe to sway the senators and been a political opponent in every sense of the word. *From this stock sprang our gray-eyed Diana? A wonder, if true. They seemed near collapse even in my day.*

Gaius shook his head, running a well-trimmed nail down page after page of lineages, births, deaths, all matter of scandal, despair, joy and tumult disguised by dryly worded fact. At length, he found the family dwindled almost to nothing, only possessing a single estate in southern Latium, and then—twenty years past—nothing. No children, no legal records. A dying clan guttering out at last.

"Hmm." Gaius rubbed his nose. "Is she the last of a disgraced, bankrupt house?" He wondered who would know her antecedents—*the Duchess, of course, but I cannot ask her!*—and began to trace the linages backwards, through the contorted branches and leaves of a sprawling, often-intermarried family. He sighed, wondering how long he would have to wait in this hot, close place.

Evening advanced and an elderly man entered, a heavy basket of scrolls tucked under one arm. He pushed through the workmen, exchanging greetings with a few, to stand at the bar beside Gaius. The old Roman put away his papers. The woman behind the slab-shaped counter lifted her head in question.

"Pickle, fish sauce and nut custard, please." Nilos' voice was marked by a distinct "Palace" accent and tinged with exhaustion. Gaius felt a twinge of sympathy—the basket of scrolls was not for show, but the man's uncompleted work from the day, being taken home to be copied or reviewed by lamplight.

The woman nodded, spooning a gooey confection of pepper, cracked nuts, honey, rue and raisin wine in egg white into a hand-sized cup from a bowl built into the countertop. One of her assistants scurried off to draw pickles from a huge vat in the back of the shop and pluck a jar of Hispanian fish sauce from one of the shelves.

"What news from our father's house?" Gaius made the statement to the empty air, though his voice was low and barely audible among the bustle and chatter in the common room. The workmen saw each other every day and most lived within a block of each other, yet there was never any lack of conversation or dispute.

Nilos did not look at him, but gratefully accepted the bundle of custard and pickles wrapped in cheesecloth from the proprietress.

"Thirteen," she said, wiping her hands on a dirty gray rag. The secretary counted out a handful of copper coins and left them on the countertop. He nodded to Gaius in a friendly way as he turned, saying softly, "Some cousins are coming for a surprise visit, one Briton and three German."

"What?" Gaius Julius caught the man's eye, voice a bare, sharp whisper. "Our *cousins* are coming? We don't have a *British* cousin!"

Nilos shrugged, trying to push past, but Gaius caught his elbow in a tight grip. "Ay," hissed the Greek, still trying to ignore the Roman. "Leave go! That's all I know—the orders were cut today and are already gone by courier."

"Where does Pater expect to find an entire Legion in Britain?" Gaius turned the Greek bodily to face him, using the man's head to block sight of his lips. So far, no one in the *coupona* had paid any attention, even the woman behind the bar bustling off about her own business. "He's already stripped the garrison to the bone."

"I know!" Nilos' face flushed as he wrenched his arm free. "The province is on its own. He's recalling everyone, even the governor and his clerks."

Gaius Julius blanched, staring in open horror at the secretary. "What about Germania?"

"Almost the same," Nilos allowed, shrugging. "There are

only five Legions along the entire Rhenus, and three will be here in four weeks, maybe less." The Greek slipped away while the old Roman was grappling with vivid, overwhelming visions of cataclysm.

Gaius Julius finished his wine abruptly—a poor vintage fouled with silt and bitter, clashing tones—and set the cup down on the counter. He left two coins before climbing up to the street. The sun was just setting and he blessed the architects who had raised such a bulk of marble and concrete atop the Palatine. The street in front of the temple of Claudius was already in shadow, allowing a minute fraction of the day's heat to recede.

Fool of a fool, Gaius thought, walking quickly north towards the vast marble cliff of the Colosseum. *Did he hear nothing the prince said? He'll throw another four Legions—five with Alexandros' Goths—to the Persian butchers for nothing.* He turned left in the plaza surrounding the amphitheatre, hearing a muted roar rumbling within. The evening games—nothing special, really, just tyro gladiators trying their skills—were already underway. *We'll lose Britain and Germania and Gaul all in one useless, stupid throw of the dice. . . .*

Sunk in depression, he failed to note a young woman standing in one of the vendor's alcoves piercing the outer ring of the Colosseum. She, however, did not fail to notice him and after he had passed by she bundled up a knitted rug covered with charms and trinkets and followed him at a prudent distance.

The dying sun painted the walls of the bedroom with gorgeous streaks of orange and red and purple. Maxian stuffed a spare shirt and some tightly bound papyrus scrolls into his old *medikus* bag, squinting against the flare of light. He had changed his tunic, cloak and leggings—finally realizing they had acquired a particularly stiff aroma of molten iron, coal dust, marble grit and sweat. The prince supposed he could have made them new again, but the maids in the town house were forever slinking around, looking for things to clean and mend.

"I want to come with you," Martina said, fighting to keep a whine from her husky voice.

Maxian shook his head. "I've already told you what I intend. Though your company would be welcome, there's no need for you to spend weeks sleeping beside dusty roads on the way south." His hand searched among a collection of bronze and iron knives, finding an ancient dagger stained with a glossy green patina. As he touched the worn ivory hilt, he could feel a commanding shout ring from the iron and glimpsed a man in old-style Legion armor standing in a line of men under a brassy, bright sky. *You will do,* he thought, sliding the blade into a common leather sheath and stowing it in the bag.

"Fine," the Empress said, crawling onto the bed, silk rustling as she moved. Her feet were bare and her formal stole and veil were discarded carelessly on the floor. She grinned up at him, arching her back and wiggling her taut bottom from side to side. "Shouldn't you keep an eye on me, lest I get into trouble while you're gone?"

The prince looked at her quizzically, then a slight frown drew his lips down. The setting sun turned cold in his dark eyes. "You would never get into trouble," he said in a flat tone, turning his attention back to the odds and ends he had arranged on the bedspread. Martina flashed him an angry look, then her eyes widened and she stiffened. For a fraction of a grain, she was perfectly still, then she blinked and sighed again.

"I'll miss you," the Empress said, curling both feet under her. Tapering fingers plucked at the hem of her silken gown, rolling seed pearls and tiny golden pomegranates over her nails.

"I know," Maxian said, favoring her with a distracted half-smile. "There are some things I need you to do while I am away. Get your notebook."

Obediently, Martina padded from the bed to fetch a heavy wooden plaquette from her dressing table. The covers were edged with wear-blackened leather and sheets of parchment oozed from the sides. Opening the heavy book, she frowned prettily, searching for an empty page. Finding space to write, Martina drew a fine brush from the thicket of gleaming curls behind her ear. A small copper cup, plugged with wax, was affixed to the spine of the book. Dipping her brush, the Empress looked up, sleek hand poised to write.

"Nine of the iron drakes in the foundry at Florentia," Maxian began in a brisk, concise voice, "are ready to fly. Winnow the pilots down to eighteen and send them south to meet me in . . ."

He paused to think. "Eleven days. Tell them to find me on Aetna—they shouldn't be able to miss the mountain if they can find Sicilia itself."

He closed the bag, snapping a clasp worked with the serpent and caduceus of his order. "You remember Cenni—our young artist? He's made some builder's drawings for me, when I could tear him away from casting scales and ever-more-frightening eye shields for our sky serpents." The prince laughed indulgently. "I want you to split the workshops into two projects— divide the artisans by skill, and set half and half to work—one group on the next set of iron drakes, the others on the 'turtles.' Cenni should take charge of the workshops and foundries—he knows my desire."

Martina nodded, hand moving quickly over the paper.

"There is another matter as well—Gaius Julius will be able to help, I think—we are using more iron ore, copper, coal, tin and lumber than the harbor facilities at Pisae can easily support. Moreover, a great deal of our raw materials come from Illyria and Gothica." Maxian sketched an arc in the air before him. "Which means the ships must sail all the way round Italia to reach our port at the mouth of the Arnus. Now, there is currently a half-surfaced road over the mountains to the north of the city, which goes to Bonnonia on the Po river. I want you to arrange a levy to widen and repair the road and prepare for the movement of goods, men and supplies directly from Illyria through the port at Arminum."

Martina continued to write, now continuing on to a second page. Maxian scratched the edge of his jaw idly, thinking. "We will need to expand the foundries and put in more workshops as well. There are several blocks of flats and tenements to the north of our current *fabrica*. Have them all torn down to make way for new buildings."

The Empress looked up in concern. "What about the people living in the apartments?"

"Build them new ones," Maxian said, frowning. "On those hills south of the river. They can double-bunk in the workers' dormitories until then."

Martina nodded in agreement and continued writing, her head tilted to one side.

* * *

Galen entered his private rooms, closing the heavy ironbound door behind him. The Praetorians in the hallway nodded good night, wary eyes watching the hallway for assassins. The Emperor—who usually shook his head in dismay at their paranoia—took a little solace from their vigilance tonight. The prospect of a knife stabbing from the dark, or a sudden rush of feet in the avenues of the city, now seemed quite likely.

Once he would have left such matters in the care of his Praetorians, trusting Anastasia to watch them in turn. Now—with the Duchess and Gaius Julius each plotting against one another, and losing valuable magical devices over what he was *sure* was a personal dispute—he didn't trust anyone. *We could have used another telecast,* he thought, though his mood was much improved. *But I do not think the Persians gained from our loss.*

A number of candles burned in his study and in the bedroom, each wick fluttering in a cylinder of bubbled glass. They cast a warm, watery light on the domed ceilings. Galen kicked off his sandals, letting his weary feet find solace in the deep piles of carpets covering the floors. With a conscious effort, he set aside thoughts of his office.

"Husband?" Helena did not look up from her writing desk. "Where have you been?"

"In the room of the telecast," he said, shrugging his heavy toga to the floor.

"You spend too much time watching that . . . thing," Helena said as she looked up. Her dark eyes widened in pleased surprise. "What happened to you? You look . . . you look well!"

Galen laughed, feeling the last of his cares driven away by the perplexed expression on her face. He collapsed on the bed, head towards her. She rose from her desk and sat beside him, thin fingers tracing the line of his face and neck. "I feel refreshed," he said, and in truth he felt almost giddy.

He had walked through the winding hallways of the Palatine with a spring in his step, greeting surprised clerks and ministers with a cheery wave and smile. Some of the men had shrunk away from this glad apparition, scarcely able to believe the evidence of eyes and ears. Galen slid his arm around Helena's waist, drawing her close with a sudden, pleased squeak.

"Husband! What are you—*mmmpph* . . ." The Empress found herself drawn down into a lasting embrace and kiss, Galen's hands sliding up under her blouse. "Galen . . ." Helena found her attention occupied again and was delightfully forced to momentary silence.

Some time later, the Emperor propped his head up on a pillow, watching his wife rooting around among a great deal of discarded clothing, searching for her earrings and bracelets. Somehow, they had been stripped from her arms and neck and rolled away under the writing table, the bed, even into a side room where the privy seat stopped one particular bauble from complete escape.

Feeling his gaze, Helena looked over her shoulder with a coy expression. She fluttered her eyelashes. "Yes? Is there something you want?"

"Not right now," he said in a lazy, satisfied voice. "In a glass or two, I might find the strength to rise again."

The Empress flipped her hair, flipping shining auburn hair over her bare shoulders. "Oh," she said, "I *doubt* that!"

Galen smiled, but the thoughts of the day intruded and he groaned in disgust. *I should forbid all thoughts of the State within these four walls! But could I follow my own rule?*

"Don't start," Helena said, groping under the bed for her slippers. "I'd prefer this strange interlude to last as long as possible."

"Have I been so foul?" Galen made a face, guessing the answer.

The Empress's head rose up over the edge of the bed with one eyebrow eloquently raised. "Have you? I am shocked to get anything from you today but grunts and an aura of exhaustion so complete, budding flowers wilt as you pass by. What happened to . . . ah . . . perk you up? Is there good news?"

"No." The Emperor laughed, smoothing back his hair. "In fact, the Persians are not stopping. They are coming right at us with a fleet and an army." He sighed. "Send a letter to Marcellus tomorrow, telling him to empty your summer house and move everything up into the hills."

"What?" Helena found her blouse and tugged the fine linen over her head. "Why?"

"The Persians plan to land their army at Catania," Galen said in a wry, almost disbelieving voice. "No more than a mile from your villa. I think the gardens will be fairly trampled, if not outright destroyed."

"Ah!" The Empress made a foul, disgusted face. "And you're happy?"

"Not about that, no." Galen felt the giddy edge to his thoughts fade. Even the warm, happy afterglow of tumbling his wife was fast receding. He scratched his left eyebrow, feeling an old, familiar pain hovering. "Nothing about the war pleases me. I would gladly trade the villa at Odyssea Akra for peace, but . . . I think the house will just be destroyed, like so many other things. But we can rebuild a house. I feel good because—because Maxian used his power to banish my exhaustion and fatigue." The Emperor nodded to himself in wonder, sitting up.

"He did what?" Helena unraveled sweaty knots in her hair, staring at him in surprise.

Galen spread his hands. "A green flash—and weeks of little sleep and too many worries are a distant memory. At least for a moment."

"Hmmm." The Empress's eyes narrowed in suspicion. "I suppose he'll be making you more muscular next, with a better nose . . ."

"Hah!" Galen started to laugh, then raised his fingers to his eyes. "Oh. He did fix something . . ."

"What?" Helena made a horrified face. "I thought you seemed . . . *larger* . . . but that is just unnatural!"

"No!" The Emperor swatted her thigh. "My eyesight was shortening—I didn't even notice—but now I can see the faces of the senators on the steps of the Curia from my office."

The Empress shook her head, regarding him with a wary, suspicious glare. "I would not trust your bother's judgment, husband. You see what he's done to poor Martina . . . she's . . . she's *artificial!* And I don't think she remembers a difference between how she was and how she is."

"She's happier," Galen said, chewing his lower lip. A black thought disturbed his momentary contentment. *What could our piglet do, if he put his mind to mischief?* "Or, at least, she seems so."

"I don't think," Helena said in a sharp voice, "he asked her first."

The Emperor shook his head. He had no idea. "Helena . . . I need you to do something for me."

"Again?" she said with an arch look, running her hand up his thigh. "I thought you needed another glass to recover. . . ."

Galen caught her hand and raised her palm to his lips. "Not that," he said, feeling grim reality assert itself and she sighed, seeing his face change. "I want you to take Theodosius and his nurse and your maids and leave the city. Tonight, if you can, and secretly. Tell no one—in fact, take only little Koré—you can find a new wet nurse in—"

"No," Helena said softly, pressing her fingers to his lips. Her eyes were very large. "I won't abandon you here among these wolves."

"Please," he started to say, but she stopped him again.

"I will not," the Empress said firmly. "The Persians will not reach the city. They will be defeated—and I will not stay away again, distant from the battle, wondering and waiting, listening for the sound of a courier's horse to bring me the news of victory or defeat." Her lip began to tremble and Galen took her in his arms, holding her close.

"Helena, I'm not worried about the Persians. We have enemies in the city."

The Empress stiffened in the circle of his arms, raising her head. "Who?"

Galen shook his head. "I've only suspicions, love. I know nothing yet. But I want you away from here, and somewhere safe. Narbo, perhaps . . ."

"I won't," she said, pushing him away. Grudgingly, the Emperor let her go. Helena wiped the corner of her eye, leaving a black smudge on her temple. "You're saying there is a plot against you. Some overmighty lord desiring the red boots?"

Galen managed a barely perceptible nod. She responded with another icy glare.

"Well, then, *husband*, you can have me gagged and bound and bundled away in a sack to Narbo to sit—in chains!—in your drafty old house where there is nothing to read and holes in the ceiling and then—and then—you can worry these conspirators have crept up and kidnapped me at the other end of the Empire, where you'll have no idea if I'm well or sick or dead or having an affair—and don't think I won't if I find a strapping young shepherd lad—and I *could* be here, in your own apartments, where you can find me each night, waiting patiently for you to come home, and rubbing your feet and making you feel better—and you would know that I am safe, and our son is safe and everything is all right with the world." She finished with a sniff and looked away, arms crossed over her breast.

Galen stared at her for a moment, opened his mouth, then closed it again. "Well . . ."

Helena turned her head, eyes bare burning slits and gave him such a venomous look the Emperor said nothing, then or later.

A long time since I've ridden this road. Maxian let the horse set her own pace, trotting along the grassy riding path beside the Via Appia Antica. The road struck south from the city, regular as a mason's rule. His spirits lifted as the spotted mare ambled along. The moon was rising, casting deep shadows below the rows of cypress and poplars lining the highway. Fields and farmyards stretched away on either hand, quiet under the night sky. Even the temperature was pleasant, the heat of the day fading and cool winds tousled his long hair.

The simple act of leaving Rome lifted his spirits. The city was close and hot and filled with sullen, dispirited people. Maxian made a conscious effort to ignore the voices whispering from the air. They wore on his temper. *Gaius Julius can fend for himself*, the prince thought, *for a time. He certainly doesn't need me looking over his shoulder. And what would I see? Ledgers, accounts, long litanies of works and favors and debts. Bah!*

Maxian supposed he should feel a little guilty, thinking of the binding he'd placed on Martina, but his husband's heart was eased to know she would not—could not—stray while he was gone. *She is terribly efficient*, he thought, pleased with his solution, *and now entirely delightful company. Everything I could desire.*

The prince rode in darkness for a time, enjoying the solitude, waving genially to those few pedestrians he passed, walking quickly along the canted surface of the Appia with paper lanterns hung on long poles. A mile out from the city, he was alone with a soft breeze and the distant lights of scattered farmhouses. The mare did not mind the dark, following her nose along the horse path.

Thoughts of Martina and Gaius and his brother and the whole irritating business of war had grown quite remote by the time he reached a crossroads and found a man standing beside the road. Here, the paving stones of the highway were heavily grown over with grass, making a circle of green turf under overhanging cypresses. A tall milestone gleamed softly in the moonlight, covered with ivy and climbing vines. The single numeral *II* was chiseled into the smooth face of the stone. Maxian reined the horse to a halt, though she did not want to stop, and nodded in greeting.

"Ave," Maxian said, leaning on his saddle horn.

The soldier saluted, his mouth moving silently. He was young, with barely a fringe of beard lining a strong chin. His hair glowed in the moonlight, ruffled by quiet night wind. Like the legionnaires of his day, a long pole lay across his shoulder-bades, kit bag hanging from pinewood. A single, solid metal plate embraced his chest, the rounded surface catching a reflection of the moon. His shield was oval and carried over the back, a pot-shaped helmet secured by a strap at his shoulder. Maxian could see the outline of the paving stones through the dark pits of his eyes and mouth.

"Well met, Lucius Papirius," Maxian answered. "I ride with the writ of the Senate—there is war in the south and every Latin is needed to drive back the invader. Will you join me?"

The young legionnaire nodded, grinning, and stooped to gather up his javelins and stabbing spear from the ground. Maxian turned the horse in a circle, watching the night. Faint lights gleamed in the orchards and woods all around.

"Rome needs you," he called out, raising the ivory staff of a tribune above his head. "The Senate and the People are in danger, our ancient traditions threatened, our honorable name blackened by defeat. I am riding to war, men of Rome. Will you ride with me?"

Without waiting for a response, the prince turned the mare to the southern road and let her take an easy trot. Behind him, the young legionnaire jogged after, easily falling into the steady, ground-eating pace of the professional soldier. The stars shone on his shield and the moon wavered in the ghostly firmament of his hair. Maxian did not think he would tire, no, not even if they marched without a halt to the world sea beyond the horizon.

Again, the prince's thoughts turned far away and he barely noticed when a second man was waiting beside the highway and then another and then three brothers, oval shields scarred by axe and fire. Like the young soldier, they proved tireless and they marched south under a vast, star-filled sky, soundless voices raised in a marching song to while away the miles.

CONSTANTINOPLE

)•(

"The latest dispatches, my lord." Alexandros nodded to the messenger—a Gothic youth, his tunic damp with sweat—and took the leather bag with mingled interest and dismay. The morning's appearance of a sail in the straits had caused great excitement in the city, but now the Macedonian stared at the bundle of letters with mounting disgust.

Over the past two weeks, he'd received a string of missives from Rome, invariably carried in Imperial dispatch pouches, one set from Emperor Galen and one set from Gaius Julius. Alexandros wondered—he often wondered, sitting up drinking with his officers—if the two men were aware of the effect their conflicting commands had on the soldiers out on the sharp end of the war.

"I don't think they have any idea which end is the business end," Alexandros muttered, sitting back in a leather camp chair. The long arcade along the seaward side of the Buchion palace was very cool and dim, the air stirred by a constant breeze out of the north and the Macedonian had moved his command staff, servants, equipment and messengers into the undamaged buildings.

He cut the dark red twine sealing the first packet with his boot knife.

"So, what does Galen have to say today. . . ." Alexandros began to read, then shook his head. The fleet gathering at Tarentum was still delayed, but the Emperor expected them to leave port for Constantinople within the week of his writing. *Two weeks ago*, the Macedonian thought, checking Galen's scribbled date at the end of the missive. "And this one?"

Gaius Julius' note was not under an Imperial cover, but the parchment was of similar fine quality and the ink was even darker—*must be a better grade of octopus*, Alexandros noted in amusement. The old Roman's strong, clear hand urged the Macedonian to immediately march his men west along the old highway running across Thrace and into the mountains of Epirus, to Dyrrachium on the coast of the Mare Adriaticum.

I've been that way before, Alexandros thought, idly tugging at a lock of hair dangling across his forehead. *But not on such a fine road as these Romans build.* "Demetrios! A moment of your time . . ."

The Eastern officer hurried over, rubbing ink-stained fingers on his tunic. "Yes, *comes*?"

"Fetch out a way map of the Via Egnatia, if we have one."

The Greek raised an eyebrow in surprise. "We're marching west now?" He sounded incredulous, which greatly mirrored how Alexandros felt about the whole matter.

"It seems so," Alexandros said, gritting his teeth. "Round up the quartermasters as well—we'll have to steal all those wagons, mules and horses back!"

Stupid Romans, he thought savagely, feeling ill-restrained temper rise. *March east, march west, sail south, march west again . . . the war will be lost by the time we find the enemy!*

〉〈

Heavy yellow dust smeared across the sky, borne by some zephyr turning across leagues of desert. Khalid al'Walid strode purposefully along the harbor road, most of his tanned face covered by the wing of his kaffiyeh. Flying grit stung his face, but the Arab's long lashes kept most of the dust and sand from his eyes. In any case, he was used to such weather, though the Egyptian workers laboring in the port complained bitterly. The Eagle passed rank after rank of mule-drawn wagons, each cart stacked high with the dusty, withered remains of the dead. Thankfully, these were old, dry corpses scavenged from tombs scattered at the edge of the desert and they exuded only a faint, spicy smell.

Not every corpse—even those stirred to unnatural life for the attack on the city—would suit this new endeavor. Each body, as Khalid was now far too aware, needed to have a certain . . . composition . . . to allow stowage in the holds of the fleet. The corpses of those freshly slain still maintained cohesion, if they had not been torn limb from limb or gnawed to the bone. The ancient dead—almost petrified by ages in the dry air—were equally suitable. The rest, threatening to spread disease to the living and foul the air with rampant putrefaction, had been consigned to enormous fiery pits dug outside the city walls. The ditch in front of the Roman wall had proved very suitable.

Khalid struggled against a constant, inner chill when he focused on anything beyond his own booted feet. The fall of a city usually generated plenty of captives—officers to be ransomed, men to be recruited or repatriated in exchange for one's own prisoners taken by the enemy, hapless merchants caught taking the wrong coin, mercenaries eager for new contracts. But not this time. Instead, the animate dead—the *gaatasuun*—

had been driven by a whip-like will to hunt down and kill every legionnaire.

Dangerous, very dangerous. How will the Romans treat us, if we fall into their hands? Khalid thought to himself, though at the same time he grasped the cold, calculated reality of the act. The bodies of the Romans had been carefully gathered, re-united with their arms and armor—weapons tied to the corpse-limbs with hempen twine, helmets nailed to rotting scalps—and sent aboard the fleet. The young Arab trotted up a ramp of broad sandstone steps and found the man he had been seeking.

"My lord," Khalid called to the hulking, powerful shape of Shahr-Baraz. The King of Kings turned, raising a bushy eye-brow at the young man.

"Lord Khalid, what brings you to the port today?"

"Good news, I suppose," the Eagle answered. He failed to banish a sickly, pained expression from his face. "The last of the . . . the harrows are filled and ready to load onto the fleet." Khalid made a vague gesture encompassing the sweep of the harbor, the outer breakwater, the enormous towering shape of the Pharos and the busy docks. The waters, shimmering almost white in the full summer sun, were crowded with countless ships. Their sails furled, the fleet made a confusing forest of polished masts, rigging and canvas shades suspended over open decks. Odenathus' latest count placed their number at just over two hundred vessels considered reliable for the open sea.

The King of Kings nodded, his own expression ambivalent. He scratched the base of his chin thoughtfully and Khalid gained a distinct impression of a man struggling with unwel-come duty. "Will loading the *kameredha* be complete today?"

Khalid nodded, focusing on the shining, white-marble sides of the lighthouse. Heat rising from the water made the build-ing—only a mile distant—shimmer in slow, rolling waves. "By nightfall, I hope. I do not think the longshoremen will work af-ter the sun sets."

"Nor will this cargo be disturbed by thieves. . . . Our living crews will go aboard tomorrow morning." Shahr-Baraz fixed the young Arab with a piercing, considering stare. "You seem out of sorts, young general." The Persian did not smile, though a faint amusement sparkled in his deep-set eyes. "I must say, for myself, I never expected to command a *Roman* army in my life. But the lord of the world is not without his own grave humor."

Khalid started, turning pale at the jest. "Do you find this amusing?"

Shahr-Baraz nodded, hooking his thumbs into a broad, tooled leather belt. He sat up on the stone railing around the observation platform. "You're young, Al'Walid. The enmity between Rome and Persia must seem eternal to you. When *I* was young, I fought alongside men of the Eastern Empire in our war against the usurper and legionnaires marched in the streets of Ctesiphon with flowers wound in their helmets as the common people cheered them as saviors. That, young Eagle, was an odd circumstance."

Khalid nodded jerkily, his forearms resting on the warm, smooth stone. "I have heard the stories. I just . . . this war of sorcery is not . . . what I wanted, when we set out from Mekkah."

"What did you want?" Shahr-Baraz' rumbling voice was almost quiet. "Honor? Clean glory, won over a lance or sword, in fair, open struggle? Two champions facing one another over dusty ground—and victory turning on the outcome of a single passage at arms?"

Khalid looked away, unable to meet the older man's too-understanding gaze. "I guess . . . I did."

"Like in a song or story. I had those dreams myself, long ago. But this is the way of things—you chase a half-glimpsed hind and find only sticky, painful reality in your hands." The Boar chuckled. "But *our* deeds will be a song—if not already—all the smell and stink and sleeplessness and terror winnowed out, never to trouble the thoughts of the young."

"Yes." Khalid felt his heart shrink to agree and a pit opened in his stomach at the prospect of such a cruel end to his dreams of glory. With an effort, he turned his thoughts away from the ruin wrought by circumstance. "How many living men are we taking?"

"As few as I can manage," the king said, one big scarred hand tugging gently at his long nose. "The ship's crews and longshoremen, my own guards, ourselves. I am thinking—the Queen agrees—but you should know, to leave Jalal and Shadin in command of the Egyptian garrison. They are reliable old dogs from what I've seen, and they will not lack for work in our absence."

"Good," Khalid said, feeling his gloomy mood lift. "They can command the Sahaba in my absence. I . . . I was thinking to leave them all here, all of the men who came up from Mekkah and the Nabateans and most of the Palmyrenes, save those we need to pilot and steer and crew the ships." The younger man's voice almost trembled and he realized he was on the verge of begging.

"I agree," Shahr-Baraz said softly, clapping Khalid on the shoulder. "The Queen has already seen to the assignments and ordering of our fleet and army. She has some experience in these matters." He leaned close. "The Serpent will take his Huns and that wolf C'hu-lo to command them in battle and his cold servants and I will take certain picked men of the *pushtigbhan* and those we must, but I am sending most of the younger men home, and others will garrison here and there, out of harm's way."

The young Eagle's eyes widened and his hand moved in an abortive sign against ill luck. Despite the fallacy of keeping anything secret if the Serpent turned his attention directly upon them, Khalid's voice fell to a whisper. "You . . . you and the Queen think we will lose?"

Shahr-Baraz' face twisted into a rueful grimace. He tilted his head to one side. "What if we win? Would that be any better? In the end, all that matters is for the Serpent to live as long as possible. I am growing tired of seeing my men die in his service."

The king looked up at the huge white disk of the sun, shading his eyes with one hand. He sighed, feeling the warmth flood his bones and settle into his chest. Motion in the upper air caught his eye and he squinted, lifting his chin. "Look."

Khalid stared upwards as well, relieved to look away from the wagons rattling past below, each heaped high with rope-bound bodies and gleaming white skulls. An irregular *V* of birds drifted on the upper air, heading south. At this distance, they were pale cream against a cerulean sky.

"Cranes," Shahr-Baraz said. "The first to head south for the mountains of Axum and Ethiop. Soon, there will be thousands upon thousands. The seasons turn, lad, regardless of what we do."

"Yes," Khalid said, finding no solace in the sight of the glossy, white creatures. "I suppose."

Shahr-Baraz tossed his head, letting heavy black curls shot with gray fall over his shoulder. "Your mood will lift, I think. See—here is a man whose ugly face will cheer you." The king pointed down the steps with his chin.

Khalid turned and saw a tall Persian climbing the stairs, armor gray under tattered desert robes, solemn face creased by the smallest possible smile. "Patik!" Khalid stepped forward, clasping forearms with the big Persian soldier. "Or Prince Shahin, I suppose I should say."

"Patik is better," the diquan replied, crushing the Arab's arm with a powerful grip. "The Serpent Lord is no longer pleased with the great prince Suren-Pahlavi."

"What happened?" Khalid looked to the king in alarm and found the Boar nodding in dour agreement.

"I failed to find our sorcerer his ancient trinket." Patik rubbed his neck. "Though I believe I caught a glimpse of the cursed thing once, at distance."

"Too bad," Khalid said, trying not to grin in delight to find his old friend still alive. "What about your men?"

Patik shook his head dolefully. The young Arab sighed. "I'm sorry."

"Another failed hunt," Patik said, bowing politely to Shahr-Baraz. "Your pardon, Great Lord."

The greeting drew a sharp bark of laughter from the king. Shahin's new sense of humility was far preferable to his old hauteur, which had only gained him contempt. "You look well, Shahin, and I am glad you live, though I begrudge even the deaths of your flea-bitten desert jackals. Particularly in Rustam's service."

"Thank you, my lord." Patik looked out at the fleet. "The Queen sent me to find you. She says everything is in readiness, waiting only upon the wind and tide."

Shahr-Baraz stepped away from the wall, settling the leather harness and straps holding his diverse weapons. Swords, maces and dagger clanked against each other. The king squinted at the eastern sky, then to the south. "The fishermen say there will be a morning breeze as this dust cloud turns and we will make good headway out of the harbor." He looked to the west, his expression hardening. "And we shall see the mountains of Sicilia in a week, or ten days at the most."

⧼◌⟩─◌─⟨◌⟩─◌─⟨◌⟩─◌─⟨◌⟩─◌─⟨◌⟩─◌─⟨◌⟩─◌─⟨◌⟩─◌─⟨◌⟩─◌─⟨◌⟩─◌─⟨◌⟩⧽

ROMA MATER

⌖

"M istress, you must wake up!" A small, firm hand gripped Anastasia's shoulder and a flare of candlelight fell across her sleepy face. The Duchess blinked, recognized alarm in the girl's voice and struggled to clear her mind of sleep. Yawning, she sat up, throwing back a light sheet. She had slept poorly—the night was too warm for comfort.

"What has happened?"

Constantia ducked her head nervously, a candle bobbing in one small hand, the other holding back gauzy netting draped around the couch. The maid was half-dressed in her nightgown and the sleeping porch was entirely dark. Anastasia made a face, seeing the waning moon high in the sky. *What time is it?*

"One of your watchers came to the garden gate," Constantia said, words tumbling over one another in a rush. "The Praetorians have marched out of their camp without horns or trumpets, weapons muffled in cloth, cloaks drawn over their faces."

The Duchess came entirely awake, the fog of sleep blown away. The cantonment of the Imperial Guard was on the northern edge of the city. No more than two hours march from the Forum. "What about the Urban Cohorts?"

Constantia licked pale, pink lips. "Another runner came—the Urban Prefect sent his men home last night, their barracks are locked and deserted."

"Oh, black day," Anastasia grunted, rising from the couch. "Get me clothing—quickly now, child! And boots, not slippers.

And a watchman's lantern. Maxentia!" The Duchess's clear voice rang through the pillars and halls. "Where are you?"

Without waiting for her maids, Anastasia hurried across an octagonal gazebo redolent with orange blossoms and into the villa itself. By the time she reached her winter bedroom, both girls had returned and the cook stuck her head in one of the doors, holding a lantern high.

"Good," the Duchess said, seeing the older woman. "There will be trouble in the city today," she said briskly, "and perhaps riots. Mallia, everyone must get out of the house before the sun rises—scatter the slaves to our farms, and everyone else should go stay with their relatives. Everyone should discard any token of service to this house, or to the Archer! Constantia, where is my purse?"

The maid pressed a heavy leather bag lined with silk into Anastasia's hands. She considered the weight of metal, wondering how badly things would go. "Maxentia, dress for travel and take one of the horses down to Ostia port before the city gates are closed to all traffic—which will be soon! Tell my agent in the port to close his shop and warn off any of our ships making landfall. Anyone in port should go to . . . to . . ." She scowled, failing to think of a safe harbor. ". . . to safety!"

The Duchess sat, tying back a cloud of unruly hair, her legs sticking straight out. Constantia buckled riding boots onto her mistress' small feet. Anastasia glared at the cook and the other maid. "Go! Now! There is no time to waste. Not today."

Wiggling her feet into the boots, the Duchess nodded. "Good enough. Now, Constantia, there are many papers in my study and I have to leave immediately. You must take everything marked with blue twine away to the house on the Ianiculan Hill—I will meet you there later—and all other correspondence must be burned and the ashes sifted. In particular, you must destroy *all* of the pay records. Do you understand?"

The girl swallowed nervously, but nodded. Anastasia fixed her with a steady glare, plush lips tightening in consideration. *Will she do this properly? I hope so. There's not time for a more thorough evacuation . . . and Betia is not here. Curse the snip of a girl for haring off on some useless adventure!*

"I will be back later," the Duchess said, waving Constantia away. "Get busy, child!"

When the maid had run off down the hallway, Anastasia knelt and dragged a heavy wooden box from under her bed. Inside, she found a sheathed knife and the leather and wire apparatus of a spring gun. Gritting her teeth, the Duchess hid the knife in the girdle of her tunic and stola. The oiled leather arm brace of the spring gun still fit on her left arm—which surprised her, so long had it been since she donned the weapon—and the release ring fit snug to her thumb.

The glass is spilling too fast, Anastasia thought as she pushed the garden gate closed. The sky was still dark, without even a hint of the sun behind the eastern mountains. Hushed voices and the clatter of men and women moving baggage followed her down the narrow alley.

"Halt! Who goes there?" A rough shout filled the night. A young man on a well-traveled horse reined in, letting the stallion puff and paw on the street pavers. Torches flared, casting a wayward red glow on the faces of soldiers barring the gate. The young man pulled back the hood of his riding cloak, revealing rugged features and light brown hair.

"My name is Ermanerich," he called to the legionnaires milling about in the courtyard of the house of Gregorius Auricus. "I've just arrived from the north with messages for Master Gaius Julius. Is he here?"

"He is!" boomed a commanding, glad voice. "He is here, young prince!"

Gaius Julius himself pushed through the crowd of soldiers, face brimming with a smile. The Goth swung down from his horse and tentatively embraced the unfamiliar Roman. Gaius brushed dust from the prince's riding cloak and raised an eyebrow at Ermanerich's stubbled chin and vexed eye.

"Well met, my lord," Gaius Julius said, "a propitious night for you to come, but I'm surprised—"

"To see me?" Ermanerich glanced around, puzzled by the appearance of the legionnaires standing at arms. They were dressed differently than the Eastern legionaries or even his own Goths. They were taller, stockier, with fur-lined cloaks entirely unsuitable for the Roman summer. He leaned close to the older man, still unsure why so many men would be out—armed and armored—at such an hour. "Alexandros bade me find you straightaway when we reached Rome . . . should I return at another time?"

The old Roman winked saucily, shaking his head. "Tonight, you need to be here with me, and I bless the gods who set your impatient feet on the road to Rome. What of your men?"

"Still a day's march away," the Goth growled, suddenly impatient. "I have received many letters from the Emperor, urging speed. Are we truly supposed to be in Messina *now?* Is it true the Persians are landing at Sicilia?"

Gaius Julius made a quieting gesture. "Pax! This time of year, you're only three days from landfall at Messina by sea. If your Goths need be there, I will arrange ships to carry you."

"Fine. Who are these men?" Ermanerich kept a hand on his horse's bridle—the stallion was tired, but still game, and the young Goth was not a man to mislay fine horseflesh. Particularly not among these Roman scoundrels. Everyone seemed on edge and there was a harsh, brittle smell in the air, reminding him of the last hour before battle.

"These are men from the Legio Eight Augusta," Gaius said, moving towards the gate, his voice rising as he moved. "These Gallic Bulls have come down from Germany as reinforcements—and never more welcome than tonight!" The old Roman hopped up on a step just inside the wall. "Soldiers of Rome," he called out, drawing the attention of every man in the courtyard. "You've come to answer your Emperor's call to battle, ready to throw the Persians back and seize victory for the city, the Senate and the people. But tonight—as your officers and I have just learned—you've a more desperate task." Gaius looked around, resting one hand on Ermanerich's muscular shoulder. A hundred men, or more, looked back, tense and attentive. "We've learned there is a mutiny among the Praetorians in their camp beyond Tiburtina. Rebellious cohorts are marching on the Palatine, intending to murder the Emperor Galen and acclaim their own tribune, Motrius, as king instead!"

A hoarse shout and a growl of anger answered the bold words and Gaius Julius nodded, gauging the men's response. "Yes—a black act of treachery against the Senate and the people, against *you*, whom Galen has always favored, always supported. Who has seen your pay raised? Galen! Who has increased the size of the retirement allotments? Galen!"

The legionaries answered him with a fierce shout, some clashing their spears against breastplate or shield. The old Roman swung his arm, pointing south across the city. "But we will not let them spill the blood of the Princeps or his family—no! We march to the Palatine ourselves, with haste, and we will find these traitors and we will cut them down like dogs, scattering their weak limbs, their corrupt hearts as grain is cast upon the threshing floor!"

"Aye!" boomed the legionaries and their officers were among them, shouting for order and quiet and a column of twos. Gaius Julius hopped down, flashing a quick smile at Ermanerich, who gave him a suspicious look.

"What is this?" the Goth whispered, clutching the dispatch bag to his chest. Everything seemed to be losing focus, as if the earth under his feet turned unsteady. "What are you doing?"

"Come on, my young friend," the old Roman chaffed, grasping the saddle horn of Ermanerich's horse. "This nag will take two riders!"

Shaking his head, the Gothic prince led the horse from the gate, letting the column of troops jog by, then mounted, reaching down to pull Gaius up. As he did, Ermanerich leaned close. "Where are these troops from? From Germania? How many are here?"

"Not so many as I feared, thank the gods," Gaius answered, settling in behind the Goth. "I managed to convince two of the Legion tribunes to turn around and march back north. These men are part of the lead elements of the Eight."

Ermanerich glanced over his shoulder in surprise. "Who watches the Rhenus, then?"

"No one," Gaius Julius answered, his face bleak. "No one at all."

Her skirts clutched in one hand, Anastasia bolted up a flight of stairs, taking them two and three at a time. The way was dark and very narrow, forcing her to turn sideways at each turn, a sputtering lamp burning her hand. The top of the passage was closed by a door and the Duchess paused, catching her breath.

No time for subtlety, she thought, measuring the ancient termite-carved wood. She braced herself, then slammed a shoulder into the panel.

Old plaster moldings squealed and cracked, shattering and spraying dust and paint across a tiled floor. Anastasia kicked the splintered boards clear, thankful again for taking proper cavalry boots reinforced with iron strips in the uppers and soles. Bending down, she squeezed through the opening into a short, richly appointed hallway. To her right, a painted, carved door swung open.

The Duchess darted forward, catching the edge of the door and stepped inside. The woman opening the door cried out in alarm and staggered back. Empress Helena—like Anastasia before her—was still waking up, barely clad in nightclothes. The Duchess slammed the door behind her and threw the locking bar.

"Get dressed," she snapped at the Empress, who was staring at her in befuddlement. "Go on!"

The Duchess leaned against the door, concentrating, listening for alarms or noise. Grimacing, she drew the knife from her girdle and settled the heavy bone hilt in her hand.

"What—what is happening?" Helena found a quilt and wrapped the patterned cloth around her thin shoulders. Anastasia, seeing her bare feet, became very irritable.

"Put on some shoes," the Duchess hissed, casting around the room for something suitable. "Good ones, not those flimsy slippers you're always wearing." Her eye lit upon a pair of stoutly built sandals. Anastasia snatched them up and threw them to the Empress, who fumbled the catch but then managed to gather them up. "Where is your son?"

Helena pointed wordlessly at a connecting door as the Duchess's grim tone and bared weapon finally registered. Anastasia eased the side door open, hearing a warning hiss. She stepped back, pushing the door wide with her boot. The nursery seemed empty and dark, but the lamplight from the bedroom picked out a pair of blazing green eyes crouched under little Theodosius' bed.

"Come, we'll have to leave quickly." The Duchess made a sharp gesture, her tone brooking nothing less than obedience. The eyes blinked, then a little girl—no more than six—darted out, unkempt black hair falling glossy around scrawny shoulders. Koré held Theodosius on her back, his round fingers clutched about her neck. The boy was almost as large as the girl, but the maid had no difficulty carrying him. "Do you need shoes?"

Koré shook her head, sidling along the wall towards the door. Helena caught her hand, white feet dwarfed by the pair of sandals. Anastasia realized they must be Galen's. "There's no time to do anything but run," she whispered, striding to the outer door. "Where is the Emperor?"

"I don't know," Helena replied, her voice tight with fear. "He left a little while ago—there was an urgent message . . ."

"Put out the lamp." Anastasia could hear a commotion through the door.

Darkness folded around the three women, Helena shaking soot from her fingers.

Grunting with effort, Ermanerich ground his spear into the Roman's chest, iron scales snapping under the pressure, blood oozing between armor plates. The Praetorian gasped, crimson flooding from his mouth and the light in his eyes died. A cavalry spatha clattered from his nerveless fingers. The blade was nicked and chipped, ornamented with a long streak of red. Silence suddenly replaced the clash and din of men grappling in combat. Gaius Julius stepped into the chamber, waving back two German legionnaires poised with javelins at his side.

"These are the last of the traitors, I think," the old Roman pronounced gravely. Making a show of careful consideration, he stepped among the bodies of the dead, turning some over with his boot. "We were just in time," Gaius Julius said to the men crowded into the doorway of the Emperor's study. The corpse at his feet had long, dark hair and sun-bronzed features. "This was Motrius himself, now sent to Tartarus as he deserves."

Ermanerich wrenched his spear from the dead Praetorian against the door, letting the body slump down the gold-chased panel. The thrust had scored the wood, leaving a dark smudge. Gaius Julius tested the latch, finding it solidly closed.

"They did not have time to break in," he said, waving back the Germans. Two of their officers were staring around in awe—at the busts of past Emperors and philosophers, at two grand paintings on wooden panels held up by bronze tracks on the facing wall. Gaius was fond of them too—one showed the triumph of Aëtius the Great over the Huns in vibrant, almost living color, the other diabolical Odysseus before the shattered walls of Troy, accepting the surrender of Priam and his noble house. "Carex, take your men and search the floor for survivors—some of the traitors may have escaped. Phalas, your maniple should go downstairs and secure the main hall. The servants and slaves will be in a panic, I'm sure. Calm them down. Tell them order has been restored."

Both officers nodded, then rousted their men out of the hallway and outer rooms. Somehow, a great deal of damage had been done in the brief melee, with crockery shattered on the floor, and tapestries and drapes torn down. Gaius watched them depart and was sure every man had managed to scoop up *something* valuable in the brief confusion.

"No use counting the silverware," Ermanerich said ruefully, watching the closed door, his spear held lightly in both hands. "They'll be carting out the statuary next."

"They won't have a chance," Gaius said, keeping his voice low. He was carrying a gladius, still sheathed, in his hand. He had not drawn a weapon in anger for a long time, but believed in the healthy exercise of caution. "My men will escort them back out of the city within the hour and see they're well supplied with food, wine and women." The old Roman smiled tightly. "Their pockets will be heavy enough with the Emperor's gold, in gratitude."

Ermanerich nodded absently, still watching the door. Alexandros had warned him to beware the Romans and their politics. The young Goth felt much, much better to have a weapon in hand and the prospect of a solid, material enemy to fight. "Is there another way out of here?"

"Perhaps." Gaius Julius shrugged. "This mausoleum must be riddled with hidden passages. Every Emperor wants to keep his secrets." He tested the latch, then raised an eyebrow at the Goth. Ermanerich nodded in agreement, then both men set themselves and slammed into the door together.

Wood splintered with a *crack* and the panel gave way. The door bounced back from the wall, and Gaius Julius stepped into a darkened passage. Broken bits of wood crunched under his feet. Ahead, lamplight glowed in a richly appointed chamber, and a familiar man was standing at the foot of a bed heaped high with pillows and silken quilts.

"Master Gaius," the Emperor said, drawing his own sword with a soft rasp. "And . . . you must be Prince Ermanerich of the Gothic nation."

Pale smears of light streaked the eastern sky as Anastasia crept from behind a hedge. She listened carefully, but heard nothing but the distant crash and rumble of delivery carts on the city streets and the thin squeaking of bats fluttering through the stone arches of an aqueduct rising a hundred feet to her left.

"Quickly now," she whispered to the two women behind her. Koré crouched at her knee, little Theodosius swaddled in a rug and pressed tight to her breast. Helena knelt behind the maid, short hair loose around her neck and hanging in her eyes. Anastasia glanced around again, then hurried down a path between long ranks of cypresses. Their feet crunched on gravel and then padded on dirt. The path descended steeply, running down a long strip of garden flanked by the monumental platform of the Severan Palace on the right and an *insula* of exclusive flats on the left.

"Where is my husband?" Helena's voice sounded drained, coming from the darkness like a ghost's cry. "Where are we going?"

"Somewhere safe, I hope." Anastasia slowed, searching with her hands along the wall to the left. After a moment, she found the outline of a door and pushed. Old leather hinges creaked and she smelled lye and soap and hot water. "Galen will have to find his own sanctuary, I fear."

Koré ducked past the Duchess and into the dark passage. Helena stood on the path, her face a barely visible oval delicately touched by the first reflection of dawn. Anastasia beckoned. "Helena! We must get away from here quickly before events sweep you and your son away. If you are taken, Galen will be a captive to your safety even if he remains free."

"Who did this?" The Empress's voice was hoarse. "Is this mutiny?"

"Conspiracy," the Duchess answered, tugging at Helena's sleeve. "Which may have failed by now—I sent warning to the right people, I think—but we'll not risk being seen until I know how things have played out."

Stumbling and listless, the Empress let herself be led into the passage and Anastasia shoved the door closed behind them, hoping no one had marked their hasty exit from the palace.

Ermanerich stepped lightly into the bedchamber, automatically drifting to the left to clear the door, while Gaius Julius stepped to the right, giving the Goth room for his spear. The Emperor watched them with a faint smile on his thin face. His habitual nervousness had dropped away like chaff. For his part, the young Goth felt even more at sea than before. The flurry of events following his arrival in the city had left him dizzy. Only the steady, solid presence of Master Gaius—a man whom Alexandros had said he could *trust, absolutely, in all things*—kept Ermanerich from fleeing in terror. He'd never been on the Palatine before, not without his father in attendance. Everything was so . . . huge.

"We discussed," Gaius said, thumbing the loop away from the hilt of his gladius, "sending you into exile, to tend a plot in some remote province, far from Rome and the centers of power."

"Cabbages?" Galen turned slightly, tension draining from his shoulders as the air in the room grew sharp. "I detest them, fresh or boiled, though I appreciate the thought." The Emperor tilted his head slightly, watching Gaius Julius directly, though Ermanerich remained in his peripheral vision.

"There is an air of tradition to such a fate," the old Roman said, sliding his blade from the sheath. "But I am afraid simple mutilation would *not* keep you from trying to reclaim all . . ." Gaius swept the gladius around in a sharp arc, ". . . this. We cannot afford any disorder, not now."

"What is this treachery, then, but chaos unbound?" The Emperor's voice was sharp. "Do you expect mutiny and murder to save you from the Persians? To reclaim our lost provinces?"

"This is already over," Gaius Julius replied, trying to keep his voice level. "You, sir, though a noble Roman and a fine gentleman, are too blind and shortsighted to be allowed to rule. You have sent the State rushing toward oblivion by appalling judgment. Our only hope to succor the Empire is to set you aside!"

The Emperor laughed, unable to believe his ears. "And you—the new Emperor, I'm sure!—will conjure victory? How? Where are your armies?" Galen made a violent motion with his sword and Gaius and Ermanerich both stepped back in alarm. "You will grapple with the same constraints of men, time, ships, taxes . . . every burden that has weighed upon me, will weigh on you threefold. The Legions will not accept you as Augustus and God, dead man, and there will be civil war. Then how will you keep the Persians from marching through the Forum in triumph?"

Gaius sighed, casting a sidelong glance at Ermanerich. "There will be no civil war," Gaius said, turning his attention back to Galen. Now the old Roman felt tired—drained by the rush of events—and he was in no mood to explain himself. *Yet,* he thought, *I do owe this man something for his courtesy and trust.* "Within the hour, there will be a new Emperor, acclaimed by the Senate and accepted by the army. Life will go on. Taxes will be collected, tribute given to the gods . . . all as it was, and shall be."

Galen started to speak, but Gaius Julius moved—quickly!— and his blade was at the Emperor's throat, the shining tip pressed against the side of Galen's carotid. Ermanerich flinched, his spear rising reflexively, but then the iron point wavered.

"What is going on?" he asked plaintively. "Who is this man?"

"I wanted to wait," Gaius Julius said, ignoring the Goth's question. "There seemed no reason to rush—twenty years could pass without inconveniencing me—but you . . ." Trembling anger finally cracked the old Roman's controlled tone. ". . . you have become such a dangerous, meddling fool! You've stripped the German frontier bare, abandoned an entire province to the Gaels and Picts! What in Hades were you thinking? To send more Legions to the butcher's mill down in Sicilia? To give the enemy *more* corpse-soldiers!" A finger stabbed at Ermanerich, who almost flinched in reaction. "You ordered the Gothic Legion to Catania, to oppose the Persian invasion. Are you mad?"

Understanding flared in the Emperor's eyes. "I did not summon the Rhenus Legions to Rome to *fight the Persians*, you ass!" A sneer curled across his face. "The Goths were ordered to Messina, to stand in reserve in case the Persian fleet broke past Maxian and his flying machines! I hoped they would be reliable in the face of the enemy, giving my brother support on the land if his efforts in the air failed."

Gaius Julius blinked. The Emperor's eyes narrowed. "The Rhenus Legions were called home because I feared a conspiracy—and now I can guess whom you suborned on my staff . . ." Galen spit on the floor. "Bastard of a Greek . . . I freed him myself. A pity I didn't know the Eighth was already here or our situations would be reversed." He sighed. "I should have listened to Anastasia."

"You ordered those Legions to Rome to suppress . . . *me*?" Gaius Julius licked his lips. The point of his gladius dropped away from the Emperor's neck.

"I should," Galen said in a brittle voice, "have had you and Alexandros killed as soon as I knew of your existence." The Emperor nodded politely to the young Goth, who had stiffened at the threat to his friend and sword-brother. "Your pardon, Prince Ermanerich. I fear you've fallen into the company of traitors. . . ."

"Why didn't you?" Gaius Julius feel a queer pressure in his temples and tiny black dots swam in the corners of his vision. He felt unaccountably grainy, as if the air itself were wearing against him. "The Duchess, at least, must have told you who I was if you'd not guessed yourself."

The Emperor's face changed, revealing deep melancholy. "You were *my heroes*," he said, voice thick with emotion, "Daydreams of youth remain even with the old, and you are both here—giants out of history—throwing down all enemies, conquering nations, driving back the darkness of barbarism. When I learned who you were, Gaius, I was . . . so pleased. Here is my idol in living flesh, and I can speak with him; discuss literature, history, politics! What a joy!"

A faint, bemused smile flickered across the Emperor's haggard face. "No greater surety has a king, than knowing Alexander of Macedon commands his armies in the field. I worried about Aurelian every day, but never about the Gothic Legion, never! My faith was unshakable, for he is *Alexander!*"

Gaius Julius started to speak, then felt a trembling at his chest. His hand clutched on the prince's amulet, still on a silver chain around his neck and found the metal burning hot. "Ah!" He stared around the room, suddenly cognizant of a black mist filling the corners and darkening the shadows. "The Oath!"

Ermanerich's eyes were quick, darting from the old Roman slumping towards the floor to the Emperor to the spreading discoloration on the floor around Gaius' feet. *Sorcery!* his mind screamed, flooding with fear.

Without thinking, the Goth lunged forward, powerful arms thrusting and the leaf-bladed spear plunged into Galen's side. The Emperor gasped, face draining of color, and Ermanerich felt the spear point scrape between bone. For a moment, everyone was transfixed, a tight little tableau of a dying man and two murderers looking on. Then, with a sigh, the Emperor slipped from the spear and crumpled to the floor at the foot of his bed. A thin stream of blood fluted from the spear point.

Gaius Julius staggered, clawing at the air, then fell down himself. The Goth leaned over him in concern—nothing *seemed* to have touched the old Roman—but his face and hands and neck were withered with age. A hot, bright spark glowed on his chest and smoke curled up from the prince's amulet. Ermanerich's fingers moved towards the peculiar object, then jerked away.

"It's burning!" he blurted, stunned. Reflexively, the Goth made a sign against evil.

A grain passed, then two. A cough wracked the old Roman's body and his eyes fluttered open. "Ermanerich . . ." he wheezed. "Carry me to the Senate building, to the Curia. There is work to be done."

"Not dead, are you?" The young Goth approached Gaius Julius cautiously and prodded him with the tip of his boot. "What happened?"

"Help me up!" The old Roman tried to lift a hand and failed. He closed his eyes. "While we were each certain of our cause, the Oath let us settle things ourselves and neither Galen nor I intended anything but the best for Rome." Gaius coughed wetly, scowling at fresh spots of blood on his sleeve. "By the gods, he nearly had me with pretty speech. . . . I'd almost changed my mind."

Ermanerich lifted the old man. He was very light, barely skin and bones. "Watch your head." Turning sideways to get through the door, the Goth edged down the hallway and into the study. A group of heavily armed men loitered in the outer room, though none were legionnaires. Each wore, however, a dolphin sigil in silver on his breast.

"Sad tidings, my friends," Gaius Julius proclaimed, letting Ermanerich stand him up. Gaius' guardsmen stared at him with interest. "Guard these doors and let no one enter! A bleak day for Rome, but not one without hope. The Emperor lies sadly dead, but before the sun rises, the Senate shall acclaim another."

As it happened, the sun was just climbing among the peaks of the Appenines when Gaius and Ermanerich and an ever-growing crowd of guardsmen and supporters reached the doors of the Curia. Down in the maze of buildings around the Forum, only the rooftops were glowing apricot with the first touch of dawn. Two ranks of Praetorians blocked the entrance to the Senate House and the Goth slowed, seeing the legionnaires held bared swords and spears. Standing nearby, a brace of men in crimson cloaks and high, horsetail-plumed helmets surrounded a woman in regal garb.

Martina started with surprise when she saw Gaius Julius' troubled face in the torchlight.

"What happened?" she exclaimed, hurrying through the ranks of her own guardsmen. Gaius Julius managed a wan smile, but his weight was almost entirely supported by Ermanerich's powerful arm and shoulder.

"There was fighting in the palace," the old Roman said in a loud, carrying voice. The men on the steps of the Senate tensed and their officers moved forward, recognizing the Eastern Empress and the visage of one of the Imperial ministers. Gaius clutched Martina's proffered hand and bowed his gray head over her rings and bracelets. "Empress, I am surprised to find you here, and afraid I must give you poor news in public."

Everyone grew quiet; the tradesmen rising early to attend their shops and workshops passing through the Forum Romanum slowing their pace, eyes and ears drawn by the torches and grim-faced men arrayed on the steps of the Curia.

"Motrius, commander of the Imperial Guard, attempted to take the princeps Galen hostage tonight and claim the purple for himself." Gaius' voice grew stronger as he spoke and he winked at Martina. Relieved, she squeezed his hand in return. "By good luck, the guardsmen within the palace remained loyal and their valiant sacrifice bought time enough for news to reach me and allow some cohorts of the noble Eighth Augusta to run to the Emperor's succor."

A murmur ran through the crowd and behind the ranks of Praetorians on the steps, the great ivory doors opened a crack. Someone looked out, listening.

"The traitors have gone to a just reward," Gaius continued, his voice ringing from marble facings and pillars. "But we came moments too late. The Divine Emperor, our Lord and God, lay dying, though the dog Motrius had fallen as well, struck through by the Emperor's own sword, which has ever been ready in the defense of justice and freedom and against tyranny in all lands."

A stunned silence followed the words, and Gaius Julius bent his head, as if he hid tears with the folds of his bloody toga. For a moment, no one moved, and then one of the centurions among the Praetorians stepped forward.

"Who will lead us now?" the grizzled veteran asked of the crowd. "We are at war and the Emperor's son's too young to take up the laurel crown. Someone must lead Rome while we strive against Persia." The man turned to Gaius. "Did the Emperor say aught, when you found him?"

Gaius Julius shook his head, grief plain on his old face. "No, my lords. He breathed his last as we fought to his side. He said nothing."

"What of Aurelian?" Someone in the crowd called out. "He is Caesar, though absent. He will rule!"

Many of the tradesmen and passersby shouted in agreement, but the commander of the Praetorians—now joined by a clutch of senators newly dragged from their beds—shook his head. "A double tragedy," the centurion said, "for news has recently come from Egypt. Aurelian is dead, slain in defense of Alexandria itself."

"No!" A great moan rose and many of the senators on the steps cried out in fear and alarm. Men in the crowd gathered on the plaza ran away through the streets, shouting the news. Gaius Julius frowned after them, and motioned with his head to some of his guardsmen. The mercenaries loped off, hands on their knives.

"Do not despair!" Gaius Julius climbed the steps, one hand on the small of Martina's back, dragging her along. The Empress flushed, then hurried to catch up. Ermanerich was happy to remain in the crowd below, leaning on his spear. Exhaustion from the long, endless night was beginning to wear upon him. He'd ridden ten leagues, seen his men encamped, then plunged into this. . . .

"Emperor Galen was a wise man and foresaw many paths fate might take. Beyond brave Aurelian, he also titled his younger brother Caesar. Now, with Theodosius an infant, the law says Prince Maxian should rule until his nephew is of proper age."

"But where is the prince?" the crowd murmured in response to the plaintive cry.

"Fear not, my friends," Gaius responded, pitching his voice so even the washerwomen at the back of the steadily-growing crowd could hear. "Prince Maxian has taken the field in Sicilia, where we have lately learned the Persians plan an attack. But the prince and his Legions wait in ambush, where the Persians do *not* expect them. He will seize victory from the jaws of the Cylcopes and bring home many captives, and much tribute, to honor great Rome!"

The frightened muttering died down a little. Gaius Julius turned to the senators clustered before the doors of the Curia. "Noble senators," he said, drawing their walleyed attention. "I abhor haste in all things, but this dawn we must move swiftly to assure and ease the troubled minds of the public. I call on you to open these doors and let the Senate enter, so Maxian—the young prince—may be proclaimed Augustus and God, Emperor of the Romans!"

Watching from below, Ermanerich pursed his lips in a slow, thoughtful whistle. At the old Roman's words, the Praetorians herded the senators back inside and Gaius and the Empress Martina entered, flanked by a hedge of men in armor, swords drawn. A great commotion rose inside the building, which was filled with the light of many lamps. *It seems the headmen have already gathered*, the Goth thought, allowing himself to be pulled along by the crowd surging up the steps. *How did they know? Lest they were told aforetime. . . .*

Gaius' singular voice rose above the din, filling the hall with calm surety and determination. Senators milled around in a white cloud like so many sheep adrift on a hillside. Ermanerich forced his way out of the crowd, taking up a vantage just inside the doors. The Praetorians had recovered themselves and now began shouting and pressing back the common citizens who wished to look upon the deliberations of the mighty.

What geese these men are, the Goth thought sourly. *This Gaius is a shrewd man—yet I would take care buying a horse from him! Aye, and count all four hooves and tail too, before silver left my hand. . . .*

The doors closed with a heavy thud and Ermanerich settled in to wait. These Romans had seemed prepared to deliberate and debate while the day came and went and the sun rose again. But he did not leave quite yet, though his men marched southward at a steady pace, for Ermanerich wished to be sure of events before he went once more to war.

"A thousand years is not too long to wait," Gaius Julius said sotto voce to Martina, who sat beside him on a marble bench, "for proper respect." The old Roman clasped the hands of one of the Senators, who emerged from the crowd in the Curia, muttered something about his "sympathies" and confided his support for the prince's imminent deification. Martina looked demure and grief-stricken for her brother-in-law's demise, answering the man's politeness with her own.

The crowd moved and the Empress stole a moment to glare at Gaius. "You didn't have to kill him," she whispered, rosebud lips twitching into a very pretty grimace. "I liked Galen! He was always polite to me and kind to my son."

"I did too," Gaius answered from the side of his mouth. "Necessity makes its own demands."

"Very well," she said, forcing a smile for the next of the magnates circulating in the crowded, hot room. Outside, the sun was well up, making the Forum shimmer, and even a system of constantly rotating fans suspended below the ceiling did little to alleviate the heat. "*You* can tell my husband what happened to his brother. A brother," she said, voice cracking a little, "he loved very much."

Gaius started to say, *it was him or me*, then restrained himself. He had a very good idea where the Empress Martina's priorities lay and they did not necessarily include an old Roman dictator who happened to have escaped death by a very fine hair. Instead, he nodded somberly. "I will tell the prince. He will judge these events as he will."

One of Gaius' guardsmen approached, nervous without his weapons; the Praetorians had recovered something of their equilibrium and now surrounded the Senate House with a double ring of armed, angry men. The man bobbed his head, trying to draw attention without interrupting.

"Over here, Verus. Stop that, you look like a duck." Gaius Julius turned away from the Empress, leaning close. "What news?"

"Not good, sir." Verus screwed his face up. The old Roman gave him a withering stare. "We've searched the Palatine from top to bottom—" The man's voice dropped like a stone into a well. "—there's no sign of her or the boy. None. Like she just . . . vanished."

Gaius Julius grunted, his face sliding into careful immobility. He pinned the man with a furious glance. "How long," he said softly, "have Empress Helena and her son been missing?"

"Since . . ." The man gulped. "Last night. One of her maids says she went to bed at the usual hour!"

One eyelid flickering, Gaius Julius turned away, waving his hand in dismissal. Martina was watching him, her perfect face tinged with feigned concern. Her limpid brown eyes seemed very cold. "Well? What did he say?"

"Nothing we can do anything about now." Gaius Julius felt his stomach slowly unclench. *This is what haste gains you, my lad*, he chided himself. *But our nets will scoop her up*. "Your good friend Helena, in her grief, has disappeared."

"Has she?" The Empress of the East's lips curled back from white, white teeth. One smooth hand drifted across her breast, coming to rest with long fingertips on her clavicle. "She'll hide with friends, won't she? Where else would she go?"

Gaius nodded, spying a storm cloud of perspiring senators bearing down on him. He stepped away from the Empress, smiling genially, yet with the trace of profound regret appropriate for such a terrible day.

"Good," Martina said to herself, wondering how much longer she would be forced to endure this heat. She began to smile, spirits lifting. "Their names will be on one of dear Gaius' lists and when the arrests and executions begin, they will beg for their lives and she will be yielded up, trussed like a . . . a summer sausage!" Then her face fell again and she had to fight against gnawing on a nail. *I never meant Galen ill! Stupid, reckless Gaius Julius!* She sighed, feeling very lonely. *I miss my husband*, she thought morosely, but the image in her mind was neither Maxian nor Heraclius, exactly.

THE WASTELAND

)−(

Y ou are Mohammed," the wounded man said in a weak voice, forcing his eyelids open. They were caked with grime, dried blood and crusty yellow crystals. The rest of his face—once darkly handsome—was no better, his eye sockets surrounded by glassy scars, his scalp lacerated by jagged cuts. "You were selling cups and plates; a whole caravan of beautiful red pottery. . . ."

"Yes," Mohammed answered, lifting the Egyptian from the black sand. The body was very light, but still had some weight. Ahmet had been a strong man with a powerful build in life. "Is my caravan the last thing you remember?"

"I . . ." Ahmet turned his head weakly, an expression of bewilderment working its way across his wounded face. He did not seem to recognize the wasteland of broken, black stone and weathered spires. "I remember roses climbing a plastered wall

and . . . and a woman." He stopped speaking, his body clenching convulsively into a tight ball. Mohammed let him shudder,
holding Ahmet close while he climbed carefully out of the pit.
There did not seem to be any weather in this place—the flat,
black sky remained still and unblemished by clouds or wind or
even a celestial body—but instinct bade him find shelter.

One of the jagged boulders harbored an egg-shaped opening
in one side, the largest among hundreds of cavities and pits
eroded from the glassy stone. Mohammed ducked inside, finding the floor covered with the same obsidian-colored sand as
the plain. He noticed, but was no longer surprised by, the directionless, ambient light picking out every detail. There was no
sun—the air itself seemed to be the source of this queer, febrile
radiance.

He laid Ahmet down, letting the Egyptian's body uncurl at its
own pace.

"Do you remember her name?" Mohammed sat on the sandy
floor beside his friend, the staff of fig wood leaning against his
shoulder. "Do you remember the golden city?" *Do you remember the siege?*

Ahmet managed to nod, though he seemed very weak. "I remember the last day. A dreadful shape rising above the
towers . . ."

"You fell," Mohammed said softly, "and your body was
stolen by the enemy. I searched among the ruins, but you had
been taken away. Do you remember what happened after that?"

Convulsive shuddering wracked the emaciated body again
and the Quraysh waited patiently until the spasms passed. This
seemed to take a long time, though Mohammed noticed he did
not tire, or grow hungry or thirsty. He began to wonder if time
had any meaning in this place, wherever it was. *It may not,* he
considered, *if this plain is beyond life and death alike.*

The Egyptian lay still again. Mohammed waited until the
man's eyes opened. "Do you remember now?"

"Yes." The word was flat, and dead, and laden with enormous, inexpressible weight. "I do."

"How did you come to be here?" The Quraysh tried to restrain his curiosity—*there is time enough to be patient, or is
there?*—Mōha had claimed time did not pass in this place, but

what if he had lied? What if the perception of timelessness were part of the trap, the prison?

A dry, rasping sound shook Ahmet's body and the Quraysh was heartened to recognize a feeble attempt at laughter. "I do not know what this place is. I became aware of this desert when you touched my shoulder. Before that . . . I was . . . I was in Egypt."

Mohammed frowned. "Egypt? What do you mean?"

Now the withered, scarred lips twisted, trying to smile. "I sat in a great temple—not the Serapeum, but one looking out upon the sea and the harbor—and the multitudes came before me, bowing, offering tribute and sacrifice." Ahmet's hands moved, groping around his head. "Hard to see what they dragged before my altar through the mask, but there were screams . . ." His lips fluttered, broken teeth making a *click-click-click* sound.

"What kind of mask?" Mohammed squatted, trying to make out the croaking words.

". . . there were many priests and they wore the casque of Set and the lords of shadow . . . There were statues—new statues— of me . . . She was seated at my side, I could smell her hair!" Ahmet's eyes flickered open, filled with shock and surprise. "I can *still* smell her, hear them, hear the screams of men on the breaking block!"

Mohammed shook his head in confusion, then remembered something Zoë had once done. "Ahmet," he said, grasping the man's shoulder and feeling a chill shock as his hand started to pass through the wiry muscle and bone. "Ahmet, you are *here* with me, with your old friend Mahammed, the caravaneer. You are *here*, not there, not in Alexandria in a temple." Flesh stiffened and the Quraysh sighed in relief, seeing his friend become solid once more. *Time is short*, he felt. *This interlude cannot last.*

"Open your eyes," Mohammed commanded, putting steel in his voice. "Tell me what is happening in the world you saw."

The Egyptian focused again and the Quraysh thought he saw awareness flare in the dead eyes before hopelessness dulled them again. Ahmet lifted a hand, his dusty fingertips brushing Mohammed's face. "Hah. Are you real? I can touch you—but any sensation may be deceived. How did you find your way into my prison?"

"I am a prisoner too," Mohammed answered, now sure time

was pressing. "But I cannot see out into the living world. You can—is your body, your true body, in Alexandria?"

"My corpse, you mean," Ahmet said, voice strengthening a little. "Yes. A puppet, moved by a dark, implacable will."

Revulsion and disgust twisted his expression. "The Serpent's army has taken the city and my . . . my shape, for there is no better word, sits on a throne like Pharaoh and dispenses fear and terror in place of wisdom and judgment."

"Who else is there?" Mohammed felt oddly adrift. *The Persians in Alexandria? What happened to the campaign in Thrace? Did Constantinople fall? Did Shadin and his little army overcome the Roman garrison?*

"She is," Ahmet groaned, starting to curl up again. Mohammed pressed his shoulders down with both hands. A cold suspicion was growing, just under his breastbone. Bits and pieces of . . . of *everything* were beginning to come together in his mind.

"Who is *she*?"

"The Queen, my queen, my beloved," Ahmet whispered. "She sits by my side and her voice is gracious and sweet as she pleads for mercy. We make a fine pair—one to distill fear, the other to offer hope—each on a golden throne."

"Zenobia?" Mohammed felt the chill blossom into a deadly, breath-crushing flower. "Or Zoë?"

"They are one," Ahmet gasped, hands clutching on something only he could see. "One more horror laid at horror's feet. . . ."

Mohammed sat back, mind roiling with fury, despair, realization; a whirlwind of emotion. He grasped the staff for support, pressing his forehead against cool wood. A regal voice echoed in his memory: *You are being deceived.* He'd recognized the clear soprano then and ignored her warning. *I was a fool*, the Quraysh thought. *I am not the voice, I am not infallible.*

"How . . . how did Zenobia—" Mohammed stopped, realizing what had happened. "No, I understand. The Queen's mutilated body was a trap. Zoë took her corpse from the mountain tomb, and her mind become ensnared . . ."

Ahmet nodded, knocking his bare skull against the sand. "*He* is fond of innocent-seeming lures. By our heart's desire we are captured and bound." The Egyptian managed another hoarse, rattling laugh. "He is strong, but made stronger still by the desires of others bent to his will."

Mohammed grasped Ahmet's hand. "This 'he'—the same wizard you fought on the plain of towers?" The Egyptian nodded. "Is he a spirit, a god, or just a man?"

"He was human once," Ahmet said bleakly. "He let a power enter him—one of the pitiless, inhuman Great Old Ones who were worshipped before man, an incalculable power beyond comprehension—and has been transformed. Only a tiny fragment of his master's strength can pass through him—but that is enough to make him formidable beyond all others. . . ."

Mohammed tried to voice a question, but his mind grappled with a sudden realization. Mouth working soundlessly, he took a breath, then managed to speak. "Are these . . . Old Ones . . . opposed? Are they the wellspring of evil?"

Dead lips stretched over rotted teeth and Ahmet barked another hoarse laugh. "Evil? A human conceit, my friend. Do you remember our discussions round the campfire? The wise thoughts of the philosophers and sages? They are no more than rubbish, the prattle of children too young and shortsighted to grasp the truth of the world. There is no good and there is no evil." Ahmet shuddered. "But there are things—powers—which dwarf the works of man and have lived so long in the abyssal spaces between the stars, death no longer touches them or makes them weak."

Mohammed recoiled from the despair and nihilism in Ahmet's voice. *This is not the man I remember! He had faith and a good heart, unbowed and unbroken.*

"You have abandoned hope," the Quraysh said, changing the subject a little. "You think *he* has captured you, lured you into his service, bent your neck to the yoke."

"He has!" Ahmet rose, eyes blazing. "His will rides me like a ghoul, moving my limbs to murder, my power to strike—so many dead have I heaped at his feet I cannot remember their names! He sees with my eyes, speaks with my lips. I am no more than . . . a container for his desire. A tool to be picked up at need."

Mohammed's eyes glinted hard, his suspicions confirmed.

"He holds the Queen—Zenobia—before you as bait, making you dance so you might see her once more, hear her voice, feel her touch? And too, now you fear death, don't you? You think there is nothing beyond the portal save annihilation and you cannot abide the thought of nothingness?"

Ahmet's face blanched and he lifted a skeletal arm to hide his face. "There is *nothing*," he groaned hopelessly. "I have passed beyond death—my body died on the steps of the palace, exhausted in the last effort of defeating the *dhole*—and there was nothing, only an eternity of darkness, before *he* summoned me back from oblivion." The Egyptian's voice faded to an almost unintelligible whisper. "Even this half-life is better . . ."

Mohammed's fierce expression faded, replaced by gentle understanding. He looked around the little cave. "You are not dead," he said in a matter-of-fact voice. "Nor were you before. Your body may have perished, destroyed by the forces unleashed in defense of Palmyra, but your spirit has not completed its last journey." The Quraysh looked down and found Ahmet watching him with a peculiar, fixed intensity. "You are trapped in the borderland, in the margin between death and life. Our enemy has great strength and a cunning mind. He has—he had—blocked the gate through which the dead must pass."

The Egyptian tried to speak, but could find no words.

"This place is illusion," Mohammed said abruptly, rising to his feet. His visage became stern and he raised the fig-wood staff with an abrupt, defiant motion. The wooden stave broke through the stone ceiling and light flooded into the cavity. Stones and shards of obsidian crumpled away, falling up into the sky, driven by the power of the blow. A faint rumbling sound trembled in the air. "Another trap, laid by a master of snares."

The ground did not heave or split, but shivered, and Ahmet gaped to see entire spires and boulders begin to fragment, splitting apart. Each shard, released from some strange gravity, tumbled up, filling the sky with a black, spiraling cloud. Mohammed ignored the fantastic scene, holding out his hand to Ahmet.

"You weld your own chain," the Quraysh said, lifting his friend to his feet. "You bind only yourself and you may free yourself."

Ahmet, hunched, unable to stand straight, stared fearfully at Mohammed, who now seemed to loom enormous against the rippling, unstable sky. The broken stones, monoliths, spires, boulders—they plunged into the perfect darkness arching overhead—and as they fell, spit fire and meteors, shedding a terrible orange-red glow. Ahmet's eyes burned in reflection. "No! I will never see Zenobia again, never taste life again . . . I will cease!" The Egyptian was crying, though he had only dust for tears.

"While you cling to this half-life," Mohammed said, "you bind her as well. She has fallen into the same trap, bound by love and desire and—most of all—fear. While you live, you do countless harm, trampling the weak, throwing down the strong, spreading evil with either hand." His voice rose to a sharp snap. "And there *is* evil in the world and good too. You know the difference, in your heart."

"Yes," Ahmet gasped, clubbed by the harsh words. "But . . . but . . . have you *seen* what lies beyond the gate? Can you tell me what will happen? Truly?"

Mohammed shook his head, meteors streaking in his flashing eyes. "No. I have not made that journey. But I have *faith* and trust to the lord of the world, who made all things, all powers great and small, and whose provenance none can deny, not serpents or dead gods, or even the great ones who prowl the abyss among the dead suns."

Ahmet stood at last and looked into his friend's face and saw an incomparable strength shining there. "You have changed," he said. "You are not the man I knew—lost in his heart, confused, searching always for some answer beyond the next city, town, hill—what happened?"

"I grew still," Mohammed said, leaning on his staff, "and I listened."

Ahmet's face changed, growing pensive. "What did you hear?"

"Wind rattling the leaves. Stone groaning in the heat of the day. The voice of the world."

Ahmet let his hands fall to his side and closed his eyes. "What did the voice tell you?"

Mohammed smiled slightly. "The truth."

With a sigh, the Egyptian collapsed backwards, falling a little to the side. His body struck the ground in silence and the wasteland of shattered stone was gone. Only the black, perfect sky remained, now conjoined to an endless, glassy obsidian plain. Mohammed looked around, a bemused look on his face. "Good-bye," he said to the empty air. "My friends."

A look of determination and purpose came over him and the Quraysh reached up with one hand, grasping the sky and—with a powerful motion of his arm—tore open the firmament with an impossibly loud ripping sound. A blaze of light flooded down on his face, coupled with the roar of the sea and men shouting and the cry of gulls wheeling against an azure sky.

⊡≻0≺0≻0≺0≻0≺0≻0≺0≻0≺0≻0≺0≻0≺0≻0≺0≻0≺0≻0≺0≻0≺0≻0≺0≻0≺0≻0≺⊡

MESSINA, SICILIA

)╫(

Alexandros stepped up out of the street and into a doorway. A wagon heavy with meal bags and pottery jars rumbled past, axels squealing, wooden wheels rattling on stone paving. A column of Gothic pikemen followed, helmets slung at their shoulders, backs bent under round shields and netted bags of clothing, food, personal effects.

The men marched past in silence, faces sharp with weariness, shining with sweat, the *tramp-tramp-tramp* of their boots barely audible over the din of the wagons. Most sported bile-yellow streaks on their scaled breastplates. Alexandros' doubted few of his men had been to sea before, and the ferry passage from Dyrrachium had been rough, with a harsh, gusty wind quartering out of the southeast. The Macedonian nodded a greeting to the column syntagmarch as he marched past, then stepped down and made his way into the forum. The squad of peltasts Clothar Shortbeard had sent to find him dogged along behind, bearded faces slack with exhaustion.

The plaza was crowded with marching soldiers, supplies, wagons, lines of unsteady horses. Late-morning sun picked out shining details, though heavy clouds covered most of the sky.

Alexandros was glad of the shade, for the day only promised to get hotter and wetter. He hoped the rain stayed away long enough for his men to disembark. Masts crowded above the rooftops to the east, where the harbor was crowded with every barge, trireme, grain ship and coaster Alexandros could beg, borrow or steal. A constant din of shouting beat at his ears, but he was used to the racket of armies on the march. Without pausing, he climbed the steps into the city temple devoted to the Capitoline Triad, weaving his way through a maniple of archers sleeping in the shade.

Within, long tables crowded the nave and the Legion battle banners made a red, gold and iron thicket beneath a frowning, marble Jupiter. His officers were busy stuffing their faces with roasted fish, garlic, lentil soup—anything the commissary could confiscate—and Alexandros forced himself to nod in greeting to those men who looked up at his approach. Clothar was snoring—he'd heard *that* a block away—his tousled head resting on Jupiter's feet.

"Any news?" An irritated snap in the Macedonian's voice woke some of the younger men, but they fell back asleep—heads on their bedrolls or helmets—after a bleary glance in his direction. Alexandros' temper was near frayed to the breaking by the confusion, chaos and delay outside.

"Here, sir!" One of the Eastern tribunes beckoned from the rear of the temple. The man had a queer, frightened look on his face. Alexandros started to snarl a curse as he paced between the fluted columns, but he controlled himself. He knew the look. Something out of the ordinary had happened and the man was half-pissed with fear of his general's reaction.

"Another batch of letters from Rome? If I see one more Hades-cursed Imperial Order, I'm going to—"

Alexandros stopped dead, his eyes adjusting to the dimness. The rear half of the temple had been partitioned to provide for storage. Juno and Ares watched silently over on the Legion's pay, stacked in heavy iron-bound chests. Standing below the shadow-dappled statues was a lean, dark-haired man. The Macedonian blinked. "Lord Prince?"

Maxian turned to look at Alexandros and the Macedonian was stunned to see the young Roman's face grown old and wan.

At the same time, there was an unexpected, compelling weight to his presence, as if Alexandros had stepped into the presence of one of the ancient heroes. "What has happened?"

"My brothers are dead," Maxian replied, his voice ringing with barely concealed power. The Macedonian staggered, forcing himself to remain standing by catching himself on one of the trunks. The Eastern tribune cried out and fell to his knees in a clatter of iron scale. "The Emperor was murdered last night, even as my men crossed the strait."

"Your . . ." Alexandros rallied himself, denying an urge to bow to the prince. "You've brought reinforcements?"

"Yes," Maxian said, stepping forward out of the shadows. As he did he seemed to shrink and the pressure in the air eased, allowing Alexandros to stand without effort. "I've brought at least three Legions across from Italia. They are already on the road to Syracuse. What of your Goths?"

"We're still unloading the fleet," the Macedonian replied, a little stunned, feeling as if he were suddenly a length behind in an unexpected race. "Another day and everyone will be ashore. Luckily, the Eastern troops are familiar with ships or we'd be here for weeks trying to get everything untangled."

"Good. I know you've received conflicting orders from Rome." The prince's face twisted into a remarkably sour expression. "This will not happen again. You will march south along the Via Pompeiana as quickly as possible. Do not tarry here." In brighter light Alexandros could see Maxian's cloak was tattered and torn, tunic badly stained, his boots fouled with dust and mud. Every sign spoke of a long road march, though the prince did not seem exhausted at all. His eyes blazed with irresistible command. "The Persians will be landing within days. You must meet them on the beaches below Catania if we're to have a chance at victory."

"I . . . see. My lord, if the Emperor is dead, then who . . ."

Maxian stiffened, his thin lips curling back from white teeth. "Who struck him down?"

"No," Alexandros managed to say, though the pressure in the air was rising again. *I don't care who wielded the knife, you young fool, that's no matter to me or my men!* "Who now rules in Rome?"

"I am Emperor." Maxian deflated again, the words hoarse with agony. "My brothers are dead, used up in this endless war." The prince swayed, then mastered himself. "Only I am left."

Alexandros was silent, his whole attention fixed on the prince. A dead, sick feeling was trying to gain a foothold in his gut. The man in front of him seemed to vacillate between supernal power and ashy exhaustion. After a moment, the Macedonian said, "My lord, if your brother is dead, then what has happened to . . . to the guardian?"

"The what?" Maxian tried to focus on Alexandros' face and failed. He slumped against the nearest chest, but the Macedonian caught him before the prince could fall. Maxian's skin was hot, almost hot enough to burn. Alexandros drew back, alarmed.

"*Ayy!* You've not just a fever—more like a furnace!"

"Yes," Maxian whispered, a ghoul-like smile stretching his lips. "Do you remember the night I tried to raise Octavian, tried to shroud him with the Oath and shatter the keystone?"

"I remember." Alexandros did. A night of destruction, raging with fire and lightning. Even this half-life had seemed precious then, when annihilation was only a hairbreadth away.

"Now I am the keystone," Maxian said, his voice a mere breath. Alexandros leaned closer, barely able to make out the words. "The Senate has acclaimed me Emperor, princeps, guardian of the Republic. And all the strength I tried to overthrow—it presses on me, Alexandros, crushes me like a vise!"

The Macedonian felt cold again and the sick feeling inside him grew stronger. He knew what it was like to rule men, to hold the power of life and of death over a vast domain, over millions of human souls. But even when the Persians had acclaimed him as a god, as a living deity, he'd never felt such pressure as this young Roman must feel.

"I can feel them all, a constant, raging noise . . ." Maxian's breathing grew ragged, his head rolling back. Cursing, Alexandros caught his shoulders, ignoring the heat.

"Lord Prince!" The Macedonian shook the Roman gently and Maxian's eyes blinked, focusing on him. Alexandros gave him a fierce glare. "How do you know the Persians are landing at Catania?"

"We saw . . . Galen and I saw them planning through the telecast." Maxian seemed to gather himself. "The Persians and the rebellious Greeks put a great fleet to sea. Their full strength will strike here. They plan to come ashore in strength, then turn either north to Messina or south to Syracuse and capture a port."

Alexandros clenched his teeth, thinking of his exhausted troops. If the Legions who'd marched down from Rome were in better shape, they might have a chance . . . but from looking at the prince, the Macedonian didn't think the legionaries were ready to fight schoolchildren, much less the Persian Immortals. *And then*, he thought, *there is the real enemy . . .*

"My lord . . ." Alexandros's tone was harsh with suppressed fear. "I've spoken with the survivors from Constantinople— they say the Persians have a sorcerer with awesome powers— how can I fight such a creature?"

"Yes," Maxian pushed the Macedonian's hands aside. "He is coming. I can feel him."

The prince stood, his movements weak for a moment, then filling visibly with strength as he gathered himself. Alexandros stepped back warily.

Maxian smiled grimly and a plainly visible corona of cold flame limned him, silhouetting his head, outlining his arms. Every trace of weariness, of exhaustion and grief, washed away in the spectral light. "Our dear friend Gaius has done me bitter service, Macedonian. His plots have murdered my brother, spilled the Emperor's blood, forced upon me unwanted honors, a crown . . ."

Alexandros' quick mind leapt ahead of the prince's words and the Macedonian's handsome face split in a feral grin. *At last, the boy begins to think like a king. The first good news I've heard since entering this life!*

"Yet now I've strength enough, and more, to face this Persian and his servants, be they two, three or a multitude." Maxian's grief was plain on his face, matched with a newly found steel.

Alexandros lifted his chin in challenge, his spirits entirely restored. "Wouldn't your brother give his life to save Rome?"

"He has," Maxian answered, teeth bared. "I will not waste his sacrifice."

)•(

"H*sst!* Get back." Betia retreated slowly from the street corner, making a shooing motion with her free hand. Thyatis backed up, left hand tense on the hilt of her spatha, glancing over her shoulder to make sure Shirin had caught the warning. The Khazar woman was already two paces back, watching their back trail. The lane was narrow and badly paved, scarred by gaping potholes and overhung on both sides by three- and four-story buildings. Even at midday—with a perfectly clear blue sky above—the passage was dim and grimy.

Betia eased into a building entryway. Even with the litter of rinds and broken wine bottles and discarded chicken bones underfoot, she did not step wrong or make a noise. Thyatis filled most of the space with her broad shoulders, while Shirin occupied the rest, enveloped in a patched gray cloak. All three women were sweating, for the heat today was particularly fierce and the city was slowly baking in a humid mash of sweat, rotting garbage and wood smoke.

"There's an entire cohort of legionnaires on the street ahead, breaking down the door to someone's house with a ram." Betia's voice was clipped and precise. "I don't think we should go that way."

"Our destination?" The redheaded woman looked thoughtful.

Betia shook her head. "No. Next door. A house of the Gracchi, I think." The girl frowned. "You saw the broadsheets posted on the port notice boards?"

Thyatis nodded. She had, though at the time she'd been more concerned with guiding their longboat through the maze of canals in old Ostia without running into someone or something and pitching them all into the fetid, gray-green water. "There are proscriptions."

"What does that mean?" Shirin's voice was tight where Thyatis had assumed a slow drawl. Everyone had their own reaction to the tense, frightened atmosphere in the city.

"Lists of traitors," Betia said, keeping her voice low. Thyatis could hear the crash of wood splintering and people screaming now, even with such a goodly distance between themselves and the house of the Gracchi. The streets were entirely deserted and silent, she realized.

"When there is trouble," the girl continued, "or the Emperor needs gold, lists are posted of those who have committed crimes against the state. They must defend themselves in court, which costs money of course, or they are executed out of hand and their properties confiscated. But nothing like this has happened for decades."

Thyatis felt grief welling and clamped down hard on the useless emotion. "Not since Galen became Emperor," she bit out, though she'd had no intention of speaking.

Betia nodded, her own face shadowed. Shirin kept quiet, though she'd seen the black bands on the arms of the legionnaires in the port and at the city gates. Even the temples they'd passed had been silent and in the rare occasion they met someone on the street, no greetings were exchanged and the passersby avoided eye contact, hurrying on as fast as their feet allowed.

"We need to get into the house," Thyatis said, forcing herself to action. "If only to see if it is empty. The Duchess may have fled elsewhere and left a sign."

"How?" Shirin looked up at her friend, and Betia frowned also. "The street . . ."

"Up. We're on the same side of the street, right?" Thyatis said, stepping to the heavy, four-paneled doorway behind her. Her fist tested the latch and found the door barred. She felt around the edge, pressing at the cheap wood with powerful fingers. "Keep an eye out," she said over her shoulder, one hand reaching under her woolen cloak.

Shirin backed up, biting her thumb. Thyatis produced a iron pry bar and sighted one end—fitted with a shovel-like spike—just above the latch mechanism. "Anyone coming?" she muttered.

"No," Betia said. Thyatis swung the bar in a short, controlled blow. Wood *thumped* and screeched as she bent her shoulder into the bar, twisting the iron down and sideways. Splinters screwed away from the wood and Thyatis grunted. There was a popping sound, and she levered the bar down. Something went *clunk* in the passage.

Smiling faintly, Thyatis pushed the door open. The corridor beyond was quiet and dark. She stepped inside.

Leading with the point of her spatha, Thyatis glided across a plain tile floor, flitting from doorway to doorway. Despite a heavy, encompassing quiet, the house did not feel empty to her. Frightened to silence, but not untenanted. Shirin followed, her feet bare and then Betia, a dark gray ghost who barely disturbed the air with her passage.

Thyatis paused at the head of a stairwell leading down to the cellars and her long nose twitched. She jerked her head towards the opening and the other two faded into the gloom of a nearby alcove. The tiny statue of Pan did not mind their proximity and Thyatis crept down the stairs, feeling the slowly building *tic-tic-tic* of bloodfire coursing in her veins.

A moment later, her head appeared on the stairs and she beckoned her companions down.

"Hello, mother," Thyatis said softly, stepping between two stout pillars streaked with brown water stains. Anastasia's head jerked up as if she'd sat on a nettle and an incredulous, glad smile bloomed in her tired, pale face. The redhead grinned broadly, making a sketchy bow towards the other woman lying on a cot against the wall.

"You . . ." Anastasia squeaked, crushed in a powerful hug. Thyatis held the Duchess close for a long moment, her eyes stinging. ". . . I can't breath!" Anastasia managed, though her own embrace was just as tight.

"Sorry." Thyatis let go, holding the Duchess at arm's length. Her face settled into a concerned, grim mask. "I'm sorry we're late. The winds were against us for the return voyage from Alexandria."

Anastasia tried to tuck back her hair—grown entirely matted and snarled—then gave up. "I had hoped you wouldn't come here," she said, dabbing at the corners of bloodshot, violet eyes, indicating the house, the city, Italia. "But I'm glad you're alive." The Duchess peered around Thyatis and then she did start to sniffle. "Oh, Betia—you're here too—and you must be . . . Shirin." Anastasia put her hands over her face and sat down abruptly, only managing to gasp for breath between uncontrollable tears. "I'm sorry, I'm so sorry . . ."

"Empress?" Thyatis knelt beside the still, quiet shape on the cot. Helena did not respond, though her eyes were open, staring at the ceiling. The redheaded woman turned, saw Betia and Shirin sitting on either side of Anastasia, trying to give her a handkerchief, arms around her, heads bent together. "I heard about the Emperor," Thyatis said softly, taking the Empress's hand. The fingers were very cold and clammy, like a fresh-caught fish. "I'm sorry he is dead. He was a fine man."

Helena's eyes moved, tracking slowly, and she mustered a breath, though the effort seemed enormous. She met Thyatis' troubled gaze with her own and the younger woman stiffened. There was such a depth of sorrow and grief in the dark brown eyes, she could barely stand to meet them herself.

"Hello," the Empress said, the sound rising from a great, unguessed depth. "You are Diana, aren't you?" Her attention seemed to focus, though again the effort was slow. "You were filled with rage . . . and sorrow. I remember you, in a garish room clouded with lotus smoke and scented oil."

Wordlessly, Thyatis nodded, remembering a wild, desperately lonely night.

"You must take my son," Helena said, a feeble gleam of light sparking in her dead eyes. "You were swift on the bright sand, striking down your enemies like a whirlwind. You can take him away from all . . . this."

Thyatis half-turned, searching for the Duchess. Anastasia met her eyes and nodded, lifting her hand. "Little Theodosius is here." She beckoned with the damp handkerchief. A young girl appeared from the gloom, tiny, sharp hands on the shoulders of a toddler, guiding his steps over the uneven paving stones. "But we are all who have survived, so far."

"What about the servants in the villa of Swans?" Betia's young face seemed old and grim.

"Gone." Anastasia made a motion with her hand—casting grain upon the waters. "Some safe, I'm sure, but others . . . there have been many executions." Her voice faltered. "The morgues are too full to hold them all," she said in a despairing voice. "Wagons fill the streets, jumbled with the dead. They are burning them in the fields south of the city. In the rubbish dumps." The Duchess stopped, unable to continue.

"Who is doing this?" Thyatis clasped her hands over the Empress's cold fingers.

"The dead make more of their own," Helena answered and the tiny bit of strength in her voice grew. "The histories say he was ever generous to his enemies and openhanded and rescinded every edict of banishment, pardoning all crimes—real and imagined." She managed a hollow laugh, holding only the bare memory of her cutting peal. "Sulla or Tiberius never made Rome bleed as he does. . . ."

"A man named Gaius Julius rules the city, in the new Emperor's name," Anastasia said quietly. "He has the support of the Praetorians, the crime syndicates, the Urban Prefect, even the Senate. Yet he is being thorough, ensuring no living enemy will oppose his rule."

"Who . . . who is the new Emperor? What happened to Aurelian and Maxian?" Thyatis shook her head in disbelief.

The Duchess's lips quirked into a cold smile. "Aurelian lies dead in Egypt and Maxian is our Lord and God—though I doubt he knows yet. The young Emperor, who we once seemed to know so well has gone south to Sicilia. We have heard . . ." Anastasia shrugged her shoulders. ". . . he has gone to deal with the Persians 'once and for all.' Or so the gazette says, if anyone will dare the Forum to read what is written there."

"Sicilia?" Thyatis and Shirin exchanged a puzzled glance. "The *Paris* passed Messina only days ago—there was no sign of battle or war." The redheaded woman scratched her ear. "Though there were many galleys in the port."

"Rumors," Anastasia said. "My networks of informers and spies have been devastated by Gaius' purges—one of the reasons, I'm sure, he's being so brutal. He must be searching for me, for us, with every man he can trust."

"How long have you been here?" Thyatis let go of the Empress's hand and stood up.

"Too long." Anastasia sighed, clasping her hands together to keep them from trembling. "It took us a good two days to get here from the Palatine—the streets are thick with informers and patrols—and we had to rest. So four days in all." She smiled at the little girl, who had settled beside Helena, letting the sleepy little boy crawl into his mother's arms. "Only Koré had the strength to get over the wall and let us in."

"We had better leave," Shirin said, rising from the cot. "They're already going house to house in this district."

Thyatis nodded, considering both Helena and Anastasia with a worried expression. "We'll go as soon as it gets dark. Koré seems to have the boy in hand, Betia can scout, and you, Empress, I will carry on my own back."

"No," Helena said, clutching her son to her breast, one hand slowly stroking his hair. "I am not well. I've never been an athlete and these last two days have used me up. I barely have strength to rise from this bed, much less manage flight. But my son—you *will* him get out of the city and out of Italia." The Empress raised her head, fixing Anastasia with a fierce glare. "The Duchess knows a safe place, I think. One far from Rome where a little boy will be safe from his enemies. Send him there."

Anastasia stiffened, face pale as bone. She said nothing, only staring aghast at Helena. Her expression brought an almost-normal laugh from the Empress, who laid her head back down afterwards, exhausted.

Thyatis looked from one woman to the other, but neither said a word. She turned to Betia and Shirin, who shrugged. They didn't follow the aside either. "Right," muttered Thyatis, poking at some pots and pans filled with cold oatmeal. "Let's find a place to make a hot meal before we go. Never know when you might get one again, eh?"

)(

Freezing winds roared and lashed around the vast shape of a *byakhee*, forcing Dahak to crouch low against the stupendous body. A forest of black, frond-like tentacles gripped him on either side, keeping the sorcerer from being flung from the monster's back as it turned, bifurcate wings cleaving the air in a sweeping arc over a glimmering bay. The sight of so much water—so much seawater—wheeling below him made Dahak's lean fingers dig deeper into plush, thorny fur.

The placid, sun-dappled face of annihilation yawned up at him, stretching from horizon to horizon, a sheet of sparkling glass. Only the enormous, sloped cone of Aetna offered him any hope of survival. The mountain dominated the island landscape, rising thousands of feet above the rumpled hills and sharp ravines spread at its foot. No other mountain on Sicilia, or even in Italia, matched the height of the volcano. Snow covered the truncated crown, white mixed with streaks of dark gray. Steam boiled away from the summit, though the throb of the mountain's heart—perceptible even here, at such a great height—was steady and quiet.

Down, the sorcerer commanded and the *byakhee* slewed sideways with terrific speed, plunging towards the curving tan line of a beach barely visible below. Dahak swallowed a scream, worming his way into the living, writhing fur, shutting his eyes against the blaze of the setting sun upon the water.

The creature boomed across the bay, wheeling like a kite, and landed on a broad, white beach. Sand billowed up in a great cloud and a line of trees a hundred yards back from the surf line creaked and bent, battered by a tremendous gale. Talons crunched in loose gravel and a dark mist of tendrils descended onto hard-packed sand, searching for food.

Staggering and weak with reaction, Dahak tumbled from the

monster's back and fell heavily onto the hot sand. Long shadows stretched from the nearest trees and the air took on a golden quality as the sun settled towards the western rim of the world. Shaking himself, Dahak turned away from the waves lapping on the shore and staggered into the cover of a thicket of witch hazel.

"Go," he growled at the *byakhee*, which had found a colony of clams under damp sand below the high tide line. Thin, prehensile tubes distended from the rugose, insectile body, digging into the beach. A wave of dull hatred radiated from the thing's mind at Dahak's command—*hunger . . . eat*—yet it could not disobey his will or the compelling sign he raised in the hidden world. With a vast rushing sound, the ground trembled and a whirlwind of grit and sand and gravel clattered against the trees. The servitor leapt into the sky and was quickly gone, only a dark speck against a cerulean sky and then nothing.

Hiding in the thicket, glossy green leaves tickling his neck, the sorcerer waited, his own rage and fear simmering. He did not like this place. But then he turned his attention to the bright sea and calm relief fell over him. The bay was filled with white and cream and brown sails. The Persian fleet arrived, driven by unseasonable winds, covering the sea from shore to shore. They could not miss their landfall, not with the vast cone of Aetna rising towards the heavens, visible for a hundred miles in clear weather.

The lead wave of galleys surged towards the shore, white spume leaping from their bows, sails taut with vigorous zephyrs. Three enormous grain haulers advanced in the center of the fleet, dwarfing their companions as a bear might tower over her cubs, black hulls rising like mountains from the blue sea. Already, as the sorcerer watched, the lead merchantmen were lowering longboats filled with men.

My Huns and faithful C'hu-lo, Dahak saw with relief, recognizing their topknots and darker skin, their black armor and furred cloaks. He remained in hiding, tense and alert. For the moment, it seemed, he was alone on the beach, but Roman patrols—if there were any on this placid stretch of agricultural coastline—would not have missed the thunderous arrival of the *byakhee. Or my great fleet*, he thought smugly. Sleek galleys nosed towards the shore, brilliant eyes shining in the setting sun; round-bellied merchantmen leaned with the wind, anchor chains rattling into the deep, sailors shouting commands as they turned painted sails; everywhere there was busy industry as the fleet entered the broad, white bay.

A high deck rode above gleaming green water, the depths below thronged with striped fish, then shining white sand and fluttering strands of kelp and sea grass. The sun was almost on the mountaintop, letting the last lucid rays plunge down into the beckoning sea, brilliant on burnished shields and helms, casting a forest of stars against the darkening shore. Two great chairs were moored to the deck under a canvas shade, and a terrible king sat in one, a beautiful queen in the other, flowers and gold wound in her raven hair.

Every eye aboard was turned to the shore, a long band of white between deepening blue and the lush green and brown of the forest. Water meadows glinted beyond the foaming strand, filled with vineyards and planted fields ripe with summer grain. Stands of black poplar clustered along streams rushing down from white-capped mountains and even at sea, on the great-hulled ships, the lowing of kine and the bleating of countless goats carried on the evening wind.

A rich, lush smell reached out from the shore and those living men on the ship were minded of home and family and the turning of the seasons.

No one marked the jackal-headed king's cloak—gray on gray, fine linen and silk—sprawling loose across the arms of his chair. The jackal himself sat with his bronzed arms on the seat, his mask staring at the shore. A pocket in the fabric jumped and twitched, yielding a square of gleaming black cloth that fell onto the deck behind the throne. For a moment, the material lay still, then—with dizzying speed—the square unfolded into a rectangle, then again, then again, then again. Man-shaped, the dark, lustrous material soaked up the last rays of the setting sun and split open, head to toe, a powerful hand wrenching the cloth aside.

Mohammed sat up from darkness, then rose from the deck, naked save for a tall staff of fig wood held in one hand. Wind gusting from the white-capped sea tangled the glossy cloth into an unruly wad. Fluttering, the scrap of black silk lifted from the deck, whirled past the feet of the Queen's guardsmen and disappeared over the side of the ship.

The Arab, chest covered by a flowing white beard, took in the vista of ships and sea and mountain, keen eyes counting masts, gauging the seaworthiness of the fleet. He saw many ships flying the twin-palmed flag of Palmyra and more with a familiar green banner snapping in the wind. He saw two thrones facing away from him, surrounded by hard-faced men in desert robes. No one was looking in his direction and Mohammed regretted the fate that had brought him here. *I am among the enemy*, he realized, *though many names and faces are familiar to me*.

Someone called from the foredeck and Mohammed's eyes flickered in recognition. *Our young Eagle*.

Turning, he stepped to the railing, looked down into the darkening sea, and dove—pale body flashing into the water with an abrupt slap—and he was gone. Ceaseless waves rolled past, obscuring the trace of his passage.

Wind tangled in the Queen's hair, rattling jewels and gold. The *Asura* pitched in a heavy sea, her rigging and mast creaking in gusting wind. She turned her head to look upon the dark, still shape of the Jackal sitting beside her in gray and gray, with a torc of silver around his neck and iron bracelets upon well-muscled arms.

"My lord?" she said quietly. The passage of time and many days spent in close company—both in Pharoah's court and upon the fleet beating up from Egypt to this abandoned shore—had dulled a little of the pain his visage brought, but not all. The Queen found the jutting ears, the snarling muzzle entirely repulsive, the mockery of a man lacerating her heart. But now the signal had come from the shore—hundreds of Huns arrayed on the beach, the black banner rippling with ringed serpents raised high—their master had reached the isle and commanded their presence. "We must go ashore."

Her entreaty was met with silence and a strange, half-felt emptiness. Forcing herself, the Queen touched the jackal's hand and found the brown flesh cold and inert. She stiffened, rising halfway from her seat and a fierce young voice spoke sharply in her thoughts.

Let me see him! Zoë surged forward, swelling in Zenobia's suddenly crippled thoughts.

The girl forced white hands to touch the cold, mottled iron of the mask, then press against a broad, muscular chest. The scars and puckered wounds under her fingers yielded nothing, neither life nor the dreadful semblance imparted by the sorcerer's will.

He is gone, Zoë said, voice sighing in wonder. *He has escaped!*

No! Wailed Zenobia, cringing away from fate and the dead, now truly-lifeless corpse of her lover. *No! He cannot leave me alone! I waited for him, I waited . . .*

Drums boomed across the water, interrupting the Queen's despair. Both minds turned, the body's eyes mixing blue and brown as they both struggled to see. On the shore, men poured forth from longboats and skiffs, galleys grinding to a halt in the shallows. The dead were waking, crowding the decks of every ship, sightless eyes turned to the beach. A long arc of the beach was dotted with companies and regiments gathering, the banners of Persia and Nabatea and the Decapolis snapping in the stiff, offshore wind.

Zoë made their body rise, hand rising to shade brown eyes. *There will be fighting! The Romans are here!*

Already? How can . . . Zenobia stirred, quick mind canvassing the fleet—still so many ships waiting to land, more than half—and then the wooded fields. The last ruddy rays of the sun gleamed on metal—helmets, spears, marching shields—and instinct and long-held command carried her to the fore.

"We must disembark," the Queen cried, striding forth from her throne. The guardsmen turned, faces brightening with the thought of battle. Khalid was first among them, and he too had spied the Huns running towards the trees, bows already lofting arrows into the ranks of the enemy. "Launch every barge and boat! Let the dead walk or swim ashore—they've no need to breathe—battle is swift upon us!"

Is the Roman prince here? Zenobia demanded of Zoë, though the girl was still focusing the bright core of her perception, preparing to enter the hidden world. *Can you feel him?*

No, Auntie, Zoë snapped, *I've only just started!*

The Queen restrained a curse, struggling for patience.

)H(

"There she is," Vladimir whispered, curly dark hair bound back behind his head, heavy iron scales wrapping his powerful shoulders and back. "The house with the high gate and a moon carved in stone above the lintel."

Nicholas eased his head around the corner, eyes narrowed in falling twilight. He saw nothing, only an empty alley, untenanted even by cats or wild dogs. "I don't see anything," he growled, though softly. Their informer had only given them a vague location, based on a half-heard whisper in the bustling port of Ostia. The Latin was trusting the Walach's uncanny nose for the rest.

Vladimir's long face twitched with a smile. "No, she's a flighty doe, that one, with a soft tread and quiet ways." Something turned in his gruff voice, steeped in grief. "But she loves the smell of pine and juniper and sweet flowers. I can smell her, even from here."

"Good," Nicholas looked away from his friend, avoiding the Walach's wounded expression. "Centurion—post a cohort at each end of this alley, then take your men *quietly* round to the front and break down the door. Bring the other ram up here. We've run this ship aground, but there are captives aboard our master needs alive."

Vladimir continued to watch the gate while Nicholas dispersed his men. The Walach felt cold, though the dusk was very warm and a vision of Betia leaning against the railing of a trim ship, the blue-green sea framing her tanned face and fine blond hair filled his thoughts.

"Quit mooning about," Nicholas said, thumping his shoulder with a mailed gauntlet. The Latin's scent had changed, spiky with anger and frustration. Vladimir looked up, seeing a tense, bitter expression on his friend's face. "They're inside and I want to finish this. We'll wait just a bit, until the others are at the front door."

"Empress . . . time to leave." Thyatis knelt beside the cot, scarred fingers brushing short brown hair out of Helena's face. The older woman's eyes flickered open at the touch. Thyatis allowed herself only the briefest frown at the dull expression. The Empress's eyes slid away from hers. "Very well." Thyatis stood, then bent down and scooped Helena up, the thin body almost weightless in her arms.

"No," the Empress protested, though her voice was even fainter than before. "Take my son . . ."

"We're all going," Thyatis muttered, hoisting the woman onto her back, arms loose around her neck. "Let's go," she called to the others in the cellar.

Shirin was right at Thyatis' side, flashing a warm smile at the Empress and a frown at her friend. "You're very inconspicuous this way . . ." The Khazar woman's nimble fingers rearranged Helena's grip on Thyatis' chest and tied the two together with strips of cloth. ". . . but we can say your mother is sick, if we have to."

Thyatis caught Shirin's hand and drew her close. The Khazar woman fell silent, lifting her face and Thyatis kissed her soundly, crushing Shirin's slimmer frame to her with one free arm. After a moment, they broke apart and Thyatis managed a rueful smile.

"We're all going together," the Roman said, leaning close to her lover. "But if anything happens, you take the boy yourself and get away." Thyatis' voice settled to a flat, hard tone like iron pig. "Go home, if you can. If we're separated, I will make my way to Itil."

Shirin's luminous eyes widened and she snuck a look over her shoulder at Betia and Koré and the Duchess, who were waiting by the foot of the stairs. "What about . . ."

Thyatis pressed Shirin's hand to her face, turning her cheek into the warm palm. With a quiet sigh, she said, "he has to get out of the Empire and *no one* knows you're here. They'll be watching all the Duchess's ships and agents and the sea road west." Shirin grimaced, but nodded very slightly.

"Let's go," Thyatis said in a louder voice, holding onto the Empress with one hand and picking up her scabbarded spatha with the other. Betia led, darting up the stairs with Shirin on her heels. Koré scuttled along next, little Theodosius cocooned against her chest with braided cloth. Thyatis shifted in her boots, then took the steps one at a time, letting the Empress's weight settle against her. Helena groaned a little—she was sore from head to toe, though she'd barely moved for a day—then her thin hands clutched at Thyatis' tunic, fingernails catching on the mailed shirt beneath. "Come on, Anastasia."

The Duchess looked around the cellar for the last time, then snuffed out the wick of the single remaining candle and hurried to follow.

Thyatis loped out into the main atrium of the house and turned to the right, heading for a flight of stairs rising to the second floor. Almost immediately, she saw the others had not gone the same way. She skidded to a halt. Anastasia slowed up, looking around in alarm. "Where . . ."

"They went outside," Thyatis snapped. "Go get them—we daren't leave this house on the ground! There are informers and patrols everywhere on the streets."

The Duchess nodded and ran off through the columned hall toward the garden. Thyatis snarled to herself, then bounded up the steps, past an internal door, to the top of the staircase. A short balcony opened from the landing, leading to two bedrooms. One side of the passage was open on the garden court at the center of the house and Thyatis leaned out, seeing three figures near the ornamental pool.

"This way," Thyatis called down, as softly as she could. Shirin looked up, her face a pale oval in falling twilight. Clouds had started to gather over the city as the sun set, and the light of myriad fires and lanterns below cast a dim yellow radiance on their white backdrop. Anastasia appeared in the courtyard and everyone ran back inside.

A dull *boom* echoed from below and Thyatis fell her heart skip, flutter and then beat strongly again.

"What was that?" Helena whispered in her ear.

"A ram," Thyatis said grimly, taking two long steps back to the top of the stairs. Koré bolted up the steps two and three at a time, her glossy black hair framing a determined, fierce expression. Thyatis stood aside, letting the little girl dart past. "The end of the landing," Thyatis called after her, "crawl out onto the roof, then to the north wall, just the way we came in!"

Without looking to see if the maid understood, Thyatis stepped down the stairs, her spatha rasping from its sheath. Shirin and Betia scrambled up past her and Thyatis growled. "What were you doing?"

"The garden gate leads into an alley . . ." Betia hissed, short of breath. "There's no one . . ."

Thyatis turned, fury building in her face. "Did you come back from your errand that way?"

"Yes—" Betia fell silent, seeing Thyatis' lips twitch into a flat, hard line. A heavy crash boomed up from below, followed by the sound of splintering wood. Distantly, men shouted.

"Go!" Thyatis jerked her head. Betia, flushing, was gone. Shirin tarried, her hands on the long knife she carried in her girdle. Thyatis fixed her with a piercing glare. "Take care of the boy."

The Khazar woman nodded, face dark against the fitful light outside. Her hand brushed Thyatis' cheek, leaving a tingling warmth and she ran the length of the landing and swung easily over the little wall. Terra-cotta tile creaked under her hands and feet as she scrambled across the roof.

"Anastasia!" Thyatis took another step down the stairs. The Duchess appeared in the doorway, hair coming loose, her long gown tangled. Face grim, the older woman swung the panel closed with a bang, then groped for a locking bar set against the wall. "Leave it!" Thyatis shouted.

Wood shattered, sounding close, and the baying of a dozen throats hot on the hunt rang and echoed in the main hall. Anastasia grunted, shoving the bar down against the retaining slats. One end stuck and she struggled to fit the bar properly into the groove.

Thyatis cursed, but the Duchess whirled as she prepared to leapt down to help her. "Get out!" Anastasia's face was a blur in the dim light, but the snap of command in her voice was unmistakable. Thyatis felt her heart wrench, then turned and sprinted back up the stairs.

* * *

Nicholas loped across the main hall—ears pricked for the sound of running feet on tile—and heard a clank of wood against wood off to his left. He turned swiftly, Brunhilde bare in his hand, her eager voice keening in his ears and the flicker of blue-white along her edge showed him a short flight of orna-mented marble steps leading up to a door. "Vlad, the door!"

The Walach burled past, powerful shoulders swinging, the long-bladed axe in his hands whipping around in a tight arc. The blade crashed into the door, shattering gold-painted panels and knocking a big section out of the frame. Someone shouted in alarm on the other side—a female voice—and the Walach slammed an armored shoulder into the wood. A splintering crash followed and the entire door frame tore away from the wall. Vladimir stumbled inside—he hadn't expected such flimsy construction—and Nicholas caught a glimpse of a woman in a formal stola and gown, her left arm stiff and swing-ing up at him, thumb twisting.

Blind instinct threw him to one side as he rushed into the doorway. Vladimir was down, sprawled on the floor in a ruin of broken panels and splintered wood. There was a sharp *twang* and something snapped past the Latin's head. Snarling, Nicholas lunged, the tip of dwarf-steel blade catching the woman under her raised arm. Steel sank into soft flesh and the woman grunted, thrown back against the wall. Without think-ing, Nicholas wrenched the blade free with a half-twist and smashed her down with the armored point of his elbow.

Behind him, there was commotion as the legionnaires poured into the house and torchlight flared on the walls of the stairwell. Nicholas saw on opening at the top and leapt in pursuit of the enemy, blood slicking away from Brunhilde's blade.

Vladimir tore his shoulder free from the remains of the door and rose to his hands and feet. Nicholas had disappeared up the stair-case. Directly in front of the Walach, a woman was sprawled on the steps, her mane of curly dark hair matted and tangled, one hand pressed against a deep wound in her side. Blood spilled be-tween white fingers, slicking the curve of her breast.

"Ahhh, it's cold," she gasped, barely able to breath. Vladimir crawled forward, wondering if this were the Empress they sought. He saw she had been blessed with a nearly perfect oval face, hawk-wing brows and plush, rich lips. *The Empress has shorter hair*, the Walach remembered. He hissed, seeing the depth of her wound.

"Who—" The woman opened her eyes and Vladimir felt cold, stunned shock burn through him. They were a glorious pale violet and his nostrils twitched, taking in a heady smell of blood, sweat, myrrh and honey. *She smells like . . .* His hand—moving with its own purpose—brushed back the tangle of dark curls around her face. *She is beautiful. This must be Betia's mistress, the Duchess Anastasia.* The too-familiar smell registered and he slumped back, stunned beyond measure.

"Vladimir," he said, barely able to speak. "I'm Vladimir. My lady . . . I'm sorry."

The woman tried to smile, but blood welled from her mouth and she stared to choke. Gently, Vladimir turned her head, letting the fluid pour from her mouth. Her skin was very warm under his fingers. Desperately, he pressed hard on her wound, trying to stop the flow of blood. "Thank you, Vladimir," she managed to say and a genuine smile lit her features, shining through sweat and blood. "Betia . . . *cough*. . . . said you had a kind heart."

The Walach felt his guts twist. "Nicholas didn't mean . . . he wouldn't have. . . ." Vladimir stuttered to a halt, unable to express the enormous, overwhelming feeling of grief crushing his chest. "He didn't know you were his sister!"

The Duchess's brows drew together and for a moment the agony seemed to fade, leaving only a puzzled, beautiful woman. "I've no bro . . . oh—oh, I remember—the collar hurt his neck and made him cry . . . his eyes . . ."

"Are yours! Your faces—your smell—everything . . ." Vladimir twisted, trying to see if anyone had come into the house. "I'll send for a healer, mistress, it'll only be a moment!"

"Vladimir," Anastasia's voice was barely audible and the Walach could feel a chill mounting in her chest like rising water. Already her legs were heavy with death. "You must take care of Betia," she said, face turning pale. Her hand closed tightly over his. "This is only misfortune . . ."

She started to choke again and Vladimir tried to roll her over, but she shuddered in his arms and grew entirely still. The Walach started to weep and his tears mixed with the blood fouled in her garments, leaving thin silver trails on the side of her neck and face. Gently, he laid Anastasia down upon the steps and straightened her gown and stole, crossing pale arms across her chest.

For the first time, the smell of so much fresh blood did not spark hunger in his breast.

Thyatis ran lightly along the roof ridge, her weight making the curved tiles creak and splinter. The sun had set at last; leaving the city sprawled below her dark save for the slow appearance of glowing windows and bonfires in the public squares. Low clouds drifted across the sky, shining with a reflected orange glow, letting her see just a little. On her back, the Empress wheezed in pain with each jarring step.

Thyatis reached the wall at the end of the roof and raised her head. On the floor above in an adjoining building, Shirin's tense face stared down between sections of crosshatched wooden lattice. Upon entering the Duchess's safe house, they had taken one of the lattice sections out. Thyatis waved, then halted, gauging the distance. Coming down had been easy—a light drop after hanging on the lip of the upper balcony—but getting up was going to be difficult.

"Hand her up," Shirin hissed, reaching down with both hands. "I'll lift—" The Khazar woman's head jerked up and her eyes went wide in alarm. She scuttled backwards out of sight. Thyatis spun, feet sliding on the tiled roof, her spatha flickering into guard position.

Nicholas advanced towards her, his heavy boots cracking tile, sending slivers of red pottery bouncing down the sloping roof. The Empress's hands tightened on Thyatis' armor and her legs scissored tight around the younger woman's waist. Thyatis felt a great calm come over her—her peripheral vision fading to gray, shutting out the sight of the garden below her on the right, now filling with armed men; and the two-story drop to the street on her left. She took the spatha hand and hand, remembering the power in Nicholas' shoulders and arms.

The Latin advanced, footing unsteady, his boots finding purchase difficult on the rows of terra-cotta, but the blade in his
hands was steady, flickering with a sullen, half-hidden light. He
said nothing, but Thyatis could feel his fury radiating like the
glow of a banked oven.

"Cut me loose," Helena whispered in her ear. Thyatis shook
her head. She shifted her footing on the tiled roof, the pressure
of the Empress's weight vanishing as bloodfire kicked through
her veins. With slow grace, she turned in line with Nicholas,
blade swinging back and up. He matched her motion, but again,
his footing was precarious.

For a moment, they froze, each in balance, watching and
waiting. The legionnaires in the courtyard fell silent as well,
their rude cries dying down. Tense expectation settled on the
rooftop; the warm, humid night drawing close around them.
Thyatis realized with faint regret she would have to kill every
man in the house if she were to escape.

Nicholas attacked, the gleaming blade flashing at Thyatis'
face. She blocked the blow away and down, steel ringing high
and clear, then there was a blur of cut and counter-cut. He gave
a step, then two, back foot sliding on the tile and she reversed,
whipping the spatha at his exposed knee. Grunting, face
streaming with sweat, Nicholas parried, catching her blow
inches from his leg. Thyatis bore down, forcing the shimmering
blade into the tile with a squeal of metal.

The Latin struggled to rise, failed, then wrenched his sword
away. The spatha sprang back with a ringing sound and
Nicholas rolled away. Almost immediately he slid, clattering
down the rooftop, fingers clawing at the tile, terra-cotta shattering under the impact. His foot fetched up against a drainpipe
along the edge of the roof and he slammed to a halt. Nerves
singing, Thyatis darted towards the balcony. Legionnaires began to shout and there was a commotion as the men in the
courtyard scrambled into the house to cut her off.

Only a single figure remained in the courtyard, a silver-
haired old man in patrician's robes, his face turned to the skyline. Thyatis skidded to the end of the roof, then slid sideways,
one hand catching an overhanging eave to stop her. She bent
down, preparing to swing onto the landing.

Vladimir was waiting, axe poised, his pale face framed by unruly waves of hair. He looked dreadful, face mottled and streaked, but his hands were firm on the haft of the war axe. Thyatis saw him and stopped, searching his face. The Walach advanced a step, teeth gritted, eyes enormous and filled with anguish.

"Don't . . ." he managed to choke out, licking his lips. Thyatis was very still. Boots clattered on the stairs, mixed with sound of shouting. Torches flared in the passage.

The Roman woman smiled, catching the Walach's eye with her own. "Be well, Vlad," she said and scrambled back up onto the spine of the roof. She came up, one hand out of balance, the spatha drifting out of guard. Nicholas rushed forward, his blade glittering with pale color and she grunted with the effort of swinging the cavalry sword into the path of his blow. The impact knocked her back, one leg twisting under her and the spatha shrilled, metal screeching as Nicholas caught her blade square on edge. The spatha rang like a bell, iron cracking end to end and the sword splintered. Iron fragments zipped past her face, one scoring her cheek. Thyatis' arm shuddered, stunned, and she could barely make nerveless fingers fling the useless hilt aside.

Nicholas windmilled a second cut, his blade cleaving the air where her head had been. The Empress screamed, crushed under Thyatis' armored weight as she fell. A wild hand groped at the side of the younger woman's face. Thyatis rolled aside, trying to spare Helena, feeling tile shatter and crack as her feet groped for purchase. Broken tile cascaded toward the street. Nicholas crabbed down the incline, the tip of his sword punching the air. Thyatis scrambled aside and the blade sheared through three layers of terra-cotta with a *crack!* Nicholas started to slip himself, staggering, trying to catch his balance.

Thyatis scrambled back to the roof ridge, one hand steadying her, the other drawing a dagger from her belt. She glanced sideways and saw Vladimir crawling out from the balcony, his feet bare, the axe clutched in one hand. The lone man was still standing in the garden below and she risked a look over her shoulder at the adjoining building. The Empress's breath was harsh in her ear.

No one peered down from the trellised balcony and the section of crosshatched wood had been replaced. Thyatis hissed in dismay, though her heart leapt with the hope her friends had escaped. The sound of creaking tile snapped her head around and she scuttled back, the dagger feeling painfully small in her left hand.

Nicholas did not delay, rushing in, his face contorted with a cold, determined rage. Thyatis lunged forward, the dagger slashing left to catch the glittering sword, her right fist swinging at the man's nose. The two blades met and the lighter dagger twisted away. Gasping, Thyatis felt her arm wrenched aside by the blow, the longsword thrusting past as her fist crunched into the side of Nicholas' face. His head snapped to one side, but he did not go down. Time seemed to slide to a halt, Thyatis tottering back, sandals slipping on the loose tile, Nicholas recovering. His blade ripped back in a savage sideways cut and Thyatis felt the blow as a massive concussion to her side. Breath rushed from her mouth, metal squealed, mailed links shattering as the dwarf-steel sword clove through Helena's outflung arm and into Thyatis' ribs.

She crashed backwards, the Empress crying out, and slid sickeningly down the roof, tile shattering and splintering. Both women hit the edge of the roof, the gutter—poorly fired pottery—disintegrating and they fell, limbs cartwheeling. Thyatis tried to twist into the fall, but hit the top of a vine trellis with her chest, crushing the last breath from her and everything went black in a roar of shattering wood, falling tile and then a dull, wet *crunch!*

One last tile slithered from the roof and spun through the air, shattering on the paving below. Gaius Julius blinked but did not flinch away from the sound. With a sigh, he returned his gladius to the leather sheath with a soft *click*. The sounds of men running echoed from the house, but for the moment the old Roman was alone in the courtyard. Repressing an urge to vomit, Gaius picked his way through the ruins of the vine trellis. Bending down, he lifted shattered, twisted wood and foliage away from the two twisted bodies in the garden plot. Helena's pale face stared up, eyes sightless, framed by crushed roses and lilies. Her body was hidden under the bulkier, broader shape of her protector.

The old Roman surprised himself with the strength in his arms, straining to move the heavy, armored body aside. Beneath her, the Empress lay contorted, one arm ending abruptly in a severed forearm. A sluggish flow of wine-colored fluid spilled from the mangled limb and Gaius Julius felt his stomach roil as he sagged into the mushy, blood-soaked soil. Trying to keep his fingers from trembling, Gaius touched her pale, unmarked neck. The skin was growing cold, *Oh, no,* he thought mournfully. His thumb peeled back an eyelid, revealing the sightless stare of the dead. *Dead already from the loss of so much blood . . .*

The old Roman pressed a hand to his mouth, taking a breath, and then another. *Why have things ended this way*? he wondered, feeling all of his plans and intrigues turning sour. There was no joy in this—he had never intended for anyone *important* to die. Some of the lesser lights could be snuffed, to show he meant business, but Galen and Helena? They had entertained him at dinner, listened to his stories, even laughed at his jests . . .

"Well?" a thin, strained voice echoed down from above. Gaius Julius looked up, seeing Nicholas silhouetted against the softly glowing clouds. The old Roman tried to speak, but had to cough, clearing his throat before he could respond.

"She is dead," he said, feeling anew the pain of such bald words.

"And the other?" Nicholas' sword shifted, pointing, a pale brand against the darkness.

Gaius Julius managed to turn the armored body. The face was revealed, matted with mud, scratches tearing one eyelid, a cloak and mailed armor shattered and wadded around the woman's chest. The old Roman felt another shock, a cold, icy blow stunning his troubled mind to stillness. *Diana? My Diana? No . . . Thyatis. Her name was Thyatis.*

He wiped mud and flower petals away from high cheekbones, bloody fingers leaving a smear. Her skin was clammy. Gaius Julius bent his head for a moment, remembering the fire in her brilliant gray eyes as she wrenched her hand from his grasp in the garden of Gregorius Auricus. A brief vision of her dueling on the white-hot sand of the arena tormented him, slowly replaced by her slack, pale visage in this ruin and mud.

"Dear Amazon," he whispered, "how could this happen to you? Aren't you invincible?"

Gaius felt his knees and supporting hand sink into the garden mud, finding himself beyond caring for his ruined garments. He struggled against hot tears, shocked to feel such grief for an opponent. *Why is my heart so stricken?* Gaius struggled to think, though his thoughts seemed to crawl where once they had sped. *Are these dear enemies so precious?*

Then he felt a fluttering breath against his hand. Gaius Julius froze, staring at her bloody face. Thyatis' lips seemed to move slightly and her eyelids twitched. *She lives?*

The old Roman pressed long fingers to the side of her neck and there—faint, but unmistakable—was a thready, uneven pulse. *She does, but not for long, if my young friend's anger is let loose upon her.* A cloud of wild thoughts distracted him for an instant, though his heart had already decided what must be done. Gaius Julius looked up. Nicholas was still crouched at the edge of the rooftop, staring down with a hard-set grimace.

"She is dead," the old Roman said, rising to his feet. "What about the boy?"

"Gone," Nicholas answered. Vladimir stood behind him, shaggy mane stirred by the night wind, a black outline against the dim sky.

"Find him," Gaius replied, despair curdling to anger in his breast. "Search the neighboring buildings, cellars, closets, everywhere! Find the boy and bring him back to me alive!"

The Latin nodded as he turned away, one hand on Vladimir's shoulder. The Walach stared into the courtyard for a moment, then followed. Gaius Julius looked back down at the bodies at his feet.

"Sir? What should we do with them?" The centurion in charge of the cohort loitering at the edge of the garden stared at him, face drawn and pasty white behind the slash of his chin strap.

"Take . . . the Empress to the Palatine and set her beside her husband." Gaius Julius' voice grew colder with each syllable. "Treat her gently, Claudius. Make a bier from your spears and quilts taken from the house. One cohort shall march before and one behind. Let no man will speak until you have laid her to rest."

The centurion nodded jerkily. The old Roman's eyes dragged towards the other corpse.

"She. . . ." Gaius Julius felt his loss as a physical pain, a pressure in his chest. He turned away with obvious effort. *Perhaps your goddess will watch over you, protect you, if you've even the least chance at life* . . . "Put her in the wagons with the other traitors. Let them burn her, in the abattoir beyond the city walls."

Vladimir searched along a kitchen wall, the axe tight in his hands, heart thudding wildly in his chest. Nicholas stalked behind him, the dwarf blade in his hand humming with excitement. The Walach tried to block out the wild voice ringing from the steel, begging for slaughter. *I've had enough death today. . . .* The smell of so much fresh blood had set his mind reeling and he could only move in a crouch. With a fierce effort, he kept himself from running on all fours, but his sense of smell unfolded, showing him ancient trails of mice, the passages of men and women through the kitchens and bedrooms of this apartment. The flood of sensation was overpowering.

He stopped abruptly, drawing an alarmed hiss from Nicholas. Vladimir sidled up to a wall, sharp talons scratching across a wooden door. Stagnant air moved beyond the panel, carrying a ferocious stench. "Here," he said, tasting Betia's sweat and a young human needing to empty his weak bladder.

Nicholas waved him aside, then smashed in the cabinet door with his iron-shod boot. A gaping, dark opening was revealed and a noisome, thick odor rolled out. The Latin peered down the stone-lined shaft.

"Bring a light!" he barked and one of the legionnaires following along behind passed up a watchman's candle lantern. Holding the light out over the shaft, Nicholas stared down. "A rubbish tip, into a sewer," he said, voice muffled. "But there is a ladder, which has been recently used."

Without waiting for a response, Nicholas passed the lantern back before swinging into the opening and descending the ladder with reckless speed. Vladimir followed, though the foul miasma clogged his noise and made his head hurt.

At the bottom of the pit, they stood ankle-deep in slowly moving water. The walls dripped with humidity and thick green

slime. Vladimir coughed, trying to breath. Nicholas seemed unaffected by the stench.

"Which way?" the Latin growled, jabbing to the right with
his sword. As before, in the absence of any greater light, the
blade began to gleam a soft blue-white. The Walach stared
around in disgust, but saw nothing like a track or sign.

"Betia knew I would follow." Vladimir coughed, feeling his
throat clogging with the awful smell. "I can't make out anything down here. We'll just have to pick a direction. . . ."

"You go to the left," Nicholas replied with a curse, his jaw
clenched tight. He splashed away to the right, leaving Vladimir
in steadily growing darkness. Above, the legionaries stared
down the shaft, their lantern casting a fitful dim glow on the
ladder. Vladimir stared after his friend, shaking his head slowly.
The Walach was no stranger to death—he had taken innocent
lives when he could no longer control the pain in his bones—
but Nicholas seemed transformed, all pity leached away, his
heart wounded by Thyatis' betrayal. *Cruel fate digs her claws
deep*, Vladimir thought mournfully. *He is blind and sinking
deeper into such a hell . . .*. Standing in the sewer tunnel, half
bent under the low ceiling, the Walach resolved never to tell his
friend—*he is still my brother in blood and arms!*—who he'd so
carelessly murdered in the hallway. *I will spare him the stain of
kin slayer, at least*.

Mind still wild with bloody deeds, Vladimir slung the axe
over his back and scuttled off down the tunnel, finding surcease
in going on hands and feet, as generations of his forefathers had
done. After a hundred feet, the way split, one arched passage
tending down the hill, the other rising. Brow wrinkled in debate, Vladimir turned towards the descending passage, then
stopped shock still. The hackles on his neck stiffened and he
growled in alarm.

The K'shapâcara Queen! his mind gibbered, filled with
atavistic fears. *How can the Dark Lady be here?*

He tried to press on, but the rank smell brought harsh memories to mind and after a moment of dithering, Vladimir backed
away and began climbing the rising tunnel. He glanced behind
him often, nerves still taut with fear, but he saw nothing.

* * *

"He is gone," Koré said softly, yellow-green eyes glittering in the darkness. Shirin relaxed a little, though her flesh crawled with the clinging taint of the sewer and the sharp fear of pursuit. The little girl moved past, one hand tucked around little Theodosius, the other tapping along the curving wall. "If we go this way," Koré hissed, "we'll reach the river. Perhaps there will be a boat."

Filled with disquiet, Shirin followed, keeping close to the girl. They had descended through two joining chambers—where other pipes fed into the main sewer—before she realized Betia was no longer with them.

"What other body?" Gaius Julius looked up in the darkness of the main hall, sluggish thoughts stirring to slow motion. An earnest-looking young legionary stood atop a short flight of steps, in an opening filled with the splintered remains of a door frame. "No, I'll see for myself."

The old Roman stepped onto the staircase and looked down. The sight of more blood failed to move him—he felt numbed—but the sight of this face and body sprawled in unkind death forced a groan of dismay from his lips. The legionnaire drew back, Gaius Julius waving for him to leave.

"This is a cruel winter," he muttered, kneeling beside Anastasia's body. There were welts on her white neck where a necklace had been torn away by greedy hands and her left wrist was scored with deep cuts. Her rings and bracelets were gone. Gaius' fingers drifted over the signs of looting, then to the serene, quiet face. Even in death, with her lips parted and a thick trail of congealing blood puddling on the steps under her mouth, he could see her beauty linger. "So many blossoms withered, so many buds cut down by sudden frost."

He turned the corner of her stole over the face and composed her hands and feet as best he could in the cramped confines of the stair. All light seemed to have fled, leaving him entirely in darkness, accompanied only by the pale corpse, her raiment gleaming in the night. Gaius Julius sat on the step, chin on his folded hands. *What a bleak world*, he thought, overcome by terrifying emptiness. *Where every fair enemy is struck down and nothing bright remains*. He had felt something like this before, when he had achieved victory over Pompey the Great at last and the world lay in the cup of his hands. An end of challenge, the cessation of everything that fired his blood to life and moved his agile mind to delight.

"No one can deny," he said at last in a choked voice, harsh sound echoing in the empty hall. The legionaries had carried the bodies away, leaving him entirely alone. . . . "that during the civil war, and after, Caesar behaved with wonderful restraint and clemency. Whereas his opponents declared all those not with them enemies of the state; Caesar accounted every man not against him, his ally. He forgave all crimes, pardoned all prisoners, returned their properties, sponsored their children, made good their debts . . ."

Overcome, Gaius Julius covered his face with his cloak, unable to speak, wrinkled old face streaming with tears, his thin shoulders shaking.

Vladimir heaved himself up into a brick chamber, his long fingers scraping through a thick, gray slime clinging to the lip of the pipe. The cavity was very dark and he groped across the floor, fearing another pit yawned before him. His outstretched fingers touched something warm and he became very still. The sensitive pads on his fingertips traced the outline of a toe, then another, then a slim foot.

"Who is there?" he breathed, barely able to raise his voice. A familiar smell tried to separate itself from the foul miasma in the tunnel.

"Hello, Vladimir." Betia drew back a heavy cloak from her face and his sharp eyes found her outline—a faint reddish smear against the cold walls. "You've caught me."

"No!" The Walach's exclamation was abrupt and unplanned. "Betia, you should flee . . ."

Her fingers pressed against his lips, then her gentle hand caressed his short beard, the side of his face, his powerful neck. "I am tired of running away," she said, crawling to him. "Take me to my mistress, she'll need me in captivity."

A groan escaped the Walach, his free arm crushing the girl to his chest. He buried his face in her hair, breath hot on her neck. "No . . . you must fly away from here, far away."

"What happened?" Betia's voice changed, catching his anguish and her small hands framed his face, her lips brushing against his. "Where is the Duchess?"

"Dead," Vladimir managed in a choked voice. "An accident . . ."

The girl stiffened, her forehead pressing against his. "Truly?" Voice was very faint, but then she shook her head. "You must come away with me," she said. "I know where a ship is waiting. . . ."

Vladimir shook his head slowly, though his heart leapt to say *Yes!* "I've sworn an oath . . ." His fingers pressed against his chest, feeling the prince's amulet. The metal was a little warm, comforting against his hand. Like her body conforming to his, her arms around his neck. "I . . . I cannot go with you."

Betia's body slumped against his and she sighed in exhaustion. "Take me with you, then."

"With me? But . . ."

"No one will notice a servant," she said, head buried against his chest. "No one at all."

⊡◘O◘-O◘-O◘-O◘-O◘-O◘-O◘-O◘-O◘-O◘-O◘-O◘-O◘-O◘-O◘-O◘-O◘-O◘⊡

THE CATANIAN SHORE, SICILIA

)I(

"Where are we?" Alexandros shouted, his strong voice carrying in the humid afternoon air. He rode at the head of a column of his Companions—the Gothic knights astride heavy warhorses, armored from head to foot in the Eastern style, great bows jutting from sheaths on their saddles. Two of his scouts emerged from a thicket of dusky gray brush on the meandering farm track ahead. The Macedonian spurred Bucephalas the Black forward, the stallion catching his master's tense mood. "Where is the sea?"

The scouts stared back at him in alarm, their faces red with the sun and scratched by low-hanging branches. One of them—

with the shoulder flash of a file leader—swallowed nervously and jogged up to Alexandros' stirrup. "My lord! We thought *this* was the way to the beach!"

"Who is behind you, then?" The Macedonian's voice came in a harsh snap.

"The whole of the sixth syntagma, my lord," the man answered in a rush. "The syntagmarch said march away from the sun, great lord, but we've gotten turned around in these lanes . . ."

Alexandros stopped the man with a raised hand. His eyes glittered in fury. "Climb a tree, now!"

Moments later, the younger—lighter—scout was swaying in the branches of a tall poplar, shading his eyes against the last gleam of the day. He stiffened, one hand clutching the thin trunk. His free hand stabbed out, pointing left of the farm track. "There," he shouted, "a fleet! A whole fleet! Hundreds of sails!"

"How far?" Alexandros bellowed, while the cavalrymen behind him stared nervously into a dense boscage of vines, creepers, silver-barked trees and thorn between them and the presumed enemy.

"Less than a mile, my lord," the scout replied. "This track turns and swings towards open ground and grassy bluffs."

"Double-time," the Macedonian roared to his signalmen and file captains. Without waiting for the scout to clamber down from the tree, he urged Bucephalas on and the horse thundered down the lane, Alexandros leaning close to the stallion's neck, branches whipping at his shoulders. The earth trembled as the rest of the column kicked to a trot. Dust boiled up from the dry road, coating the horses' chests and making men blink.

The lead scout jumped out of the way, crushing himself against a stand of holly to avoid being trampled. His own column was only moments from marching onto the road, pikes and axes swinging and there would be a Fury's own mess if the two groups collided. Ignoring his junior, who was swinging precariously in the treetop, the lead scout crashed off through the tangled undergrowth, bawling "column halt!" at the top of his lungs.

Attend me, beloved Arad! The Lord of the Ten Serpents turned his attention from the land, where C'hu-lo and his Huns were gathering in a lean, dark circle around the copse of trees where Dahak had made his temporary command post. T'u-chüeh archers laughed in the shade of intertwined trees, unpacking long curved bows they had carried ashore wrapped in leather and waxed cloth. The sorcerer felt much at ease, knowing he would not be taken unawares. He squatted at the base of a tree, his banner flapping smartly in the wind only paces away. *Have you come ashore?*

The mental query was met by unexpected silence—more than the attenuation of distance or the interference of the sea— but an emptiness, a void from which Dahak's tendril of thought did not return. *Arad?* The sorcerer's lean head stiffened, turning to face the glittering water. Triply-lidded eyes flickered, focusing on the rakish shape of the Palmyrene flagship. The *Asura* rode easily at anchor, her sails furling as sailors scrambled in the yards, dragging in canvas. *Where are you?*

Dahak realized he had not felt the mournful wail and lament of the Egyptian priest's mind for some time. He concentrated, feeling a sickly, cold fear welling up at the back of his own thoughts. *The Queen, the Boar, the Eagle, the Sixteen . . .* he could feel all his servants, even the least, the *gaatasuun* and their harsh, singular thoughts of blood and sharp teeth crunching through flesh. But not the first tool he had made with his own hands.

Arad? Faithful servant? Dahak wailed, reaching out into the emptiness. *Gone? Gone? How could you escape these bindings? These chains?* Rage flared in the sorcerer's heart and he leapt to his feet, the air around him darkening with malefic power. *Return to me!*

There was no answer, though the tall poplar at his back shriveled and cracked, suddenly dead leaves falling in a drifting rain around him. "Arad!"

Shahr-Baraz splashed ashore, hairy feet bare on clinging black sand, low waves rushing past with a *hiss* of spray and foam. Riding boots hung around his neck on a leather thong—a cumbersome, heavy weight of leather reinforced with strips of iron—but worse still if they were wet. The soldier Patik was only a pace behind, followed by a crowd of Immortals, bannermen, trumpeters, runners and aides. The Boar found his footing on drier sand and picked up the pace, massive thighs propelling him up the beach without pause.

The shoreline itself ran in shallow, then rose up at a line of hard-packed dark sand mixed with debris from passing ships and storms. Beyond the tide line, a hundred feet—or less—of rumpled sand dunes slanted up in a gentle shelf and then the shore proper began, with scattered grass-covered dunes, stands of cork trees and the lower, marshier outlets of streams.

Shahr-Baraz found the banners of two regiments of Persian footmen standing above the tide line, surrounded by a mixed crowd of soldiers. Thousands of *gaatasuun* were crawling from the sea in complete disorder, wandering aimlessly in packs, forcing the living men to form a barrier of steel and wooden shields around the banners to protect themselves. Officers were shouting, trying to make themselves heard above the rush of the sea. The following wind, which had driven the fleet from Alexandria with such speed, snapped the banners taut, throwing sea spray and sand against their backs. The Boar growled, drawing the attention of those nearest to him and stormed into a cluster of men in peaked helmets and sunflower insignia.

"Who commands here?" he roared, grasping one *diquan* by shoulders and setting the surprised man aside by main strength. "Why are you standing about?"

A portly nobleman in the etched, fluted armor of the Kushan-shahr highlands stepped forward, making a deep bow to his king. "King of Kings," he declaimed in a serious voice, "we're trying to rally our men, and gather our companies, but—" The man waved his arm to encompass the long sweep of the shore. Everywhere, there were ships—some run aground, others standing offshore, soldiers piling into longboats—and the beach itself was no better, with the sodden dead crawling through the breakers, while men came ashore in dribs and drabs, as skiffs and barges could manage. The gusting wind made the sea rougher than Shahr-Baraz had expected and as he watched, a longboat turning away from the beach took a breaker abeam. Sailors tumbled into foaming white water as the boat capsized, oars splintering against the sandy bottom.

"—everywhere there is confusion. Only a handful of my

levies have found me." The Kushana finished, his own impatience and concern showing.

"Don't worry about that," Shahr-Baraz boomed, making every man in the group of officers start in alarm. "Take these men and push inland! Where you see the *gaatasuun*, drive them before you! Take any soldier, no matter his clan or house, under your banner. *We must* get off this beach!"

The Pashtun chief nodded, forked beard making a sharp shadow on his breastplate, then turned away, his own bull-like voice raised in command. "Men of Herat—with me! Persia, with me!"

The living soldiers crowded around the banners answered with their own shout, taking heart from his bold words and the entire mass of men began slogging inland through the deep sand. The Boar gestured for his own officers to attend him. "Here, you lot," he boomed, his powerful voice overreaching even the sea and the wind. "Patik—where is Prince Rustam?"

Patik had been surveying the beach, eyes shaded against the setting sun. "We've drifted north before this wind, my lord," he replied after a moment. "I see the prince's banner—he's a mile away or more south . . ."

"Go to him," the Boar snapped, his tone brooking neither delay nor disobedience. "Tell him to master his dead servants and send them inland. They're useless for fighting in formation, so they might as well bring confusion and despair upon the enemy."

Patik nodded, then jogged off through the sand. After a hundred paces, he swerved towards the waterline, where the footing was firmer. Shahr-Baraz immediately forgot him, turning to his other officers. "Piruz—you're a likely lad, beloved of my daughter—take a dozen men and move along the beach. Tell every officer and lord to take what men he can find and move inland with all speed! There's no time to muster properly, not in this chaos, so every *diquan* and lord must show boldness and daring, striking at the enemy with every means at their disposal."

The prince of Balkh nodded, sharply, his expression hungry for battle and glory.

"You boys," the Boar growled at the spry young lads he used

as couriers. "The rest of the *pushtigbahn* will be coming ashore somewhere near here. . . ." Shahr-Baraz waved a huge, armored hand in a vague circle. ". . . find them and send them to me. We will take yonder hill—" A empty grassy mound rose behind the beach, two hundred yards away. "—as our command post. Off with you!"

The Boar grinned then, drawing his own blade, a massive length of steel that measured more than most men could lift. He swung the sword inland, bellowing: "The rest of you, with me! Forward, to victory!"

Bucephalas burst from the trees and galloped across a swale of high grass. The rich, dark soil of the bottomlands turned to grainy obsidian-colored volcanic sand. Alexandros breathed a sigh of relief to see the green ocean swell before him and to get his cavalry free of the constricted lane. Then he cursed, the stallion slewing into deep, loose sand. He reined in before the horse broke a leg and pirouetted back onto harder ground. In the brief moment, he had looked down on the sweep of the beach and his heart froze with alarm.

The sea was black with ships, the dull gray strand swarming with Persians, their banners a forest, their spears glittering stars. He drew Bucephalas to a halt, the stallion snorting in disgust, and the Macedonian took a long, hard look up and down the beach. The rest of the Companions trotted out of the orchard lane, spilling to his left and right, automatically forming a loose, irregular line. The Gothic knights unlimbering their lances, preparing for a charge.

"All sections, halt along the verge," Alexandros shouted, turning so his captains could hear him and repeat the commands. "Dismount, send the horses back. Form two ranks! Philos—find the pike syntagma those scouts were talking about and get them up here, now!"

Immediately, there was confusion as men swung down from their horses, one in five grasping bundles of reins, hurrying to tie leads to the following mares. The grassy sward filled with a huge crowd; more men riding up from behind while others tried to move back. The Gothic captains and centurions were hoarse, screaming at their dull-witted charges, trying to form ranks while men rushed this way and that. Alexandros ground a fist into his saddle. *This is very bad*, he realized; nervous, quick eyes scanning the beach.

A mob of Persians moved slowly uphill towards him—he doubted they even realized his Companions were shaking out a confused, disordered line—they were certainly in no better order. But there were a great many of the enemy and there were so many ships offshore, crowding the sea with dozens of smaller craft. He glanced to the north.

In the distance, outlines shaded by humid air, he could make out the rooftops of a small town rising on a rocky headland. *Catania*, he thought, wishing suddenly he'd stopped the army in the little city at dawn. They had marched down from Messina with heedless speed. A day and night's march toward the looming cone of Aetna had been draining to men and horses alike. Now, today, they had put on another burst of speed—the prince had said the enemy would make landfall on "the beaches"— and here they were.

Seeing their numbers, the Macedonian felt a cold chill in his bones. *If we'd regrouped at the port, we could advance like a scythe, from north to south along the beach and slaughter these lambs as they came ashore, our lines orderly, our wings entirely in my sight.* Now, Alexandros was all too aware he'd scattered his forces piecemeal among the farm lanes and tracks behind of the beach. *Where is my vaunted skill now?* he thought harshly. *I should have been patient and sent out my scouts to spy the land and the positions of the enemy.*

Alexandros felt his stomach roil. He'd advanced recklessly, trusting to speed and surprise to overwhelm the enemy. "Krythos was right," he muttered under his breath. "I need to stay back."

"Orders, sir?" A captain of the Companions was standing at his foot, grizzled face looking up expectantly.

"Two ranks deep, Ostrys, and extend the line as far on the flanks as we can. Keep the Persians from getting off the sand." Alexandros squinted at the sky, taking some faint hope from the dwindling light. "When the pike syntagma gets here, form three ranks deep and advance in a wedge." He pointed down at the beach. "Cut your way to the waterline, then hold. If more men come up, expand the wedge to the left and the right."

"*Ja*, my lord." The Goth grinned. "Keep them in the sea, where they can drown before our shield wall."

"Yes," the Macedonian said sharply, "and keep them from gathering their forces!"

Now where should I be, Alexandros thought as he turned Bucephalas away from the sea. *I need to find the rest of my army.* He rode towards the thicket, though slowly, the big black forcing his way through a countervailing flow of pikemen. Long spears danced around him, a thicket of ash and iron, and the footmen swung past with a grin and a rousing shout. They were glad to be out of the claustrophobic trees as well. *How am I going to find anyone?* The Macedonian clucked, nudging the horse to the side of the road. A new column of men jogged towards him in the golden, late afternoon sunlight, through sparkling clouds of dust. He realized there was literally no way he could find anyone else—Chlothar, Krythos, any of his commanders—in the sprawl of hedges, meadows, streams and orchards behind the beach.

Grunting in dismay, Alexandros turned the stallion, then stopped abruptly, his eye hanging on something passing strange. The approaching column tramped smartly out of the lane, three banners—a golden hand, a silver eagle and a square plaque bearing a horned ram—leading the first ranks. These men were smartly equipped, oval shields slung on their arms, long spears in hand, feathered conical helms snug under shaven chins. A Roman officer—he could be no other, not with such a proud nose and grim expression—paced them on the left and Alexandros found himself staring down in surprise at the man.

"Who are you?" the Macedonian asked, feeling a chill to see the man's iron breastplate no more than shadow or mist and his speaking mouth like glass, showing trampled leaves and mud.

First Legio Roma, the ghost answered, saluting smartly. The centurion's eyes were dark pits, without even a gleam in their shadows. Pale teeth showed in a grin. *The Consul said the Epirotes are coming ashore? We're ready for another go at them, by Mars! We've waited a long time to even the score for Ausculum.*

"The . . . yes, they are landing from their ships, just over there." Alexandros pointed over the downs towards the sea. "My men will hold the center. You . . . take the right flank."

Ave! came a soundless response and the centurion turned away, broad hand chopping at the air. The ghostly ranks clashed spears silently on bronzed shields, then jogged on, a long, ceaseless line. The Macedonian watched them with slowly mounting fear eating away at his composure. By his count, at least four thousand men marched past, not one more than a pale outline, casting no shadow on the sunny ground, but in the dimness under the trees, they seemed almost solid.

Unwillingly, Alexandros looked to the sky and saw the sun touching the mountain peaks to the west. *It will be dark soon,* he thought. *Will I hear their battle cries then?*

A brace of Palmyrene sailors, stripped down to loincloths, bronzed limbs flashing in the water, ran the longboat ashore. The Queen swayed a little as the keel breasted on the sand, then her men braced the boat and she stepped down into shallow water. More boats followed, carrying her guardsmen from the *Asura.* The cool water felt good on her bare feet, splashing against armored greaves covering her trim calves. Zoë stood ready in the back of her mind, the center of a glittering dodecahedron of shifting light and half-seen patterns. *Can you feel him yet?* Zenobia asked.

No, but something is happening . . . there is a veritable army of lights snaking towards the beach from inland. Not men—not living men—but not these husks the Serpent has stirred to life either. They are very angry, I can feel that much!

"The Romans are coming," the Queen called to her captains. She saw the Palmyrene sailors and pilots had done well, keeping their flotilla together, the ships anchored to form a barrier against the wind. The Persian fleet—and she allowed herself a cold, satisfied smile—was in confusion, ships yawing against the breeze, some fouled in another's anchor chains. "Skirmishers and archers forward in a screen, form up the *qalb* and the *maimanah* as they come off the boats. Lord Khalid!"

The young Arab turned, brief anger flitting across his face at her preemptory command. The usual gang of Sahaba was around him, all younger men culled from the cities and towns of the Decapolis. His recklessness had turned many of the more experienced Arabs from his faction. Odenathus was first among Khalid's confidantes, but the Queen knew his friendship restrained the Eagle from openly flaunting her authority.

"You must command," she said firmly, raising her voice to be heard over the rattle of oars and men shouting as they unloaded. "Lord Odenathus and I will be busy in the hidden world. The Romans are sending some power against us, not just mere legionnaires, and we must turn our attention away." Zenobia singled out two of the Sahaban captains of heavy foot. "Malik, Duraid—you must watch over us while our minds are distant— find a hundred men and form a square, girding each of us in a fence of steel."

Both men nodded sharply, then set to work gathering up likely men. The Queen beckoned Khalid close, though she had yet to step out of the rushing surf. The day was hot and the sea pleasant between her toes. "Our armies are scattered," she said as the young Arab approached, "and everywhere I see confusion. Victory will be more likely won today by clear thought than bravery or strength of arms. The footing is poor on this sand and we have no horses, so we must strike inland as quickly as we can."

Khalid nodded in understanding, looking sharply to Odenathus and then back to Zenobia. "Will you each ward a flank, north and south? We may be attacked from either side . . ."

"We will," Zenobia nodded, and then—with a sigh—let her mind fall back, yielding hands, eyes, legs, even the beat of her heart to Zoë. The girl surged forward, filling the body with her quick energy. "Here they come," she cried, spying the glittering flight of arrows and javelins lofting into the afternoon sky. The Arab skirmishers were already among the higher dunes. Her hand sketched a complicated sign and a wavering gleam filled the air as the wind rushed into a near-solid barrier before the advancing army.

The Sahaba surged up the beach, voices booming like the sea, crying *Allau, Allau ak-bar!* Horns and trumpets wailed, answering the skirling call of the Roman bucians. The men of Mekkah were used to running in sand and they loped towards the enemy with glad hearts. Every step taken away from the un-steady sea raised their spirits.

Zoë walked forward, surrounded by a ring of armed men and she stretched her power, feeling the heavy blue strength of the sea behind and shining red streams of power in the earth ahead. "This land is strong," she cried, though Odenathus was now be-yond earshot.

A huge shadow suddenly rushed overhead and Zoë yelped in alarm. Shocked, she looked up, catching a glimpse of vast wings, a snaky head and a sinuous tail lashing in the air. Stunned, she and the men around her saw the *thing* roar past, the sound of its passage deafening everyone and snap into a tight circle over a stand of trees a half-mile away. Flame vom-ited down, spewing from gaping, black jaws and the entire copse burst into flame, men fleeing in all directions, the trailing black banner of the Serpent Lord engulfed in a blast of greenish-white fire.

The Queen heard a piercing howl echo in her mind and stag-gered, clutching her ears in pain. The cold, clammy touch of the lord Dahak faltered and she felt him struggle, wrapped in flame. In a single, crystalline moment, his control slackened, lifting iron chains from her will.

Cousin! Zoë screamed at Odenathus, her thought leaping across their battle meld, mind and mind meshing violently into one. The young man's mind was awhirl and he groped to match her thought. *We are free!* Zoë's shouted giddily.

Not yet, Zenobia forced herself into their meld, unexpectedly filling the apex of a triangle she'd not known existed between them. Odenathus recoiled, but then she felt glad wonder touch her like the glow of a warm fire on a cold night. *Hello, nephew.* Zenobia thought wryly. *Zoë—the Roman prince?*

The girl's exultation faded, dashed by chilling reality. *Yes,* she thought in unison with Odenathus. *It's him!*

Zenobia recoiled, faced with a secondhand image of a storm-dark titan astride a steed of iron, wreathed in rippling flame, circled by flickering blue-white signs and glyphs. A con-stellation of bright spirits whirled around him, shrieking with rage. Power cracked from his hand like the stroke of a forge hammer. Her body's hearing shuddered in response, the air thundering with a long, echoing crash. Lightning stabbed along the beach, darkening the air.

Our men come first, Zenobia snapped, capturing the stunned attention of the two young wizards. *We must protect them!*

The Lord of the Ten Serpents writhed on the ground, flames roaring around him, scaly limbs glowing cherry-red with intense heat. The copse of trees roared, slender trunks wrapped in greenish fire and the sandy ground bubbled and popped, turning to a glassy slurry under the sorcerer's feet. Wailing, barely able to breath, Dahak lunged away from the sea, bounding up into the air. Power wicked around him, the tormented core of his mind struggling to ignore the searing pain stabbing from ruined flesh and summon a shield of defense.

Gusts of wind slammed the sorcerer to the ground, sending him crashing into a stand of brambles. The iron monster in the sky banked sharply, wing rolling over and a searing trail of phlogiston smoked in the air. The viscous fluid streaked across the ground in a long arc. Dahak rolled away from the tongue of flame. Everything—trees, brambles, sand, old tufa—lit with brilliant greenish-white fire. Smoke roared up, climbing to the heavens in a thick, black cloud. The iron drake shrieked upwards, gaining altitude.

Coughing up soot and burning ash, the sorcerer scrambled down the dune. The sandy crown burned fiercely, streams of molten glass spilling after him. The T'u-chüeh fled, leaving smoldering corpses scattered under the trees. Dahak wailed, a long, sobbing moan escaping his seared throat. He'd only felt such dreadful pain once before and he splashed desperately into a muddy pond, crying in relief as cool water hissed against his skin. Taloned fingers plunged into the mud, feeling strength throbbing in the rich soil.

A rising, hurricane shriek snapped his head around, the sorcerer catching sight of the flying machine—now he could sense gears and wheels, cunning skeletal limbs sheathed in hammered copper and bronze, a blazing crystalline heart—sweeping towards him. Even the brief respite had been enough, letting his mind settle, confusion flee, and power rush into his body from the living earth.

"Now we'll see, stripling!" Dahak turned, one black hand slashing across the pale blue sky. The sun had settled behind the mountains, but the heavens were still flush with day and the rising smoke was only a smear against a perfect field of azure. Lightning leapt up with his motion and the iron drake plowed into a massive, earth-shaking discharge. A thunderclap smote the ground, shaking leaves from the trees and making the surface of the muddy pond jump.

The machine staggered in flight and Dahak felt his enemies' surprise. Iron plates glowed bright, groaning as iron expanded in the wake of the strike. The sorcerer rose from the pond, delighted to see his opponent veer away, a spiral of smoke hanging in the air. He scrambled out of the pool, eager to gain some high ground.

Smoke hissed away from the turning drake as it rushed through the upper air and then petered out. A faint blue-white flash rippled across the massive head, deep-set eyes blazing orange and red. The machine banked around with a shriek, the wind of its passage bending the trees.

Dahak cursed, summoning every power and ward he knew. A wave of darkness rushed away from him, killing grass, flowers, trees in a great circle. "Come then!" he screamed at the sky, "test my strength!" At a great distance, the door of stone quivered, feeling binding signs upon the ancient granite weaken and fray.

Stunned, the Sahaba raised their heads from the sand, every man's eyes wide in fear. The Queen was already standing, searching the sky with liquid brown eyes, her lips a harsh line. Three more of the great creatures plunged towards her from the west. Against the sun-bright sky, they were almost invisible, but the earthshaking roar of their passage rolled before them like the clash of a massive drum. Zoë grasped the air, her fingers tangling in the last rays of the sun. A hazy wall flickered above the dunes, fierce zephyrs rushing over the ocean hurrying to her aid. "Keep down," she managed to shout as the first of the enemy cracked past overhead.

The drake's wingtip, tending low towards the ground as the leviathan body slewed into an *S*-curve towards the fleet, clipped the trembling, near-invisible wall. Zoë was slammed back into the sand, breath driven from her body and the shield of wind disintegrated in a whirlwind of sand and dust and debris. The iron machine cartwheeled unexpectedly, flame spilling away from a twisting snout, and slammed at great speed into the merchantman *Der'a*. The colossal impact broke the ship in half, iron wings tangling in the mast, planks and keel shattering with a roar. A huge spout of water fountained up, vaporizing to steam as the drake coughed up a bellyful of phlogiston. Fire rained down in blazing droplets, engulfing the broken foredeck of the *Der'a*, and spreading on the tossing sea in great, hissing sheets.

"Dusarra's brass teat!" Zoë cursed, scrambling to her feet. Two more ships caught fire in the space of her exclamation, their sails bursting into yellow flame, rolling black clouds surging across the water. The iron monster struggled in the wreckage, tangled, massive claws shredding the hull as it fought free. Steam boiled up with an ear-splitting hiss, obscuring her view. The surf glowed red, catching the light of the inferno roaring around the three ships.

The other two iron drakes had broken away, veering left and right from their unexpectedly fallen brother. Zoë's heart fell as the bat-winged monstrosities shrieked over the fleet, triangular heads dipping down, sending sheets of green flame drifting down over the massed ships. A rippling series of booms echoed across the water, dry cordage and canvas catching alight. Dozens of ships were aflame in moments.

Odenathus, Zoë called, feeling her cousin rising woozily from the sand. *Give me your strength!*

Her fist clenched in the air, whipping through a tight circle. Giddy power rushed from land and sea and air, coalescing into a shimmering, blood-red cube clasped in her ghostly hand. Grim brown eyes followed the swooping flight of one of the machines as it pulled away from the stricken fleet, wings roaring in the air, clawing for altitude. Odenathus' power joined hers and the cube multiplied fourfold. Now the simple shapes split and re-formed, tearing and extruding new surfaces with dizzying speed.

The iron drake executed a sharp plunging turn and shrieked

back across the bay. Zoë canted her arm, then flung the power she'd gathered like a javelin, leading the massive, onrushing metallic shape. The girl staggered, drained by the enormous gradient she'd released, then armored hands caught her from both sides. A spray of brilliant crimson duododecahedrons snapped out in an expanding cone.

The machine slammed into the cloud and the sky lit with a concussive, blinding *crack!*

Smoke and fire bloomed in the air, a roiling black cloud. Metal screamed and the drake burst free, one wing torn away, the head smashed, white smoke billowing from rents in the scaled flesh. Zoë shouted in triumph, and the men around her cheered wildly. One massive wing still beat the air, and the machine tilted to one side. Zoë turned to find the other drake, catching sight of it sweeping inland, rising on titanic wings.

Look out! Odenathus shouted over the meld. Zoë spun back—just in time to see the crippled drake slam into the shallow water a hundred yards away and crash through a burning barge, sections of iron hull flaking away from the skeleton. Zoë sprinted away, her guardsmen wailing in fear, and the enormous machine bounced—wreathed in flame—onto the beach behind them. A whoomp of flame jetted out and the creature blew apart. Zoë felt something lift her up, then she smashed into a sand dune with a sickening *crack*. Fire roared around her and she blinked smoke from her eyes. Dazed, she tried to roll over, but her arm failed and groaning metal drowned out her weak cry for help.

Something blotted out the sky, toppling over, and she caught a glimpse of an intricately detailed iron wing rushing towards her before searing pain washed consciousness away.

Dahak leapt into the air, tearing free from the burden of gravity and a thick, scaled tail slapped the ground where he'd stood. Trees shattered, limbs torn away, filling the air with flying splinters. The sorcerer twisted, a crackling blue-black flare leaping from his outstretched hand. The blast seared the drake's head and shoulders, iron plates groaning with the impact and the creature whirled away. Wounded, the machine bounded for the open sky.

Something rose out of the smoke, surrounded by whirling points of white light and Dahak drew back, drifting in the sooty air, eyes narrowed in surprise. His enemy came forth in the flesh at last and the young Roman's aspect was vastly different than he'd seen before.

You have grown strong, the Lord of the Ten Serpents hissed.

Maxian rushed forward, suspended in a shifting sphere of sullen glyphs and whirling, frenetic bright sparks of living flame. His lean face was dark with strain, but the sorcerer could feel power moving to the boy from every direction. The hidden world twisted, contorting around the strength collecting in the Roman. Even Dahak felt the tug, a steadily steepening slope wicking his own *mana* away.

No! Dahak howled, and mustered his own vigor, sapping the land, sending thousands of his *gaatasuun* collapsing to the ground, yanking tendrils of guiding thought away from his servants, opening his heart to the power dwelling in the empty spaces behind the moon and the sun. Incandescent with rage, he met the prince's charge with his own blow—a flickering, swift sign bursting new-formed and whole from the air—darkening the afternoon sky.

Jagged patterns clashed, lightning licking along impossible surfaces and a coruscating blast of fire, wind and deafening sound rolled away from the two wizards. The sea heaved, more Persian ships capsized or the flames raging on their decks were snuffed by the overpressure of the blast. Thousands of men threw themselves to the ground in fear, some blinded. The soft bottomland convulsed and heaved, entire orchards and meadows flattened or swallowed by the uneasy earth.

Dahak slashed in, howling unholy words, splintering the prince's wards like eggshells, dispersing glyphs, striking at the power flooding from earth and sky. They grappled, a whirlwind of searing blasts rippling along the edge of their conflict. The prince strove to drive Dahak towards the sea, but the sorcerer did not yield. His reptilian eyes blazed red, curdling beams lashing across Maxian's pattern. Defenses flaked, splintering under the blow and the prince staggered.

The Lord of the Ten Serpents grinned, bearing down, his will closing like a vise.

Maxian slammed back, ultraviolet lightning crashing against Dahak's shields, bleeding through layers of swirling defense. The sorcerer felt his ties to the earth weaken, then a raging inferno enveloped him, hammering with heat and light at his concentration. Gasping, desperate to recover himself, Dahak leapt away, soaring across the empty sky, high above the line of the beach, towards the harbor of Catania itself. *He's too strong here*, the sorcerer thought wildly, dimly perceiving some enormous pattern building behind the prince's ever-mounting attack. *I've been lured into a trap!*

The prince gave chase, roaring in pursuit, a roiling cloud stabbing with lightning hot on his heels.

Run, old snake! The prince's grim thought arrowed after the sorcerer. *You can't find a hole deep enough to keep me from your throat!*

A howling mob stormed against the Roman lines, withered corpses screeching, skeletal hands clawing against shields and grasping at the stabbing spears. Alexandros trotted great Bucephalas behind the third rank, screaming encouragement, ordering men up from the reserves when he saw the line weaken. The dead swarmed up the slope in waves, throwing themselves heedlessly against the Gothic shield wall. Red-bearded men hacked with axes, hewing away brittle arms, throats, hands. The pikemen stabbed overhand, crushing the chests of corpses, yet still the dead surged against the line, trying to break through with main force.

The Gothic line sudden split open, a wedge of waxy faced legionnaires crashing through, swords slashing wildly around them.

"Hold! Hold!" Alexandros waded into the fray, slashing down with his cavalry spatha, splitting open the skull of a desiccated Roman. The creature's hands scrabbled against the blade, trying to wrench the sword from his hands, but the Macedonian kicked out, shoving the corpse away. The dead man was immediately trampled underfoot by a wave of his fellows, oily yellow guts squishing under hobnailed boots. A noisome stench rolled before the *gaatasuun*, choking the air and making living men faint with nausea. "Reserves! Reserves here!"

Bucephalas reared, striking out with flying hooves. Steel sparked on rusted armor, smashing two half-rotted ghouls back. The dead went down, tangling the legs and arms of those behind. Alexandros swung with the horse, slashing the head from another undead Roman. The legionnaire continued to fight, methodically hacking away in front of him, even though no one was there. Grimacing, the Macedonian leaned down and slashed the backs of the thing's mottled gray legs. The corpse toppled, arms still swinging.

Another rush of the dead boiled up the slope and Bucephalas screamed. Spears jabbed at the horse's face and he reared. Alexandros, unprepared, toppled out of the saddle, hitting the ground with a clang of armor and metal. The stallion whirled, kicking with his back feet, shattering the dried, fragile skulls of two more assailants. The dead pressed forward, black ooze spilling down their archaic armor.

Whinnying, Bucephalas bolted back out of the line of battle. With only a moment to spare, Alexandros managed to get to his feet and was immediately beset by two headless spearmen. Their leaf-bladed spears jabbed at him in eerie synchrony and the Macedonian slapped one weapon away, then grunted, the other scoring across his breastplate at an angle.

"Reserves!" he screamed, hacking down with his spatha and cleaving the exposed arm in twain. "Hold the line!"

The other spearman lunged and Alexandros twisted, catching the point on his shield. Iron squealed on the laminated wood, then the Macedonian stepped in and smashed his blade down on the thing's exposed collarbone. Ribs splintered, black-and-gray dust spewed from a dozen ancient wounds and the thing collapsed. Alexandros stepped back, drenched with sweat, gasping for breath. His sword arm did not feel exhaustion, but his mind struggled to break free from the melee surging around him.

"Hold the line!" he screamed, falling back a step. Two legionnaires with oval shields filled his space, and Alexandros felt a peculiar chill as one passed through him like mist. "Hold . . ."

We'll hold, growled a sharp voice in his mind. The ghostly centurion stepped past and a maniple of his men flooded into the gap. As insubstantial as their spears were, they crushed back the crawling dead, bright blades licking down to pierce spines or hew legs from under the walking corpses.

Alexandros staggered back from the line, then flinched away from the sky.

A colossal blast thundered overhead and two burning figures streaked past in the upper air. The Macedonian's head snapped around, trying to follow their flight to the north and he suddenly realized the sky was choked with cloud, vast plumes of steam rising from the bay, the forested lands behind the beach engulfed in a spitting, crackling forest fire. The sun had set, but the land was lit by wavering flame on land and sea. High up, beyond sight, he could hear the roar of some monstrous creature quartering the sky.

Stand fast, bellowed the centurion and Alexandros was at his side, staring down the slope. A wedge of men—living men—in gleaming armor jogged towards them under waving sunburst banners. The furious attack of the dead had drained away, those few remaining animate wandering aimless or crawling on the ground like enormous snakes. The Macedonian stared in surprise, recognizing the enemy banner, then drew himself up.

"Romans! To me, to me!" His spatha swung down, pointing at the advancing men. "Great Persia comes! Let us show him what Roman valor means!"

A bellowing shout answered the Macedonian as he wiped sweat from his eyes and settled his battered shield. He had never expected to face the war flags of Achamaenid Persia or the golden-masked Immortals again—yet here they came at a run, straight up the shallow slope at him. His grip tightened on the sword hilt.

Epirote scum, echoed the ghostly centurion's voice. The man was almost solid now. *Where are your fucking elephants now?*

)H(

Maxian swept through smoky air, long, dark hair flying out behind his head. With the Persian sorcerer driven before him in panic, the prince turned his attention aside for an instant, eyeing the fleet scattered across the bay. Many of the ships were afire—some had already burned to the waterline, leaving ghostly hulls half-visible below the choppy water—but more remained. The wind continued to bear unseasonably from the southeast. A few of the surviving Persian merchantmen were tacking away from the shore, wakes bright in the dying, ruddy light. Some of the remaining ships continued to unload, sending more boats filled with men towards the beach.

Alexandros is in trouble, Maxian thought. A chorus of voices rose in his mind, clamoring spirits eager to gain his favor. Their whispers resolved into a litany of coherent thoughts: *the Roman army is too small and trying to fight in too many places at once*. The prince grimaced, slowing his headlong flight through the air.

The dark shape of the Persian disappeared among the jumble of houses, temples and imposing theatre of Catania itself. There were no fires burning in the town and the fading light cast the streets and avenues into shadow, but Maxian—with a cold smile—thought he'd have no trouble running the sorcerer to ground when he needed to. *He's out of play for the moment . . . and that is enough.*

Frowning at the enemy fleet, the prince turned his attention to the sea and the vast web of forces and powers at work above, on, and below the waters. He could feel—would see, if he cared—the glittering forms of two Persian wizards still active on the beach itself. But their light was dim in comparison to their master and Maxian set his thoughts of them aside.

Their fleet is too numerous, Columella's dry voice whispered. *You must not give the Persian too much time—he will recover his strength, set fear aside, devise stratagems to defeat you. Let Lord Alexandros deal with these matters.*

"No," Maxian said aloud. He drifted in the air, surrounded by potent signs and the ceaseless, shimmering motion of his patterns and wards. Hundreds of feet below, waves swept in long, foaming arcs against the shore and men struggled and died, pierced by iron or steel, over sandy ground. He could feel their spirits flash bright, then vanish as blood spilled and breath fled. "A Persian army ashore, intact and ably led will be more trouble than we can afford."

His eyes lifted to the vast, smooth cone of Aetna and a grim, almost mischievous smile came upon him.

Great Lord, you cannot . . . Columella grew silent, feeling a spark of anger flare in the prince's mind. *The citizens . . .* The old ghost's voice trailed away feebly.

Maxian let sight expand, shedding the immediate pressures of flesh and the wind and smoke biting at his nostrils. A sullen red core slumbered far beneath the mountain, tendrils of glowing crimson slowly rising, percolating through the veins of the earth, finding release from subterranean pressures in gouts of steam and a constant, rumbling *hiss* that threw a column of flattened smoke away from the mountaintop. The prince felt his irritation mount—time *was* pressing and he could feel the Persian's sharp-edged pattern growing stronger—the mountain was quiet, without the vast lode of power Vesuvius once held. *The Oath is not trying to bottle this one*, he realized.

One of the pale lights whirling around him flared, and the prince saw a brief, fear-etched vision of a massive wave roaring up out of the sea, smashing ships to kindling and then raging against a shore studded with ornate houses of stone and brick.

"Well done." Maxian grinned, favoring the mote with a moment of his attention. He could feel the Oath trembling around him; a deep, superbly complex matrix of memories, traditions and the living citizens of the Empire. His intent flashed out, leaping from Aetna's dark, trembling heart along a fissure running out to sea. Swiftly, his will sped, burrowing beneath the earth, finding black fumaroles boiling in the vasty deep, splintered rock grinding against crushed limestone.

Here is some power! he exulted, a diamond-bright pinpoint lancing down as he commanded, spearing into a tight green-and-blue balance of vast forces. There was slippage, weakness and then drowned mountains ground violently against one another, making the ocean floor heave and pitch. The sea shivered. Thousands of feet above, where the water was falling dark with the flight of the sun, a dimple formed on the surface, then collapsed, sending jets of spray hundreds of feet into the air.

The prince laughed in delight, casting a pitying look upon the ships crowding below him. He turned abruptly, speeding north, the sky rumbling behind him. Fey lights played in his hair and the whirling orbs surrounding him brightened, becoming almost visible in the waking world.

Catania swelled below him, whitewashed buildings passing by, temple roofs red with tile and bright ornaments. The streets were empty, every shutter locked tight. No one could be seen or felt. Maxian drifted past a temple of Poseidon—marble columns glowing pale in the twilight—his sense of unease growing. A dog barked wildly in a yard below. He reached out, captured the fragments of the Oath lingering in the ancient town and felt his battle-shield wax strong. His brow furrowed, feeling the tenuous fabric pervading the Roman city fray.

Something flared in the hidden world—a dark spike of power—and the prince cursed, leaping high into the air. Below him—to the right, hard by the port and the sea—the shape of a grand amphitheater rose, strikingly done in alternating slabs of dark volcanic rock, red brick and pale yellow marble. Three terraces of columns and arches, with boxed seats, surrounded an oval floor. The tiers of seats and the sandy floor were covered with thousands of fallen men, women and children.

They fled here when word of the battle came, Columella whispered sadly. *Seeking safety. The old city walls were torn down for building materials in the time of Emperor Trajan.*

Ebon hues played among the statues lining the top deck of the amphitheater. Maxian slowed to a halt, the roof only inches below his feet. Flat, rust-colored tiles splintered as he drifted across them, the strength concentrated in him distorting the waking world. Ghosts prowled around him, empty eyes vigilant for the enemy. He could smell the acrid stench of death in the air and the queer, trembling vibration in the hidden world when lives were taken to grant power. Maxian shuddered, feeling the urge to consume rise in his throat. His mouth stretched in a feral snarl. Some of those sprawled on the sand still lived . . . the prince darted down to the theater floor, a black crow with ragged wings stooping over the crumpled body of a young man.

"He's not—" Maxian staggered, the counter-rotating spheres around him lighting with a tremendous flash. The Persian stormed out of a tunnel mouth, a whirlwind of black lightning slashing at the prince's shield. Layers of glittering blue-white shuddered, then cracked, darkness surging against the barrier of drifting glyphs. Ghosts swarmed into the breach, wailing piteously, their frail remnants dissolving in a mad rush. The sorcerer stamped down with a scaled foot and the sandy floor erupted with a *boom!* Maxian flew backwards, crashing into the retaining wall circling the amphitheater floor. His physical body bounced back from the tufa wall, blood flying from his mouth.

Mind distracted, his shields weakened, straining to hold back stabbing bolts of indigo, the prince spat to clear his mouth, forcing himself to his feet. The last of the ghosts congealed before him in a wavering wall of lights, but their numbers dwindled with each attack. The sorcerer clapped his hands together, eyes blazing, and the stone behind Maxian groaned and split, showering him with needle-like shrapnel. Physical pain cut into his focus, but the prince had no time for such trivialities.

Faintly, he could hear a roaring sound rising to swallow the world.

Maxian crouched down, letting the last of his brittle shields fail, the sign of Athena guttering, overwhelmed by darkness and he pressed his hands against the sandy ground. He closed his eyes, ignoring the blood and sweat dripping from a forehead scored by deep cuts. A familiar, debilitating cold flooded around him, leaching his strength, drawing his breath out in trailing white mist. The Persian's laughter rolled and trembled in his ears, as the stone walls of the amphitheater creaked, crumbling to ash and dust.

Shahr-Baraz ran up the dune, his boots dragging in soft, black sand. His breath came in rasping gulps, though his stride did not waver or slack. He was the Boar and his strength of limb and will was without limit. Armored hands grasped the hilt of a heavy, straight blade half-again longer than the longest carried by his guardsmen. Another man would find the sword taxing to lift, much less wield in combat. Shahr-Baraz had sparred with a weapon like this—either a sword or mace or axe—since the first whiskers sprouted on his chin.

The *pushtigbahn* loped alongside their captain, each man laboring through the loose sand, weapons held high, shields riding on brawny arms. They did not waste their breath in shouts of rage or war cries; each was a veteran, selected from the ranks of the great nobles for valor, for courage, for skill in the saddle and afoot surpassing all others. Among them, the dark, cloaked shapes of the Shanzdah strode like hunting dogs, silent and intent. The ground firmed and now there were drifts of shattered bodies, legs hewn from hips, arms cast awry, rotted skulls caved in by axe and spear.

Shahr-Baraz saw the army of the dead had broken upon the Roman lines and the enemy was waiting, shields locked, three—perhaps four—ranks deep, every face set, weapons ready, poised to accept their charge. Shahr-Baraz raised his massive blade abruptly and the trumpeters and drummers slowed to a halt. "Sound," the King of Kings shouted, keen gaze sweeping the line of battle.

A brassy honking shocked the air, quickly joined by the rattling of drums. Clouds of smoke drifted in from the sea, glowing with the reflection of the burning, wrecked fleet. In the dim, shifting half-light Shahr-Baraz ran forward again and now the *pushtigbahn* gathered themselves, many men snapping down the golden masks covering their faces.

The Romans braced, the first rank of men going down on one knee. Javelins and sling-stones pelted the charging Persians. Some went down, struck by a lucky blow, but the Immortal's armor shrugged aside most of the missiles.

Swinging the huge sword over his head, his mighty voice at last roaring a challenge, the Boar leapt among the enemy. His Immortals howled in on either side, hewing with their long axes, maces, swords. Legionnaires stabbed back underhand with their short blades and spears. Shahr-Baraz swept his shield aside, knocking down two spears and a sword thrusting for his vitals. The longsword smashed down, cleaving through a tilted shield, splitting the laminated pine with a stunning *crack!* Blood spattered as the Roman went down, goggle-eyed, his plated helmet shorn through. The Boar roared in exultation, wading into the Roman ranks, his blade ripping sideways, tearing a man's arm clean off. Crimson spewed, blinding a legionnaire in the second rank. Shahr-Baraz smashed his fist into the man's face, feeling metal bend and break.

A broad-chested Roman officer stabbed in from the left, slipping the tip of his gladius past the Boar's shield. The sword point slammed into plated iron, skipped across two curved plates and wedged violently against one of the wire joins. Shahr-Baraz bellowed, feeling the tip pinching his side and crashed the shield into the man's chest. The blow lifted the Roman from his feet, sending him careening into another legionnaire struggling hand-to-hand with an Immortal. The collision left both men pinned against the locked shields of the third rank.

The Boar spared not a grain for the fallen officer, bulling forward into the third and fourth ranks, smashing about him with the long blade, clubbing men with the spiked face of his shield. Two more Romans went down under his rush, and the Immortals crowding in behind him smashed down the struggling men with their maces. Shahr-Baraz waded in blood, his longsword running red.

He laughed, a huge, booming wild cry, laying about him with maniac strength. The *pushtigbahn* began to chant his name, a rolling, rising shout, and they pressed harder. Among them, the Shanzdah wreaked terrible havoc, ignoring mortal wounds, their ebon blades reaping a rich harvest. The Boar traded blows with a centurion, barely noticed the man was half-transparent, then plunged the gore-slick sword through a fury-crazed face. The ghostly centurion shattered like a glass bead ground under a sledge.

Open ground lay before him and Shahr-Baraz whooped with delight.

Drenched, the Queen struggled to rise, arms straining to push aside a section of iron plating pinning her to the beach. Surf rushed past, filling her armor with sand and grit. Hissing fires eddied in the shallows where the iron drake's belly had split open, spilling oily flame across the water. She could see curving ribs rising above her, black silhouettes against a purplish sky streaked with rising columns of smoke.

"Sahaba, to me!" she shouted, forcing her water-clogged throat to work. The ironwork burned her fingers, the plate glowing red with trapped heat, but she continued to push. For a moment, the massive weight trembled, then moved an inch. Now she could turn her hip and push with her leg as well. Creaking, the etched panel shifted. Zenobia gasped, feeling muscles burn, then the plate fell aside with a wet, smacking sound. She crawled from the wreckage, immediately coming across a fallen, sodden body.

"One of ours?" Zenobia coughed, forcing herself upright.

Yes, Zoë answered weakly. The girl had suffered a heavy backlash when the shield of the winds collapsed. Then she'd tried to protect them from the concussive blast of the machine blowing apart on the beach. They lived, which Zenobia accounted a victory. The Queen patted the dead Sahaba's shoulder and limped towards the high-tide line.

A deep, groaning sound caught Zenobia's attention as she clambered out between two hissing, popping iron ribs. She turned towards the sea, wondering if one of the big grain haulers had caught fire. Her fingers clutched steaming iron in shock, brilliant blue eyes widening in horror.

The water was still crowded with ships, many burning, but others made headway towards the beach. The serpentine shapes of two of the flying creatures circled in the dark air, jets of flame licking down from gaping jaws to set more ships alight.

But the sea in the broad, wide bay had grown strangely flat. Wind still gusted over the waters, tangling the Queen's hair and tugging at the linen shirt over her armor, but the whitecaps and breakers were gone. Instead, the sea was running out, hissing across the sand and galleys that had lately been moored in shallow water creaked and groaned as they settled on the exposed bottom.

"What . . ." The Queen felt the winds turn, shifting wildly from side to side and then a vast, unimaginably deep groaning sound rose from the waters. The eastern horizon—already plunged into purple twilight—now turned dark in a broad swathe across the mouth of the bay. She felt the ground under her feet shift and settle, little puffs of air jetting from crevices opening in the sand.

Run! Zoë stormed into her paralyzed consciousness, the girl seizing control of their body. *The Wave Lord is coming!* The Queen leapt between the smoking iron and sprinted up the beach, legs flashing, sand spurting away from blurring feet. Zoë reached out desperately, forcing her battered will to wing ahead of the body, rippling through the soft sand, making a hard-packed surface. Zenobia fought the urge to look over her shoulder, keeping her concentration focused solely on speed and flight.

The groaning sound welled up and up and up, shaking the sky. A vast, crashing sound boomed right behind and a grinding, splintering undertone was swiftly consumed by a roar that shook the ground and sent hurricane winds lashing ahead of the angry god's advance.

Zoë wrenched them free from gravity's cruel bonds and the Queen sprang ahead, soaring over the line of dunes. Below her, startled soldiers turned from their deadly play of iron, then shrieked in horror. The roaring deep rushed up, swallowing everyone on the beach, driving jumbled wood, canvas, cordage and stone cast up from great depths against the land. Lesser waves surged between the high dunes, boiling up the shallow streambeds and foaming in the river mouth.

The Queen turned at the top of her leap, heart in her throat, and saw the great fleet crashing to ruin on the shore.

Many ships had ridden out the sudden wave, but more were shattered wrecks, some still afire—for even Poseidon's wrath could not quench combusting phlogiston—and they glowed and smoked, far beneath the raging surface, shining stars drifting into the abyss.

Weeping for her sailors—many Palmyrenes served aboard the fine, trim ships—she fluttered out of the sky, an armored harpy, circled by quick winds. Sand crunched under her boots as she landed on a slope strewn with the dead. A sunflower banner leaned drunkenly not far away and the Queen looked down into a vale behind the dune ridge, where men still clashed, raising a great smoky din, blades and spears flashing in the dimming, flame-shot light.

More of her allies—a motley band of Huns, Sahaba and Persian land knights—climbed past her, their grim-faced captain aiming to join the battle.

"Fools," she growled, seeing the mighty shape of the King of Kings rampaging among the melee.

A snapping crack of thunder drew her attention and the Queen turned to the north. Light blazed in the air over a town, even now inundated by the rushing waves. She drew back, feeling enormous forces unleashed, making the sky ripple and shake. Her blue eyes went wide and a great, dreadful chill settled in her heart, making her limbs weak. *The stone door is breaking!*

The earth bounced under Maxian's hands and he let the shock fling him to his feet. The Persian sorcerer was taken unawares by the violent motion and spun in alarm. A towering black wave crashed against the seaward side of the amphitheatre, foam boiling through the pillared terraces and arched tunnels. Maxian let the full power of the Oath rush into him, opening his heart to sixty million striving lights, his fist dragging through suddenly thickening air. The sorcerer screamed in fear, seeing a wall of surging dark water spill across the amphitheater floor. Dahak sprang into the air, conveyed by a ghostly cloud of winged spirits.

Maxian snarled, lean face splitting with a furious grimace and leapt up himself. His blow cracked into the Persian's shields, splintering wards visible and invisible alike. Wreathed in lightning, his fist smashed across the serpent's temple. Stunned, the sorcerer flew into the first rank of seats, smashing through marble and brick and lava stone. His shields flickered and the prince bounded into the ruin. Lightning roared up from the earth, catching the Persian as he staggered to his feet.

Howling, the creature writhed in torment. Maxian stabbed in, fingers stiff in a sharp, cutting sign. The Persian's chest dimpled with crushing, irresistible force. Another shriek of agony pealed from an inhuman throat. Ghosts blew away in a sparkling cloud, unable to resist the prince's advance. Haloed in whirling, incandescent fire, Maxian forced a burning hand towards the sorcerer's scaled neck.

Squirming away, the Persian clawed at the prince's face with razor-sharp talons. Black fingernails bit into Maxian's neck, but the skin healed as fast as they tore, stiffening into dark hide-like armor. Maxian slammed his fist down, crushing the serpent's shoulder. Bones and scales popped, blood spattered on the marble seats and the Persian gasped, unable to breath, collarbone cracking.

Floodwaters broke on the lower seats, fountaining back from the retaining wall. Across the oval, pillars tore loose from their moorings, vanishing in the foaming sea. Statues of the gods and heroes toppled from the upper deck and the entire edifice shivered, bricks splintering. The sea rushed back, cresting, and the eastern wall of the theater collapsed with a grumbling, sharp roar. Bricks, stone, timbers, marble, blocks of tufa larger than a wagon—everything was swallowed by the sea.

Maxian's eyes blazed bright, the power of an entire Empire shining from his mouth, his skin, every pore. The Persian tried to turn away, seeing his destruction in the terrible brilliance. The prince pinned him, one knee cracking a weak arm against the stone floor. His fist opened, flames lashing the sorcerer's broken face and Maxian forced his fingers—spread wide—onto the Persian's forehead.

"You," Maxian growled, savaged throat barely able to form the words, "will never threaten my city again!"

Dahak screamed, a long, wailing, unending cry of torment, his body thrashing violently, every limb loose in abandoned, unhinged motion.

"Rome! Rome and victory!" Alexandros lunged forward, fighting his way through struggling men. The line of legionnaires and Goths had broken open, letting the Persian Immortals pour into the gap. A giant of a man was in their midst, howling like a titan, laying about him with an impossibly huge sword. Even the ghostly centurions fell back before him and the Macedonian saw the heavily armored *pushtigbahn* widening the gap with brutal efficiency. "With me, men of Rome!"

Alexandros loosened his grip on the shield in his left hand. Shouting wildly, he sprang in front of the giant, throwing a high cut at the man's head. The giant spun—so nimble for his great size!—and blocked effortlessly. The Macedonian tried to slip the blow, letting his sword bind on the longer, larger weapon, but so great was the other's strength the spatha was nearly torn from his hand. Alexandros scrambled back to avoid losing his head. The shield was held only by a single strap in his fingers.

The Persian champion rushed in, his blade flickering in tight, controlled slashes. Alexandros blocked hard, swiping sideways to catch the blurring tip and felt his arm rock with the blow. He threw the shield at the man's feet, all of his strength in the motion. The giant hacked down, catching the Macedonian's sword and driving the blade into the sand. Alexandros rolled away, suddenly weaponless, and the man shouted in pain. The flung shield had smashed into his trailing foot and he toppled, going down to his knees.

Heedless, Alexandros plowed into the Persian, slamming his armored hip into the man's face. The golden mask crunched, skewing to one side. The Macedonian followed with a kick to the giant's throat, then gasped, his own foot snatched from the air by a blurring hand. He slammed down on the sand, breath punched from his breast. Alexandros rolled, sand spraying, and a massive fist smacked into the ground. The Macedonian twisted, cracking his vambrace-encased arm across the dented mask. The giant grunted, his tree-like neck barely moving with the blow.

Alexandros scrambled to his feet, sliding back. One of the Roman centurions pitched him another sword and the Macedonian caught the spinning blade from the air. In a single motion he grasped the hilt, flipped the scabbard away and fell into a guard stance.

The giant rose as well, wrenching the golden mask and helmet from his head. Enormous mustaches, dripping with sweat, jutted into the air, and keen, bright eyes looked down upon Alexandros. A huge grin split the man's face.

"A worthy foe, by Ormazd!" he shouted in a basso roar. "The very likeness of the Greek devil Iskender!"

"I am the very *Macedonian* devil," Alexandros snarled, feeling his muscles waking to the task. "And you the greatest of the Persians, I wager?"

"I am," Shahr-Baraz growled. One of his men threw him a spear, which smacked into his meaty palm. He spun the shaft end for end, settling the weapon's balance to his satisfaction. "Then let the gods judge!"

Maxian's fingers dug into the sorcerer's neck, crushing muscles, tendons and veins. His other hand burned white-hot on the creature's forehead and Dahak struggled anew. Blood sprayed across the seats, dripping smoking hot from the prince's face.

Now I have you, Maxian raged, feeling the last of the Persian's defenses crumble. The world groaned around them, stone and brick shattering, the sky wavering with an aurora of brilliant, ghastly colors. Winds raged in the heavens, lashing the clouds into a maelstrom. The flesh on the inhuman face shriveled, burned down to a bony core. Fangs jutted from blackening gums, then splintered. *You end, now!*

Dahak twisted, still trying to break free, and found annihilation only a heartbeat away. Every atom in his body was in torment, spiked with lightning, dissolving in acid. Such an enormous pressure weighed on him, encompassing half the world, focused by the shattered walls of the amphitheater like a lens, he could see nothing but destruction before him. "No!" he wailed, the last fragment of his power shredding in the energy storm whirling around the Roman prince. "If I die . . . the world dies!"

Maxian's eyes darkened, hearing pure fear and terror in the creature's voice. "Show me," his voice boomed, ringing from the heavens, driving columns of smoke into twisting vortices. The fingers of his right hand, still burning white-hot, sank into the Persian's elongated skull. Dahak's scream soared beyond human hearing as bone and membrane parted.

The prince looked, and saw *a portal of stone, massive granite cut from the heart of a mountain, etched with a thousand lines of prayers, glittering with every seal and potent sign. The door was shaking, blazing with sullen yellow light, a force building beyond the portal beyond human comprehension.*

Flakes of stone and dust rained down from a distant ceiling, the living rock shaking in time to a colossal heartbeat.

A fragile, frayed pattern bound the dying sorcerer to the stone door and Maxian perceived the slender thread arcing arrow-straight over the eastern horizon. His thoughts whirled to a halt, the light shuddering from his skin and face dying. The prince looked down on the dreadful, shattered face. "Show me what lies beyond." His voice was cold and emotionless.

Dahak quailed, but Maxian's fingers were deep in the gelid mass of his brain, rippling with power, keeping life in his ancient limbs, while the Persian's secret thoughts and every plan and strategem were peeled away, the cracked shells of countless eggs.

The prince looked, and saw *a void of darkess, filled with bubbling chaos, a leviathan shape blotting out the stars, countless worlds rendered down to dust, the shrieking of nightgaunts hunting the black abyss, a lake of obsidian under a sky filled with so many stars it seemed day; a twisted, malefic tower looming over a city composed of a single, endless building.*

"They are waiting," Dahak croaked, torn lips fluttering, "beyond the threshold. If they enter . . ."

Maxian rose up, looking down with a grim, implacable face. His eyes were black pits reflecting the horrors he had seen in the creature's eyes. Tiny motes of light drifted around his head, some shining bright, some bare gleams. "You are the key in our deathless lock," the prince grated, venom and scorn dripping in his voice. "You stole from the gods and now they are rightly angry." Black, fathomless eyes narrowed and Maxian withdrew glowing fingers from the serpent's skull. "You will live."

Dahak collapsed into the dust, shuddering with relief. He closed his eyes, translucent lids lowering one by one. The prince's face did not change, seeming cast from iron and plunged in blood to temper.

"Instead, you will serve." His thumbs ground down on the fluted skull and Dahak stiffened, broken limbs taut, mouth gaping, eyes wild and open in horror. An intricate sign blazed on his forehead, among pebbled black scales, and then faded into the skin like the light dying on the sea at sunset.

"Rise," snapped the prince, standing himself. His clothes—

ripped and torn, burned by fires and scored by blasts of fury—
shimmered, knitting anew around his lean body. Maxian looked
to the south, ghosts whispering to him of battle and fury and
men wading deep in slaughter.

The prince ascended, rising into the troubled sky, and the
withered, broken body of the sorcerer followed. Together, they
sped along the shore, the wind bowing before them, columns of
smoke bending away from their passage and those few men left
alive in the wreckage below stared up in awe.

Alexandros darted in, slashing with his sword at the haft of the
oaken spear. The giant danced away, grinning like a madman,
and the leaf-bladed tip whipped round at the Macedonian's
head. Alexandros leaned to the side, feeling the breeze of metal
passing, then reversed his stroke, steel belling on steel. Shahr-
Baraz grunted, the blow knocking him back.

"Well struck!" he called, slashing at the Macedonian's legs.
Alexandros leapt and spun, striking and parrying in a whirlwind of motion. They drew apart, panting, and the Macedonian
began to grin himself. *Here is a worthy opponent!* He circled,
blood singing, looking for an opening.

The wind gusting among the dunes fluttered and then stopped.

Alexandros looked up, gray eyes widening in surprise. He
saw a lone figure—a woman in gleaming armor and a tattered
white tunic—standing on the ridge above them. She was facing
the north, her unbound hair fluttering in some distant breeze.
The men of both armies had grown still, and everyone turned,
even the giant, who slowly lowered his spear.

A man approached in the turbulent air, shining like the sun,
his raiment glowing with inner fire. A crippled *thing* followed
at his heels like a dog, barely alive, leaking blood and dark
fluid. As the shining figure passed over the top of the dunes, the
woman bowed her head. Alexandros, standing below amid the
armies of Rome and Persia alike, watched in awe. Golden light
washed across the ground, shining on the fallen bodies, broken
spears, cloven shields. Withered trees stirred and new growth
sprang from charred limbs. Tiny blue flowers bloomed across
the protected, landward face of the dune. Spring did not touch
them, but the power radiating from the beneficent face did.

The giant knelt and the remains of the Persian army bowed down, pressing foreheads to grounded weapons, averting their eyes.

Alexandros felt a great sense of peace wash over him and he too collapsed to his knees. His spirit struggled, trying to force him to his feet, but every bone and sinew responded gladly to the silent command. The legionnaires stiffened, raising their arms in the Imperial salute, and every eye blazed with proud delight.

"I am Maxian," a stern voice rolled and crashed in the sky. "Put down these weapons. Let there be peace in the world."

Alexandros, teeth gritted in a furious effort to control his hand, felt his fingers open and the sword fall to the sandy ground. Not more than a pace away, the giant king let his spear drop, though his neck bulged with effort.

"This is ended." The prince settled to the ground, waves of silvery light shining in every face. Then the radiance faded, leaving only men and women—wounded, tired, exhausted from the day's struggle—standing in a darkened hollow between the turbulent sea and burning land. Alexandros slumped, falling onto his hands, and felt every muscle in his body trembling in reaction.

Even I will be sore tomorrow, he thought. *This Persian has Herakle's own strength in those arms!*

Maxian stood on the crest of the dune ridge, his lean, dark face silhouetted against the distant glare of Catania. The city was burning fiercely, billowing clouds rolling up into the sky, obscuring the slopes of the great mountain. The stars had come out, shining down fitfully through drifting ash and a gritty, bitter-tasting haze. The prince faced a handful of men and one woman. His face was in shadow, though a single green ember burned where one eye would be. The distant voice of Gaius Julius faded from his thoughts.

"My brother is dead and by the acclamation of the people and the Senate, I am Emperor of Rome." The young man's voice was flat, leached of every emotion. "I rule and within the reach of my hand there will be peace."

No one spoke, a fugitive breeze tugging at their hair or hissing across scored and dented armor.

Maxian placed his hand on the withered, broken shoulder of

the creature crouched at his feet. "This is Dahak and he is the first of my servants. I have made him loyal, for in his flesh rides the life of the world."

Light blazed from the sorcerer's eyes, mouth, seeping from myriad wounds. He shuddered, overcome, and then stood, body whole, skin rippling with scale, his elongated skull dipping in obedience. Obscure glyphs flared on his body, covering every inch of skin, even the darting black tongue. Then they faded. Maxian stepped to the next man.

"You are C'hu-lo, yabghu of the T'u-chüeh, the Great People."

The Hun nodded, swallowing convulsively. His high cheek-bones were scored with ash, his arms lashed with wounds. He leaned against a broken spear, one leg lamed by fire. Maxian brushed back long, oily black hair, and the man's skin cleared, flesh knitting without blemish or scar. "You will rule in my name," the Emperor said, "khan of khans, in all the lands under the Rampart of Heaven. Your armies will be as leaves of grass, without number, your flocks plentiful and the strength of your race unbounded."

Maxian stepped before two young men, each wounded, armor spattered with blood, faces gaunt with exhaustion, leaning on one another for support. They were alike as peas in a pod, fierce, noble faces turned to the Emperor with dread riding in their dark eyes.

"You are Khalid al'Walid, the last son of the Makhzum," he said to the first. He set his hands to both men's cheeks, inclining his head towards them in greeting. "You are Odenathus, son of Zabda, prince of poor, dead Palmyra, like your friend, the last of a noble line."

The Emperor smiled and both men straightened, weariness banished, their eyes brightening. "You will build anew," he said, "and your cities will grow great, radiant with learning and knowledge, filled with cool gardens and shining marble. Those lands, you will hold in my name, and guard wisely."

The young Eagle knelt, pressing Maxian's hand to his lips. "In your name, great lord."

"What is this," the Emperor said, raising a hand to beckon a dark shape from the shadow of the hill. "Which hides its face from those of living men?"

A harsh, armored shape stirred unwillingly, then stepped before Maxian, cloak thrown back, a dented iron mask catching the gleam of the burning city. The Emperor looked upon the captain of the Shanzdah and his shadowed eyes took the measure of the thing and its purpose.

"Even in an empire of light," Maxian said, his voice untroubled, "there will be work better done by night than by day." The shape stiffened, then knelt to the ground, making the proskynesis in the Persian style, forehead to the ground, hands outstretched. "You and your brothers please me," the Emperor said, touching the iron crown of the helmet with his fingertips. "With such devotion."

A giant man loomed over Maxian, long mustache sweeping from a craggy, bloodied face. Arms like old roots crossed the chest of a titan or a god. A beard shot with silver covered a laminated steel breastplate. In Shahr-Baraz' eyes, there was nothing but defiance and ancient pride.

"Have you drunk deep enough of war?" The Emperor's voice softened for the first time. "Is your thirst quenched? Where are your sons, the friends of youth, your brothers?"

"Dead," growled the King of Kings, the word forced from his mouth against his will, face twisting in despair. "They are dead."

"You are Shahr-Baraz, the Boar, shahanshah, lord of the Medes, master of the Persians." Maxian's voice cracked sharply. "You *will* rule Persia in my name and yours will be a realm at peace, where a wise king rules from a throne not drenched in blood, but founded on order." He lifted his hand and the middle-aged man tried to turn away, but sighed—a long, exhausted exhalation—when the Emperor smoothed back his wild, tangled hair. Years lifted from the man's face and his beard curled dark and lustrous again.

"You, I know." Maxian looked upon Alexandros with a grim smile. "By your tread, I will measure the circumference of the world." The Macedonian flinched, his heart quailing away from the pressure in the shadowed eyes. Maxian grasped his shoulders and Alexandros felt weariness fade, spilling out on the ground in an invisible stream. "India is waiting and beyond her—who knows what wonders might lie?"

The Macedonian pressed fingertips to his forehead, and bowed, as the others had done.

Only the woman remained, standing a little apart, her face turned away to the east. Wind tugged at night-black hair, cascading in waves of curls down her back. The Emperor looked upon her and his mouth tightened. "Who are you?"

The Queen turned, looking over her shoulder. Her face matched his for cold composure, showing neither fear nor despair. The glow of the burning city shone in sapphire eyes and her chin lifted. "I am Zenobia Septima," she said tonelessly. "My city is ruins, scattered bone and rock. I have no kingdom, no subjects, nothing save sand and wind."

"Palmyra the Golden will rise again," Maxian said, brow furrowing slightly. "White towers will rise and countless gardens bloom. Silver will fill her coffers and her ships will ply the wide sea, holds filled with silk, spices and every luxury. All will look upon your beauty and rejoice!"

Zenobia did not respond, the corners of her mouth tightening. Sweat beaded her neck. The Emperor waited, remaining entirely still. She swayed, then straightened. Long fingers stiffened and her oval face became pale. Maxian remained still, watching her, implacable and irresistible. The Queen gasped, staggered and fell.

The Emperor caught her with gentle hands and he bent close, whispering. White fingers clutched tight on his arm and he stood while she knelt in homage.

"Now," Maxian said, "there will be order in all the world, and peace."

SOMEWHERE ON THE COAST OF SICILIA

A single star burned bright in the eastern sky, the first to spring alight with the passing day, and cool light shone down upon a rocky shore. Twin headlands jutted out, enclosing a sheltered cove where the violent sea had passed, leaving wrack piled high among glistening black rocks. Mohammed crawled from the sea, foam streaming from his chest and thighs, long white beard plastered to a muscular body blessed with powerful arms and mighty thews. Spitting brine, he used a staff to aid his tired feet and climbed up, out of the rocky strand to a shelf thick with olives and dwarf pine.

"A welcoming cave?" the man said aloud, testing his ragged voice. "Dank with sea mist . . ."

A faint, attenuated rumbling drew his attention and Mohammed turned, keen eyes piercing the night, looking out to the north across the long sweep of Catania's broad gulf, where of late so many ships had perished, swallowed by the vengeful sea. Night was full upon the waters and great clouds and storms rode the upper air. Yet despite all these obscuring veils, the Quraysh saw flame shining in the darkness.

He leaned against the staff, his head bent in weariness. The night wind moved among the trees, making their soft leaves rustle and shake and the sea sighed against the headland shore. When Mohammed lifted his face, letting the pale stars gleam upon him, determination and knowledge filled him with a clear light.

"Now," he said, "all powers are unmasked and a daunting task set before me. But I will not turn away."

Yes, came a voice from the clear air. *Your purpose is revealed. There is your enemy, shining dark, a deadly sun. Here is your great test, for which destiny has chosen you.*

The Quraysh leaned against his staff, long white beard luffed by the sea wind. "I accept this fate," he said to the night, and the stars, "I submit myself to the will of the lord of the world. But I am not ready, not yet . . ."

No, answered the voice, *but you will be.*

)·((

Gaius Julius scowled, his fists knuckling on either side of a stack of tattered parchment sheets. They had been touched by fire, the edges charred and split by heat. Columns of figures—*payments*, he thought, striving to clear his mind of grief—and names filled each page. "These were all your men found?"

"Yes, sir. The Duchess's servants had set the rest afire." Nicholas stood opposite, hands clasped behind his back, narrow face tight with ill-concealed tension. The man's armor was spotted with blood, his leathers creased and worn, dark with sweat. Gaius Julius nodded absently.

"These names," the old Roman said, "will lead us to others. Gather your men and set them upon the trail—question these . . . traitors . . . closely, but do not use them up." Gaius flashed a hard glance at the man and Nicholas nodded stiffly. "They serve our purpose best by leading to more interesting prey." His fingers traced the shortened, abbreviated names in the left-hand column. "Bait, Nicholas, bait. Find me a larger fish."

The Latin bowed his head in understanding, though the old Roman could see his angry thoughts clearly enough: *Why coddle traitors and conspirators? Why not purge the city of their taint, root and branch alike?* But he would obey. In time, Gaius hoped, he will learn some circumspection. Perhaps even forethought. An endless vista of labor stretched before them.

"Has Vladimir returned?"

Nicholas nodded, though his lip twitched in something like disgust. "He has."

Gaius Julius raised a gray eyebrow in response. The Latin squared his shoulders. "The child escaped with . . . two others. One, at least, was the Empress Helena's maid, a child named Koré. They entered the sewers on the Ianiculian hill, thwarting our Walach's sense of smell. I have the Urban Cohorts searching every mile of every adit, channel and tunnel. Boats filled with our men patrol the river, and the city gates are closed."

Nicholas paused and Gaius saw he wanted to say more, but restrained himself. The play of half-hidden emotions made an interesting play on his narrow face.

"Vladimir found nothing in the tunnels?"

The Latin shook his head sharply. "No, my lord. Nothing at all."

The old Roman regarded Nicholas with a considering, prolonged stare. After a time, Gaius Julius made a dismissive motion with his hand. The Latin strode out, obviously relieved to have escaped without hearing his master's opinion of the night's events.

Well, Gaius thought, leaning on the desk again. He was very tired—his body did not yearn for sleep, but his mind was exhausted by the relentless passage of events—and longed to sit somewhere, undisturbed for hours or days, watching the sun pass in the heavens. *I shall find a dead boy of the proper age and features and bury him beside Galen and Helena.* The old Roman nodded to himself, finding the solution at least practical. *Should Theodosius turn up again . . . he will be an impostor, a rogue, a false pretender. Such things have happened before.*

He bent, scribbling a note with a fine brush. "One more thing to do," he grumbled.

"My lord?" A breathless voice accompanied the clatter of boots in the doorway. Gaius Julius looked up. One of his Praetorians stood in the entrance, wiping sweat from his brow. "There is a . . . a dragon landing in the gardens of Domitian!"

Our master? Gaius Julius straightened, feeling the air in the palace change subtly, as if a stone had fallen into a still pool. "Send an honor guard to meet the Emperor," he snapped, looking down in disgust at his soiled robes. "I will be there in a moment."

A phalanx of legionaries, breastplates shining silver, their horsetail helmet plumes stiff, lined the top of the staircase. Gaius Julius climbed swiftly, looking neither right nor left, and entered a tall, vaulted hallway on the upper floor. Niches lined the walls, each one holding an Emperor's bust. The old Roman ignored them, even the smug face of Octavian, and paced down a long Indian carpet to a half-open door.

Knocking softly, Gaius Julius heard a strange voice say "enter."

Maxian stood on a balcony, wooden doors swung wide to either side. The city lay before him, lights sparkling yellow in the darkness, the long oval of the Circus Maximum barely visible below, outlined by lamps set around the periphery of the track. Beyond the racecourse, the Aventine loomed as a dark mass and the sky behind the hill was thick with smoke. Countless fires lit the slowly billowing clouds with a ruddy, red light.

The funeral pits, Gaius thought as he entered the chamber. He had attended many meetings here, while Galen was Emperor of Rome, and he had never felt such a chill, disturbing air in the room as he did now. A handful of legionaries stood against the walls, their faces sallow with fear. The old Roman frowned, feeling icy drafts swirl around his ankles.

Then he caught sight of a *thing* standing in the shadows just inside the balcony doors. A tall, stooped figure clad in long dark robes. Firelight gleamed on an elongated, inhuman skull. Long-fingered hands, tipped with glittering black nails, peeked from the cloak. Gaius' heart thudded in alarm and he slowed, dragging his feet. A chaos of thoughts raged, foremost among them the overriding desire to draw the sword hanging from his belt and thrown himself upon the abomination, striking until there was no strength in his arms and the *thing* lay dead. *And cast the remains into fire!*

His fingers twitched towards the hilt, but Maxian raised a hand from the balustrade. Gaius Julius froze, feeling his master's displeasure. He moved his hand away from the blade, though he could not bring himself to look upon the grinning charnel face of the creature standing in the shadows.

"My lord?" The old Roman found it difficult to speak. His flesh was crawling with suppressed horror.

"We are victorious," Maxian said, continuing to look out upon the city and the distant charnel fires. "The Persian fleet has been destroyed. Their king, their generals . . ." The hand moved, indicating the creature. ". . . even their overlord have bowed down before me. Order is restored throughout the world, and there will be a Roman peace from the pillars of Hercules to the gates of India. Alexandros has taken charge of matters in Sicilia, though I have brought loyal Dahak home with me. I am sure you will become great friends."

Sickeningly, the thing in the shadows bared needle-like teeth at Gaius Julius and the old Roman knew—he could not say how, but the truth struck at his heart like a well-flung javelin—he had been replaced by a new favorite. The world tilted on its axis, but Gaius had not survived the collapse of the old Republic without a canny mind and a quick tongue.

"Hail Caesar," Gaius said, his mouth dry as dust. A dreadful pressure seemed to fill the room, pressing in on him from all sides. Without thinking, he knelt, bending his forehead to the floor. As he did so, he caught sight of the Praetorians also kneeling, as did the creature in the shadows. Words hissed from his mouth, unbidden but undeniable. "Hail Maxian Atreus, Augustus Romanorum, Emperor and God, Protector of the Romans, Master of the World."

Maxian turned, the fires burning beyond the city glowing against the cloudy, dark sky behind him. His face was in shadow, but Gaius could see a faint, pale light reflecting in the man's eyes. The Emperor stirred, a hand shrugging his cloak into a clean line.

"Yes," Maxian said, softly, in final, full awareness of himself and the world. "I am a god."